Philip Boast is the author of *London's Child*, *London's Millionaire*, *London's Daughter*, *Gloria* and *The Foundling*, all set in London. He is also the author of *Watersmeet*, a West Country saga and *Pride*, an epic novel set in Australia and England. He lives in Devon with his wife Rosalind and their three children, Harry, Zoe and Jamie.

City

Philip Boast

HEADLINE

First published in 1994
by HEADLINE BOOK PUBLISHING

First published in paperback in 1995
by HEADLINE BOOK PUBLISHING

10 9 8 7 6 5 4 3 2 1

ISBN 0 7472 4726 9

Printed and bound in Great Great Britain by
Cox & Wyman Ltd, Reading, Berks

HEADLINE BOOK PUBLISHING
A division of Hodder Headline PLC
338 Euston Road
London NW1 3BH

For my daughter
Zoe

15   And in those days Peter stood up in the midst of the disciples, and said . . .

16   Men and brethren, this scripture must needs have been fulfilled, which the Holy Ghost by the mouth of David spoke before concerning Judas [Iscariot], which was the guide to them that took Jesus.

17   For he was numbered with us, and had obtained part of this ministry.

18   Now this man purchased a field with the reward of iniquity; and falling headlong, he burst asunder in the midst, and all his bowels gushed out.

19   And it was known unto all the dwellers at Jerusalem; insomuch as that field is called in their proper tongue, Aceldama, that is to say, The field of blood.

The Acts 1

CONTENTS

Jemima Fox's Family Tree
as known to her on
9 December 1870

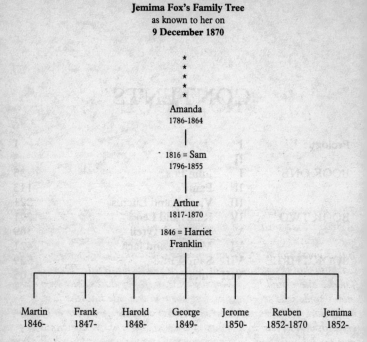

*
*
*
*
*

Amanda
1786-1864

1816 = Sam
1796-1855

Arthur
1817-1870

1846 = Harriet
Franklin

Martin	Frank	Harold	George	Jerome	Reuben	Jemima
1846-	1847-	1848-	1849-	1850-	1852-1870	1852-

PROLOGUE

I

Thus in the seventh year of the reign of the God Claudius, the traveller in Judea continued his long journey home by sea, for good fortune giving a silver piece into the tabernacle, the box that stepped the mast. But a great storm arose, and the traveller's ship fell among mighty waves so that the mast was broken. The sailors muttered, 'This man is Jonah,' and would have thrown him over if they dared, but even this man's smile was cruel, seeing into their hearts. He had the face of a barbarian, yet he wore the purple cloak of a prince. A citizen of Rome, yet with his red beard growing as long as a Jew's. A strange mixture of a man. A band of red fox fur encircled his upper arm, and in Celtic or Roman tongue his name meant Son of the Fox.

He stood alone on the forepeak of the storm-tossed vessel, and they feared him.

When the wind calmed, Fox joined the sailors, offering libation to the God-Emperor for their salvation, then the Arimathean tin trader knelt with him in Christian prayer, and finally Fox burnt an offering to Teutates, great god of the water. But still the ship was sinking.

Then Fox pointed with his sword, and they saw land closing from every side, except behind them. Swept upriver by the rising tide of the full moon, the dark countryside slipping by them was a map of islands under its silvery, haunted glow. They passed the City of the Sun before midnight, not a light showing. The British slaves were set to oars, and the vessel moved through banks of pale mist drifting on the black waters.

A military bridge, its trestles bound with rope, glimmered ahead of them. On Fox's right a raised gravel causeway crossed the marshes

1

towards two low, moonlit hills. Behind a palisade of stakes he spied a few leather tent tops and thatch roofs. That was all.

He reached up to touch the raised drawbridge as the vessel was swept through the gap. Tilting, sinking, the hulk grounded on the soft mud of the south bank.

Fox had come home to his land.

The Arimathean crept forward. 'Tiberius Claudius, what is this dreadful place called?'

John Fox replied, 'London.'

II

Friday 9 December 1870

Evening had fallen, dark with rain, and it was the same old London story: Jemima's train was delayed by stuck points near Spa Road. For an hour she stared from the foul third-class railway wagon over the rooftops of Bermondsey below, planning her escape. Her long red hair had fallen over her shoulders, but she dared not pin it up in case she drew even more attention to herself, or look at her dead father's pocket watch in case it was stolen. The bench she perched on and the London and Greenwich Railway windows she stared through were dirty as a disease. She had never realised people like the travellers clustered around her existed; for the first time in her life the cloth caps had faces beneath them, purple-veined, hairs jutting from nostrils, eyes staring at her, the man lounging opposite chomping his way toothlessly through a stump of cheese, and everywhere the fug of sweat, sour clothes, tobacco smoke and cheap sweet cider. The girls with their smooth, careless faces, faded as flowers, scratched their hair and, like her, gazed through the window at London below.

Jemima Fox had left Holywell Manor for the last time, and soon, she feared, she might be just like them. She remembered her grandmother's favourite saying: 'Something always turns up. You never can tell, Jemima, you never can tell. Lucky is as lucky makes.'

At last the train lurched forward, but nobody cheered.

Jemima ran out of London Bridge Station holding her expensive velvet skirts hitched up in her fists to keep ahead of the other folk streaming from the train, everyone hurrying anxiously after her through the steam and smoke to make their connections, none of them looking each other in the eye, first breathing through their noses, now their mouths, not wanting to be beaten by a girl. The third-class wagons were placed in the smokiest, most dangerous place, behind the engine, so she was well ahead of first and second; and she had jumped running onto the platform before the train had stopped, tripping over her skirts and only saved from falling headlong by a grunting porter. 'Sorry!' she called over her shoulder as the competitive sea of cloth caps, toppers and upraised umbrellas flowed after her.

Puddles splashed her ankles as she ran for the last remaining horse-omnibus serving the previous train, the bony nags steaming in the rain. Up top the driver sat hunched in wrappings of coats and mufflers that seemed made of solid grease to keep out the rain, water trickling from the brim of his hat in a steady stream between his knees. At the back the oilskinned cad was cheerfully shoving people inside with his tarry shoulders. The fare board contained the magic word 'Piccadilly'.

'How long will you take?' she panted.

The cad eyed her merrily, wiping the beaded drops from his nose. ''Ow long will *I* take?' Jemima stamped her foot – these folk always answered a question with another question. 'Well,' he pondered, smearing his hand down his cape, 'this is the busiest time o' the evenin', wot wiv some lucky folk leavin' work early no doubt.' He paused for thought, then shook his head. 'An' it's a Friday, too, miss, which makes it the busiest evenin' o' the week, since yer asked. So I 'as ter reply honest-like, "It takes as long as it takes." ' He brightened. 'Give yer a bunk-up, miss? Schedooled service, an' if yer believe that yer'll believe anyfink. "Fast" is these knock-kneed brutes's middle names! Why, just *look* at 'em!'

'Listen to me, it's very important that I reach King Street in St James's by fifteen minutes past five.'

'Wery, *wery* important, is it?'

'I have an appointment and most important family business to conduct at Spink's, the coin dealers.'

'Then, miss, I got ter tell yer, yer missed yer homnibus.' The cad pointed with his finger through the rain to the gaslit clock hung beneath the station eaves. The wrought-iron hands pointed to sixteen minutes past five. With a click they advanced another minute.

4

'Oh!' Jemima said, and stamped her foot, which splashed.

An old gentleman with curly white sidewhiskers, panting from his exertions, thrust his umbrella past her to claim the last seat on the bus, and scrambled aboard. Squeezing into the last possible space on the bench, his knees tucked halfway to his chin, the enormous hat brims of the ladies beside him and opposite him almost meeting over his head, he grinned down at her in toothless victory. Beside Jemima a drenched flower girl slipped from the shelter of a hoarding, her basket empty but for a few broken stems, and nudged with her elbow. ''E's a rude blighter, ain't 'e? Tell 'im it's fer bleedin' Bermondsey.' That was the exact opposite direction from Piccadilly.

'It's for Bermondsey!' Jemima shouted in her well-educated voice.

The cad banged with the flat of his hand to start the vehicle. 'Spink's'll be closed by the time yer got there,' he tossed back at her, but not unkindly, swinging onto the step. 'Try Slippole an' Murge, 'ard by the Monument.'

'Bermondsey?' cried a muffled voice from inside the bus. 'But I'm for Piccadilly.'

'This is fer Piccadilly, just give us yer fare.'

'No, no, you're not getting *me* like that!' There was a commotion and the old man's figure squeezed out through the narrow doorway. 'I wasn't born yesterday, you know!' He jumped down, then stared, his umbrella half up, as his bus swayed into the dark down Southwark Street towards Waterloo and Piccadilly. He threw his umbrella into the puddle.

'Better clear the view,' the flower girl warned in Jemima's ear. 'Pecooliar, some o' them old gents are.' But the old man ran towards the Southwark Street cab stand as a hansom drew up there.

Jemima looked down Long Southwark to the Tabard Inn. She was wet and cold, and the urge to give up and wait for her brothers by a warm fire was very strong. But then the station clock advanced another click, and she clasped her embroidered handbag tightly, feeling the hard, circular shape inside.

'Missing the bus was a blessing in disguise!' she decided in her forthright way; what was lost was lost, and there was no use in crying over spilt milk. Meanwhile the flower girl was sizing her up with practised ease. Her mum called her Betty, or Betty 'Ow

5

Much Yer Get Us Terday, until Miss Betty Owmuch was the name in all honesty she gave the crushers who arrested her and the magistrates who fined her.

'Wot's yer name then?' she demanded, and Jemima told her innocently, when you should never give anything away for nothing. 'Yer spoiling yer dress,' Betty said in disgust. Already the fine purple velvet was speckled black by raindrops and the expensive shoes soaked and muddy, but this pampered young lady didn't seem to care. Betty was fifteen – though she didn't know it, being able to count only to twelve, the number of pennies in a shilling and the most a flower girl needed to know. She had never had a new pair of shoes in her life and never expected to, and the way Jemima took hers for granted was offensive; especially as Betty had an eye for someone on a slippery slope, often knowing before the person herself did. That velvet would be nothing but wrinkles come morning. 'If I 'ad a pair o' shoes like yers,' Betty lectured angrily, 'I'd look after 'em, an' I'd take 'em off an' cuddle 'em while I slept just ter keep me warm, luvverly shoes like that.'

'I suppose so,' Jemima said, drawing back into the shelter. She supposed she must save every penny she had now. It seemed so odd not being able to buy whatever she wanted, having to purchase an embarrassing third-class ticket to travel on the train, even having to realise that by walking she could save herself a few coppers on the bus. She had always taken money for granted and now she had nothing to put in its place.

The clock's hand clicked down another minute and Jemima shook herself. 'Where is the Monument?'

If it hadn't been such a dismal night, Betty knew that the stone column, taller than anything except St Paul's, would have been in plain view across the river. 'I'll show yer,' she offered kindly. 'I live wiv me mum in Candlewick Ward, so it's not too far out me way.' She dodged out and snatched up the umbrella the old gentleman had chucked in the puddle, erecting it with a dripping flourish. 'Let's travel in style! Yer look like yer used ter being dry.'

'I was,' Jemima said, 'but my life has changed.' Again she clasped her bag tight. She hadn't given up hope yet.

'Well then,' Betty said brightly, 'yer'll just 'ave ter learn ter be like me.'

6

'Hurry up!' Jemima said, putting her best foot forward. She was within a few days of her eighteenth birthday, accustomed to giving orders and not yet prepared to be anything but the leader. Betty hustled after her with the umbrella and her flower basket, worrying that the rain was easing off and she would no longer be needed. As they hurried across London Bridge they saw the East End like a vast glimmering dullness on their right. The new roads winding to the docks were gaslit and every pub flaunted its own brilliant gas globe over the door, so it was the meanest and poorest districts that gleamed, from this distance, most like jewels; the Thames, bare of bridges below this point, showed the outline of the Pool and the river's loop into the distance round the Isle of Dogs, revealed by the thousands of ships' riding lights.

'Don't rush it so fast,' puffed Betty as they trudged uphill from the bridge. 'It's not a blooming race. It's all right fer yer, but I bin working all day.'

'Give the umbrella to me then.'

'No. An' I ain't 'ad nuffink ter eat neither.' Betty stopped. 'Wot's got into yer? Life's too short ter 'urry, an' I got this nice umbrella. I'm off 'ome ter me mum,' she called as Jemima kept walking. 'If yer want a roof over yer 'ead tonight just ask fer Smith's in Crooked Street, the blue door. We got a Guy's medical student wot lodges, our 'Enry Summers, poor as a church mouse.' She added spitefully under her breath, 'An' 'e speaks just like yer.'

Jemima, too busy searching for the shop to have patience with the girl, or to acknowledge what she said, found she didn't need the umbrella, it had stopped raining. She hurried up Fish Hill Street, a scandalous area smelling of fish and blood from Billingsgate below it. By the clock advertising a watch repairer's, she saw it was nearly five thirty. The sky was clearing and now she saw the Monument looming over the rooftops, but no sign of any coin dealers round the little square. She ran across into Pudding Lane, and found the place at once. A doorway was set down some steps and above the lintel she made out a faded signboard, gilt letters on dark blue: 'Slippole, Murge and Son, Coin Dealers, Expert Valuations Undertaken, Gold and Silver Purchased'. In the bow window a small sign was hung, *Open*. As she watched, a hand appeared and turned the sign over, *Closed*.

7

'Wait!' She ran down the steps before the hand could turn the lock, and pushed open the door.

She went down two more steps into the shop, and closed the door carefully behind her. It was like entering another world. The air was dusty and smelt of old waxed wood. The dust came from the bare floorboards, but the counter by the black window was immaculately polished, holding the reflection of the old man behind it. The only light came from the lantern beside his hand, scrawny as a chicken's claw. Jemima could see plainly he was dying; his strength was almost gone.

Jemima thought she knew all about slow death. She had witnessed her father's. She knew the lies men told themselves to keep going.

'Can't you see we're closed!' he said.

Two paces brought Jemima to the counter, where she put down her bag. 'Do I have the honour of addressing Mr Slippole or Mr Murge?'

'I am Mr Elias Slippole, but we are *closed*.' Women did not come into his shop to buy, and being a good businessman Slippole waited for her to make the first move as a measure of her desperation.

'But your door was open, sir,' she said, 'and I have something that will fascinate you.'

'You all say that,' he informed her haughtily. 'Come back tomorrow.'

She looked at him with pity. There was not an ounce of spare flesh on him and his skin resembled waxed paper. She recognised that transparent look. His wasted frame supported a large, rounded head; mutton-chop whiskers curled as thin as spun sugar round his jutting cheekbones. Above them his pale steady eyes surveyed her with the automatic hunger of a long life in a lean business. Elias Slippole did not see her for herself but for what he could make out of her.

Jemima remembered her father on his deathbed begging her to bring him one last little one, for pity's sake, but she saw no such humility in Slippole's cold merciless gaze; he was not quite so near death.

'Sir, tomorrow will be too late,' Jemima admitted. Tomorrow they would all be gone.

She looked past him as the curtain to the back room moved. Perhaps there was a draught.

'Very well, show me,' old Slippole sighed impatiently, having asserted himself. 'I have seen everything, you know.' He propped his withered hands flat on the counter, leaving a space between them, waiting. Jemima took the coin from her bag and placed it there.

She did not know what she expected, but she knew what she hoped: she hoped that Slippole's sad, sly old face would light up, his mortal cunning drop away, and he'd examine the coin with lively eyes, growing excitement, childish enthusiasm. That head, large as a memory-man's, must contain whole catalogues, a lifetime of accumulated facts.

But Elias Slippole gazed at the coin without a word, unimpressed. He felt himself beyond surprise. After a long lifetime as an acknowledged master of his trade, he'd seen it all, knew it all.

The curtain moved again and Jemima was sure that younger eyes were watching her shiftily between the curtain rings – nearly seven feet off the ground, he must be standing on a chair – studying her body as the old man studied the coin, but with a good deal more interest.

'It's old,' Slippole grunted, without moving his hands. 'And it's big – big enough to fit in the palm of a man's hand. Wouldn't get many in his pocket, would he? *Would* he?'

'No, sir,' Jemima agreed. 'I've never seen anything like it.'

Slippole peered closer at the coin, showing her the lice crawling in the pink crown of his hair. 'No, wasn't made for pockets,' he mumbled. 'No denomination, wasn't meant to be money. Struck for presentation, then. Out of pure silver, apparently.'

'It's been in my family for many years,' Jemima talked the price up. No sign of attention from that crawling globe of spun-sugar hair. 'My father and my grandmother, and she could remember *her* grandmother . . . probably much longer than that.' She hesitated. 'Nobody knows. We never needed to know before.' No movement. Jemima licked her lips. 'It's something, isn't it?' she asked. 'We children always called them the talents – and probably my great-grandparents did too, when they were children. It's been a family tradition for . . . for ever.'

Slippole raised his head and looked at her, then gave a dry

snort. 'You need not pretend with me. Family this, heirloom that, sentimental value. Sentimental claptrap!' he cackled. 'People only come in here to know how much a thing is worth.'

'No, sir, I am – we are all – interested in it for itself.' Jemima tried to sound confident. 'Is it worth . . . how much?' Her voice trembled. She was not even convincing herself. She and her brothers, having been born to fortune, now needed a further stroke of good fortune desperately, more than anyone who had not already been lucky would understand. A way of life died hard.

Looking into her eyes at the vulnerability that she was trying to conceal from him, Slippole was too exhausted to smile at the girl's frailty. She had a strong face, and that red hair lay in strong coils on her shoulders, but she couldn't lie to him and he knew he'd get this for almost nothing in the end, take it or leave it. The baubles, each with their story, he'd been offered in his day: tawdry medals on mothy strips of ribbon, the proudest moments in the lives of husbands who would never return exchanged for a meal or a week's rent for the family left behind; medals and medallions ten a penny, even a pathetic girl selling a Victoria Cross for a song, but what did she know of gallantry, or honour, or heroism? He never paid tuppence where a penny would do. In his prime he'd twirl his whiskers and bark out a price, no negotiation; they'd come in brave-faced as lions but creep out quiet as lambs. He'd paid pennies for a load of dross just for the Newark half-crown he spied in it; and once a lovely Queen Anne shilling with roses and plumes caught inside a medal ribbon. This was how he had to make his living. 'Fourpence ha'penny the lot!' Done.

Old Mr Murge, now, that man had been a romantic; that was why the name Slippole, who had joined second, was now first on the shop board.

'It is true that my father is dead and we have fallen on straightened times,' Jemima recited her rehearsed lines clearly. 'I do not mean by that admission that I would sell this talent, or consider accepting a lower price than its true value.'

Slippole twitched his shoulders without weight, his equivalent of a shrug, knowing he could eat her alive at this business. 'A thing is worth what someone will pay for it.' He glanced at last towards the curtain. 'Young Mr Murge! Shop, if you please!'

Caught out, Slippole's youthful partner, Murge, fumbled the

curtain aside in feigned surprise. 'I didn't know anyone was here,' he lied, and Jemima knew it was his eyes she had felt peeping all over her. He was tall like a beanpole, he didn't need a chair to spy through the curtain rings. She looked up into a long sharp face and shy, luminous eyes and all but laughed at him. His baggy black suit could not conceal scrawny white ankles and wrists that showed every vein, and his black hair was slicked into a fashionable kiss-curl on his high forehead. He bumped his head on the curtain pole as he ducked through.

Murge smoothed his ruffled hair, aware of his loss of dignity in front of her. Tall though he was, he lived in Slippole's shadow.

'You'll oblige me with your clear eyes, Mr Murge. The young lady claims this is a talent!' scoffed old Slippole with a demeaning flick of his fingers.

'It's very beautiful,' the young man murmured in his light, melodious voice, with hardly a glance at the coin. From upstairs came the sound of a baby crying, then footsteps went creaking above their heads and the crying stopped. Murge dragged those large eyes, which lent his face distinction, from Jemima and he caressed the coin with his fingertip, as if assaying its value by touch alone. 'Yes, most beautiful.'

'That doesn't drive the price up,' Slippole told Jemima with an angry look at Murge.

'You see, Miss . . . ah . . .' Murge began.

'Fox.'

'You see, Miss Fox, a talent simply means "beyond value". Like beauty. The parable of the talents just says "For to every one that hath shall be given". Abundance, the full weight. The more you have, the more you get. That is the way of the world, is it not? Some people seem to have every advantage in life, don't they?' Those staring eyes seemed to probe every contour of her face. 'Strictly speaking it was not a unit of money so much as a burden, the weight of silver a donkey could carry on its back all day. The weight of a man, perhaps, depending on whether you go by the Old Testament or the New.'

'Of the Bible?' Jemima was amazed. 'But that's old!'

'I'm sure this thing is not,' Slippole put in quickly.

'Every culture gave the talent a different weight,' Murge went on. 'Romans, Greeks, Babylonians, Assyrians, the Jews—'

11

'Mr Murge is too clever for his own good,' Slippole interrupted. 'You are boring the young lady with your rambling, Mr Murge. Now, let me assess—'

'But it always meant beyond value,' Murge said.

Slippole gave an angry, warning rap with his knuckles on the counter. But Phineas Murge was a young man who could not stop his tongue, he blew with the wind and swam with the tide, just like his father, blinded by his enthusiasm. They had no sense of personal advantage, that family. Slippole despaired at the thought of the profits of his labour eventually passing into those hands. Murge had no grasp of the one thing that must dominate a coin dealer's life: the value of money.

'You'd never hold a man's weight of silver in your arms, miss, would you?' Murge laughed, hoping to see Jemima laugh, but her expression remained pale and serious. 'Sometimes it was even taken to be a state of mind – of will, or desire, or of . . . other things.' Two spots of colour appeared on his cheeks. 'Passion.'

'Or *anger*,' warned Slippole peevishly. 'Thank you, Mr Murge, that will be quite enough.'

But Murge could not stop. 'Roman coins are ten-a-penny, miss, mudlarks and sewer-hunters are always fishing them out of the Thames.'

'Just what I was going to say!' exclaimed Slippole with relief.

But Murge, watching Jemima's face, suddenly plucked up the coin, taking it seriously for no better reason than because she did. 'Actually, Slippole, it *is* rather interesting. Have you seen this?'

'I've seen enough,' Slippole said through tight lips.

'Mint condition.' Murge fiddled an acetylene lamp from under the counter. 'Look out!' He lit it, and they all shielded their eyes from the brilliant white glare, then blinked at the coin flashing between his fingers. 'Facing to the right, that's unusual. And a cruel old face it is too.' Murge rotated it to read the inscription. ' "TI.CAESAR.AUG." Tiberius Julius Caesar, Augustus – which means Emperor, ' he explained for Jemima's benefit. ' "DIVI F.AUG PONT.MAX." Son of the Divine Augustus, and Grand Pontiff too.' He grinned at Jemima. 'Some fellows have all the luck, don't they?'

'The Emperor Tiberius was a man of most unattractive tastes,' Slippole informed her censoriously, as if this unpalatable

12

information must drag down the worth of the Roman coin still further. 'He was the Caesar of the Gospels: "Render therefore unto Caesar the things which are Caesar's." Still, that dates the thing between AD 14 and 37, more likely the latter part of his reign, given his apparent age.' He screwed a magnifying glass into his eye and Jemima watched the two experts examine the face closely, both obviously fascinated but confused by what they saw, their voices muttering between themselves in the thick, dusty air – the acetylene glare picked out each swirling mote. She listened with all the patience she could muster and a church clock chimed slowly, then a lantern flickered across the darkness of the window-panes – someone being shown home. 'Please hurry,' she said, and both men looked at her, startled, the light flinging deep shadows into their faces, then went back to their mumbling.

'Your opinion, Mr Murge? Too big for a denarius, surely, and there's an Eastern influence. . . .'

'Minted to the Greek Standard, Mr Slippole? Tyre or Antioch, perhaps.'

'Too big even to be a stater coin, Mr Murge.' Slippole turned it over. 'That does it. Look at that! Forgery, plain and simple.'

'We are not accusing you, miss,' Murge said hastily, when Jemima coloured. 'It's just that – well, look.'

He traced his forefinger over the shape on the reverse, and when Jemima leaned close a strand of her hair fell across his hand. 'A candlestick with seven branches?'

'The Menorah, an important and complex Jewish symbol of the Light.' His gaze travelled over her face and rested on her mouth as she swept back her hair. 'A celebration of the Law. The Menorah was hammered, not cast, from a talent's weight of gold and kept in the tabernacle. By the time of Christ it was in the Holy of Holies of King Herod's great golden temple in Jerusalem, dazzling in the sun.'

'Politics in those days was just as difficult and complicated as it is for us, no doubt!' chuckled Slippole indulgently, slipping Murge the secret sign to shut his mouth and find something better to do in the back room.

'The Jews didn't have politics. They had religion.' Murge was still looking at Jemima. 'See this Hebrew inscription. Glory in the centre, Kingdom to the left, Power on the right. Some men believe the Menorah guides us to the order in which the Apostles were seated for the Last Supper – I mean the real Last Supper, Miss Fox, not the da Vinci painting. If that sort of distinction means anything to you.'

'Now, now,' Slippole hummed. 'This is not suitable talk for young ladies.'

'But if this coin is nearly two thousand years old,' Jemima said, 'surely that makes it very valuable.'

'It is almost worthless,' Slippole interjected quickly, 'because it is certainly a forgery. It purports to have been struck in Jerusalem by the Jews towards the end of Tiberius's reign. This word JEB is for "Jebus", the ancient city of Jerusalem captured by King David. The land belonged to a primitive clan called Jebusites; its use may symbolise, or propose, military victory.'

'It may be a coded reference to David as King of the Jews,' Murge amplified. 'Descendants of King David were still around during the New Testament, you know, fallen on hard times but living in hope of great days again. The Essenes. Awaiting their Messiah. Perhaps this reflects that fact.'

'The Jews struck their coins in Caesarea,' Slippole said flatly. 'There was no Jewish silver mint in Jerusalem. This is a forgery and, worse, an ignorant one. Two thousand years old? No more than I.'

'Perhaps they made an exception for some reason,' said Jemima hopefully.

Both men laughed. Slippole showed no mercy. 'At that time the Jews struck coins only in copper or bronze.'

'And not many of them,' Murge said. 'So few that even their half-shekel temple tax was paid in Greek drachmas and God knows what. That's why there were so many moneychangers in the temple – they were the only ones who knew what everything was worth.'

Slippole grinned, understanding such men. 'There were no Jewish silver coins until their great rebellion of 66, thirty or forty years after the purported date of this clumsy forgery. It cannot possibly be real, Miss Fox. You and your parents have been fooled by a fake.'

'But silver was very special to the Jews,' Murge said thought-fully. 'In the Bible it sometimes symbolises the purifying effects of suffering.'

Slippole made his offer. 'Miss Fox, I can give you a silver shilling for it. Not a penny more,' he said arrogantly.

'But why should a forgery be made with such a heavy weight of silver?' Jemima appealed to Murge. 'And why should anyone make a forgery so easy to detect?'

Murge was silent. He couldn't meet her eye.

'We don't have the answer!' Slippole said, handing the coin back. 'Whatever you have here, Miss Fox, it is not money, and we're shutting up shop now. I'll melt it down for the value of the silver, no more. Mr Murge, if you would see to the door.'

'I won't sell.' Jemima clenched the coin in her palm. 'I don't care what you gentlemen say. I don't care if it *is* false.' Her voice rose. 'It's been in our family for as long as anyone knows, and it's lucky, I *feel* it, and nothing you two can say will change my mind.' She stared at them defiantly.

Slippole shrugged and went to the back room, then glanced round his knuckles on the curtain. 'Remember, a silver shilling. I've made my offer.' The curtain swung closed and his voice came from behind it, muffled and weary. 'Good night.'

Murge obediently went up to the steps to the door. Jemima slipped the coin back in her bag and wiped the corner of her eye with her fingertip, then went quickly past him. Suddenly he reached out and caught her wrist in his long, mobile fingers.

'Miss Fox?' He cricked his neck upwards as again the baby cried above them, and footsteps went creaking across the ceiling.

'Well, Mr Murge?'

Outside, the rainclouds parted to reveal the moon gleaming off the cobblestones. 'May I talk to you for a moment?'

'I am in a great rush and late already.'

He took a pace after her into the night. 'These streets are dangerous for a young lady alone.' He looked her in the eye. 'If I may light your way, I would take it as an honour.'

'Thank you,' she said bitterly, 'but it seems I have nothing worth stealing.'

'You have you.'

She stared at him, then turned away abruptly.

'Don't go,' he begged.

'You are being foolish, Mr Murge.' In the yellow window above them she glimpsed the silhouette of a mother cuddling her baby.

'I have been foolish all my life, until now.' But he saw she would

15

never stay with him, or let him accompany her. 'I overheard . . . I could not help myself . . . I overheard you tell old Slippole that as children you and your brothers called *them* the talents. Are there more?'

She looked surprised. 'Yes, there are six others, one for each of my brothers. They are our inheritance, all our father could not drink. By legend there were once twenty-nine, but the rest have all been lost or destroyed. Probably melted down by people like you.'

'I'm not like that,' he said yearningly.

'Our family ends tonight,' Jemima Fox said. 'None of us will ever return to Holywell, where we were children and happy. Now I don't know what will happen to us all. And the coins are worthless forgeries.'

Phineas Murge stood alone in the doorway with his tall head bent. He watched her figure hurrying away from him through the moonlight and blue shadows.

'I wish I had a penny for every girl we've had in here like that,' came Slippole's voice from behind the curtain, then the sound of the kettle bubbling, and Murge hated him. 'Well, my young Phineas, you managed not to blurt out the answer to her question. Why should anyone make such an expensive forgery so easy to detect?'

'Because it's real,' Murge said. 'It's as real as real can be.'

'She'll be back,' came Slippole's yawn.

The kettle whistled.

It was now or never. Murge bent his long body behind the counter and pulled out his stovepipe hat. He doused the lantern and crept out, closing the door softly, then put on his hat and ran. He ran with both hands holding down the hat brim, his coat tails flapping, past the Monument, until he came to Fish Hill Street.

Jemima hurried through the glowing pools of light beneath the gas lamps down Fish Hill Street. The darkness between them was made deeper by its contrast with the glinting river which curved round Southwark and Rotherhithe, reflecting the light of the moon which had emerged from behind the rainclouds. She paused to look behind her, grateful for the tread of a passing policeman with his bull's-eye lantern at his belt. He moved on a woman and three children huddled in a doorway, and Jemima remembered her father once telling her that such lost souls were sometimes found dead of hunger outside the West End hotel where he and she had just eaten for two pounds a head. Her father knew about lost souls. He was one, enjoying nothing without feeling guilty afterwards.

She walked quickly onto London Bridge, looking down on the banks of mist drifting through the spans beneath her, the moon going in for a moment and London rushing down like a dark cloud around her; then her eyes adjusted and she made out the glimmering gaslights once again. City clerks pattered past her, going home to their wives and children, but the traffic was thinning, the life of the day losing its pace, night-London coming out as though a coin had been flipped, as different from the London that she knew as night from day. Jemima looked behind her several times as she walked down the far slope of the bridge, thinking she heard footsteps, but saw nothing to worry her. At last she came back into Southwark. Men were crouched round a road-mender's brazier pitching coppers, calling penny heads, penny tails, but they did not raise their heads from their game. Jemima heard a girl laugh, slouched with a sailor in a grimy doorway, her wrists on his shoulders, but he had eyes only for Jemima.

She hurried past the railway station, now almost deserted, then down Long Southwark. The moon came out again, throwing this side of the Borough High Street into darkness.

The archway leading to the Tabard Inn had a house, number 75, built over it, and the crooked wooden gates beneath were patched with rusty iron. Jemima slipped between them into a long courtyard filled with chalky light, carts and drays stored everywhere in heaps of shadow, a tall coach rotting in a little-used corner with 'William Parkhurst and Son, Daily Stagewagons to the Tabard Inn, Borough' still visible on the canvas hood. The railway had killed off coach trade in the last thirty years or so and the Tabard was running to seed, the stables mostly empty, though the smooth round balls used to keep the horses apart in busier days had been left dangling from their chains, as though the place expected lively crowds to return any moment. A wing of outbuildings, tall and tottering and full of shadows, jutted across the courtyard from the tumbledown main structure – a farrier's workshop, the Garrns Brothers warehouse, hop stores, a tiny cottage, then another small courtyard opening beyond. Above and around them all rose the overhanging wooden galleries and cranky staircases of the Tabard, bound with bands of iron where the planks were giving way, climbing to a mess of high sloping roofs and cock lofts. Higher still, the many chimneys against the moon streamed cold blue smoke mixed with a few merry sparks.

Blowing on her hands – the temperature was dropping rapidly with the clearing sky – Jemima crossed the yard and ducked indoors.

Inside was the usual warm, human confusion of smells and pushing, shoving people that she could not yet accept as normal, a whole new world to her: everything dirty, every armchair sag-bottomed and every bench worn smooth by its customers, even the low oak beam scalloped into a curve where everyone banged their heads, the squeaking floors crooked and the walls dark yellow with generations of pipe smoke.

A girl saw Jemima and ducked down behind the counter. No servile waiters in white jackets here, only sluttish barmaids who surveyed her with half-closed eyes. Jemima pretended she knew it all and went through the rooms, one after the other, her nose assaulted by the smell of tobacco, beer and boiled vegetables, soiled sheets, bad teeth and unwashed feet, down hallways and up stairs that seemed to lead in every direction to dead ends, parlours and taprooms. Snatches of lantern light slanted through low doorways and she heard rough talk of trade, then passed a dark room with no one in it but the pale shape of a small boy crying on a bench, his swinging feet not touching the floor; Jemima took a candle from the corridor and left it on the table so that he would not be so frightened. Across the landing, silently watching her from a private parlour, three old ladies sat in wooden chairs drinking tea.

Jemima hurried on, three steps up, then three down, and the corridor turned to her right. The Tabard must be very old, older, by its appearance, than Holywell. It seemed to have grown in an organic way, spreading itself a room at a time, filling it, moving on to the next. Sam, her grandfather, had been born here, and perhaps his bloating heart (apparently he had put on weight dreadfully in his last years) had always remained within these walls. Jemima did not remember him, only the indomitable, passionate, repressed figure of Amanda, her grandmother, at Holywell, her grace and delicacy concealed beneath the awkwardness of her body – she had been born, tragically, with a club foot – and an upper-class reserve cast of iron. Jemima had admired her desperately, but now she was quite sure that if her grandmother had ever visited her husband's birthplace here, it had not been more than once. Jemima stopped, lost. Then she heard Reuben singing.

She turned back on herself, retracing her steps, and found a doorway she had missed. As she opened the door, Reuben's voice was suddenly loud – no, *rich*; he was a fine tenor. Before his voice broke he had been sweet even on the highest notes in the St John's choir, much better than a small parish church knew what to do with. Their father forbade a private singing master, then even turned down a scholarship, and for the first time the older children – Martin, Frank and George, anyway, because Harold and Jerome always kept their own counsel – began to realise that something horrible was happening. 'I'm sorry, I'm sorry,' Father had stormed, dragging them all down with him like a drowning man in his despair, 'it's just the way things are.'

The room Jemima came into was not large, but even so her six brothers gathered in a semicircle round the fire looked small and lost. The handmade firebricks of the chimney breast were crumbling with age, red as blood where flames had not blackened them, loading the room with a lurid flickering light. Reuben's voice fell silent. Martin, the eldest, caught feeding the conflagration from the coal scuttle, hid the tongs behind him thinking she was the landlord.

'Oh, Mimmy!' he exclaimed. 'Where in heaven's name had you got to?'

'Don't call me Mimmy,' Jemima said tersely, 'and your britches are on fire.'

He pulled the tongs away and slapped his backside in case she wasn't joking, but Reuben came to her holding out his arms and hugged her to his stiff salty peajacket. 'She's freezing!' He pulled her to the fire, rubbing her hands. 'Welcome to the Pilgrims' Room. We've been worried about you.'

'There was no need, Reuben,' she smiled.

Jerome took the long clay pipe from his mouth for a moment, tapped it lightly on the iron firedog. He had a degree in theology from Spurgeon College and he was training to take Holy Orders. 'There's never any need to worry about Jemima, we know that.'

'She wants to look after herself?' Frank shrugged. 'She won't get a husband.' He was the second eldest son after Martin and carried a train ticket for Liverpool in his pocket: in ten days his ship would be steaming up the St Lawrence towards a new life in the Canadian wilderness. On a map his pin had found a place north of Ottawa called Paradise, and to convince himself of his commitment to the endless forests, he had already bought an axe, less in resolve than lest his resolve should fail.

'Are you all right – really?' Reuben studied Jemima's eyes.

'I had it valued.' She turned to the fire and warmed her hands.

'*More* good news,' Martin said, tossing the tongs back into the scuttle.

'Good news,' said Harold, the gentlest of them and the lucky one, 'is something that happens to other people.' By putting it like that he was trying to keep in touch with the constant disappointments of his brothers, yet he was the only one of them who was going of his own free will, not because he had to: his girl, Kate, an only child, lived with her father in a farm on the Waldingfield road near Sudbury in Suffolk. She and Harold were bumped together on the crowded train to Kent where she was visiting an aunt, and in her Harold had met all he wanted from life.

'Tell us what happened, Jemima,' Reuben said kindly, taking over command from Martin, who was too careful and methodical to give this youthful wreckage of the once proud family the lead they needed. Reuben was only eleven months older than Jemima, and it was his cheery, amoral recklessness that she would miss most. He had signed on as a deckhand aboard ship, sailing at dawn from the St Mary Overie dock by London Bridge with a cargo of ironware for the Baltic. 'I'll soon have a girl in every port,' he had bragged to Jemima. 'I'll marry them all, take over the shipping company and staff it with my children.' But he should sing. 'I'll have a fine voice for shouting orders over the gales,' he'd laughed at her concern.

'Just give the girl a drink,' George said, pulling a hip flask from his pocket and splashing a generous measure of whisky into an unwashed glass, holding it up to her without wiping the rim. He was blowing the last of his money on an hotel and a saucy girl tonight, then shipping on a wool clipper to Australia. It was his intention to step onto the Fremantle dockside without a farthing to his name, living each day as it came. Jemima drank. 'Go on, finish it.' He leant back in his chair and propped his feet on the arm of another, his leather boots creaking.

'I think I'd better call the meeting to order,' Martin said.

'Let the girl speak,' George said. Jerome pushed his feet off the chair with his own. 'I wouldn't hit a man of the cloth,' George threatened him, 'unless he was my brother.'

'I'm not of the cloth yet.'

'One day, Romeo, you'll have that parson's nose.'

'Many are called,' Jerome said, 'but few are chosen. You'll be sorry when I'm archbishop. And if you kick me again I'll muddy your boots with my dirty soles.'

'Souls,' Martin punned. His quick intelligence always picked up on that sort of thing. Being far too clever, he had lost almost all his authority with the brothers.

'Give me my whisky,' George appealed to Jemima, 'before my dear sainted Jerome makes me repent and pay the landlord corkage.'

'The talents aren't worth anything,' Jemima told them, handing back the glass. 'I missed my appointment at Spink's but I found this other place near the Monument, called Slippole and Murge. Perhaps not trustworthy, but quite expert, and I think the young one had his heart in the right place – and he did not contradict the older man's offer. But he hardly took his eyes off me,' she blushed.

'True love,' Jerome said.

'Not a suitable suitor at all!'

'You'll have to find someone rich to marry,' Harold said.

'Those worthless trinkets have always meant something special to you, haven't they, Mimmy?' Martin shrugged. 'I'm sorry you're disappointed. Myself, I never had a hope.'

'How much for the last piece of family plate exactly?' George demanded.

'A shilling.'

'Strewth!' George rummaged in his pocket and flicked her something that came flashing through the firelight. 'Have mine, go on. Remember me for old time's sake.'

She turned his talent over in her hands, taken aback that he had given it so easily.

'It's all Father left us. It's lucky.'

'Yes, I noticed how lucky we've been recently,' said George with heaviness. 'At least my liver hasn't given out, and I don't pee steam.' Jerome caught his eye disapprovingly. 'Sorry, Jemima.'

'What do you mean, "all", Jemima?' Frank picked up.

'They're not *all* Father left us?' Jerome said. He looked round the semicircle of their faces. 'Oh, hell.' He covered his mouth. 'I mean, there's been some mistake. Surely?'

'You were busy with your work,' Martin said, 'I was up to my eyeballs at the College of Pharmacy, and you others were coming and going, except Jemima and Reuben who were too young. We should have listened to them.'

'It wasn't your fault, Martin,' Reuben said. 'None of us really understood how much Father was getting through until it was too late. It's unbelievable how cunning he was.'

'After he had passed away, Reuben and I found bottles everywhere,' Jemima confessed. 'It was awful. Worse than him dying almost.' Reuben hugged her with one arm, nodding. 'We found them hidden under the stairs, under stones in the garden, even crammed into the old hollow tree. It turned out the drawers in his desk were full of empties, not papers – we could hardly get them open. Even the ornamental fountain had whisky bottles sunk in it. Nobody had the faintest idea until old Jake drained it to clear the dead leaves.'

'Thank God our mother never lived to see it,' Martin said glumly.

'I thought the pool was supposed to be bottomless,' Frank said, always ready to nitpick.

'That's the fountain,' Jemima said distractedly. 'The pool's only eighteen inches deep, what do you think the water lilies grew from?'

'Everything in this old country is a lie,' George said, refilling his glass. 'I won't be sorry to shake the dust from my feet.'

'Everything's not a lie,' Jerome said.

'Father was,' said Frank bitterly. 'He was a lie. He lied to us.'

Martin shook his head. 'He was such a wise man. I don't know what made him go so wrong, taking such pleasure in destroying himself.'

'It wasn't pleasure,' Jemima said quietly, 'it was an agony. Don't forget Reuben and I were with him at the end, when he was bedridden. He knew he had thrown everything away. I can imagine what it cost him to start begging me for liquor, can't you?' She shivered. 'Just a sip at a time, towards the end. And that sip was all he was.'

She took the pocket watch from her bag and put it on the table. Frank reached out and examined it, opening the case, putting the movement to his ear.

Martin rapped on the table with his knuckles. 'I call the meeting to order.'

'I've got a train to catch,' Frank reminded him.

'Order!' Martin snapped. 'To summarise. Father's investments: there were no investments. Mother's jewellery: sold.'

'What about her rings?' Jemima asked.

'Gone. Father burned the receipts, because he was so ashamed, I suppose. We don't even know where he got rid of them, one of those little backstreet shops in Greenwich probably. Either he missed these talents,' Martin sighed, 'or he knew they were rubbish. He even sold his childhood toys, mementos. Then he started on the library – and there were books in there that were written by hand, four or five hundred years old, from before printing. I don't think anybody knew everything that was there. First editions, everything the family had gathered together and cared about and built up. Sold to buy bottles.'

'Don't drink any more,' Jerome told George.

'Don't worry, you won't get me,' George said.

'You'll get like our father.'

'That's enough,' said Jemima.

'Order!' Martin said, coming to the worst part. 'He mortgaged Holywell in its entirety: house, grounds, the Mickfield, everything.'

'Spare us, just give us the cash realisation,' Harold said.

'Mortgaged to the hilt.'

'Lock, stock and barrel?' Frank demanded furiously. 'Not one penny left over?'

'The house was locked this afternoon,' Jemima said. 'The

bailiffs chained the gates, had the house sealed, posted notices. It's theirs.'

'Not one penny!'

'All you care about is money, Frank,' said Reuben. 'We're all in the same boat.'

'Exactly,' Martin agreed. 'We share equally, even with Jemima though she's a girl.'

'Share nothing equally!' laughed Reuben. 'How much is there?'

'He overlooked a few books. Some items of furniture, porcelain, armour. They might fetch a little. On the other hand there were wages due, and solicitors' bills. The farm owed tithes,' he glanced at Jerome, 'but we paid the Church in pigs.'

'You can't expect me to start a new life in a strange land with nothing in my pocket,' Frank said.

'Nine pounds, six and eightpence each.'

'That's something!' Reuben laughed. 'That makes me richer than any other deckhand I know.'

'And the seven talents,' Martin said gloomily, 'one each, to do with as you will.' George winked at Jemima. 'Father's gold pocket watch. I vote Frank has that, he's always in such a hurry. A cutthroat razor and badger-hair shaving brush. . . .'

His voice filled Jemima with exhaustion. She leant her head on the great oak beam, blackened and gnarled with age, that supported the weight of the chimney breast above them. The flames below flickered through her closed eyelids, and Martin's voice droned on, and on.

'There's nothing left for Jemima,' Jerome said.

'She's a girl,' Frank said.

'You got his gold watch, Frank,' George pointed out, 'that was the best thing going and what you wanted, so give Jemima something she wants.'

Frank stared blankly. 'Oh, this?' He fished out his silver coin from his pocket, tossed it to her without looking at it. 'She can have that to remember the past by. The rotten worthless past.' He kissed the gold case of the watch.

'But why should a forgery be made with such a heavy weight of silver?' Jemima repeated, looking round their faces. 'Why should anyone make a forgery so easy to detect? And this one seems to have whorls and marks melted into it, as if by burning fingers.'

'You're a silly, romantic little girl,' Martin said, kissing her forehead.

'I should have thought our father's terrible death would have beaten that stuffing out of you,' George grunted.

'But I'm *not* romantic or silly.'

'You're a girl.'

'You don't understand,' Jemima said. 'None of you do.'

'Why's this so difficult for you, Jemima?' Harold frowned.

'It's just a feeling.'

'A woman's feeling.' George patted her shoulder, patronising but meaning it kindly. 'Well, it's getting late, I must set off,' he said, and began shaking hands with his brothers for the last time.

'I'm afraid,' Jemima whispered. 'Once we were together. Now we're setting off on our travels to I don't know where, and I don't think we'll ever come back.'

'I told you this is the Pilgrims' Room,' Reuben smiled. 'I chose it specially for you. From this inn, from this very room, Jemima, Chaucer's pilgrims started their once-in-a-lifetime journey to Canterbury, *anno* 1387.' He pointed, and for the first time she noticed the splitting wooden plaque hung from a greasy black chain high above the fireplace.

' "In Southwark at the Tabard as I lay," ' she read, ' "ready to wend on my pilgrimage to Canterbury, at night was come to that hostelry nine and twenty in a company, sundry folk, by chance fallen on fellowship, and pilgrims all. . . ." ' Her lips moved. 'Nine and twenty. The same as the number of the talents, once.'

'It's just a story,' Reuben said, hugging her goodbye. 'Probably this room wasn't really even here then.'

Jemima stared upwards. 'We aren't pilgrims,' she said, 'we're emigrants.'

'Jemima, Jemima, don't take it so seriously. Look after yourself,' he added in a whisper, for herself alone. He kissed her lips looking into her eyes, then turned away lightly on his heel, the usual Reuben again who behaved as though he would never grow up, pretending nothing touched him. 'Must rush!' he laughed to the others. "Bye, everyone! May good fortune attend you all your days, in all your ways!'

Martin said goodbye to Reuben then crossed the room to Jemima. 'He's just like you, Jemima,' he tried to joke. 'Always late. Where will you stay tonight?'

'I'll think of somewhere, Martin.'

'I'm at the Pharmaceutical Society in Bloomsbury Square. If you want to get in touch, they'll have my address.'

'Martin, if there's any chance you don't want—'

'It's mine,' Martin said possessively. 'What's mine is mine.'

'I just wanted something to remember us by,' she whispered. The fire was dying down, filling the room with darkness. 'Remembering when we were all children at Holywell, and Mother and Father were with us, and we were happy.'

'That's all over now,' said Martin.

St George's beat out ten chimes, and Phineas Murge waited.

Opposite the Tabard Inn, in the middle of the road where once a church had stood, was set an island of shops and the London and South-Western Bank, with Counter Street like an alleyway running between them, and it was here that he hid.

Murge blew on his long fingers; they were numb with cold. He folded them in the dark beneath his pointed chin, squeezing his lapels together to hold what was left of the warmth in his thin body. His mother, God bless her memory, had never been able to feed him up however hard she tried with steak and kidney puddings, fat pork crackling, always the best, and vast indulgent scoops of broad beans swimming in butter, so that his earliest childhood memories were of how different he was. And as an adult, how much more he deserved. He was always hungry.

He could not get the girl out of his mind.

This side of the street was fixed in brilliant moonlight, which made the shadows very deep; a man lurching down the narrow alley pissed a pale stream on the bricks within ten feet of him, and never a clue. A slut strolled by giggling on the arm of her swell, then said, 'No, don't, it's too cold,' and he said, 'I know 'ow ter warm yer up.' From further away a woman was scolding her cat, then a window slammed.

Still Murge waited, but the girl did not come. His mind was so fixed on her that he was hardly aware of the life going on around him in the dark.

Two portly types in hats almost walked him into the wall, talking. 'Yes, sir, and if my aunt had been an uncle, she'd've been a man. . . .' Their voices grew. 'Balls under her arse, that one.'

Murge shrank back at the last moment, close enough to touch, but they passed by with no idea of him.

Again he nerved himself to peep round the narrow shop front on the corner of Counter Street, almost opposite the Tabard here, but sheltered by the island of buildings. Through the Tabard gateway an enormous man waddled into view, his shadow flung in front of him, an apron strapped over his bulging belly, his legs dropping so thickly to swollen ankles that he seemed balanced on feet as petite as pigs' trotters. He yawned and drew in a deep breath, exhaling a stream of vapour before turning back. In the gateway he bumped into a willowy young man coming out, who apologised and hurried away towards the railway station. Two more followed, the landlord raising one plump arm, a table leg carved of fat and muscle, to let them pass between his body and the wall. A door slammed closed.

Murge couldn't get the picture of her red hair out of his brain, lying coiled on her purple velvet shoulders like nothing he could have imagined. Red and purple, a dangerous and sublime combination of colours, and her deep brown eyes. Miss Fox. Her lips white with shame or anger, he'd guessed, at what she had come down to, having to deal with people like him. One look at her and he'd known he would never forget her, and he had hated old Slippole's shameless wheeler-dealing and the tight little shop suffocating him, everything with its price. When Murge touched her coin it was the silky coil of her hair he felt, her eyes the colour of earth that he saw. Then he'd heard the crouped baby crying again upstairs. His wife's weary footsteps, down-at-heel, no longer special – how he hated her shuffling walk, her hands propped on the back of her hips, her belly protruding under her sagging breasts and dull face, and another mouth already in the oven.

And so he had run out into the dark after this girl like a madman, as if he was leaving nothing behind him, throwing everything away to chase a dream.

He had seen her slim figure slip through the gateway into the Tabard, and he crouched obsessed in the night, waiting for her to come out. He would wait until dawn if he had to. A baby cried and his head snapped round, but it was only someone else's. Candlelight crossed a window and the crying stopped.

The slim figure of a young man in baggy slops and peajacket appeared in the gateway. How many brothers had she said she had? This one blew through his teeth at the cold, chuckled as though he had not a care in the world, then buttoned tight and put up his collar. Murge watched him walk away to the left with quick footsteps, his silhouette flashing into view past every moonlit arch, shrinking towards the river.

Murge tucked his fingers under his armpits, shuddering. There was no heat left in him, he was made of ice.

Suddenly the inn door slammed again and her running figure came into view – no mistaking the swirl of those skirts. She paused for hardly a moment before setting off after her brother. Murge stared aghast; he had been determined to put himself in her face – saying anything, bettering Slippole's offer just to hear her talk, offering any price to keep her attention, but her haste caught him out. He shilly-shallied, listening to her shoes pattering out of hearing along the pavement, then came to life and hared after her, running pell-mell but not forgetting his cunning, following the middle of the road so that the mud and horse droppings muffled his running footsteps.

He paused outside London Bridge Station, but heard nothing for the thunder of steam and smoke – a train was leaving.

Slowly silence returned. 'Reuben,' he heard her voice calling.

The broad river gleamed over the Borough Market buildings on his left, and he saw their black figures down there. A train seemed to fly straight towards him through the sky past the four pinnacles of St Saviour's Church, sheeting sparks from the wheels and tall funnel, shaking the houses and roadway on which he scampered below, then curved above his head towards the station. Murge held down his hat with both hands as he ran.

'Reuben!' he heard her voice again, echoing between the buildings, and this time the man's figure turned in surprise, waiting for her. Murge leant his shape against the wall of a pub with half a dozen others. He wasn't cold now, he was hot, and his lungs panted at his ribs. The dwelling next door was held up by posts, and through the open doorway a man roasted a herring over a bonfire of broken door panels, fat dripping from the skin, making the flames hiss.

Murge drew a deep breath. He slipped after them quietly.

How he envied them for holding hands. As he crept closer he

saw how grief-torn they were to separate, the boy and the girl, and listening to them talk – he'd had no sister to learn closeness with – he wished he could share her grief. There was no Holywell Manor left to hold them together, Martin would be a shopkeeper, Jerome taking Holy Orders, Harold marrying a Suffolk girl . . . the names meant nothing to him. Frank bound for Canada, George for Australia. But what was *her* first name?

'Aren't you superstitious at all, Reuben?' she was asking as they crossed St Saviour's churchyard.

'I'm a sailor now,' came his sad voice. 'You ever know a sailor who wasn't superstitious, Jemima?'

Jemima! Murge pursed his lips, as if sucking her name between them.

'You're just pretending,' she said, pulling Reuben's arm affectionately, 'pretending you don't care about anything.' But he wouldn't stop. Masts and rigging were visible like cobwebs between the rooftops of Hibernia Wharf now; they had almost reached the inlet of the St Mary Overie dock. 'You're as hurt as I am,' Jemima said.

'Not me!' Reuben laughed. 'Glad to get away from the old place!'

'Look me in the eye when you say that,' Jemima told him in the moonlight. But still he wouldn't stop. She ran after him between two buildings and Murge followed like her shadow. Soon she would be alone and he could talk her over to him. He would escort her up the steps to the main road, string it out to ten minutes beside her with luck, winning her with his tongue. He knew that she had noticed him in the shop, liking him because he was kind when Slippole was beating her down. In ten minutes his silver tongue would find where she was lodging. His young lady.

Murge stopped, realising suddenly how far his infatuation had brought him. He was mad. Everything had changed for him, and she had changed it; he felt as though he really had left his old life behind. Remembering back to this afternoon was like looking the wrong way down a telescope, everything tiny and unimportant. He had been wasting his life. He might go back to the shop, but only to think of her. He might lie beside his wife, but he would be thinking of Jemima. She filled his mind like the fog rising off the water.

'Lucky is as lucky makes,' Jemima was telling her brother. 'Go on, run away to your girl in every port if that's all that matters to you.'

They were standing at the water's edge, a ship's bow jutting over their heads, askew because the falling tide had grounded the vessel on a slant, her masts unstepped, not a light showing among the bollards and mooring rings along the quay. Murge tripped over the snaking ropes then slipped behind a baulk of imported timber, unloaded today and too big to steal. 'There's more to you than that, Reuben,' she said.

Somewhere in the alleys a pub door slammed, and a few cheers rose in self-congratulation, followed by singing, and Murge cursed them because he could not now hear what was being said: Jemima had gripped Reuben's elbows and her mouth was moving.

Murge drew back into the shadows as the party of drunks rolled genially past his hiding place. They had their arms round each other's shoulders and they were singing 'Spanish Ladies' in slurred, tuneless, heartsick voices. A light was uncovered and flashed over them for a moment across the water – a four-oared galley of the Thames Police lying in wait for the thieving tier rangers, lumpers, and cunning dredgers that infested the river. These were harmless drunks; the light was muffled and with only a soft creak of rowlocks, bound with leather for silence, the duty boat returned from the inlet to the river, and Murge breathed a sigh of relief.

'Something to remember you by,' came Jemima's voice, 'since you are not superstitious.'

Reuben reached into his pocket and took out a handful of coins. He let the modern money slip back and looked at the heavy, glittering medallion left in his palm without any affection; after all, he had been brought up to expect a fortune. But then, even as Jemima reached out, he shook his head and smiled. 'No, I'll keep it for myself. I shall believe it's lucky, Jemima, because you believe it.'

'But people can't believe things for other people, can they?'

'Because you asked for it,' Reuben laughed, 'it's no longer a worthless trinket to me. I shall keep this close,' he clenched his fist round it, 'for old times' sake, that's all, and it will bring me luck, because you say so.' He opened his fingers. 'Kiss it for me,' he demanded.

At first she wouldn't, then she bent her head and touched it with her lips as he had asked.

'There,' he said casually, 'now I'm the luckiest man in the world.'

'We'll keep in touch,' she said, standing on tiptoe to be kissed.

'Aye, aye, cap'n.' Reuben gave her that careless hug of his and kissed her cheek farewell, his eyes already turning to his ship. He walked away with a wave, coming right past Murge at the end of the wharf, but neither seeing him nor sensing him.

Murge could not take his eyes off Jemima. It seemed that she waved to him, not to Reuben, and he crouched there simply desiring her, in love with her, filling his senses with her. The smell of sawn pine timber and iron and wet rope all around him, even the sickly stink of mud and faeces, made him realise now that he had not really been alive before.

Jemima lowered her arm, then turned and walked away towards the street. As soon as she disappeared round the corner, Murge slipped after her from his hiding place, everything he would say primed ready on the tip of his tongue.

Footsteps pattered behind him, figures swarming out of the shadows around Reuben. The drunken sailors had been thieves waiting for their chance. Murge dropped behind a bollard and wrapped his arms round the cold iron as if to become part of it in his terror. He hunched his shoulders over his ears but the terrible sound of men struggling without giving voice never seemed to stop, their shoes scuffing on the cobbles, fists thudding, breath gasping, clothes tearing. Murge peeped, shuddering. A knife flashed in a man's hand, then Reuben fell with a noise like a wet towel dropped on the stones. For a few moments more the shapes of the men plucked at him busily, money, shoes, peajacket, taking everything he had, then flopped him over the edge of the wharf and scattered.

Nothing moved in St Mary Overie.

Murge got slowly to his feet and looked over the edge.

Reuben lay on his back in the mud below, arms and legs thrown apart. The moon made his staring eyes look blue. His throat was cut neatly from one earlobe to his windpipe, then raggedly where he had struggled, cutting his shirt to the armpit in a jagged line.

31

The severed windpipe stared up like a black eye, slowly exhaling the last breath.

His clenched hand slowly relaxed in death, dropping something shining into the mud. Murge stared at it, his mind racing, caught between greed and what he thought was love.

Suddenly he jumped down and squelched to his knees in slime. He half fell, but his hand closed over the shining medallion as he saved himself. Standing there up to his thighs in Thames mud beside the body, Murge examined the coin in his palm, wiping the mud from it with delicate sweeps of his fingertips until the silver face appeared to look back into his own.

He clenched the talent of Reuben Fox in his hand.

Murge heaved himself back onto the wharf and tried to run after Jemima, so tightly was his mind fixed on her, as though nothing had changed. Then his footsteps faltered and he stopped in horror. It would look as though he must be the murderer: he held the dead man's coin, he was stained to the groin with slime, he was distraught with lust and desperation.

Marked like this he dare not follow Jemima; by seizing the coin he had lost the girl he loved, just when he thought he had found her.

Yet he could not throw the chance away.

He stumbled towards an alley, then began to run on his long stalky legs like a crazy man. His muddy shoes slithered on the paving stones and his mud-caked coat tails slapped the backs of his legs as he ran; his hat flew off his head, lost, windows opened above him and sleepy insults followed him, dogs yapped and lanterns were lit, but Murge could not stop.

Above him Jemima came into view high on the arch of London Bridge. She paid no attention to the wild figure stumbling along the narrow streets and winding alleyways of Bankside below. She sensed that there was always some such sight in London, for eyes that looked. As the dogs fell silent, she drew in like a deep breath the vast and peaceful night over the tangled city, down there the tiny dock of St Mary Overie pointing like a shining finger of water and mud between the tight-packed houses, the steeply-cranked rooftops of Victorian London drifting with smoke below her. Over her head the steady moon illuminated the silver loop of the mighty River Thames, appearing motionless and eternal, as it curved into the distance round the dark island of Southwark.

BOOK ONE

I

John Fox

John Fox's Family Tree
as known to him after
19 September 47

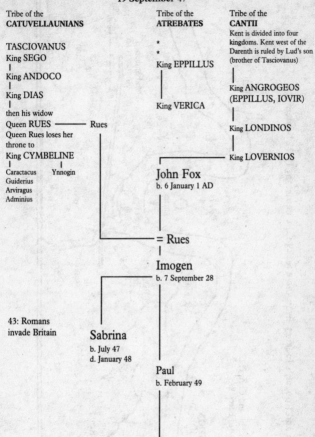

Tribe of the
CATUVELLAUNIANS

TASCIOVANUS
King SEGO
King ANDOCO
King DIAS
then his widow
Queen RUES ———— Rues
Queen Rues loses her
throne to
King CYMBELINE

Caractacus   Ynnogin
Guiderius
Arviragus
Adminius

Tribe of the
ATREBATES

*
*
King EPPILLUS

King VERICA

Tribe of the
CANTII
Kent is divided into four
kingdoms. Kent west of the
Darenth is ruled by Lud's son
(brother of Tasciovanus)

King ANGROGEOS
(EPPILLUS, IOVIR)

King LONDINOS

King LOVERNIOS

John Fox
b. 6 January 1 AD

= Rues

Imogen
b. 7 September 28

43: Romans
invade Britain

Sabrina
b. July 47
d. January 48

Paul
b. February 49

John and Imogen's Journey from the wreck to the nemeton, 19–21 September

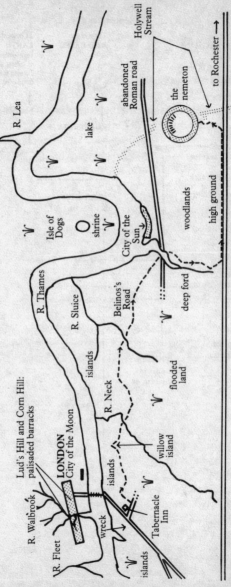

Tuesday 19 September AD 47

'Yes,' John Fox murmured, 'this is London.'

The moon, which had lifted the flood here into the inlet where tidal waters never usually reached, illuminated the silver loop of the mighty River Thames, seeming motionless and eternal as it curved round the dark island where the vessel had struck.

The boat bumped once more, turning on the flood, then stuck firmly in the mud, and Fox did not think she would move again. Behind him the Arimathean braced himself on the tilted deck but said nothing, rubbing his foot through the split in his sandal. He was standing behind a man who had lived his life more apart even than the Jews, and such isolation frightened him.

'In my tongue we called this place *Luan-Dun*,' Fox said, still without turning, or taking his booted foot from the small wooden casket on which it rested. 'City of the Moon.'

Then he heard the voice of a girl singing, and knew he was almost home.

But the great city that he remembered was gone. Not a lamp was lit, the vast church between the hills was as empty as though it had never been; not a soul was to be seen beneath the moon. Even the woman's voice, forced to chant a crude soldiers' song about blood and breasts, was muffled inside a building somewhere, blasphemous on this night. All around the vessel the arm of the risen sea stretched out silver fingers into the marshlands as though grasping to reach the ring of moonlit hills, exhaling mist like breath, but still no worshippers came. Spiders were spinning cobwebs like silver hair between the bulrushes, almost hiding the hulk in the inlet as it settled into the slime. The night sounds of London filled the air around him: the whirr of an owl, a frog croaking, then the splash of a salmon or trout almost beneath his feet, or a pike perhaps, gape-mouthed for her prey.

The flood was at full height and the moon poured down its

radiance like a libation over the heads of the two men, a fine sacrificial light, but Fox saw no priests standing one-legged like cranes with their toes dug into the water's margin, no horns were blown or offerings sent spinning and plunging into that river of beaten silver.

Even away from the water's edge he discerned none of the homely round houses he remembered, each with its porch, and steep useful roofs for the rain and snow to run off, leaking smoke through the thatch from the sociable hearths below, women shouting and cursing and laughing and children scampering everywhere. No open city surrounded by fields and allotments, no meeting hall at the centre where the four kings of Kent, including his own father from the City of the Sun, could meet to talk and exchange gifts with the kingdoms to the north and west while their people bragged and traded. No granaries on stilts, no store huts dotted among the skin and wickerwork boats pulled up along the strand for the river's trade, no temple held up by its colonnade of oak trunks, or Druids in their leached white cloaks to take upon them the sins of the people. No bonfires, no fights, no sparks sheeting from swords. No marriages would be celebrated beneath the mistletoe tonight. The life Fox had missed in his exile was gone, and now he was too late; that perfect time had ended even before the Roman invasion, with Cymbeline's triumph over the kingdoms, and those days were fled into memory like his youth. Fox was forty-six years old, no longer young.

His eye followed the strange, foreign bridge sewn like black thread across the shining water to the north bank. Above the reed beds with their heaps of pontoons and military debris, beyond the new Customs House on the site of Belinos's Gate, of which there was now no sign except its name in his memory, the land rose in the steep gravel terraces left by earlier floods, useful natural fortifications, towards the two hills that the Romans had enclosed within their wooden palisade as if they owned them. There they had placed their alien encampment, the leather campaign tents that must shake like the furies in a northerly gale now gradually being replaced by modern sharp-edged barrack blocks. Their whitewashed walls were aligned along the road, which now ran straight where the British lane had wandered, their roofs flat enough for Mediterranean tile when the legion's tile kiln was built but in the meantime dressed with local reed. White stones marked every path and junction. A Roman barracks was a man's world, strict and safe, with no women or children or disorder allowed. A place made for men to live without love.

Fox's keen ears picked out the footsteps of the Tyrian ship-master coming forward and he touched his sword, but the man was only whispering to the Arimathean for orders. Should he set the brutes to baling out the water they had shipped? Fox answered. 'There's no point.' He half turned, enough to show the hilt of the illegally carried sword through the front of his cloak. 'Repair your vessel when the tide falls, you won't get another as high. To refloat her you must kedge her back across the mudflats to the water, if you can.'

The master would not look the Jonah in the face. 'I've had his sack of stuff thrown ashore,' he confided carelessly in Aramaic to his employer, thinking a Gentile would not speak the tongue, 'and I'd just as soon that pot of shit threw himself after it.' In response the Arimathean lifted a finger. 'Your sentiments do you credit, Captain,' he murmured smoothly, 'but I have done what I said I would do.' The shipmaster grunted and thumped back to the stern, slapping a few backs with a rope's end on his way. Fox was staring at the moon.

'Yet you trust me behind you, sir,' the Arimathean said. He was a religious man who had retired, disgusted, from the politics of religion. A man of simple belief and total conviction, once he had made up his mind, he was a merchant and traveller again in these times of faction and despair, when all that the Christ had won was lost. It was the worst of times to be a Christian, when every sacrifice seemed worth nothing. Joseph of Arimathea despaired of his fellow men.

'I know you,' Fox grunted. 'You walk with a split in your shoe.'

While John Fox watched London, remembering how it had once been, the Arimathean watched him.

'Our Roman friends have changed everything, Tiberius Claud-ius,' he commented, to stir this dangerous barbarian out of his reverie, wishing only to wash his hands of such a passenger and cut his losses after so terrifying a voyage. 'They change every-thing, don't they, sir?' His voice rose and Fox knew the old man was ranting under his breath against the Romans again, though they were the source of his fortune, sure a Gentile would not see into his heart; yet the Romans tolerated Christians, who were persecuted by their own folk – only a couple of years ago the apostle James had been executed by the King of the Jews. But Fox understood pride.

He turned and clasped the Arimathean to him in farewell, lifting the old man's sandals from the deck with the ferocity of his hug, acknowledging the years between them.

Two decades had passed since the Arimathean, trading Samian pottery, wine, fish paste and the latest Empire fashions into every coastal nook and cranny from Dover to Kingsweston, where he had been shipwrecked and wintered rebuilding his boat among the lakes and islands of Glastonbury, had sailed Fox into exile on the continent, far from the arms of the woman he loved: a glowering barbarian prince to add class to a cargo of tin, Atrebatian slaves and hunting dogs as savage and incorrigible as he. As a young man, tall and strong, with hair as red and curly as the shimmering sun at sunrise, Fox had been proud, clever, wilful to a fault, determined to think only of himself once he was exiled from his princess. Age had not weathered him, only intensified him, but cruel treatment had made him cruel in turn and loss had withered his soul. Everything he had done wrong, and his was now a face that wore a life of sin clawed deep into its lines, he had done wrong because of earthly love. The only love that mattered to him had been taken away, so he had thrown away everything. Watching him, the Arimathean sighed. Both men knew love, it formed and simplified each of them and dominated the life of both, but it was a different love and they would never be friends. As fellow voyagers, however, they had shared, for a while, sincerity between them, and trust.

Fox sniffed the air. 'No, Joseph, nothing changes,' he said in Aramaic with a terrible sadness. The sound of the girl's voice was gone, whisked away on a whim of the night breath as though she had never been. Yet it was enough. Like him, somehow she had survived, she was here.

Fox had not at first believed the rumour; then he could not bring himself to believe anything else. He had lived with his hope night and day since that nervous pecking at his door in Rome. The ragged informant, an escaped British slave shivering at the stylish gate of Fox's villa on the Clivus Argentarius, conveniently near the meeting of four roads, had promised the major-domo priceless information for the ears of Tiberius Claudius Loverni-anus alone. 'Your ears are forfeit if it is not,' Fox drawled when the man was pushed in. But priceless information it was indeed, and Fox, not as drunk as he appeared, rewarded him beyond price as agreed. The fool was caught trying to exchange the priceless coin from Fox's belt at a cheap clothing stall instead of using it cleverly, was returned to his owner to be killed, and Fox got his money back.

Ever since his years in Judea he had been prepared to believe in the impossible.

Rues was alive. She had been seen.

He promised his squealing girls a big party that evening, left them plucking their armpits and smearing halcyon cream on their florid, lascivious faces, layering saffron round their eyes; but by evening he was far away on horseback leaving his mortgaged villa and the mountain of debts with tailors, dressmakers, jewellers, perfumiers and suppliers of vintage wines behind him.

Throwing it all away again, all for Rues.

He polished his hope as long and as carefully as some men polish their swords.

He changed horses and names at every staging post on the Aurelian road, passing the shadow of the Alps on the second day, losing himself in the waterfront quarter of Burdigala on the Atlantic coast of Aquitania within the week, a driven man, a man come alive again, no longer cleanshaven, washed, or displaying Roman manners. He was a true Celtic aristocrat, wild-eyed, something of the cocky peasant about him; Tiberius Claudius Lovernianus, unable to admit his Roman citizenship by which he – and his debts – could be traced, had ceased to exist. Then by chance on the quay he met his old acquaintance from many years ago, and for a moment Fox had slipped back into his sloughed Roman skin with a reassuring smile and a persuasive arm round the Arimathean's shoulder. At dawn the vessel set sail for Britain against its owner's better judgement, Fox's coin beneath the mast for luck, and the storm came whipping down.

What brings him back? wondered the Arimathean. Why does a man throw his life away – for the second time?

Fox stared into the still London night. He sensed her here with his heart and with his soul.

'Nothing changes,' he repeated in Aramaic.

The Arimathean swallowed. 'I didn't know you spoke my language.' He was so rattled that he forgot to say 'sir'.

'When I began my exile, I was in Judea where you left me,' Fox reminded the little man mildly, towering over him by a head and a half. 'I stayed there for five years. You didn't think I would be drunk all the time, did you?'

'I only know you later became a citizen of Rome, sir, and that now you can speak Latin moist and dry like a Roman.'

'I survived.'

'Did you? You spent years on the island of Capri as a crony to the Emperor Tiberius himself, before he became a god.' The Jew's voice dripped contempt for the Imperial Cult. 'Such high friends no doubt earned you a great fortune.'

'I earned no money, I simply spent it,' Fox grinned, taking his foot from the cedarwood casket which he strapped to his belt with quick jerks of his fist. 'And the more I spent, the more I was believed to be rich.' He jumped down into the waist of the ship, his greasy woollen cloak swirling behind him and the soft leather of his boots making no sound on the deck, but the Arimathean called after him.

'And the empty life you have lived has not changed you at all.'

'Skin deep,' Fox shrugged, peering over the side for the best way down. 'Now I am my own man again.'

'Then you have learned nothing. A man who has been baptised is transformed and knows there is more than this,' said the Arimathean devoutly, high on the bow, and Fox threw him a sharp look in the moonlight. Again he was reminded of the Christians, as they were called, one of the hundreds of sects struggling for air in Judea, whose beliefs had survived the death of their founder, a wise man and a doer of wonderful deeds.

'Tiberius Claudius,' the Arimathean called down, 'I promise you this. If you believe in nothing, you are nothing, merely a man of the world. Is that all you are?'

'I believe in what my eyes see and what my heart tells me.' Fox swung himself over the bulwark and stood balanced on one of the oars, then squinted up at the Arimathean's head haloed by the moon. He saluted him with the Christian farewell. 'We shall meet again.'

The Arimathean shook his head. 'A man who prays to many gods is heard by none.'

'Listen, my brother,' Fox said angrily. 'Did you never wonder what happened to me after you left me on the beach near Caesarea, with only the clothes I stood up in? Among your folk I am called John, an unusual name, after the man who baptised me in the Dead Sea.' Fox laughed at the other's amazement. 'Why not? I paid my half-shekel in the boat, an uncircumcised celibate Gentile of the ninth grade. Only one species of fish is to be found in that lifeless sea: the human species. My new name was inscribed on a white pebble from the River Jordan and tied round my neck. On the other side of the pebble was the symbol of the fish now used by the Christians. The group of us, a hundred full members and fifty novices like myself, and the three leaders, toppled into the water and waded ashore to be "fished" by the priest on the jetty. I was one of the one hundred and fifty-three fish brought to salvation at the feet of Jesus Christ.'

The Arimathean ran down and stared at him. 'God preserve us,' he whispered, 'how can you not be changed? You're as far from Him as a dog is.' He turned from the steady gaze in John Fox's oval eyes and looked into the darkness over the marshes, realising. 'You don't believe she's dead. You've come back for her after all these years.'

With a sigh for the foolish dreams of men, and his own, Fox bundled his cloak over his head to keep it dry and jumped into the shadow of the boat. Cold water splashed his bare legs, his feet sank into the slime below; he felt an eel slide against his knee, then it wriggled and was gone. His hearing adjusted from the level of human conversation to that of the night, the wildlife taking advantage of the moon to hunt: the soft, heavy rustle of an otter, the lighter scuttle of a rat. Somewhere a dog barked across the marshes, then yelped and was silent. Lifting aside the ropes trailing in the water, pushing away a spar still attached to its rigging, Fox waded to the bank and heaved himself up between the reedbeds.

He was in his element again: alone.

He crouched for a moment, panting through his open mouth to make no noise, hearing the splash of baled water behind him and the grunts of working men, but the hulk was already concealed by reeds and shadows. He wasted no time probing with his fingertips for his kitbag; wherever the Tyrian captain had thrown it in his spite the mud would have swallowed his few personal possessions by now.

Parting the reeds, he slipped between them with only his memory to locate him. He came to a low gravel mound and stood upright. The water on his hands tasted sweet; the tide was no longer rising and the sea must be pooling back the fresh water flowing downriver. Looking around him, he saw that the marshes of the south bank were now a spreading silver lake three miles across, dotted with islands as far as the hills of Grien-wich, City of the Sun, that touched the river's course. The huge low island that had lain immediately to the north of that point, where his father's hunting dogs had once been kept and exercised, was entirely drowned but for the low hummock of oak trees near its centre, a shrine.

Fox looked up at the moon. The face wore a halo of haze, warning those who had eyes to see of rain coming, as though the flood was not high enough already.

Not so far away stretched a chain of low mounds covered with scrub. In several places the intricate channels between them had been abruptly bridged by blunt causeways, Roman work, joining them like a clumsy string threading its way towards London's bridge. The largest island, a low spine a few hundred yards south of the river's usual course, had been cleared of bramble and hawthorn and what he thought was a dark jumble of buildings there was confirmed when a flash of light showed as a door was opened. A sad snatch of song carried to him, not a drinking song this time but the haunting, familiar lament about the blackbird. Fox's lips moved. *Blackbird on a branch in the deeply-wooded plain. Sweet, soft, peaceful is your song.*

The light went out and a few moments later the slam of the tavern door closing carried to him, then there was silence.

He waded to the next islet and strode quickly, following the chain of sandy, thorny islets barely above the water, splashing through the shallow channels between them until he came to the causeway. Getting a foothold on the massive timbers, he pulled himself onto the smooth crushed gravel of the new imperial roadway, alien as the bridge, running like a pale arrow from Thorney Island to the west, the upstream ford. Fox sat in the middle of the road as though he had not a care in the world, and emptied the water from his boots.

A dozen slaves watched him from the doorway of a nearby dormitory or warehouse, trying to keep their scrawny white feet out of the water lapping the step on which they sat, their eyes entirely without curiosity or even the comradeship of their shared misery. Watching Fox smooth his cloak with the palms of his hands, they hung their heads again, hoping he would ignore them. He took a bone comb, its spine finely worked into the figure of a nude woman, from his tunic and ran it through his hair and beard while he watched them, then approached the crossroads.

'What are you men doing here?' he asked in Roman.

They jostled one another like birds on a rod, but none replied.

'Did you hear the singing?' Fox went on in British, his accent marking him out as an aristocrat, one of their own race, not the foreign military man his cloak and short sword suggested – it was against the law for a civilian to wear a sword, even a citizen. He touched the gold ring-necked pin that secured the cloak at his throat, British work.

The men elbowed one of their number until he was elected. 'No sir. We don't know nothing, sir.'

Fox purred. 'How did I know you'd say that?'

'We don't know nothing about her, sir.'

'When did you learn to lie?'

'When I caught a spear through my sword arm, sir, that's what it advised me to learn.'

There was no point in trying to hurry a humiliated man who somewhere inside himself remembered being a warrior; Fox hid his impatience.

'At the Medway River, was that?'

'Two days on our feet, sir, and then our own folk from east Kent crossed against us wearing Roman armour, the treacherous bastards, just when we was giving them other bastards a good licking. Bloody foreigners. I never did trust that bunch from east of the Stour.'

'Bad luck, then.'

The man shrugged his chains.

'Whose property are you now?'

'It's one of them funny names, sir, Paretes, from Palmyra. Par-ee-tees. Not a very funny man, sir. Don't crease you up laughing, none of them merchants what saw their chance do. Speaks like one of us, been trading from Calais for years. I remember meeting him man to man in better times, but now I lick his spittle.' He lifted the shift on his shoulders, showing the stripes of flogging. 'Going to rain, sir.'

'What's your name?'

'Briginos, sir, in our British tongue, but,' he mimicked the hard Roman *g*, 'Briginus, to our new landlords.'

'Then Briginus is wise.'

'And this here piece of scum is Eberesto, and this is Rianorix—'

'And you were listening to her sing.'

'Who would that be, sir?'

'You know who, my friend, and you knew the song too.'

All the men shook their heads. 'No, sir, we're just keeping our noses above water.' Briginus's voice trembled with longing. 'See, when we sleep we dream of our children, sir. All of us do,' he added, and Fox nodded, realising how terrible the shock of their defeat and disgrace by mere soldiers had been to these warriors, turning them into mice. During the battle the leaders above them had probably had the sense to change sides, and the peasants below them would have been back at their fields and ploughs the very next day with their lives probably changed not at all, except paying taxes to a Roman bureaucrat instead of a tribal warlord, but these men had been left in the middle with nowhere to go. Three or four years ago in the aftermath of the invasion, their youthful strength, and the fact that they were more accustomed than most Britons to taking orders, would have made them valuable slaves. But they were unskilled at everything except fighting, so it made commercial sense to work them into the ground. There would always be wars, and always a supply of such men after them.

'You're lucky men,' Fox said. 'I have no children.'

'Then you must be afraid, sir.'

There came a burst of laughter from the largest building nearby, the other side of the crossroads – small in itself, with crooked walls of unbaked clay in fawning British imitation of Roman style, and a hinged wooden door that didn't fit. The place was surrounded and built up on three of its sides with a higgledy-piggledy of outhouses, stables and byres; even tents huddled against the walls away from the road, and lean-to's roofed with pieces of reed fencing held up on sticks. The original dwelling had obviously grown into the centre of domestic life on the island. The pigs grunted and splashed alone in their slimy sty, but in every other scrap of shelter, human forms slept or sat sleepily among the sheep and chickens, or with their arms wrapped round their dogs for warmth, or using them as pillows. No one loved their dogs like the British, and Fox inhaled the homely reek of it all, and the smell of that beechwood smoke, the warm comforting scent of his childhood.

'What's that place?'

'It's a tavern, sir,' Briginus said, 'called the Tabernacle. That's the thing on a boat what holds the mast, sir, so you see it's a brothel. Them foreigners can't do anything, even make love, without organising it first, if you ask us.'

Fox put his foot on the step of the dormitory and his elbow on his knee, then pointed at the place, speaking close. 'Are they legionary soldiers in there?'

'No sir, auxiliaries.' Briginus spat. 'Batavian long-hairs from the low lands, and very at home they must feel with this water over their feet. It's common sense that the proper legions are all away in the west and north, hanging on to all they've stolen, not that we'd say so to their faces, you understand. They call London a vexillation, sir, a garrison left to hold conquered land.'

'And you still say she's not in there.'

'Property of Paretes, sir. Not for the likes of you and I, if you get my meaning. Well, not for the likes of me, anyway. We're kept apart from the women, at least the pretty ones, we can't imagine why.'

Fox clapped Briginus's shoulder and stepped back. The door of the Tabernacle banged and a man staggered out, followed by laughter. Wearing leathers and a dagger, hardly a uniform, he dropped to his knees with deep belly-wrenching gurgles, so that at first they thought he had been stabbed, but then he held his hair away from his face and vomited between wall and road.

'Paretes's special beer,' Briginus said wistfully. 'Two parts barley and three parts piss.' The man clutched at his crotch with a groan, vomiting over his hair a second time, then staggered back inside and the door banged. Then it was slammed again to make it shut properly.

'If you was to ask for a general piece of advice, sir,' Briginus said as Fox stood up straight, 'I wouldn't go in there, particularly.'

'I didn't ask.'

'That's fair enough then. I'd be afraid to touch the beer, though.'

Fox glanced back. He smiled. 'You asked me earlier if I was afraid.'

The men waited eagerly. They loved nothing better than eloquence and a riddle. 'And are you, sir?'

'Well, I'll tell you this,' Fox said. 'I'm afraid the sky will fall on my head.'

He nodded respectfully to the gods of the crossroads then went over safely, his long strides crunching on fresh gravel not yet worn smooth. To his left the road from London's bridge approached and swept past the Tabernacle before branching like legs at the islet's southern end. The important road towards the supply bases of the south coast and the loyal client kingdom of King Cogidubnus, Verica's heir, leapt the marshes on a huge causeway, but he saw that the branch to the east was unfinished, slumping into the moonlit swamp amid piles of pebbles, timbers and half-submerged carts. Probably most of that road was being tackled from the Medway end, where stone was more plentiful. The line the Romans had chosen ran considerably to the south of the old British lane, and for a moment Fox hated them for their stupidity and wastefulness.

He had wasted twenty years of his life among them, almost become one of them, but now everything had changed.

Cloud covered the moon and at a stroke the tavern disappeared, becoming part of the darkness. He saw no windows, no illumination from the Tabernacle to guide him, only the small fire tended by the pig-man keeping an eye on his pigs. Out of the dark to his left came a low cry of pleasure or pain, then a giggle, and he stepped forward knowing exactly what was going on. Camp followers and tradesmen were never allowed within shouting distance of a Roman fort for obvious reasons – the men would have got no peace; like other soldiers, auxiliaries were not allowed wives or children until they retired from the army with citizenship and perhaps a grant of land, but no one supposed they lived celibate lives. Few survived to reach the promised retirement, and even fewer had legitimate sons to inherit the precious citizenship; that was the way the system worked. Off duty, the garrison came to the camp.

Fox reached out into the dark. His knuckles touched the door and he slid his hand across at the height of the latch, finding the thong. He banged the ill-fitting door open and stepped inside.

The stench was usual. It was the smell of soldiers enjoying themselves.

These places were the same the world over. He was standing at the end of what seemed to be a long room full of fog, the fire in the centre casting brilliant flashes through the smoke swirling into the roof and down again. The men watching the flames with glowing faces streamed solid black shadow from the backs of their heads. Behind them the lower orders, kept separate by a low screen, sprawled and staggered over the earth floor, pissing, vomiting, lying dead drunk, gambling with hanging heads, not knowing by now whether they won or lost, having a fine time. Girls with exhausted faces had been sent among them to clear up, not hurrying about it, hoping for a pair of groping hands and a penny or two for nothing.

The older men reclining watchfully on couches by the fire were the ones. They were waiting for something, played to by a young man plucking the strings of a lyre, helping themselves with their fingers from bowls of tiny fish in sauce, pickled onions, plates of Lucanian sausage – Fox could smell the cumin spice – that were brought to them from time to time by the ugly serving girls. Fox closed the door behind him with his foot, not taking his eyes off these men.

He circled through the shadows, stepping over the forms lying along the wall, black tallow dripping on them from the tapers set here and there. His foot touched someone who had passed out clutching a quart mug of British beer to their chest, and Fox bent at the knees without looking away from the group at the fire,

51

helping himself before spitting out a mouthful: halfway down it was thick as porridge, the good stuff had been on top. The flames crackled and somewhere he heard a baby crying. He was near the men at the fire now, a shadow in the shadows behind them.

He could feel their growing anticipation, their excitement. Something was about to happen. He felt it in his skin, like a quickening of the air, he could sense it in the palms of his hands.

'Come on, Paretes!' someone shouted, and the other older men took up the chant, 'Par-ee-tees! Par-ee-tees!'

At the far end of the room was a serving counter bent under the evening's debris of chipped jugs and beakers, and Fox narrowed his eyes as if to pierce the smoke, discerning the dark doorway behind it where the serving girls came from. The curtain was pulled aside and a boy scurried through carrying a red Samian flagon, real quality, and dispensed wine into the mugs of the men in a half-circle round the fire. Then he knelt ready to refill them without being told, these favoured customers who were pretending to be gentlemen – Fox could tell by their accents and the hang of their togas that they were Belgic, not Roman. The lyre player was jumbling his notes but no one knew to say anything.

Suddenly the curtain was flapped aside and a fat-faced smiling man made an entrance, plump shining hands outspread in smiling apology from the creamy folds of his toga, but an angry sweat slid like grease down the grooves beside his hawk nose and his eyes were thin. 'Gentlemen, gentlemen,' Paretes greeted them, speaking Roman to them to compliment their aspirations, 'a thousand apologies, but you know what women are like when the milk is flowing in their breasts and their hearts are full.'

'Get her back, Paretes,' yawned a silver-haired man.

'And her eyes are full of weeping,' Paretes said. 'She could not stop herself from weeping. Look at my poor hands, red from beating.'

'Then make her sing a different song,' someone suggested. 'It was the last one that did for her.'

'If you can't thrash her into shape, Paretes,' promised the silver-haired man, 'we'll oblige.' The other men laughed, so Fox marked him as the leader. Paretes was laughing too, but flicking his eyes from side to side. The woman must be more than very difficult to cause this man trouble; she must be very valuable.

'What do you expect, good sirs, of the daughter of a queen,' Paretes bragged, making one last attempt to turn his obvious difficulties to his advantage. 'I have broken her spirit, I assure you, but still she remembers . . . remembers the way things were.' He bowed his bald head, then backed away with a flourish. It was the signal for the girl to be pushed through the curtain.

Fox stared.

He stood in the dark, watching the fireglow light her face as she surveyed the men who had come to watch her flaunt herself, her long chestnut hair, sprinkled with golden glass beads, falling past her shoulders, the sort of hair a man longed to slide his hands into. But then you saw her eyes, deep brown and slanted upwards at the outer edges, fierce and contemptuous. She had not aged by a day since Fox last saw her twenty years ago; through the years of his exile she had remained as perfect and changeless as in his memory.

'Rues,' he whispered, and her footstep hesitated, raising her hand to the silver flash at her neck, but he knew she did not recognise him, and thought she could not see him beyond the glow of the fire.

She wore only a strip of pale leather that contained her breasts and another round her loins, laced six times up the side. Her skin was white as wax, her long legs flawless and her movements as graceful as a girl's, yet she was the same age as Fox. What magic had she used? How could a woman defy age? But Rues had.

When she sang he watched her, marvelling, remembering.

Blackbird on a branch in the deeply-wooded plain. Sweet, soft, peaceful is your song.

Imogen sang to the men she despised. The newcomer had the cruellest face she had ever seen, yet she had never seen anyone fuller of life. She ignored him, but his long red hair and beard stood out like a beacon in the firelight as he moved forward, his intense stare filling her attention, disturbing her concentration as she drew breath to sing.

The usual types were beginning to crowd at the barrier behind him, peering round his shoulders, pushing for a place as they always did, pulling their girls with them as if those lumps had her body, her voice. But he was different, his eyes held the flame like a cat's, watching her without movement. He was not with the others in the inner circle, and her eyes were drawn back to his gaze even while she tried to ignore him. He seemed to look right inside her, yet she was sure she had never seen him before in her life.

She tried to look away. Sabrina was already crying again, and Imogen was terrified of what Paretes might do this time. He might do as he had threatened and cut his losses.

Sabrina's cries rose and Imogen glanced behind her, remembering the soldier – like one of these – who had taken her, grunting his lust as casually as a man relieving his bowels, feeling the hot flush of him and his sword point pressed at her side, smelling the stink of him in her bones. By the round houses her girl friends and the other slaves lay ripped in the mud, and after it was over Imogen had huddled herself against her mother's body in the dark and wished the same fate was hers.

She was not dead, and it was worse.

At dawn her weeping had attracted a travelling merchant to the ditch, a plump Palmyran at first as kindly as an uncle, who kept his slaves in chains. His name was Paretes. 'A pretty girl,' he had told her appreciatively, flicking his eyes over her bloodied clothes, 'is always assured of friends.' Even before he heard her sing – and she sang of her life that had gone before as hauntingly as a trapped songbird – his flabby hands had dressed her in fine Sudanese cotton and a golden-brown woollen cloak that matched her eyes. He saw his opportunity with her in London, swarming with soldiers paid cash and nothing to spend it on, not even a tavern in those first days. His slaves threw up the first place in a week, placed amid the busy southern roadworks, the crossroads that everyone must pass going to and from the bridge. Paretes had struck his goldmine at last, and became insistent as well as kind. For as long as her looks allowed, Imogen had sung for the soldiers, wondering if one of them was the father, singing more beautifully than ever in her distress, because there was not a day she'd not felt her tightening belly and hated the baby growing inside her. Meanwhile the Tabernacle had grown and grown, its rooms knocked into one another until the original hovel was almost hidden under the jumble of huts and outhouses that it supported – that *she* supported. Here Imogen had suffered her unborn child, swearing she'd not look at it when it came, not allow it to be placed to her breast, not have it live.

But the old woman whom the impatient Paretes had found to attend her lying-in, the sort of dreadful raggedy creature who always appeared from the edge of camp to clear up a mess, plonked the child to Imogen's breast as though that was that. At once the baby's lips had sucked the warm milk, and Imogen watched the colour come into her daughter's cheeks. 'There,' the old woman had said, 'now give it to me and I'll chuck it away.' But Imogen had shaken her head, and the old woman shook her head too. 'You've fallen in love,' she'd said victoriously, but Imogen had denied it. Even when, with her own hands, she had shifted her baby from one breast to the other, she had denied it.

Paretes had not interfered. She was slim again. She could sing.

Except for the baby Imogen had grown to love, Paretes could never have controlled her. For her, motherhood was a kind of madness, a desperate need to give love to her child as though it was more than her own enslaved life, and Imogen, who had never loved, began to comprehend a little of her mother's emotions.

Sweet, soft, peaceful is your song. Tonight her sudden tears, her dash for the kitchen, had made a fool of Paretes in front of the officers he was wooing; he'd lost face with people who mattered, and that was one thing no hot-blooded Palmyran forgave. He would indulge her wilfulness no longer. But his stinging slaps and pinches had not made her submissive, she had glared into his eyes even while her lips quivered at the pain he was inflicting on her, but when he'd picked up the crying baby she went instantly meek, promising she'd do anything he said, and Paretes's snarl had stretched into his honey-lapping grin of triumph. Killing the baby would break her spirit, and his hold over her, but he might yet be provoked to the point of thinking it worthwhile. He had come close to thinking it tonight.

He'd handed her the baby to comfort and Sabrina's cries stopped at once. 'Now go and squeeze the last farthing out of them,' he'd ordered, making her hand the baby to the witless crone Brica, who hardly knew which end to hold.

'*Rues,*' the stranger's voice had whispered, and Imogen had faltered, her hand flying to her throat.

A silver-haired man took out a knife to cut a lemon, extraordinarily expensive, as a symbol of his status. He passed a quarter to a second man, who nodded and squeezed it into his wine, then pressed it to his lips. Neither of them had spoken. Behind them stood the man with the red hair, a band of red fox fur encircling his arm and his eyes fixed on her.

From the kitchen Sabrina was making that hicking repetitive cry of distress, not loud but needing, the sort of cry that pierced a mother to the bone. Imogen could hardly concentrate, she felt her eyes filling with tears and she was terrified her voice would begin to choke again. She sang trembling notes to the lusting faces of the old men in the circle of firelight which illuminated her, struggling for self-control. Paretes watched her with a face as fixed as bronze. The awfulness of her life washed over her; she was terrified, for herself, for her infant. She could hardly think. The baby screamed. That idiot Brica was doing everything wrong.

'I can't!' she shouted at Paretes.

The man with the red fox fur leaned forward and touched her.

'You know what to sing,' he murmured in her ear no louder than the crackling of the flames.

Imogen could not make a sound. Her tongue was locked to the roof of her mouth. He wanted the song that had caused all the trouble, her mother's song that brought back memories of her happy childhood and all she had lost. She could not bring herself to do it.

'Go on,' he smiled.

Imogen opened her mouth. Incredibly, for him, her voice came out sweet and clear as the stream from Quarley Hill where she had lived with her mother under King Verica's protection.

Blackbird on a branch in the deeply-wooden plain. Sweet, soft, peaceful is your song.

'You're the woman I remember,' he murmured, stopping her, 'and yet you don't remember me, do you?' He touched his finger-tip to the tiny coin that she wore by Celtic tradition at her throat, a keepsake, a memory, and an oath.

Fox watched her struggle with her feelings. Through the curtained doorway her baby gave a piercing cry and she looked frantically at Paretes. Around them the circle of men was muttering impatiently, and Paretes raised his bunched fist to the girl's face, but he was glaring over her shoulder at the doorway, not threatening her but her baby; so he was not the father. But he was pushing the girl too far and Fox waited for what she would do. She might simply cry weak tears, or she might run. But she surprised him, lashing out at Paretes's fist with the flat of her hands, then raining down slapping blows on his head and shoulders. The drunks behind the screen cheered, but when Paretes slipped his hand into his toga, Fox knocked the girl back. Her feet came off the ground and she went down, then rolled over quick as a flash, running for the back room, her hair flying, her toes digging into the earth floor – she'd lost her sandals. Fox knew the only thing she was aware of at that moment was not her danger, but that her baby was crying.

Paretes started after her, his right hand pulling out from the folds of his toga the dagger concealed there, but Fox trod on his feet then wrapped his arm round the fat man's shoulders like an old friend and reached down to seize the wrist, entirely at his ease, grinning broadly. 'Falernian wine all round for these gentlemen,' he ordered the boy.

'But that's four times the price of ordinary!' squealed Paretes.

'And mark it on my friend Paretes's account, boy.'

'Do I know you?' hissed Paretes. 'Let me go!' He struggled as he was lifted. 'Let go of me!' He gasped as the air was squeezed from his lungs.

'Let's talk,' Fox said cheerfully.

All Imogen heard as she rushed into the kitchen were the cries of her baby. That useless crone Brica sat snoring with her toothless mouth open like a fish, her clawed hand rocking the crib on the table in front of her even in her sleep, heedless of the shrieks from the bundle inside. Imogen was terrified one of the cats that the Romans had brought with them, now running wild everywhere, had crept in and coiled itself over Sabrina's little face the way everyone said they did. She drew a deep breath of relief, seeing that the wool blanket was rucked up into a mound by the baby's own fretful movements, that was all. She snatched her up and Sabrina burped, then fell silent feeling her mother's warmth, questing for milk as usual. Imogen could almost persuade herself that everything was normal. Perhaps if she stayed quiet it would be all right. Later, she knew, the warm kitchen would be crowded with slumbering forms so that you could hardly find a place to step between them, but for now only the huddle of early-bird girls was curled up as usual in the plum spot by the warm brick arch of the stove, the charcoal glowing ready for the bread they must bake first thing. They had left an iron pot bubbling forgotten on the gridiron – it took a thunderstorm to wake those miseries. Imogen took it off absent-mindedly. Her eye was caught by the row of kitchen knives of every shape hanging along the wall, deep curved blades, long thin blades, scalloped blades, all of them glinting by the light of the bronze table lamp. Brica's sleepy rhythm had not changed, her hand with knuckles swollen as large as pebbles from age continued to rock the reed crib as though Sabrina was still in it, still crying, instead of cuddled in quiet contentment to her mother's breast. The spell broke and Imogen ran for the door at the back, secured against thieves by an oak bar. It wouldn't budge.

'You can't lift that beam with one hand,' came a gentle voice from the curtained doorway.

She struggled, then stood quietly with her forehead against the wood.

'Unless you put down your baby,' the stranger's voice suggested. 'Then you can use both hands.' She wouldn't risk doing that, as he must have known. She squinted at him curiously as he swung Paretes politely through the doorway, sweeping him forward without a pause in his long strides to the table, the Palmyran bobbing beside him like a plump, vindictive bird. His silence meant he was biding his time, Imogen knew.

'He always carries a dagger in his clothes!' she blurted.

'I'm sure not,' the stranger said. 'You don't, do you, Paretes?'

'Of course not, my friend, she's lying,' Paretes said.

'Paretes is a man of his word, a businessman, a very successful man,' the stranger nodded. 'Should I take the word of such a man, or believe the accusation of his slave girl?'

Imogen kissed her baby's cheek, stroking Sabrina's fine hair, trying to forget either man existed.

'Trust me.' The stranger's hand startled her, she had not heard his footsteps come close, and the baby sucked from his little finger. Imogen thought she had never seen a face she trusted less, seamed with cruelty and suffering and strong living, but his eyes were dark and steady. That long purple cloak gave him an air both regal and military, though it smelt of the sea, and hemp ropes, and hard travel. Yet there was something almost gentle about him. While she wavered uncertainly, the stranger reached out his other hand and pulled the bar off the door. 'You have no clothes on,' he said quietly, 'and outside it's raining and pitch dark by now. You choose. Would you rather stay and listen to what I have to say?'

She couldn't make him understand about Paretes. Men were all the same, and she knew she was going to die. 'You won't change anything,' she said wretchedly.

'Come, come, my dear,' Paretes said, and the stranger's eyes twinkled at Imogen, for her alone. He was back at the table in two quick strides, then sat on the corner and pulled up a three-legged stool with his foot, gesturing Paretes to sit. 'A thousand thanks for your help with the girl,' Paretes said insincerely, still on his feet. 'I'll deal with her now.'

'Sit.' The stranger's tone was casual, but Paretes sat at once. 'We're businessmen, let's talk business. She's for sale, am I right?'

Paretes looked startled, then cunning. 'Indeed, one is always open to offers. But the price of such a one. . . .'

'You had a difficult auction.' The stranger went to the curtain and glanced through it before returning genially. 'Gone. Perhaps you can persuade your classy gentlemen to return tomorrow.'

They certainly wouldn't be back, and no one knew that better than Paretes. 'Tonight was unfortunate, but I can afford to bide my time, can't I, my dear?' he purred to Imogen. 'She is beautiful and talented,' he explained, 'and of course those ones are always the most difficult to shift, because they are the most expensive.'

Fox helped himself to a strip of carrot from a bowl that had been returned half finished. 'A girl with a baby is impossible to sell. No man buys two birds singing.'

'I have been too gentle with that one, sir. I should have had the weakly child put away tonight, but that is my generous nature for you,' Paretes said winningly. 'Usually it is better to keep the separation until after the sale, grief takes the life from a woman's face so.' He splayed his hands long-sufferingly.

'What's her name?' Fox asked without looking round.

'Imogen,' she said, putting herself in front of him, one hand on her hip, her other clutching her baby defiantly. 'My name is Imogen.'

'Imogen.' Fox scratched the tabletop thoughtfully with his fingernail. 'That's a good British name.'

'Daughter of a queen,' Paretes repeated proudly.

'Rues,' Fox murmured. 'Yes, she was brought up to be queen.' Paretes raised his eyebrows, he neither knew nor cared. Fox looked directly into Imogen's eyes. 'When were you born, Imogen?'

'Nineteen years ago, exactly.'

'How do you know exactly?'

'Because it was the autumn equinox like today's.'

'And did your mother truly die in childbirth, as I was told?'

'No, sir. She lived eighteen years in quiet retreat, it was a condition imposed by Verica who dared not provoke another war with Cymbeline's kingdom north of the Thames. As it was, half our goods were paid for in Cymbeline's coinage. Rues was permitted to take no part in politics. In the end Verica fled to Rome and . . . and . . .' Her voice broke and she turned over her wrist to show the brand. 'Cymbeline's brother, Epatticus, took us as slaves.'

'Simply that Rues was alive was politics in those days,' Fox said. 'I never knew of it. My father's emissaries lied to me.' He put his hands to his face. 'I have been more foolish than any man who ever lived. I believed my father, I believed *in* him. I have wasted my life. I have gone nowhere.'

'We should talk of money now,' Paretes said soothingly, taking in the expensive Tyrian cloak and those soft kid boots with sharp flicks of his eyes, knowing the price of everything. 'Without money, talk means nothing, does it?'

Imogen watched the red-haired stranger anxiously, puzzled by his words but knowing her life depended on him. 'Yes, yes,' she urged, 'give that fat fool his money, whatever he asks, I'll pay you back.' She meant she would run away at the first opportunity.

'Your baby's wet,' he remarked.

She laid her girl on the table beside the snoring woman and changed the towel quickly. Paretes looked away, disgusted.

'You should know my name,' the stranger whispered, interposing his bulk between her and the Palmyran, leaning his hands on the table beside her. 'I am John Fox.'

Imogen stared. 'But you're dead.' She shook her head. 'The

man my mother knew died abroad many years ago.'

'In a way that's true,' he said. 'But now, as you see, I have come back.'

What hurt John Fox most was that she obviously didn't know what to make of him. She was enchantingly young. She had no choice but to trust him right now but he knew that would last only until she could run away. She would have been brought up in the company of women, and probably the only man she had known as a person, apart from servants, was Paretes. She even acted as though her air of innocence and contempt made her unattractive to men. He doubted she'd been married, she was too concentrated on the baby who had taken over her life. Imogen was in extreme peril but Fox saw that her mind kept turning away from them to the baby; she hardly listened as he and Paretes decided her fate. In Imogen, he decided, her grandmother's implacable will had been tempered by her mother's gentleness, and he loved the way she cared for her child. Everything in her life was for that pale baby now wrapped up warm in a dry towel, and he was sure that if the choice he had offered her at the door beam had been life for her or the child, she would have forfeited her own life.

John Fox knew he was being weak. Rues was dead, there was nothing for him here. Imogen saw him only as a stranger with a sword, a man of such power that he must be submitted to, appeased, denied, used, thinking of herself and her baby, not him, seeing him only as a lesser evil than Paretes, and she would get rid of him when she could. But he knew he could not stand aside. Her cloak was folded at the far end of the table, he saw her looking at it; she must be cold. She would need shoes too, preferably boots, and there were several muddy pairs left to dry by the fire, but she made no move towards them. It was obvious that she had given up hope.

He looked towards the boots and she followed his eyes. 'Everything will be all right,' he whispered, then before she could resist he lifted the baby and settled her comfortably in his arm. 'Trust me,' he repeated, and nodded again towards the boots. At last she caught on and pretended to be busy, throwing the soiled towel into the corner, taking a fresh one from the cupboard kept warm by the fire.

Jogging the sleepy baby in the crook of his elbow, Fox went back to Paretes and sat comfortably on the table corner. 'I'll take them both off your hands,' he said.

'Kind sir, can a man carry enough gold to buy so rare and valuable a girl?'

The baby sucked Fox's finger and he smiled. Imogen watched him fondle her, as gentle and full of care as though he held his own child.

'No, a man cannot buy a life,' he murmured. 'Who can value a life?'

'I can,' Paretes said quickly. 'Five thousand pence for the woman, five hundred for the baby.'

He was demanding an extraordinary price – a day's work cost a penny. John Fox sighed, shaking his head.

He was aware of Imogen stepping into the best pair of boots that had been left by the fire, the sort with lengthy straps above the ankle, winding them in crosses up her long white legs and tying them off just below the knee. She found a girl's red-brown tunic drying too, still stained with foam from an accident with a flagon of beer, and pulled it over her head.

Fox drew his fingertip from the baby's mouth and with two sharp jerks snapped the knots holding the cedarwood casket to his belt. With a sigh of relief as the awkward weight was taken off him he thumped it on the table. Opening the bronze hasp with a small forked tool, he banged back the curved lid.

Paretes leaned forward eagerly to see inside, his mouth open as though in hunger.

At the far end of the table Imogen had unfolded the cloak and clasped it to her neck, her eyes widening at what she saw in the box. John Fox lifted a single heavy silver coin from the glittering mass that lay within, turning it slowly, then pressed it into Paretes's palm.

'It's *heavy*,' the Palmyran murmured. 'It's warm.'

'Keep it, it's yours. Even if we don't do a deal,' Fox smiled. 'Go on, keep it. Give me the girl.'

'My baby comes too,' Imogen interrupted.

But Paretes didn't hear her, rubbing the coin anxiously, filled with doubt. 'Can it be real?'

'King Solomon's silver, pure and unalloyed,' Fox said patiently.

'It doesn't mean anything. It's not money, Paretes, though the God-Emperor's head is on it. It's only a gift. A talent. Make of it what you will.'

Paretes's hand closed over it. 'One is not enough.'

'Then we have no deal.' Fox dropped the lid with a bang, clicked the hasp closed. The rope was still looped through the bronze hoops and he picked it up, pulled the casket towards him across the table.

'All of them, John Fox.' Paretes slammed his hand greedily onto the box, stopping it. '*All* of them, and she will be your very own.'

'No.'

Finally Paretes sat back. 'Have it your way,' he sighed, raising his thumb: a deal. 'She's more bother than she's worth anyway. Take her, take her, she's yours.'

Fox held the baby out to Imogen.

'Paretes let me go too easily,' she murmured as she bent to take the child. 'You know he doesn't mean what he says.'

'Get the crib, we're leaving now,' he ordered, catching her eye. 'And say nothing.'

'Leaving so soon? Rest awhile,' suggested Paretes. 'It's the depth of night and there is no hurry, surely. Some wine.'

'I promise you he has a dagger hidden in his clothes,' Imogen hissed.

'Your slave insults me,' Paretes said.

Fox slapped Imogen with the flat of his hand, drawing a red flush from her temple to her jaw. Her eyes filled with tears. She looked away, then kissed her baby. Fox's fingers did not pause as he strapped the box to his belt, shrugging his cloak to hide it. He shoved Imogen at the door but she hung back rebelliously, sulking.

'Farewell, Paretes,' he said genially, filling a mug with sieved wine and handing it to the Palmyran. 'You've made the best deal you ever made in your life. Be satisfied with it. Be satisfied, Paretes.'

He pushed Imogen's glowering form ahead of him to the door, pulled it open, and they stepped out into the night. 'Oh!' she said as her boots splashed in water, then 'Oh!' as she realised it was pouring with rain. There seemed to be no sky, no land. He dragged the hood of her cloak over her head and pushed her ahead of him through the mud towards the pig-man's fire, the only spot of light in the darkness. The pig-man's black silhouette was hunched by the flames in his lonely vigil. A pig-man had no friends to share his fire, even on such a night. His rickety shelter had no walls, the thatch roof was held up by four sticks, water pouring off it all round. They ducked through the rain to the shelter, gasping, peering through the swirling orange smoke. Imogen pressed her hand to her mouth thinking she would be sick. 'What's *that*?'

'Pigshit,' Fox said. 'Put your hand over your nose and breathe through your mouth if you want it to smell any better.' He drew his sword and put his face down to the pig-man. 'Go away!'

Imogen listened to the man scrambling into the dark. 'Do people always do as you say?'

'No.' He looked around him, keeping Imogen between himself and the fire. She could hear the snorting pigs outside, see their pale, washed shapes as blurs moving behind the wattle fence. They loved the rain. '*You* don't. You didn't keep your mouth shut when I asked you to,' he pointed out.

'Why should I? Paretes had a dagger, I wanted to warn you. But all you did was slap me for insulting him.'

'Not for insulting him.'

'You did!'

'For telling the truth,' Fox said patiently.

She stared. 'But of course I told you the truth.'

He paced like an animal, keeping her between him and the fire, then used his sword to poke the flames into a frenzy of sparks, kicking the pig-man's whole night store of twigs onto it in one go, so that the flames leapt up and she feared for the roof. She turned to him, shielding her eyes from the glare.

'What exactly are you doing?'

'What does it look like I'm doing?'

'You think I'm stupid,' she said.

'I think you don't know much.'

She lifted her baby until the tip of her nose touched Sabrina's face. 'You have no idea,' she said, 'what I have been through.'

'Keep quiet,' he said. 'Look at the fire.' He gripped her shoulder in his left hand. 'Don't look round.'

'I can hear something. I think the pig-man's coming back.'

'No he isn't. Keep looking at the fire.' But she did look round of course, and her eyes widened. He slid his hand from her shoulder into her hair, pushing her head against him, forcing his mouth against hers in a long kiss. She struggled but could not move. The footsteps splashed closer, entered the shelter.

Fox turned, sweeping up his sword as the dagger came down. Paretes had thrown a cape over his toga, but it was too short and his skinny white legs stuck down beneath it, splashed to the knee with trickling mud. They seemed too spindly to support such a round weight. The rain was running orange with firelight down his face, catching his expression, earnest, nervous, full of greed. Even in the last moment when he saw the raised sword he could not stop himself, thinking he was too quick. His arm sliced with squealing bones down the honed edge of the blade, the hand dropped from his wrist into the fire, the fingers still clenching the dagger tight.

Paretes stooped to the fire in horrified disbelief, then lifted the stump of his forearm with his other hand, his mouth stretching wide into a scream that would wake the dead, as well as the dead drunk. Fox jabbed him beneath the fifth rib into the lung and the scream emerged no louder than bursting bubbles. His braced feet on the slippery ground, Fox swept the blade from side to side through the internal organs, which felt no pain, and Paretes left his life with nothing more than that terrifying expression of disbelief on his face.

The body fell forward on the sword, levering it from Fox's grasp. He bent down and pulled, but the point had caught in the spine or a shoulder blade, and came out with the tip snapped.

'He's broken it,' Imogen said.

'Finest Austrian steel,' Fox said bitterly. 'Are you all right?'

She had pressed her hand over her mouth, jiggling the baby with her whole body, and he didn't know whether she was laughing or going to be sick.

'What's so funny?' he growled. 'Next time do as you're told. When I tell you don't look, *don't look*.'

He crouched, searching for something on the earth floor, then plunged his hands into Paretes's toga, the naked flesh beneath still as warm as though it were alive. There was only the belt that

65

had held the dagger and the usual oddments, a couple of leather pouches, one containing silver coins and the other gold. He tossed them to Imogen and moved on without a pause.

'He wanted me back so badly,' she said. 'Poor old Paretes. I'm complimented.'

He glanced at her and rolled his eyes.

'That's not the first man you've killed,' she said.

'And you're not the first girl I've kissed.'

She put her head on one side. 'It's exciting. You're exciting to be with, and yet horrible, too. I don't know what to call it.'

'It's called life, Imogen, staying alive. Are you going to help?' He looked towards where the eastern horizon must lie. 'We have very little time.'

'What are you looking for?'

'What Paretes died for. It wasn't you, Imogen. Sorry. You'd better start sulking again.'

He crouched, shielding his face from the heat with his arm, and prodded the fire with the broken blade, rolling the hand from the embers. The heat had tightened it into an impenetrable claw, the point of the dagger looked red-hot. He trod on the palm and used the flat of the sword blade to prise open the fingers. 'Here we are.' He used the hem of her cloak to lift out the silver coin, blew on it, then dropped it into a pouch.

The fire was dying down rapidly now. Working quickly, he slipped the severed hand into the folds of the toga, lifted Paretes under the armpits, and dragged the body across the wet mud towards the pigsty. He could hear the pigs' grunts following him along the other side of the wattle fence. Pigs were a good way of getting rid of unwanted bodies but they would not have finished their meal by morning, and Fox had another plan. The pen drained towards the far corner and he backed cautiously now, then stopped dragging his burden as his outstretched foot felt nothing but a thick, soft slurry. He lowered his leg to the knee over the edge of the pit without finding bottom, then turned and slid the body into the pig-cess without further ceremony. No bubbles rose.

'What a terrible death,' Imogen said.

'His choice.' Fox pulled her hood over her head again against the pouring rain; she would have stood watching him until her hair was drenched, not moving or thinking of herself, he was sure, though he had noticed she was holding the baby dry beneath her cloak. 'You're an odd one.' He shook his head, then fetched the crib from the shelter and took her elbow, hurrying her past the outhouses slumped against the rear wall of the Tabernacle. A faint glow showed round the kitchen door, and without realising that they shared the thought they both imagined the old woman asleep at the table, the bronze lamp guttering on the last of its oil beside her, rocking an invisible crib with her hand.

He looked again towards the east; still dark, but the rain was easing off. A sudden firmness beneath their feet told them they had come to the crossroads, and he pulled her to the dormitory on the far side where Paretes had chained his male slaves. A voice spoke out of the night.

'Sky fall on your head yet, sir?'

'Yes, Briginus, I think it probably has.'

'You must've drunk the beer,' Briginus said. 'Thought there was a bit of a row.' He peered. 'And a woman involved, of course.' A faint glow suffused the misty air around them, the first of first light. The chains that held the crouching men on the step were looped round a longer chain, allowing them limited movement as long as they kept in the same order. Fox drew his sword and smashed it down, then again. The chain parted at the third blow and they heard the sliding, tinkling sound of loops slipping down the links, then the rattle of them on the boards. The men gazed at him uneasily, shuffling their feet.

'Run,' Fox said, pointing to the west. 'Freedom.' He whacked one of them with the flat of the broken blade to break their thrall, and they scattered, their footsteps splashing as they jumped down into the marshes until only Briginus remained.

'See you again one day, sir,' Briginus said steadily. 'For the moment I'll do exactly what you say.'

'West,' Fox said, and Briginus gave a sharp nod, taking his orders like a warrior. He dropped down onto the road leading westwards to the ford at Thorney Island, running stiffly at first, then picking up speed. His running figure disappeared in the mist between the tall reedbeds within a minute or two.

Fox took Imogen's elbow and hurried her down the road leading south over the spine of the island. At the end, at the junction with the unfinished road sliding down into the marshes to the east, he paused. 'How long before my grandchild needs her feed?'

'What?'

'How long before my grandchild needs your tit?'

'She'll probably last for an hour or two.' Imogen began to cry. 'What do you mean, your grandchild?'

'You don't suppose I go to this trouble for every brown-eyed girl who looks like the woman I love?'

'I don't know,' she said fiercely. 'Do you?'

He hesitated, caught out by her sharp insight of how he had wasted his life, yet also aware how far from her he was in age, in sex, in knowledge and experience. But her fierceness persuaded him.

'It seems . . .' He cleared his throat, then continued, 'I am your father.'

Imogen wouldn't admit that she was still crying. John Fox hadn't noticed her tears or taken her in his arms to comfort her, so she comforted the baby beneath her cloak instead, jogging the tiny warm bundle against her breast, staring after Fox as he jumped down into the water and went sloshing away between the reed-beds. The reeds looked like charcoal strokes drawn against the pale mist. They jostled and creaked as he pushed between them, closing behind him with soft clicks, and he was gone. The rain had given way to a soaking drizzle. Imogen jogged the baby nervously, then swallowed as a honking, booming sound carried to her out of the mist. She'd been in London long enough to know that the river was the life of the place; without it there would be nothing here. The Romans had brought their new gods, but they were much the same as the old gods, and she wondered if the sound was a spirit moving in the holy waters, perhaps finding a way into the marsh channels on the flood. She went backwards to the middle of the road. 'Fox,' she whispered, comforting Sabrina for all she was worth.

A robin landed on a bulrush, surveying her bright-eyed, and she wondered which spirit that bird represented here.

The dawn light was growing, but the landscape of marshes that she knew must lie around her was formless mist. She was enclosed in a perfect foggy circle that contained her gritty patch of road, lapped by black water in every direction except the way they had come. She backed against a roadbuilder's cart abandoned with a broken wheel. 'Fox . . .' she called, then drew a deep sigh of relief when his figure reappeared sloshing towards her between the reeds, knocking them back with his hands. In the water to his waist, showing no sign of cold or discomfort, he reached over the road's edge and held up his arms to her.

'You're certainly old enough to be him!' she said.

'Quick, this mist won't hold for ever.' He beckoned impatiently. 'I've found the old lane, stop making such a noise.'

'I never knew my father,' Imogen told him with trembling lips, 'but I know he was a kind and loving man, and he would have been a king except that he loved my mother.'

'Is that what Rues told you? Am I really being uncaring?' he demanded. 'Haven't I saved your life and don't you owe everything to me?'

'You're not like him at all,' she said miserably. 'You're not at all like I always imagined you, or like she said.'

He glanced towards the mist that hid the inn. 'Shall we stay here all day?' he hissed, and she glowered at him. Then she knelt obediently to be lifted. 'No, not you!' he said. 'Give me the baby.'

He held the bundle against his chest and pulled Imogen down without ceremony. She splashed to her thighs in the cold water, then felt it creep slowly over her waist as her legs sank in the mud. 'Ssh,' he muttered, pulling her among the reeds. The robin flew up over their heads and Imogen tried to dry her crying, but it was hopeless, the whole world was wetter than tears. She had to drag the heavy weight of her sodden cloak and tunic after her whenever the water grew shallower, then fight her tangling clothes as she waded through the deeper parts, gasping from the cold. Above the waterline she was soaked from the drizzle and mist swirling around their heads.

'Stop crying,' he said without looking back.

'I won't do anything you say,' she told him rebelliously.

'Pretend you're a man,' he said, pushing ahead, and soon all she saw of him was the reeds closing behind him. Her eyes widened as that booming call came again. She splashed faster, suddenly coming out of the reeds into a clear stretch of water. Fox was standing above her in the middle of it, wet only to his knees.

He jiggled the child. 'She woke, but she must sleep a little longer.'

'I suppose you've put a sleeping spell on her or something.'

He looked at her sharply, then put out his hand. Imogen let herself be dragged from the deep water up the gravel sides onto a flooded path winding between the rushes, and instead of mud she now felt timbers and tightly-bound bundles of reeds beneath her feet.

'Belinos's Road,' he said. 'I've never heard of it being flooded before.'

'You make it sound like it's been here for ever.'

'Four hundred years,' he said casually. 'It was Belinos who raised the gate and tower by the river's ford at Greenwich, and founded the City of the Sun. Boats paid customs dues at the quay beneath Belinos's Gate, and pilgrims waded across the Thames there on holy days, making offerings at the sacred grove on the Isle of Dogs. But the river grew too deep. In my father's time dues were paid at London, by then the head of the river, though the new quay was still called Belinos's Gate.' He gazed around them at the watery landscape revealed by the thinning mist. 'The river's always growing deeper, that's why the Romans had to build a bridge over the old London ford there.'

She splashed after him along the path. 'How can you know these things?'

'Do you doubt everything I say?'

'Yes,' she called at his broad back. 'I doubt that you are my father.'

'How can you?' he laughed. 'Look at you! Listen to yourself!'

She was taken aback. 'You're not the father I dreamt of.'

'Rues remembered me as a young man, and for a young man everything is different.' He slowed his walk, the water splashing only to his ankles now, each reedbed towing ripples behind it as the level fell. 'You see, we were in love, your mother and I, we saw nothing but each other, the rest of the world did not exist. Years later no doubt she remembered, in mourning, my best features to you, and forgave my faults. I, too, probably remember only the best of her. If we had really been reunited, which I longed for with all my soul when I began my long journey home, would it really have been the same between us? Exchanging memories and feeling our grey hairs instead of passion.' Fox turned with sudden sincerity, stopping her. 'Instead I have found you, her youth alive in you, Imogen.'

The baby cried suddenly. 'Milk,' Fox said, and she snatched her baby back, irritated that he had understood the cry. He took her hand lightly. 'You can rest soon, there's a place nearby.' He pointed at the blue circle of sky growing above them, the mist that had protected them slowly clearing. 'We must not be seen, and movement shows.' They made better time now, the path winding in front of them almost dry, the water gurgling down between the reedbeds that bordered its sides. That booming cry came again, not at all frightening in sunlight. 'A bittern,' he said, glancing at her. 'A bird fit for a king's table.'

'Why?'

'Why do you always ask why?'

'Because I'm young and I want to know everything. Why fit for a king's table?'

He sighed. 'All voice and no meat. It's just a show.'

'I wish you'd told me earlier,' she said with feeling.

'You would not have followed so quickly.'

'You were carrying Sabrina, of course I followed!' she said. Then she added grumpily, 'I would have come anyway, I don't want to be hunted down. Slaves who kill their masters are crucified.'

'No. For women it's worse.'

'I know.'

His eyes crinkled with amusement. 'Where people are concerned, I always like to make sure, Imogen.'

'You know a lot about people, don't you? You know how to make me come along with you. I didn't stand much of a chance once you'd made up your mind, neither did Paretes.'

'He made his own fate. So did you.'

'How did you know he'd follow us outside?'

'As you pointed out, I know a lot about people,' he said heavily. 'I had to learn something during those long years abroad.'

'Will I walk with you all day?'

'You'll walk all night. I haven't slept and neither have you, and there may be a hue and cry today. I don't think so. They'll think Paretes has simply upped sticks for reasons unknown, taking you and his male slaves with him, and they'll loot the place for

71

whatever's left. If they find the body somehow, or get suspicious about the broken chain, the escaped slaves blundering west will be a lot easier to follow than us.'

'You freed those men and deliberately sent them in the opposite direction to attract any attention away from us.'

He shrugged. 'Fair exchange.'

'Where did you learn to be the man you are?' she asked nastily beneath her breath, but he heard.

'I learned it when I was separated from your mother nine months before you were born, Imogen.' Fox stopped his walk, fixing her with his eyes, ignoring the crying baby. 'When I was excluded from my country because I would not marry a woman I did not love and secretly married Rues, your mother. Because I thought I could not live without her. Because I was told she died in childbirth, and our child too. You, Imogen. You and Rues made me the man I am.'

'What happened to you abroad?' she whispered, staring. His eyes were flecked brown ovals, so like her own yet so different, with fire and movement deep within them. It felt as though she was looking deeper than she wanted into a part of herself.

'I lived,' he said, 'without love.'

Suddenly he gave a grunt of satisfaction and pointed off the path. A clump of weeping willows showed their broad green tops out of the mist. He pushed ahead of her through the screen of reeds and she followed him onto a low island of tree roots and tussocky grass, above the highest level of the flood, still dry beneath the trees. Fox ducked beneath the fronds and laid his cloak against a tree trunk. 'Feed your baby.' He took her golden-brown cape and spread it in the sun to dry. Imogen settled herself and at last Sabrina was silent, suckling contentedly. Fox paced up and down for a while then yawned, stretching his arms. The bulrushes concealed everything closer than the blue, shimmering hills that surrounded them, the village and fort of London visible only as a few threads of smoke about a mile away. The baby slept and Imogen basked sleepily in the sun, putting up her hair into a ponytail.

Her voice carried to him softly. 'Are we safe?'

'Safe from everyone but ourselves, Imogen.' Fox sat and leaned back against the tree beside her, propping her wrists on his knees.

'How do you know so much?' she asked.

'I'm older. I keep my eyes open.'

'Tell me.'

'I have told you exactly.' He shook his head. 'You're already half a Roman, aren't you, Imogen? Fashion, that's how they always get the women.' He touched the Celtic beads in her hair, which in his youth every woman wore. 'These aren't you any more. Paretes was selling you as a barbarian princess – look, she has barbarian glass beads in her hair! Sings barbarian songs! Soon he would have had you tattooing the sacred faces on your skin, to increase your curiosity value. But inside yourself, Imogen, you're already a bit of a Roman. Your cloak has a braided hem, the latest fashion. And golden brown is this year's colour – all the girls were wearing it in Burdigala.'

'What's wrong with it? King Verica, whose protection we were under, was more Roman than the Romans, that's why his people hated him. He escaped to Rome, wore the toga, made sacrifices on the Capitol, all but begged the new Emperor Claudius to invade.'

'And you've put your hair up like a Roman girl.'

'It's practical,' she justified herself.

He laughed and smelt her. '*And* you take baths, and wear oil too.'

'Go to sleep,' she said. 'You're tired. You're hiding it, but you are. How long since you slept?'

'Three night, four nights. Before the storm.'

'You need rest so badly. Will anyone come along Belinos's Road?'

'Not without me seeing them.'

'Don't you ever sleep?'

'No.'

The warm sun waved frond shadows across their faces. Imogen stroked the heat from her cheeks, tired but restless. 'How can you *know* that Belinos built it – however long ago you said.'

'Four hundred.'

'All those years ago. How can you possibly know that?'

'Because I remember it.'

She stared at him, then laughed uncertainly.

'You've forgotten,' he said sadly. 'The Romans you secretly admire write everything down, their speeches, their laws, even

73

their commercial transactions, so you think it's the only way. What of the power of real words, Imogen? The rhymes that girls learn on their mother's knee that they never forget, that never lose their power to move? *Blackbird on a branch in the deeply-wooded plain. Sweet, soft, peaceful is your song.*'

'That's how you found me,' she murmured. 'I couldn't help remembering home and everything I had lost. The soldier with the flames reflecting on his sword and helmet, my friends screaming. I'm nineteen years old,' she said plaintively. 'More than half my life gone.'

'Men learn the epics, fighting songs, religious hymns passed down round the camp fire from father to son, from son to father to son. Our parents, grandparents and all our great-grandparents never die, Imogen. They go on to another life, but their old lives live on with us in words. Whoever lives never dies; whatever happens, happens for ever. They have become memory, and it is the job of some of us to remember . . .'

She sat up respectfully. 'You're not a priest, are you? Which religion do you prefer? I'd love to see the temples in Rome! In London they're already putting up a temple to Diana on one of the hills . . .' She stopped, realising he was asleep. He'd put back his head against the tree trunk, his face full in the sun.

If she really wanted to run away from him, now was the time. But she had nowhere to run to. The water was already creeping back towards the island. 'Where are we going?' she whispered.

'A safe place,' he said, and she jumped.

But she remembered what he had said earlier. 'Safe from everyone but ourselves.'

He was snoring. She reached out to brush a fly from his forehead, then stared. His eyelids must have been covered by a thin white grease which was melting in the heat, sliding away. He was staring back at her with the bright blue eyes that had been tattooed on his eyelids.

Imogen woke with a start. The tree root against her back seemed to be digging its way into her spine. The sun had moved around the sky, the rising water had fallen, and Sabrina had been turned round and laid against her other breast, suckling contentedly, the sensation that had woken her. Fox was standing with his back to her. 'Dark soon,' he said, pointing at the setting sun.

But she could not forget his eyes. She made herself say casually, 'And then?'

'The moon will show us our way.' He fetched her cloak, now dry, flapped it to shake out the wrinkles, then bent and wrapped it round her shoulders. 'The air will be chill. The moon will rise in our faces.' He even spoke like a master of the lore.

'I know now what you mean when you say you never sleep,' she told him respectfully, then added, 'I know who you are. I saw.' She bowed her head for his blessing, like a child. 'You are a Druid.'

'Not only a Druid,' he muttered. 'I left that behind me too.' He shook his head. 'How amazing, that after all these years of concealment my own daughter is the first to truly see me. But I can't bless you, child, I'm no longer that man.'

'What you are is against Roman law. You have the blue eyes that see the gods.'

'That's just superstition.'

She couldn't believe what he was letting slip. 'But everyone knows—'

'I've seen ordinary men, barbarians from beyond the Rhine, who have blue eyes.'

'But you don't feel the cold, and you're not frightened. You've been trained to be what you are. The Romans would have killed you if they knew,' she said earnestly. 'How have you lived with that for almost twenty years?'

He stood up, a dark silhouette against the colours in the sky.

'I wear a sword, and that's against the law too.' He shrugged without turning to her, speaking to the marshes. 'A blessing is more than a benevolence, it's open-ended, who knows where it may lead? Sooner or later there's what the Romans call a *quid pro quo*. You don't get anything for nothing, and the price may be higher than you think. Best if we were just ourselves, Imogen. Would you feel happier on your own?'

'No.' She shivered, drawing her cloak round her throat as the evening chill approached. 'I most definitely would not.' But still she was looking up at him expectantly, and he sighed, then slid his fingers into her hair, the top of her head warm in the curve of his palm.

'I bless you,' he said.

75

Her tummy rumbled. She was starving.

'Tonight we have three rivers to cross,' he said, lifting her to her feet. 'The Neck, the Sluice, and the Raven. We must cross the deep ford on the Raven before the moon pulls up the tide again, and then we shall reach the City of the Sun at dawn.' He put out the crook of his arm for the baby, a curiously feminine gesture. 'You must be hungry from feeding her. I'll carry her.'

He took Sabrina and settled her while Imogen looked at him thoughtfully. He was intimidating, but she was getting through to him, and underneath he was kind.

'Come on!' he said irritably, and she smiled.

Following his long strides, Imogen glanced back to see the island was already lost behind them in the reeds and twilight. She wished they could have stayed at such a pleasant place.

When they came to the lane, Fox pulled her up the gravel sides and turned left, setting a cracking pace over the uneven surface while the sunset behind them still cast a glow, and she hurried after him. 'I don't know if there are really any gods,' he was saying, almost as though he was talking to himself, 'but it's safer to believe that there are. People who believe in them see them.'

'But you don't?' She trotted to keep up, her feet catching in her cloak.

'I used to, Imogen. But it's all rubbish. Claudius has issued his edict against the Druids and we are killed on sight. The old lore can't be written down, it's only breath and memory, it's gone into the air as though it was never real. We're human animals and that's all there is to it. I won't live again after I die. I don't really believe every place has its own little god, or each heart a soul. I just go through the motions, I live as it comes. I bless you, I bless you, I bless you – there, it's easy for me. I believe in everything these days, and nothing.'

'Yet you came back for my mother,' Imogen called. 'You gave everything up for Rues, twice.'

'I know,' he grunted over his shoulder. 'That's what disturbs me.'

Imogen ran to catch up, holding out her arm affectionately, but she tripped and all but landed in a puddle, saving herself on her hands. Suddenly, beneath her nose, the water stirred and splashed. She screamed, seeing a serpent in there. Fox was back

76

in a flash. He pulled her up by her arm and shook her furiously.

'Don't you ever give us away like that again!' She saw such ferocity in his face that her eyes burned.

'Don't you talk to me!' she said furiously.

They stared at one another, both as angry as could be, then Fox laughed, his grip on her elbow becoming gentle. 'There's enough for us to fight,' he said, 'without fighting ourselves. Pax?'

'Don't shout at me again.'

'I promise.' He handed her the baby then reached into the puddle, snatching up an eel as long as his arm. 'Trapped by the tide. Good luck for us.' He split it with his sword, skinned the chewy, succulent flesh between blade and thumb, then sliced it in half. They ate as they walked.

'But bad luck for the eel,' Imogen said, and he laughed again, then held up his hand as a rushing sound carried to them. It was almost dark now and they felt their way forward to where the path dropped into rushing water. A tree had fallen down between the steep banks, swaying uneasily in the ebb flowing back to the Thames. Fox stood with one hand on the roots, waiting for the trunk to ground firmly as the level dropped.

'Tell me,' she said gently, 'why you're angry, and why you laugh.'

Night was complete now. His voice came out of the dark, as though blindness made his words easier. 'I am . . . I *was* the favoured child.' She had never heard such bitterness. 'I was taken to the Druid nemeton the day I was weaned, schooled in the Druid mysteries and the poetry of blood and fire. I have no memories of my mother. I can't see her face, and I never felt anything for her . . . I don't know how I could. And my father was not my father, he was the king. A king cannot be close to anybody, least of all his son who is next in line. He was a powerful and wrong-headed man.'

'You were educated – what is a nemeton?'

'A nemeton is a sanctuary, Imogen, the clearing within a sacred grove, the holy of holies. The discipline and ritual of the special school absorbed my childhood. You see, in me all the omens came together. I knew from the youngest age that I was born to be king. Usually it isn't so simple because of kinship and the choice among cousins, the interwoven families going back four generations. Our succession is agnatic, a king is chosen from among the male descendants of a common great-grandfather. I am the son of King Lovernios, son of Londinos, son of Androgeos and his queen Lovernisca. These were not the only kings of Kent west of the Darenth during that time, but you see my point: I am both the son and great-grandson of a king. On my father's death my election would be certain. As a child I always knew this, I was trained for the moment all my youth, to the exclusion of everything else. Of affection. Of family. Of peace. Of love.'

She heard his cloak rustle as he flexed his sword arm.

She waited, listening to the undercurrent of emotion in his voice, fascinated by how vulnerable he was with her; but then she remembered who she was. 'But?' she murmured.

'I fell in love with the wrong woman. I fell for young Rues.'

'My mother was the daughter of King Dias and Queen Rues, and the granddaughter of Andoco. Surely two kings in her blood was more than good enough, even for you.'

'To my father they were the wrong kings,' Fox said.

The roots were quiet beneath his hand now, he could no longer feel the rush of the water. He swung himself up. Imogen's head was a shadow against the last line of sunset as he guided her silently along the fallen trunk – there was no more squeaking or silliness from her. He jumped down on the far side and searched the stars. The Pleiades were rising like a patch of shimmering mist from the hills ahead of them, but the constellation of Perseus twinkled high and pure. He swung Imogen down. Now that they knew its direction, they could just make out the path in front of them, following the curve of the Thames.

'The Romans call Britain an island, but it's not,' Fox sighed as they walked. 'It's many islands.' He took Imogen's hand in his own, seeing ahead of them like a cat in the dark; or maybe, she thought, he had trodden this road many times in his youth. 'Each tribe was its own island before the Romans came, with its own customs and way of life. My people of Kent were very different from the Atrebates to the west, and the Atrebates were different from the Catuvellaunians north of the Thames, and . . . everyone from everyone else. Now all that's gone. The Iceni are still hiding out in their fens and swamps, and Cymbeline's son Caractacus is hiding out in the mountains of the west, but the Romans cannot afford to fail. Soon we'll be one people, one province.'

'They will bring peace and prosperity.'

'The Romans, Imogen, bring Romans. Their only interest is Romans. They invaded Britain to make money for Romans. We have corn, cattle, slaves, precious metals, and harbours on every side to ship them off to the markets of Rome.'

A white glow stretched along the horizon, clearly showing the broad notch the Thames had cut through the hills, and the stars were fading. 'All I remember of the old days,' she said softly, watching as the top curve of the moon, harvest orange, rose into the glow, seemingly large enough to touch, 'was the men fighting and bragging while the women did the work. You didn't invent those useful pottery jugs with a nipple on the side for feeding babies, or think how useful olive oil is, or store it in those clever amphorae sealed with pitch so that it keeps. The Romans did. You just told us how wonderful you were and we believed you.'

He looked at the child he carried. 'I thought you hated them.'

'One Roman soldier. But I love Sabrina, she's the one who's important to me, not who her father was.'

'You'd do anything for her,' he said.

'I would have killed Paretes. And I've come with you without asking exactly where we're going.' She waited, then said loyally, 'I banged my knee when you swung me down from that tree trunk but I didn't make a sound.'

'Good for you.'

He put out his arm to stop her. They had come to the Sluice, a deep cleft worn through the mud, almost drained of water now. He found the narrowest place, where part of the bank had collapsed, and swung her across. They heard a trickling sound coming from the direction of the river and water slid beneath them, going upstream. They watched the flow increase, swirling with bubbles. The moon had risen two handspans above the hills, casting a fierce silver light in their faces, and the tide had turned. Fox went faster than before, but this time he held her upper arm where he could take her weight if she fell.

'Before you can know where you're going, Imogen, you must know where you've come from.'

She laughed as he lifted her over a decayed section of track.

'Oh! It's just like flying!' She glanced at him under her eyelashes, changing her tack with him, almost mocking. 'Druids are supposed to be able to fly, aren't you?'

'I'm telling you about yourself, Imogen, who you are. Your mother's ancestors were Catuvellaunians, the strongest tribe. They had a strong king in Tasciovanus – the brother of my great-grandfather Androgeos, incidentally. Tasciovanus made himself lord over the Trinovantes too, who faced us across the Thames estuary. But when he died, fifty-seven years ago, his empire fell apart. King Sego could not hold it together, so he was killed by Andoco. Andoco was killed by your grandfather, Dias. But Queen Rues was the more formidable half of the pair, and when Dias was poisoned, Queen Rues ruled in her own right, an implacable and ambitious woman with dry breasts and the face of a man. But in those days men were more proud than they are now, and many would not follow Queen Rues. Also she had given birth to a daughter not a son. The rebels were led by Cymbeline and he proclaimed himself King after a butcher's battle. Queen Rues fled south across the Thames to Atrebatan territory, safety, and obscurity – the condition on which King Verica gave her refuge, not daring to offend his powerful neighbours. But the queen gave her daughter, then ten years old, her own name, an old woman's dream of another Queen Rues one day on the Catuvellaunian throne. Meanwhile Cymbeline extended his power. Fifteen years later, when I met young Rues and gave her my head and my heart, he was in his prime.'

'Why was loving my mother such an evil thing?'

'Because my father had come to believe that the only way of preserving his kingdom was an alliance with Cymbeline. Both hated the Romans even as they followed Roman fashions, buying Rhodian wine and showing off Austrian cutlery and selling slaves to pay for it all. But at the same time Cymbeline was as greedy for territory as the Romans, and if my father was to keep his kingdom, and London an open city, the meeting point of the four tribes, I must make a political marriage, an alliance, with Cymbeline's daughter Ynnogin. She was a great beauty but I did not want her. Instead I was blind for Rues, the daughter of Cymbeline's enemy. You can't understand. All our life was love; common sense and duty did not compare. You know what young men are like. I threw away everything I was and all I'd learned, I would have paid any price to have Rues. And I did.'

Imogen looked up into his fierce face in the pale moonlight. 'Yes,' she said, 'I can imagine you doing that.'

'The forests are limitless. I married us, secretly, beneath the mistletoe, and we lived in a turf cottage deep in the oakwoods of the Weald. Above all I longed for a male child,' Imogen was startled by the deep, possessive glare in his eyes, 'not only for myself but as a token from the gods to justify my love. But it was not to be, and my union was perceived to be not blessed. Rues's barrenness was taken as a punishment to me and a warning to the tribes of Kent.'

'You, you,' Imogen said. 'You only talk of you, you're just like all the other men.'

'We were betrayed,' he went on, ignored her gibe. 'Rues was condemned back to the boredom of Verica's kindly care, but I was put in chains and dragged to my father's court at the City of the Sun, brought back to my people as though I was mad, a traitor for falling in love. After all my training and all I had been taught, my privileged and favoured treatment, I had put myself before my people. And still I would not marry Ynnogin. So I was exiled in disgrace. Eventually one of my cousins, Postumus, had the kingship dangled in front of him and married the girl, and a merry dance she led him, by all accounts.'

'And you never saw Rues again.'

'Until I saw you.' Then Fox shook his head. 'Of course, I did meet her once more. The captain of my guard was a friend, and on our way to the port near Glastonbury he turned a blind eye to my last night in Rues' arms at Quarley Hill. The ship taking me into exile set sail at dawn. My feet did not touch dry land between the muddy quayside in Britain and the boiling sand of a beach in Judea.'

'And when you heard the lies about her death in child-birth—'

'I believed that I had killed her.'

She touched the corners of her eyes.

'What's the matter?' he asked.

'Don't you realise how awful it is, what you're saying? How did you live?'

He stared at her face. 'You're crying tears for me.' He wiped her cheeks. 'Me? Thinking she was dead? I lived accordingly, Imogen. I cared only for myself.'

The moon hung high over their heads and the tide was in full flood now, tugging at their boots, so that they trailed long silver ripples upstream as they waded across the shallows. The marshes were again being inundated, the floodwater pouring along the channels, making them look like a huge silver web rising out of the earth.

Fox paused as he went in over his knees. The next step took him in to his thigh. 'This is the deep ford across the Raven,' he said, 'but I've never known it like this. We'll be trapped if we don't get across soon.' He waded back to Imogen and handed her the baby. He pulled his cloak forward in two wings over his shoulders to keep it dry if he could, then did the same with hers. He crouched on his knuckles. 'Up you get. Shoulders.'

She hitched up her tunic and locked her long white legs round his neck. 'This is fun!' she giggled as he swayed to his feet.

'You're heavier than you look,' he grumbled, 'and you have your mother's sense of humour.'

'She kept to herself. You knew her very well,' she said, keeping her balance with wicked little tugs at his hair.

'Even better,' he said, looking half round, 'than this.'

The water was flowing upstream fast and he leaned into it as the level rose over his waist, wet Imogen's feet, reached his chest. As it came to her knees she fell silent, feeling him struggle beneath her on the uneven stones of the creek bed. She could not swim, and if he dropped her she and the baby would probably drown. In the middle, the flow reached his chin, then for a brief moment bubbled over his head, but still he kept going. She did not doubt him for a moment. His head reappeared gasping below her and she said nothing now, stroking his wet hair between her legs. And he had said he cared only for himself.

He heaved himself up the far side, staggering forward with increasing speed, then dropped her on her feet. He rolled over and put his head between his knees, spluttering. 'All right?'

'We're just fine. Not a splash on her,' Imogen said, resting her hand on his shoulder. That cloak needed wringing out. 'You rest awhile, John Fox.'

But he was on his feet in a moment. 'Not much further now.' He parted the reeds, then stopped. 'Look.'

She came up beside him and looked. In front of them lay flooded ground with a Roman road running straight as a rule across it towards the creek, where it stopped. There was no bridge, and the road did not continue on the far side of the creek. This route would never reach London Bridge now. On their left they saw the wide steady sweep of the Thames round the Isle of Dogs; on the other side of the abandoned road, marshland petered out in a scattering of small rectangular fields, their outlines curving upward into silvery foothills overhung by dense black forest.

'Let's get our feet out of the water,' he said.

There were no fences; they crossed the Roman road and rested on the slope of a ditch and embankment thrown up to mark the boundary between two sets of fields, different properties. A muddy lane ran along the bottom, and Fox found a tangle of brambles for them to rest behind. He took off his sodden cloak and they lay with their arms round each other for warmth, the baby between them. Several times Imogen cleared her throat as if to speak.

'What is it now?'

'Am I really like her?'

He chuckled. 'You smell different. Rues didn't use Belgian rouge on her cheeks, or wear Capuan perfume.'

'I had to, for Paretes,' she said seriously. 'And this white lupin-seed skin powder. I must look a sight by now, don't look at me.' She touched her legs. 'Blotchy.'

'What else did you do for him? Were you his concubine?'

'He wouldn't touch a soiled woman,' she said, caressing the baby. 'He was funny, kind in his way, and fastidious.'

'Is that how you think of yourself, soiled?'

'Because I am.' She stroked Sabrina's head with her slim fingers. 'Not her. She's perfect.'

'Rues was always brown from the sun.'

'He kept me prisoner, it's not my fault I was never allowed out.'

'You're not my prisoner.'

'Thank you, John Fox,' she said tartly. 'I know what you mean by free, look at how you treated those poor men, freeing them to be chased and hunted and draw attention away from you.'

'*Us*.'

'You're a dangerous man, the worst sort, I mean dangerous to the people around you.'

'Around *us*.'

'I don't want to talk about my mother any more!' she said with sudden fierceness.

He reached up and plucked a blackberry from the bush above them, and they realised it was growing light, mist rising from the marshes into the haze. He touched the small silver coin at her throat. 'When our last morning came it was like this, misty.' He wouldn't stop. 'I gave her that to remember me by, the way people do. It's one of Cymbeline's, all I had, a ship coin: here's the ship with sails and rigging, and if you look on the other side . . . what is it?'

'We used to see those all the time,' she said in a small voice. 'It's one of those clever patterns with a man's face hidden in it, if you look in the right way. There. Long hair and moustache. Just like you.' She tugged, then gave an embarrassed laugh when the chain would not break. 'But he was a young man then. He'll never come back because if he did he'd find everything's changed. The woman he loved is truly dead now and his home is gone, he's a hunted man and he's lived too long and seen too much.'

Fox shrugged, tossed a blackberry into the air then caught it in his mouth. He was incorrigible. 'Maybe he hasn't changed inside,' he said. Imogen turned away from him and fed her baby.

Fox scrambled to the top of the bank. 'Look at this,' he whispered, gazing. There was something different in his voice. With the child still at her breast, she scrambled up after him.

The sun was streaming through the mist, highlighting the desolation of the scene ahead of him. There was no smoke of camp fires, none of the busy signs of a new day. Jutting from the water Fox saw the stumps of landing stages, dragged down by ropes and broken up. The white skeleton of a horse looked ridiculous and horrid. Only round black circles remained of the houses that had straggled for miles along the shore, and the timbered hall by the lane called the Straightsmouth was also burned. The ash circles were long cold now, flattened and run like black stars by rain and flood, as if they had been dropped from high in the air. Even Belinos's Gate, the royal mausoleum where the Straightsmouth came to the river, was burned as though it and all its kings had never been. The destruction had been methodical and Roman, the granaries looted before their stilts were broken. Through the mess the Roman road angled down from the hills as straight as an arrow, though now itself already covered in weeds and brambles. Whatever had happened here was years past.

'Is this the City of the Sun?' Imogen whispered.

'Greenwich. It was.'

Many of the fields that they had glimpsed by moonlight they now realised were overgrown, run wild. It seemed no young men at all had been left alive in the City of the Sun, though a few children and older women picked through the ripe, damaged crops tangled with weeds, bolters and brilliant scarlet poppies. Where the river curved closest into the foothills, a green pasture led upslope. Holy ground. Many of the burial mounds and barrows were broken open, and the dead were truly dead at last. Empty dene holes made chalky circles here and there, though not enough were revealed to show the celestial pattern. Sunken lines in the turf showed where some of the network of tunnels deep below had collapsed. The hill fort was undefended and already almost invisible, its earth banks overgrown or dug away by the road builders for sand.

Fox's face showed nothing of his feelings, but she was sure they were there because he did not move when the creak of wooden wheels carried to them or respond to the slow clop of the donkey coming into view along the boundary lane below. Imogen stared at the strangest vehicle she had ever seen, a battered war chariot stripped of its ornamentation, pulled by a white-muzzled donkey.

She pinched his hand.

'I know,' Fox said. 'There's no hurry. I know these people, they were my own. This early the farmer is asleep and the nirrup,' he pointed at the donkey, 'knows the way.' He slid down to the path, gathering a handful of grass which the donkey stopped to eat when it reached him. Fox drew his sword and walked down the side of the chariot, noting that the hobbling blades were broken from the hubs and the rocky wheels missed spokes. The ashwood frame was sound, but lightly built for speed, not strength, bending under its load. The open platform where the spearman once balanced with his feet thrust into leather thongs was now matted with compost. A mould-board plough had been heaved aboard, its heavy iron share resting on a bundle of cut reeds. Beneath more reed bundles, for thatch or field drainage perhaps, the farmer snored comfortably with his head against the wickerwork side of the chariot.

'Stop pretending you're asleep,' Fox said. 'I can see your eyes moving. Got your harvest in, have you? Going out to plough?'

'You're British?' the man exclaimed, and Fox laughed, knowing he was near home: Kentish folk always answered a question with another question. The farmer rubbed the palms of his grimy hands, pink with relief, then held out his arm to be helped up. He was wearing the grubbiest tartans Fox had ever seen. 'Thought you was foreigners. I'm a free man, a landowner,' he warned them, jumping down, broader than he was tall, looking up at them with a genial unafraid face, 'and my lads will be along shortly – why, I can hear them now.'

'Slaves, you mean,' Imogen said.

But the droveway remained empty in both directions. Fox sheathed his sword.

'See, you stood like Romans,' sighed the landowner in his relief. 'And she talked before she was spoken to, just like them Roman women. Your slave, is she?' His sharp eyes had already noticed the brand on her arm, he was no fool. 'Hard times, eh? They're hard for us all. I've nothing worth stealing, sorry to say, but if I had fine dry clothes they'd be yours.'

'Are you an honest man?'

'Well, sir, I'm as honest as the day is long!'

'Then I shall make sure every day is midsummer for you.' Fox jerked his head at the ruin of the town. 'What happened there?'

'Some young men kept their pride and made trouble, sir, that's all. Painted themselves in war colours, lot of screaming. Not like us sensible old rogues what survived. We're working for new masters under Roman law, and we pay a land tax and have to borrow money at userers' rates, so you see nothing's changed much, but a wise man can increase his holdings in times of confusion.' He spat. 'Not aristocrats, are you?'

'Why?'

'Them what sold us out.' There was real anger in the man's voice now. 'They got their fine villas in reward, no doubt, and wine with every meal. No, I can see you're not. They say they lie on beds when they eat, and they always smell of fish, and they have teachers to make sure their children don't learn British. But you've been swimming, you two have, and she's your slave.'

'I am not!' Imogen said.

'Yes she is,' Fox said with a warning glance to her, then shrugged tolerantly to the farmer. 'And you, my friend, what do they call you?'

'Vagnius, sir, and I must say things are a little better for me than what they have been, not that I'd admit it if you asked. I have a few investments and I know the value of money. Deeper than it looks back there, ain't it? Lost everything?'

'Vagnius, I need your nirrup, your cart and everything on it, and I'll pay you whatever you want for them.' The farmer stared at him in astonishment.

'What's your name, nirrup?' Imogen asked the donkey.

'And there are other things,' Fox explained gently to the man, 'which you will want to fetch for me.'

Vagnius braced his hands on his broad hips, laughing, shaking his head.

Fox held out Paretes's pouch and let gold coins spill into his palm. 'You see what I mean,' he said as Vagnius fell silent, awed. 'You may claim the larger half if you return, alone, before sunset.'

'I always trust a man who admits he's a rogue,' Fox called back through the rain pouring like a veil round the edge of his broad-brimmed hat, 'because at least he has that much honesty.'

'I spent all day expecting him to return with a cohort of troops.' Imogen watched Fox sliding and slipping in the mud of the forest trackway winding uphill ahead of her, holding himself up against the donkey on the leading rein. 'Ow!' she complained when the wheel of the chariot banged over a stone, but he paid no attention to her. The slope was steepest here, water splashing across the gravel to the River Raven foaming below. Fox slithered to his knees, then dragged himself up, pulling as hard as the donkey. The chariot lurched around Imogen, its battered wickerwork creaking loud enough to be heard even above the rain and wind whirling beneath the trees. But for the baby she would have preferred to walk, muddy though it was. In here she had too much time to think.

'You trusted him with *our* lives,' she called petulantly beneath the front rail where she was trying to protect Sabrina from the worst of the bumps, 'not just yours. He could have betrayed you, just as Paretes did.'

Fox chuckled and shook his head, sending water splashing onto his filthy cloak. 'Paretes never betrayed me, he did as I counted. He was a greedy man and he made his own fate. You see, I had no money then. Not a penny.'

'You certainly didn't behave like a pauper! You're a wealthy man, aren't you?'

'Only what Paretes gave us at the cost of his life. The bag of gold coins and some pennies.'

She stared at Fox, chilled. 'Where did you learn to look inside people so?' she whispered. 'What do you see when you look at me?'

'I trusted Vagnius because what he said was true, Imogen. He was a rogue but an honest one.'

'You're a rogue too,' she muttered under her breath, but he must have heard, because he turned back to her, smiling, his teeth looking very white in the failing light.

'He knew the value of money.'

'Well, you don't!' she said. 'I wept when you poured all your money—'

'Our. Our money.'

'No, don't you try and get me in on it! Poured all those gold coins that you killed Paretes for into his hand.'

'Paretes killed himself,' Fox insisted patiently. 'Hope, Imogen. Hope is what I see when I look at you.'

'Vagnius had your measure though. When you offered to exchange the whole lot for one of your fancy silver things, he looked so offended, as though you were trying to cheat him!' Imogen couldn't help laughing, even though wet leaves were sticking to her cheeks, as she tried to mimic Vagnius's earthy voice. 'That's a purty pretty piece of metalwork, sir, but money it's not.'

Fox stopped the donkey and came back. 'Salt of the earth,' he yawned. Vagnius had given full value for the small fortune he had been paid: the chariot was dangerously overloaded with the goods that he'd found or stolen for them, battered pots and pans, a stone hand quern, very worn, for grinding grain, a small iron fire box with glowing charcoal inside, a rotating wheel for need-fire should it go out, and a whole mess of other bits and pieces. On top of the rushes that protected Imogen and her baby from the worst of the rain a wicker chair was propped like a wobbly throne. It had certainly seen better days, but it retained its British ornamentation in tight-bound patterns of straw of beautiful workmanship: the seat was the face of the sun, and horse heads made the arms. Imogen hoped the rain would not ruin it.

'Are we stopping for the night now?' They'd reached the top of the slope and she saw dull clouds driving beyond the thinning treetops ahead.

'We won't stop at all tonight, Imogen. The new Roman road is just ahead of us. I don't want to travel it in daylight.'

'Do you think they're looking for us?'

'No!' he said impatiently, then picked aside the fold of her cloak with his fingertip, grinning at the baby.

'You're besotted with her,' Imogen said gratefully. 'Mind you don't get her wet.'

'Babies are used to being wet. Just you mind you keep her warm enough.'

She lifted the brim of his hat so she could see his face. 'What did you mean,' she asked softly, 'hope?'

'A better world,' he said, then laughed. 'You don't think I'd be here if it wasn't for you! I'd be pleasantly drunk back at the Tabernacle, warm and snug, with a slut snoring in each armpit.'

'No you wouldn't, you'd own the place by now. That's how you do things, you liar.'

'Now that's one thing I never do,' he said. 'I never lie.'

He tipped a stream of water off his hat, then went back to the donkey. Imogen ducked her head beneath the rail. 'I'm sorry,' she called.

'The truth is a terrible thing,' he said without looking round. 'As terrible as love.'

He took up the leading rein, opening his palm with the tempting green acorns, and the donkey followed him eagerly out of the trees onto the plateau. 'Nearly at the road. Too late for travellers now.' Fox used the last of the light to hack a way through the dense underbrush of thorns and shrubs growing up since the forest was cleared – the military would not tolerate trees close to a highway in case of surprise attack, and encouraged the bramble tangles for the same reason. Fox tempted the donkey up the steep camber and turned left along the centre of the road, which had been cut straight as a spear through these high woods. Imogen's voice came yearningly from the chariot.

'I don't think I can ever feel what love is.'

'People die for it,' Fox said. 'It's what you feel for your baby. You'd die for her, wouldn't you? If by your death she'd live. That's one of the things love is.' He shivered, and she could just discern his eyes in the dark as he glanced back. 'Years ago I was offered a ceremonial death or exile. I've always chosen life.'

'Do you regret it?'

'It's all there is, Imogen.'

The donkey plodded forward at an even pace and the moon rose slowly in front of them. To Imogen these woodlands were a featureless tangle of black and silver bordering the straight and steady road, but several times Fox looked into them as though reading exactly where he was from the shape of a tree, a small stream, a boggy pond. She watched him sniff the air and thought how like a wild animal he was, always so in touch with the world around him, caring only about surviving. The vehicle rocked soothingly and her eyelids drooped.

'That's the second time you've used them,' she muttered sleepily. He was walking beside her with the moon above his head. 'Your talents. Where did you get them?'

'A talent is a gift that must be repaid. No, not the second time, Imogen,' he said grimly, 'or even the third.'

'What gods inhabit them?'

'None.' He sounded surprised. 'They have no power. Like Vagnius said, just purtty pieces.'

'How many do you have?'

He thought about it. 'Twenty-nine.'

'What an odd number.'

'I've never lost one I've given away.' He made a joke of it. 'Bad pennies always come back in the end.'

'You mock them,' she murmured, 'because you're afraid.'

'I'm not afraid of anything that walks on the earth.'

'You're a little bit afraid. You stole them, didn't you?'

He went striding on beside her for some time without

answering. 'No. They were willingly given to me.'

'They have gods,' she muttered, trying to keep her head from falling forward into sleep, 'and these woods have gods too.'

She woke with a jerk. The baby had found her nipple, drunk her fill, and was asleep again, soaking wet. The vehicle had stopped its creaking, jolting progress and grey light filled the misty air. Fox, carrying a long stick, slipped out of the woodlands like a ghost, ducking back to her through the brambles without a sound. 'It's all right, it's me. You were sleeping. The donkey's asleep too.'

'Where are we?'

'Home.'

She got down. The rain had stopped, but water showered off the brambles as Fox lifted them with his stick, making an archway for her to get through, then led the donkey after her. Beneath the trees it was still almost dark and heavy drops thumped from the vaults of high branches into the ferns and moss of the forest floor. Imogen changed her baby into the last dry towel, then ran to catch up with the chariot, walking alongside as it bumped over the tree roots. Fox strode ahead as though he saw a footpath here, but everything looked overgrown to Imogen. Nobody had been here for years. She cried out as he almost dropped from sight, the ground falling away steeply in hanging woods.

He held up his arms to help her down. 'Leave the donkey here for the moment.' Their feet crunching on acorns, they slithered down between the moist tree trunks, the largest oaks she had ever seen. Regularly spaced like enormous footsteps, they had been deliberately planted so long ago that the idea frightened her.

'Oh,' Imogen said, hanging back, 'I'm not coming in here. This is sacred ground.' Sensing her fear, Sabrina began to cry, and Fox climbed back to them.

'Sacred and potent,' he said, 'and *past*. It's past, Imogen. Today is what matters. How long are you going to stand there letting her cry?'

Imogen hesitated, then allowed herself to be led down into the valley. Fox knelt and dug into the warm, living moss: water gushed out between his hands and he splashed his face, laughing at her. Imogen looked around her, listening to the dense birdsong. He took off his cloak. As they went further down, standing stones appeared between the massive trunks rising on every side, the ley stones of a pattern too large to be seen. Circles and wheels had been worn into the crumbling surfaces, the shapes of faces and flames. 'Don't be afraid,' Fox said. 'That's very important. *Don't be afraid.*'

A stream bubbled beside them, foaming into a pool at the foot of a stone, but she saw nowhere for the rippling water to run. Fox tugged her forward. Between the tree trunks ahead of them, slants of sunlight appeared.

'Where is this?' Imogen whispered, looking around her in the silence as though the trees were listening, looking down on them.

'We're coming into the Druid nemeton,' Fox said. 'This is the sanctuary where I was a child.'

'Now I understand! You can't seriously think we can live here!' she cried. 'There's no shelter. There's nothing . . .' She was really crying now, and he looked at her in surprise, then took her in his arms, baby and all, hugging her. 'You had such high hopes,' he murmured, his lips in her hair, holding her until her tears had subsided to hiccups. 'I thought you knew how hard it would be.' His voice became rougher, almost mocking. 'You'd rather go back to London and give yourself up. You're soft. Yes, maybe that's all you're good for.'

Her colour rose. 'I'm as tough as you are,' she said fiercely. 'I've pulled my weight, *and* I've had to look after the baby too.'

He grinned at her anger, because the tears were still on her hot cheeks, then offered his shoulder for her to wipe her nose on his tunic. She blew on it too, just to teach him.

'This way,' he said, taking her hand and leading her forward into the sunlight. Their eyes narrowed at the brightness of the open space, and Imogen saw the three of them as if from above: herself the young girl, her unbound hair falling down her back, a dark, reddish chestnut, cradling the baby who was crying because *she* had been crying, and standing beside them the much older man, his curly red hair and beard catching the sun like fire.

Their three figures moved forward slowly across the open, level heath. The ground fell away steeply on three sides of the knoll. If there had been buildings here, they were gone and all sign of them overgrown with shrubs and weeds. The ancient oaks had been planted in a perfect circle, towering up behind them like a wave, curving past them then falling away down the slopes, curling round the sides of the knoll so that ahead of them they saw only the tops of the trees completing the circle. Above the treetops they looked down on the fields of the City of the Sun laid out below the level of the impenetrable forest, the ruined dwellings no larger than black dots at the river's edge, and the Thames making a brilliant blue chain of lakes towards London. The encampment was almost lost in the vast bowl of green hills, the military bridge little more than a black thread sewn across the stream, but they saw that the drawbridge had been raised for a slow white sail to pass through. The Tabernacle was visible only as one line of smoke out of several rising into the still air. Rooks flurried from the treetops, suddenly close.

'Whatever was here,' Imogen said, 'it's still here.'

'No,' Fox said. 'I remember ten thousand people here, priests in white robes held by golden torcs round their necks, women in black beating their breasts, driving out the spirits, and young men with painted faces. I remember the sacrifices screaming as the fires were lit and the spirits fled into the flames, into the mouths of the burning people there, standing on each other's shoulders, hundreds of them burning in the shape of a huge, hollow wicker-work man. And the gold knives of the priests on the altars below and the smell of holy blood, holy flesh, purity. And the screaming faces in the hollow man. The holy water flowing.' He shook his head. ''Tis my earliest memory, so long ago and so much a part of me that it feels like an emotion rather than something remembered. I would have been four years old.'

'And they all burned?'

'Yes. It was for the best.'

'Which was stronger in those days, fire or water?'

He stared at the Thames below them. 'Water. Water below, fire above. Fire all around us here on the grass.' He looked about himself like a man waking from a dream. 'It's gone. All these things have grown up now.' He gestured at the bracken, hawthorns as high as their heads. 'It's yours and mine now.'

She tugged his elbow until he looked at her, and for a moment the look in his eyes was as if he saw a different person wearing Imogen's flesh, looking through Imogen's eyes.

'What matters most to you?' she asked.

93

'You,' he said. 'You aren't my slave, Imogen. You're a free woman.'

He left her in the middle of the nemeton feeling very alone, clutching a stick, watching his confident strides taking him back to fetch the donkey by an easier route round the side of the knoll. Changed and grown up though the place undoubtedly was in the twenty years since he left it – her whole lifetime – Fox still seemed to sense his way around like a man navigating comfortably across the back of his hand. He was right. Childhood would always be the strongest force in a man of instinct such as he was. Here was his home. He had known no other, and she would just have to come to terms with that.

But he hadn't thought about all the practicalities that concerned her. He was thinking in the way that men think – something would turn up, he'd go hunting, strike lucky, or at least live on the hope of striking lucky. But what about her? A woman had more immediate concerns, like picking some of these elderberries for supper, finding a place they could rest. She would not allow her baby to go a third night without shelter, and they could not survive much longer without proper sleep. He'd have to find firewood – at least there was bound to be plenty of that here. What happened if it rained? How would he keep the fire alight? How would they keep dry? Would he build her a little roof of reeds on sticks like the pig-man's? Was a man like him really prepared to live like that? Autumn was almost upon them, the air unexpectedly chill out of the sun and soon the leaves would fall, and then winter would come. What then? How would they dry their clothes? They had no servants, no slaves, how would they achieve even the simplest things? What then?

The weight of her worries threatened to crush Imogen, and the more she worried, the more she found to worry about. There was that whole mess of things in the chariot – if Fox could get it down here in one piece – but she couldn't remember if there was an axe in it, or a proper iron cooking pot on a chain. If there wasn't, what would they do without it? Her life would be an endless drudgery, they would be grubbing for food like the lowest peasants, outcasts in their own land, their feet bundled with straw, groping for acorns beneath the snow.

The sun was hot on her head. 'You're not my slave, Imogen,'

he'd said, but of course that was exactly what she was. She had no choice but to stand where he had left her, clutching her stick at imaginary dangers, her baby lying between her legs in the crib of woven rushes. Imogen worried about a beetle or tick crawling from the ferns onto her daughter's face, and flies were beginning to buzz around them too. The dawn birdsong had abated and the sun felt like a solid weight, making a heavy green shimmer of the trees around her, trapping the heat within the circle. When the undergrowth rustled close by she raised the stick in both hands. 'Ho!' she cried as threateningly as she could. But it was only a hare sitting up on his haunches, brushing his whiskers, so indifferent to her alarm that a laugh was jerked out of her. Sabrina hicked and complained, woken by her cry, then coughed. The hare hopped away in search of more interesting things.

Still Fox did not return, and the place felt very empty without him.

'Fox!' she called. 'John Fox!' Her voice echoed around her, amplified by the encircling trees. They had chosen their place well for their lessons and chants, those old Druid schoolmasters. She picked up the crib to find some shelter from the sun and the flies, forcing her way across the tangled, waist-high expanse towards a clump of dense, quick-growing laurel trailing shadow where the slope dropped away. The apparently flat ground was covered with little bumps and clefts, as if there had once been much more here than now remained.

Imogen rested the crib gratefully in the shadow.

As she straightened she felt an odd sliding sensation beneath her foot. She gave a cry, feeling herself going down. The stones gave way and her leg dropped into the ground as though there was nothing under her at all. For an awful moment she thought she would go all the way in, and as she pushed the crib away from her, Sabrina shrieked. Imogen dug her fingers into the earth as she was sucked down past her knees, trying to pull herself out of the hole, but she dropped further in. Roots snapped in her fingers as the soil gave way beneath her hips and she slid inside.

Her feet banged on stone. She stood there with her head sticking out of the ground, screaming.

'Fox!' she shrieked. 'Father! Father! Help me!'

Panting, she stopped. Her heart was going like a hammer and

her ears were ringing from her own cries, but she heard no reply. She put her fingers to her mouth, forcing herself to be quiet, imagining the envious spirits that lived below ground, close enough to touch but hidden in the earth, coming together in the thick darkness round her legs. She could feel blood trickling on her chin and realised she had bitten her lower lip, which was a fault of hers, one her mother always used to scold her about. 'Bite your lip, your smile will rip,' she would say, tickling Imogen's chin fondly.

Imogen took a deep breath. You're a free woman, she told herself. There'll be lots of times when he won't be here to help you. You've got to face your troubles and work them out for yourself.

But that hadn't worked before. It hadn't worked with Paretes, only earned her slaps and pinches to make her behave better. She hadn't freed herself from Paretes; Fox had. But still there was no reply.

She whimpered, knowing there was only one way to deal with her fear. Working her shoulders into the earth, she pulled her head down and crouched in the gloom underneath.

Light from the hole above revealed stone steps leading downwards. She was kneeling near the top of the slope, and she guessed that once the stairway must have been at least partly open to the sky and only hastily covered with stones and earth.

She took a step or two down, gathering courage, and the light streamed past her full onto the screaming stone face of a devil-god guarding the doorway below.

'You've found it, well done,' came a cheerful voice from above. Fox was lying on his elbows, dangling his head through the hole. 'You're a plucky one. I heard you shouting. Why don't you call me John?'

His head snatched upwards and Imogen waited with her hands over her heart, panting. After what seemed for ever his legs appeared and he dropped down. He was carrying a bundle of rushes and the fire box.

'It's a silly name, that, John,' she said furiously. 'I've never heard of a name like John. It's as if you're a foreigner.'

'It's not foreign here,' he said mildly, then gave that cruel smile of his and a gentle squeeze of his fingers on her arm, and she realised he was pleased with her. Taking a small piece of glowing charcoal, he bent his back and touched it to the bundled torch. The flames spread in a slow flare. He went down past her, held up his forearms respectfully to the stone face, then handed her the torch.

'Don't call me Father. In some parts of the world it's what priests are called.'

'You are a priest,' she said.

'Not now. John will do.' He climbed back past her and she turned, alarmed. 'I'll get your baby,' he said.

'You're not leaving me alone down here?'

'I should leave her alone up there? The donkey is kind-hearted but a fool, and no fighter.'

'Are there wild animals round here?'

'Yes,' he said economically, and pulled himself out with his arms. He widened the hole with kicks of his feet, sending earth and stones bouncing down around her, then he lowered the crib to her and jumped after it. 'Come.'

Taking the torch, he led her step by step down the long ramp. Instead of growing darker, the light increased; after the first few paces the dark compacted gravel gave way to walls of white chalk that reflected the torchlight, and the air smelt clean. The steps ended on a level floor and as the walls widened out around them, Fox held up the blazing torch.

The debris of a hurried exit years past lay scattered in the cavern: a sandal, rubbish, a few animal bones tossed down around the kicked-out embers of a last fire, gouge marks where something heavy had been dragged out across the chalk floor.

'This was the holy of holies, wasn't it?' Imogen whispered. 'What's down here?'

'Nothing, unless you believe in it.'

Fox walked round the cavern, his shadow dashing and flickering along the rough-hewn walls.

'This is the first room. There are six others, three of them as large as this, three smaller.' He took her hand, leading her through them one by one, the open spaces like the links of an invisible chain binding the earth. 'Our winter quarters.'

'That wasn't what they were used for,' she said decisively.

'No one knows who dug this place, except that it was here long before memory, and they used antler horns to dig it out – you can still find fragments. What a task it was. The gods must have helped them. It must have been a shrine even then.'

'What's that noise?'

'What does it sound like?'

'Running water,' she said.

He lit a fresh taper, holding it up as they came to the final cavern. The flame flickered in a faint gust of air. This room was much larger than the others, the roof lost in darkness above them, the floor sloping down into clear water filled with ripples. They glimpsed chalk boulders shimmering in the depths, but the flame glittered and flashed off the surface like a mirror, defying their sight. From a crack in the far wall a fresh stream poured, the source of the ripples and the sound of water.

'But it's beautiful,' she murmured. 'It's wonderful.'

'What did you expect? I've done what's best for us.' He shrugged. 'The best I could, anyway. Rues knew the power of this place.' He looked at her accusingly. 'This is a holy well,' he said, 'if you believe in it.'

He waited, watching her. 'Of course I believe,' she said wearily. Her baby would need another feed soon, and Imogen herself was trembling from hunger. There were loaves of bread somewhere in the chariot, and a pot of Rhodian wine, and she felt faint at the thought of them.

'Then everything will be all right,' Fox said. 'They have cosmetic surgeons who will do this for a fee in Rome, but this is better.' He wedged the taper in a crack between two rocks and drew his sword, the broken tip making a jagged flash in the dark between the flames and water.

'What are you doing?' she said.

'I swear by the gods by whom my people swear.' He held out his hand for hers. 'Give me your arm, Imogen. Not that one, the one with the slave brand.' He swept the steel carefully across her skin, slicing away the tattoo between the blade and his thumb before she knew it was done. He took her arm and plunged it into the icy water.

'Now you really are a free woman, Imogen.'

Imogen knew she would never be free of her father.

Throughout her childhood, though she'd never seen Fox with her own eyes, he'd dominated her life through her mother's memories, her mother's feelings, her mother's love. And he, it seemed, would never be free of her mother. In her, her mother lived on. She saw it in his eyes whenever he looked at her.

What a strange, haunted, frightening man he was. And yet how fascinating he was too. Sometimes it seemed he'd known all there was to know about everything, experienced everything, tasted everything. All she had to do was trust him. Allow herself to be swept along with him, like a second childhood, a return to seeing things innocently with him here on the knoll, like a child.

But she was not a child, and neither was he. She could no longer believe, even if he could, in the childish things.

I don't know if there are really any gods, John Fox had said, *but it's safer to believe there are. People who believe in them see them.*

Yet Imogen couldn't believe. She paid lip service to such a reassuring idea, and she thought it would be nice if they existed, at least the good ones, but when it came down to it, she did not believe there was anything there. But she had to admit the skinned place on her arm had healed. *Nothing, unless you believe in it*, Fox had said.

But their lives were so prosaic and humdrum that there was no time for anything more to Imogen's life than work. The elderberries she'd eaten had given Sabrina an unforgiving bout of diarrhoea, mother and daughter were both exhausted, and beneath the towels, however frequently they were changed and washed, the baby's skin became a glowing rash. The poor thing cried at night, fretting at the irritation with her little hands, and Imogen bit the tiny fingernails to stop her scratching herself. Fox took matters into his own hands and lowered Sabrina naked into the freezing waters of the holy well. The mite clung to his hairy arm like a desperate little animal as she was dunked, her eyes fixed appealingly on her mother. 'You're hurting her!' Imogen cried, snatching at her.

'Hurting her to do her good,' he replied in that invulnerable voice of his.

'Leave her alone, she's *terrified*. Don't you care?'

'She's my blood too,' he said gently.

Perhaps Fox was right about the curative powers of the holy

well, for Sabrina's rash improved and disappeared, but Imogen wasn't going to admit it, putting her faith in the small jar of olive oil she'd found among the stuff in the chariot. Her baby was her life, and she knew no one could love and care for Sabrina as much as she did, and she didn't like John Fox getting between them. Her happiest times were when he was out hunting or feeding the wild pigs and she was alone with her daughter, the firelight flickering on the chalk walls, Sabrina gripping her finger and cooing, a quiet, intimate interval of peace that went into Imogen's soul. Everything else that happened in the long, busy, humdrum day was a pale shadow by comparison with that fierce personal delight.

Had gods really once inhabited this place? Had their forms once really come shifting and rippling inside these white walls, their goodwill or malevolence called into being by the chanting priests? Was the holy water really holy, or was a snail shell of olive oil just as good? Perhaps it was Imogen's fault she saw and sensed nothing supernatural, nothing here in the dark. She hoped there was something, and sometimes in the smallest hours of the night, lying awake looking up at the flickering corbelled roof, she could imagine something was there, even pray to it or them for hopes and favours – please, wind, don't let the last of the barley blow down and rot before I can thresh it, please let my baby's cough be better in the morning. She made small, secret, personal sacrifices, leaving aside a spoonful of the barley porridge in her bowl as an offering although she was hungry, bringing inside a piece of strangely-shaped broken bough whose whorls and creases seemed shaped like a woman, then other pretty ornaments that caught her eye outside, which she arranged in a chalky niche. But did these comforting shapes really contain spirits? No. She talked to them because she was lonely, and afraid.

Sabrina coughed, and the weather was growing colder. One day all the treetops uphill from the clearing were white with frost. When the wind got up later in the day, dead leaves blew everywhere.

By following his stings, Fox had found the old pottery beehives still swarming in the woods and laid in pots of mulberries from the old tree below the knoll, preserving them in the honey, and gooseberries and cranberries too. Imogen knew she would not have survived here without him, would have crawled back to London probably, accepting her cruel fate. No local people trespassed in these haunted woodlands, cloaked in Druidical mists when the high forest of the plateau above them was in the clouds. In these undisturbed combes where the grunting of the wild pigs seemed to echo from every direction, he knew where to find hazelnuts and stone-pine nuts, and how to steep hips and haws in vinegar, which mushrooms were safe to eat, all the basic skills a princess had women for. Below the knoll, barley, spelt and oats for animal feed had run wild from the long vegetable field, and he'd found the old apple trees too, pulling Imogen after him through the undergrowth with the baby bouncing on her hip. 'Decio apples.' He pointed at the laden boughs with satisfaction. 'We'll store them in layers of rush mats, they'll keep us going through the winter. It's all here, Imogen. All around us for the taking.'

'How do you even know what sort of apples they are?' she laughed. 'There isn't anything you don't know, is there? It must be because you're so old!'

'I'm not old.' He hated her jokes about his age, and her irreverence, but that just made Imogen more determined to keep civilising him. She pulled at his furs. 'And your awful tailor.'

'It's more important to be warm. You'll see.'

'And you're stuffy.'

'We grew the apple trees for the mistletoe,' he said with dignity, remembering how different everything had been, the intense sense of order in this place: school, monastery, shrine, sacrificial altar, remembering the whole disciplined chain of life he had given up for love, for a single woman. 'It grafts on them as a parasite – the apples were a bonus.' She yawned, and he knew she was still worrying about her baby – he had sensed her awake most of last night. 'They were brought by Veneti merchants from Normandy, more than two generations ago – over eighty years.' Like the Jews, he counted royal generations as forty years, those of ordinary people as twenty-five. But he was surprised when she looked blank, never havi .g heard of the Veneti. 'They were seafarers who held the monopoly on trade in those days,' he said, then sighed. 'Almost everything is being forgotten, it's slipping away from us.' He watched her looking at her white-faced baby, obviously not listening to him, yet she seemed to ignore the coughing, even covering the flecks of blood on the lips, as though not seeing them would make the illness go away. 'You're right,' he said sadly. 'All we should care about is what's happening now.'

That night they sat together on the side of the fire where the draught kept them out of the smoke, staring into the flames. 'I'm afraid,' she admitted, 'that's why I'm silly sometimes.' In their early lives both of them had often seen the children of other people fall ill and die; infants under four were the only group permitted to be buried in towns. He knew she was coming to terms with losing Sabrina, but her guilt that her love alone had not saved her child would stay with her. He put his arm round her, just as she had her arm round her own child.

'Some men believe love rules the earth,' he whispered. 'They believe love is limitless.'

'I've been wrong,' she murmured. 'You've seen it, I haven't been loving her as much as I could. I can't face it if she dies.' The word was said.

'She won't die,' he said arrogantly.

'There!' she said, as if he had frightened her again. 'Most of all I'm afraid of you.'

He thought she meant she was afraid of not wanting to survive, of being overwhelmed without having lived. Without her child she had no hope, no reason. Nothing he could say or do would comfort her.

'You must think I'm a fool,' she said miserably. 'You knew she probably wasn't strong enough to stand her first winter.'

'Who can tell? Life is a miracle and you aren't the first mother to love a child for herself, Imogen, wherever she came from.' He stroked her pliant back, closing his eyes, again remembering.

'I know what you're thinking,' she said angrily, putting her face against his chest. 'If I believed, she would live.' She shivered, glancing up at his bright blue gaze, the all-seeing eyes tattooed on his sleeping eyelids. 'I'd do anything for her, but I *can't*.'

As winter closed in, the ground turned to iron above them, and the end came quickly. When Fox returned from hunting, the first thing he saw was Imogen's uncomprehending face. He waited, knowing what had happened. She was kneeling uncomfortably by the fire, holding her dead baby propped in her arms as though the little thing was still alive. He watched her change the towel, then clasp the body tight, blowing on the blue cheeks as though to bring the colour of life back into them.

'Imogen, your little girl is dead.' Fox shook the snow off his clogs, moving around to claim her attention, laying his bow and quiver of arrows in the corner, blowing out his breath in clouds in the warm damp air of the cavern. 'It's not your fault.'

'You promised me she wouldn't die.'

'Imogen.' He fetched her deerskin and put it round her shoulders, letting her talk.

'I can't live here any more. It's this dreadful place,' she fretted in that dull voice. 'I want her above ground. You know how to do these things properly, don't you?'

He held out his arms for the burden. 'I only know we must treat her with respect, Rues.'

'Rues,' she gasped. 'You called me *Rues*.'

'Did I? It's the expression in your eyes,' he breathed sadly. 'The last time I saw your mother . . . Loss. Neither of us knew what she carried inside her.' He gave a crooked grin.

'Don't,' she said. 'Don't look at me that way.'

'You've grown up, Imogen. You're a woman like your mother.'

'We can't go on living here like this,' she said, 'like animals.'

He took the tiny body of his grandchild. 'Stay here if you wish.'

'I'll come,' she said.

'Then carry her yourself,' he said harshly, turning away, 'and cry.'

Imogen followed him up the ramp into the white glare of the morning, holding the baby's face against her chest, lest the sun should hurt her eyes. She plodded after Fox across the deep, fresh snow of the clearing to the edge. The treetops below them were stark as claws. It was low tide, the Thames a blue line wandering through vast black marshlands towards London, where a couple of dozen misty strands of smoke rose into the air to about their level before fanning out like a white anvil.

'Sing,' he said, getting to his knees and breaking the frost with a small shovel, digging as deep as his arm into the earth. Imogen could not find her voice. She whispered the words staring out at the smoke drifting in the distance, encircled by the bare white hills of London. *Blackbird on a branch in the deeply-wooded plain. Sweet, soft, peaceful is your song.*

'Kiss her,' Fox said. 'Give her up.'

She did as she was told.

Fox took the body reverently and cut off the head, then knelt and laid both in the ground, placing the head carefully between the knees. 'This is so that she will be reborn. She has died, Rues, but she will live again.' Taking out the cedarwood casket from beneath his cloak, he opened it without looking at her, and held it out. 'Choose two.'

'But – but they're valuable to you.'

'Any two,' he said.

The talents all looked the same to her, freshly minted, identical silver circles without character or individuality. She took two and he closed the lid with a bang. When she handed the coins to him he reached down into the hole and placed one over each eye of the child. Imogen found comfort in the old, old ceremony. Finally he placed an acorn in the hole.

'She will grow into the sun.' He opened his blue eyes in prayer. 'She will feel the summer and the winter, the spring and the harvest, the wind and the dew, and she will shelter and provide for us.'

Imogen looked at the circle of full-grown oak trees standing around the knoll, more than she could count, their planting going back hundreds, perhaps thousands of years, and suddenly she understood.

She knelt beside him and they replaced the earth in careful handfuls.

When it was finished, Fox stepped back and dusted the soil from his hands.

'We can't know anything,' he whispered. 'But we can feel.' He dropped his head, turning away from the view and the trees, each one a human soul, of the shrine surrounding the clearing. 'Now let's get down to work.'

Imogen worked as though she would die, but not for the reason Fox thought, punishing herself, working to forget. In a way the opposite, something wonderful, had happened to her that day on the edge of the knoll. She had begun to realise that this was her land too; it belonged to her just as much as to him, and perhaps more. This land would be her life, she would never leave here; she would grow old here, be buried here, grow here. This was *her* place.

Each day she slid downhill to the long strip of the old vegetable field, the lingering bounty that still sustained them with finds of turnips and parsnips beneath her earnest, probing hoe, nibbled or wormy though they often were. It was patient work that Fox had no mind for; he could not do it, he did not have her delicacy of touch, he stabbed the ground impatiently then made an excuse to find some more congenial task that he was good at, usually hunting. The hares only came hopping out when she worked alone. Each day she dragged herself back uphill almost crying with the cold and how little her efforts had won, but victorious, because she was finding, not happiness, but satisfaction. She was proud of herself, learning which little winter flowers poking through the slush she could eat without making herself sick. She was not quite starving. *My land*, she thought, chewing the bitter bulbs, and she no longer raised her eyes above the horizon of trees.

She no longer cared to talk to Fox about his travels. He had seen sunset at noon, and a man raised from the dead, but his fingers were not sensitive enough for the work that was important now, sorting by touch the mess of seeds they had brought inside in such a hurry last autumn to protect them from frost, the clubwheat, rye, barley and spelt that had run wild in such confusion. Next year would be harder than this. In the evening, by firelight, long into the night, she separated the sprouting seeds from those less advanced, organising them into proper piles. Afterwards she huddled into the warmth of his sleeping frame, his greasy purple cloak thrown over them, and her golden brown cape too. Already the expensive lambswool felt as soft and far away as those days; she could hardly remember them, or the spoiled, weak girl she had been. It seemed incredible that she had let that fat little Palmyran merchant exploit her as he had.

'You smell,' she told Fox when he woke. 'That's the smell of you. The smell of feet.'

'Sleep on the other side of the fire then,' he said, but she slapped him. 'I'm not going to wash at this time of year, Imogen. It isn't as if we were Romans keeping elegant company in a warm climate, and we don't have a bath-house.'

She was silent. 'Yes, we do,' she said, throwing the cloak off him. 'And look at your tunic, it's disgusting.'

'Don't start this,' he said with a withdrawn face. 'They always start this.'

'Who?' she asked sweetly.

'Women. They always push too hard.'

'I'm not like other women!' she laughed. 'I'm your daughter.'

He had no answer to that, but he laughed ruefully. 'I'll bathe when the ice is broken,' he said.

'Promise. And don't call me they.'

'I swear and vow and yield to you personally, Imogen.'

'More than that.'

He looked at her seriously. 'Yes, my dear, I promise. I'll wash!'

'Good,' she said. 'I'm not going to let you forget that.' And she didn't.

The snow melted and there was little more than moss and bulbs to eat, but she ate what there was. There were weeks when it rained day after day and she could hardly bear to go out, because once wet through her furs never really dried. Everything in the caverns stank of smoke and damp, rotten apples, their own flesh.

They lay on the greasy straw palliasse by the fire, more smoke than fire. Imogen sat up and poked at it.

'It's going to get worse, isn't it? We're going to be what we've always been, fugitives. We're going to be fugitives here all the rest of our lives, aren't we? But getting smaller and weaker and further from what we were all the time. I never see anybody.'

He pulled her down beside him. 'Are you afraid I'll die?'

She squeezed his hand, then picked at her own. The blisters from hours of hoe work had turned to stiff, yellow calluses, and she realised that a couple of days ago, before the wet weather and mists returned, her forearms had been browned by the growing power of the sun.

'Summer's coming,' she said. 'It *is*.' Then she lost her smile. He probably knew the date to the month and day.

'It'll be hard for you this year,' he said, 'but it will get better. In a year's time we'll be able to trade, a pig or two maybe, a little grain, buy some oxen to pull the plough.'

'You always know what you're doing.'

'So do you.'

'I still miss her,' Imogen admitted. 'I miss her like a real, actual pain, just here.' She pressed her elbows against the hard muscle of her tummy.

'I know,' he said in a low voice.

'You've never felt guilty about anything, have you?'

'No,' he shrugged, then he said, 'Yes. Yes, I feel guilty about believing my father, when he sent word that you and your mother were dead.'

She wriggled against him. 'Oh, I'm not dead.'

'But I believed it,' he said sadly. 'I lost my faith, my faith in her. For twenty years I believed . . . in nothing. In death.'

'And you lived accordingly,' she remembered his words and repeated them. She peered into his eyes. 'I thought Druids didn't believe in guilt.'

'No, because we didn't believe in love.' He lay back. 'But both exist. Flip the coin, the other side of love is guilt. I don't think there's one without the other, Imogen. The name they've given it is sin. But . . . but the God of love forgives sin.'

'Which god is that? Venus?'

'She's the goddess of sex, fertility. I meant another love. Love.'

'I prefer the first sort,' she said.

He lay without speaking.

'What happened to you,' she asked him quietly, 'out there?'

'Nothing, nothing,' he said.

'Today is the feast of Beltain,' came Fox's voice roaring over the clearing, 'the first day of May!'

Imogen hopped among the nettle beds that were sprouting everywhere, stifling new life in their dense tangles just as effectively as the shadows of the ferns or the piles of impenetrable brambles running riot. His figure in the distance waved to Imogen, then he beat on a cowbell with a stick while she did the same, hallooing as they advanced across the clearing, sending hares bounding out of the bramble thickets to the safety of the surrounding trees, birds flying up, butterflies whirling in the breeze. He threw away the bell, laughing, then held up a flaming brand in his left hand, the need-fire, and came striding towards her through last year's old, yellowed undergrowth. He was wearing only his tunic which flapped as the wind gusted, and his hair and beard made a fiery circle round his head. His feet and legs were bare to the knee, covered with deep, bloody scratches that he ignored. He broke into a run, holding out his right hand. 'Run with me!'

She gasped as he pulled her along with him, plunging the torch into dry bushes as he passed. She could hardly keep up, he was running like a man possessed, shouting and yelling himself breathless. She began to fear that he'd fall and drag her down with him into the thorns, but then he let go of her and she found herself running after him. Perspiration stuck her tunic to her spine, her lungs hurt, and although she was wearing boots, the brambles scratched her thighs, which were no longer white but red with the sun and nettle stings. The ritual of Beltain was preordained, they ran following the direction the sun took in its travels round the sky, the river first in front of them and now behind, flames leaping up after them round the cool, shadowy perimeter of oak trees that stood like leafy sentinels of the ancient ceremony. Not ten thousand of them now, only the two of them left to race the wind. She had nearly caught him up, his form dancing ahead of her, then the wind took the smoke and blew it over them. She stopped to wipe her watering eyes, then when the smoke cleared he was standing almost close enough to touch her.

He bent over with his hands on his knees, watching her.

'You're puffed,' he said.

'You're too old to catch me,' Imogen said.

He moved suddenly, three short paces to the grass where she stood, and from between her feet picked up something thin and long, marked with dark brown diamond shapes down its back. He held the curling adder delicately behind the head, then crossed the ash and laid it in the mossy safety of the trees, came back and kissed her full on the lips. The taste of smoke on his tongue filled her mouth.

He pulled back, looking at her furiously, and she knew exactly what he was feeling, the bond between them was that close. They were the same blood, needing no words, closer than strangers could ever be. Sure of her victory, she kept her eyes down. Fox took deep breaths. She listened to the wind sighing in the trees, then looked up at the leaves made green and silver by the sun, the grey clouds of smoke streaming away from them, leaving blackened, fertile, controllable earth. She knew what would happen.

Not here, she thought.

She took his earlobes between her fingertips and pulled his head down against her, as if she could pull him into her own head, feeling his hard cheekbones on hers, his nose still hot from the sun, his lips.

He grunted, feeling for her as she drew back, then swept her into his arms almost reverently. He was not seeing her. He was young again though there were white strands in his hair. Clinging to her, he half-carried her down the ramp to the cavern below. Kicking a brand from the fire that always burned there, he bent and picked it up, scorching his hand on the embers. His other hand enfolded her breast, his fingers kneading her nipple as though he was already milking her. *Not here*. He took her stumbling through the second cavern, then the third, until they came to the entrance to the final chamber, and the flame flickered in the draught coming out of the darkness, burning brighter.

They entered the holy well, the sound of running water echoed all around them, and he plunged into her at last.

The child cried at the shock of the icy water.

'I call on Uquetis, Sequana, Quariatis,' Fox intoned the blessing in the ancient holy tongue, his cloak floating round him in the water, 'I call on Belatuqadrus the Bright Shining One . . .'

Imogen stood in the gloom, remembering. The names he was chanting meant nothing to her, washed over her. Here in this cavern she had lost her identity, become a woman, nothing more, nothing less. It had been easy, as easy as being a bed, or a pillow, or a wife. The chalk floor beneath her, his body on top of her, his seed spurting the moment he parted her and they touched, so that for a moment she thought her gift was wasted, but then the slipperiness slid him deep inside her, and with all her force she had pulled him tight.

She'd stared at his face in wonderment. He really had loved her mother, and Imogen realised he had given life to her again. The tears had flooded into her eyes as well as his, understanding his need and tenderness, knowing what she would never have. She would never have love. Her nose had snuffled at the thought of it and he had kissed her, licked her, taking her again. Whispering her name, Rues. Rues. Lifting her gently off the cold chalk, thinking of her tenderly because he was thinking of *her*.

The same cold chalk Imogen now felt beneath her feet, their child's booming cries making the sound of running water seem no louder than a trickle. Fox was holding the baby as though he'd never held one before, not supporting the head enough, as if even a baby must be strong, but she knew better than to interfere.

'I'll never love another man,' she murmured to the sound of the falling water, 'and I'll never feel guilty.'

Here she had willingly rolled over and lain on Fox, smelling the fire on his skin, the smoke on his greasy tunic. Her father's collarbone had been a hard line beneath her ear, her knees cradling his hips. His arms round her. He was keeping her warm, and she knew he would look after her. She was as happy as she ever could be. Her knuckles on the chalk, the limp fingers of her right hand lapped by the water. She'd sucked them thirstily.

'Your knees are hurting,' he'd said, standing and lifting her with him. The taper he'd jammed between two rocks still cast its flickering light, and he'd looked into her face, her eyes. Nodding, taking off his tunic, he'd plunged into the icy water, emerged blowing spray, rubbing the dirt from his body, and Imogen had gasped.

She saw him as he really was. John Fox was a painted man. From shoulder to thigh his body was a mass of tattoos, the whirling patterns of a Celtic puzzle, faces cunningly concealed among the shapes, and the more she looked, the more she saw. She even thought she saw the outline of a fish cutting across the other shapes, as primitive as if drawn by a child; she remembered seeing such a fish at the Tabernacle, imprinted on the seal ring of a trader from Ephesus.

'There,' John Fox had mocked her. 'I have sworn and vowed and yielded to you – and bathed, as I promised.' He'd held out his arms. 'Now you know me.'

But it wasn't special like that between them ever again. Their lovemaking became ordinary, as if they were just animals, or husband and wife. A few moments on the edge of sleep, or waking in the night feeling one or the other of them moving, a momentary comfort that she treasured. She hated this place below ground, but she'd wanted it to start here. In the dark. Out of sight.

'You do feel guilty,' he'd marvelled.

Imogen had not been sure about the baby until high summer,

guelder roses quickening around the edges of the clearing, butcher's broom and wood anemone tangling among the trees. They had teased the green shoots of barley and breadwheat from the blackened, fertile soil, watching them grow golden, then darkening, yellow-black, ready for the backbreaking toil of harvesting; but Imogen had felt even more of a change in herself. When she was certain, she wouldn't let him touch her again, and her thoughts turned inward. 'I won't be another woman for you any longer,' she told him, and he touched her belly for the last time, knowing.

In the morning she heard the sound of the axe cutting among the pollards, long saplings growing from the stumps of chopped trees, returning with lengths as thick as his leg across his shoulder, throwing them down gasping with the effort. He dug post holes in a circle in the ground, bracing the roof poles against one another to make a peak, and she remembered watching the structure taking form, growing to a conical outline three times the height of a man, standing among the crops near the middle of the clearing, thatched before autumn: the house where her baby would be born.

'You too are my harvest,' Fox had bragged. 'It doesn't matter where they come from, only that they are loved.'

He saw things in such a different way. He saw another world out there, not just the clearing, the house, the land. He saw above the treetops to the river rising towards London, where a sprinkling of white buildings with proper orange tiled roofs had appeared on the two hills within the stockade, smaller than nail parings at this distance, probably more barrack blocks for soldiers. He saw that there was much more shipping on the river, not only galleys but also the laden barges, dirty square sails set and thatched huts built over the stern, inching towards London with cargoes of Kentish ragstone; and the Customs House near the bridge had been rebuilt and extended. Even when winter set in there was always a boat or two to be spied on the black water.

But all she thought of was the child inside her.

Imogen jerked. Her lids had closed, but even with her eyes open it was hardly lighter here in the cavern that she now hated, the holy well. After today she never wanted her son to return here, the place where he had been conceived. She was ashamed, and she didn't want him to know of such things.

Fox chanted to his gods. Apollo, Maponus . . . everything went through him. He saw only himself, the man, as important, but he was wrong. He saw the child as his property, but he was wrong about that too. He would be an old man when Imogen and her son were still young. And he was still not holding her child properly, but Imogen bided her time.

'John,' she called. 'Husband.' But he ignored her, his head bowed over the baby.

'Andraste, Belenos and Taranis, Esus, and Teutates, Mars Rigonemetes, king of the sacred grove . . .' The names droned on. Fox was calling on everyone he could think of to look after his son just to be on the safe side, she guessed, whether good or evil she did not know. All she knew was that everything would be all right when her baby was returned to her arms.

He turned towards her and for a moment his seamed face lost its cruelty and strength, even the love went from his eyes, leaving him looking more sad than he could utter.

Then he plunged the baby deep beneath the water.

Lifting him up, Fox wiped away the drops with two strange motions of his hand, a symbol Imogen had never seen before.

'And in the name of the Father of Love I baptise you,' John Fox said, 'and I name you Paul.'

II
Paul

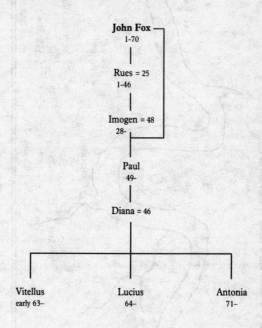

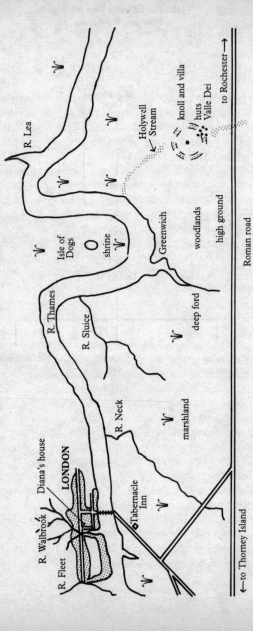

John Fox and Paul's visits to London, 61

Paul had always known he was a very special boy to his parents, and the knowledge was a warm glow that wrapped him round and never left him. Although their lives were so hard, it made everything easy for him.

It left him safe to take risks.

He would be handsome too – as handsome as his father, one day. But Paul was clean. His mother insisted on it; like a Roman woman she made him wash his face before letting him out into the fields, and she taught him Latin words as though he was a gentleman.

Paul looked over his shoulder as he climbed into the woods to bring the pigs down before night. Her figure in the doorway of the round house waved to him and he waved back. Then he saw her pull her tunic round her as though she was cold, and her face already wore its withdrawn expression; she hated the night, he knew. Imogen believed in cleanliness and sunlight, really *believed*, as if by believing strongly enough they would become true and everything would be pure. She allowed no shadows into her life or Paul's. Often in the evening she would shush his father's rambling stories with her hard, warming smile, and Paul would watch her lips pull back as tight as a snarling animal's if Father did not stop at once, that baleful protective light in her eyes, a mother defending her cub. She was sweet and gentle with him, but it was the ferocity she was capable of that Paul loved most. It made everything safe.

His father knew about shadows.

'Don't frighten him, Father,' Imogen would smile, then turn to Paul, tender and indulgent for him alone, excluding John Fox from her relationship with her son.

It wasn't that his father was their enemy; not quite. But Paul understood that his mother was the one to run to, that whatever happened he would always find safety in her arms. After a fall, a grazed knee, a bee sting, she would always be there to pick him

117

up and cuddle him in her warm arms and lap, Paul drawing up his long legs as though he was still a baby, the feminine scent of her enfolding him, sinking comfortably into his bones: dried herbs and wood smoke in winter, apples on her breath, the fragrance of the sun in her fine hair falling around him if it was summer. He would remember these feelings always, not so much memories as emotions, colours, flavours. The pure magic of being a child.

But Paul was growing taller.

Imogen denied it. Paul would never lose his innocence, she was determined on it. Her gangly, flushing boy would never be too old for a kiss and a cuddle from his mother, or a smack if he needed it, but even the flat of her hand carried love in its sting. And she would always get in first, as though to interpose herself between Paul and a beating from his father.

She did not love John Fox. She had taken what she needed from him. She did not even like him now that she had Paul.

Paul was completely her own child.

The tension between the two grown-ups was easy for a child to sense; Paul felt it filling the air, as hard and heavy as iron. He realised that they were separate people as well as his parents. Though they were so alike in some ways, even in looks, the colour and shape of their eyes, and sometimes, extraordinarily, in the bodily mannerisms of a shrug or a sigh, Paul realised his presence kept them apart instead of bringing them together. Paul wondered what he had done that was so wrong.

When he was twelve, he saw that the answer was obvious. *He* was wrong. The bad things were his fault. He had been born guilty.

When his mother hugged him in front of his father, she was doing more than giving Paul love; she was claiming him, too.

Imogen hated Paul's longing looks after his father as the lonely figure set off alone on the dawn journey down through the woodland paths to Greenwich, carrying whatever they had saved to trade: a little grain, honey, a sack of apples on his back, maybe driving a couple of pigs in front of him with a stick. That had been the hardest period for them, barely able to survive, each winter at the nemeton bleaker than the last. The donkey had been sold almost before Paul was old enough to remember it, and the marvellous old chariot lay abandoned, green with mould in a corner of the long field, everything that could possibly be of use stripped from it, even the spokes from the wheels to make chair legs. Paul, his imagination racing, holding invisible reins in his hands, would wait by the chariot for his father to return in the evening, climbing wearily into view, grunting and pushing on his knees up the steep hill. On his back would be strapped one or two iron goods, hoe heads, knives, a jug of oil. Paul would run down without shouting (which would have warned his mother), to walk back the last few paces beside him, as though they had been the whole way together.

When things got better, his father came back with a nanny goat, old but still in milk. Once he took down the old patched bronze saucepan which Imogen called her Vagnius pan, exchanging it for a newer, bigger, patched one, but it didn't make her any happier with him. That was the time he brought back a pot with a perforated base, too, whose purpose mystified Paul.

'It's a cheese press,' his father explained. John Fox made even the most ordinary statement sound formidable, and Paul just nodded quickly, two men together, as though he knew all about cheese presses. 'So next time, Paul, I'll take some roundels of goat's cheese to trade too.' John looked at his son seriously. 'You're a bright lad,' he said, seeming to feel both sadness and happiness at the same time. 'Too bright, perhaps, just like your mother.'

Paul risked saying, 'And just like you too, Father.'

John tousled the lad's fox-red hair, his son and grandson. Paul had his own dark chestnut eyes – and Imogen's. But she had kept him soft and unformed. Paul's skin was pale, scrubbed too clean, and he had no smell. His gaze was clear and shallow, merely boyish, without suffering. John sighed, rubbing wearily at the harsh engrained lines of his own features, the wrinkles that crowded round his eyes, feeling all his sixty years. Every son, without knowing it, and without being able to do anything about it, carried his father inside him. Add half a century to today and Paul was looking at himself, unless Imogen managed to shelter the lad from everything that would shape him. 'Yes, Paul, when I was a boy I was just like you.'

'I don't believe that,' Paul said.

'I knew it all. Then when I was a young man I knew love was

119

greater than anything. Now . . . now I don't know. It's better not to be too bright, Paul. Take things as they come, and swim with the tide.'

'What's the tide?' Paul asked in a flash. He'd seen the fishing boats pulled up like dots along the beach at Greenwich, and he'd noticed that sometimes there was no sand showing and the boats swung from mudweights. He reckoned his father was not to know how sharp his eyes were.

'One day, Paul,' John promised, 'I'll show you the tide.'

Paul longed to accompany him to Greenwich tomorrow, but his father glanced at his mother and both males knew better than to ask.

One day John came back leading a plodding ox, stronger and bigger and more massively horned than young Paul had ever imagined an animal could be, and Imogen had hurried him inside, begrudging the older man's increasing pull on Paul's thoughts. But still Paul escaped her one way or another, slipping down to the weedy wreck of the chariot to await his father's return with hopeful fascination – this time a set of solid wheels that he could not make himself, next an iron coulter for the plough, finally a second ox to haul the plough through the stony, rooted earth. All through the winter John whittled with the small bronze axe and a square-ended knife to make harness poles and an ashwood frame, allowing Paul to help when Imogen ran out of chores to keep him away.

'You can't own the boy,' John said reasonably.

'No, but that's what you want to do,' she snapped back.

The wheels were fitted before the snow melted, and there it was: a sturdy ox cart. Paul understood the change this would make to their lives. No longer would they be limited to the weight his father or the oxen could carry on their backs, but only by the much greater weight they could pull. Paul stared at his father in awe.

One evening Paul was sitting on the only part of the chariot's frame that had not rotted into the earth, sucking a stem of the trailing honeysuckle that covered it, when he heard voices down the hill. People were coming. He hid under the honeysuckle, shooting frightened glances down the rutted track, then heard the familiar creak of the cart's wheels. His father did sometimes talk to himself, or sing nonsense songs in the old language. But this time a man Paul had never seen before walked beside the heavily-laden cart. Paul stared. The stranger was no taller than he was, but middle-aged and sinewy. He never stopped talking, looking up at John so that his feet kept tripping over stones and roots and it seemed he must turn his ankle in the deep wheelruts any moment. He must be talking so loudly and cheerfully to hide anxiousness, Paul thought.

At a respectful distance behind the two men sauntered the dirtiest woman Paul had ever imagined. His experience of women was limited to his mother, and Imogen always kept herself as clean as her pots – Paul thought that somehow she even boiled herself inside with soured milk, the same way she cleaned their pottery. This big, voluptuous, sleepy-eyed girl had red hair hanging in tails down to her breasts, and she slid her filthy hands inside her greasy woollen shift to scratch her hips in a very bored way while the men talked. Watching Paul watching her from beneath the honeysuckle, she slowly dropped one soot-blackened eyelid, catching him out. Paul scrambled out and followed them, itching with curiosity.

'Look who I found stealing at the market!' John called across the clearing to the hut, clapping the stranger on the shoulder like an old friend, but Imogen held herself back by the doorway, looking as disapproving as a thundercloud. 'It's Briginus!'

Imogen's frown deepened.

'You remember me, mistress.' The ex-slave eyed her nervously. 'Us lot chained up over the road from the Tabernacle that night—'

Paul had never heard of this.

'I remember him,' Imogen said quickly, interrupting Briginus. She didn't want any reminders of the past, or for Paul to know about it. 'So they didn't catch you, Briginus,' she said coolly, 'despite my husband's best efforts. You can't stay, we have nothing to spare.'

John knew how to deal with her. 'Tell us what happened to you, Briginus,' he said firmly, offering him a seat on the tree trunk hospitably.

'Ran like a stag!' Briginus told him proudly, sniffing the air, making himself at home. 'No hard feelings, master, we all of us hid out on Thorney Island until we found someone to rid us of

121

the fetters.' He slapped his knees as though it had all been great fun. 'Me and Rianorix drifted north, sold our sword arms to one of them Iceni chieftains, prickly lot, a sneeze and a fart and you've insulted the whole blooming tribe of 'em, and when the Roman governor ordered 'em to throw away their precious spears and swords and whatnot you can imagine they went up like wildfire, painted themselves in blue and the women ran around screaming. Didn't come to nothing, bit of splashing about in the marshes, but then that clever sod Ostorius sent in his bastard Batavian auxiliaries from the lowlands, what have got webbed feet and are used to living up to their balls in mud, so old Antedios reckoned he was going to lose and cooked up a peace just when it was getting interesting. That did for him with his people, but the Romans installed that bumbler Prasutagus as king, whose job it is to get walked over and give everything away with a smile, make the Emperor his heir, you know how it goes. But they've got a woman and a half for a queen now, acting on behalf of the king's daughters, and I'm not having that, am I, sir? So I drifted back south again, reckoning things would be quiet here with the legions in Wales, and brought this nice piece of northern skin and bone to keep me warm.' He slapped the girl's generous rump affection-ately, showing off his catch half his age. 'Tacita, this is. That's not a Roman name, mind, it's British all through, and so's she, aren't you, my love? Yes, she is,' he answered his own question. 'Strong shoulders, big tits and broad hips, a man's dream.'

'You'd find it would improve you to practise Roman manners,' Imogen said primly, 'as we do.'

'Believe me, no one admires what they've done more than Tacita and me does, mistress,' Briginus said earnestly. 'We'll speak the language, anything. I'm settling down, master,' he assured John Fox, adding with a wink, 'Little ones.'

'You can stay as long as you work,' John said decisively, and that's how the matter was decided, over Imogen's head.

'John!' she exclaimed furiously. 'You cannot!'

'You can put me in harness,' Tacita said, embracing her little man cheerfully, and Paul watched his father laugh. Tacita stuck her tongue out at Paul to make him her friend but he didn't know whether to laugh or cry, torn between his father and the newcomers, and his mother. Imogen, smartly dressed in her pressed tunic with the sleeves painstakingly woven as part of the garment, a heavy overfold at the waist secured with a braided belt, could not have contrasted more sharply with the other woman, whose unpinned shift was crawling with lice. Imogen held out her hand for Paul to come round without getting close.

'So you married that one, master,' Briginus smiled. 'She's as pretty as you're handsome, sir, if you don't mind me saying so, and the same light of battle as your own in her eye, if I'm not mistaken.'

Imogen pulled Paul inside, and the last thing he heard through the thatch was Briginus saying, 'There's others of us, master. Rianorix is down on his luck, and there's Baculo who's found his daughter Pluma, who speaks Roman sweet as a bird.' He dangled that like a tidbit after Imogen in the doorway. 'And there's the other good plain sorts used to taking orders and living respectable, Vernico and his wife Coventina, widowed three times . . .'

That night Imogen, unmollified, broke her pots. They were the only things of value that she had. She threw her knives out into the night, then kicked her straw bed to pieces. 'Are you satisfied now?' she shouted at John.

'I had no choice,' he said calmly. 'We can't manage alone.'

'You're so *weak*!' She turned on him, slapping at him with her hands. 'Get away from me. Go away!' She burst into tears. 'Everything was so good here. You've just spoiled everything! We didn't need them. You were managing. You could have done it all alone. You *could*.'

He picked up a broken shard by its point. 'Mind you don't cut your feet, Imogen.'

Unable to stop newcomers intruding on *her* land, *her* home, *her* son, Imogen at least made sure that their huts were positioned well apart from her own, over by the trees, and she kept Paul aloof too. Because she believed he was better than those dirty urchins who swarmed, more every year, around Tacita and Pluma, Coventina and the other women of childbearing age, he believed it himself. And because he believed it, so did they.

'You're my good boy,' Imogen said once, hugging him tight for no reason, smiling her bright smile with the tears shining in her eyes.

Now Paul, climbing the slope, looked back once more from the shadows of the trees. She was still standing in the doorway and he waved again, but obviously she could no longer see him; she turned and went inside. He felt very alone without her. Smoke filtered from the vents round the peak of the house down there on the knoll – she must be stoking the fire. By the other round houses, not as large as his father had known how to build, knocked together in an irregular clump nearer the edge of the clearing, mothers were calling their toddlers inside with weary voices, hands braced on their hips, yawning, getting the toddlers' elder sisters to do the work if they could. Their calls, and the cries of one baby who had found a nettle beneath one of the grain stores on stilts, sounded very small in the odd, gigantic circle of trees that surrounded them. Nobody knew the reason for it, if there was one, or who had planted them. He remembered asking his parents one evening. 'It was probably just an accident, Paul,' Imogen said, with a warning glance at his father. 'Coincidence.'

But Paul had caught that speaking glance. 'Do you think so, Father?' he asked.

'John,' Imogen warned, 'you mustn't worry the boy.'

'But I like the stories,' Paul said excitedly.

John simply turned his seamed, rugged face towards his son. He was sprawled on a log with a cloak thrown over his shoulders, poking the embers of the fire with a stick. 'Maybe I'll tell you when you are older, Paul.' Paul looked at his mother. She was smiling her smile, and he knew what that meant: she'd make sure it never happened.

John put his hand on Paul's shoulder. 'For now, whatever your mother tells you,' he said, 'must be right.'

'Yes, sir.' Paul bowed his head.

Imogen had taken Paul's other shoulder. 'Time for sleep,' she'd whispered, with a wink to make herself close, and he'd yawned instinctively.

Getting him away from his father.

Paul understood that now.

Now that he was twelve he saw her from the outside, as a real person, not only as a stream of endless love, endlessly forgiving, to be manipulated but obeyed. She was staying the same, an adult, but Paul was changing, no longer a child, but not yet a man.

Yet still he knew he was special, because he was his father's son,

124

and his father was special. All the other men deferred to him. His father knew everything that Paul longed to know. Deep in the night before sunrise he could point to the starry notch in the hills where the sun would awaken, and he had travelled to the mysterious faraway lands beyond the clearing, beyond the river, even beyond the sea. Paul drank in every word, but his mother always called him back to do some task or other, separating them. His father believed in magic, but his mother denied it, saying, 'Don't listen to him, it's only old man's nonsense. Just you put your mind to helping me clean these pots, right now.'

Paul had listened to her and obeyed her. He was frightened of his mother. But she didn't know where the sun rose; she didn't know all those things he needed to know.

Paul climbed deeper into the woods, following the path made by the women to fetch water from the pool, realising how much time he had wasted with his thoughts – darkness fell quickly at this time of year, the height of summer. There was no one about, it was too late. He came to the pool, by the foot of the stone with the strange markings, which never overflowed despite the stream trickling into its rippling waters. The women, who always moved in sociable groups and chattered happily here as they filled their pots, made it a friendly place, but now Paul hesitated. Alone, it was very different.

His mother always said there was nothing to be frightened of, but there was, if you were alone. The sight of the patterns worn into the standing stone, shifting in the rippling, reflected light from the water below, bothered him. Maybe his father knew what they meant, but he didn't. He traced his fingertip along the wheels and lines that Imogen would have scoffed at had she been here. The sun was in the tops of the trees now, a green glare over the shadows in which he was crouched. He stood up, looking around him uneasily.

Briginus had found him here once, staring up into the trees, listening dreamily to the overwhelming silence. 'Who planted them, boy?' he asked, dropping his filthy hand on Paul's shoulder, looking up reverently into the treetops. 'You must have wondered.'

Paul had shrugged off the older man's superstition. 'Why should I? I expect they just grew.' Briginus was uneducated.

'That's what trees do, isn't it?' Paul lectured him. 'They just grow!'

'They say the gods planted these trees, boy,' Briginus whispered. 'You know what the Romans call this place? Valle Dei.'

'Valley of the gods,' Paul translated self-importantly.

'You're right, sir.' Briginus nodded wisely. 'That's why they don't bother us folk, unless some well-off toga or other travels from town to make an offering in the old well here. For good health, or a lost loved one. Or something worse. A curse, maybe.'

'You're trying to frighten me,' Paul said uncertainly. 'There's no such thing.'

Briginus laughed. 'Woooo,' he called in an eerie voice. The common people were a superstitious lot; they'd believe in anything, the more frightening the better. Only the upper classes – who, like the Fox family, were not necessarily rich, but knew how to behave – favoured particular gods, and apparently there were several special buildings used as temples in London now.

'The gods are good,' Paul insisted.

'That's right.' Briginus winked, turning away with the deferential smirk of a man who has just enjoyed himself. 'If that's what your mother told you. It's a comfortable idea, you stick with it, lad.'

Obviously, Paul reassured himself now, Briginus had been trying to scare him for a bit of fun, the way adults like to scare children. He assured himself that he was too grown up to be frightened by such fantasies. Besides, whatever Briginus and the others had once believed about these mighty oaks, that had not stopped them from felling what they wanted to build their houses or make space for crops.

Paul looked up, shivering. The sun had faded from the treetops, and it was dangerous to be out late. Whistling for the pigs, he rattled the small satchel of grain that they adored, but no response came from among the shadows that were growing up everywhere. Because he was determined not to be afraid, Paul made himself kneel slowly and drink a cupped handful of water from the pool, then another, wiping the drops from his lips with his fingertips. He decided that the pigs were foraging up near the road again and reckoned he would have to go all the way to the top to fetch them. It would be dark before he was home and his mother would be frantic with worry. With a smile because he would really be all right, he climbed the slope, using his hands to pull himself up.

It was not new to Paul, this daring himself. Nothing bad would happen, the worst that Valle Dei had to offer were the adders that sunned themselves on hot days in the clearing, near the nettlebeds Imogen had preserved for their wine and to tenderise her cooking, but she'd had most of them killed. The brown bears that had once roamed these woods were also gone, hunted to extinction lifetimes ago. But Paul had yawned, unimpressed, at that story. How could his father remember anything so long past? That was another of the secrets they kept from him – he'd intercepted that warning glance from his mother to his father. And suddenly Paul, staring first at one adult then the other, had realised his power.

Since then his life had been twice as good. As the only child, the centre of attention, his parents revolved round him like the sun and the moon revolving round the earth, and he could do whatever he wanted. If he got caught, he knew he could play them off against each other. If he was punished by one he could run to the other. He could even invent bad treatment, setting his parents against one another for twice the love and half the beatings. He'd hardly noticed the wise look in his father's eye studying him, as though he knew exactly what Paul was thinking.

Not long afterwards, it had been Paul's turn to catch his father out, or so it had seemed at the time.

Paul had always slept by his mother. She'd arranged it so that his father slept on the other side, furthest from the fire – they never lay together. It was as if she feared he would molest her boy if she did not keep herself between them. But she was a deep sleeper, and Paul had been woken very early by the crackle of straw. His father, who usually moved so silently, was rolling to his knees, getting up. Standing, he pulled on a loose-fitting tunic and the old-fashioned tartan trousers he liked to wear, then put back his head and fixed the clasp pin of his cloak at his neck with a loud click. Through slitted eyes Paul had watched him push aside the thatch door and go outside, not dropping it back quite properly in place, so that a bright gap was left. Careful that his knees did not crackle his own straw bedding as his father's had, Paul slipped across to the door and peered through the gap.

Outside he saw that the dawn was red, signalling bad weather to come later, but for the moment the sky was cloudless. His father knelt on the beaten earth by the pig pens to strap on his sandals, scratched the head of the goat that had been hobbled nearby, then walked away from the hut without looking back. When he was far enough away, Paul slipped through the door and followed him on bare feet, still wearing his nightshift, moving from the shelter of the pig fence to the shadow beneath the grain store, then crouching behind the trunk of an apple tree. As he peeped round the rough bark, his father's head and shoulders moved behind – no, *among* – the tall growth of nettles that protected a clump of new-planted saplings from the goats and sheep. It was such an extraordinary sight that Paul almost shouted out.

John Fox's head ducked from view, and did not reappear.

Nothing could have been more calculated to rouse a boy's interest.

Paul waited, staring, hardly aware of the cramp creeping up his legs, or that his mouth was still open in amazement – and excitement. He realised he was on the very edge of solving a mystery, one of those adult secrets his parents kept from him. He could hardly wait.

But nothing happened.

When he could bear the pain of his knotted muscles no longer, he risked hopping to a better place of concealment, behind a pile of firewood, and leaned back rubbing his stiffened legs. No one else was out so early, the embanked field strips that would later be busy with men and oxen, followed by clouds of mewling seagulls, were all deserted, and no children cried or bawled by the huts clustered by the forest's edge.

John Fox's head rose into view among the nettles as though he was being born from the ground. He walked calmly through them, unstung in his thick clothes, followed by a thin line of smoke from the burning taper upraised in his hand. Peering between the logs, Paul waited in a frenzy of impatience as his father emerged from the green stalks about fifty paces away. He threw the taper onto the compost heap, and brushed off the dew and nettle spores that had stuck to his clothes. He nodded respectfully at the young oak tree which grew from the slope below the knoll, now about fifteen years old and twice as tall as a woman. The respectful dedication was something else Paul didn't know the reason for, and he bit his lip petulantly, realising how little he really knew about his parents. Once that old man had been thin and quick as he himself now was, itched with these same feelings, curious, angry and unsatisfied as he was now; a young man like Paul.

John Fox pissed in the nettles and then, with a glance at the woodpile, wandered off downhill past the single oak tree, dropping from sight below the brow of the knoll towards the long field. Paul scampered out and picked up the guttering taper, blowing on the thread of smoke that remained until a tongue of flame appeared, then examined the place where his father had emerged from the nettles. A nettlebed was the last place he'd have looked for a path, but there it was, perfectly obvious once he knew it was there, a faint track outlined by the disturbed nettle leaves and trickling dew. Half an hour later, as the sun burned off the moisture, no trace would have remained.

Paul pushed between the tall stalks which bobbed their stinging heads painfully against his bare arms, while below the knee his bare legs were lashed by new growth. This had better be worth it, he muttered, pushing forward with gritted teeth but no thought of turning back. His father hadn't given up; neither would he.

But the path went nowhere.

Paul stared around him. He could see only nettles and sky.

The ground creaked beneath him, and he stepped back in alarm. When he tested the patch with his foot, the ground creaked again, bending slightly. Dropping to his knees, he dug his fingers into the grass and earth, feeling sticks woven together beneath. He found the edges and lifted the cover aside, then crouched, panting, gazing into the dark inviting hole that had been revealed.

The cries of children carried to him from the woodland's edge, and he realised the settlement was waking up. The taper wouldn't last much longer, either. Should he go down or waste this opportunity? He made his decision straightaway.

Paul slid down the hole.

He dropped onto a flight of rough stone steps, more than he'd ever seen before. Wherever he was, it was big. Sunlight poured down around him from above, but when he turned he almost screamed: a stone face leered at him out of the dimness, carved so long ago, and so softened by age, that it seemed part of the

129

dark that lay everywhere down here.

When the hammering of his heart had eased, Paul forced himself to laugh at the disgusting relic. Nothing had happened.

He slipped past it, patting it on the nose, then went forward with more confidence into the cave, the taper flickering its light back to him in gleams from the streaks of mica and quartz in the chalk walls. Paul rubbed the chalk between his fingers, barely able to contain his excitement, then stumbled over the ruins of a fire, old rubbish, broken pots. People had eked out an existence down here. Then he picked up a piece of pottery handle, recognising it as modern by the fluted shape and red colour of the glaze: Samian ware, imported.

He had discovered something about his parents' origins. They had lived here.

Paul chuckled. This would be something to twit them about, if he dared!

Why had they concealed it from him? Were they ashamed of once not having lived as well as they now did? Or did they think of it as simply part of the past, irrelevant?

Perhaps they had been happy here.

To Paul, twelve years was a whole lifetime, but it was only one-fifth of his father's life. He had so much to learn, even at this age when it felt as though he knew everything.

The taper flickered warningly. He was running out of time. He went quickly through to the next cave, then the next, marvelling at every piece of discarded debris he glimpsed by the failing flame, even a piece of broken shelf – the authentic touch of his mother, surely. It seemed incredible he'd never guessed of this amazing place, hidden only a few paces beneath his feet as he crossed the sunlit earth between the woodpile and the hut. In fact, he must be just about under the hut now – and he looked up, imagining he could see through the rough, gouged chalk, through the stones and gravel and soil to his mother's form curled sleeping above him, and his chuckle turned to laughter at the thought of it.

At least, he hoped she was still sleeping.

Squeezing through to the next cave, he heard the sound of running water. Shielding the flame with his hand, he followed the sound until a final cavern opened up around him. This one was much bigger, darkness at the top – he must have gone deeper beneath the ground that he'd thought. From high in the far wall a small waterfall spouted, not much faster than from a pouring jug, into the pool below. Paul's throat tightened. Many people believed in the power of holy water. His mother didn't, of course, and he knew better, too.

Paul forced a mocking shout from his throat, breaking the trickling silence of the place. He kicked spray across the pool. The flame flickered and almost went out, and he blew on it quickly, feeling a horror of being left here in the dark. The flame grew back, but smaller than before. It was time to go. He turned, and saw the casket.

He realised at once that this was not a piece of rubbish carelessly thrown down and abandoned, but something that had been carefully placed in the darkness between two boulders, where it could not be seen – he never would have spied it but for its reflection, a chance flash from the ornamental metal that bound the wooden corners and decorated the curved lid.

Kneeling, he examined the box so closely that his nose almost touched the fragrant, resinous wood – the scent, to his imagination, of faraway lands. Too hard for his fingernail to scratch, the workmanship was beautiful, finer than anything he could have thought of, and there was a hooked bronze rod to open it with. He was not sure how to use it, and the flame guttered alarmingly, almost out. He was about to give up when he tried lifting the lid anyway, and it effortlessly swung open under his hand.

He had discovered his father's secret, and it had not even been sealed.

The casket was full of faces.

Silvery light spread over Paul's features, thrown up from the box in reflection of the flame he held. He'd never seen money, but he had a boy's instinct for treasure. Between his fingertips, delicately, with reverence, he picked out a single silver coin from among the mass, staring at it in wonder, realising how beautiful it was. The face stamped on it made him think of of how his father might have looked as a younger man – if his father had ever worn the toga, or his hair in Roman curls, a picture so different from anything he knew of John Fox that Paul giggled. Letters were stamped round the circumference; he traced them with his nail. The Emperor Tiberius, Grand Pontiff.

Paul was holding the face of a god.

He inhaled the heady scent that clung to his fingers – the coins had been anointed and the perfume made his head spin.

So this was what his father did when he went down here. He came down to look at these coins, to hold these gorgeous things in his hands. Paul glanced down at the other pieces gleaming in the casket, each raised silver profile trailing shadow, changing shape as he leaned forward and the light altered its angle, each face flashing a different expression with the swinging of the shadows, so that Paul for a moment seemed to be looking down into the faces of a living crowd. He drew back with a gasp.

The light flickered and went out, the darkness rushed in.

Paul clutched the coin he held to his chest, both hands clamped over his heart. The emotion he felt lasted barely a heartbeat, but he knew he would never experience such a deep feeling again, and he would never forget his sense of loss, as though he had felt his death.

Then he reached down and breathed a sigh of relief to find he'd only wet himself with a sticky emission. That explained the sudden rush of his emotions, and he cheered up, feeling quite proud of himself and not at all afraid of the dark. He wiped off his thighs with a handful of water from the pool.

Just one, he thought. My father won't miss just one.

He knocked against the lid as he got up and it dropped down with a bang. Clenching the coin in his hand, he stumbled back through the dark caves guided by the glow of daylight at the entrance. Pulling himself up, replacing the cover carefully, he returned home whistling as innocently as though he'd been out to relieve himself. His mother was only just waking, and his father was down at the bottom of the long field, digging out the spring that soaked from the boggy earth down there to make a proper drinking place for the animals. Paul slipped the coin inside the sewing of his belt as he dressed – his personal talisman, all the sweeter for being stolen, the first thing he had ever really had all for himself.

Later in the morning he tolerated his mother's lessons with a smile, and when his father returned in the afternoon, his face looked so dull and hot, exhausted by his day's labour and completely unsuspicious, that Paul, doing his chores, could hardly conceal his elation. He'd got away with it. He was free and clear. What fools his parents were.

It was the late evening and the day had lost its colour by the time Paul reached the top of the slope and emerged from the beechwoods. He brushed the dirt from his knuckles and whistled for the pigs. The cleared heathland bordering the road was wider every year as Londoners, at first carrying baskets on their backs, then leading pannier mules, used the highway to come into the country to collect firewood for their hearths. Nowadays, in winter, men made a living chopping the trees here, overloading their carts with more than half a ton of logs, taking advantage of the downhill run to market in town. Up here where the trees fell back the weather was cold and windy, and the new growth could not penetrate the ferns and brambles quickly enough to survive. Paul pushed through the underbrush, the wind fluttering his tunic, until he came to the roadway. He stood on its crown as though he owned it. Its perfect line was arrogant and bewitching; straight as an arrow, it ran for miles into the twilight on each side of him, smooth white gravel levelling the ugly bumps and clumsy hollows of the ground. He thought he had never seen anything so beautiful.

'Yi-yi-yi!' shouted a driver's angry voice.

Paul jumped to the side then watched deferentially as the wagon of the Imperial Post rumbled by, a lady in a pinned cream tunic sitting in the back. Her husband or father must be very important to have got her a place on the official vehicle, and he stared after her in awe: she was the first lady he had seen. As little as two or three hours ago, allowing for the weary haul up the hill, she had been in London. London! She would not arrive at the staging post by the river at Crayford until well after dark, but he knew she would arrive safely. The Romans believed in personal property and their laws against stealing were strict. They had been written down so that everyone could understand them, even in different districts of the country, and justice was the same everywhere.

Paul whistled urgently for the pigs now. His father would be angry; he kept no supper aside for Paul when he was late, but he knew his mother would contrive to slip him half a loaf and some thin beer later. In fact Paul was looking forward to driving the sows downhill in the dark, making a challenge and an adventure of it – the silly creatures were bound to try and lose themselves among the tree trunks. But he knew he could do it, and that though his mother would be angry at first when he arrived home, then weep a tear, she would be proud of him really. Nevertheless, it was worrying that the herd had roamed this far – they always used to stick close to the settlement, but now that there were more people, there were more pigs. The thinned trees no longer made a natural fence, and the herd was no doubt finding food harder to scavenge than his father remembered from when there was only him and his mother here. Paul shook his head impatiently. At last he heard a sow squealing and set off along the road after the sound.

Now he heard them all squealing. They squealed as loudly and frantically as though they were being butchered. The sounds of heavy bodies blundering through the undergrowth carried to him.

'Who's there?' he called. It might be lads from the village playing about, and if it was, they'd be sorry. He knew them all by name, and his father knew their fathers.

Paul stopped as the pigs came running out of the trees towards him, squealing and kicking. He counted three short, and held up his arms to make them stop so that he could fetch the others. But, panic-stricken, they didn't stop, and Cupita, the old dame who was the leader, knocked him flying as she rushed past.

For several seconds Paul just lay there on the roadway, too surprised to move. It did not occur to him to be afraid. He felt angry because the scattered, stupid herd was too important for someone not to get the blame, and it would be him. His father would beat him half to death, and Paul knew that this time his mother would not be able to stop him. The pigs were all they had of any value. Worse, he would never live it down if the village lads heard old Cupita had run right over him. He might as well be dead anyway.

He rolled over as Ylas, the prime sow, but with only one of her piglets scampering after her, went trotting by him. Blood was streaked along her flank, her ribs sticking from the wounds like broken teeth.

Paul had never seen such a terrible injury. 'Oh no,' he cried. He stared as Ylas tottered, lowering her nose tiredly onto the roadway to rest. Then she quivered as though gathering all her strength. But she could not raise her head. Instead, she keeled over with a heavy thud that Paul felt in his bones. The piglet nuzzled into the carcass, suckling eagerly.

'Ylas, get up,' Paul said, blubbering openly.

He looked around him, realising how alone he was. Not one of the herd had returned to pilfer the grain spilled from the satchel by his fall. Then to his horror he saw that the precious satchel had split, and not along a repairable seam either, the leather itself had burst. He put his hands to his head in despair.

He was being watched.

Paul turned slowly. At first he thought he was seeing one of his father's mystical spirits, a shadow detaching itself from the darkness of the trees. He saw the gleam of tusks from the triangular head in front of the enormous shoulders. The flat nose grunted like a pig's, but a whippy tail, splayed with stiff hairs at the end, stuck from puny hindquarters.

The moment its dim eyes saw Paul, the boar charged.

Paul ran. He ran as slowly as in a nightmare, clutching the useless satchel to his chest, spilling a seam of grain along the road behind him. He voided his bowels down his legs, then his urine too, and his throat closed up with terror so that his breath whooped. He dodged from side to side, but the boar was too old and cunning to fool. Whooping and gasping, Paul flung the satchel away, making a terrible mistake by looking over his shoulder in his terror. The boar closed in a rush, and Paul screamed, knowing he was going to die. He tripped and tumbled into the ditch. As he rolled a tusk caught his tunic, tearing it with a loud ripping sound. Paul screamed again, clutching at his ribs with a vivid mental picture, but they were not sticking out.

He scrambled up the far side of the ditch into the undergrowth, heaving himself forward through the brambles with all his strength, feeling them shake around him as his ferocious pursuer plunged after him. Nothing would stop the boar. Paul dropped down, drawing up his legs and worming frantically beneath the tangle towards clear ground beyond. It was the bravest thing he had ever done.

But it wasn't clear ground. His situation was worse. What he had taken for grass was a slimy moss, and his elbows and knees sank through the decaying surface into sticky mud. He staggered to his feet and struggled through a marsh dotted with reeds. The mud sucked at his feet, his shoes were gone, his legs trembling as he lifted them. The boar went crashing past and this time he smelt the creature, as sweet and dark as blood.

Paul had one clear thought. His only chance was among the trees. He struggled, wet and filthy, towards the mossy bank that was the edge of firm ground. He was weeping. The boar came round, pivoting on the massive shoulders, white hairs bristling among the grey, and came for him again.

'Why do you hate me?' screamed Paul at the top of his voice, but heard only a whisper. He was finished. All the strength had left him and he stood planted with his feet stuck apart in the mud so that he would not fall, so weak that his body trembled all over, shaking with sobs.

His father's hand reached down to him. 'Paul.'

Paul stared.

'Give me your hand, son,' came John Fox's voice. He jerked his fingers impatiently and Paul almost laughed, it was such a human gesture. He reached up and the hand clamped round his own, pulling him up with a force that made both men's shoulder joints crack. Mud sprayed over them and Paul felt bristles scratch his bare foot.

He dropped onto the mossy bank, and lay looking up with a shock. He'd not noticed before how white his father's hair and beard were becoming; against the shadows that surrounded them he looked as old and indomitable as the boar.

John Fox unpinned his cloak and drew his sword. It was the old rusty one with the broken point. As the boar charged, he dropped the cloak over its head and let the beast's own weight drive the blade into its body. John let go of the sword as the handle was rammed into the ground. A terrible muffled squealing began. He drew his dagger and chose his moment. Silence fell.

The boar twitched one last time. An owl hooted. Leaves rustled in the darkness.

John pulled his cloak from the beast's head like a man reclaiming his property. Paul lay still, too exhausted and afraid to move. His father came back cleaning the blade of his dagger.

'Father,' Paul groaned, knowing he would never be forgiven for

136

the loss of the herd. But John knelt and embraced him.

'You're with me, son,' he murmured. 'I've got you. You're with me now.'

'But – the herd—'

'Oh, they won't go far. We'll find them tomorrow.'

Paul clasped him tight, shuddering. His father's cloak stank of the boar, dark and bloody, filling his senses. They searched for his shoes together, but they were lost in the dark. Paul's belt felt as though it had been driven into his hip, and when he touched the edge of the silver disc he had stolen, he found it pushed through the sewing, the curved edge pressed deep into his flesh. It had almost killed him – or perhaps back there in the ditch when the boar had actually caught him, it had saved his life.

Biting his lip, Paul levered it out with a jerk of his fingers. He wished dearly that he had never stolen the thing. He was ashamed of himself. But he could not put it back. It was his now, blooded by him, his as much as his father's. He wept weak tears.

'You'll learn to be strong, Paul,' John Fox said fiercely, 'as strong as I am.'

'But Paul's too young to go with you,' Imogen said, 'he's only a boy.' She had kept up this steady complaint all day, following them around to bitch at them as the two men piled the smoked hams round the cart, ready for loading.

'Paul is coming with me,' John said patiently, 'and you can wear your smile or your frown, Imogen, it's no difference to me. The lad's more than old enough, and that's that.'

'I am old enough,' Paul said.

But she wasn't having it. To her, he was still her own little boy, not his own man. He was amazed what his mother would do to keep him.

'I could tell him some things about you,' Paul overheard her threaten his father angrily, but John shrugged. He knew he had won.

'What did she mean?' Paul asked later. 'Things about you?'

'Oh, you know what women are like when they don't get their way.'

'Absolutely,' Paul said wisely, and the subject went no further.

But Imogen crossed her arms and refused to prepare their main meal, eaten the Roman way in the mid-afternoon. Paul had to go without his eggs and meat, and she had always made sure he ate every last mouthful. His father laughed, but Paul's tummy rumbled, and he had to make do nibbling the stale wedge of yesterday's wholemeal loaf. Later Imogen changed her tack and fussed after him, slipping him a hard-boiled egg when she thought his father wasn't watching, brushing the grease of smoked meat from his shoulder, telling him not to work so hard.

'She's afraid of losing you,' John explained, heaving a side of bacon onto the clean straw that floored the cart. The muscles stood out in his arms and back, and Paul knew he would never have muscles like that.

'But she hasn't lost me,' Paul dared to try to explain to his father, chewing the hard-boiled egg, then putting it down with embarrassment. 'She's still my mother, she still loves me.'

'That's why she wants power over you,' John said, brushing his hands and surveying the half-loaded cart with satisfaction. 'She loves you, so she hates losing even a little bit of you.' He checked the harness on the oxen, then drew a deep breath. Paul finished off the last bite of egg behind his hand. 'I may have made a mistake, Paul. I've allowed you to be brought up in a way I was not. You know your mother and love her.'

'I suppose so.' Paul swallowed.

'You see, Paul, I never loved my mother. I was sent away before I was old enough to love her, or even feel loss at not knowing her.'

'But you must have felt . . . it must have affected you.'

'No.'

Paul was amazed. 'Where were you sent to?'

'A school, here.'

'A Roman school?'

John hesitated. 'No. Before the Europeans came.'

'I can't imagine that,' Paul said, staring at London in the distance, a crown of white buildings on the two hills, and the sails of craft of every sort dotting the river. He shook himself out of his reverie as his father leapt aboard the cart. 'We can carry much more than this to Greenwich tomorrow, can't we, Father?'

John winked, then cracked the whip. 'We won't be going down to Greenwich any more, we'll get better prices in London. Yes,' he laughed, 'I thought you'd be pleased!'

Paul jumped up beside him, but looked back. A few days ago

his father had chopped down the nettlebeds that concealed the secret entrance, protecting the saplings with rings of stakes instead. Paul had walked over the ground. He had found no hole or any sign of one. His father had filled it in as though it had never existed and was forgotten. Did he know that Paul had discovered his secret?

Paul was certain of it. And there was something else. His father admired him for it. He wanted Paul to be close to him, manly like him, a younger version of him, for there to be no difference between them.

Even only half-loaded, the footpath winding up the Valle Dei was a fearful struggle for the oxen, the cart bumping over tree roots, in danger of rolling back, and Paul had to push at the wheels with his shoulder. Reaching the plateau they stopped within the tree line and made a cache of the hams and bacon, covering them with fern, leaving Briginus's boy Matugenus to keep an eye on them while they returned for the second load.

But Imogen spied them returning past the huts of the freedmen's village, Rianorix lazing while old Vernico chopped down one of the oaks to make beams to start his granddaughter's house, and realised where they were going.

'London?' she said, aghast. 'But that means you'll be away two days at least! Oh, John, you can't!'

John nudged Paul. 'We thought . . . I mean *I* thought,' Paul said as they followed her into the house, 'that we could bring you back one of those square cooking pots you wanted, an *angularis*. That would be easy to find in London.'

'A cooking pot!' scoffed Imogen. 'What a wonderful exchange! And can't I just guess whose idea that was!' She glared at John. 'You want to make him just like you, don't you?' Then she burst into tears. 'I hate this place. I want to go! There's so much I want to do!' She stormed out.

'Don't worry, Paul,' John said, 'it's her time of life.' He clapped his son on the shoulder: us two together. But still Paul looked back as they left the house shortly before sunset. This time his mother did not come out to wave goodbye to him through the failing light.

Little Matugenus, his eyes gleaming as wide and round as snail shells at the sound of their approach, was pathetically relieved to see them. He was sure the woods were haunted – Paul could guess what terrifying stories old Briginus, who had tried to scare Paul – must have spun his own son. Perhaps they were true, too, Paul thought now, perhaps his father was right to believe in the gods, or at least right not to disbelieve. Such terrible things happened, like Matugenus's younger sister being born with a hare lip, that they must be deliberate, a punishment and a sign, perhaps from a mother-goddess, or a goddess of fidelity. The other women had at once concluded that the mother, Tacita, had been sleeping with more than her own husband, and cut off her beautiful red hair to the skull.

Paul watched Matugenus disappear running down through the woods like the wind, then helped his father fill up the cart to capacity with the half-load they had dumped here earlier. They slept between the wheels wrapped in their cloaks, except that Paul was too excited to sleep. He woke his father as soon as the planet Venus touched the tree line beyond the road, and they were on their way, shaking the dew from their cloaks and blowing on their hands, by the time the first grey line of dawn lit the horizon behind them.

The oxen plodded with agonising slowness, and the cart jolted unmercifully even on the smooth road, so that soon Paul was glad to get off the hard wooden bench and walk beside them. He had never been further than this, and he looked round him eagerly, seeing everything for the first time: the trees falling back from the road, the cleared heathland growing broader all the time. By dawn gangs of slaves were out already, cutting timber, and there were a few huts of the poorest sort, often with a much better one nearby. Later they passed a small villa, built with straight walls and a tiled roof, looking unbelievably strange to Paul's eyes. There was even a stable with painted walls and a thatched roof, horses in the yard, and teams of oxen hauling stumps to clear fields on the property.

They pulled off the road as a cohort of soldiers came marching up behind them with a steady tramp, hard-eyed men wearing leather armour and polished leather helmets. 'Auxiliaries,' his father murmured. 'Those are Batavians. Others come from all parts of the world.' Paul was disappointed not to see legionaries.

'You'll see enough legionaries,' his father said, chewing a straw. Other carts were bumping along with them now. They began the long plodding descent from the plateau, London shining in the morning sun now far away on their right, across the marshes and the river. The lower they descended, the further away London appeared to be, the high hills and moorlands rising behind the town dwarfing the line of tiny terracotta roofs below.

'I feel like an outsider here,' Paul said.

'We are outsiders,' John grunted. 'We were British, and this was our land.'

'And because of our names we're even more outsiders than the others.' Paul jumped up beside him, but his father wouldn't hand over the reins.

'What do you mean?'

'In our village there's at least half a dozen boys called Bellicus, and two or three little girls named Boudica, but there's not a single Paul or John.'

'They're common enough names in some parts of the world, boy.'

'But—'

'You ask too many questions. Stop thinking. Get down there on your feet and give those lazy animals a whack with the stick!'

The sun was hot now, shimmering over the marshes as they came to a broad causeway cutting across in front of them. The junction was busy with traffic from Thorney Island joining an awkward mass of laden carts from the south, men and women on foot bent beneath heavy loads winding between the stalled vehicles, carts carrying barrels of fresh oysters in sea water, farmers driving stock ahead of them with the help of scampering boys. Paul stared, astonished to see so many people. 'It's the busiest time of day.' His father spat over the wheel, unimpressed. He cracked the whip, forcing the cart into the stream of traffic, then put up his feet, placed a rag over his face against the sun and dust and closed his eyes, trusting the oxen to keep their faces against the bottoms of the beasts in front as the traffic slowly moved forward up the hill.

Paul saw that there were headstones everywhere now they had come to drier ground. Cemeteries stretched on each side of the road: wooden plaques at first, gaudily painted, the names carved and painted in another colour; now of painted stone, including some mausolea the size of small houses, one or two sheathed in brilliant white marble with a brightly-coloured statue of the deceased on top or in a niche. Then abruptly there were no more – they must have passed the town limits. Paul was technically in London, but he saw no houses yet.

A column of soldiers came swinging along the centre of the road, the officer on horseback in flashing armour and clean cloak, the troops filthy with dust, sweat running in sunburnt runnels down their harsh faces, their callused hands favouring the straps that held up the heavy kit on their backs, wooden planks, shovels, rolls of leather and canvas, weapons. They grunted rhythmically, like one long animal, as they passed. John slipped the cart into the clear space they left behind them, following the unit as if part of it. He looked bored, as if all this life and bustling action and city cunning was familiar to him and beneath comment. If you think these are roads, Paul, his bored eyes said, you should see the highways of the mainland; this is a village compared to the white canyons of Rome. But Paul looked around him, marvelling at everything he saw.

'It's wonderful!' he said with shining eyes.

'Stop dancing about like a country cousin,' his father told him tersely, 'or people will take advantage of you.' He didn't even look at an inn called the Tabernacle as they passed, the smart types, some of them in togas, drinking imported wine and watching the passing crowd with sleepy, calculating eyes for what they could sell, or might buy, if the price was right.

'Why don't we sell to them?' Paul came prancing back.

'Don't be a fool,' his father said.

Paul saw men buying pies and peas in the gloom inside, eating them on the counter with their own knives and spoons. Older men sat outside, their stubbled faces turned to the sun. Stables and pens for the temporary storage of livestock, for rent at a price no doubt, were scattered around the back of the building, field after field of them reclaimed from the marshes. On each side of the inn stretched a jumble of stalls and brightly-painted huts, all of them in the continental fashion, with straight walls pierced by windows, though the frames and shutters were painted sky-blue, as if in concession to British taste. None of them looked as if they would stand up to a decent gale. 'Is this a street?' Paul asked.

'I suppose you could just about call it that,' his father replied, looking slightly irritated by Paul's continuous enthusiasm.

'And we aren't even in the town yet,' Paul breathed.

The troops broke step as they came to the bridge, only barely wide enough for two carts to pass abreast between the wooden balustrades. The central drawbridge had been lowered and their boots crossed it with a hollow roar, the cart swaying after them onto the north bank. Timber quays followed the line of the beach, some standing on piles in the water, barges canted around them on the gravel, being unloaded, other vessels waiting for the tide. Men dragged on ropes to swing the cargoes up onto the wharf, more men heaved the sacks and bales through sliding double doors into long storehouses, which ran in a neat line from the bridge downstream as far as the Customs House at Belinos's Gate, where vessels declared cargo and paid dues. Workmen were busy on building work everywhere along this north bank, even upstream of the bridge, orange to their knees and elbows with London clay, working like ants shifting gravel and fetching timber pilings on enormous four-wheeled carts, while deeply-laden barges delivering cargoes of Kentish ragstone clustered at the mouth of the Walbrook and along the quays of the River Fleet beyond.

'Look, Paul.' His father pointed up the slope steepening ahead of them. 'We called this the Corn Hill – it was fields in my day.' The rise was topped with a fortress now, of wood and embanked earth, with a big white building at each end of a long gravelled parade ground. An open drain ran down from it, clotted with refuse and smelling of human soil, waiting for the next heavy rain to wash it to the river. Although Paul walked beside the oxen beating them with a stick, they could not keep pace with the soldiers' steady tramp uphill, and he was intensely disappointed when his father turned left before reaching the grandest part of the town on the hill. 'Only soldiers and administrators there,' John grunted. 'Not for us.'

The road they followed, still being made up and bordered only by low thatched dwellings, followed a level terrace along the slope, the river below and the town above. This was a growing district, the walls here were very white, very new, many of the dwellings left unfinished by the speculators – just holes for windows, and tiles not yet placed over the chimneys against the winter rain that was still some months away. The children of families who were already renting ran beside the cart, banging the wheels with sticks and begging for money. The mother of one screamed at her child in a foreign tongue, then put her hands in her hair and went back inside. They began to pass buildings that were being converted to two storeys. Piped water was being laid to them and the pavement rose a foot above the dusty roadway, which must turn to mud in the winter rains, judging by the stepping-stones a foot high for pedestrians to pick their way across – the wheels of the cart slipped neatly through the gaps. What had been side roads became alleyways winding between steep walls, and the houses were open at the front. Paul saw that you could walk off their verandahs straight into them, as if you owned them.

'Shops,' his father explained. The ground dipped towards the River Walbrook and they passed tiny open-fronted shops selling cheap goods of every description – mass-produced pots and kitchen utensils, inexpensive cloth, necklaces made of seashells, tweezers for plucking unwanted hair. Paul could hardly take in all he was seeing. A man gripped his arm, selling him the services of a scribe to write a letter. Another begged him to try the finest Medway oysters. The next shop sold nothing but lice combs and hairpins, thousands of them, white bone or black jet, copper, silver, with every sort of decoration or none at all. Paul gaped at a lady choosing a pin whose bone head was carved into a hairstyle that exactly matched the piled up fashion of her own hair. Her girl-slave paid. The lady returned Paul's stare with amusement, then interest, at his youth. Then two more slaves, young men, lifted her and carried her away in a sedan chair.

'You'd better come up here with me, Paul,' warned his father from the cart, and Paul jumped up. For a moment he thought he saw a strange envious light in his father's eyes, as if he was jealous of Paul who was seeing everything with such eager innocence for the first time, and being noticed for the first time. 'Don't let them take advantage of you, Paul.'

But Paul wasn't listening. As they came to the Walbrook, he saw that the river banks were lined with shrines to every sort of deity, and fine shops had sprung up to take advantage of the crowds, selling statuettes of every shape and size, charms and amulets to be worn, offerings to be placed in a shrine. Paul pointed at one old woman scratching something on a pot with a nail, then she bobbed respectfully and flung it into the sluggish stream, her head bowed as the splash came. 'Is she making a wish?'

'Or a curse,' John said. These shops were not built of wood and painted plaster but of white ragstone, some of them along the frontage of much larger buildings, the businesses of bankers and import-export negotiators, and living quarters. Paul studied each doorway closely as they passed – a cutler's display of bone-handled kitchen knives, finely made and beautifully ornamented, and very expensive; a greengrocer selling imported lemons, pomegranates, melons, figs and dates which would go down well with the foreigners on the hill. Narrow, deep shops with big men leaning in the doorways sold gold and silverware, copper bracelets, dress pins worked with precious stones and metals. The owners fawned on any person of quality, and ignored everyone else. The next shop, opposite a popular shrine, sold pricey Cumaean pottery and red Samian crockery. The distinctive plates from Spain, of every different colour, glittered with bright flecks of mica for even greater effect. This was obviously the shopping street where the rich people came. There was red ribbed cloth from the north moors, Welsh wool and herringbone twill, cotton from Sudan, glowing silks from China, pearls from India, rare spices. One shop was stacked with pointed amphorae, the elegant necks sealed with pitch, alluringly advertised: the best fish paste from Antipolis, the finest olive oil from Baetica, vintage wines. Further on, past a fishmonger, John spied a shopfront festooned with every imaginable sausage: dark red Lucanian sausage, pale almond sausage, pork and bacon sausage speckled with pepper and lovage, cured sausage of every colour between black and white hung in rings or loops, all displayed swinging from strings to tempt the eye.

'This is what I'm looking for.' Stopping the cart, John jumped down and carefully brushed the straw from his tunic and tartan britches. He unfolded a clean cloak from the back of the cart, not the one he had slept in, and swept it over his shoulders, pinning it with a haughty flick of his fingers. With the ease of a traveller used to blending into different backgrounds, yet still commanding respect, he had become a different person before Paul's eyes.

Paul wished he could be like his father.

'Stay up there on the cart, Paul,' John growled. 'Don't let anyone steal anything, and don't let that curiosity of yours get you into trouble.'

'Yes, sir,' Paul said obediently, clutching the whip tight, and gazed down on the heads of the crowd flowing around the cart. One shrewish woman gave him a look for parking so inconveniently, another complained that the cartwheel had brushed against her new shawl, marking it, and what was he going to do about it? An old man tried to sell him something, but he learned they couldn't reach him up here, and ignored them. He watched his father saunter across the verandah to the butcher's shop as confidently as if he was the landlord. He braced his hands on his hips, staring at the display.

'Your sausages look all right, butcher,' he grunted in fluent Roman to someone Paul could not see.

'I am not the butcher, sir, I am the owner!' came the stilted reply, through a thick British accent. The man who thrust himself heavily through the broad doorway almost filled it. Nothing about him was soft, his shoulders were powerful and even his belly, tightly corseted, looked hard with muscle. But his plump hands and chins gave him away, they looked slack and shiny, and his watery blue eyes peered from webs of puffy skin. He did not walk; he pivoted himself forward over each leg. 'Dumnius Pomponius, sir, at your service,' he said grandly. Paul thought he was more than ugly, and he was frightening too, even though he was stretching his rounded face into a smile of welcome. 'My slaves, sir,' claimed the smiling shop-owner in a high phlegmy voice, 'do the menial butchery work.' Despite those eyes and his smile, his weight gave him an implacable air, and though he had denied his trade, from one hand dangled a skinning knife, so familiar a friend that he had forgotten it.

'I see that you are a man who knows his business,' John said, touching his finger to the blade of the skinning knife. Pomponius dared not move a muscle lest he give injury.

'For my best customers only.' He smiled using his whole face, though his eyes remained the colour of ice. He disengaged the knife with infinite care, then tossed it through the shop doorway where it landed without sound in the sawdust. John stood

146

perfectly at his ease in the hot sun, examining the sausages shadowed beneath the eaves, taking his time. 'Dumnius' was a made-up name, he knew. Probably this ambitious, intelligent Briton had started life as a lowly Catuvellaunian named Dumnogenus or Dumnorix, and he'd never have achieved anything under the old system. Now he was rich, and his children, if he had any, and if London prospered, might rise to be citizens of the curial class – local aristocracy. But poor snobbish Pomponius never would speak Roman properly, though not for want of trying. What in his inexperience he called civilisation was really servitude.

The big man tried to find a patch of shadow to stand in, then flourished his bloody, sweating hands, each plump finger bulging flesh round a ring that shouted his new wealth. 'If you do not see the goods you require on display here—'

'I would speak to you of more than sausages,' John said.

'Ah,' Pomponius said with relief, getting down to business. 'I have you now. You mean my representations on the municipal council. I am of course qualified by property and considerable financial interests. I supply the army, which I am sure you will agree demonstrates my trustworthiness.' He paused impressively. 'I have it on good authority that London will soon be awarded the status of *colonia*. I have been, as you may have heard, lobbying on behalf of the shopkeepers in my ... our ... street for a local assembly room to attract persons of deserving quality to this district.'

'Obviously you are an influential and important man,' John said patiently.

Pomponius's civic pride, the route to local influence even for a non-citizen, knew no bounds. 'And then there is my plan to raise a subscription for a public baths,' he confided. 'Ah, but money is desperately short. Wait, you!' He intercepted a slave arriving with a cage of thrushes from the aviary, counted the number against the tally and signed with a symbol, then nodded for them to be taken inside. 'Yes, desperately short. The huge loans that got things going in the early days are over, foreclosed or recalled to Rome since the death of the God Claudius.' He made a brief genuflection at a brightly-painted statue on a podium on the other side of the river, the head wearing a fresh laurel, probably replaced there every day by acolytes. 'So, the centurions are plundering the colony – most understandable, in those regions beyond the reach of civilisation,' he added loyally. 'The sky-blue savages must be taught a lesson.' Twenty years ago he had himself been one of them. 'It's for their own good. In the old days, listen to me, we British so ate ourselves up—'

'Not in your case,' John said, slapping Pomponius's broad belly.

Pomponius gave a polite but barking laugh. 'So much effort put into fighting one another that our German mercenaries seized power over friend and foe alike, don't deny it. The Romans saved us from that; the energy we put into fighting we now put, my friend, into making money. The governor terrorises the people, and the procurator terrorises our purses, but at least they're organised about it, we know where we stand, don't we?'

Paul heard a door close somewhere inside the shop, then the sound of wood-soled shoes on stairs. The cart's seat put him on a level with the sunlit tiles of the verandah roof. No doubt because of the hot day, the shutters of the first-floor window had been opened, one side thrown all the way back for ventilation, the other only halfway for the cool shadow it cast. In the room beyond, the head and shoulders of a girl appeared. Paul blinked.

'But of course,' droned Pomponius's voice, 'London is too important as a financial centre to be too plundered by the tax collectors, because confidence is the oil of money. They dare not.'

'You must be right,' Paul heard his father's voice.

The girl crossed the cool, shadowed room. She was carrying something Paul could not see. She must be a year or two older than he was; he could see the swells of her breasts moving beneath the creamy pinned pleats of her gown. Paul swallowed; he had never seen anything so beautiful. The pleats, tight at neck and waist, secured by expensive glints of gold, broadened suggestively over her curves. Her hair, which must be very long, was piled up in chestnut waves, requiring yet more gleaming gold pins; instinctively Paul knew it was the latest fashion.

Beneath the verandah roof, Pomponius's worry burst out of him. 'But the Iceni are a civilised people – I mean the nobility, of course. The men take their families everywhere with them. Yet Decianus Catus has revoked their tribal taxation agreements with the old emperor, and he's threatened to have the queen flogged if she doesn't pay up. Of course, he wouldn't be so stupid as to really go ahead with it . . .'

Paul had not taken his eyes off the girl in the room. She came to the window and he saw that she was carrying the dish called a *boletarium*; it was piled with the largest, whitest boletus mushrooms he had ever seen. She couldn't be going to eat them all. He grinned as she unfolded a small pocket knife, then, hugging her elbows to her sides with an expression of secret joy that Paul understood perfectly, she speared one of the mushrooms and twirled it in the wine sauce. Closing her eyes luxuriously, she slipped the mushroom into her open mouth. Her eyelids fluttered open, and their eyes met.

Paul risked it. He smiled his broadest smile. She gave a flustered half-smile in return, then giggled at herself for being so caught out.

Below, Pomponius's voice trailed off. He had noticed John's tawdry homemade footware. There were half a dozen shoemakers within sight, any of whom could expertly draw round a foot and produce a shoe in wood or leather, with uppers of any style and almost any colour or decoration, within the hour – for a price. Pomponius turned, seeing the cart, and put two and two together. 'This thing's yours?' He strode over to it and pulled off the blanket covering the back. He stared at the smoked hams and sides of bacon lying in the clean straw. 'You've fallen a long way,' he said, dropping his awkward Roman for British, speaking fluently now and with contempt.

'And you've risen far, if I'm not mistaken,' John said.

'Don't expect handouts from me. You fooled me, you liar. I'm a great man around here!' Pomponius pushed John's shoulder angrily. 'And where did you learn to get your tongue round Roman grammar like that, you son of a whore?' He had to use the Roman word; these latest foreign imports, prostitutes registered with the magistrate and taxed by the Emperor, hung about along the street, near one of the temples of Isis, at the inn between the bath-house and the public toilets. They wore short colourful tunics, their lips painted cinnabar red and their hair loose to signify their trade. Pomponius shook his head. 'Times have turned against you, old man, and they won't come back.'

'No, master,' John said meekly. 'You're right, master.'

'Anyway,' Pomponius said haughtily, sticking his thumbs through his belt and hanging his fingers from his enormous waistline like sausages, 'where did you come from to waste my time?'

'Along the Rochester road, master.'

'What good's that to me for the supply of meat? It's summer, I have to use the stuff like lightning. On a really hot day pork spoils in an hour, you idiot! I don't want to kill my customers.'

John reached into the cart and pulled out a ham, brandishing it in front of Pomponius's face. 'Alexandrine,' he said, meaning finest quality. 'Smoked on oak chippings, keeps for months. You can sell more than sausages in summer.'

'Space is short,' groused Pomponius. 'You must know how difficult warm weather makes my life. I have to keep my week's supply of chickens alive, in an allotment, and pay a boy to watch over them, and still they get stolen. And I have to beat the value out of his hide and it exhausts me. And then there is the wringing of their necks and the slitting of their gullets, though the blood fetches a fine price. I'm not going through all that aggravation with pigs, there's no room for them. Look, see how I must work!' He gestured into the shadows of the shop, busy elbows working at the chopping blocks. 'Two trained slaves – trained to be lazy, I say. I should turn them to cash and get out of this trade entirely.'

'I do all the work,' John said patiently. 'The boy delivers weekly.'

'What boy?' Pomponius said, and both men stared up at the empty seat of the cart. Paul was gone.

Paul couldn't help himself, it was as simple as that. He'd knotted the reins round the verandah post, the two men's talk mumbling past him behind the rows of sausages. Then, standing on the seat and reaching up, he had got both elbows and one knee onto the tiles, and pulled himself up onto the verandah roof. The hard tiles dug unmercifully into his ribs and hips as he struggled to spread his weight, then he almost slipped off the edge. Despite his fear, he realised that he still wore his fixed smile.

'Greetings,' he said in Roman, trying not to grunt with discomfort. 'I'm Paul.' She gazed at him from the open window without speaking, still holding the bowl of mushrooms and knife; he was sure that at any moment she would remember to put them down and slam the shutters.

'You're going to fall off, doing that,' she said, her curiosity bringing her into the afternoon sunlight; she must be at least fourteen, but her voice had a deep, mellow tone quite unlike her father's, though she had his blue eyes. Paul noticed dark roots in her hair; she used henna for the coveted red colour, an advantage he had over her, and he risked sweeping a hand through his russet locks. 'You're a show-off,' she said scornfully. 'Go away!'

It was now or never. Paul wobbled to his knees. The tiles didn't seem to be nailed down at all, grating under his weight, but they didn't slide off. Placing the balls of his feet on the curved piece of terracotta joining two tiles, which would be the strongest part, and balancing forward on his knuckles, he scuttled up the shallow slope to her window. Settling back on his haunches, hanging onto the sill with one hand, he winked cheerfully at her, then panted victoriously.

'You look like a monkey,' she said. 'What you are doing is very dangerous, you know.'

'I haven't fallen yet,' he said cockily.

'I meant that I only have to scream.'

She would, too. She had something dark in her eyes. Perhaps that was what he liked about her; and she wasn't afraid. He took a breath, then stopped as he recognised the perfumed scent of her flesh. It was the same heady scent that had clung to his fingers in the cave when he touched the coins. For a moment his head spun.

'Have I frightened you? Careful you don't fall,' she giggled.

'You're special,' he said. 'Stop it.'

She stared at him.

'Giggling down your nose like a little girl,' he said. He pulled himself up onto the windowsill and sat swinging his legs carelessly. 'Scream, then, if it suits you.'

'You're so sure I won't,' she said, spearing a mushroom and eating it.

'Those are the best-looking, biggest mushrooms I've ever seen in my life,' he said.

She softened, flattered, then confided in him. 'I grow them myself, downstairs. Is this all you're getting yourself into such trouble for?'

'Am I in trouble?'

'Yes, when I have to call my father.'

'Just one,' he begged. 'Then I'll go.'

She shook her head, her hair catching a slant of the afternoon sun beautifully. Either she wanted to keep all the mushrooms for herself, or she didn't want him to go.

'You have a lovely straight nose,' he said. 'It's Roman. And your perfume.'

She preened. 'Do you really think—'

He stole a kiss from her lips.

'Now it's worth it,' he said.

She put down the plate on the low table, frowning. 'What?'

'When you give me away.' He winked at her, daring her to scream.

'Paul?' called John Fox's voice along the street.

'Quick, inside.' The girl took his arm in her soft white hands, pulling him into the room. 'If my father finds out you're here, he'll kill you. I mean it.'

He looked at her seriously. 'Is that why you didn't scream?'

She hurried him through to the inner doorway, looked both ways along a narrow landing, the stairs leading down to the shop at one end.

'Are you frightened of him?' Paul whispered.

She glanced at him, then led him across the corridor to the room opposite. 'Quickly.' She opened the shutter, revealing a long, thin yard below, the sunlit backs of houses beyond. He tried to snatch another kiss to show he was unafraid, but she pushed him away, looking fearfully over her shoulder. Paul crouched lightly on the windowsill.

'Tell me your name before I die.'

'Diana!' she said, then went to the door and peered round it into the corridor, flapping her hand for him to go.

'I love you, Diana,' he called. She jumped as though he had pinched her leg, then glared at him, putting her finger to her lips: some people just wouldn't be helped. Paul slid down and hung at arms' length against the outside wall as the sound of heavy foot-steps approached on the stairs. Then he kicked off and dropped lightly into the yard. Running past the pens of chickens and a sleepy old horse tied to a post, he vaulted over the fence at the far end.

He crossed the dusty building lot that lay beyond, his lips pressed tightly together to fix the taste of Diana in his memory: white mushrooms, red wine sauce, and fresh green coriander. He sniffed his fingers where they had touched her, dangerous and irresistible, remembering the perfume she wore.

He jumped the railing at the end of the building lots without using his hands. He never wanted to use them for anything but holding her. She flavoured his lips and fingers, he could see her in his mind as clearly as if she was part of him. He tripped over a pile of bricks; a kiln blasted more heat past him into the hot air, the sun struck his eyes as he came back to the gravelled road. He wanted her with a desire that was more than desire, a kind of rage he had never felt before, a reason for living: love. And he had her name. 'Diana,' he said aloud.

'Over there, chum,' called one of the workmen, with a jerk of his head. 'Working on her last week, I was.'

Paul gaped at him, then looked across the stream to the hill rising on the other side of Walbrook, Lud's Hill, where the extraordinary statement was explained. A number of white buildings with pillars and porticos dotted the gardens of the slope. At the summit was one still being built, higher than the others, a temple to the goddess Diana.

Paul paused thoughtfully, then returned to the butcher's shop, pushing through the group of whores as though he was returning from the public lavatories built over the stream. His father and Pomponius both looked at him suspiciously, but Paul rubbed his backside and grimaced to explain his problem.

'Help me carry the hams and bacon inside,' John said. 'You'll be delivering here weekly from now on, while the summer lasts.'

Paul feigned disappointment.

'Monthly in the winter,' Pomponius said. 'Fixed prices, remember, and penalties for late delivery. I'll have a scribe draw up the contract. And don't forget, my trade's quality, quality, quality.' He pushed his thumbs into his belt and watched them work with great self-satisfaction. 'My wife passed on and never saw how great a man I have become, but my daughter will marry a three-named citizen of Rome, and my grandchildren will be three-named citizens and sit on the council, or my name's not Dumnius Pomponius.'

There had been an accident at the end of the street, blocking the right turn. Two carts passing in opposite directions had locked wheels and were jammed together in a mass of splintered wood;

one cart had lost its wheel entirely and fallen over, almost toppling into the stream. A man was swearing it could not be his fault, he had been hardly moving. Obviously the mules had panicked and bolted, for one of them was stretched on the ground almost strangled by its awkward harness. Paul heard the owner negotiating with a group of men who had gathered, hoping for pennies, to lift the mule back onto its feet and not to cut the precious leather.

To avoid the blockage, Paul drove over a bridge thrown across the stream. The road cut through farming land that intense demand had subdivided into allotments, and dusty paddocks where sheep and cattle were awaiting slaughter amid dumps of household and building rubbish. His father sat beside him counting a handful of small bronze coins. 'The truth, now. Don't tell me you went in the shit-house, Paul.'

'You mean you saw me climb on the verandah roof,' Paul said.

'I mean you didn't have any money to pay the old lady for a sponge to wipe your arse on.' He flicked a coin with his thumbnail and Paul caught it: his first money. 'You can thank your lucky stars it was I who heard you on the roof, not that horror Pomponius.'

Paul cleared his throat. 'He has a daughter.'

'Paul, every girl looks beautiful at your age!'

'She *is* beautiful. And she has . . . something else. In her eyes. And she wears perfume.'

'I didn't bring you to London to get you into trouble, or for you to get her into trouble. Anyway, you don't stand a chance with that class of people, Paul.'

The cart bumped and lurched on the gravel but, empty, moved uphill easily.

'You don't understand,' Paul said. 'I love her.'

John sighed. He glanced at Paul and saw the expression there. Paul's lower lip was set into a tight line, an expression John recognised from himself – and from Imogen. He leant back and covered his face ruefully with his hands. 'You're my son all right,' he said.

'Then you would have done exactly the same thing,' Paul said. 'You *would*,' he insisted with frightening intensity.

'You'll grow out of wanting what you can't have, Paul.'

'Will I? Do you love my mother, does she love you?' Paul raged. 'You don't love her, do you? Why is she so much younger than you? Where do we come from, Father? Why are we born?'

John searched his son's eyes. 'You idiot, you really are in love,' he said.

They came to the top of the rise, stopping by the white ragstone colonnade that workmen were clothing with marble. Below them a scattering of Mediterranean-orange rooftops sloped to the broad blue river. 'When I was your age,' John murmured, 'this was a city of reeds.' Beyond the marshes of the south bank his eye followed the river's loop to Greenwich and the vivid hills of the nemeton rising behind: the countryside which overlooked London like a mute green witness.

'You can't stop me,' Paul said, but his voice trembled. He knew his father could make life impossible for him, and then he would have to run away. Either way, he couldn't see how he could attain Diana.

John sighed, as though the same thought had passed through his mind. 'My own father tried . . .' He cleared his throat. 'Love is the most powerful force in the world. When we're young we'll do anything for love.'

'And what about when you're old?'

'Sometimes old men forget, I suppose. I can hardly remember what it was like back then when I was young. What it was *really* like. So I won't help you, but I won't stand in your way. What did you say her name was?'

'I didn't. Her name is Diana.'

'Diana the huntress, the virgin – the silver goddess.' John laughed, realising where Paul had brought him, and pointed through the colonnade of the temple. 'All right, leave your prayers in there, my boy, and your money. Who knows!'

Paul could hardly wait for next week to arrive. Every night, and most of his waking hours, he spent in a dream where Tuesday came and he hoisted himself effortlessly onto the verandah roof, and said all the right things to make Diana laugh, in exactly the tone of voice to make her admire him, and looked deep into her blue eyes, and inhaled her expensive perfume . . . He spoke Roman as well as his father, which was rather better than Diana did, and surely that must count for something between them. In Roman he overcame her father's objections effortlessly . . .

'What have you done to him?' Imogen grumbled at John. 'I knew this would happen. You've changed him already. He doesn't hear a word I say to him.'

Tuesday dawned at last. As before, but alone this time, Paul passed the night beneath the loaded cart on the edge of the bleak heathland beside the road, but when he woke there were no stars visible; it was pouring with rain. As soon as he could see anything at all he dragged the oxen to the road and climbed up miserably onto the seat. Hours seemed to pass before first light filtered through the heavy clouds clinging to the treetops. The oxen splashed sullenly through the puddles while he sat cloaked to his feet by his long *byrrus* of heavy wool, the rain pattering on the hood. He hoped the smoked hams and bacon, covered only by canvas, were not getting drenched. How small the Roman villa looked this time, he thought as he passed the place, smaller than a British round house. The painted plaster walls of blues and scarlet looked very dull and drab, darkened by the pouring rain. As he came down to the junction at the south works, he was again greeted by a queue of carts struggling in what seemed like every direction, livestock and mounted riders and people on foot all travelling at a different pace, pushing and shoving to make the worst possible confusion. A flock of sheep had got loose in the roadside cemetery, and barking dogs ran among the headstones sending sheep this way and that.

Lacking his father's experience, Paul failed to find a column of troops to slip in behind, and half a dozen others snatched the opportunity to push in front of him when the swaying, banging wagon of the Imperial Post swept past, pulled by horses that were replaced every thirty miles. Paul hunched miserably over his knees, listening to the pattering rain, thinking of Diana. He hardly noticed London.

Walbrook Street was deserted, a few dark carts bumping along pale watery ruts, but the sheltered verandahs were a crowded mass of *byrri* and women in cloaks, many of them speaking with a Gallic accent. They were probably the wives of Romanised administrators, Paul mused, brought in from the continent until sufficient numbers of British rose through the career system to replace them, or be sent abroad – to his horror, Paul saw that the upstairs window was shuttered. Diana wasn't there.

The bottom dropped out of his world.

In his misery he was hardly aware of the rainwater pouring down the gutterless roof in streams over him. Pomponius appeared and stared at him from the shop doorway, suspiciously, Paul thought, remembering the footsteps he had heard thumping on the stairs.

'Is it dry?' Pomponius rumbled. Paul stared at him blankly, the shining image of Diana only slowly fading from his mind. 'Not you, my consignment, you sopping fool!' Pomponius roared, crossing the verandah with his great weight and boxing Paul's ear. 'If it's wet I'm not accepting it, boy. I won't buy mould!'

Paul swallowed his pride. 'I'm sorry, master.' He moved the cart from the streaming roofwater, wondering where Diana was, how he could ask, and lifted the canvas to show that the cargo was dry. To his horror four large legs of ham were missing, pilfered. He searched frantically, but there was no mistake. He stared aghast. It must have happened in the traffic, hands slipping busily under the flap while he was sitting with his back turned and his mind a million miles away, thinking only of himself and Diana. The whole settlement at Valle Dei had sold stock to his father to make up this consignment, and John would be honour bound not to let men who had trusted him – Vernico, and he'd taken everything Briginus had – lose by it; he'd have to look after them somehow. Paul felt sick, but still he couldn't help glancing up at her shuttered window, and he was hot in the belly. He must be out of his mind to be thinking of her now, but he was. 'Bring that one here, boy, so I can examine it!' bellowed Pomponius. Paul's foot skidded in the mud and he fell, twisting himself under the ham he was holding so that he, not the precious meat, was muddied and bruised.

'I don't like you.' Pomponius looked down on him.

'Yes, master.' Paul scrambled to his feet.

'Is that clear?' Pomponius said.

Paul hopped from one bruised leg to the other, thankful that his suffering was not witnessed from upstairs. 'Yes.'

'I beg your pardon?'

'Yes, master.'

'You've wet that ham. Half price, or I'll take none of them!'

The first-floor shutter swung half open, revealing a girl's hand

and face. Paul could not bear to look at her. His humiliation was complete.

Afterwards he drove up to the temple and sat in a haze of misery. He would have to get the cart off the streets before sunset, but he hardly knew where he would find the energy. And he did not have the money to buy the *sartago* frying pan, which doubled for baking, that he had promised his mother, to go with her *angularis*. Everything would have to go to pay Briginus and Vernico.

He glanced round at the approach of a sedan chair carried at a steady tread by two slaves between the shafts, their sandals splashing in the puddles. As it passed, the curtain which hid the occupant was twitched aside, and he saw Diana looking at him from the interior.

Those blue eyes took in every detail of him, his mucky boots and his *byrrus* streaked with mud from the hem to his shoulders, the rain speckling his face. She put her finger to her lips: don't talk, the slaves will hear. Then, seeing his despair, she smiled. The curtain dropped down, the slaves continued on their way, and Paul almost passed out with desire.

He slept in the woods that night, and dreamt of her as vividly as though she lay beside him.

'I know I got it all wrong,' Paul confessed anxiously to his father when he got home. The round house smelt very much of earth and wet thatch to him now, comfortable though it was, and he hated the primitive hut shape of it with the walls sloping up to the central peak. Imogen had tried to fit it out with shelves and couches, and the classical interior looked distinctly odd. Paul knew she wanted a proper house, but John showed no inclination to change. 'Please let me go again next week,' Paul said eagerly. 'I'll make it up to you.'

'Redeem yourself with me, you mean?' John said shrewdly, gazing into the flames. 'Or were you thinking of someone else?'

'What happened wasn't Paul's fault,' Imogen said, taking advantage of his adversity to give Paul a hug. 'It's yours for sending him out, John. I told you, he's just a child.'

'That's just it, I'm not!' Paul said.

'The boy's right,' said John. 'And you're right too, Imogen, I shouldn't have sent him alone. I was asking too much of him, but

Paul has learned by his experience. Next week you'll take a lad with you.'

'Then you'll let me go again!' Paul exclaimed with relief.

'Don't you like us here or something, Paul?' Imogen asked. 'Why are you so keen to leave here?'

Paul shrugged. There would be the most awful fuss if his mother knew.

'He's fallen for the girl who lives above the shop,' John said.

But Imogen did not explode. 'How nice,' she said at last. 'I'd like to meet her. You must tell me all about her, Paul.'

John stared at her.

'You remember what it was like to be in love, don't you, John?' Imogen murmured sweetly. Paul missed the flash of implacable hatred in her eyes, but John did not. He looked stunned.

'You'd love her, Mother,' Paul said earnestly. 'She speaks Roman, and she has proper white couches in her room.'

Little Matugenus quivered with excitement as the cart came down the hill to the great road junction, but this was the third time Paul had made the journey to London and the wonder had gone for him. He yawned as they crossed the bridge, and Matugenus gazed at him with admiration for being so calm on the extraordinary structure, surrounded by marvels, storehouses, quays and vessels; Matugenus kept pointing at all the things to see.

The weather was kinder to Paul today. The sky was overcast but showing gleams of sun, and he had no intention of alerting the butcher to his presence before he had conducted certain other business closer to his heart. He had it all worked out. He stopped the cart at the place he had decided on, behind the building lots.

'Stay here,' he ordered Matugenus briskly, 'and sit facing the cargo where you can see if anyone tries anything funny. Don't take your eyes off it!'

'I won't, Paul,' Matugenus promised, old enough to be responsible but young enough to be obedient. 'Where are you going?' he called after Paul, but there was no reply from the running figure.

Cutting across the building lots, Paul counted the windows at the back of the shops until he came to Dumnius Pomponius's fence. Clambering over, he slipped along the yard. The old horse had gone, but there were twice as many chickens awaiting their fate in the pen. Paul saw a blood-spattered barrel against the back wall and climbed on it. Being full, it did not wobble. He could hear Pomponius's voice in the shop, talking to a customer. He was bullying and ingratiating at the same time, but the customer knew what she wanted and was obviously getting the better of him.

Paul reached up to the window above, opening the shutter with his thumb. Getting a grip on the frame, he pulled himself up, using his knees and ankles to lever himself up the painted plaster. The small storeroom was dark but for the slant of light from the opened shutter. He rolled inside and padded to the door.

'Diana?'

The corridor made him nervous; in fact the whole network of vertical walls and tiny rooms made him nervous, it was so foreign and unnatural, and he found the smell odd, too: not grass and smoke but plaster dust and oiled wood. It seemed overbearing, closing in on him.

He crossed the corridor in one bound, and stood silently in the doorway.

Diana was sitting by the window. She had placed her basket chair where she could see along the street, the shutters open and her head with its tall hairstyle silhouetted against the swarming activity below. She knew it was his day to deliver, she was waiting for him! On a board in her lap, rather than use the shale table and risk marking the linen, she was occupying herself with a glass smoother to press the washing wrinkles from a plain undertunic, similar to the one that peeped its creamy line at her neck and below the hem of her pinned gown. Her ankles were crossed on a wicker footstool and her lips were moving. Perhaps she was making up conversations with him, as he was with her! The chair creaked as she worked, but she didn't look out of the window again.

Seeing her so contented with herself, bitterness welled up inside Paul.

'I suppose you don't want to see me,' he said, hating himself for desiring her so much, 'now I'm not wet and miserable.'

She jumped up with her hands over her heart. 'What are you doing in here, you idiot?' she exclaimed, delighted, then made herself frown. 'How did you get in? You must be mad!' She waved him out of the way and glanced along the corridor. 'What sort of girl do you think I am?'

'You saw me make a fool of myself last time,' Paul said, behind her, 'and you just stood there at your window and watched.'

'You grovelled!' Then she pushed the door almost closed and whispered, 'Do you really think I'm like my father?' Her eyes took in his neatly arranged, clean clothes and she could not help a glint of amusement at the care he had taken for her.

'I don't care about anyone else,' he said, reaching for her hands. 'I just want you to be you.'

She snatched her fingers away, but with a certain pouting pleasure in scolding him for what she wanted him to do. 'There you go again – grovelling.'

'I'm not!'

She gave a bored yawn. 'Then you should be,' she said.

'Then I am.' This was going dreadfully wrong. He stopped awkwardly, afraid to look into her eyes. He thought he had never suffered so much; he was tongue-tied with her and she was making him feel ridiculous. He was sounding exactly like someone he was not, acting out how he thought she wanted him to be, making a lie of himself for her. 'I admit I don't know you,' he confessed. 'I only know what I feel for you.' Suddenly what he was really thinking gushed out of him before he could stop himself: 'What are you wearing?'

She looked at him uncertainly, smoothing the palms of her hands down her Gallic gown, unwittingly revealing the outline of her body to him, silhouetted for a moment against the bright window.

'Your smell,' he said.

Her face, blank with surprise, turned to laughter. 'Oh, Paul, it's very expensive! You couldn't possibly afford it!' Her expression became tender, almost curious. 'You're such a funny boy, I can't make you out at all. My father says your father was a great prince once.'

'He doesn't talk about it. It's all lost.'

'But it *isn't*, don't you see?' Diana clapped her fingertips together, her eyes shining. 'The way he walks, his bearing, even the way he speaks. As if he owned all he saw, even the people. And he looks like he's seen everything before. Beside him my father stands like a peasant. And yet here he is, working for us!'

Now Paul understood. 'Is that the only reason you see me, Diana? So that you can humiliate me as your father humiliates mine, making a sort of family business out of it?'

'You're silly,' she said lightly.

'Yes, I am.' Paul was fierce.

'Stop staring at me like that. That's silly too.' She was trying to sound superior.

'Stop talking like that. You know what I feel for you,' Paul said.

Startled, she tried to shrug, but he shook his head angrily. 'It's not fun for me, Diana, I can't help myself. It's real, and that's all there is to it. *You* are real, despite your Roman talk and saffron round your eyes. I'm not one of your suitors in a toga invited by your father so he can arrange a good marriage for you, for him. He's trained you well, hasn't he, Diana? What do *you* feel?'

At last her eyelashes gleamed. 'How can you be so unkind?'

'Because it's the truth. You'll never marry me but I'll always love you.' He was close enough to inhale her perfume with every breath he took. 'Why are you hiding? Where's the real you, Diana?'

'I'm not being false,' she said tearfully, and a single saffron-coloured tear trickled down her cheek. 'It's my favourite perfume, that's all, and I saw you noticed it last time. That's why I wore it again.' She saw how her honesty moved him. 'Apple balsam. It's distilled from Apples of Jerusalem, and comes from a monastery called Qumran, somewhere thousands of miles away.'

Paul put his arms round her lightly; she was almost as tall as he was. This time he did not have to steal a kiss – and this time her lips were not flavoured with coriander. Her hands touched his shoulder blades, then her soft embrace tightened. He had no idea how long the moment lasted.

Footsteps sounded along the corridor and they pulled apart. Diana turned wildly but there was no escape. Paul held her tight and they listened as the footsteps approached, seemed to pause, then went past the door. He winked and let Diana go, opening the door a finger's width. Through the gap he saw that it was not Pomponius after all, only a slave going along the corridor on some errand or other. But when Paul looked back into the room, he saw that Diana had pressed herself into the corner, and he would never forget the expression on her face. She was terrified.

He clasped her tight.

'Go,' she said. 'Go!'

Reaching into his belt, Paul took out the coin there. He held it, warm in his palm, stolen, then drew a deep breath. 'This is from me to you. It's not mine, but it's all I have. It's ours.'

She turned it over in her fingers, admiring the heavy silver, then put it agreeably inside her gown.

'It means I'll always love you,' Paul said.

As he cut back across the building lot, the foreman, who recognised him from earlier, shouted at him to get off his land and not come back. Paul jerked his fingers in a rude gesture, which was promptly returned. When the foreman, cursing, sent someone running after him, Paul ran faster, vaulted the fence and repeated the gesture with both hands. He found Matugenus sitting on the cart looking exceedingly grateful to see him.

'This is an awful place,' the little boy quavered. 'There's evil spirits and everyone's out for themselves and I don't know what.'

'Your sort always believes in evil spirits.' Paul didn't bother to climb up. Cracking the stick on the hindquarters of the oxen to get the brutes lumbering along, he ran in front, then tapped their chests to make them stop at the butcher's. 'Stay here.'

Paul ducked beneath the multi-coloured strings of sausages, detesting the sight and smell of them. Inside, the slaves recognised him and let him past. Two women were working in the kitchen behind, talking busily, a cauldron of fat bubbling on the fire. They fell silent as Paul came in, then jerked their heads at the rear doorway: he's through there.

The back room was actually a dining room and Pomponius was skinning a hare on the low wall round the cold hearth. He glanced round and grunted. 'What are you doing back here? Make your delivery and get out. What's keeping you? You don't want me to hold your hand for you, do you?'

'No, sir.'

'Learned your lesson last time, did you?'

'I know you'll check my delivery with an eagle eye, sir.'

'Sir? A little more respect is due. To you my name is *master*.'

'I ask for the hand of your daughter in marriage,' Paul said.

'What? You must be crazy,' Pomponius growled, bunching his fists.

Paul repeated what he had said.

'Look what that awful man did to him!'

'Paul was lucky to get off with only a beating,' John said, and Paul could almost hear his shrug. His father didn't think Diana was good enough for his own flesh and blood.

'I want my son to have everything I never had,' Paul overheard his mother say simply. Her voice was muffled by the sloping thatch wall yet so full of feeling that Paul stopped. He had limped outside last thing before turning in, and she thought he could not hear. He paused in the dark, the dewy grass brushing his knees and the stars in a huge arch above him, arrested by her urgency, realising how deeply his mother still loved him even though he was, at least to himself, a man now. She was still fighting on his behalf. Paul's bladder was full, he was aching to bathe his bruises and the purple swelling on his cheek caused by one of Pomponius's rings, but he was curious enough to turn back and put his ear to the thatch.

'I've never been in love,' came Imogen's voice, with a terrible sadness in it that struck Paul's heart. 'John, I want him to be in love. A proper wife, a proper house, a proper family.'

'Haven't I done enough for you?'

'No one has ever loved me. Not you. When Paul was conceived, it was not my name you shouted. It's horrible.'

Paul waited for his father's reply. When it came there was no rage in his words, only weariness. 'We both knew what we were doing, Imogen, even though you deny it now.'

'I don't deny it,' Imogen said seriously, her voice fading as though she had moved closer to him, and it struck Paul that for once they weren't arguing or simply living in silence. He frowned, straining to hear what his mother was saying. 'I can't deny that we have a son.' Her next words were clogged by the thick thatch. 'A son by my father.' Paul was never sure if that was quite what she said, or what she meant by 'father'. The thatch creaked as he leaned on it, and he held his breath.

'But you do feel guilty now, Imogen.'

'I want more for him than I have had. A life without love.'

Paul felt himself tugged in both directions, first to his father, then to his mother.

His father's voice came, lower and deeper. 'It isn't love that Paul feels, Imogen.'

'Isn't it?' she said loudly.

'It's infatuation. He's in heat.'

'What about *her*? Does she love him?'

'How can she know her own mind, any more than Paul does?'

'You sound so old!' said Imogen scornfully. 'You've been in love, John Fox. Or have you forgotten?'

'That was long ago.'

'You were young, just as Paul is. Look what an opportunity you have. You don't have to push your son to an arranged marriage for political reasons, money, power, as your father pushed you. Give him happiness. A marriage simply for love.' Paul could almost see her putting her fingertips together, a mannerism she had, as though completing an invisible circle. 'Beautiful. And grandchildren.'

'Mine as well as yours.'

'The whole family is yours, more than any man has a right to claim. You've had your way! Give me my little piece of it. And Paul too! Let him choose his own life.'

There was a pause, and Paul held his breath again, lest the thatch creak. Finally his father's voice came again, very low. 'What are you proposing, Imogen?'

'You know,' she said urgently. 'Dig it up. Show him. Do as you did before. Overawe Dumnius Pomponius with what a man you are, having such a treasure in your possession, and yet living as a simple farmer. Use them!'

A long silence. 'I don't know that I can any more, Imogen.'

'If you won't do it for Paul, do it for yourself.' She let him think about it. '*Use them for yourself.*'

Paul pushed himself away from the wall. She meant the coins, and it was impossible now for him to return the one he had stolen and given to Diana. He hated the thought of his father using them, devaluing his gift. And he did not want his father's help in winning her hand, but he knew it was impossible for him to refuse.

Paul relieved himself in the cesshole and washed his face by the light of the rising moon, then returned to the hut. 'I'll be accompanying you next Tuesday,' his father said, pushing past him, and went outside. Paul knew where he was going. Imogen looked self-satisfied and victorious, but Paul went to bed uneasily. He dreamt of the boar chasing him.

He was still uneasy when Tuesday came, riding beside his father through the August heat haze into London. The streets were more crowded than ever and several times they were stopped by the crush of people pushing past them. There was an atmosphere of gaiety that had been absent before, and the workmen on the building lots had downed tools and were hanging around in groups, drinking cheerfully. Paul was too apprehensive to take an interest in the reason for it – a military victory, apparently. Diana was not at her window, and in the abrupt rush of despair that Paul felt at not seeing her the jostling, grinning crowds merely irritated him with their good cheer. His father's face was set in a haughty frown, and he looked neither right nor left.

'I wish to speak to you,' he said, brushing past Pomponius into the shop. Paul followed them into the dining room, shadowed from the heat and glare. John came straight to the point. 'I will forgive the beating you gave my son,' he told Pomponius, 'because he did not address you with proper respect, according to the proper forms. He was hasty and I apologise.'

'I'll hear it from his lips,' Pomponius said, unable to let an advantage go by. 'I've never been so insulted, the good name of my daughter—'

'I'm sorry,' Paul said.

'Lay a finger on him again, Dumnius Pomponius,' John said, 'and I shall kill you.'

Pomponius dismissed the threat with a laugh. 'What have you got in there?' He pointed at the casket. 'Nice piece of work. Judean cedarwood? I thought they were all chopped down.'

John took the wooden box from his belt. Paul watched nervously. He would never forget what he had seen inside, and he flinched as his father pulled open the lid. The coins' perfume wafted out around them.

Pomponius, still laughing, reached inside. His reaction was the opposite to what John must have expected. 'What sort of a joke is this? You're trying to impress me with a few shekels?' His frame heaved as he chuckled. 'Is this all that is left of the great man you once were?'

'On my death,' John said, 'they will be Paul's. And his wife's. And their children's.'

Pomponius shook with amusement. He slapped his chest for breath, and a few coins fell from his fat fingers, tinkling on the floor. Paul bent to retrieve them. 'And what do *you* think of this great inheritance, my lad?'

'I only know what I feel,' Paul said.

'You're wasting my time,' Pomponius said, unimpressed. 'Both of you.'

Paul looked at the greedy, contemptuous expression on the butcher's face, the silver in his hands, its reflection in his eyes. And then he thought of Diana and the coin he had pressed into her palm, the lovely silver flash as she turned it over in her delicate fingers. That gift to her had meant everything to Paul, because she did. These other things were worthless compared to that. He did not dare to look at his father's face, at the dismay and confusion he knew he would see there. John Fox had walked into the shop absolutely confident of his power to sway the butcher, and he had failed. Worse, he had made a fool of himself. Paul, head down, swept the coins quickly back into the box. His father moved like a weary man, and needed the arm that Paul put round his shoulders.

'I don't care what you say,' Paul told Pomponius, 'I'll always love her.'

'That's all right,' Pomponius said agreeably, 'just keep your distance, that's all, and know your place.'

Paul helped his father out to the cart and did all the unloading himself. John sat bowed on the seat, his elbows on his knees and his head hanging, exhausted by his failure. Could it really be that he had been lucky enough in life never to have lost at anything he set his mind to? What a wonderful life that would be! But now, as if he had been struck in the face, he had aged by ten years in front of Paul's eyes; he looked like a man weighed down by seventy years or more.

'By the bye,' Pomponius called out to them with some pleasure, 'up in Colchester that idiot Decianus Catus I told you about, the tax collector, finally went too far. He had Queen Boadicea of the Iceni stripped and flogged in nothing but her red hair, and her daughters raped, and got back the money he said was his. Teach them a lesson! Instead, what happened? A mob of British traitors, the *incolae*, herded the garrison into the Imperial Temple, massacred them to a man, and burnt the place – and the city too, some say. So the fool's achieved the impossible, he's stirred up the British upper *and* lower classes, but they're bigger fools than he is, just a rabble of ordinary folk led by a woman. The Ninth Legion's marching their way, infantry and cavalry both, so the British don't stand a chance. Reinforcements are expected here with the governor any moment.' Pomponius rubbed his hands in gleeful anticipation. 'And of course they'll need feeding! Oh, we live in fine times. So keep your noses clean, you two,' he tapped his nose wisely, 'if you know what's good for you.'

Paul looked up at the shuttered first-floor window. He was sure that Diana was being kept prisoner by her father. At least, that was what he wanted to believe.

John sat without moving, his head bobbing wearily with the motion of the cart returning home to Valle Dei. Paul had loaded up with an iron cauldron needed in the village, an iron chain, various bronze tool heads – they would fit the ashwood hafts themselves – and the extra weight made the hill up to the plateau a hard drag for the oxen. He doubted they would reach the summit tonight. The farmers who walked out of London to work in the fields all day, preparing for the harvest, and the teams of slaves digging drainage ditches to reclaim yet more fields from the marshes, had been streaming back past the cart for some time. Their numbers thinned as darkness fell, the stragglers hurrying to get back across the river before the ceremonial raising of the drawbridge for the night by troops in shining helmets and a plumed officer on a white horse. After that time a man must find a place to sleep by the Tabernacle, usually on the hard ground at the mercy of thieves and ruffians, or pay the ferryman and risk a dangerous river crossing by coracle in the gloom.

The second time Paul rested the oxen on the slope, he decided without asking his father that they could go no further tonight. He wedged a rock beneath the wheel and turned to look at London Bridge in the distance behind them. His keen young eyes could just pick out the raised drawbridge, but he saw no sign of the ceremonial guard or the flaming torches that usually accompanied them. John wrapped himself wearily in his cloak and lay down beneath the cart, but Paul stayed stretched out on the seat all night, dozing, staring sleepily at the lamps showing here and there in the town across the marshes. When the moon rose, so late that it was almost morning, the marble colonnade of the temple of Diana threw back a pale lunar gleam from the top of Lud's Hill.

As the lights faded with the first glow of dawn, Paul saw a column of soldiers crossing the bridge. Nearly an hour later he pulled well off the road to let them pass, tired men grey with dust and fatigue, a few with minor wounds, their heads lolling with the harsh rhythm of double time – and not many of them, only a few hundred. These Romans had come from further away than London, and they were heading in the direction of the broad Medway River. Paul dared ask nothing of them, but hurrying in their wake came the women, the first of a few dozen camp followers.

'What's happening?' Paul called out to a British girl, her red hair made spiky by being washed in lime. She struggled past with her clothes and whatever else she could carry roped to her back, a dark-haired child running beside her. 'Is something wrong?'

'How should we know!' she cried. Later another group of the desperate creatures, fearful of losing their living, went straggling by, one with the sandal already flapping from her foot, but their answer was always the same, and after mid-morning the last of them had gone. 'What do you think?' he asked his father.

John merely shrugged. 'What does it matter?' he sighed, and Paul, gazing along the empty road, and at the slaves working contentedly in the fields around the walls of the Roman villa, supposed he must be right.

When they arrived home, bumping down the track between the trees, the children left the women washing clothes at the pool, rubbing the fabric on the standing stone, and scampered beside the cart. John did not respond with orders or throw a few copper coins as he usually did when he had been trading; he remained sunk in his reverie, and Paul slapped with his stick to send the children flying back to their mothers, then pulled hard to stop the cart by the house near the edge of the knoll.

Imogen ran out to greet them. The hope faded from her eyes as she looked from one to the other, then John pushed past her without a word. Paul went quietly to water the oxen, and Imogen followed him.

'Paul. Paul!' She grabbed his elbow.

'What, Mother?'

He was surprised by the yearning look in her eyes. 'Did he let you see?' Imogen whispered.

'See? There was nothing much to see. I saw my father make a fool of himself. In fact, he made fools of us both,' Paul said. 'He told Dumnius Pomponius they'd be mine one day.'

'Yes!' Imogen said eagerly. 'And—'

'And Pomponius laughed. He *laughed*!' Paul raged in his disappointment, shaking off her hand. 'I'm not surprised. What did Father expect? A little box with a few worthless shekels! Now I don't know what I'm going to do.'

'I'll finish watering the animals,' Imogen said.

Paul ran down from the knoll and flung himself into the grass beneath a young oak tree. He sat up slowly. Far away a haze of smoke hung over London, though it was a hot day and past time for baking. Below him, barges carrying ragstone for the building of public works were moving upstream, raising their square sails against the blue water as they rounded the Isle of Dogs, taking advantage of the southerly wind. In London, which they could not see, but which was only a blink of an eye away for Paul, he saw ships pulling into the river under oars, straining to move downstream, although the tide must still be in the last quarter of the flood. What a phenomenal effort lay behind that slow progress, and what a waste, when the ebb would sweep them effortlessly on their way in only a short while!

A ship with noble purple stripes along the side and a white curve on the bow that Paul reckoned was a figurehead in the shape of a swan, ran aground on a mudbank. The crew got her off once, then she grounded a second time, caught in the maze of shallow channels. She wouldn't float again this tide. No larger than dots, the crew scrambled across the treacherous mudflats, taking to the reeds and marshes, and he didn't see them again.

Paul heard movement behind him and looked round. His father

was working a hoe in the long field, the back of his neck already red from the sun and his naked shoulders coated with perspiration, a dark figure toiling up to his thighs in a haze of golden barley. He did not raise his head as Paul fetched a hoe and started in from the other border near the herb garden. It was very hot. Paul stripped the tunic from his shoulders but left it tied to his waist, and soon the calluses on his hands showed raised, hard edges as he laboured, the skin between them turning to soft white blisters. He kept glancing at his father but there was no response, even when a hare dashed between them. His father worked head down as though he hated the earth, rooting out the weeds and bolters with the edge of the hoe and flinging them to the side of the strip. Jab, cut, lift, throw. He would not stop, even though he was clumsy with weariness, the sweat running down him, scratchy seeds from the ears of barley sticking to his reddened skin.

Imogen's herb garden was beginning to run wild: medicinal rue, fennel, dense growths of parsley and towering over them all the stalks of elecampane, taller than a man, their leaves flavouring the air with aniseed. Paul found a piece of rag in his belt to tie round his forehead, keeping some of the sweat from his eyes. His wet hair felt as though it would scald him. At last he threw down his hoe and went down to the well his father had dug out of the boggy area at the bottom of the field. The ground was waterlogged no longer, and the well, lined with wicker, had slowly filled until now it overflowed into an irrigation ditch. The ditch was becoming a proper stream, flowing busily even now at the hottest time of year. Kneeling, Paul splashed the cool moisture over his burning face and shoulders. The water must come leaking beneath the earth, he thought, through the holy well, from the pool uphill of the knoll. He drank, then looked up sharply as the sound of approaching hoofbeats carried to his ears.

A single horseman came riding through the field, forsaking the easy sloping path from Greenwich, knocking a ruined swathe through the precious barley. Paul ran at him, outraged at their hard work being trampled, and the rider gave a shout of terror to see the wild-looking, sunburned figure running after him. Bending forward, showing pricey cotton underwear, the Roman kicked his heels with a will, but before he could send his mount galloping uphill Paul grabbed the simple grazing bridle with both hands, pulling the horse's nose into his shoulder, and as the animal dragged back, the rider swayed and almost fell.

'What d'you think you're doing riding through our crops!' Paul demanded furiously. 'Is this your horse?'

The young man was riding bareback, his hairless thighs rubbed raw, and he was clinging to reins knotted of strips torn from his cloak. He was wearing a dagger but he didn't look as if he knew how to use it – he hadn't drawn it. His fringe was crimped into curls like the Emperor's, his cheeks scraped smooth of beard, and though he was finely dressed in a cream woollen tunic with a pattern woven round the hem and armholes, he was as sprayed and speckled with mud as though he had run through the mud-flats along the river.

'British?' he croaked. He looked at Paul with eyes made sick by fear. 'Are you loyal? Take it, it's yours.' He threw down the dagger, scabbard and all. 'Everything's yours! Let me go!'

'You've nothing to fear from me,' Paul said.

The young Roman straightened his back, eyeing the dagger lying in the dirt. The hilt was pure white, with none of the yellowing of bone; it was ivory.

'Who are you?' Paul demanded.

'You have the honour to address C. Petronius Urbicus, on the procurator's staff.'

John had joined them. He stood behind Paul with his hands hanging at his sides. 'Procurator? You mean you're a tax collector. I thought your master was in Colchester.'

'He had to leave by ship.'

'He escaped, you mean. And so hastily that a few of the unimportant ones got left behind in the confusion.'

'I am hardly unimportant. I am C. Petronius Urbicus—'

'And he has an ivory handle on his dagger,' Paul said.

'Actually I'd rather like it back.'

'I think not,' Paul said in equally polite Roman, and Petronius looked at him with new respect, and some confusion: Paul's face and shoulders were red like a slave's, burned as red as his hair.

'The rebellion will be stamped out to the last woman and child,' Petronius said, his courage flowing back now that he was not looking over his shoulder. 'The Ninth Legion . . . No one knows what has happened to the Ninth, but it's a disaster.' He closed his eyes, his bravado deserting him again.

'Go on,' Paul said.

'The governor of the province, Gaius Suetonius Paulinus, returned to London last night, but found all the troops gone and the British tribes on his heels.'

'Led by the woman who was flogged?'

'People believe in us, they believe we can save London. But we who were there know what those brutes did in Colchester.' He looked round urgently, but the peaceful evening scene below them, a shepherd strolling behind a flock of sheep into the shadows, the sun setting over London in a glare of smoky light, did not reassure him. He pulled nervously at the makeshift reins.

'You mean the governor's still in the town?' Paul asked. 'He's going to defend the town?'

'No,' John said.

Petronius gave a high, exhausted laugh. 'When I arrived this afternoon, the governor had already kicked up his heels and gone! He's taken with him any man able to fight and cleared himself out of the way, going to wait it out. He'll let the British loot the place and do the usual trading to get captives back. Most of our British have stayed, of course, they're safe enough, and the women and children, and the old folk who've got too fond of their homes to leave.'

'The governor's sacrificing them,' John Fox said.

'I see you're a man who understands the realities, sir. They'd only slow him down. And if there was a panic they'd block the roads. This way London slows Queen Boadicea and gives him time to regroup.'

'But you realise what this means,' Paul said to his father, who shrugged. The three men looked back through the gathering dark, the camp fires spread across the far hills looking like burning straw around the glittering, welcoming bonfires of London.

'Those aren't bonfires,' John said calmly. 'They're burning the town.'

'But Diana . . .' Paul turned furiously. 'How can you be so calm!'

'I'd have done the same myself if I and my family and my people had been treated as Boadicea's have been. She knows she must strike south of the river next, secure the Roman ports, or she's lost.'

'But Diana,' Paul groaned.

'Think of your own skin first,' John advised. 'If that woman crosses the bridge, those fires will be burning here tomorrow night.'

'I don't care!' Paul shouted. He hauled at Petronius, who squealed as his skinned, stiffened thighs were dragged from horseback. 'I'll take his horse!'

'It's too late tonight,' John told him. 'Whatever Diana's fate is, it's in the lap of the gods by now.' He held out his hand to Petronius. 'You'll sleep with us tonight.'

But none of them slept. As the camp fires on the hillsides and moorlands to the north of London died down and became part of the darkness, the glittering fires in the town grew in number and brightness, joining together, drawing in towards the centre like a tightening fist of flame. Paul was reminded of harvest time, the hares and other small shy animals driven into the middle of the field by the work of the reapers cutting and beating around them, until in the end a terrified knot of survivors hopped and scrambled over one another in the final stand of the ripe crop, right at the centre. Then his father would burn the stand with the need-fire, the ritual since the beginning of time.

The fire did not cross the bridge. Dawn revealed nothing to them of the town on the north bank, only a pall of smoke. Occasionally dark red flames licked in one place or another, then died down, and again there was only smoke. The bridge still spanned the river, and Paul, who had the keenest eyes, thought that the drawbridge had been let down, presumably by people on the north bank frantic to escape to the south. Yet when he climbed up through the trees to the road, he found it almost deserted, not crowded with refugees fleeing the destruction as he had expected, but only a trickle of people from outposts and remote farms on the south bank, who knew less than he did. Paul returned to the knoll where everyone in the settlement, even the women, had gathered along the rim of the slope, staring out. The children still played around them, but no one was joking now. The wind changed during the morning, blowing towards them so that the air carried a smell of wood smoke. It reminded everyone of food, and they began to drift away.

Briginus stayed, sharpening his old notched sword, and

Petronius stood on his own, his sore thighs smeared with a foul-smelling ointment of olive oil mixed with assafoetida, recommended to him as silphium by his personal Greek physician of better times. Imogen had been fascinated and they had talked for hours, but now Petronius, his ivory-handled dagger reclaimed and thrust bravely through his belt, had come to try to rejoin the men.

'She hasn't crossed the bridge,' he opined, for the benefit of anyone in the small group around John and Paul who would listen. 'She's lost the war.'

Briginus, still sharpening his sword on the stone, spat over the blade.

'I've got to go there,' Paul begged.

'Not today,' said John. 'Today the men will be sleeping it off while their wives and children go into town to scavenge whatever hasn't been burnt, and load it into carts. When they wake up tomorrow, they'll be on their way. They'll find plenty of other new Roman towns to plunder to the north-west, as rich or richer than London – the vast estates of Sullonius at Brockley Hill, or the place they call Verulamium.'

'Then I'll go tomorrow,' Paul said, and no one could argue him out of it. 'I'll take the horse.'

'You'd better get your fill of sleep tonight,' John said. 'You got no sleep last night, and you won't tomorrow night either.'

'Why?' Paul asked, but his father just looked at him. He had guessed what Paul would see in London.

Refreshed by a long, dreamless rest, Paul was up before dawn, but John was up before him – the scent of war had taken a few of the years from him, and he tried to move with a spring in his step like a younger man. He gave Paul his cloak, almost black with grease and use after all these years, but warm. The heavy close-woven wool felt as thick as armour to Paul as his father laid it over his shoulders. He finished his beer and swung himself up onto Petronius's horse, still clutching the wedge of bread given him by Imogen. 'One more thing, Paul.' John handed up his sword, the one with the broken point.

'You didn't even clean the rust off!' Imogen said.

'It was mine,' John told Paul. 'Now it's yours.'

'Thank you, Father.'

'Good fortune, son.'

'You eat every last mouthful, now,' Imogen called as Paul rode away, and watched until she could no longer see him; and then she watched where she imagined he was, timing his journey.

Paul passed a few people camping out in the trees, but the road across the plateau was empty, a pale spear in the early light. The horse, which Petronius called Avita, was obviously British bred, with short sturdy legs and a surprising turn of speed, but Paul held her back to a slow, rocking canter that she could keep up all day. In no time at all, by comparison with the inching progress of the ox cart he was used to, he reined in where the road turned downhill by the Roman villa. There was no one to be seen, but it had not been burned. Staring across the marshes, he could make out that the drawbridge on London Bridge was definitely lowered, but he saw no movement across the structure.

The sun was hotter than ever on Paul's sunburn, and the cloak itched his shoulders unmercifully as he rode down to the junction. He found the normally busy crossroads deserted but for a few broken vehicles, some guarded by dogs which crawled out of the shadows beneath them and barked at him, lunging viciously on their chains. Paul skirted them with caution, wishing they'd be quiet: if anyone lurking in the roadside cemeteries or the apparently unharmed buildings dotted along the street ahead of him had been unaware of his approach, they certainly knew of it now.

The Tabernacle Inn stood empty, its windows dark and outhouses looted, just a few chickens rooting in the dust by the open doorway. Paul dismounted, pulling Avita after him, and called into the shadows inside, but there was no reply. He was very thirsty but rather than risk going inside, he drank a cupped handful from the trough and let Avita have her fill, then rode to the bridge.

He gave a low whistle at what he saw.

The townsfolk trapped on the north bank had lowered the drawbridge to flee across, pursued by the British no doubt. Men from the Tabernacle and the other buildings here in safety on the south bank had cut the timbers between the shoreline and the first pier. Paul stared across the empty space, thirty-five feet at least, the tide swirling round the weedy cross-braces. The naked body of a man hung down between them, his long hair rippling in the water, his body so shafted with arrows that he must have been used as target practice by the men on the south bank, once the worst of the danger was over. Other bodies lay up on the bridge, but because of the high angle Paul could see little more than bundles of cloaks piled between the handrails, the hafts of spears sticking up at every angle, crows and magpies fluttering among them.

Paul drew back as the falling tide revealed bodies stuck in the mud at his feet, and he realised a second wave of British troops, probably attacking under cover of dark, swimming or wading, had almost succeeded in taking the south side; the defenders had fled, not realising their victory.

Paul hauled on the reins and sent Avita galloping back past the Tabernacle, then turned right and set her pounding along the road to the west, upstream. Passing an inlet with a broken mast and the rotten sternwork of a wreck sticking out of the muddy water, he followed the causeway across a lake, Llyn Din. Wild duck rose into the air all around him, which made him set his lips grimly; no one else had been this way today. The lake was separated from the Thames, looping round in front of Paul, by a long sandy island. As he reined in on the shallow rise, the road ahead of him sloped into the water. He had come to the ford at Thorney Island.

He saw no one on the other side, and Avita was pleased to take to the broad stream chuckling over the gravel bank, beyond the reach of the brackish tide, and snatched mouthfuls of the fresh water as she crossed.

Paul turned to the right, along the wooded path that followed the river's loop downstream, catching glimpses of the blue curve bordered by its beach of dirty sand. He saw no boats pulled up along there, no fishermen or itinerant families who were usually to be found in such places. A hut was still burning, and for the first time Paul heard the crackle of flames and felt the heat. He drew his sword and rode on, the smoke streaming past him, towards the town of London ahead.

Paul never came to terms with what he saw.

Avita's hooves crunched loudly on smouldering ash. Beneath the gravel, the road had been constructed of timbers painted with pitch to make them last in the wet ground, and they had burned. Beside the roadway, men hung from crosses, only one or two at first, then as thickly as trees, their clothes burned off and the bodies roasted dark brown by heat and smoke. Some had died still taking their weight on their toes, but many of the crosses had fallen over, planted too hastily. Paul wrapped the cloak round his mouth and nose, but still the stink came through. He couldn't believe what he was seeing. These people were not Romans, they were British. Why had the British done this to their own people?

He pulled Avita off the road and slipped from her back, walking beside her in the marsh as they came to the River Fleet. The bridge was burnt, so he waded across, tugging the horse after him up Lud's Hill. Logs had been heaped in the temple of Diana to make the stone burn, and the roof had gone, but the colonnade remained, pointing like splayed fingers at the sky. Paul saw that what he had thought were logs were in fact the cindered bodies of men, and older women, and children too young to work, and the bundles of charcoal were babies. The British had burned the temple with Londoners.

'Why?' he shouted.

No echo came back, only the crackling and popping of the bodies, and the meaty stink of them. Paul vomited what was left of his breakfast.

He stumbled downhill beside the horse. The allotments had been cleared of every vegetable, ripe or unripe, and the stock pens were broken down and empty, the livestock driven away. He forced himself to stare across the valley to Corn Hill, but all he could see was smoke streaming away from him, the smoky outline of the streets glimpsed by the broken or burnt-out buildings that had lined them. He saw that the circus at the edge of town, the oval track that the British loved better than anything for horse racing and whatever they could find to gamble on, seemed to be crowded with spectators. All had been crucified, many of them back to back to make the most of the available timber. Other bodies lay around them, beheaded. Then for the first time Paul saw people alive, moving slowly between the motionless shapes, working among the birds. Women were stripping the bodies and the men were throwing them into the Walbrook. No one looked at him.

Paul had come to find Diana. Now he dreaded that he might.

The bridge over the Walbrook was intact, though it creaked

alarmingly under the weight of the horse, and the stream, backed up by the number of corpses that had been thrown into it, was overflowing its banks among the shrines. Paul splashed along the street. He was very close now.

The women taken in this street had been treated as collaborators, their hair shaved, their bodies speared to the men they were found with. Some had their breasts cut off and sewn to their mouths. Others, caught alone, stood upright, transfixed on long stakes hammered into the roadway, their feet standing in the cold dirty water, their eyes staring past him.

Paul left the horse and threaded his way between them, carefully at first, flinching when he touched someone, then knocking them aside, banging at them with his bare hands, finally scrambling onto the verandah with his breath screaming in his throat, his forearm pressed over his mouth.

He looked back, but he didn't see her face.

He didn't dare call her name.

It seemed at first that only the doorway remained of Dumnius Pomponius's shop, and his figure dominated it in death as it had in life. He had been crucified across the entrance, his head bent down cruelly by the arch, his entrails hanging between his legs.

The floorboards beneath him were covered with bloody bare footprints where looters had ducked through to plunder the shop.

Paul knew what he would find in there. He would find Diana's body.

He wanted desperately to turn back, but then, reaching up, he gripped Pomponius round both shoulders and pulled him down. The body slipped against him, then fell with a heavy thud that set other, smaller sounds tumbling and clinking through whatever ruined structure lay behind.

Paul went slowly through the doorway.

The roof was open to the sky. Only blackened beams remained of the first storey, but the brands that had been thrown in through the windows hadn't caught properly. Sunlight slatted the ground floor with shadow as Paul picked his way across the debris that had fallen from above. As a piece of lath slid aside, the plump legs and heels of a girl stuck out, white with plaster.

'Diana,' he whispered.

He reached out. He thought he had never touched anything so

cold as this human flesh. As he tugged, the girl slid sideways, revealing a hole in the floor.

He drew a breath, and made himself look at her.

He did not recognise her face; she was a slave. He let her roll from him and crawled to the lip of the hole.

'Diana?'

There was no reply.

He moved his head so that the sunlight slanted past him. It illuminated no floor below him, only darkness, then as his eyes adjusted he saw a broken wooden tray and mushrooms spilt from it. He was looking down into a mushroom cellar, and now he saw that there were mushroom stalks scattered over the cellar floor by someone who obviously ate only the tender caps.

'Diana!' he called.

Hearing a footstep, hope filled Paul in a single intoxicating rush, and he never forgot the feeling ever. Hope.

He laughed as her pale face came into his view. Diana had brushed the plaster dust from her hair with a comb she must have taken down with her into her hiding place. She looked up at him calmly.

'Paul,' she said, putting her hands on her hips. 'You're such a fool. I knew if anyone came back it was bound to be you.'

He reached down his hand. 'Marry me now,' he said.

For a moment her slanty blue eyes flickered in her broad face.

'So there's no one left to say no.' Then without further hesitation she reached up her hand.

'Now your life is your own,' Paul said over his shoulder. The horse plodded slowly towards the junction at the Tabernacle Inn. It had taken them half the afternoon, riding two up, to get as far as this, yet the two hills of London, burned and hardened to the colour of terracotta across the Thames, seemed almost close enough to touch.

'If I am your wife,' Diana murmured, 'I have no life of my own. We clasped hands, but I brought you no dowry. My father and my uncles are all dead, even my girl slave.' She put her soft arms round Paul, her palms pulled flat against his chest, resting her cheek in the hollow of his neck. 'As a woman I can't own property or control any children we may have. You can divorce me any time you like, by a simple statement of renunciation.'

'I'd never do that,' he grinned.

'Why shouldn't you?' Her chin quivered.

'Don't you understand?' he said confidently, not catching her look. 'I'd shown how much I love you, and you knew I'd come back.' He reached behind his hip and squeezed her knee. 'You didn't doubt me, did you?' The horse rocked soothingly beneath them.

'And I suppose you will take all decisions for me,' Diana murmured, 'because in the eyes of the law, a woman remains a child all her life.'

'Roman law.'

'The Romans will crush the British now,' she said venomously. 'Savages!' But again her tone became beguiling. 'How *could* I know it would be you who came back, Paul?'

'You thought it might have been any one of your other suitors?' he joked.

She hugged him, laughing.

He half turned. 'Do you still have it?'

She frowned, then smiled. 'Oh, that.' She reached into her gown and pulled out the silver coin he had pressed into her hand only nine days ago – a lifetime ago.

'It's *ours*,' he said. 'It links us for ever. Didn't you think of it like that?'

'Yes, of course I did, Paul.' She held it out, and it flashed in the low evening sun streaming behind them. 'I had it pierced and put on a silver chain. Real silver. It came back from the silversmith the day . . . the day that . . .' She sobbed quietly, remembering.

'I gave it to you to show I meant what I said,' Paul told her. 'Because I'll always love you.'

'But you hardly know me,' she said nervously.

Paul realised how tired she was, and knew they had to rest soon. He had buried Dumnius Pomponius in the mushroom cellar with all the respect of which he was capable, but hurriedly, because he was anxious not to stay in the town after dark. The wind had risen during the afternoon and several times he had heard a thudding sound like weakened houses falling, and once there were screams, running footsteps. Diana had done her duty and shed a tear for her father, but it was Paul she had been looking at. She stood beside him squeezing his hand as, dusty and covered with sweat, he said a eulogy of a few words: 'Dumnius Pomponius, never a citizen of Rome, as he'd aspired to be, but a loyal citizen of London.'

'That was kind!' Diana had said, surprising him with the warmth of her glance. 'You're quite soft inside, aren't you, Paul?'

She was soft outside; he'd caught his breath at the supple beauty of her that he'd felt as he lifted her onto the horse. He'd brought the mare round the back of the empty building lots so that the sights in the street would not disturb her, but she must have an inner strength that was like iron in her belly, because she hardly seemed to notice the terrible desolation all round them. All her concentration was on him; even as he'd lifted her and the growing wind had loosened her hair and blown it round his face, she'd laughed and looked him boldly in the eyes, before untangling him. Unbound, her henna-red hair came down to her waist; she'd pinned her cloak across it to keep it down, and Paul had swung up onto the horse's back in front of her.

The wind had blown in their eyes with a smooth force as Avita plodded to the ford, and did not slacken with evening and was now fluttering Paul's cloak in front of him, as though to speed them on their way, as they came to the road junction. But they could go no further tonight. 'We have to rest,' Paul said over his shoulder as they came up to the Tabernacle Inn, the wind snatching the words from his lips. He felt her nod in agreement. He jumped down and tied the reins to a water trough; in front of him the inn door banged loudly.

Drawing his sword, Paul went inside, finding himself alone in a large, empty communal room smelling of sour beer and strong meat. The wind whirled straw and rubbish among the tables with each slam of the door. He turned back to help Diana, but she had already slipped down and was watching him carefully. 'It's ours,' he said.

'Oh, Paul,' she said, slipping her arm through his. 'You will look after me, won't you?'

They found a wing of small rooms joined by a side corridor, with proper tiled floors and painted walls, and couches smelling of wine and olives. She sat, then half reclined, looking at him under her eyelashes. The roof, too, was of terracotta, Paul noticed, in the Roman style; the wind, muffled by the thick thatch of the old quarters, here roared above the thin tiles. Diana lay back tiredly, her knees raised and the back of her hand over her eyes, showing the milky curve of her breast. When he was sure his absence would not wake her from her doze, Paul went out quietly and found hay in one the stables. He stuffed some in a net to feed the horse, then returned to the inn round the back way. In the kitchen he picked out pots of olives, dried peas and, hanging from a shelf, loops of thin Lucanian sausage. A glowing ember left in the ash of the fire sufficed to light a lamp. Putting the food on a platter, he carried supper to their room. Diana was already sitting up, her blue eyes reflecting the warm glow of the lamp.

'You forgot the wine,' she said.

He returned to the kitchen and found wine in a large covered jar, and selected two goblets from a row. Diana insisted on serving him on the couch. Paul did not talk as they ate, too drained by the experiences of the day. He did not respond as she arranged herself on the couch in his view, her elbow on the bolster, her fingers to her cheek. She watched his eyes flutter closed.

Paul slept.

Diana looked down at him. He was really a very nice looking boy, and she knew she could make him do what she wanted. Hunger filled her, she felt empty and unsatisfied despite the meal in her stomach. She poured herself more wine – he'd brought cooking wine, but he would learn. As she drank she wondered how much he had beneath his clothes. The wind roared and sent an olive stone skittering across the floor; she lifted his tunic as though the wind had done it, teasing her breath on his warm, male-smelling flesh as though she too was the wind.

'Husband,' she whispered, but he did not respond.

She put her lips close to the lamp's flame and blew once. The only light came from a small window high in the wall, with real glass in it, the moon among the ragged clouds glowing in soft gleams across the room. The coin round her neck swung from the silver chain as she lifted her gown and straddled his warm hips with her own. A man was supposed to be experienced on his wedding night, a woman to know nothing, but a girl could not live three doors from a temple of Isis and hear the calls of the courtesans there without knowing – or so she thought – almost everything. All Paul knew was love. She looked down tenderly at his innocent features and, bending her face close, blew her perfume into his nostrils.

'Husband,' she said, more loudly this time, taking her weight on her knees and stroking him with the heat of her opened flesh, arousing him in his sleep, just a boy. What did he know of love? she thought to herself, sinking down on him, taking him as he woke. Here was the real power of love, she exulted, sweeping them along, making him do what she wanted.

'Wife,' Paul said, his voice hoarse with passion, both of them unpinning her gown to show him all of her in the moonlight. She pulled his face between her breasts, throwing back her head with a hiss of desire. But he cried out much too soon.

She leaned over his limp body on her elbows, only their sweat joining them, but she could not arouse him again, and the harder she tried to grip him within her loins, the smaller he became.

I want something I can hold, she thought, each word forming in her brain as hard and dark as a pebble. I want a family.

They saw no sign of any buildings being put up in London that winter; even the Customs House was left in ruin. Paul, looking up from his work, thought that the great burnt mounds of Corn Hill and Lud's Hill, sticking up like two bare red breasts, might remain barren and deserted for ever. Meanwhile Petronius Urbicus, when he was not teaching the women table talk, shook his head and spoke of shattered business confidence, but his father in prosperous Brescia, overjoyed to hear word that his only son was alive against all the odds, sent a large reward in silver *sesterci* to Petronius's astonished hosts.

On the high road above Valle Dei, ragged children in skins, and not a few hungry adults, stayed in hiding behind the trees and watched the imperial troop columns pass, thousands of legionary infantry soldiers landed from Germany, auxiliary infantry and auxiliary cavalry streaming from the harbours of the Thames mouth, all heading north across London Bridge, hastily repaired, without waiting for supplies. Then the road was empty again. The war and its terrible revenge had passed by Valle Dei, almost close enough to touch, and down in the valley the people thanked their lucky stars then got on with their busy lives as usual.

184

The villagers in their round houses rooted secretly for the British side, but on the knoll the Fox family knew the Romans could not afford to lose. Only John Fox thought it would make no difference in the end. What will be will be, he said. Nothing will change because, he said, human nature never changes.

But no one listened to that old man nowadays.

'Do you do *everything* she says?'

'She's my wife,' Paul said patiently, unrolling the twine and pegging it to get the level, sighting between the marker posts for the next course of bricks. He had been taught to do this by their visitor, Toherus, from the peaceful Dumnonii tribe of the south-west, born of a long tradition of builders. He had been returning home from Trier, where he had studied as a master builder, when his cartwheel broke. His bad luck was the Foxes' good fortune. He knew how to calculate roof loading and could feel the strength in a piece of timber by eye. 'And her name is Diana, Father,' Paul added, straightening.

'You've let her get the upper hand over you,' John Fox grumbled. 'A man must make sure his wife knows her place, or before you know where you are they don't treat you with respect.'

'Talking back at the dinner table,' Paul muttered, adjusting the height of the twine by the thickness of a fingernail; Toherus was a hard taskmaster, though he rolled his broad Dumnon vowels like a yokel.

The old man glared balefully, not sure if Paul was joking. 'Making your life a misery with their hard faces and dry breasts. Ow! Be careful, Imogen!' He rubbed his arm, burned by the long-handled baker's peel Imogen was withdrawing from Cabriabanus's roaring tile kiln, which made a magnificent oven. He gave her loaf a dissatisfied rap with his knuckles, as though the fresh, hollow sound it made was not as good as in his day.

'You're the old misery round here, John Fox!' Imogen flashed at him. She put him down in such withering terms quite openly nowadays, all pretence at respect for him gone.

Though the sun had melted the frost, the air was chill away from the kiln. More than a year had passed since Paul had returned from London with his new bride. Paul was the one with the energy now, it was Paul and his young wife who set the pace on the knoll. Imogen knew she had won him back from his father, those broad shoulders at last beginning to stoop, and the old man had taken to muttering his thoughts to himself as he shambled about the place. He had no clear idea where he was going in life now, she thought, or what he was trying to achieve, but Imogen was not yet in her fortieth year, probably stronger than he was. Impatiently she elbowed him aside, sending the loaf skidding from the flat iron disc onto a tray, and puffed her hair out of her eyes.

Just as John Fox returned home, long ago, in the prime of his life to build a safe haven for his daughter and exhausted himself doing it, she was now giving in turn to her son. Standing back, Imogen stared at the building site all around them as proudly as though it was her own, which in a sense it was. She was the driving force behind the place: it would be Paul's home. But where he now busied himself with levels, hammers and twine, she had used motherly love and cunning to get her way, and a certain amount of sacrifice. She had even welcomed Diana into her son's heart.

That Paul thought he was doing all this for Diana gave Imogen nothing but pleasure. She had immediately formed an alliance with the girl. From the moment she first clapped eyes on Diana, looking around her shyly as Paul walked her out of the oak trees of Valle Dei onto the broad cultivated knoll, a sophisticated town girl obviously out of her depth in this rustic setting, Imogen had determined that they should work together. Diana said she would die without a bath-house nearby; Paul, at his mother's urging, built a hut by the well downhill, and both women used it. At their request a corn drier, which Imogen had long desired, had been erected round the back of the kiln so that grain no longer sprouted and bread was good all year round. When Petronius spilt salt at dinner, the two women followed his Roman example by flicking a pinch over their shoulders for good fortune, and Paul copied them with a good-humoured smile; and, again like Petronius, they pierced their empty eggshells with the special pointed handles on their eggspoons for the same reason. They had another set of spoons called *cochleare* for the edible snails that were to be found everywhere in the grass after rain. The travelling cutler did good business with the two women on the knoll.

Paul learned that when Diana was happy, he was happy. What

186

his mother could not tell him, he would hear from Diana; when words were no use, he was brought round by his wife's caresses in bed, and in the end Paul congratulated himself that everything was his idea. Only when he dug in his heels, as over the bath-house, were sulks or tears used against him, and the caresses, which had previously been so willingly given, denied. But that never lasted long.

Diana became pregnant in the early summer.

Rumours filtered back from the outside world: a great battle somewhere in the north, eighty thousand British men and their women killed, twice that number fleeing in chaos, the disciplined legions marching steadily after them, systematically killing the survivors wherever they made camp, burning the land. The queen had taken poison and been given a magnificent burial by the last of her followers, no one knew where. None of that was important in Valle Dei.

What the two women wanted of Paul was simple. They wanted a proper house for the children to grow up in, and that meant a Roman house with straight walls, separate rooms, tiled roof: a villa, paid for in Brescian silver.

Toherus's work began to rise. Nothing like it had been seen in the valley before. The village boys came down each morning and stood in awe – until they were threatened with work – watching the house grow. First a rectangle of ground was levelled on a prominent position on the knoll, then the footings were dug in, the youngest children scratching the ground with sticks in imitation, older girls already set to work weaving the rush mats that would take the echo from the rooms to come. Carpenters fashioned the timber frames for the walls, and now the slaves were placing unfired mud bricks between the wooden uprights under Paul's direction. To begin with, the neat, slow progress was dwarfed by John Fox's large British round house nearby, but now the precise sharp-edged geometry of the dwelling made the thatched house look shaggy and tumbledown – primitive – by comparison.

Best of all, as far as the women and their high-born and finicky house guest Petronius Urbicus were concerned, the new house looked fashionable even by Roman standards. Despite its small size, its uniqueness in the valley as well as its expense, proclaimed Paul's status and thus their own. Besides, Toherus had built it with growth in mind – if more children came along, for example.

'You're just doing what the women want,' John persisted, shaking his head.

'But I want it too,' said Paul. 'Nothing's worth an unhappy wife.' He smiled, but could not make his father laugh.

The roof was tiled just in time before the first snow, sheltering them to finish off the inside work during the winter, facing the interior walls with clay by the warmth of a fire in every room, using rollers to stamp a pattern as a key for plaster, then getting in a slave who was trained and owned as a professional plasterer to perform that skilled work. Labour was still easy to come by, and cheap, despite the works started in Colchester to rebuild the temple of the Imperial Cult. Prices would soon go up, Petronius said. He was no good with his hands but he always seemed to know the latest gossip, and effortlessly enchanted his audience at dinner.

Events beyond Valle Dei hardly touched its inhabitants, but a ripple did eventually reach Petronius. Suetonius, his vengeance wreaked and his reputation wrecked by a damning report on the rebellion from the new procurator, Julius Alpinus Classicianus, a Gallic Celt, had been packed home to Pisa by Emperor Nero. The new governor was Publius Petronius Turpilianus, a nephew of Claudius and an old general whose family had a long history of moderation – his father had successfully kept the Jews from each other's throats in Caligula's day. Sent to mend fences with those Britons who had remained loyal, he had served as a consul and was an extremely important man, not least because he was patron to Petronius Urbicus's father. A senior post was smartly arranged for Petronius.

The evening before his departure, Paul held a dinner party, the first time they had all gathered in the dining room of the new house.

It was John Fox's house, not his son's; John was still the head of the family, not Paul. But the front door was not opened, the curtains that hung over the interior doorways were not swept aside, they did not hear the creak of his muddy fur boots on the matting. The party waited awkwardly, Petronius in the guest's place at the top of the table, the women at the smaller tables on each side facing each other, the eyes of everyone nervously skirting the empty place at the head table. There were no curtains over the windows and they imagined him looking in at them from the cold shadows outside, making them out through the thick green glass, his white eyebrows drawn together with anger, ferocity, and envy. Envy at their youth.

'This is ridiculous!' exclaimed Diana, only a month from her time, kneeling uncomfortably on her low couch, made irritable by her condition. She pushed back on her knuckles with a groan, giving Paul a fixed look that turned to a frown as she rose: do something. But Paul was chatting amiably to Petronius. Diana offered him the red Samian bowl of *gustatio*, holding the snacks in front of Paul's nose until he took one – a giant olive from northern Spain, imported before trade collapsed, kept in an amphora sealed with pitch and now very precious, as was the Narbonne wine they mixed with water. Petronius followed suit and tucked into the cubes of lamb fried in fish pickle with gusto, licking his fingers.

'Your father isn't coming, Paul,' Imogen said. 'You know he isn't.' He accepted it from her, nodding obediently for the empty place to be taken away. She looked at him fondly as the main course of Kent oysters stewed in white wine was brought in from the kitchen, congratulating herself on her successful influence during Paul's childhood. Marriage had polished the rough edges of adolescence from him and he had become a genial and content adult: her own son, fashioned by her, sunny and pliable. There was nothing threatening about Paul, he and Diana made the ideal young couple, showing few deep feelings except for each other, like most young people expecting the arrival of their first baby. To them even the recent past was already a very long time ago, experienced intensely but quickly forgotten. Diana appeared to be quite undisturbed by what she had seen in London – although those strange dark blue shadows moved in her eyes as she talked of what she had heard and felt down there in the mushroom cellar, eating nervously while looters ransacked the rooms above. 'I must have stuffed myself with pounds and pounds of mushrooms!' she laughed now as she helped herself to an enormous chestnut omelette sweetened with honey, in preference to the shellfish.

Paul's attitude was equally straightforward and reasonable. 'I can understand why the British murdered their own people –

I can see both points of view now, I think,' he said. Clean tables were being carried in after the second main course and more lamps set out to banish the darkness. 'The Londoners felt they had no choice but to collaborate with the Romans, learn ways that were foreign to them in hope of better lives, send their children to foreign schools—'

'But all they learned was servitude,' John Fox said from the doorway. He held up his hand as Paul poured beer into a quart pewter mug for him. 'No, save yourself the trouble.'

'Servitude, but to a superior culture,' Petronius argued insensitively, nodding at the walls painted dark red and green in the shape of windows, the built-in cupboards, bronze lamps and comfortable couches, the thermospodium that had kept the food warm. He patted his full belly – he had put on a lot of weight from Diana's cooking.

'I agree with you, Petronius,' Imogen said, but then she never agreed with her husband about anything.

'Yet you can see the point of view of the British who regarded their folk as traitors,' Paul said, helping himself to another glass of Narbonne wine. 'I'm not defending their behaviour, but—'

'You make death sound so reasonable!' John said, his sandals slapping on the plain red mosaic floor as he crossed to Paul's side, resisting their Roman table talk, staring down with trembling muscles at Paul's locks cut short and crimped like Petronius's, their good manners, all that he had left behind him long ago. His own hair was totally white and reached below his shoulders. 'Didn't you see anything in London, Paul?' he demanded. 'Or did you just see the point of view of it all?'

'That's unfair,' Paul said.

'I never meant us to be like this, Paul.' His father's back was bent and his grey face dragged downward with haggard lines. 'Oh, if only we could fight women in the same way we fight men. What's to become of me?'

Paul stood and put his arm round his father. 'This is your home now.'

'That's just it,' John Fox said. 'It isn't. It isn't.'

The old man didn't get better. He got worse. The arrival of the baby brought him no joy. White-haired and dirty, prowling in the snow outside, his fist braced round a stick as high as his jaw, he listened for the mother's screams.

In the small room at the end of the house a cheerful beechwood fire crackled in the grate, illuminating Diana's spread thighs. She was held back in the wickerwork birthing chair by Tacita's strong arms clasped under her breasts, that ravaged face and decay-laden breath sweeping over her like a warning of mortality. Diana panted the other woman's breath and heaved from side to side, grinding her teeth to make no noise against the agony she felt, but the chair creaked like a ship in a gale. 'Don't break it! Easy now girl,' Tacita said roughly. There were no social barriers during a childbirth. 'Lucky to have the chair, you are,' she said for the third time. 'Both mine came at harvest, at the field edge. Luxury, this is.' Her boy Matugenus, who spent most of his time kneeling in the corner looking frightened, scampered to put more wood on the fire, then broke into a broad happy grin when Imogen gave him a nod of encouragement.

Imogen was much more worried than she showed. She knelt between Diana's legs, her knees frozen by the concrete signinum-work floor beneath the mat, worried that this labour was going on too long, even for a first baby. She had cut her fingernails short but she wished she had longer fingers; she could feel the baby's head wanting to come but she couldn't get a grip. There were no doctors – all doctors were Greek, and all had been crucified in London. The only proper midwife in the village was a witch and neither Diana nor Imogen had wanted anything to do with her. But now Imogen was not so sure. She had started off encouraging Diana by promising her the baby would be born before dark, but now it was the deepest time of night. Still, Diana was terribly strong, though her contractions still felt like iron bands clamped under her flesh.

'I can see its hair!' Imogen said.

'Oh, let me see,' Diana said. 'What colour is it?' She groaned as another contraction built up, pressing her head back into Tacita's shoulder.

'Red. It's a beautiful dark red,' Imogen said. 'Almost there. Next one. Get ready. *Push*!'

Tacita blew through her fat lips, making a blubbery sound.

'Here it comes!' Imogen cried, the tears starting in her eyes.

191

'That's it. That's it! That's it, my dear!' And Diana screamed.

Outside, John Fox grunted, his head turning like a questing hound's towards the flickering light showing through the green.

'Don't push! Don't push now!' Imogen hissed. The baby's face appeared behind a spurt of fluid, sliding into her palms, then the rest of him followed in a rippling rush, and he was perfect.

They even gave him a Roman name, Vitellus, pronounced the Roman way, with a W: Witellus.

Afterwards Matugenus fetched the leather bucket and sluiced the chair down, trying not to look at the blood. 'Ready for next time,' Imogen said with a weary smile. Matugenus grinned then settled down beside the fire, resting his head contentedly on his elbows, fading to sleep.

In the morning Paul held his swaddled son in his arms, then handed him to his father. 'Here he is. Your grandson.'

'Ten Roman pounds and a few ounces,' Imogen said. 'I weighed him on the kitchen steel.'

'He'll be strong,' Paul said.

John Fox stared down. 'But he's got blue eyes, boy!'

'Babies always have blue eyes,' Imogen snorted irritably, taking back the baby firmly and giving him to Paul. 'Don't you remember?'

But these blue eyes of birth stayed blue.

'He's not a Fox,' John Fox said to himself, sitting alone in the doorway of his round house. 'Vitellus – Vitellus. He doesn't look like me!'

By the time Vitellus was old enough to stand, albeit on wobbly, chubby legs, with frequent falls on those hard floors so that his knees and hands were always scratched, Lucius was born. This second child arrived easily, almost gracefully, and kindly chose the best time of day to enter the world, a sunny mid-afternoon, so that his mother's first contractions did not start until after a good night's sleep. After her short labour, Diana finished off the day with a little supper, with newborn Lucius, just under eight pounds, tucked in on one side of her, where Paul laid him, and Vitellus on the other. You could not ask for a more involved and thoughtful father than Paul. The women shushed him out at once.

The next morning John Fox sat on a tree trunk by the round house he had refused to pull down, dominating the low tiled roof of the villa with its shaggy peak – how that must irritate them! – and waited for the new child to be brought to him for his approval.

'Here he is, father,' Paul said, holding out the new child. 'Lucius has brown eyes, like your own.'

So, John Fox thought, he has not forgotten what I said about Vitellus a year ago – Vitellus, the firstborn, with his eyes of Pomponius blue, who will inherit this land and everything in it. He looked at Lucius but did not bother to touch him. Paul handed the child to the nursemaid, who took him away.

'Paul, my boy. Sit down.' John patted the trunk for Paul to sit beside him, and broached the matter that increasingly lay closest to his heart, that he fretted and worried over during the long hours of the night, sleeplessly kicking memories of his youth back and forth, memories that now seemed so much more real than the present time. He had no one to share his thoughts with since Imogen had moved into the new house. Not that he missed her. Not for one moment. Those two women getting their heads together and running the place their way, and Paul doing nothing about it. John Fox trembled with rage.

'You don't like Diana, do you?' Paul said without warning, having seen the shaking hands and read the signs. 'We're happy, don't you realise?' He swung out his arm. 'We've got every-thing—'

'*We*? Your wife is as important as you, is she, young man?'

'We have everything we could want,' Paul said patiently. 'Two wonderful children, a fine house, and the land is now in law our own property, registered officially in our own names, thanks to Petronius. After the procurator Julius Classicianus's death, he was transferred to the governor's staff and dropped a word on our behalf.'

'Owned,' John said, 'and so taxed, you idiot. No one knew about us before. We got away with it!'

Paul stared out through the clear April air, the angle of the sun illuminating the new white threads spreading along the lines of the old roads of London: new buildings. He replied quietly, 'That situation may have suited you, Father, but it couldn't have lasted for ever. You were lucky at the start. Now I have been lucky again.'

'Your choice!' snapped the old man. 'Luck, that's all it is, is it? You'll have to live with it!'

He doesn't make good sense these days, Paul thought sadly.

What was once mysterious and powerful about him is just gibberish now. His mind's going.

'The estate is profitable, Father, we can afford to pay our way,' he said. 'And it's our duty, after all.'

'My only duty is to myself.'

Paul tried to find a topic that would not infuriate the old man. 'I've sent the slaves who built the house to London,' he smiled brightly, 'where their skills are much in demand since the rebuilding started, and that's also profitable – it's in cash, too.'

'And your *clever* wife—'

'Father, please don't.'

'Ambitious, too. Given them all fashionable Greek names,' the old man barked contemptuously. 'Do they take your orders, or hers?'

'Mine, through her.' Paul kept his temper level, wishing he could hug his father, hold his hand, simply be friends with him. But John Fox had excluded himself from the life of the estate. Paul searched for something to say that would not provoke the unreasonable, incoherent anger in his father. 'We've kept their children here, and they'll receive an education they otherwise wouldn't have received. They can't marry, of course, but in due time we'll breed from them – Diana says it makes sound commercial sense. Next year we'll start sending timber to London. There's talk that the town will be awarded municipal status, and the broad spans of that forum roof they're planning will require oak. We have some of the finest oaks close to us here, you know.'

'Yes, I know.'

Paul breezed on. 'It may even be possible to roll whole trunks downhill to be shipped upriver! Where the trees have been felled we'll improve the ground with sheep and cattle.' His voice trailed to silence, and his tongue felt frozen to the roof of his mouth. His father was giving him such an odd look that Paul didn't know how to deal with it. The truth of what he was hiding behind this conversation blurted out of him. 'Why do you exclude yourself from our happiness, Father? Why do you hate us?'

The worst possible thing happened. John Fox's eyes filled with senile tears. He leaned forward, groping for Paul. 'It's not because I hate you. It's because I love you.'

This was embarrassing. It was deathbed talk, the sort of thing that could not be said between father and son during a lifetime. 'We love you, too,' Paul said, clinging awkwardly to the dry, shivering hand, but all at once guilt over the coin he had stolen as a child filled his mind. He must say something, but he didn't know how. The hand fell from his limp fingers.

His father spoke first.

'Paul. Listen to me. If you don't have Vitellus and Lucius baptised, they will go to hell when they die.'

'They'll be punished for something *I've* done?' Paul struggled to grasp the concept.

'No, something you haven't done.'

'Baptised?'

'Anointed into the Christian Church. You were. You belong to me, just as I belonged to the Baptist. Others belong to Apollos, or to Peter, or to Jesus. I saved you with my own hands, in the holy well. I can do the same for your children,' he said eagerly.

'I thought you believed in many gods. All of them. I thought you felt it wise.'

'Only one.'

'I know of no such single church. Neither does Diana, I'm sure. Or any holy well.' Paul lied badly. 'You mean the well by the bath-house?'

'Don't play the innocent with me,' John Fox said.

He knows I followed him down there into the cave, Paul thought. He knows I saw the treasure that he had hidden there, which one day I will inherit. And after me, my eldest son. The box of silver coins smelling of apple balsam. But he doesn't know that I stole one of them. He never counted them – because he never really cared about them, just used them to get what he wanted. Until they failed him.

But now, in the twilight of his life – what does he want now?

'Is this—' Paul croaked, 'is this talk something to do with that fellow Apollos who passed through here last year?'

'No, Apollos is head of the Order of Ephraim, followers of John the Baptist. Of the myth of John the Baptist. He teaches that the Baptist was murdered but that his head was rejoined with his body, and he rose from the dead.'

'Do you believe that, Father?'

'No. It's impossible for a man or a woman to rise from the

dead. Everyone knows that. Apollos brought news that James, the younger brother of Jesus, had been stoned to death, and he did not rise from the dead. Yet . . . and yet . . . More and more as I grow older I think of things I have seen in my life. Memories, pictures of things once unimportant to me, or of no more importance than anything else . . . Now they fill my eyes when I sleep.'

Paul stood up, disturbed. He had a mountain of work to do; he must make sure the men were doing a good job painting the nursery, and one or two people were bound to be waiting by his study to ask favours from the clients' chair. But still he hesitated. He was quite sure his father was mad.

The nursemaid had gone back into the house and no one else was close by, only a few youngsters chasing away rooks and magpies from the fields.

'Father,' Paul said, standing, 'I hope you won't worry Mother or Diana with these thoughts of yours.'

'I won't,' John Fox murmured. 'It's between us, Paul. Our secret.' Then as Paul turned away he called, 'But I know now what I saw. I saw a man raised from the dead.'

'Oh?' sighed Paul over his shoulder. 'What was his name?'

'The first man was called Lazarus. And now I'm not sure if the second was a man at all.'

Paul shook his head and made his way through the bright morning sunlight to his new house.

Overnight, it seemed to John Fox, Vitellus was running about the place, little Lucius crawling after him, then toddling with his hand wrapped trustingly in his elder brother's, then running together, always muddy, always having fun, always being bleated after by their ineffectual nursemaid with her Greek name . . . he couldn't be bothered to remember it. Five years old, now seven, racing as fast as horses, driving him crazy. You could take bets on them, except that Vitellus always won. What did they have to be so happy about, those children?

The days passed by John Fox in an endless moaning stream, hardly worth remembering, for each of his days was the same, but year by year the sun grew dimmer and the wind harsher. Food was hardly worth the effort of eating, he had almost no teeth left. No one cared about him, they only brought him his food on sufferance! He pretended he could not hear them when they came knocking, so they had to leave the plates outside, and he took to his bed when they tried to move him from his house. They wanted to knock it down, he knew; his roof was spoiling their view. Yes, how he must irritate them! When the wind blew in their direction, he stoked his smoky fire.

Yet his mind was sharp as nails and he was as active as a goat, no spare weight these days. Death gradually ceased to obsess him, he thought only about life. Life meant women. The women he'd had! Probably thousands of them. There had been someone he'd loved, but he couldn't remember her name. Thousands, on Capri or in Rome – those were the days!

Rues.

He wrote it down, but the next day found the loop of paper and stared at his scrawl, wondering who she had been.

He could not remember her; she was nothing, he could not remember her at all.

Yet she had been important. He was sure of it. Once, long ago, she had been the whole world to him.

When his mind cleared he cried, realising how much he was losing, then the shadows closed in again. He lay listening to the children's joyful, playful shouts, hating them. Despite his jealousy he could not remember their names.

People avoided him when he went out, or perhaps he was not aware of them, filled with thoughts of all his women, no faces, no wasting any time with talk, just their pale cloven bodies to possess. He glimpsed Diana in the distance, shapeless in her gown pinned only at the neck, on the path to the bath-house. He could walk as fast as lightning, his stick led him where it would, and suddenly he was there. There by the bath-house wall.

The slave had lit the fire and departed; steam puffed out round the door as Diana closed it. He gave no sign of his presence. He did not like Diana, and she did not like him.

He looked around suspiciously, but no one was watching him, so he pressed his eye to the gap.

She had unpinned her shift and it fell away to reveal a pair of enormous milky-white mouthwatering breasts.

Between them hung *his* silver talent.

One of *his*, his very own, which he had never given away without it coming back to him sooner or later.

Diana leaned forward towards him, her arms up to do her hair, and he watched the silver disc slowly spin, flashing, as it swung between her dark, carmine nipples, from one to the other and back again. His lust evaporated in outrage. He raised his fists to beat the door down, to scream at her. *How did you get that? Mine, all mine!*

She was singing to herself or she would have heard him mouthing his fury. What an overconfident fool he had been to trust Paul with the knowledge of the cave, he told himself bitterly. The boy hadn't waited for him to die, couldn't wait for it all to become his. Thieving his own birthright! Worst of all, he had stolen it only to give it, in the British tradition he had now rejected, to that fat breeding-sow of a wife!

The old man fell back from the door and put his knuckles to his mouth. His eyes began to move cunningly from side to side.

It was dark that night.

It was darker in the hut. John Fox moved his bed and began to dig down. His strength seemed to grow as he dug, at least that was what he believed, and he could not stop, though his muscles cracked and his back felt as though it would break. He had worn himself out by dawn. Struggling to drag himself from the hole he had dug, he lay flopped on his bed, biding his time through the day, gathering his strength, knotting a ladder from lengths of rope, his mind too busy to sleep. Though the two children played catch by the edge of the knoll and their voices were no louder than the birds', he put his hands over his ears; their laughter was driving him crazy, and he was hardly able to contain his hatred of Paul until dark.

He dug all night again, lifting out handfuls of chalk, hiding them behind cupboards, spreading them across the floor when there was too much, then went back to work in the hole. The bottom had acquired a hollow sound, and he was ready for it when it gave way beneath his feet, pulling himself up on his elbows, his feet swinging over nothingness. Kneeling on the edge of the hole, he threw the rope ladder down into the dark. The sound of running water came up.

He took the lamp and dropped, swinging, into the empty black space. Almost at once he felt something hard beneath his feet – he was on top of the pile of boulders that tumbled down to the holy well. He could see the glitter of the water below as he picked his way carefully down from rock to rock.

The cedarwood box remained where he had thrown it in his despair the day he had returned from London nine years ago, and sealed the place up for the rest of his lifetime, knowing that his son would know where to find them when he was dead. But Paul had abused his trust and put the knowledge to his own use!

The old man chuckled. He wasn't beaten yet. There'd never be another John Fox!

He tied some twine round the box. Holding the harsh strands between the gums of his toothless mouth, which soon began to bleed, he climbed up the rope ladder and inched himself out of the hole. He lay on the ground, spitting blood, his whole body trembling with exhaustion, the muscles of his arms quivering, but exultant. He didn't have the strength to fill in the hole, and he could tell by the paleness of the eastern sky beyond the doorway that he had little time left for what he must do: farmworkers rose at dawn.

No one must see him.

For the last time, John Fox opened the box and counted the silver coins, laying them in his palm, then on the ground. Once he forgot the number and started again. He counted twenty-six. Again he counted them: twenty-six.

There had been twenty-seven left, before Paul stole one.

Carefully replacing his talents, he tucked the box under his arm and went outside into the thin grey light. Mist clung knee-high to the flat ground of the knoll, only the field boundaries showing, a green grid stretching away from him. No smoke came from the blue-painted villa chimney. Everything was silent but for his own wheezing breath as he crossed to the edge at a particular point, finding the place where the slope fell away steeply in a gully, wet only in the heaviest rains, long choked with undergrowth and brush. No one ever came here, the place was supposed to be haunted. He looked around him carefully, then quietly pushed his way among the brambles and nettles, his feet sinking into the soft soil, ivy slithering over his shoulders. Dropping to his knees where some wild roses grew, twining their stems among the gooseberries and blackcurrants, he pulled aside the mat of weed and grasses and reached behind him to continue his work – but he had forgotten to bring his shovel.

No matter. He dug his hands into the soil, pulling back the excavated earth between his knees, moving round to another angle when there was too much piled up. Faintly he could hear cockerels crowing up in the village – Diana refused to have them near the villa, she was a late riser – and the sun cast an orange spoke through the tangled vegetation around him, then dozens as its brightness grew, until it seemed he was surrounded by a net of shadows rather than by light.

He paused as two men called out greetings to one another on their way to the long field, holding his breath until their voices faded away downhill.

Deep enough. He dropped the box into its new hiding place, letting handfuls of soil patter down on the lid until it was covered. Chuckling to himself at his cleverness, he pushed the earth over the hole with his palms until all sign of it was gone, then stood up and on his thighs wiped the dirt from his hands, hissing as a bramble thorn embedded itself just under the nail of his fore-finger, the most painful place. He returned home sucking his fingertip, knowing it would be better in no time; in fact the whole of him was feeling better already, and he walked with a spring in his step – and without his stick! – for the first time in years, congratulating himself on his revenge. He felt strong enough to live for ever. Perhaps the box would be sucked down deeper as the land breathed, and never be found. Perhaps it would be exhaled slowly to the surface and in a hundred years someone would dig it up again; but not Paul, the thief.

John Fox lay down on his bed, sucking his finger like a baby.

While the day grew warm, he slept, then woke with his finger still in his mouth, but he couldn't get the bramble thorn out from beneath his nail. He worried at the place with the thumb and forefinger of his other hand, but the digging had worn his nails blunt. *I feel strong enough to live for ever.* During the night the pain grew worse, but squeezing his fingertip between his gums relieved him somewhat, and he looked with interest at what daylight revealed: white and wrinkled, softened by his saliva, his flesh had swollen round the nail. He put it back in his mouth, and slept.

During the night he woke up and stayed awake, getting angry with his finger for its throbbing which would not stop. At dawn he stood in the doorway examining the blotchy, purple flesh. The finger was swollen to twice the size of the others, the nail dark grey, undoubtedly infected, and hot. In the afternoon, when his meal was brought to him, he roused himself in the gloom and shouted through the door that he didn't want it, and like yesterday's food it was taken way. They didn't leave it outside for him any more to take in himself with dignity. Yes, they'd be glad to be rid of him! But he wasn't going to give them the satisfaction.

The swelling had spread into his hand now.

He looked at his swollen knuckles and wanted to laugh, the situation was so ridiculous. Infections always cleared up. He sucked at his nail, and it came off softly on his tongue.

He licked and squeezed at the square of naked flesh, but still he couldn't find the thorn.

He must have dropped off to sleep, because some time later he woke with a start, not sure what day it was, but quite clear in his mind that it was day, because he could see his finger. It was black. He heard himself moaning, because it hurt like hell, the pain throbbing up his arm to the elbow.

What should he do? Call out to Paul for help? Not likely.

He rolled over and took his meat knife from his belt, unfolded the blade, and bent his finger, finding the joint of soft cartilage that joined it to the knuckle. Inserting the point of the knife, he began to cut.

When the frightful task was over he wrapped the puffy mound of his hand in a rag.

He woke sweating. The pain was intense now, unbearable. The rag binding his hand looked tight enough to slit, dark blotches spreading through it from below, and it smelt like a dead body. He would have to cut it off to save his arm, but he trembled at the thought. A hand was connected to a wrist by many bones, ribbons of soft cartilage, wiry tendons. And without hot pitch to seal the stump, he would be bled of his life force, and die.

Die. He couldn't believe it.

'Paul,' he called weakly when his evening meal was brought. After one peep through the door the terrified slave girl screamed, dropped the small portable table she carried, and ran for Paul.

When Paul came into the hut his face changed. That was the only word for it. He changed. His hands rose as though to cover his nose or his mouth, but then he dropped to his knees beside his father – they came down so hard on the packed chalk that John Fox heard them crack. 'Mind you don't hurt yourself,' he admonished mildly. 'You'll soon get used to the smell.'

'Ye gods,' Paul whispered, appalled. 'What have you done to yourself?'

'Do it for me, will you?' John said. 'Only as far as the wrist, mind. Cut off my hand, then let me get better. No further than the wrist.'

Paul sent to the village for the blacksmith, Cymbarrus, a large gentle man who breathed through his nose. 'The elbow, at once,' Cymbarrus sniffed on coming inside, 'and he might die even so.'

'Wrist, or I curse you for ever,' the old man quavered.

Paul leaned close. 'Do you understand what you're saying, Father?'

'I'm not hurt,' grinned John.

'Only to the wrist,' Paul told the blacksmith, and Cymbarrus didn't bother with niceties: his axe swept down, the stump of the forearm was thrust into a bucket of hot pitch taken from the fire. When John woke, Imogen was bathing his forehead, her face tender.

'Don't you dare forgive me,' he said. 'Don't give up.'

She looked at him, seeming very tired, with dark crescents under her eyes, and he wondered how long she had been here watching him.

'Oh, stop pretending,' she said. 'Be honest for once in your life.' But he just grinned at her, as though he was not in dreadful pain.

'For pity's sake, take the thing off at the elbow,' Paul begged.

'Too late.' Cymbarrus grunted as he moved his hands up the cold, ballooned flesh of the arm, hardly touching the splitting black skin, though the old man screamed and screamed. 'His shoulder's red-hot, you know.'

'Then do what you have to do,' Paul said.

'You need a butcher for that, not a smith,' said the amiable Cymbarrus. 'He's gone rotten inside.'

'Listen to me,' John Fox said clearly and calmly.

He had been lying quietly on his left side for as long as he could remember, coming to his senses without pain, without anything except a faint tickling where his right arm and shoulder blade had been; the side of his head was propped up on a bolster of straw, so that his cheek pushed his left eye closed and pulled up the corner of his mouth, distorting his face and making talking extraordinarily difficult. He wondered if they would understand what he had to say. He thought not.

Looking around with his right eye, he'd seen he was in his hut, that they hadn't moved him to their house. Good. He would die at home.

But first, he'd try and tell them the truth.

'Paul?' he slurred.

'Here, Father.' Paul's face swum into view.

John rallied his strength. 'Diana with you?' It came out as 'Dinerwicher?' and a tear squeezed helplessly from his eye.

'Here I am.' He'd seen her fat fingers squeezing his good arm, which stuck out from under him at an awkward angle, but he hadn't felt her touch, nothing at all.

'I can't see you properly.'

Paul reached out his hands, taking the strain off his father's face, moving his head until everyone was in his view. 'Is that better?'

'The nurserymaid is looking after the children,' Diana said anxiously. 'We've been here all the time. We haven't eaten or anything, or drunk a drop, since . . .' Her voice faltered, those round blue pupils of hers flickering towards his missing arm and shoulder.

But his mind had already moved on. 'Imogen here?'

A rustle of clothes, and she came to kneel beside him, those crescents beneath her eyes darker than ever, her hair tangled.

'You don't look your best,' he said.

'Neither do you,' she murmured, giving him a sip of water. 'No, don't swallow!' Wiped his forehead with the ball of her thumb, soothing him, the tiny coin he had given Rues glittering at her throat as always. Watching her, he began to remember everything, every day of his life, as a brilliant light surrounded by darkness.

Hardly moving his lips, he said, 'Do you still hate me, Imogen?'

'You're a wrong man,' she whispered, leaning so close to him that her breath tickled his eyelashes, both his daughter and his wife. 'I think everything you ever did was a wrong thing. You were wrong to go away, you were wrong to come back. I pity you for what you did to me. No, I don't hate you.' She stroked his forehead with her hands, her lips almost touching the tip of his nose, none of the others could hear these hard words of hers, so softly spoken. 'I had a fine son, doubly yours, but doubly mine too,' she whispered. 'I have beautiful grandchildren. That's all I care about. Of course I forgive you. But everything you ever did was wrong.' Then she sounded so irritated with him. 'You could have had a happy life, John Fox!'

He drew a deep breath. 'Listen to me,' he said clearly, moving his left arm from beneath him with an effort he did not feel, holding out his open hand. 'Listen to me, all of you.' He grasped Imogen's slim hard fingers, reached out to the others. 'You too. Put your hand in mine.'

Paul and Diana glanced at one another, then did as he demanded.

John sighed.

'When I was twenty-seven years old, I was exiled by my father from Britain to Judea, for falling in love with the wrong woman. This you know. And you know it was the end of the world for me. I went not caring if I destroyed myself, and that was how I lived, taking each day as it came, treating my liberty as a licence to do whatever I wished. But now I'm dying, and I want to tell you about the most important thing that ever happened to me. Sometimes a truth is so obvious you just don't see it, it's right in front of your nose and you don't see it. I saw with my own eyes, and I didn't believe. I was one of the five hundred, but I just didn't care. Not then. But now I must tell you what I saw.

'Listen to me! Imagine . . .'

'Imagine the sun, not much larger than a small silver coin, sending brilliant rays past you across the dark sea, illuminating hills ahead of you as white as bone. I was assured by the merchant who stood beside me on deck that once they had been green and covered with trees, but men had lived here for thousands of years and built camp fires, and furniture, and iron foundries, and copper smelters. I listened without interest. It was their promised land, he said, a holy land, built on religion and their belief in a Jewish nation, though they were ruled by the Romans. Why should I care? The sun was high by the time I jumped onto the beach, the sun burning my head and the sand burning my feet, but my heart cold as a lump of metal. I had no reason to live. I was nothing, a hollow man.

'But I was surrounded by people who had everything, even the meanest of them, because they were Jews. They were fired by the divine spark. Their valleys were green, the women's tunics were blue, everyone was hoeing the flax. Their faces were the same, and the faces of the men too, and their bodies moved in the same rhythm as they worked: one motion, one people. Their cities, glaring white in the sun, pink and yellow in shadow, were a pushing, shoving babble of religious chatter, hot as steam blowing all around you. And full to bursting with people. People waiting. You saw it in their eyes even as they worked, in the way they struck bargains, in the way they shook their heads, in the way they stepped round you – because they sniffed out the smell of a Gentile a cubit away. Waiting.

'They waited for their Messiah, and their waiting had made their dream solid. Every day was holy in one way or another, you never saw so many priests, such a massive hierarchy, and so many rules for everything. A man could not possibly be perfect, because he could not possibly observe them all flawlessly. The priesthood worked with the Romans, and so received the support of the Romans on condition they kept their people in order, and so they learned submission. But I wandered among street-corner, back-alley preachers by the hundred, common sorts with rough manners and dirty beards, not trained patiently all their childhood for their vocation as I had been, but on their feet because they *believed*. They could not keep their garrulous mouths shut. They grabbed you by the elbow and shouted over your head, drawing others in. Most hated the Romans and believed violence was the way to freedom, though a few preached patience. They all knew a day fulfilling the prophecy of Isaiah would come, they had waited eight centuries for it, but they did not know when. Such a huge system of calendars and dates to predict their Messiah! They worshipped only the one god, called God, but they had splintered into as many sects as we have gods, and each sect, rather than each god, had a name: the Sadducees, the Pharisees, the Palestinian Zealots of Galilee who were against everyone, the assassins called *Sicarii* who mingled with festival crowds to murder priests and devotees, the Essenes of Qumran meditating on their lonely hilltop above the Dead Sea. These were the ones I knew but there were many, many more.

'Everywhere I was treated like a dog, an unclean animal, because I was a Gentile. And so I became an animal; I did not care. I was robbed, so I stole food and drank water from streams. I was not allowed in the house, so I cuckolded the farmer with his wife in the barn. In June I harvested barley with a copper sickle for a loaf of bread and cup of wine in the evening, except on the Sabbath, when I drank myself to sleep in a ditch. I did not rest my head in the same place for two nights. I was attached to no place, no one, no self.

'On windy days my arms helped with the threshing, sending the straw flying down the wind, and I moved on in that direction the next day, with a wife or daughter's heart in my pocket if I could, or some small thing thieved, spreading hurt everywhere I could because I had been hurt. In September I spread misery along the foothills picking fruit, figs, pomegranates, grapes. It was the Law that you could eat all you wanted but not carry anything away in a container, so I stuffed my stomach fit to burst and took anything else I could get away with, so great was my unhappiness and despair.

'I told a hundred women I loved them, and they believed me.

'It was not a bad way to live, if you must live. In December I learned ploughing, and came plodding to Jerusalem across the snowfields, crossing the bridge from the Mount of Olives. As I came down the slope the stone octagon of the Roman fort seemed to sink behind the temple, glowing with gold in the low midday sun. Beyond the throngs at the moneychangers' tables, rich and poor were throwing their offerings into the Treasury. Forced to cover my head, I stood in the Court of the Gentiles listening to the preachers along the colonnades, hearing no words, only the babble of them because there were so many. It was death for me to go further. I turned away into the hovels of the streets, and no one saw me go, even when I pulled the rags from my head and walked bareheaded.

'During that winter I robbed and was robbed a dozen times, and when it got too hot for me, with cash jingling in my pouch I wandered up to Capernaum by the huge Galilean lake – a sea of fish crowded with fishing boats, and around it the richest farming in Palestine. Everything was green under the spring sun, and forests were still on the hills. At sunset a preacher used the flat calm of that time of day to amplify his voice, talking from a boat to the fishermen mending their huge seine nets on the beach, his captive audience. Believers, mostly women and not all of the best sort, had gathered in a crowd to listen to him. Some had dragged their husbands along to hear, mostly bored-looking men picking their teeth who wished they were at work or the inn. A few threw pebbles, which was another reason he was in the boat. He wasn't so popular with the men, but he appealed very much to the ones who didn't matter.

'I forget exactly what he was saying. Without faith, you are nothing, that sort of thing. It's as common as can be from preachers, for obvious reasons. But he was the sort of man you noticed because he noticed you. He certainly seemed to know me and I wondered where I'd met him before. In Britain? Jerusalem? I suppose I was too busy trying to remember to listen. Too late, I realised he had been talking in metrical tercets, groups of three, as I had been taught in my childhood, and the tears came to my eyes. He was talking to *me*, standing with my arms crossed on the sand, even though I was a Gentile . . . I suppose he must have been talking to everyone really. I'd grown my beard like a Jew's to fit in and fooled some people as long as I didn't talk, but he saw through it. I couldn't help smiling at my own foolishness, and he smiled too – not with his mouth, with his eyes. Big eyes, pale brown and intelligent, an oval face, about my age but looking much younger – no lines, no suffering, nothing worse than loneliness. A scholar's face, without oil. His beard was neatly trimmed, like his nails, and his hair was combed. His gown was woven of white linen in one piece, even the arms. See? I could even see the sweat stains in his armpits as he blessed us. *Without faith, we are nothing*. It was as if there was no distance between us at all, no water, no boat, no sand.

'People drifted away, some shaking their heads, cuffing their children as they rounded them up against approaching night, and the fishermen lay down to sleep on their nets. A Zealot bodyguard rowed the preacher ashore and he disappeared up the road to a fine house with lamps and a courtyard. The gate was shut, and that was that.

'I heard about him from time to time at inns and the farms where I worked. His friends called him the carpenter, the son of Joseph – the heir to King David, in other words. His enemies called him Yeshu ben-Pantera – Pantera being a Greek name. His mother had been one of the seven nuns of the High Priest, a temple virgin and an Essene, who believe sex defiles. According to the whispering campaign she had been got with child by a Roman auxiliary soldier, a Greek. Whatever the truth of the rumour, in Nazareth the innkeeper knew the family well, and I overheard him sneer to another traveller that even the preacher's half-brothers called him "Mary's son". She'd been determined to have the child, nothing would put her off; she refused to have him adopted or exposed in the wilderness at Mird. The family's story was notorious in the village, growing in the telling no doubt. Nearly thirty years ago their father, at that time recently widowed, fell for Mary's beauty and her strength of personality. Although her condition was obvious she insisted she was innocent of man, and in Joseph she found someone able to believe her. He was an Essene scholar, an Ebionite, meaning that he was a member of the ascetic Qumran community on the Dead Sea. Outside the commune he worked as a carpenter as his humble duty to the poor, which was what brought them together, and he never doubted her word. Even if he had not loved Mary, theirs was almost an ideal match. Like him, she was of the royal line descended through Nathan from King David; a child of their own would be doubly David's son, doubly of the royal line from whom the Essenes believed their Messiah, the Christ, would be born. They were married under Essene rules, which command two ceremonies, at the second of which the woman is three months fallen, so they need make no secret of the illegitimate child.

' "Trouble came later," I overheard the Nazarene innkeeper winking to another traveller. He was pouring out his cheap home-town lees as though it was finest vintage wine, in the manner of innkeepers the world over. According to the innkeeper, Mary had other sons by Joseph, his second family. She'd probably thought he was past it. But being legitimate meant the youngsters took precedence over their elder half-brother in the view of the strict new High Priest in Jerusalem, Caiaphas. Joseph had died five or six years earlier, after being the David, the most senior of the royal line, for about a decade. Mary had had to choose between James, her eldest legitimate son, and her firstborn who called himself Joshua, or Jesus, which means Saviour. Some people said he was the Son of God, and the Angel Gabriel told Mary so, but according to the innkeeper that was just a mother speaking. I mean, she would say that, wouldn't she? Anyway, Caiaphas's ruling meant Jesus couldn't be Priest and Pope over the Essenes, or even be acknowledged as the David. Mary had to accept the reality of the situation. Her best hope of keeping the family influential was to stick with James, for him to be the David; she couldn't be seen with Jesus. But he wouldn't give up, wouldn't admit his illegitimacy mattered, so everyone was against him, they called him the Man of a Lie. "He's given us a bad reputation," the innkeeper complained, "and people say things like, can *any* good thing come out of Nazareth? It's bad for business, I can tell you. He's desperate for friends, even befriends Gentiles, they say, and he's trying to strike an alliance with that wild man, his cousin the Baptist – brilliant speaker, you should hear him, though he won't touch wine or women. But all John the Baptist whispers in his ear is, 'Are you the One?' And that," said the innkeeper, "is a rather dangerous question to answer."

'Later, from their talk, I learned Qumran is an easy day's walk from Jerusalem, lying east of Bethlehem. I followed a shady, winding path between brightly-coloured fields of fragrant Jerusalem Apple, a pilgrims' road bearing the tracks of many sandalled feet in its dust, but now empty of movement. According to legend this was the site of ancient Sodom. Then I came across a dead mule, still in harness but already buzzing with flies, and round the next corner found a man in a striped tunic sprawled face down in the middle of the road. He lay in the full heat of the sun, the back of his neck burnt raw even through his long red hair. His eyes fluttered when I lifted him. He was Celatus of Ancyra, a Galatian of the Celtic race like myself. He had travelled many days from his country, but anyone could see he was going no further. He begged me to drag him into the shade of an apple tree, which I did, and there he died. I closed his eyes and availed myself of his heavy gold coins carried in a secret pouch in the small of his back, and a hundred silver half-shekels carried openly, and went on my way.

'In the evening, climbing to the crumbling plateau above the Dead Sea, I was greeted like a brother by the crowd at the monastic camp outside Qumran's eastern gate, the broad area still called the potter's field, after the pottery kiln and workmen who used to live there. Unleavened bread and roasted mutton was pressed joyfully into my hands by the pilgrims, and I was welcomed as Beloved Celatus. All one hundred and fifty-three of us in the tents were Gentiles. We each paid one hundred half-shekels for our initiation. I went along willingly, it was no skin off my nose, and who can tell if someone is a believer or not, if he obeys the laws? At this Zealot outpost of Qumran you did not have to be a Jew to be baptised, an astonishing and unorthodox step, but inevitable. More numbers than the Jews could muster would be required to successfully rise up against Rome, overturn what they saw as pagan gods and achieve the religious freedom under Jewish Law symbolised by their seven-branched candlestick, the Menorah. They would need the help of converted Gentiles. It was whispered around the tent pegs that Yeshu ben-Pantera, the Jew, even helped and healed Romans. If so, he believed that not all who followed him need follow the Torah. He was going very, very far ahead of his friends.

'The money must have come in useful, of course. This busy, fortified centre of the Essene Law under their spiritual leader the Pope, Simon Magus the Samaritan, with his assistants Judas Iscariot, Thaddeus, Jacob, Matthew and Thomas, was expensive to run, though they were rich men. Judas was a tax collector while the followers of Simon, also known as the Zealot, believed he had magical powers, and their devotion had made him wealthy. But still, the rooms of scribes copying old scrolls and their assistants stretching new skins to work on had to be paid for, so Qumran turned to refining and distilling precious perfumes, for which it had become famous – apple balsam from the Jerusalem Apple, olibanum from frankincense trees, myrrh. Yet I found it a dry, dusty and unappealing place. It felt as though its stone walls were blowing away on the wind even as I watched. But the pilgrims looked at it through the eyes of faith and saw an entirely different view.

'We were woken in the darkest hour and taken down to the Dead Sea to embark on a boat. At a precise time, at a precise distance offshore, the Baptist and his workmen plunged us over the side. It was no easy ceremony, our eyes and lips burned from the salt, we could hardly be held beneath the water. We were fished to salvation at the feet of the priest called the Father, standing on the end of the low jetty as though on the surface of the water. By claiming this authority, in this the only place in Judea where he could hope for political support, Jesus had declared himself the Prince of the Congregation, the Christ. I recognised that shadowed yet open face, the way the beard was combed fastidiously round the small, sensitive mouth, the wide, knowing eyes. A new religion, the Christians, had been born.

'Anyway, it was *his* fight. In Judea there are many messiahs, a new one proclaims himself every day. It was nothing to do with me.

'Afterwards, quietly on the beach, he told us a story about a rich man who travels far away from his home, leaving his talents of silver in trust with his servants, an enormous fortune. Some used them well, made them grow, but others were too shy or frightened of the responsibility. I forget how the story ended, being up so early I must have fallen asleep, and when I woke I was alone.

'I slipped back to Jerusalem and spent my gold in ways you can imagine. For a wretched year I never knew where I'd wake or who I'd wake beside, their dirty flesh huddled against mine. I was as drunk all morning as the night before, and spent the afternoon on the lookout for opportunity, a penny or two to buy me oblivion again.

'Then by chance I saw him three times in little more than a week. By then there were crowds wherever he went, joyful shouts, mimes, the usual poor and sick trailing along behind that you find everywhere, desperate to believe in anything or anyone that might relieve their affliction. They wouldn't leave him alone, peeping over the wall even when he was at a Pharisee's house having a good meal, the lady of the house serving him herself and in a nervous state about whether the bread was as he liked it or if

211

there was enough wine. That was the day he raised Lazarus from the dead, but some scoffed that it was just a mime, and some said they didn't actually see it themselves, though later they claimed they did because it impressed people. I saw it but I didn't believe it. I thought it was a trick somehow. But some people did believe it was true, and it was said some cripples threw away their sticks and walked, such was their belief in him.

'Jesus had risen a long, long way in a very short while, and I think everyone knew it was too good to last. Something had to give. The common people loved him, calling out "*Maranatha, Maranatha!* Our Lord, come!" But mobs are fickle and he was attracting the attention of powerful, entrenched, established enemies who saw their power slipping away. The nationalists demanded a red-blooded messiah, not someone who worked through Gentiles and thought decades ahead, paid taxes to Caesar and renounced a kingdom in their lifetime, like our Yeshu. Yet the Romans feared a King of the Jews and the priesthood was terrified of the Romans' retribution. It would be worth sacrificing one Jew, the High Priest reasoned, for the sake of many Jews. The Baptist was dead by now, but many still whispered his question: "*Is he the One?*" It could not be answered by words, only by action. Our Yeshu went as far as he could; he said he could knock down the temple and rebuild it himself in three days, but he did not do it, and he said that the way of the future lay in simple faith, not money or armies, but that was no more than words either. Yet if Yeshu ben-Pantera drew a sword against the organised might of Rome, as it was feared he would sooner or later, the priests of the Sanhedrin knew the rebellion must fail, and a bloodbath ensue. There was only one solution, reasoned the High Priest: this upstart against organised religion must lose his followers while he was still vulnerable and die alone, discredited. Politically it was a simple calculation, though expensive. A traitor must be found or forced or tempted from among the Twelve Apostles, the inner circle. Everybody has a price – that's only human nature. In darkness, haste, rumour and confusion, the circle would unravel for long enough.

'For the Passover, Jerusalem swells to five times its normal population, pickpockets and garrotters aplenty, not a room to be had unless you're someone special, and plenty sleep in the gutter – the streets were soft with slumbering forms, believe me.

Outside, tents in every nook and cranny, and the owners of every little strip of dusty land, every inn and shed and stable, were coining money hand over fist. No place for me, and the religious police about. So I was beyond the Damascus Gate, and that's where I saw him, on Golgotha. Despite all these people swarming under shelter within a mile or two, the hilltop was almost deserted because of the storm – the priests had been lucky. The thunder kept the few who were on the hill quiet, standing about as if they'd been drowned, though it hadn't rained yet. The crew was experienced, they'd nailed his heels together and hammered him by his wrists to the crossbar in case his hands split and he dropped off. The others crucified suffered just like him, but noisier, screaming in whispers, begging for their legs to be broken to kill them. It was so dark with the storm clouds that they kept thinking it was night, and by Jewish Law they had to be taken down dead before dark. It must have seemed endless. I didn't risk going near him, in the middle, in case the soldiers took me for a follower, and everyone else felt the same. Even his mother didn't turn up till almost too late. He died after sucking from a sponge, and later some people said it was snake poison. But after he was no longer there, so to speak, the spectacle lost its interest and most of us drifted away, leaving the weather to the soldiers. I found a garden to sleep in.

'A few days later, however long it was, an innkeeper said he'd been seen again, but someone said it was a mistake for his half-brother James. No, the innkeeper insisted, the risen Christ had shown Himself to Peter – some thought it was Peter who'd given Him away because he'd looked guilty, others that it was Judas the *Sicari*, who was such a committed nationalist. They said Judas had been offered leadership of the Essenes, that "buying the potter's field", in other words being put in charge of the community, was the price of his betrayal.

'Then I heard He had appeared to the Twelve, and I didn't believe it even though I was drunk.

'You *can't* believe that sort of thing's true, you see, because rising from the dead turns everything upside down. Once you believe *that*, you have to swallow everything. But I don't think the Twelve believed what they were seeing either, at least not at the time. Thomas didn't.

'I didn't believe it myself, when I saw Him.

'There were at least five hundred of us moving along the road from Jerusalem, and we all saw Him at the same time. He was saying no more than any other traveller, and behaved no differently. I mean, you'd have to *know* that what you were seeing was extraordinary. The same thing I remember from Capernaum though: you didn't see Him first, He saw you. He didn't slow down, but I could have run to catch up. It was the road to Qumran, everyone returning to their homes after the Passover, the fragrance of Jerusalem Apple blowing all around us. And I said to myself over and over, snake poison, snake poison. It was the only thing I dared think. Anything but the alternative: that He was truly risen from the dead. One by one the travellers with me turned off to other villages, following other roads, and at eventide I arrived at Qumran alone.

'Nothing moved, only the wind, the dust blowing past me across the dusty buildings, my long shadow trailing over the precipice, and the Dead Sea so far below that it looked as black as a well, except that it was wrinkled where the wind touched it. I saw no one on the plateau, the gates were closed, the tents removed from the potter's field and only the tent posts left standing, like a naked forest. If He was inside, nothing showed. I unplugged my wineskin and sat on a wall as the stars came out, black and white.

'When I heard a gate banging I knew that Qumran, if it hadn't been empty before, was empty now. There wasn't a soul there to stop that banging, and it punctuated my stupor, so that I woke up when it stopped. The full moon, high and tiny, shone down but the wind had not died away, and a man walked by, dark as a shadow, the dust of his footsteps blowing over me – he didn't see me pressed against the wall.

'I watched him cross between the tent posts, looking up at them, stepping over their shadows like a superstitious man.

'I watched him throw a rope over a post as though pitching his tent, lifting his gown and standing with one foot on the wooden post cleat to reach the top, breathing between his teeth. He had long red hair. I didn't call out or help him, and as he stepped down I saw he was carrying something, a piece of baggage, not a tent. It was heavy, it took all his strength to heft it.

'Sitting, he tied it carefully to his legs to weight himself, then

214

climbed back onto the cleat, pulled the noose tight round his neck, and stepped off without a moment's hesitation.

'I'd never seen that before, a man choosing death without honour for himself, by a dirty rope, the loneliest and most pitiable death imaginable. He dropped a cubit or less, his toes touching the ground, and dust blew as he kicked. After a minute or two he was still kicking.

'I moved closer and I recognised him: the gaunt tax collector, the *sicari*, Judas Iscariot. He, the nationalist, was the traitor. The moon shone on the tears sliding down his cheekbones as he struggled, and the silver tied to his ankles jingled like a goatherd's bells with his kicking.

'The Temple had paid such a rich and committed man a mighty prize; but Iscariot had seen the risen Christ, and knew he had bargained away his soul.

'Coming forward, I wondered, staring up at him, if anything was going through his mind. Behind that blackening face, had he seen confrontation between Jesus and the priests as a way of provoking Jesus into asserting his leadership of the Jewish people? Only if he believed that Jesus was a man, capable of being manipulated. So he had doubted Jesus was in fact the Messiah.

'Judas had betrayed his Lord and everything he believed in – for what? You had only to look at his face to see he knew the truth.

'He hung without moving. I took my knife and slit the rope tying the leather bag to his legs. Still he didn't move, only his eyes. Inside the bag was a box, small but weighty, though not heavy enough to break a man's neck. I thought he groaned as I opened it, but the sound must have been the wind, considering the tightness of the rope round his neck.

'Inside I found thirty pieces of silver.

'Not *denarii* – pence – for our rich, doubting Judas. These were big coins, gorgeously worked. Made to fit the palm of your hand. Made for using. But to what use would you put them? Made you feel warm just to hold them. Worth having just for themselves, just to look at. I expect he thought so. I took mercy on him.

'The wind moaned again and I took my knife and plunged it in him to the knock, slit him from his breastbone to his crotch, stepping back so his guts and blood falling out didn't splash my clothes. I didn't want him coming after me, ever.

'On my knees I counted them again. Thirty. Blood money. That's a one-way transaction that can't be undone. They couldn't be given back any more than an hour can be relived a different way, or a life returned. What I held felt neither guilty nor sinful, quite clean of hatred, just innocent silver coins, their use a matter for the hand that held them.

'As I put them back into the cedarwood casket, before tying it under my cloak and heading west from Aceldama towards the Mediterranean, I examined them one by one. I don't think I ever looked at them so carefully again. I grew to accept them, but later I always looked into the eyes of the people seeing them for the first time, seeing myself there, remembering the rich man who travelled far from his home, leaving his talents behind him. An enormous fortune, beyond value, and yet meant to be used. I soon learned I did not have to pay for what the talents bought.

'Holding them up to the moon, I realised how beautifully made they were, and the subtlety in the design, the face of the present time on one side, the rule of Caesar, money. And on the reverse side, the future: the Menorah. Freedom.

'They're not coins, my children. They're promises.'

'Promises,' quavered the old man. His voice faded. He tried to point, but he had neither arm nor finger. Paul leaned close, holding his father gently, hearing the death rattle. 'Promises. . . .'

They all stared at one another.

'At last!' Diana broke the spell with a yawn, stretching her porcine white arms. 'I thought he would ramble on for ever,' she said with astonishing insensitivity. 'I'm sorry, Paul, but I thought he would.'

'I think he wanted to,' Imogen whispered.

Paul put his ear to the grey lips. 'He's gone,' he said.

The others rubbed the feeling back into their hands, their aching legs, after the long hours of their vigil. John Fox had spoken some parts of his story in almost a shout, at other times barely a whisper, or lain silent, marshalling what was left of his strength to carry on, and they were still not quite sure what they had heard, or what they believed.

'Is it dark outside?' Imogen went to the door, not noticing the two frightened faces of the youngsters, one taller than the other, hiding behind the angle of the thatch. The day was long gone.

Diana braided her hair quickly; she didn't want to look like a common woman, even for the short walk back to the house in the middle of the night. 'I just hope our stupid nurserymaid has had the sense to put the children to bed. She has to ask me every little thing. And she frightens Vitellus and Lucius by telling them silly stories about old-fashioned Celtic gods, and of course the poor little things don't know any better than to listen to her, and it gives them nightmares. Like your father – oh, Paul, you *don't*. Surely you don't believe a word he said! He was dying. He was dreaming.'

Paul closed his father's eyes. The shut lids stared up, Druidic, sky-blue, pagan. The painted body was clotted with blood, but the child's drawing of the outline of a fish was still visible, and the Greek symbols, *Cho-Rhi*.

'No, of course I don't. You're quite right.'

'I always am,' she said agreeably.

He glanced at her, thinking of what she wore round her neck beneath her gown. In some way the old man had implicated them in his story, and Paul wished with all his heart he'd never given Diana the silver bauble he had stolen. To her it was just an innocent piece of jewellery between her breasts where only he would see it, worn to please and tantalise him. But for Paul it was different. It obsessed him, it was his only unhappiness. Sometimes he dreaded making love with her because of what lay between them. He thought of it all the time he was in her, perhaps because she was only a pale shadow beneath him, more felt than seen, whereas the talent glittered in any available light and seemed more real than she was. Nothing touched Diana deeply, Paul concluded in sudden despair, not even him. He loved her and would do anything for her – and he had – but slowly he was realising that she had her house, her children, her own life, and nothing else mattered to her.

Yet he was happy. He was determined to be.

Diana moulded her arms round him and kissed his forehead, then patted his shoulder in her businesslike way. 'You're the paterfamilias now, Paul, the head of the family. It's best we think about all this tomorrow.' She meant not think at all. 'In the morning we'll wash him and lay him out properly.'

'Wash him,' Paul said, nauseated, looking at the mess of congealed blood in which the body lay. He put his hands to his head, close to exhaustion. 'What burial rites should we use? He said he was a . . .' He searched for the unfamiliar word.

'Christian.' Imogen came back from the door. 'A Christian, at the end.' Her sad voice covered the sound of a pair of footsteps running back to the new house; Vitellus and Lucius had long ago learned to run as one, so perfectly matched were they. 'Just do what you think is right, Paul.'

'He would have wanted to be buried by the holy well,' Paul said.

The next day, shifting the bed, Paul found the hole and the rope. Old Briginus had been hanging around in the hope that some small task would be found for him; he had worshipped John Fox, insisting he owed him everything, his whole life and his happiness. Paul swore the garrulous old man to secrecy and together they lowered the body into the hole, and dug a grave at the edge of the pool. Then Paul sent Briginus back up.

Search as he might, Paul could not find the box containing the talents. It was not where he had last seen it, between the rocks; it was gone as though it had never existed.

Paul was relieved. Perhaps Diana was right. Everything was for the best.

He climbed out and ordered the hole to be plugged with stout timbers. Then mortar mixed with pebbles and shards of broken tile was poured on top, several feet in depth. When it had set rock-hard, rubble and earth was poured in until the ground was level. No sign remained.

John Fox was dead and the talents gone with him.

The hut was knocked down and the villa enjoyed its proper view over the valley, the busy river, and London rebuilding. Soon the villa was extended with stables and a barn, Paul's plans for a colonnade and a central garden came to fruition, a daughter was born, and their lives continued on an upward spiral of achievement. Everything bad that had happened seemed such a very long time ago. With his father's days almost forgotten, Diana even felt safe to return to her old refrain in bed whenever Paul's optimistic brightness, which was what she liked most about him, inexplicably gave way to his depth of silence and brooding.

'You don't think he was really telling the truth?' she'd chuckle, circling her fingertip on his chest, irritating him to draw him out.

'Oh, Paul, you *can't*.'

'I believe that my father believed he saw what he saw,' Paul admitted.

'But you don't believe it,' she persisted.

Paul stared into the dark.

'No,' he said.

III

Vitellus and Lucius

John Fox's Family Tree continued
Summer 75 – Midsummer Day 138

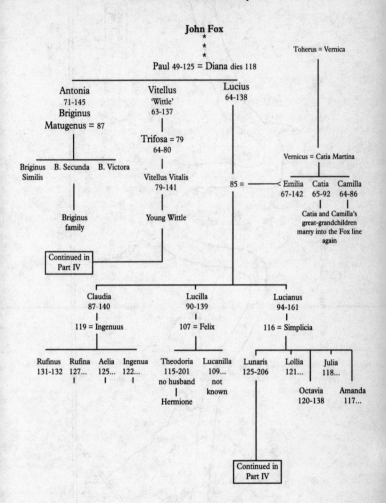

John Fox
★
★
★

Paul 49-125 = Diana dies 118

Toherus = Vernica

Antonia
71-145
Briginus
Matugenus = 87

Vitellus
'Wittle'
63-137

Lucius
64-138

Trifosa = 79
64-80

Vernicus = Catia Martina

Briginus   B. Secunda   B. Victora
Similis

Vitellus Vitalis
79-141

85 = < Emilia   Catia   Camilla
        67-142   65-92   64-86

Briginus
family

Young Wittle

Catia and Camilla's
great-grandchildren
marry into the Fox line
again

Continued in
Part IV

Claudia
87-140

Lucilla
90-139

Lucianus
94-161

119 = Ingenuus

107 = Felix

116 = Simplicia

Rufinus   Rufina   Aelia   Ingenua
131-132   127...   125...   122...

Theodoria   Lucanilla
115-201   109...
no husband   not
             known

Lunaris   Lollia   Julia
125-206   121...   118...

Octavia   Amanda
120-138   117...

Hermione

Continued in
Part IV

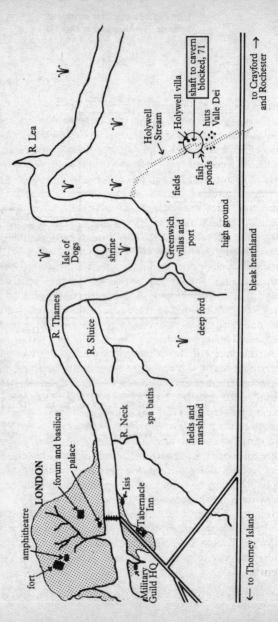

London and Valle Dei, 122

LONDON

amphitheatre
forum and basilica
palace
fort
Isis
Tabernacle
Inn
Military
Guild HQ

R. Thames
R. Sluice
R. Neck
spa baths

Isle of Dogs
shrine

Greenwich
villas and
port

deep ford

fields and
marshland

R. Lea

Holywell
Stream

Holywell villa

shaft to cavern
blocked, 71

huts
Valle Dei

fish
ponds

fields

high ground

bleak heathland

to Crayford
and Rochester

to Thorney Island

But of course there was a difference between the inseparable brothers, Vitellus and Lucius. It ran deeper than the angry Pomponius-blue eyes and high-blooded face of the older boy, Vitellus, whose hair was so dark it was almost black. With the first hints of his beard, rigorously plucked, and his muscular stance, the village girls soon noticed him and put a swing in their walk – though he was not quite old enough to notice them openly. There was something attractively rough about Vitellus, alluring; some of the cliques of older women sniggered that the fall of Diana had come before the fall of London. Stand Lucius beside Vitellus and you would hardly know they were brothers. Lucius was not only smaller but slighter, pure Paul, and Imogen longed to fuss over him. Lucius's thoughtful brown eyes were large and gentle beneath an unruly mop of red hair, through which he habitually ran his fingers, making it even worse, spikes and curls everywhere. The mannerism was so like John Fox's it gave Imogen a jolt to see it repeated in her grandson.

At the moment the boys were trying to get away from their determined little sister who pestered them back and forth in the entrance hall, her demanding cries echoing on the new picture-mosaic floor (ordered by pattern book from a firm in London). Vitellus was red-faced, trying to learn his Greek which he should have been studying last night, while Lucius, well-versed, was droll and quick to correct Vitellus's declensions. Slowly Vitellus grew more infuriated, smacking at Antonia, who just wanted his attention, yelling along the corridor for her nurserymaid, who was probably trying to catch up on her chores and had grown cloth ears where her charge was concerned.

Imogen, on her knees in the villa's central garden, busy with the herbs she was planting while the morning air was still pleasantly chill, looked through at the children fondly. For all their faults and strong points they were part of her, and she felt for them all.

225

They were part of John Fox, too; he lived on in them, and would continue to live on in their children – and probably also in the various little bastards Vitellus would no doubt soon start fathering in the village. Vitellus was Diana's favourite, a down-to-earth son for a practical mother, they understood one another perfectly. Lucius was Paul's boy, slim and mild but with deep reserves of determination. Like his father, once he started something he didn't give up. And what he started himself, Lucius finished himself, whereas Vitellus usually stormed off impatiently, his temper as short as his patience. Even their Greek pedagogue Soter walked softly with Vitellus.

In little more than a year Vitellus would be fourteen. At that age he would officially become a man. By Roman law the boys' inheritance, when the time came, would be shared equally between them, and their sister would have a sum set aside for her dowry if she had not married by then. But equal division could cause endless trouble and argument, with houses split in half, estates broken up and subdivided. Not everything Roman was better, Imogen had to admit now she was no longer so young herself. The broad-backed, dark mass of British people had their own ingrained traditions and rights which conquerors could not easily overturn. Women still ruled the home and had much more authority indoors than Roman wives. In the village, British women conducted business and owned property just as they always had, quietly shaking their unwashed hair at even the idea of paterfamilias and the Roman custom whereby mothers, sisters, nieces were packed off dutifully to live in separate households.

Vitellus would inherit the villa. The living quarters around the central garden weren't as big as they looked, being only one side of the hollow square and half of another; the rest was the cheese dairy and milking parlour for goats and sheep, stables, small barns and servants' dormitory, all given the same appearance as the living quarters, with fake windows and the same decorative tile courses, the outside rendering painted with white lead. He would inherit the field barns and byres and the cottages, together with everything and everyone in them. The good-will of most of the villagers as his clients would be his, and much of the responsibility for them. He would inherit the working capital, the neatly worked fields, the hoes and ploughs, the slaves and their children. His word would be law, with power over life and death. He would inherit the investment in the land which was being so busily cleared up and down the valley, the thud of axes always to be heard, the creak of timber, the shouts and whips of the ox drovers whose teams strained to drag the massive stumps from the ground. Half the remaining estate profits of these good, peaceful times, after costs and Antonia's dowry, would be Vitellus's; the other half of the cash would go to Lucius, and he would come into the small estate at Vagniacae that Paul had bought. It lay next to the much larger, richer property of the widower Vagnius Vagionius, whose single daughter Campana was the same age as Lucius and would make the perfect wife. It was all arranged. Lucius did not know of it, but Vitellus did; he was a boy given to friends who came and went, whereas Lucius kept to himself.

Imogen waved to Paul as he returned from his morning ride. She dusted her knees and went to greet him – Diana was still in bed. It was no secret that Diana wished her mother-in-law would find a new husband, meaning another house to move to, leaving Paul to herself. The time when the two women needed one another to get their way was long past. Imogen's ambition was satisfied and Diana could make Paul do whatever she wanted – as long as he was kept happy, and the bedroom usually provided the means. But for all Paul's outward cheerfulness, Imogen sensed a darkness beneath, something of John Fox held inside himself. Fourteen years had passed since he had been almost killed by the boar. He had never told her what he had felt that day, but she was sure it still lived inside him.

She had her own inner devils which occasionally rose up to haunt her. Last night she had dreamt what her conscious mind always denied, that she had seduced her father, his willing accomplice to conceive a child, not the victim. She had jerked awake, her hands clamped to her cheeks, and her face haggard, drained of blood.

She pushed the memory away with a shudder and entered the hall. The steward, Eutuches, obsequious with his shiny bald head and tightly closed lips, took Paul's dew-speckled boots and slipped the soft house shoes over his master's feet. Paul crossed the hall and embraced his mother.

'You smell of horse,' she said fondly.

227

'And you, Mother, smell of herbs and the earth.'

'I've been planting.'

Paul cupped a hand to his ear as Vitellus shouted angrily at Antonia, pulling his knee away from her clutching hand, his slate spinning from his fist to the floor and shattering. 'Now look what you've made me do, you miserable sheep-tick!'

'I'm not! I'm not!' shrieked four-year-old Antonia, her tunic pulled half up her back, purple-faced, her fists clenched.

'She didn't mean it,' Lucius grinned at his brother. 'It was your fault anyway.'

'Wasn't!' Vitellus snorted, then roared for the steward to get himself together and clear this mess up. Antonia ran to Imogen, burying her face in her gown, starting the grizzling cry for attention that she would keep up for hours, with the occasional whooping breath for air.

'I can't hear myself think!' Paul laughed, abandoning the situation, heading towards his study. 'I'm sure you boys are to blame, there's always trouble wherever you are.'

'It was her,' Vitellus sulked.

'Go on, go,' chuckled Paul, flapping his hand behind him as he went to his study door. 'Go and find that tutor of yours, and be quiet!'

Alone of the interior rooms of the house, his study was set apart by a heavy double door in oak, stained almost black and studded with bolts and knuckles of bronze to look even more imposing. Clients coming to request favours and keep him abreast, one way or another, of the latest gossip and rumour and the cycle of births, marriages and deaths in the village would await their turn outside the oak door suitably impressed. The anteroom was painted with wall frescoes to make it look larger, though the finest work was reserved for the study itself, in the Fourth Style, the latest fashion. Facing the desk was a perspective view of rooftops and trees receding into a distance so real that it looked like a plan for a town that might one day stand here. If it ever actually came to fruition it would make everyone in the area a rich man, and every last one of them was Paul's client.

The fresco was a statement of ambition. But it was not Paul's, he had not thought to order the work himself; Diana had commissioned it immediately after John Fox's death from a travelling company of continental painters. Paul himself stood in one doorway of the painting, Diana another, Vitellus and Lucius below them, and Antonia, not born at the time, had been added later right at the bottom, just above the row of winged Psyches, by a local hand, rather sketchily.

Paul's desk was also a gift from Diana – a gift for which, as always, he paid the bill. Constructed of citrus wood from India, it was so hard that it could only be worked on with steel tools. It had been shipped in one piece by special order from Spain, landed on the beach at Greenwich, and carted uphill by a team of eight oxen pulling in tandem. Lucius had said one elephant would have completed the task more suitably – his gentle way of saying the desk was as large and unwieldy as an elephant. Which it was, Paul admitted. But it was undeniably impressive.

He could hear the murmur of voices and knew that as soon as he signalled with a single clap of his hands his steward would show the first client in. With a hooked rod Paul opened the glass window set high in one wall, not to admit more light but for ventilation, as some of the freedmen farmers brought a powerful smell of the barnyard with them. Then from the water jar he lifted the perfect, hemispherical drinking glass, its curved base making it impossible to put down and thus allow the drink to go stale. He poured a sip of water which he rolled contentedly round his mouth, then inverted the glass and dropped it back over the long neck of the jar. At least the boys were quiet now; Imogen would have packed Antonia off to the nursery at the back of the house, where she could grizzle for attention, as she had since she was a baby, without the family having to listen. Diana had been so upset by the constant crying that she could not feed her from the breast, and the wet nurse had ended up in tears, sure her milk, too, was not satisfying. Both the women, rejected, were hostile to the child, but Paul had laughed, confident Antonia would grow out of it.

'Peace and quiet,' Paul sighed, then clapped his hands, and the door creaked open to admit the first client of the day.

Soter was not in his room. 'We can't find him, can we,' Vitellus announced, 'so all we have to do is keep our heads down somewhere nice and quiet.'

'That's not what Father meant,' Lucius said.

'You heard what he said.'

'Yes, but he *meant*—'

Vitellus padded along the corridor and Lucius sighed, then dropped the scroll he had been learning and followed his brother outside, running to catch up. The two boys slipped round the back of the house, past the men working on the new barn who called out cheerfully, 'Where you off to today, then? And Lucius too? Somewhere we don't know about then!'

There was a cackle of laughter. 'It's that Timotheus.' Lucius gritted his teeth.

'I wouldn't let them make my life a misery,' Vitellus said.

'Shame on you, young Master Vitellus,' called big, blunt Timotheus, 'leading our little friend Lucius astray. He has his studying to do!'

'Why aren't they more respectful?' Lucius said.

'I wouldn't be,' Vitellus said. 'And neither would you if you worked with the sun burning the top of your head all day.' He played truant so often he had almost beaten a path leading to the edge of the slope. He ducked from sight, then cut back because Lucius had gone a slightly different way, ever cautious, and chosen a place near the shelter of bright yellow gorse and brambles. It took Vitellus a moment to work out why.

'You're not frightened of being caught, are you?' he jeered, never admitting Soter's beatings hurt him. Lucius hated being hurt; he was sure he felt pain much more deeply than Vitellus – not the pain of the rod, the humiliation of it. By himself there was almost nothing he would not do to avoid being in the wrong, always sure he would be apprehended. With Vitellus, by a strange contradiction typical of life's irony, he told himself, he felt safe; Vitellus was rarely caught.

'No, I'm not frightened,' Lucius lied.

'One day,' Vitellus swore, 'I'm going to have children, and I'm going to do the catching.'

'Only if they're like you.'

'I know every hiding place there is to know round here,' Vitellus bragged. 'They won't be able to fool their *pata*. I'll teach them!'

'Then they *will* be just like you,' Lucius said.

'That's the idea! I think Father's soft, don't you? *Mata*'s the one with all the push, she doesn't love him, she just works through him, that's all.'

Lucius was shaken to hear the love of his parents, which he had always believed in, so matter-of-factly challenged. 'But it's a love match.'

'Of course it is,' Vitellus said sarcastically, 'on one side, anyway. That's how she's made it work.'

'But Father went to London—'

'Yes, that old story. What about her? No one asked her what *she* wanted. She just had to make the best of it. And she has! Whose idea do you think the barn was? Not his.'

'I don't know how you can say such things,' Lucius murmured weakly. He had always had a child's faith that he, and Vitellus, had been born not only because the gods willed it, but because their parents loved one another. 'Vitellus, surely you can't really think—'

'I know what's what,' Vitellus said bleakly. 'Don't bother your pretty head about it.' He banged his hand on the ground in the way he had, and the subject was closed.

After a moment Lucius yawned amiably, lying back on the soft grass of the slope, bracing his hands behind his head. He would pick over what had been said all night, but it was too fine a day to argue. The early morning mist over the river had evaporated and through half-closed eyes he saw that he was holding London between his knees, and swung them lazily from side to side, amusing himself. The day was so clear that he could make out the new forum and basilica even at this distance, the yellow squares of the parade grounds, the sandy oval of the circus seeming smaller than his fingernail. After a slow start but now reaching fever pitch, all traces of the fire were being buried beneath new buildings, an expanding grid of streets and rubbish tips; even fresh soil was carted in and spread over the burnt clay to erase any memory that might harm business confidence. A small, business-like palace, the fountains in its courtyard fed by piped water from the Corn Hill, had been built near the Walbrook for the governor and his staff, constructed like the law courts and town hall to be easily extended as the town's status grew to match its prosperity as a trading port. Hundreds of boats dotted the channel near the bridge and along the wharfs, even up the Fleet River, and every inlet was hung with a dark haze of fishermen's nets.

Lucius jumped as a cow and her calf moved in front of him, grazing, and he made a soft lowing noise. She looked at him curiously, her wet muzzle already bothered by flies, poor beast, then she lumbered away as Vitellus flicked a pebble.

'Anyway, nothing will happen for ages,' Vitellus grumbled, chucking stones at the bushes, 'because Father had us children when he was so young. I don't think it's right having sons then holding them back for *ages* while you get old. By the time this is mine I'll be too old to enjoy it.' His eyes widened and he pointed. 'Lucius, look!' The sun flashed on something below the bushes, something washed clean by last week's heavy rain.

'It's probably nothing,' Lucius said.

Vitellus held him back then scrambled down, dropping from sight, and Lucius realised that a deep gully ran beneath the undergrowth. 'I never realised this was here,' he marvelled, probing with his foot to find the way down that Vitellus had used so easily.

Vitellus reappeared below, his eyes very blue in the shadows. He put his hands on his hips, squinting up at his clever brother outlined against the sun. 'Now you know why I never got caught, you dunce!' he called. He knelt and plucked the silver circle from the mud, then shrugged. 'It's only one of those things Grandfather spoke about. So that's where he was trying to point! He was trying to tell us, daft old sod.'

'A silver talent!' Lucius exclaimed, then added soberly, 'He wasn't trying to tell *us*.'

'None of the grown-ups believed him. They wouldn't, they're so fixed in their ideas. Anyway, he's dead now, what does it matter?' Vitellus squeezed the talent in his hand. 'This changes everything. Buried treasure! The thirty pieces of silver he talked about.'

'Yes, when he was dying,' Lucius said uneasily. 'I don't like it, Vitellus.'

Vitellus cupped his hand to his ear. 'What did you say?'

Lucius decided. 'I said put it back.'

For a moment there was silence, then Vitellus flung the coin down. 'You're as stupid as the rest of them!' he shouted, enraged, his voice so loud that Lucius looked round nervously, sure they would be heard. 'Go to the barn and bring back one of the workmen's shovels, you woman,' Vitellus ordered, kicking the ground. 'There's more to be dug out here.'

'But what shall I tell them?' quavered Lucius.

'Heard any hammers lately? They're eating their bread and beer, idiot! And hurry up about it.'

Paul shielded his eyes from the sun as he came out onto the portico steps, yawning. Sitting upright on a backless stool always set his spine and made him weary. The slave workmen were resting in the shadow of the barn's end wall which had been bricked in; the timber skeleton of the side walls and roof was silhouetted against the sky. The barn would hold enough animal fodder to see the estate through the winter without an October killing and the boredom of smoked or salted meat for months on end. It had been Diana's idea, and sometimes Paul got down on his knees and blessed his luck in loving such a woman. And he did love her, desperately; needed her for everything. As a mark of his esteem he'd had a mushroom cellar dug for her, but Diana had recoiled appalled. Only then had he realised that she hadn't eaten a single mushroom, of the white-domed boletus variety or any other, since her experience in London. And she had never gone back to the town, though sometimes Paul's business took him there.

Through the half-finished barn slats, the ocean was visible like the blade of a turquoise knife pointing towards him out of the far distance, jewelled with the estuary islands and sandbanks. Such clarity in the air, with a cool breeze despite the heat of the sun, meant a change in the weather.

Into his view over the edge of the slope climbed the figure of a boy. Paul watched, frowning, then instinctively moved behind a pillar as the boy ran crouching towards the barn. Up to something! He was surprised to see it was Lucius – Lucius, who should be indoors studying under Soter. Paul's lips tightened, seeing the hand of Vitellus in this. Lucius was by nature obedient and too sensitive for troublemaking, and Paul almost called out, hating to see his younger son's innocence abused. Whatever they were up to, he would have to beat Lucius too, for the sake of fairness. Vitellus, with his fists clenched and head lowered, would show no sign of being redeemed by his punishment, and certainly would not be reformed. But poor Lucius would cringe like a dog under every stroke.

Paul shivered to think of his children growing up, feeling his own life shrinking in proportion. At their age he had been sheltered from everything by Imogen, his father's baleful influence kept at a distance. Paul had sworn never to allow the same gulf to emerge between himself and his sons, determined that his family should be as normal and happy as they were portrayed in the fresco: strong father, dutiful mother, respectful children.

Lucius crept up to the barn, snatched something that the workmen had left lying about, then showed a surprising turn of speed, flying back the way he had come on his slim legs, tunic flapping silently, dropping from sight over the edge of the knoll. Paul walked slowly towards the place. 'Where are you off to?' called Diana, coming after him down the steps. 'Where's Vitellus?' Paul shrugged irritably and walked a little faster.

From ahead of him came a muffled half-scream, half-shout: Lucius's unbroken voice, he was sure of it, raised in the most terrible cry and silenced in a moment.

Paul ran, knowing he was going to find something dreadful. Though he was in no danger himself, his bowels loosened and his cheeks flushed scarlet, ashamed.

He stopped, panting, on the edge of the knoll.

There was no one on the slope; he saw clear down to the men working in the fields below. The only place to hide was a stretch of wild growth.

He looked back. Diana was running after him, her pace restrained by the Gallic gown she wore, demurely tight round the ankles. He waved her back.

Paul ran across the angle of the slope.

He knew the gully, of course, he'd played here as a boy, but it had worn deeper than he remembered, and he stared down through a tangle of bright yellow gorse and brambles that had grown up since the trees were felled. As for the tableau that revealed itself down there as his eyes adjusted to the shadow, it required no explanation.

The two brothers had argued. Lucius lay dead or dying, his face and mouth pouring blood, his arms thrown above his head as though to ward off a blow. Vitellus stood over him holding a spade in his clenched fists, knuckles white, motionless.

By them on its side lay the cedarwood casket, broken open. One child standing, one lying, around them a mess of gleaming coins.

'Oh, my God,' Paul said.

Vitellus looked up at his father.

'It wasn't my fault,' he said, which was what he always said. Then he looked down at what he was holding in his hands as though seeing it for the first time. He dropped the spade, revealing the coin he still held.

Paul remembered the old man's dying words. *They're not coins. They're promises. Promises.*

Vitellus's eyes returned to his father above him. 'I didn't do it,' he whispered up the slope. 'I didn't.'

Paul said nothing. He could hear his blood whistling in his ears, his breath panting in his lungs. He jumped down, dislodging clods of earth.

'Is he dead?' Vitellus asked, backing away, wiping the dirt from his hands onto his tunic. He pulled backwards through the brambles, the stems clutching at him, as taut as ropes. 'Father. Please. You're frightening me.'

Paul picked up the spade.

'He couldn't find the way down,' Vitellus pleaded. 'I'm telling you the truth for once. I said, throw the spade down to me, please.' He struggled. 'All right, I shouted at him. Chuck it down, you woman! If you haven't got the guts to jump, chuck it down! So he chucked it and I started digging. He just waited on the edge. And then he took a deep breath and he jumped it all at once, like a fool, and down he came arse over head, and he screamed! Father, I never touched him, I never.'

Paul swung the spade. It made a whooshing noise.

'Father, *don't!*' Vitellus shouted. He could retreat no further. The flat of the blade caught him between the eyes, and for an instant a dent was shoved deep into his forehead, which instantly swelled and softened to a watery bruise, deep purple-red. Vitellus stared, not seeming to know where he had been hit. He laughed, then put his hands slowly to his head and leaned against a rose bush as though he could not feel the thorns, falling through it, stumbling away.

'You killed my son!' Paul yelled. He dropped the spade. 'Go!' he screamed after Vitellus crashing through the bushes. 'Get out! Get out! Get away from me!' Paul wept openly, beating at his head with his fists. 'You're not my son! Oh, my God!'

Diana slid clumsily into the gully. Without a word, she dropped to her knees and cradled Lucius in her arms, holding his lolling head to her breast as though to succour him with her milk. Her hair had caught on a branch of gorse and sat crookedly on the side of her head – a wig. Paul had never realised. She looked ridiculous yet implacable. He slumped to his knees beside her, both parents wailing their grief. Lucius's mouth still poured blood.

Paul stared. 'He's bleeding,' he said.

'He's not dead?' Diana gathered the boy more closely to her. 'He's not dead!' She turned his head so that he should not choke on his own gore, careless of the blood staining her clothes. 'He's alive! He's bitten his tongue – it's half severed, hanging off.' She thrust her fingers in his mouth, holding the tongue in place. 'Quickly!' she snarled at the heads of the slaves peering over the edge of the gully. 'Do something useful. You, you, you, get down here – make them, Paul! Carry him to the house at once.'

'Do as she says,' Paul said, his face ghastly. 'Send someone to fetch Cymbarrus, to meet us there.'

'Don't,' snapped Diana. 'His fingers are like tree trunks.' She held up her own bloodied hand. 'It's woman's work. I'll need my needles. And catgut from the kitchen.'

Lucius was lifted onto the shoulders of the slaves, who grumbled as usual, and Paul wanted to shriek at them but he held it all inside himself. Diana clambered up beside them without a shred of dignity, holding Lucius's head to one side against her, her hand still in his mouth to slow the bleeding as much as possible and stop the tongue sliding down his throat. There was little Paul could do to help; he was useless.

He stood alone in the mud, which gleamed with silver coins around him. He kicked out at them, shouting.

He leant against a trunk, panting. His mother had been wrong. Good and evil did exist in the world. There *was* something to be frightened of, very frightened. It was yourself.

Imogen spoke softly, peering over the edge of the gully. 'Paul, where is Vitellus?'

Vitellus skidded, and fell. Even lying motionless, hanging onto the grass with his hands, he felt as though he was falling, the ground giving way below his back, the sky rising higher above him. His head whirled and the sun moved perceptibly down the sky. He had never been so cold, and then so hot, the sweat streaming down his brow. He reached up to wipe it away, and put his hand inside his head.

That was what it felt like. He could feel the bones in his forehead move, and in one place his flesh was soft as pulp. There was little pain, only the falling. He looked in confusion at the coin he was still holding in his palm, then lay back with it pressed lightly against his wound, cool and metallic.

Someone was shouting.

Vitellus sat up. His face and chest were slick with vomit, straw-coloured fluid dripped from his nostrils onto his legs. My father's voice, he thought slowly.

Vitellus had never feared his father, but he had seen himself in his grandfather, John Fox, that indomitable, haggard figure sitting outside the door to the crumbling hut, only streaks of red fire left in his beard, his hair a white shock of age, and something dreadful lurking behind his eyes. Nothing that one wouldn't do to get what he wanted. He'd gone soft at the end, lost his edge when he started doubting himself. Take fifty years off him, though, and there was a man, a real man.

Vitellus slithered to the shelter of a tree as the call came again, high as a woman's with emotion. And again. Again. Each time Vitellus's lips dragged themselves thinner with contempt. You won't catch me twice, Father he thought. His thoughts echoed sluggishly, each word forming itself one at a time, but his actions were instantaneous.

He'll expect me to go downhill, Vitellus thought, already cutting uphill. He'll expect me to go downhill because it's easier. Because I'm hurt. So I will go uphill.

Am I hurt? he wondered. I don't know what I feel. I don't think I feel much. My father struck me down. I don't want the spade again.

He saw the spade swinging, the iron blade glinting, and cringed, but it was only in his head. He was kneeling by the stump of a felled oak, too massive to be pulled, split with axes and left to rot. He could just see the tiled roof of the villa, and when he lifted his head he glimpsed people milling in the portico, wringing their hands. What a show! The master's two boys dead in one day!

And there was his father, wearing blue woollen britches now beneath his tunic because it was cold with evening, and someone trying to make him wear a cloak round his shoulders. 'Vitellus, Vitellus!' his father called.

No, you won't catch me, thought Vitellus with his cunning smile, dropping back, then slipping along the enormous curve of rotten, splitting stumps that lay round the side of the knoll, the valley rising to meet him. He cut uphill of the village huts, staggering and stumbling now, falling, and a blinding headache lanced through his skull, blossoming like a slow inexorable flame. He put his fist in his mouth to contain his agony but felt as though he would burst. His body twitched, then he fell to the mossy ground and lay writhing.

He woke to the sound of water running into a pool, a hateful tinkling that jarred every sense. A terrible face was staring into his own, one of the ancient gods, carved in a standing stone, reflected in the water. Vitellus had only noticed a pattern in the stone before, but now he saw it for what it was. He drank with the face flickering around him in the water's surface, as the long-dead priests must have intended.

His breathing stopped as he heard his father's voice calling.

But the shouts came from far away downhill. Downhill!

You can search your heart out downhill, thought Vitellus. The stone infuriated him and he placed his hands against it, pushing. When it would not budge he turned his back and braced himself, heaving backwards with all the strength in his legs. The bank crumbled, slowly giving way, water flowing over his feet. Then the stone toppled into the water with such force that Vitellus almost followed it. He stared at the rising bubbles, the ripples dying to leave a flat calm mirror surface, and felt glorious.

His father's calls were closer.

He cringed, hearing the spade swinging.

Vitellus struggled uphill until he came to the road. The excitement, though he craved it, had left him feeling drained. He was so tired he just wanted to lie down and sleep. His only fear was that his headache would come back, because he knew he couldn't bear that agony.

'Whoa!'

Vitellus stared in confusion. He was standing in front of a mule cart. A small, leathery, terrified face peered at him between the mule's long ears – it belonged to the driver of the cart, who had fallen forward off his seat. He was an old man, dressed in rags and offcuts of discarded wild animal skins, badger, red squirrel, any old bits and pieces. He sniffed loudly, then pulled himself back onto the seat with all his dignity. 'Whoa!' he shouted again, as though he was in command of the mule rather than it in command of him. Driving towards the setting sun with his eyes closed against the glare, he must have been sound asleep until the stop woke him. Vitellus understood all this at once, before the words even had a chance to form their clumsy glowing trails across his mind's eye, and swung himself aboard without hesitation.

Not waiting for a flick of the whip, the mule plodded along the road. The cart creaked and jarred, the skins in the back flopping and shifting as though they were still alive.

The old man sucked his lips. 'Used to carry oysters! Big barrel, seawater, kept 'em breathing! Crayford Hill, bang, lost the lot off the back into the dust, couldn't waste 'em, ate 'em sitting on the road, took all night! Never touched one since, would you?' He didn't listen for a reply. 'Trade goes by river now.' He turned angrily. 'Don't say much, do you!' he shouted. He was as deaf as a post.

Vitellus nodded, barely conscious.

'On the run again?' the carter shouted, waking him.

Vitellus answered automatically; if he tried to think, nothing seemed to come. 'Yes,' he said.

'What?'

Vitellus put his mouth to the driver's ear. 'Are you deaf or just stupid?'

'What Can't see your lips. Daft as an eft, you are! What's your name?'

Vitellus sobered. He couldn't think of a lie. 'Vitellus.'

'What's that? Wittle?'

'Yes, I'm Wittle.'

'Greek, is that? Yes, I bet! Give me your arm, young Wittle.' He seized the boy's wrist but the flesh showed no slave's tattoo, then he drew in a breath as he spied the silver coin. 'A light-fingered boy!' he said in relief, as a precaution tugging his paltry money pouch round to the side of his belt furthest from his passenger. 'A light-fingered boy is never out of a job! Nor is someone what knows what to make of him, neither. The gods preserve me, I know just the place for you, young Wittle!'

He settled down cheerfully as the lamps of London appeared in the dusk below them, licking his lips in anticipation of the beer that would be his reward. Vitellus slept, and the mule picked up speed downhill.

'He's dead,' Diana said to Paul in the blunt, dreary voice that had settled on her since Vitellus was lost. 'He must be dead, and you killed him. I should do to you what you did to him.'

'I wish I was dead,' Paul said bitterly.

'I wish you were too,' Diana said in that tired, griefless tone of hers. How she must hate him! There was nothing he could say, or do. He had not touched her since that day.

They had never found the slightest sign of Vitellus. He had stumbled out of their lives, wandering in a delirium perhaps all night before expiring in a ditch or channel in the marshes somewhere, never to be found. His flesh had no doubt been eaten by the birds, the bones pulled apart by small toothy scavengers, the fragments licked clean to be buried by the seasons.

There was not a day they did not think of him.

Lucius, recovering in his room but still not able to speak past his stitched, swollen tongue, knew that something in his father really had died. And he knew it was his fault. If only he had not tried to prove himself as good as his brother, if only he had not jumped, showing off – look at me, I'm as good as you! But Vitellus had not even looked up from his greedy work with the spade. Since his death, Vitellus had become a sort of demi-god in his parents' imaginations, staunch, sturdy, the special child, yet it was meek, mumbling Lucius who would one day inherit the villa and farm. Lucius, the second son, would be the wealthy man.

Paul never stopped searching for Vitellus. Not a morning or an afternoon passed when he did not look for his son on the long lonely walks he took. He never asked Lucius along. He searched downhill as far as the river, asked questions at the fishing villages and at the huts by every inlet, and was told the river did not give up its dead. He searched as far as the road. He searched among the trees. He turned over the green ferns, plunged his stick into the thickets of bramble and wild flowers, quartered the fields with their concealing crops, and called his son's name until his voice was a harsh, tormented whisper. He offered a reward, though Diana warned him he would be pestered with false reports, as indeed he was. Even years later down-and-outs would turn up from time to time bending and bowing at the villa steps, claiming to have seen the boy, though he must long ago have become a man, had he lived. And always Paul lived in hope, these ghastly visits keeping his grief alive and his wound open. Once when he was riding home from Vagniacae and a woman pressed a small piece of bone into his hand, the tears rushed to his eyes, he so badly wanted to believe that the mystery was solved at last. But Diana identified it at a glance – it was only a sheep's vertebra.

At first no one except Diana blamed Paul for what had happened, but because he so obviously blamed himself other people began to come round to the same idea. If that one feels he's guilty, said the knowing glances following Paul riding through the village, then he must be guilty. That wasn't the same as being wrong. But it was Paul's bad fortune that worried them most. When the harvest failed in heavy rains, they began to worry that the gods had deserted him, and thus them. The woodland drinking pool, which had been running over in a gentle way since the standing stone toppled during the night of Vitellus's disappearance, over-flowed in earnest during the storms of the equinox, sending a stream cascading through the village and flooding some huts, sweeping out possessions, drowning a baby. The keeper of the village gods, who was Cymbarrus, made a sacrifice, and there was not a woman who did not give her household shrine a good dusting, fresh flowers and a special offering of food. But still the stream flowed, and the conclusion was obvious. Paul had indeed been deserted by the gods.

Travel-weary strangers in foreign garb were seen visiting the villa; any bearded easterner on his way to London knew hospitality awaited him at Valle Dei. The women, always the best conduit for rumour, whispered that Paul worshipped a single god, an exclusive God who denied all the others. So, they whispered, he had brought his trouble on himself. A Greek slave emptying a pot had seen Paul on his knees to a special curtained shrine in his

241

bedroom, where in an alcove the sign of a fish was drawn as simply as though by a child in the plaster. But all the men in the village were Paul's clients, they clamped down, and no one dared say anything against him openly. When a grain store was undermined and collapsed, everyone knew why, and Diana, aware of the village gossip even though her husband was not, prodded Paul the Christian into making good the loss. Paul's still a good patron, the men muttered among themselves, only made mad by his grief, and he'll pull himself round.

The new stream established a channel for itself, and did not dry up even when the rain stopped. Its course cut almost exactly through the heart of the village, which was very convenient, for no one had to walk far with a bucket any more – they wondered why they hadn't thought of digging a trench from the pool before. But still, it was a bad omen in the way it had happened, and the older women insisted on fetching their water from uphill at the pool as they always had.

Brown and soiled at first, the stream sent out scummy feelers downhill as though testing the ground ahead, soaking in but advancing a little each day, following the line of least resistance onto the flatter land of the knoll. Children tried to scratch a course for it with sticks or built little dams of twigs, but the water felt its own way forward as slowly and inexorably as a tide. Some days it paused to fill hollows here and there, taking a week to find a path meandering past the villa, about a hundred paces away.

'It's a punishment,' Paul said, staring at the stream morosely. 'You see, I am a sinner, and this is my punishment.'

'What nonsense!' Imogen said, looking over her shoulder at it as she tended the vines she was trying to train up the trellis on the ornamental south wall, above the neatly-spaced ceramic pots.

Diana and Imogen both knew they were getting the worst of the punishment, if punishment it was, not Paul; his suffering was in his mind, theirs was in the fact that the well supplying their proudest possession and greatest luxury, the bath-house, had at one stroke run dry as a bone. It was as if the greater good of the stream had to be paid for by the loss of privilege on the knoll. Now every last pint for the bath-house had to be carried from the new stream by the wheezing slave, Termo, with a yoke and two leather buckets. The old man had once done nothing more than

242

scrape the weed from the stone steps of the warm-water bath, make sure the fire was stoked and snacks laid out. His sinecure slowly turned into a torture, there was never enough water and it was never hot enough for Diana, and after several days of forgetting to put the snacks out altogether, he was found dead in the yoke before the new barn was filled with winter fodder – what there was of it, the weather being so poor.

'Perhaps Paul's right,' Diana told Imogen, as they did their hair in quiet companionship. 'Perhaps Fortune has deserted us.'

'You've got to get him to snap out of it,' Imogen said.

'I don't know how.'

As the stream neared the lip of the knoll, its rate of advance increased, and one day Paul, staring from the shelter of the portico, roused himself, realising that it would flow over the edge straight into the gully. The stream was so precisely choosing its course that it was becoming obvious that the water had flowed this way before, though perhaps so long ago that the overlooked gully had been the only sign remaining. If so, the gully would become the course again. It was a windy day, threatening rain, and Paul donned his *byrrus* and tartan hat of oily wool before venturing out. In a few hours more the water would reach the edge and go rushing down, and his last chance would be lost. He found an easy way to descend into the gully from the far side and slid down, standing with the mud thick about his boots, the gorse nodding in the wind above him. This was the place. He made a few sweeps in the mud with the toe of his boot, finding nothing. Bent and took a few handfuls, sifting it between his fingers. Nothing.

He heaved a sigh of relief.

Shrugging, he climbed back to the top and wiped his hands clean on the grass. A few hours later the gully was a brown, foaming torrent as the stream overflowed, and Paul watched it, neither sorry nor pleased. The talents were gone for ever now.

By the springtime Paul had lost thirty pounds in weight. He took no part in the Beltain revels, and forbade the great bonfires. When Imogen searched, nostalgically, for John Fox's wheel and stone for striking the need-fire, it was mysteriously gone from its place in the house garden. Diana was worried. In under a twelvemonth her husband's eyes had aged ten years, ringed by exhaustion, all sparkle gone. The bright-eyed youthful Paul who had wooed her from the verandah roof would, she feared, never return. Even his skin repelled her, dirty and flaking. She had torn her gown and wept and mourned for Vitellus, but the time for that was long past. Lucius, not Vitellus, was the future. But Paul's gown clung to him in greasy folds, unchanged for weeks and stinking, and his hand trembled. He's punishing the jug of Narbonne wine as much as himself, she thought contemptuously, and he hasn't even attempted to bring me back to his bed; he's as limp as a piece of Narbonne rope in the place that matters, no doubt.

'You're such a pathetic piece of a man,' she said, quite without warning after dinner, stopping him with her hand on his shoulder as he got up. 'You feel so sorry for yourself, wallowing in your self-pity. Why won't you shake yourself out of it?' She had eaten her fill of honeyed cakes, her belly was warm, and she couldn't help flirting a little. 'Even I don't interest you any more.'

He looked at her dully. 'How could you interest me? How could we enjoy ourselves rutting like animals when our son is dead?' He shrugged off her hand.

'But you do love me,' she murmured, her breast touching his upper arm.

'I never want to feel happiness again!' Paul said, and shambled back to his study. He must keep his drink in there, Diana thought venomously, in one of the big wall cupboards off limits to everyone except Eutuches, his steward, who knew better than to wag his tongue when he replenished the supply.

She went to the kitchen and took her temper out, as usual, on whoever got in her way. She gave the new serving girl a tongue-lashing for gutting a hare in a bucket indoors, then pulled the hair of the other doe-eyed girl for not washing the table. They ran off clutching one another in tears, and Diana stormed up and down alone, from the flour barrel to the long elegant containers of fish sauce, banging her hip on the table. Dirt, dirt everywhere, she raged; broken oyster shells crunching beneath her shoes, the charcoal store empty, not a drop in the pitcher. Doubtless Eutuches was cheating them blind. She knew it was the same story all over the estate, less money, less respect. One of the young *vernae* – slave children who automatically belonged to Paul – cheeky sometimes but harmless always, until now, had actually made the Evil Eye at her and terrified her. The place was going down because Paul was going down.

Diana stopped, forgetting even to curse and rub her hip as a dreadful new thought struck her. What if Paul carried on as he was, willing himself to die?

What if Paul died?

The thought was almost too horrible to contemplate, but Diana had never shirked uncomfortable truths. The moment she was widowed, she was finished. Roman law decreed that all women, because of their weakness of intellect, should spend their lives under the power of one guardian or another. That pipsqueak Lucius would become the paterfamilias, responsible for her in law. He would be fourteen soon and a man, and she would have no alternative but to obey him. As Diana's legal guardian, Lucius would make all decisions for his mother, and she, though infinitely greater in experience, would become his subordinate without appeal. Lucius would be awarded control over Antonia, not her, it would be Lucius who negotiated a husband for Antonia when she was old enough, and Diana would have to watch powerlessly from the sidelines. Lucius was such a green stick that she could easily bend him with the strength of her personality, as she had, with Imogen's help, Paul. But she had not cultivated Lucius, rated him as nothing compared to her beloved Vitellus. If Lucius had any sense, when Paul died he'd pack her out of the house in no time. In his shoes, she would!

She slumped her voluptuous form over one of the uncomfortable stools. If the worst did happen, she would not even be able to marry again; Paul, fool that he was, had been happy to take her without a dowry, so she had nothing to claim back and use to attract a worthwhile husband. Fortune did not smile on a penniless woman fattening even before full middle age. The soft honeyed dainties she kept by her bedside had made eating meat painful, so she ate the tiny delicate cakes by the dozen, squeezing them with her tongue against the roof of her mouth until she could swallow them, unable to stop despite her bouts of toothache. It was a relief when each decayed tooth was lost, but even she admitted she had no longer the full measure of her youth and beauty. Vagnius Vagionius had eyed her, sniffing with his warty nose, but he was rich and money only married money. Without a dowry, she could never be anything more than a concubine.

Paul must not die.

Diana dropped her head into her arms on the table and wept. She wept loudly, but no servant dared come to her. The house was silent, the windows reflected the rooms. Then Paul's footsteps sounded on the tiles of the corridor, coming slowly, doubtless looking into each room as he came to it. She redoubled her cries as he appeared in the doorway.

'Drunk,' he slurred, showing her the jug.

She wiped away her tears and heaved herself to her feet, going to him.

He backed away from her. 'It doesn't work.'

'I don't blame you for being drunk.' Stopped by the wall behind him, he looked at her gauzily. 'I don't blame you for anything, Paul,' she said, gently disengaging the jug and wine goblet from his fingers. 'Only you do. No one else does.'

'Don't start that again,' he blurted. 'There's a monster inside me. It's me. It's the real me.' He turned his watery eyes to her appealingly. 'I can't help myself. Such dreadful things happen to us.'

'Only if we let them,' she said forcefully.

'We're all sinners.'

She took him in her arms. 'It's not you,' she said.

'Who else is there?'

'*You* didn't jump. *You* didn't make a fool of yourself. It's Lucius.' She moved her shoulders, working his arms round her. 'He's the one to blame, Paul. Not you or me. I've been thinking and . . . praying. Yes, praying. I think you should have a word with that boy of yours.'

'Lucius?' Paul mumbled. 'But he's an invalid.'

'He's lazy! He hasn't done a day's work for a year. He stays in his room, wasting his life reading from a book bucket, and you're letting him get away with it. All the suffering he caused us!'

'It was I who forbade him to come out.'

'You'll have to deal with him properly, Paul.'

Paul licked his lips.

'You've let him get away with too much,' Diana purred. 'You

should teach him the most important lesson. A man must pull his weight. Like Vitellus did. He was so strong. You must force Lucius to be strong.'

'Perhaps you're right,' Paul said unhappily.

'You know I always am.'

'I've been too soft on him,' Paul said decisively.

'Make a man of him,' Diana whispered, reaching inside his gown, sliding her palm down his hairy, sticky belly, her expert fingertips finding and fondling the shapeless lump of warm putty between his legs. Against his will at first, Paul grunted, then parted her robe, panting with thin lust. She leaned back on the sideboard, helping him. It had been a long year for her, her few assignations had merely whetted her appetite, and she was so open and moist that even at half mast, the best he could manage, she sucked him inside her as slippery as a melon pip. 'Make him the man my darling Vitellus would have been,' Diana hissed, bucking her hips, and Paul cried out in the rage of his passion.

Paul went to Lucius's tiny bedroom first thing in the morning. The boy was lying on his bed reading by lamplight even at this hour, though the sun was glowing behind the closed window. Scrolls were scattered around him everywhere, on the rumpled blanket over his knees, in tubs on the tiled floor, squeezed under the couch, an endless scrawl of Cicero, Livy, the Aeneid, Homer. Nonsense, useless, worthless.

Lucius scrambled up, his smile fading to see the terrible look darkening his father's face.

'I won't touch you,' Paul told Lucius in a cold, spent voice. 'I believe in forgiveness. But you've brought such a great and continuing sadness on this family that I can see no end to it. I can never forgive you. You were the most like me.' Paul was bitterly aware that every word he was uttering exposed his frailty, his inability to cope, his need simply to shift his unendurable load onto Lucius's shoulders. 'Your mother cries herself to sleep every night,' Paul lied, trying to make the boy comprehend the enormity of what he was feeling, of how much the family had lost. 'You will remain my son, but I can never love you.'

'What do you want of me?' Lucius asked gently. 'There is nothing worse you can do to me than what you have just told me. What have I done?'

'It's not what you've done, it's what you've not done. It's not *enough*.'

'I wish I could have been as perfect as Vitellus was.'

'Your mother and I have lit a fire,' Paul said in that drained voice. 'It is in the house garden, on the stone table. You will carry your books out to it.'

Lucius could not stop his voice quivering. 'Everything?'

'The books are mine, everything written in them is mine. And the buckets, take them too, they also are mine. Every possession in this house is mine. As are you.'

Lucius trembled. 'What do you want me to do?'

'You will know when you get there.'

Lucius rolled his scrolls neatly, the writing on them blurred by his tears. Each time he looked up, his father's expression, or lack of it, did not change.

'You don't need to do this to me,' Lucius whispered. 'I'll do anything you want.'

'And my pens,' Paul said. 'And my ink. And my wax tablets and stylus, too.'

Lucius carried armfuls out to the house garden and laid them near the table where the fire was burning, then went back for more.

Paul waited until he was finished.

'I can't,' Lucius said. He turned to his mother, who watched from the colonnade with her plump arms crossed. She lifted her broad shoulders and threw him a look that said she didn't dare go against his father.

Lucius unrolled the first scroll and his eyes lingered on the text, an imaginary world so much fuller and richer than the real one. He spoke in a voice almost too soft to hear.

'But how shall I live?'

'By your own hand,' Paul said.

Lucius threw the scrolls on the fire one by one, and the buckets that had contained them, and the pens and wax tablets which fed the flames furiously, until they were all gone. When Imogen came out and saw what was happening it was too late.

'Now,' Paul said. 'Now, we'll begin.'

A light-fingered boy is never out of a job! Nor is someone what knows what to make of him, neither. The gods preserve me, I know just the place for you, young Wittle!

The old thirsty carter sold his skins to the first *negotiatores* who touted for his business on the outskirts of town, a place called the south works, a lawless encampment of tumbledown dwellings, shacks and outhouses between the necropolis and the municipal boundary, separated from the trading and usury laws of the London curial class by the Thames and the bridge. Skinned that old bastard alive, those ruthless buyers and sellers of everything under the sun chuckled among themselves outside the Tabernacle, as they watched the old man and his young attendant with the swollen forehead go into the tavern. The old bastard and the young bastard, they chuckled, always room for one more. They were perpetually on the lookout for likely business to double their money, and they were not patient men.

Inside, the carter joined the group he greeted as his friends, drinking beer from mugs closer in size to British quarts than Roman pints, playing dice on the table between them. 'Doubles!' cried one, welcoming the old fellow to the circle. 'Got your money to pay back what you owe from last time, my friend?'

'Protus, this is young Wittle.' The carter fidgeted nervously, his eyes fixed with longing on the two dice.

'Who is he?' Protus glanced into the crazy, fearless eyes of the boy, and paused, liking what he saw.

'He's a light-fingered boy, Protus. No tattoos. He'd more than pay his way.'

Protus turned fully. He was a thin man, hungry-looking, with narrow eyes, but he wore an open face which made him look genial, welcoming and honest, everything he was not. He saw that the boy understood this at once, and shook his head. 'He's trouble.'

The boy smiled. 'Yes,' he said, 'I am trouble. But not for you.'

'Whatever happened to your head?' Protus grunted in disgust. His own dark hair was neatly curled, his proudest possession, fluffed out with hot tongs to hide his bald patch.

The boy replied slowly; thoughts took him time. 'It's getting better. It can learn the trade.' His hand, which had moved almost too quickly to see, held out the money pouch from Protus's belt. Protus snatched it back before his cronies laughed him down, and for a moment his expression slipped as though an animal lived beneath his skin, showing naked murder. 'You'll do,' he admitted. 'Fetch beer, for a start.'

Young Wittle fetched beer from the girl in the back room. She was a dainty little creature with no breasts or hips, great dark circles for eyes, who did not speak.

That night and all the nights that followed, Wittle slept beneath the tables. He did not know where the girl slept, some safe little nook or niche. Since the temple of Isis was built between the tavern and the river, all service at the Tabernacle was done by boys, always dirty, always fearful. The more outgoing serving girls had joined the Guild of Prostitutes, touting for business near the temple steps, and often brought their clients of the better class here for old times' sake. It was one of Protus's little arrangements, the complex web of arrangements, Wittle soon learned, that made the Tabernacle pay, and a wing had been fitted out in Roman style to accommodate the girls and their clients. The tile floors were cracking now because they had not been properly laid, and the plaster was coming off the walls, but both Protus and the girls were careful to pay their tax to the Emperor – it was the cream of the inn's business. Below that came stabling and beer, and deeper and darker things that a boy needed to learn about.

'Wittle, fetch beer!' the call would come. 'Wittle, fetch our wine! Wittle, where are you?' But the girl in the back room was as silent as though she had no voice; and Wittle, rubbing his brow, would find the time to smile at her as he hurried back and forth. She was his only weakness.

Because here in the Tabernacle he was strong. This place fitted him like a glove.

He thought of her in the buzzing, exhausted confusion of his brain when the hostelry was quiet, in the few hours before dawn when he fell down to sleep beneath a table, his cheek on the earthen floor. The pain would begin, there in the silence, and he would lie whimpering and trying to imagine her until, to his heartfelt relief, the tavern began to fill with the chaos of a new day, drowning out his agony.

All day he was at their beck and call, the gentlemen and travellers passing through at the front tables until the sun filled the doorway in the evening; as darkness fell the barn-sized main room changed its rhythm, and he slid like a shadow bringing beer to the drunks and gamblers, fornicators, sodomites, thieves and others going down into the gloom at the back. The different worlds that hardly touched outside came together in the Tabernacle, joined by his servile presence. Here anything could be purchased for the right price: a wedding festival with garlands of flowers, a religious congregation, the finest wines, the slowest and most agonising poison. He learned that a man could buy anything he wanted from the smiling, deferential Protus with his trustworthy manner and understanding demeanour, and he would sell all you had, if you sold it cheap enough: a horse, a woman, a child, your body. Everything was in order, as long as Protus got his cut.

Wittle was at their elbows before they realised he had appeared, back with their order almost, it seemed, before he was gone. He frightened everyone with that huge empurpled hollow in his forehead, its strangeness intimidated them. But when the angry colour began to fade they all made use of him, because he learned to do anything. Wittle was as without shame or self-regard as an animal, and that was why Protus, watching him, liked him. All the knowledge Wittle had been sheltered from as a child, he acquired now. Such was his ugliness that his price would never be high, but a man was at his weakest when his gown was lifted, and sometimes, afterwards, at his most garrulous too. Wittle kept his eyes open and his mouth shut about what he learned in the back rooms – except to Protus. What a team they made!

The girl was Protus's youngest daughter. The others were married and had moved away, but this one had always been considered the ugliest. Her name was Trifosa.

Wittle observed her more and more, innocent and untouched, a familiar sight in her slim linen shift, slipping unnoticed through the busy rooms and corridors, eyes downcast. His own age less a year, she wore her long mousy hair combed straight down her back, a ridiculous style that would have had everyone staring at her in the street or in the public rooms; but she was her father's prisoner, unable to go out or be seen. Only when the place was at last shut up and deserted for the night did she appear, a waif-like pale figure clearing the tables, picking up the bowls and bones until the mess she carried seemed larger than she was, tottering into the back rooms which she haunted all day, out of sight, with her restless, silent, rebellious presence. Never once did she look at Wittle directly. Her long eyelashes and the sadness in her deep blue eyes overwhelmed the little bump of her nose, small mouth, elfin chin.

'Why do you hate yourself?' Wittle asked abruptly one night as she cleared the tables.

She gave him a hard, implacable stare, then turned away as though she had not heard him. He smiled. Got you!

The next night she returned the smile with a flicker in the corner of her lips. Victory. She would think of him during the day, too.

The nights continued to torment Wittle. That was when his pain was at its most atrocious. The hollow that disfigured his brow itched unmercifully, and several times fragments of bone had emerged, tiny hard pieces speckling his fingertip. And there was something sharp in there inside his head, he could feel it moving, clicking from side to side under the pad of his thumb, his probing making his skin crawl. And the pain would blossom like a red flower, filling his skull. He lay rigid, eyes staring, then his hands began to twitch, and his senses fled.

He was terrified when this began to happen during the day. If the evil spirit that possessed him revealed itself in front of everyone he would be finished at the Tabernacle, he would become a true outcast. Those interested glances of Protus would become frightened, disgusted; people would ward him off with the Evil Eye. So when he felt the first signs coming on, a peculiar metallic smell, lights flashing, that terrible blossoming colour, he staggered into the back room and tried to lie down. He'd wake in an entirely different position, his head and hands bruised where he had beaten them on the floor, fortunately of earth, not hard tile. He'd lie totally drained of energy, feeling dreadful, but always the worst thing was wondering if someone had seen him in that state, turned inside out in the arms of the demon, writhing and kicking, covering himself with bruises, dislocating a finger once.

Afterwards he would weep in shame and despair at himself.

The point grew, making a hard knob beneath his skin. He could not help fretting it with his thumb, working at it like a man at a loose tooth, cringing when it clicked. Tonight Trifosa was late clearing up and he had decided she was not coming, he would have to go without his fun taunting her, his only way of making her pay attention to him. The fit came on him so suddenly that he had not even time to get out from beneath the table, and he knew he was going to hurt himself this time.

He woke with his head in her lap, her workworn hands caressing his face, her huge sad eyes above him. He saw the softness in them, the gentleness. The corners of her lips moved, and then she smiled for him.

She *knew.*

She knew his secret. She had seen the demon in him.

Wittle grunted. He rolled over, crawling away from her, then stumbled into a corner where he could be alone, his arms folded over his head. He wouldn't speak to her, turned away when she approached.

She cleared the tables, glancing at him.

The next night he found himself another place to sleep. Once this part of the Tabernacle had had an upper floor but about ten years ago, just before Protus arrived, there had been a fire that consumed the second storey and thatched roof. The roof was now tile, but the second floor had not been replaced, though some of the charred floor timbers remained sticking out of the thick walls like teeth, and one or two doorways still stood above them where rooms had led off. Standing on a table, he swung himself with his strong arms onto a blackened beam, and made a comfortable niche for himself in one of the disused doorways. He even had enough room to stretch out, and a piece of timber to save him from falling.

Here he could look down on her head moving below him as she did her work. Once when he woke he caught her staring up at him, and to his astonishment she actually spoke to him.

'Why won't you let me help you?' she called up softly.

He looked down on her plain, skinny body, her awful hair. She was the only person here in the Tabernacle who was kind.

He threw a half-brick rather than reply to her, but threw it to miss. Showing weakness.

One night the skin broke and his fingernail grated on a tiny hard point of bone. Too small for the pads of his fingertips to grip and pull out, he put his hair forward to cover it the next day, then fell to working at it all the next night, biting his teeth together against the creaking in his skull, watery fluid dripping like a heavy cold from his nostrils. When the splinter at last came sliding out, effortlessly, his feeling of relief was indescribable. By the dawn light he stared at the small spear of shattered bone lying in his palm, then threw it away with a grunt of revulsion.

He did not have a fit that day, or that night, or the next.

But still he saw that sympathy in Trifosa's eyes. She had seen him as he truly was, she thought she knew him, and she wanted to help him, waiting patiently with her awful kindness and quietness and affection for the event he dreaded most: his next fit. That was all she cared about, he told himself, caring for him when he was weak and vulnerable, getting an advantage over him.

'Wittle, fetch beer!' the call came. She handed the jug to him to take out, looking straight at him with her enormous eyes, that tentative smile so easily crushed.

'What are you so happy about?' he grunted.

'You're getting better,' she said.

He went dark red with rage, but turned away without a word.

'Don't forget the beer,' she called after him, holding out the handle from that slim white hand of hers, and he had to go back and snatch it from her.

'I'm happy for you,' she called after him.

Wittle understood exactly what she meant. She didn't love him, she was *happy* for him. She pitied him, didn't she?

He was growing up, prowling around the place with ferocity, his face dark with rage at those beneath him, fawning to those above, a hard taskmaster and a respected young man, taking over the most onerous of Protus's duties. One day Protus would find him indispensable. This was the hardest thing Wittle had ever done, because such cunning required patience.

He lay in his doorway watching the girl clearing the tables below, seeing the way her hair moved, noticing how thin and white her shoulders were. She hated the Tabernacle, he realised, and she hated her father, not herself. Sometimes she glanced up at him, but said nothing.

Protus was lazy, that was his weakness.

He bothered to greet only the best customers now, and rose late, spending most of the day reclining at the table with his gambling circle, drinking his own wine. He began to wonder how he had ever managed without Wittle. The lad was a marvel, no end to his strength, Protus congratulated himself; he was no trouble, was paid board and a pittance yet never grumbled, and was careful to be friendly to the customers he should be popular with and feared by those who should respect him – easy enough with that face of his. Good work! By now he was taller than most of them, and bulky with it, which was useful. He never gave away a free drink without purpose, and he never let a customer complain without making them regret it sooner or later. Drunks liked to think they owned the place but if there was a fight Wittle was merciless with the club, there was never the same trouble twice. What a gift! Never seemed to sleep, asked for nothing, curled himself up somewhere, never bothered the working girls. Protus shook his head in wonder at such good fortune. He had not been so lucky since he won half the inn in settlement of a gambling debt. The previous owner, Eberesto, a freed slave who had apparently stumbled across the place in a near-derelict condition years before, had no proper title of ownership. A further small fire made him see the sense of giving up his claim entirely. Protus was a canny gambler who only dealt from a position of strength.

All the same, perhaps it was time to take this young man down a peg or two, he mused, before he thinks he's better than the boss.

Genial and dangerous with drink, Protus crooked his finger and Wittle came over. Wiping his hands on a rag, he ignored Protus's friends. Good boy. But there was no 'Yes master', he just waited.

'I would ask you to join us,' Protus said indolently, 'but I don't pay you enough, do I?' He laughed. 'I don't pay him enough! He's too atrocious to look at!'

Wittle looked at the laughing faces one by one, his own face going dark with blood, the way it always did when the anger that coiled inside him threatened to flash out of control. This only increased their amusement. No one had ever seen him actually snap.

Wittle smiled. His fists unclenched, he put the rag carefully through his belt. 'Thank you for asking,' he said slowly, the words as usual taking longer to form than actions. 'Thank you for your pity, Protus. It's true, I am ugly.' He dropped a silver piece on the table, looking only at Protus now.

'Solid silver,' Protus said. There was a silence. 'It's beautiful. How did a creature like you come by such a beautiful thing?'

'One day maybe I'll tell you. It's part of me.' Wittle held the gleaming circle to the centre of his forehead, covering the soft boneless concavity. 'I value it at thirty denarii. Double or nothing. Sixes.' His hand threw the dice as he finished speaking.

'You've won sixty denarii,' Protus said calmly. 'That is enough to buy in to our game.'

Wittle shook his head. 'Double or nothing again,' he said, scooping up the dice.

'The odds are against you,' Protus warned. He cleared his throat against the silence that had settled over this corner of the tavern. The bone dice rattled loudly from the cup onto the table. Double sixes for the second time.

The whole room was quiet now, heads craning, whispers asking what was going on. Someone hissed for quiet.

'One hundred and twenty,' Protus said, very calm. 'A fortune for you. Take your winnings and run.'

'*Run!*' whispered a girl's voice, and Wittle glanced at the doorway, seeing Trifosa's boyish face at the curtain. She appealed to him with her eyes. He ignored her.

'Again.'

'You can't keep winning this game, you know,' Protus warned him, very smoothly.

Wittle spat on his hand. 'Double or nothing.' The dice scattered across the table, one of them rebounding from the *duodecim scripta* gaming stone, skittering on its corner before falling as a six, and a crony of Protus covered the dice with his palm to declare the throw invalid.

'No, leave it,' Protus said. 'I'll see him fall by his own hand. Try your luck over two hundred and forty, my friend.' He did not look at Wittle as he spoke. The money did not mean much to him, but he felt sharply his loss of dignity and authority. All this was wrong, it flew against the order of things for a mere boy, sweeper of floors and carrier of wine, to win against a grown man. Protus was keenly aware of every eye in the place on him, and cursed himself for getting into such a position. As always when he was angry he

256

sweated, but of course everyone thought it was nerves or that he couldn't afford to lose.

Wittle flicked the cup and the dice rolled. A collective sigh went up.

A double six for the fourth time.

Wittle gave his smile. 'Again?' Protus recognised that smile now for what it was: a grin of pure rage. The hand that held up the silver piece shook, the black eyebrows raised in mocking inquiry round the disfigurement gave the face a horrible aspect, and the blue eyes glittered with something Protus could not quite identify. It was a kind of envy, hunger, thirst, and it was very bad. Protus shivered. He wiped a bead of sweat from his nose, drawing attention to it, laughing as though it had tickled him. His eyes were hard as stones. The audience laughed too.

'Four hundred and eighty,' Wittle said, 'I'll double it again.' But Protus's hand clamped over the cup, still the stronger. Yet he had to use all his strength, and it took all his willpower to appear calm.

'It would be churlish of me to continue against the will of the goddess Fortuna,' Protus said smoothly. He added in an undertone, 'Don't push your luck, boy.'

Wittle shrugged. 'I could throw six double sixes.'

'I doubt that would be wise,' Protus said.

Wittle shrugged again, and the fire went out of his eyes.

'What're you going to spend your money on?' someone shouted.

'Buy us a drink!' called another. 'Two drinks!'

'Five!' shouted someone else.

Wittle turned as Trifosa's voice came to him again: '*Go!*'

'But I like it here,' Wittle said, speaking slowly as always. He sounded baffled now by all the attention, staring at the big silver piece in his hand, holding it in front of his face as though he was not quite sure what he was looking at. 'You see,' he explained, carefully forming the ungainly words and getting them out one by one, 'I think I'm happy here. This is my home.'

Protus paid over his money in full view for the benefit of the crowd. 'Easy come, easy go!' he laughed, then nodded at one of his friends.

They waited until late, but not so late that the place was utterly quiet; there was bound to be a little noise, grunting, screaming. By lamplight at the entrance a couple of centurions were playing *ludus latrunculorum*, 'Soldiers', a game of skill and therefore legal, their brows shadowed by concentration as they stalked each other's counters on the marble block. A gentleman travelling with his family had retired to one of the private rooms in the Roman style, little guessing its use before and after his dignified occupancy. Courtesans were bringing their clients discreetly to the unoccupied rooms, booked in and out by Wittle as usual, and from time to time he toured the back rooms used by the cheaper prostitutes, even checking the stables where the lowest sort sometimes sneaked in for free, frightening the horses with their cries. It was a beautiful moonlit night and across the blue fields he saw the Iseum, the temple of Isis, silhouetted gracefully in black against the river's sheen. When he returned inside, yawning in the doorway, Protus was waiting.

'There is a lesson you will learn, Wittle,' Protus said calmly, nodding to his friend behind the door. Before Wittle could move, and long before he could have formed the words to cry out for help, he was seized by the arms, his head jerked back by his hair, the cold edge of a knife laid to his throat. His tunic was pulled up to his chest, the pouch of money snapped from its thongs. All three men were breathing as heavily as though they were running a race.

Wittle was dragged to an empty room and pushed into a crouching position, his knees kicked wide.

Protus kept his hands clean. He was not a man who particularly cared for boys, preferring the ladies of the Iseum. He grunted as he lifted his gown. 'You're used to this, I know,' he hissed, 'but you'll not get one penny from me. This is what I think of you.' Protus had loved his wife dearly; she had died birthing the brat Trifosa. The business of lust had long ago lost all novelty and pleasure for him.

Wittle screamed as he was impaled, but the walls were thick, and anyway Protus, in the grip of his frenzy and deliberately brutal, did not care who heard him. He would be feared the more.

He stepped back, and the weariness returned to his features. 'I am the boss, remember that.'

He crooked his finger, and both men left Wittle alone on the floor.

He crawled to the couch. The bronze lamp had a pretty little flame burning from its spout. All he had to do was tip out the oil on the couch and a fire would blossom. He could burn the place to ashes.

Wittle was not thinking in words, slow and clumsy. Protus had misjudged him. He was thinking in actions, pictures, already hobbling to the door, along the empty corridor. He had moved on from the picture of the fire and was visualising places now. Where did she sleep? Where was *her* place? In his mind's eye he saw Trifosa curled up half-sitting in a niche somewhere, her stark straight hair fallen forward to hide her face and arms, her feet poking out of the red leather shoes she wore. But she was not in the kitchen, it was inhabited only by the smell of warm fish sauce. Not in the wood store round the back. Not in the tavern's main room, also deserted, and he saw the tables were cleared; it was later than he thought. He held his hand to his forehead then stormed about, snapping his fingers. Where would a shy, dainty girl like her go? Not only to sleep. To hide. Yes, she would hide herself away to forget herself in her dreams.

The quietest place.

He lifted the trap door and dropped down the steps to the beer cellar, below ground level. Dark and silent. He came down here fifty times a day, he needed no lamp to find his way among the rows of fermenting casks. The fragrance of brewing barley with its heady undertones of cumin and honey added for British taste was strong and sweet enough to obliterate sense. His footsteps made no sound on the earth floor. A faint glimmer showed up the barrels ahead of him now. A lamp had been lit in the wine store at the end.

Here was her place. She had laid a straw mat behind the elegant amphorae jars stacked almost to the ceiling. He stood looking down at her. Wasn't she afraid of anything down here? There must be rats. Mice. Imagined creatures.

She'd covered herself with a blanket. She sat up, holding it to her, those enormous bruised eyes gazing at him. Protus's daughter. She'd put her hair up as though during the night she was free of her father, free of this dreadful place. Asleep she was herself.

Wittle pulled the band and her hair fell across her face, hanging straight and ugly. He blew out the lamp, then pulled the blanket off her with such force that she cried out. He knelt on her and took her with roughness, inexperienced, hearing only his own panting breaths, the roar of blood in his ears.

Afterwards she crawled to an opposite corner in the dark, and he leant back with his elbows on his knees, relaxed. Trifosa's quiet crying reached him through the gloom, irritating him.

He took the silver coin from round his own neck and threw it to her. 'There!' he said bitterly. 'Now you have my luck.'

The soft moans stopped, then started again.

'I didn't do anything worse to you than what he did to me,' he told her.

She stopped, then her voice came. 'Does that matter? I would have given myself to you. But you had to take it from me.'

He couldn't imagine such a gift, herself, willingly given. The very idea was suspicious. As always the words came to him slowly, he had to feel for them. 'That wouldn't have been the same thing,' he said, and she cried again. He listened to her, then took her once more before going upstairs to sleep in peace and quiet.

He bided his time, so muted and respectful that Protus was quite taken in. After some months he even invited Wittle to join his gambling circle, an honour that was courteously refused. Protus laughed, seeing the humiliation in those blue eyes, and drank his wine.

And each night Wittle went downstairs and lay with Trifosa, getting his revenge for the day by night. She could not run away, and in truth she did not seem to want to. Idiotically she tried to talk him round, to use words to make him feel something for her instead of just using her as his receptacle. She kept coming back like a kicked dog licking his hand, he told himself, fawning on him because she had no pride in herself. He yawned while she talked, recovering his desire, then left her alone.

Meanwhile Protus was not as talkative as of old. His useful friend of many years, no one better company when a knife was needed on a dark night, had himself been knifed walking back from the Iseum, and the girls would not talk. Even when Protus lubricated their tongues with money they would not talk. He took to looking behind him when he thought he was alone.

Gradually, too, he took less interest in the running of the tavern. Day after day he would sit alone in his corner where the gambling circle used to meet – he could not be bothered with that now –

drinking the wine Wittle brought him. Protus did not feel unwell exactly; he felt old. He rubbed his head, stared at the strands across his palm, more with each week that passed. He was losing his hair. At first he wondered if he'd had the curling tongs too hot and stopped using them, but still the grey, frizzy strands fell out, and gradually he ceased to care. He sat quietly in his corner, wearing a woollen cap, and when the weather grew chill Wittle put a blanket over his lap. Protus thanked him through trembling lips.

'Don't thank me,' Wittle said. He was a fine figure of a man, dwarfing Protus, growing up very broad across the shoulders, with muscular arms and those meaty hands with incongruously long, sensitive fingers. Travellers did not have to fear pickpockets in this establishment, only the establishment itself. Wittle was growing to be a master of short measures and short change; he never watered the beer too much and his wine tasted just fine. 'You see,' Wittle said, 'I haven't forgotten what you did to me. And I never will forget, or forgive.'

Protus had honestly forgotten. 'Oh, that,' he said, waving his trembling hand. 'Between friends! You'll grow out of it.'

'Finish your wine.' Protus did as he was told. 'Look what a mess you are,' Wittle lectured him, wearing his smile. 'You smell like an old dog, and you look like you're dying.'

'I am not!'

'Fight it,' Wittle grinned. 'Come on, pull yourself together. Smarten up. You can never tell when you'll turn the corner.'

It was good advice, and Protus did as he was told. He fought his illness with all his strength, dragging himself around the place, doing the tasks Wittle found for him to do such as sweeping out a room. It was exercise for his own good, Wittle would say with a smile, to build up his wasted muscles, and Protus knew he must believe him. Wittle was right. He must not give up hope. But sometimes Protus could do no more than cling to the broom handle, shuddering and holding himself up on it without the energy to do more, dreading Wittle's return, beginning to hate him. Hating Wittle's cheerfulness, his youth. It was now Wittle who welcomed the wealthy customers, taking their cloaks, snapping fingers imperiously for service. The hatred kept Protus going, struggling on quivering knees to cross a room with a beer

261

jug, making himself a laughing-stock just to prove that contemptuous young giant wrong.

'If you didn't have me to fight,' Wittle grinned, 'you'd have given up long ago, wouldn't you?'

'I wish I had,' Protus said miserably.

When the pain in his stomach made Protus incapable of eating, Wittle would bring him some wine and lift his head, make sure he drank a sip, keeping him going.

'Forgive me,' Protus begged, exhausted. 'I'm dying.'

'No you're not!' Wittle scoffed, his big red face bubbling over with good cheer. 'There's that matter of the four hundred and eighty denarii you stole from me first.'

'It was mine.'

'I won it fair and square.'

'You were too young. You did not appreciate it, you would have lost it sooner or later. You had to learn your place. I regret my method, if that makes you feel better.'

'I won't forgive you,' Wittle grinned. The words came easily because he had rehearsed them in the quiet night hours, planning exactly what would cause his dying employer the most torment. 'Everyone saw you give me that money, Protus, you can't deny it, but no one still alive saw you take it back.' His grin broadened as though an idea had just occurred to him. 'In a way, that money's as good as though I've still got it, isn't it?'

Protus gawped. 'I don't – I don't know what you mean.'

'What I mean is, I could give it to you in return for a proper piece of paper with your seal on it.' He lifted Protus's ring finger. 'This seal.'

Protus tried unsuccessfully to flap his hand free. 'Why should I put my seal to any agreement?'

'A bill of sale. My four hundred and eighty denarii—'

'But you haven't got it!'

'*We* know that, but nobody else does. You stole it. I will have the Tabernacle in exchange.'

Protus swallowed with an audible click. 'Why?' he quavered again.

'Because I want everything of yours in my hands before you die, Protus.' Wittle held out his great rough hands, clotted with dried yellow beer foam, speckled by the black lees of wine, every fingernail broken. 'And I will.'

'Never!' Protus struggled on his elbows to rise. 'Never . . .'

Wittle waited until he collapsed back into his seat.

'Take the money,' Protus whispered. 'I'll give it to you, anything. I'll send out for it.'

Wittle looked down at him dispassionately. 'I'll have the Tabernacle. But only in the unfortunate event of your death. Let's be fair, I know its worth is more than a miserable four hundred and eighty pence. The Tabernacle remains yours for your lifetime. Now, *there's* a reason for trying hard to live.'

Protus gazed up into those eyes, as blue and blank of feeling as holes punched into a winter's sky. 'How have you done this to me?' he whispered. There was no answer. Protus wept, but sent out to the scribe's stall for the agreement to be drawn up legally phrased. While they waited, Wittle poured more wine, giving a long, sad, insincere sigh to see his employer brought so low. The scribe brought in the document, witnessed the stamp, was paid and dismissed.

'Will I get better now?' Protus quavered.

'That's up to you.'

'How did you do it to me?'

'In the wine I've been so kindly bringing you.' Wittle grinned. 'Good health!'

Protus recoiled. 'Not another drop will I drink. I'll choose everything by my own hand from now on.'

'My purpose is served.' Wittle shrugged genially. 'You can trust me. You see, I have more bad news for you.'

'You can do nothing worse to me.'

'Your daughter.'

'Trifosa? Who cares about her?'

'Precisely. Not me. She's pregnant.'

Protus closed his eyes. 'You're doing this to hurt me. You didn't have to hurt her. Let her go.'

'You know what they're like,' Wittle sighed. 'She thinks she's seen a little bit of good in me, something worth saving. Whatever I do to her isn't bad enough to persuade her otherwise. Your daughter and your grandchild are mine. Perhaps you can live long enough for the birth. About five months.' He looked at his victim consideringly. 'If you try hard enough.'

'You are a demon.' Protus shuddered. He turned away and pulled his gown over his head.

Protus's health didn't improve as he had hoped. He chose his wine or beer from the tavern's supply at random, washing his goblet with his own hands, but his decline had gone too far. For a week or two he shuffled about with what was left of his proud hairstyle hanging out in clumps, a figure of ridicule. Struggle though he did, fuelled by hatred to the very last of his strength, it was not enough to sustain him. After the most excruciating suffering his eyesight began to fail, and finally his mind. Wittle asked for his daughter's hand in marriage, and Protus agreed. By now he would willingly have given Wittle the clothes off his back, anything, in return for a few more weeks of even such a terrible life, because that was human nature. He died demented by nightmares.

'Mine,' Wittle told his new wife in bed, the place he was least comfortable. His head thudded and Trifosa knew he would have to get up to work, his only peace. 'A silver talent,' he gloated, 'four hundred and eighty pence, and your dowry. The Tabernacle is mine.'

'And I'm yours too,' she said. He shrugged. She touched his cheeks, and he flinched; the strangest little things hurt him. 'I'm sorry,' she whispered. She was quiet for a while, knowing he would not stay beside her for much longer. 'Husband?'

Again he flinched. If her brat was a son, he wouldn't need her, she'd be finished.

'I have to know,' she whispered.

His voice became clumsy. 'What more can you want to know?'

'About my father.'

'Oh, him.' Wittle raised his great shoulders, yawning, showing the inside of his mouth. 'I spiced his wine with more than wormwood and bayleaves, that's how I did him! Orpiment, some folk call it yellow arsenic. Only one drop at a time, slow as a wasting illness. Fooled everyone, didn't I? And they called me the fool,' he said slowly. 'But now I am the owner of the Tabernacle.'

She smoothed his chest, feeling the baby quickening inside her. 'But towards the end he chose his own drink.'

'I laced every barrel and pot in the place.' She listened, appalled, as Wittle continued, 'It took hours, and all the new deliveries, too. We've all been drinking it, all of us, the customers, you, me, everyone.'

264

'Everyone?' She wept for her unborn child.

Such a thought had never occurred to him, she knew. Wittle thought he was master of his fate, he could do anything he liked. 'We're strong,' he shrugged, 'and it's slow. We've come to no harm. Protus was a broken man, at the end of his tether.'

She turned towards him, and he stared into those huge sad eyes that dominated her thin, waif's face. She had seen the demon in him once; he wondered if she saw anything now. He could have crushed her with a blow, yet he felt the first stirrings of lust. He saw no fear in her, and remembered how she had lain alone on the cellar floor with only the rats and mice for company.

'You aren't afraid of anything, are you?' he said.

'Yes.' She saw her whole life stretching out in front of her. 'I am afraid of you.'

Four months later Wittle's son was born.

He would hardly have recognised his brother, Lucius.

You will remain my son, Lucius, Paul had sworn years ago, *but I can never love you.*

Paul had been as good as his word, and Lucius understood his duty – even, meekly, understood the fairness of it.

He must become hard as stone.

He forced himself to become perfect, as perfect as Vitellus was, still alive in his father's grieving memory. Vitellus would never age, he would be a boy for ever. Perfectly young. Perfectly strong. Tireless. And Lucius must live up to the image. He followed Paul around the estate like his shadow, pulling his weight. He went to work in the fields and his narrow shoulders filled out with muscle, his hands became hard with calluses, and he learned the feel of the sun like a boiling wheel on the top of his head. No one worked longer hours. During the breaks when the other field workers joked or talked about women, he sat alone, impatiently, unsmiling.

Something inside Lucius had withered away, curling up inside him like burnt paper, blackened, without weight, like the precious scrolls and texts he had had to place in the bonfire one by one. Staring into the flames, his face tightening from the heat, he had accepted the burden of guilt heaped on him by his embittered father.

'If this is the way you want me,' Lucius had told his father and mother, 'then this is the way I am.'

He even forgave his mother's betrayal, that shrug of her broad shoulders, the folding of her plump white arms, taking her husband's side. Lucius understood that though his mother was hot-blooded she was cold of heart. She was in control of herself when it mattered, not vulnerable as his father was. She had her own interests to consider and she would always stand by her husband, right or wrong, because without him she was nothing. She would be stupid to do otherwise, and Lucius understood her decision and even approved.

'Now,' Paul had said, 'we'll begin. I don't want to see you in front of me again, is that clear? You stand behind me. You walk behind me. You don't speak to me unless you're spoken to. If you see me coming, you get out of my way.'

'Yes, Father,' Lucius said.

When Imogen came along the colonnade and saw what had happened, her despair knew no bounds. She wanted to shout out: *But there's no such thing as sin!* She pulled her hands through her hair, but dared not run to Lucius. She saw the way things were, that tableau by the flames with Lucius motionless, oddly calm as he listened to his father's tirade, the ferocity she saw on his face directed inward against himself; and Diana back at Paul's side, the wind stirring the bright clashing colours of her clothes, over-shadowing him with her bulk.

Imogen had turned away; she could not bear to watch them further. Like Lucius, she understood, but she did not approve. Kneeling on the edge of the gully after Lucius had been lifted out injured, she had witnessed Paul's terrible grief, his shouting and kicking, and it was she who had asked, *Paul, where is Vitellus?* She would never forget the look in his eyes, the ghastly realisation of what he had done to his son Vitellus. The guilt that in the end he had not been able to live with.

Imogen returned alone to her room. She had no religion, which was not the same as not believing in anything. If the God that John Fox had come to believe in at the very end of his life really existed and offered eternal life, it would be more wonderful and more terrible than she could imagine. But even if it were true, it made no actual difference to this life, it changed nothing, it was only belief – and she had never believed. All she could do was her best. Her respectful bob in the direction of the wall shrine was by habit, for the marble plinth supported no holy figures or household gods in the niche, only a vase of pretty flowers.

She knelt on cracking knees – her arthritis was growing bad again – and reached at arm's length under the broad wooden beams, painted white with gold chasing, of her bed. She pulled out a small cedarwood casket still with lumps of dried earth clinging to it, one corner cracked by the growth of a root, perhaps, which had lifted the box in the soil under such a slow but irresistible organic pressure that the hasp had bent and finally broken, scattering the contents that the boys had found. When Paul ran away shouting for his son, Imogen had cautiously found a way down. Kneeling in the mud, she had replaced the coins in the broken box until she was sure she had found them all.

She had not touched them since, just left them in the box which she had slid beneath her bed. Out of sight, out of mind.

But now she took them out and counted the filthy things carefully, still matted with flaking mud and strands of grass, discoloured rose petals. Twenty-five remained. In his delirium her father had sworn there were thirty pieces of silver. Tears sprang unbidden to her eyes as she remembered him young, the love he had shown, tenderly placing two over the eyes of Sabrina, her dead baby, as though she had only been asleep. In his way he had been a very gentle and loving man, but he had known too much, learned too much, seen more than his fill. Imogen dried her cheeks but slowly they became wet again, remembering. She had not wept for her pretty little girl for years, yet it seemed grief never died, it only covered itself over, became a sort of weariness and a feeling of age, of slowness, an emotion of loss.

Calming herself with a deep breath, she counted the coins again as she dropped them back in the box. Twenty-five. Perhaps now that some were lost, the remainder were not so powerful. Listen to her, sounding as gullible as the rest! Still, as she dropped the lid, she rubbed the dirt from her hands with distaste. She slept on top of the things every night. And every dreadful night to come. Poor Lucius, burning everything that had been most dear to him. What must he be feeling now?

Imogen gave a deep sigh. The talents had brought good and

evil among them, she was sure. The good and evil that Paul believed in. She remembered when she was young, how it had always been so simple under the old gods, because you always knew what you were doing wrong, and life was simply a matter of surviving.

Groaning as she straightened, she went to the wall shrine, removed the flowers, and tugged the marble plinth with all her strength, using her bent wrists to save her hands, or they would make her suffer hell tonight – Paul's hell – with every joint as painful as though it was on fire.

Behind the plinth, a gap was revealed, left there deep between the walls when the house was built, revealing a hidden stone plaque, a very private conceit carved by the builder with his name on it: *Toherus fecit*. Toherus built this house.

Without hesitation or regret Imogen dropped the casket out of sight into the secret chamber, sure it would never be found while the house stood, and if the house no longer stood, nothing would matter any more. She replaced the plinth and the flowers on top of it, arranging them nicely, and wiped the dust carefully from her hands, congratulating herself on work well done.

Perhaps Diana was not as in control of her emotions as Lucius had thought, because at first she was full of small kindnesses, smuggling the little honeyed cakes whose cloying sweetness he detested to his room, kissing his cheek and hugging him, showing him all the little details of a mother's love when the time for that was long past. He did not look forward to her brief visits, and he would not eat the cakes. She kept trying until her temper got the better of her.

'Just who do you think you're punishing by this behaviour, Lucius?'

'I should have thought that was obvious,' Lucius said without inflection. 'I am the one being punished.'

'Don't be too hard on your father,' she said, then added impulsively, 'or yourself, either.'

'But he's right. I know that I will never be good enough,' Lucius said without emotion, 'and that's the way it should be between a father and a son. It makes one . . . improve.'

'Or too hard on me,' Diana said, forcing a smile, but he didn't respond. Finally she snapped, 'You don't really like me, do you?'

'You both did what you had to,' he said patiently. 'I do understand.'

Diana tossed her head and stormed out. On her way to the bathroom which had been added at the back of the house, with its portable bath on a raised floor to accommodate the hypocaust heating which doubled as a corn drier, she glimpsed Imogen in the kitchen. Fit to burst, she bustled in. 'You know, I despair of that boy! I'm fed up to the back teeth trying to be kind to him!'

'Kindness isn't what Lucius wants,' Imogen said calmly, mixing her bedtime glass of honeyed *rosatum* rose wine to ease her swollen, arthritic finger joints, the sight of which always sent a shiver through Diana. She dreaded looking like that one day, and Imogen's increasingly obvious age made her uneasy. 'Are you asking for my sympathy?' Imogen continued. 'Lucius has made himself into what he thinks you want him to be. He'll make himself a success in life, according to your standards. You'll get what you want.'

This was not what Diana wanted to hear, so she disregarded it. 'That's all right, then,' she said, helping herself to one of the honey cakes she had brought back from Lucius's room, crushing it on the roof of her mouth with her tongue.

'But, Diana, don't you see? It's so little.' Imogen tried to explain. 'Once, like you, I thought this was everything—'

'Oh, don't go on about it, there's a dear. Aren't these the very thing? Try one.'

'*Our* land, *our* fields, *our* place,' Imogen went on. Her swollen knuckles gripped the awkward barbotine-embossed handle of the mixing jug awkwardly as she poured a glassful. 'Our position above other people, the respect they pay us, our money, our house. Our *family*. It's what I always wanted. But it isn't what matters.'

Diana gave an amazed lift of her eyebrows. 'What is it that matters so much then?'

'Love,' Imogen said seriously.

'Just love?'

'What more is there?'

Diana laughed. 'You're upset,' she said, patting Imogen's gnarled, distorted hand. 'They say old people become young again. You must be starting your second childhood. You sound like a soppy girl of thirteen, sighing at the moon.' Both women knew they were no longer close enough for such a thing to be said without giving offence.

Pain jabbed Imogen's finger sockets and she knew she would not sleep tonight. Diana's patting touch, though it was not meant to hurt, had felt like iron hammers.

'Perhaps you're right,' she said. 'Good night.' She took herself off to bed before her pain showed, then paused and looked back through the doorway. 'There's a rather beautiful song, Diana. Have you ever heard it? "Blackbird on a branch in the deeply-wooded plain. Sweet, soft, peaceful is your song." ' She let the curtain flap down and her footsteps receded.

Diana stared after her thoughtfully, pursing her lips, then helped herself to the remainder of the wine. What was that all about? Maybe it was time Imogen was packed off to a little villa on the estate somewhere. She would have to have a word with Paul . . .

And so Lucius grew up.

No trace remained of the child he had been. He wore simple, well-made clothes that suited the weather. There was not an ounce of spare flesh on him, or of anything superfluous. His movements were economical, not graceful, the gentleness in his eyes had hardened into a calculating, suspicious stare. His intelligence manifested itself in a cutting tongue and many a hapless farm worker wilted under the combination of those harsh, knowing eyes and the lashing edge of that tongue. 'Do you call that a straight furrow, Timotheus?' Lucius called down coldly from horseback, riding behind his father. 'It's as crooked as you are.' Timotheus thought he must know about yesterday's pilfering of the store grain, only a handful or two in his boots to make porridge for his son who could keep nothing else down. He began to shiver with fear, and Lucius's suspicion was confirmed. Paul asked pleasantly after the child, nodding vacantly when Timotheus stuttered how fast he was improving, keeping his head down and his hands busy on the plough, avoiding Lucius's icy stare. Lucius was universally feared by men who had once treated him with jocular contempt as a clever boy, and they knew better than to answer back.

'Privilege,' Paul said as they rode on, speaking to Lucius like a stranger. 'They must respect our privileges, respect *us*. They must be as committed to the prosperity of the estate as we are.'

'That man is a thief,' Lucius said.

'They're all thieves, I expect. I make an example of one from time to time.' He wasn't so tolerant where Lucius was concerned. 'They're good fellows at heart, I wouldn't have bought them otherwise.'

'They won't respect you.' Lucius meant *me*.

Paul rode without looking round. 'If they give too much trouble they know I'll turn them into cash.'

Lucius rode with a set face. 'I want to make an example of Timotheus.'

Paul reined in. 'Why?'

'To make the others work harder.'

'Oh, very well,' Paul said casually. He took less interest in the estate than he had; Lucius was a stickler for detail and dealt with all the unimportant daily grind. Paul waved benignly to a villager whose name he could not recall and kicked his mount across the little bridge over the stream, the hoofbeats raising no echoes from the thatched walls of the houses.

When Timotheus's hut was searched by Matugenus, busy as ever on estate work in the family's service, various incriminating items turned up: grain, a saucepan the snivelling creature could not account for, a cache of precious iron nails stolen from the building of the new house for Imogen. Cymbarrus carried out the flogging, his gigantic shoulders gleaming with grease and his belly swinging. Timotheus screamed terribly. Diana kept her eye on Lucius, who supervised the deed close enough to be spattered with drops of blood. He watched unflinchingly.

'Look at Lucius,' she whispered in her husband's ear.

'What about him?'

'It's time he was married.'

Diana was quite pleased with the way things were working out. Paul was his old self again, and getting Lucius away from him, packed off in married bliss to the estate a safe distance away at Vagniacae, would probably make him improve even further. Now that Imogen was in her own small villa near the edge of the slope, she would have her husband all to herself, and a full hand once

271

more in the running of Valle Dei. Things would be just as they should be.

'Before the weather gets bad I'll go and see Vagnius Vagionius again,' Paul decided, and Diana purred.

Next time Paul rode to his property near the River Dart, Lucius rode behind him. After only a few words with the steward who managed the place – very profitably, the land being mostly forested, the lumber rolled down and loaded conveniently from the sawmills onto boats in the Dart to be shipped to London – they rode across the bridge that had replaced the ford, through the village of Vagniacae into the rolling estates of Vagnius Vagionius. Peacocks strolled between golden, autumnal beeches in the grounds. In the huge brightly-painted villa that sprawled across the top of the low hill, Vagionius, resplendent in a robe with a fringe as ginger as his frizz of hair, welcomed Paul with a shout and a smile. Some people said his father had been a British aristocrat, others that he had been a mere peasant, but he had certainly been an excellent businessman. Vagnius Vagionius had inherited his style but not his business flair.

Hurrying slaves laid cushions and bolsters across the stone couches in the sheltered house-garden. As he clasped wrists with the older man in the large hall, Paul was sure he heard the quick scuff of a girl's house shoes echo across the mosaic of the next room. They would be overheard. Vagionius surveyed Lucius with interest. 'Got a face like a lemon.' He nudged Paul discreetly. 'Let's make ourselves comfortable.'

Reclining on a couch in a slant of the pleasant afternoon sun, Paul swirled his sweet, watered white wine in its mug. Lucius sat apart, by the house-garden wall. 'You know, of course, why I have come. It's time we formalised our agreement.'

'Taken your time about it, Paul, I must say,' Vagnius said jovially, pulling at the hairs that sprouted from his nose and rubbing his fingers. 'I've had other offers.'

'My boy's the right age now and so is Campana. I think it's time they got together, don't you?'

'Classier offers – forgive me.'

'Roman citizenship but no money,' Paul scoffed. 'Besides, forgive me, she was not as a child the world's greatest beauty.'

'Quiet, she's listening. Anyway, your lad doesn't look like an aesthete.'

'He isn't.'

'They took an instant dislike to one another as children,' Vagionius pointed out.

'What does that matter? They're not children any more. He will do as he's told.' Paul's mouth had that grim set to it that always came when he talked of Lucius.

'The estate is rather a large dowry,' said Vagionius amiably, 'though quite a large part is pledged to the Emperor in taxes after my death. Most of it, in fact. And you know that we're all supposed to buy town houses now.' Vagionius rolled his eyes. 'So that we can be taxed to pay for London's roads and temples and town walls, if there are to be any. I don't know why there should be. We're in for a thousand years of peace, you mark my words. Still, such civic trials are the burden we have to bear if we want the *tria nomina* and Roman citizenship.' He blew out through his lips, spraying wine. 'Campana's twenty-second birthday is in January. The perfect age.'

'Four months. That will be time enough for them to learn to like one another.'

'Let them meet,' Vagionius said. He loved his daughter dearly, for all her moods and bossiness. She kept him in order, pampered him, scolded him, took her mother's place everywhere except the bedroom, and tolerated his dalliances with women as young as herself as long as he was not tempted to marry them. Vagionius would miss her sorely, and he wanted her to remain within reach when she married. He genuinely had turned down much better offers of marriage for her because long ago he had seen that meek little Lucius was the best for his Campana. Gentle and dreamy boys grew up into meek husbands, whereas she had always known her mind. She'd make sure he was pointed in the right direction. None of this Valle Dei nonsense; she'd arrange it so they'd move into the little place across the river – she'd already planned the changes she wanted made, and Lucius would do as he was told. And every morning they'd wake up to the view of his much grander house above them, and Campana would come over in a litter every mealtime – no one prepared such a melting ragout of seafood dumplings as she did, or such delicious livers of animals fattened only on figs, fed by her own hand. No, Vagionius could not bear to lose her, and would not. The lad would have to learn to live with his thin belly; he was sour-faced enough for the

273

expansive Vagionius to feel no mercy.

'I don't want to marry,' Lucius said, desperation making him speak out. 'I want to live alone.'

'Your duty is to our family and you'll do what you're told,' Paul said dangerously, in a low voice. 'Is that clear?'

'Yes, Father.'

'You can't live alone all your life.'

'Can't I?'

'That's enough! You're not only letting yourself down,' Paul's cheeks flushed red with anger, 'you're letting me down.' He added in a furious undertone, 'Is that what you want?'

Lucius bowed his head. 'I'll do anything you say.'

Vagionius, who had watched with interest and pleasure to see how matters lay between father and son, broke the silence with his throaty laugh. 'My girl's a wonderful catch, you should thank your father! Simply tons of money.' He kissed his fingertips. 'And such food. You'll stay for dinner, I insist.' He clapped his hands for strong Setine wine in celebration, icy cold from the well.

There was nothing wrong with Campana, no cross eyes, no limp. She was polite but could not draw Lucius out, and so grew nervous, eventually faintly aggressive. Afterwards, when he tried to remember her on the ride back to Valle Dei, nothing much about her came to mind. Certainly nothing objectionable. They were exactly the same age. She was half a head shorter than he was. Her skin was pallid, her eyes dark, mostly taken up with looking at his clothes, which were apparently dirty. Paul thought she was very beautiful, and was enchanted by her manners and respectfulness. He had stared angrily at his son who picked sparingly at the dishes she gave him with her own hand. Their hands touched once, but not their eyes. She said nothing memorable and there was nothing Lucius wanted to say to her. 'You'll do, you two,' grunted Vagionius, sucking the meat from a chicken leg. 'You'll do!'

Paul and Lucius returned in silence to Valle Dei.

Only one person was up earlier the next morning than Lucius, who rose with the sun even in summer, and that was Imogen. Now that October was dulling into November the nights were long, and Lucius was no more than a shadow in the gloom as he led his mule past her house, so as not to wake her as he commenced his daily tour of the estate. But she was already standing on her step, her arm round the verandah post to hold herself up, watching him. She called out and he tied his mount to the gate that kept the sheep and goats out of her garden and went to her.

'Grandmother?'

Her face was so haggard that he realised she had not slept at all, her spine and hips now bent and twisted by the disease of bones that afflicted old people as invariably as the loss of their teeth and the loss of their senses. And she was old, sixty or more, her hair the same silver he remembered her husband's had been – *exactly* the same as Grandfather's, he thought. Her hands were gnarled like roots, but her eyes were still bright as the points of knives.

'Well?' she said.

'I thought something was wrong.'

'Something is wrong. It's wrong with you. Now, what happened?'

He shrugged.

'Don't you shrug at me,' she said harshly, holding out her hand for his help. 'Come on, come on!' He helped her into the house a step at a time, the small high windows on the east side glowing with dawn, then she leaned back on a tall upright chair with carved panels. 'Once I sit down I can't stand up,' she muttered absently. 'Sit your long shanks on that stool, so that I can look down at you. That's better. Now, about Campana. Does she like you?'

He looked up. 'I suppose so.'

'Do you like her?'

'I suppose I must.'

'Lucius, you really are the very picture of misery.' Imogen shook her head, very slowly, with an effort; it must have hurt her. 'Look at you.' She held up a small glass face mirror by its handle, turning it towards him, though not before a grimace of distaste at her own reflection. 'At my age one does not wish to look too closely into such things. At your age it may be a salutary friend. Lucius, look at yourself.'

He looked. 'What should I see?'

'Turn your mouth up, Lucius.'

He stared at her uncomprehendingly, and she gave an impatient sigh. 'Pull up the corners of you mouth, like *this*. That's it, smile. Use your fingers. That's right!' she said proudly. 'There! I had to force you to smile, but I've done it. Feel better?'

'I don't know what you're talking about!'

'Take your fingers out of your mouth, I can't understand you,' she chuckled, and suddenly he laughed, seeing himself as she saw him. 'There, you can do it,' she said encouragingly. The sparkle in her eyes flickered, almost died. 'No,' she said briskly, 'keep working at it, Lucius, every day of your life.'

She put down the mirror and held out her hand. 'You have ears, and a mouth, and eyes. You have the use of them for another forty, fifty years if you are lucky, long after I'm dust.' She took his hands, strong and smooth, lightly in her own. 'Lucius, do not be deaf, and dumb, and blind. Don't do that to yourself.'

The first beams of sun were streaming past her door.

'I've got to be going,' he said, panicking. 'I've a mountain of work to do.'

'Goodbye, Lucius.' She let him go, watching him scamper to the gate. He lifted off the rope and swung easily onto the back of his mule. By way of farewell she lifted her fingertips in the corners of her mouth, a smile. For the second time he gave that single bark of laughter, then set the mule trotting across the knoll on his usual circuit, ignoring his dog loping faithfully after him. Imogen watched them into the distance until the sight blurred and man and dog and mule became one. She felt tired to death, and she was afraid she had just made life much harder for Lucius, because he would think about what she had said. He was that sort of man. She leant her cheek against the doorpost for a moment, too weary to move, gathering her strength. The slave-child who cared for her, Atiliana, daughter of a poor family in the village who had sold her for a while in order to feed their other children, would soon come to help her to her bath . . .

Lucius rode up the boundaries of the long, narrow fields covering the knoll, the ploughed earth pale with chalk, some of it in stony lumps that would have to be picked out. And weeds still growing, despite the lateness of the season! How was it that weeds grew so much more easily than crops?

Coming to the bridge of split trunks thrown across the stream, he dismounted to walk across, but he let the mule drink first – the mule always pretended to be thirsty, just to get the time off, but instead of jerking him across as usual, Lucius rested his elbows on the rail, the rein dangling from his hand, thinking about what Imogen had said. Someone watched him from the trout pond that had been dug beside the stream, motionless, and gradually his attention focused on her.

She was standing in the water as deep as the top of her legs, seeming to grow from her reflection, a tall slim girl wearing only her pale green shift which floated round her waist. Her fox-red hair was so long it touched the surface of the water, seeming to ripple up from below as well as streaming down from above. The smooth planes of her skin were still brown from the summer's sun, her large steady eyes a darker tone of that same brown, just as her parted, reddened lips were a darker tone of her hair.

'Have I seen you before?' he asked, because he had to say something, aware of her steady, continuing examination of him.

'You ride past here every day!' she laughed, breaking the image she stood in, and he raised his eyes from her reflection to her face. She had fine white teeth that she was not afraid to show, and now he noticed small cheap ornaments of shell gleaming in her ears – she had shaken back her hair, the last span or so of its length spreading out, darkening, rich as blood around her in the water.

'Who are you?' he said.

'I know you. You're Lucius.' She had an advantage over him. Her tunic was dumped on the grass at the side of the pool, thonged skin boots tossed beside it, homemade and strong; then she threw her advantage away. 'I'm Emilia.'

'Catia Martina's daughter?'

'Youngest daughter.'

He pointed at the sacking she carried neatly folded in the crook of her elbow. 'What's that?'

'You've really never seen me,' she marvelled.

'Are you here every day?' he asked severely, trying to dent her extraordinary confidence.

'Of course I am. Except when it's raining.' She ruffled the water with her fingers.

Lucius frowned. 'Why except when it's raining?'

'Well, I wouldn't want to get wet, would I?' she said seriously.

They stared at one another. 'It was a joke, see?' she sighed at his slowness, ruffling the water again. 'I'm up to my crotch in water, I wouldn't want to get wet . . .'

'Oh! I see!' Lucius told himself he would never understand the complicated, excluding humour of the common people – except that nothing about her was common, however ordinary her origins. It was incredible to believe that her father, a goatherd, one of the Vernicus line, could have sired such . . . perfection. There was no other word for her. Those eyes! He could not look away from her, drinking her in like the water, and she hadn't looked away from him at all, not once. 'It must be cold,' he croaked.

'Yes, it's freezing.'

However had he not noticed her?

'You've always got such important things to think about,' she said, exactly as though she had read his mind, and he imagined himself as she must have seen him, head down, mouth down, same clothes every day, coming up the track and dismounting, crossing the bridge, mounting up again without a backward glance. Probably his eyes had flickered incuriously across her figure standing in the water or by the pool dozens of times, but he had never noticed her.

Emilia. What a wonderful name. He wondered what touching her hands would feel like.

'Your mule's wandered away,' Emilia said.

He cursed and jumped down, then realised he was closer to her and stopped, letting the mule munch the grass while he searched desperately for something to talk to her about. 'Why do you stand in the water?' he burst out.

'My older sister Camilla never liked the feel of fish against her legs,' Emilia said. 'Most people don't.'

'But you're different.'

This was dangerous talk. She was a freedwoman's daughter, she would marry a goatherd and birth half a dozen children in as many years; most of them would be sold into slavery to feed the others, and she would be too old for heavy work at thirty and dead by forty. 'No, I'm not different,' she said. The water made her voice carry with a slight echo, deep for a girl. She pulled the flap of the sacking folded over her arm to reveal kitchen rubbish, rusks of stale or burnt bread, mouldy flour, earthworms that she had picked up on the way – he imagined her bending over in the long wet grass, the form of her, the way her legs would look. He was losing his sanity. She dropped bits of food from her fingertips, and the water swirled around her, fins and mouths broke the surface as the trout fed. 'I like them, they slide against you. In the other pool we have tench, their skin feels warm and soft as a woman . . . as a woman does.'

He had never touched a woman. He could jump down into the water, feel what she felt, the icy coldness, the fish sliding around them.

'These are trout,' she said. 'Some of them answer by name, Ajax, Troy. You can tickle them.' She stroked her hands in the water, then lifted the gleaming rainbow of a fish into the shallow sunlight before letting it splash back. She laughed at him, and Lucius smiled. He actually smiled.

'Was that Ajax, or Troy?' But he didn't jump down; she would think he was mad, or he would frighten her.

'I don't know really, they're just names.'

'Could I learn to do that?'

'Jump down,' she said. But he hesitated, and his opportunity was lost. She was starting to shiver. 'Sometimes it seems a pity to eat them. They get very slow in the winter.' She waded to the side, revealing her brown muscular thighs, then the mud clinging to her white, water-wrinkled feet as she hoisted herself onto the bank by the mule. 'Do you want me to catch him?' she offered.

Lucius glanced at the mule contentedly grazing. 'Emilia,' he said, purely for the pleasure of saying her name.

'I've got goosepimples,' she said.

'I know.'

'Lucius, have you had a fall this morning?' she burst out. 'You're not anything like people say you are!'

He simply exploded with laughter and caught hold of her warm hand.

That was how Matugenus, dusty and sweating, found them. 'Lucius, didn't you hear me calling?' He caught his breath, didn't wait for an answer. 'It's your grandmother. Atiliana came to take her to her bath and found the main door of the house open, and Imogen lying slumped there in the doorway as though she was asleep.'

All Lucius could feel was Emilia's hand in his own. 'Is she hurt?'
'Lucius, I'm sorry. She's dead.'

'She isn't dead,' Paul said simply at the end of the equally simple ceremony. There had been no terrible show of grief, no professional wailing mourners or ghastly trumpets. Already the crowd, disappointed, had begun drifting away. Paul no longer bothered to keep his beliefs secret, but only a few women and older people stayed to hear the strange new words: the men didn't like anything new, and they wanted to get back to their beer.

Imogen's body had been preserved with gypsum so that it could be resurrected on the Day of Judgement. 'I don't mean she'll wake again among us in this world,' Paul hastily tried to explain as the people stirred superstitiously. 'I mean that I believe she will live in the glory of God.'

'She didn't believe it,' Lucius muttered to Emilia, squeezing her hand.

'It doesn't matter what she thought, *I* know it's the truth!' Paul shouted, overhearing, distracted for a moment by wondering who the village girl was at Lucius's side. 'A million Jews died by fire, sword and suicide in the rebellion that the Messiah refused to lead. He knew it was not the way! He has been proved right!'

'She was a wonderful woman and I loved her,' Lucius murmured, 'but he's not saying her anything like she was.'

'Ssh,' Emilia said, and he was quiet. She looked at him. 'Do you always do everything you're told?'

He couldn't look at her enough. Her hair was like gorgeous lava.

'Only when it's you,' he said. One week with her had changed his life, and suddenly his parents seemed old.

What had once been a long climb up through the trees was now only a stiff walk up the lane Paul had paid to have paved, bringing Valle Dei closer to the trade opportunities of the imperial road. The funeral party had come winding between the few remaining stands of oaks to join the village to the heath. The cemetery had grown up just outside the village boundary, mostly oak headboards already mossy and cracking, a few of ragstone, none rich enough to be carved with a likeness. And now Imogen's headstone. It had been expected that Paul demonstrate his wealth by a magnificent funerary monument for his mother, the matriarch who had, after all, founded the village. But instead of a suitable mausoleum with a large carved effigy of her standing on top, he had insisted on merely a sort of stone cross, solid but very small. That had been something else that had sent the young men of the village away shaking their heads. They had been irreverently leapfrogging it before the interment, and one lad, Remus, son of a sick Gaulish merchant, had tumbled right into the grave, standing up in it to his waist. That would bring bad luck. Even Diana felt it was time to bring matters to a close when Paul, the casket containing his mother's mortal remains only barely laid safely to rest, began to talk of love, love for everyone, neighbours, family, enemies, being the reason for the whole world.

But Lucius looked around him. Those who remained, many of them the poorest villagers, were listening raptly. Since meeting Emilia all he knew had been stood on its head. Such terrible lives some of these poor people lived! Because of her he had met them, with her he had been invited into their huts and gone into the slave dormitories, talked to those who would talk to him – and everyone would talk to Emilia. Paul offered these low folk an afterlife of joy in return for goodness and obedience in this life, but their conditions had not improved while the estate grew more prosperous. Paul was not without compassion but his views derived more from his conviction that he was a sinner, and that the end of the world was imminent. His beliefs were so strong he could no longer keep them to himself and today they had simply burst out of him.

'I want to marry her,' Lucius said as they walked home. He, too, could no longer keep what he felt inside him. Paul stopped, then shook himself like someone coming out of a deep sleep. 'I want to marry Emilia,' Lucius said firmly, pulling her forward.

'What?' Paul said, watching a crow pulling at the flattened body of a mouse on the road.

'I want to marry Emilia,' Lucius repeated. The people following on were staring at them.

'Ssh,' Emilia said, her face as red as her hair. 'What's got into you, Lucius?' she hissed. 'You're embarrassing me.'

'It's all right,' Lucius said, 'I'm asking you now, Emilia. Marry me for love.'

'Stop making a spectacle of us in public!' Diana said, one eye on Paul, who had made no response at all.

'She loves me and that's all that matters,' Lucius plunged on recklessly. 'I can catch a fish by stroking it. She taught me. She's shown me things in the village I never saw.' He groped for words, came up with them victoriously. 'I was deaf and dumb and blind before she came into my life. How can I help loving her?'

'He's lost his senses,' Diana said. 'It's all right, Paul.' She took Paul's elbow, indicating with a cock of her eyebrow the people watching and listening avidly. *Not in front of everyone*, her eyes pleaded. 'Time to go home now.' Such was her authority and the power of her grip that Paul allowed himself to be led away, stifling outrage.

'We mean it,' Lucius persisted, towing Emilia behind him.

Goaded beyond belief, Paul whirled on him, his uncoloured cloak making a flapping sound like a sail. 'You'll marry Campana and that's that. It's arranged. Not one more word.' He turned and banged into Diana, then tried to storm past her.

'Father, I won't do this for you,' Lucius said, his voice firm.

'You'll do as you're told,' Paul raged. 'I am your father, you'll do as I say. *Is that clear?*' He must have cowed the boy with those three words a thousand times in the past. 'In the ides of January,' he went on, his face flushed, 'you will marry Campana and live at Vagniacae, happily.'

'Without love.'

'Yes,' Paul spat.

'You'll have to have me killed,' Lucius said.

'Come, dear,' Diana begged Paul, 'you're both too angry to speak sense.' She turned on Emilia. 'You witch. How have you done it? You're nobody.'

'I know what he feels for me, I can see it. So can you,' Emilia whispered, eyes downcast though she was much taller than Diana, who was slumped by mood, weight and years. 'And I love him whatever you say.' Emilia looked up with those deep brown eyes of hers, her lashes freckled with tears.

Diana stared. 'You poor idiot,' she said, 'you really do.'

'I've done everything else for you, Father.' Lucius turned back and forth, torn between Emilia and protecting himself from Paul, then stood his ground. 'I've sat down when you told me and stood up when you told me. I even stopped *thinking* because you told

282

me to. But I won't be punished by you any more.'

'We'll all feel better in the morning,' Diana said, pulling Paul's shoulder. 'We can discuss this later. Leave your father alone,' she murmured wearily to Lucius. 'Can't you see he's tired? His own mother's funeral!'

'I love Emilia and she loves me,' Lucius said simply.

The anger fled from Paul's face; his skin went quite pale. He stood there with his hair fallen over his forehead.

Diana stared enviously at Emilia.

'He's right, isn't he?' Paul said, and Diana nodded. She heaved a great sigh, all her schemes flying away between the trees as though they had never been.

'Campana's no loss,' she said stoutly, 'but Vagionius will sue us, and the law is on his side.'

'He can take our estate there in settlement,' Lucius said cunningly. 'He's a greedy old man, and he'll jump at the chance of something for nothing.'

'But where will you live?'

'Now that Imogen's house is standing empty?'

'Of course!' And Paul embraced his son, almost crushing him.

'*I bless this marriage in the name of the Father, the Son, and the Holy Ghost.*'

Lucius remembered. When he was very old, he remembered being young.

The marriage had been sanctified in every way, by his father's blessing, by the exchange of contracts under Roman law, by the kiss beneath the mistletoe hung over the doorway of Imogen's house, now their own, in the ancient practice. Imogen would have watched with a smile.

And then Paul had said something very strange and awful, raising his cup of wine. 'To our friend, forever young, who cannot be here with us today, to witness our joy.' Everyone knew he was talking of Vitellus, never found, almost forgotten. But then Paul had embraced Lucius again, everything forgiven.

'No dowry again,' Diana had sighed, but then she had smiled for the two lovebirds, and kissed Emilia, because long ago she had brought Paul no dowry either. Lucius chuckled, remembering how his mother had grown closer to his father, learning to love him as her middle age turned her grey and lined her face, and made her hips as broad as a barrel even after she had given up the honeycakes.

Lucius remembered Emilia standing on the edge of the slope, her slim ravishing figure with the river glinting between her outstretched arms, London with the huge new basilica and forum showing above the mass of orange rooflines, the green and violet haze of the far distance . . . had had eyes only for her breasts really. And he remembered the feel of her sun-heated back in the palm of his hand as they went into their new house, a palace to her eyes. 'What a wonderful view, and such a good feeling,' she had murmured, 'but you see, I wouldn't mind living in a hovel again, Lucius.'

With her beauty and reckless charm, Emilia could always tell the truth, but for a moment he had doubted her.

He had searched her eyes. 'Is that really true?'

She'd laughed, rubbing his lips with the tip of her nose. 'With you.'

So Lucius, long ago, had achieved the impossible when he was only twenty-two years old, and all for love: reconciliation with his father, married bliss, his first daughter two years later, a growing friendship between his wife and his mother. An aristocrat of the Cantii marrying a commoner! Lucius, with Emilia standing beside him, eventually received Roman citizenship and the *tria nomina*, as Aelius Lucius Lovernianus, in the presence of the Emperor Hadrian in person, in London.

Old Lucius was sitting on the cross-chair in his study, behind the huge desk that had been handed down to him together with the house and the estate and all its people. He listened to the sound of his grandchildren playing in the house-garden. Through the open door he could see their parents, the grown-up children of his love for Emilia and hers for him, lying tolerantly on their couches, looking up at the occasional loud scream or shout. The mothers, his daughters Lucilla and Claudia, clapped their hands from time to time for silence or raised a finger in admonishment when there was a squabble. His eldest grandchild, Julia Loverniana, at twenty was expecting a child of her own – that girl had the big bones of her great-grandmother, and Diana's dark hair too. Lucius stopped. Memories of his mother, the apple-balsam scent of her, still ran so fresh in his mind that it was a shock to realise Julia was too young to remember her. Diana had died twenty years ago, but to him it seemed like yesterday.

Children running. How they ran!

His own little sister Antonia, who had grown up so much more formidable than Lucius and in her middle age had developed Diana's taste in sweet desserts, egg dumplings, pears sweated in cream of pistachio, had long ago married Briginus Matugenus and settled down blissfully if not always without argument. Again, with Paul's reluctant permission, the Fox family had married into the village for love, as Lucius had, throwing up the opportunity to form aristocratic alliances with people of their own sort. Now Antonia's own grandchildren were running and screaming joyously in the courtyard.

Would the children remember this sunlit day? Would they remember the old man watching them as they chased each other between the fountains, poor little Lunaris, his only grandson, hobbling after them on his club foot, trying desperately to keep up?

Slow down! Lucius wanted to call. You're all going too fast – even you, Lunaris. I'm too old, and I want this day never to end!

Once he had been like them. The older he grew, the more he became like a child again.

Life was so long, but ran away so fast. Lucius's clutching fingers could not contain all he knew, all he remembered. That bewitching apple-balsam scent of his mother – in his mind he could inhale Diana's fragrance, and something more to it, but when he tried to reach out and grasp it, the exact significance of his memory was gone.

'Well?' Emilia said.

She was standing in the doorway and she must have been speaking, but he had not heard her.

'Right away,' he said, guessing that she had been calling him to join the others; he did not tell her he had been thinking of his mother.

'Slow as a tortoise!' Emilia held out her arm cheerfully, and he took it. Lately she was much stronger than he was, and he relied on her – as he had always relied on her, he realised. Without her, his life would have been a poor thing. He stopped her before they

285

came into the colonnade, speaking to her in shadows made deep by the brilliant sunlight outside.

'I remember the day we first met. You were standing in the water and you looked so beautiful. I've always wanted to ask you one thing.'

'Ssh,' she grinned.

'You planned it, didn't you?'

'No.' Her large, oval brown eyes had not changed. 'No, Lucius. You always looked so miserable, and one thing I had sworn was that nothing was worth marrying a man who was a misery. I was not attracted to you at all.'

'You changed your mind,' he said grumpily.

She laughed. 'You smiled and I fell in love.'

'That was all it took? One smile?'

'That was enough. There was nothing more to it than that, Lucius.' She kissed his lips lightly. 'And I've never regretted my decision to marry you.'

'*Your* decision? It was mine!'

'It was ours,' she said diplomatically.

'No one ever had a happier or luckier life than I,' Lucius told her with an old man's earnestness. Their granddaughter Ingenua, looking sad, holding her mother Claudia's hand, would depart soon for married life in London. Her father Ingenuus had received a London marriage proposal for Aelia too, the second of his three daughters. Over by the aviary Octavia, willowy and wan, always offering help, was holding up Lollia's baby Amanda to see the fluttering birds, and disgraced Theodoria, who had gone crazy for the Greek merchant with the warehouses on Belinos's quay in Greenwich, held up her own baby Hermione, who must soon be adopted because she had no father; and all the other children were shouting out their names, trying to teach the tame magpie to speak.

Lucius embraced his wife as tight as he could, as though he would hang onto his love for her even beyond death.

'What's the matter, Lucius?'

'I was thinking of my mother,' he admitted.

From her gown Emilia pulled out the silver talent Diana had given her before she died.

Lucius had not seen the coins since that dreadful day when

Vitellus had yelled at him for a spade. Neither boy had paid much mind to John Fox's story, except the bloodiest bits. No one could find where he had been buried; there was a myth in the village of a holy well, but Imogen had never spoken of it and no one had ever found such a place, and if the rumour was true the only men who had known of its whereabouts, the burial party made up of Paul and Briginus, Matugenus's father, were both dead. The secret had been lost along with the other talents. Emilia held the last one swinging and flashing on her chain.

'On her deathbed your mother called me back and I spoke to her alone,' Emilia murmured. 'She said the talent was a promise. She asked me to take what she had worn all her married life from round her neck, it was for me. "*Because Lucius loves you,*" she said, "*and because you love him. It is so much more than I have ever felt, though not more than what Paul feels for me. I envy all of you so much. It's yours now.*" Lucius, she gave it to me because you and I were in love.'

'And you wouldn't give it up even when my father tried to get it back, claiming that the talent was his, because he had stolen it long ago.'

'I would not!' she chuckled. 'It's mine, and one day it will go to whichever girl our only grandson Lunaris chooses for *his* wife.' Emilia hesitated, remembering Paul calling the coins 'relics', and did not tell Lucius what Diana had told her. When Diana had spring-cleaned the shrine in Imogen's old room, the plinth had moved, and hidden in the wall she had seen the casket wedged between the bricks, still scented with the Qumran smell of apple balsam, and in its broken corners the glinting gleams whose discovery had brought the family so much grief. Diana had mortared the plinth firmly in place so that no one would ever see them. But she had whispered her secret as she died.

Diana was cremated and her effigy, complete with her favourite little dog, was erected by the road at the entrance to the estate. Paul lived another seven years, and was laid to rest beside her. For the sake of her soul he had her pagan statue replaced by a simple Christian cross, though she'd never been a Christian. Other crosses had been set up too, the family starting to reach back through the generations as life rushed onward.

In the last year of his life, Paul saw a great fire of London for the second time light up the night. Many great imperial buildings were devoured by the flames but the enormous forum and basilica were preserved. The roar of the conflagration could still be heard, like drumbeats murmuring on the wind, even over the birdsong of Valle Dei next day. The fort on Lud's Hill stayed safe behind its massive ragstone ramparts, though its new white stone was blackened and aged with smoke by the time the fire died down around it. Hugely wealthy, the town was rapidly rebuilt, showing off its pride with even larger buildings, many elegant bath-houses with curved roofs, and plans for an amphitheatre.

Paul spent his last days digging by the stream that now poured down the gully, searching for the talents he had lost. He had little strength and no real hope of finding them, and perhaps, from his dull face, he had forgotten exactly what he was searching for. When Emilia went down and gently took his elbow, he allowed her to lead him away as though it was his own decision, returning quietly to his mother's old house. The road took them past statues and arbours where once there was nothing, past the marble bath-house astride the stream, with its rumbling furnace and Oratan showers, steam room, hot and cold pools decorated with specially commissioned mosaics of dolphins, seahorses, sinuous moray eels with gold-leaf earrings, and many other wonders. Few still alive remembered the day when the bourne had not run here, or the time when the oak trees of the nemeton were a mighty enclosure like safe, strong arms round the knoll; only a few clumps remained, the larger ones given names like Nimet Wood, and a cleared field was known locally as Drunemeton, meaning a sacred grove of oaks, though almost no one now made the connection between the name and the ploughed earth. Paul, who had cut down more than enough great stands in his youth, tried to explain this to Emilia as they went by: all they had lost. And then he'd stopped, staring at a young man running after them with a spade. Paul had left it lying forgotten in the gully and the young man was returning it. Paul gazed at the panting boy as though he recognised him. Then he took the spade and turned away shaking his head.

'Who did you think he was?' Emilia asked as they walked on.

'Vitellus,' Paul replied instantly. 'For a moment I thought he was my son whom I killed, my poor dead son Vitellus . . .'

That day, by coincidence, Lucius was on his way back from a business trip to London. Maintaining no town house of his own, he stopped to have his horse watered and to refresh himself at the Tabernacle Inn. It seemed a rough sort of place to Lucius, but it had a wing of agreeable private rooms where a gentleman could rest and sustain himself with wine – the Tabernacle was well known for the quality of its cellar. The innkeeper was busy welcoming a group of travellers, great arms extended as though to trap them within the welcome of his hostelry, but for an instant his blue eyes flashed, and Lucius stopped.

'Who's that?' he asked the runtish boy who was leading him.

'That's Wittle, sir, my grandfather who bes the owner of this establishment from long afore this.' He looked Lucius up and down, reckoning his chances of a tip. 'As I will be one day, sir,' he added, 'after my father.'

The lad rushed beneath the belly of the colossus as though expecting to be dunned with great blows; and for a moment the blue gaze turned on Lucius, the eyes peering with a glazed and crafty light from raddled, boar-like features. No hair, none whatsoever, graced the dome of the skull, the face a net of broken veins. Lucius shivered, taking the other side of the room to avoid the innkeeper's great welcome, letting the boy lead him down a tiled corridor. 'And my father's name be Wittle, sir,' said the boy phlegmatically, 'and so do mine be.'

'Fetch wine,' Lucius had yawned, tired by his journey, and in the morning rode on not realising that his horse had been saddled by his nephew, or that he had seen the man his brother had become.

Lucius walked with an old man's stoop as he crossed the shadowed colonnade of his fine house with Emilia. Lunaris hobbled over to see them, Lucius's gentle brown eyes and Emilia's flaming head of hair coming together in him after a skipped generation, cheerful as a spark despite his infirmity. He was thirteen years old, and his father would soon have to think about finding a wife for him – though being a Fox, Lunaris would doubtless have his own ideas.

Lucius kissed Emilia on the lips, surprising her. 'You are my delight,' he whispered. 'Everything has been worth it.'

Emilia smiled and touched the talent she wore as a pendant.

BOOK TWO

IV

Rufus and Leo

John Fox's Family Tree continued
Spring 500 – October 516

John Fox
★
★
★
Lucius

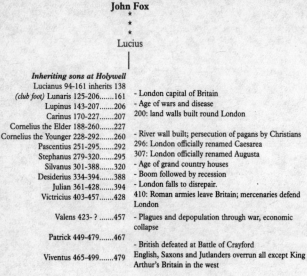

Inheriting sons at Holywell

Lucianus 94-161 inherits 138
(club foot) Lunaris 125-206.......161
Lupinus 143-207.......206
Carinus 170-227.......207
Cornelius the Elder 188-260.......227
Cornelius the Younger 228-292.......260
Pascentius 251-295.......292
Stephanus 279-320.......295
Silvanus 301-388.......320
Desiderius 334-394.......388
Julian 361-428.......394
Victricius 403-457.......428

Valens 423- ? 457

Patrick 449-479.......467

Viventus 465-499.......479

- London capital of Britain
- Age of wars and disease
200: land walls built round London

- River wall built; persecution of pagans by Christians
296: London officially renamed Caesarea
307: London officially renamed Augusta
- Age of grand country houses
- Boom followed by recession
- London falls to disrepair.
410: Roman armies leave Britain; mercenaries defend London

- Plagues and depopulation through war, economic collapse

- British defeated at Battle of Crayford
English, Saxons and Jutlanders overrun all except King Arthur's Britain in the west

Total defeat
London deserted

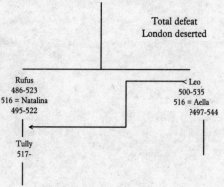

Rufus
486-523
516 = Natalina
495-522

Leo
500-535
516 = Aella
?497-544

Tully
517-

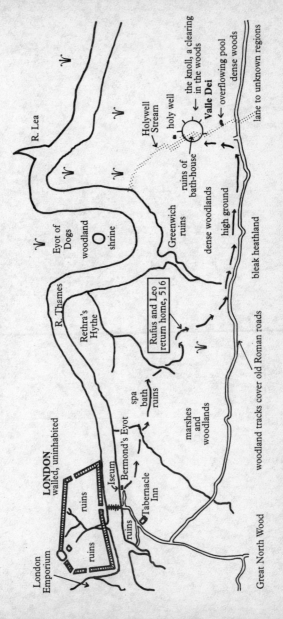

Rufus and Leo return home bringing Aella, 516

Her last scream was his first.

The baby's head emerged into the rain pouring through the green roof of summer leaves above them, the wind driving rain and mist between the gloomy green trunks that grew all around Rufus and his mother, Pascentia. He was fourteen, a grubby-faced urchin; she, with her regal way of holding her head even *in extremis*, was perhaps twenty years older, old enough to be his grandmother. Since their hut was accidentally burned down, this jagged, crumbling tooth of brick-and-plaster barn wall growing out of the swamp was the last scrap of safe shelter.

Leading the goat on a tether of woven grass, Rufus had guided, finally half-carried his mother here between the tree trunks when her time could no longer be denied, and now she lay exhausted. Even before the contractions began she had seemed terribly weak, wearied by the constant rain and too tired to fight. That had frightened Rufus more than anything, because his mother had kept her head high every day of her life. Even now her veined, smutted hands maintained their rigid, possessive grip on the rags of her old gown – it had been her own mother's, soft fabric like this was not to be found nowadays. She wore it like a badge of pride, even though it was worth killing for; but Rufus knew no one ever came down here among the trees.

Almost.

'Don't worry, little Rufus,' Pascentia had murmured, grunting as he'd settled her as comfortably as he could, then gripped his wrist tight with her broken nails, gazing at him sadly from her smoke-blackened face. 'Listen, my son. You always were a fighter. But this is one battle you can't fight for me.'

To Rufus, crouched miserably with his elbows hanging over his knees, her words sounded terrible, but worse was his feeling that she did not intend to fight. The wind rose, pushing at him so that he braced his knuckles on the ground.

'Rufus. There is one important thing. It is written,' she said, as though she could write, or read – 'it is written that you may not see the nakedness of your mother. You must not look.'

'But I was inside you once!' he complained.

'We are not animals, Rufus, we are humans. We are all children of God. Do you understand?'

'Yes. But—'

'Then I commend myself to His hands,' she said in Latin, which Rufus did not comprehend. Neither did she probably, but the old rituals were most comforting when least understood.

His mother was going to die.

'Pray for my soul,' she said, and closed her eyes.

Rufus knew that she'd said goodbye to him, and to her suffering in her harrowing life. She'd given him no jobs – fetch water, Rufus, make me a fire, a grass pillow for my head. None of it would matter. She had given up. Given up long ago, he realised, even letting herself get dirty in the last few months, when she had always been so proud of – oh, of everything. Of being clean, of being a lady, better than other people. Of marrying the husband she had. Of being a Fox.

An aristocrat.

Even though they lived in nothing more than a hut in the forest, it was more than most people had. And they owned a nanny goat and could barter young kid goats, milk and cheese for things they needed. The others paid them the respect they were due, and that sense of superiority had kept her going.

They'd slept with the goat in the hut with them though, in case it was stolen. Now Rufus was losing it all.

'You'll fight!' he told her, his voice high pitched with determination, but she just flickered that weary look at him – don't make any more fuss. Not letting him help her, that was what really outraged him; he had crossed the limit of her care and love for him, he was already alone. But he would have done anything for her.

For hours he listened to her groaning, her beating heart and panting lungs not releasing her, not letting her go even though he was sure she willed them to stop.

In the rain, Rufus walked up and down in a kind of hell. He tried to pretend everything was normal, fetching grass and ferns for her bed whether she wanted them or not, shaking them dry, making work to keep his mind off her cries, which were increasing in frequency and volume, anguished and penetrating enough now to call down trouble. Her shrieks tore at his heart. And all the time she was getting weaker and nothing was happening. She wasn't fighting for her baby to be born; she was shrinking away. Without Father, something had gone out of her. Yet still her body would not let her die.

'Fight!' Rufus shouted at her, then forced himself to say calmly, 'You've got to fight, Mother.' Suddenly what to say came to him like a wonderful flash of light. 'You've got to fight because it's what Father would have wanted.'

Her eyes flickered, then she responded. 'How do you know?'

'He would have expected you to fight,' Rufus said doggedly. 'You're our family. You're Fox.' He said in a louder voice, 'You're a Fox, and this is your place.'

'Damn you, Rufus, you urchin,' she said weakly, but that made him smile, knowing that he was right.

'I'm no urchin,' he said bravely. 'I'm Rufus Fox, and I'm your son, and I'm proud.'

And so Pascentia fought, but she still would not let her son help her. Her strength faded and the day passed its middle, but the rain did not cease its steady downpour. Rufus got a fire going, but it gave no heat or flame, just a haze of pale smoke which moved along the sodden ground among the nodding, rain-beaten heads of nameless wild flowers, butter yellow, blood red, shell pink. Over the rush of the rain he heard the growing roar of the stream, flooding now, and crossed himself superstitiously.

He listened to the panting moans of his mother dying, and there was nothing he could do. Face averted, he pushed moss and grass against her to stem the flow of stuff from under her gown.

And then her awful scream faded away, and the baby's cry began.

Rufus advanced, shaking.

In the shadows he could just see the baby's head, wrinkled and sort of a blue-grey colour, protruding from his mother's loins. Again came that dreadful half-born sound, the baby screaming and choking, both at once, then the clotted gasp for air.

Rufus had never heard a noise like that.

'Mother?' he whispered, terrified. The raindrops thudded onto his thatch of soaked red hair, sluicing down the patch of tiled roof overhanging the angle of wall, beating on him unmercifully, making it difficult for him to think. His mother now lay without movement, without sound, no gasp for air, only the wet whooping noise of the baby choking.

Rufus put his hands over his head to try and keep off the rain. He was too old to cry – he had his own sword given him by his father, though it was only an old one with nicks along the blade which wouldn't come out however ardently he stoned it, and the handle wobbled during enthusiastic practice. In his frustration Rufus drew the sword from his belt and whacked it onto some of the roof tiles lying in the grass, breaking them. It was all he could think of to do.

'Mother,' he cried, so distraught he hardly knew what he was saying. 'I'll look after it. I promise. I'll do anything you want. Only live.' There was no reply.

Suddenly his mother's legs gave a great kick, the veins rising out of the pallid skin like knotted blue cords, rainwater splashing from her raised knees down her thighs. There was no trace of the lady she had once comforted herself with being; her distorted face looked like that of an animal. She did not call on God. In terrible silence she kicked out, again and again, with such force that one pathetic shoe of wrapped sacking flew off her foot, then as her back arched, the bare white foot sank into the mud to the ankle, taking all her force. She thrust her hands between her breasts. The rain pattered into her open mouth and staring eyes.

Then the bones went out of her, and she slowly flattened out like a dead body. Her knees flopped outward and water puddled in her mouth, dripping steadily from the corner of her lip.

Rufus advanced, crying his eyes out. He dropped his sword, leaving it where it stood upright in the moss, and wiped his face with his wrists, ashamed of himself, not sure what was tears and what rainwater.

His mother was dead. In the ginger hair where her thighs joined, the baby's head and shoulders now hung half out of her like a skinned hare onto the mat of grass and flowers Rufus had crammed there earlier to slow the blood. The puddled mess was cold now, pocked with stiff circles from the rain.

Then Rufus drew in his breath in wonder. The baby had perfect hands, perfect tiny fingers with the tiniest fingernails he had ever seen. But it had no lower body, no legs, no sex; they were still locked inside its mother's womb.

Rufus looked back at the sword. He knew what he must do. The baby had no hope. It would die of cold or wet or hunger or worse. He knew what his father would have done, and done it quickly, with one kind slash of his knife; but a long time had passed since his father had gone out hunting in the strange, haunted glades of Valle Dei – and had simply not come back. No trace of him, not even of his disappearance. If he had followed a wounded animal onto the bare heath above the forest, the only really large treeless area of which anyone knew, then perhaps the marauders who occasionally used it for a camp had taken him. That race, Rufus knew from songs older than memory, had ghastly blue eyes the colour of the sky, hair like golden spray, and were seven feet tall. They dressed in one whole skin of cowhide with a hole cut through for their heads. Many years ago there had been a terrible battle on a river far away, where great-great-grandfather Victricius, the Count of the Saxon Shore, was killed – for all that he had inherited the odd blue eyes – by a giant. Those glorious days were camp-fire legends, repeated in his father's wondering, uncomprehending voice. Rufus's father might have been killed for his gold cross, or simply killed, given these Godless times; but Pascentia had prayed he might have joined his captors in hope of escape, and those prayers had sustained her. Perhaps he had been sold, or bartered, and might turn up one day, coming splashing through the Holywell bourne winding between the mossy tree trunks, the same old smile creasing his dirty face and that twinkle in his eye for Rufus, his only son.

'Mother?' Rufus whispered, not daring to touch the baby without her permission. Water dripped from the baby's big bald head – and then Rufus saw with amazement that the few strands of hair that the baby did have, plastered in wet tails to its skull, were exactly the same fiery colour as his own.

Pascentia had waited, silently losing hope, for her husband to return while her belly swelled, with Rufus's help ekeing out an existence here among the ruins, surrounded by the green safety of the forest, most of it young oaks growing wild from acorns before anyone they knew of was born. The tangled undergrowth was doubtless much more recent but equally beyond Rufus's memory. His father had claimed there was even an open field in this very place once, but Rufus could not believe it, though he had to admit that there were odd straight mounds running through the woods, almost lost but there if you knew how to look for them. Father said they were boundaries from Grandfather Patrick's time. Once all this had been broad fields, the property of their ancestors. 'That was so long ago you weren't even a twinkle in my eye,' he had said fondly, tousling Rufus's hair, 'but I remember that he had red hair just like yours, red as flame.' Twinkle in his eye! Rufus had never forgotten that, or the serious way his father had said it, as though it was really true. He gave utterance to many wonderful and dreadful things, a dreamer, whereas Mother had been a practical sort, except for her vanity, until her despair overwhelmed her. Oh, what a terrible end she had come to because of it! And the baby almost born.

'I could have helped,' Rufus muttered to himself. 'I *could* have.'

He knew what she would have replied. Without a father, without a mother – without *her* the baby stood no chance.

Rufus went back, picked up his sword, and brought it over. He stood looking down.

He swung the blade, then stopped.

Like his father and grandfather before him, Rufus knew one great, simple, overriding truth. *This was his place.* And because of that he knew one other thing: this baby was his brother, he was *family*, and Rufus must not allow him to die. They were both of the Fox blood, perhaps the last. Whatever happened to them would happen to them together, Rufus decided. And it would happen here.

Kneeling, he said sorry to his mother as he touched her body, then pulled, and the baby slid into his hands. Obviously a boy – and he felt so warm! With the nicked sword blade Rufus sliced the cord and knotted it just as they did each spring with the goat. He apologised again to his mother, then opened her clothes and suckled the baby to her flat breast. But the nipple lay shrivelled and grey against the baby's red lips. 'Go on,' Rufus said, frowning, but nothing happened; the little fellow whimpered at the dry breast.

Rufus held him up into the rain and stared at him. 'You're ugly,' he told him. 'Really ugly.' The baby stared back with a flat blue gaze, then his lips stretched into a chubby grin.

'I'll call you Leo,' Rufus announced, 'and I suppose I'll have to look after you as if you were mine.' Leo kicked his pink smeary legs and his windy smile widened into an expression of discomfort, then he gave a burp. The smile disappeared with the burp, but Rufus was enchanted. 'You *are* mine,' he said. He tore a strip from his mother's soft woollen gown and wrapped Leo in it. Then he tucked him inside his furs, leaving just a flap open for air. 'You are now, Leo. You haven't got anyone else, and neither have I.'

When he tried to move his mother's clenched hands from between her breasts, the position in which she had died, to cross them piously as she would have wished, her fingers opened and the silver amulet she had called her talent slipped from her grasp. Rufus turned the piece of silver over in one hand incuriously – it had not saved her. He knew his father's mother, Viventia, had handed it down to her, just as she had been given it on her own betrothal by her mother-in-law Tullia, the second countess, who even after Kent had fallen to the Saxons, Jutlanders, and English continued to use the title. Tullia's young husband, Valens, had rallied to Arthur's British banner in the west, but she had stayed and kept the family's memories alive while he fought for his country. She never heard of him again, only the stories. Her stewardship kept what was left of the estate going until her son Patrick was old enough to take over, but by then only the family's pride in their name remained.

There were many families like them, fallen on hard times, quietly hanging on, hoping for better days.

The charm was very old and battered, Rufus saw, worn thin and smooth by generations of skin, as though women's flesh was harder and more enduring than metal. Near the rim it had been pierced by a small hole as if for something finer than the rough leather thong that now held it. By legend there had once been a whole hoard of them, long lost.

Quickly Rufus hung the coin from his own neck, sending a cold douche of rainwater from his hair down his back. Then he arranged his mother's clothes as properly as he could and folded her arms over her cooling body, crouching awkwardly because he had to keep one arm under the swaddled woollen lump against his chest that was Leo. Then he closed her eyes gently with the tips of his fingers.

Suddenly she didn't seem so much there any more, which was good, because the night animals would come out soon, and he must go.

Rufus looked around him, shivering. It was growing dark. No animal would attack him, except perhaps a snake or a boar. The animals he feared most walked on two legs. He must think of the baby all the time now. For the baby's sake he knew he must find better shelter, but the thought of the haunted place he must go to made him shake.

The goat's tether had come loose but she trotted to him trustingly, as always, when he whistled. One hand tugging her beard, the other in his clothes supporting the baby, Rufus turned his back on his mother and went splashing away between the tree trunks. Within a few moments the rain, the mist and the trees had hidden her body. He knew he would never see her again.

The trees thinned, showing a pale glow between their trunks, and the rain grew heavier as he entered the clearing. Everything to his right was thick mist, as if there was nothing there, though he could hear the wind roaring in the treetops somewhere below. He wobbled across mounds of rubble buried under the grass and wild growth, then a large end wall leaned over him, decorated with courses of red tiles and rising to a high foreign-looking gable, providing a few moments of respite from the rain. A few bright patches of plaster still clung to it – it must once have been painted. Around it poorer dwellings made from old bricks and tiles had collapsed and the earth had taken them back; nothing more visible remained of them than the occasional beam sticking out of the mud, or patch of herbs.

'Not much further now,' Rufus told the baby, then his eyes widened as he felt his nipple nuzzled by the small warm face. 'You won't get much there, lad!' he said. It was surprisingly easy talking to a baby. 'Little bit further to go,' Rufus told him anxiously, 'don't be afraid, now.' He jostled Leo with his elbow. 'Not afraid, are you?'

Leo began to cry, a hungry cry.

Rufus swallowed, hanging on tight to the goat. Her name, by tradition, was Ylas, because that was an easy name to call at the top of your voice, but Rufus was only whispering now as he slid down the last pile of rubble, comforting the goat as well as the baby, and himself. He crossed the level ground up to his knees in mud, and ahead of him a shape began to form in the mist as he came closer: an oddly-shaped building of strange shiny stone, with curved roofs fallen inward in some places, or showing slats of mouldy wooden lath to the rain. The bourne had flooded in a broad fan in front of it, brown water with lumps of yellow foam swirling at the steps. The stream had once been contained and made deep by earthen banks, but they were hardly visible now; the water came no higher than his thighs, though he had to keep a firm hold on the reluctant goat as he struggled across.

He went up the steps.

No one came here to this strangest and most haunted place among the ruins. Whatever had hung in the gaping entrance holes had long since rotted away, and the only light filtered in from behind Rufus and down from the holes in the roof, through which streamed rain. The dark blue rooms reeked of damp, debris everywhere, fallen in or chucked in.

'Anyone here?' he whispered. Even his whisper echoed. 'It's me, Rufus. It's me and I've got Leo with me, and we aren't afraid of anything!' There was no answer but the rain.

Creepers curled dark shapes up the walls, and in several places beneath the largest holes, where the sun must fall, saplings were shooting into young trees, their tops reaching earnestly towards the light above them. Several had grown through the roof, which was splitting and collapsing round their trunks. Below, the floors were uneven, dug into deep rectangular pits, like animal traps, in which further debris lay. The innermost room had a door which looked as though it would swing, but it fell to dust when Rufus reached out. The walls in here, of plaster, were untouched by the rain, and faded wall paintings covered them: women with unbelievable hair, oval eyes, flowing gowns. The rich dark humus that had grown across the other floors had not yet reached into this room. The floor here encircling the pit was made of tiny pieces of shiny stone fitted together; even the steps down were decorated, as was the pit itself, with a mosaic of fish, as real as if they were jumping, and eels coiling sinuously among branches of weed. They looked so alive that Rufus wished he could catch them and cook them. Hunger was all he cared about, and he turned away from the useless things impatiently.

'This is *my* place now,' he said.

Leo's cries had become constant, making a terrible echoing racket, almost as bad for thinking as the rain rushing on the roof. Rufus pulled him out and held him awkwardly beneath the goat, trying to get him to suckle, but it wouldn't work. He felt inside his clothes and cut off a rough square of leather, pricked the centre of it with the point of his sword, made a pouch in one hand and milked the nanny into it. Leo suckled eagerly at the porous leather, then gave up; Rufus pricked the hole wider, and this time the baby closed his eyes and sucked as contentedly as could be. Suddenly he gave a piercing yell, and Rufus patted his back until he burped.

'For a man, Rufus,' Rufus congratulated himself as he laid Leo down in the corner, 'you're making a good mother.' His voice was shaking and his fingers trembled, and tears weren't far behind his eyes: Leo needed him.

He made sure the wool was thick enough against the cold floor and that the baby was really asleep before prowling the dripping warren for the makings of a fire. The reputation of the place had kept folk away, and he returned with bits of old cupboards to burn and tinder from the stalks of last year's grass which grew in the corners. No one knew better than he that a fire was dangerous – the smoke might give them away. But it was essential for the baby. He would never have dared come in here to these haunted baths but for Leo; looking after Leo had made him braver than he wanted to be. He gazed down at the baby with a kind of wonder at himself before going off again.

He knew that everything he was doing was probably very stupid – his father would have given him a good thrashing for it. He couldn't look after himself properly, let alone Leo as well. But as he settled down to sleep he thought of that enormous, terrifying effort his mother had made in the last moments of her life, pouring her soul into the baby to get him born, the veins rigid in her legs, utter exhaustion on her face, and yet she had kept pushing. In the end she hadn't given up, and neither would he. He owed her that.

Rufus's sleep was haunted by a soft rumbling sound, almost too deep for his ears to hear, but his body felt it as he lay on the mosaic floor, an odd quivering sensation in his tummy, and he woke sweating each time the baby cried. The first time, he milked the goat again, but Leo only coped with half, so Rufus tied the neck of the pouch and kept the rest, but the baby woke him again in no time at all, and this time slick, odourless baby shit slid stickily down Rufus's clothes.

The night was wholly dark, the rain easing off but a rising wind hooting in the holes in the roof, and still the faint rumble beneath, not enough for him to notice awake, but there beneath his knuckles when he pushed himself to his feet, like a great dark spirit stirring and muttering in the earth. Like most British people, Rufus called himself a Christian, though personally he had no idea what it meant – something to do with Latin, like Valle Dei, Romans, and other meaningless names. The Saxons, English, Jutes and other barbarians were not Christians, so perhaps it was one of their pagan spirits coming to haunt Holywell, or perhaps it had been here all the time, slumbering. It was easy to believe such things in the middle of a black night – difficult to believe anything else, in fact.

Things will get better, Rufus whispered to himself, and I will go to heaven. He wiped himself as clean as he could with his fingers, then wiped the baby too.

Sitting awake, he could hear nothing now, only the wind rising and falling, the rustle of dead leaves swirling in the eddies on the floor.

The English and Saxons, even the Jutes who mostly favoured Kent, had avoided Holywell so far, and they were said never to take over places where people had lived before, preferring to make their own homes. His mother had told him – repeating, no doubt, what Tullia had told her at his age – that the Romans had been aristocrats, administrators, soldiers, writers and readers, not ordinary people. There had never been that many of them. They changed the way most folk in Britain lived very little, and when they left the island, the British still spoke British as they had always done and lived in huts as they had always done. Rufus knew this from his own life.

But the English and Saxons were different, she said, because there were *thousands* of them, spray-haired peasants rowing ashore on any available bits of jetsam, leaving their own lands deserted and flooding, herds of common people joining together and migrating inland from the British beaches, husbands and wives and children, mostly peaceable farmers who wanted nothing more from life than to let their swords rust, raise crops and huge families and get drunk. Taxes were low and their law was free, and they often respected the boundaries of property. The British had been decimated by two plagues, their warlike spirit blunted by three centuries of occupying armies, and they had more to fear from marauding bands of their own defeated people than from invaders.

With a sigh Rufus turned his mind to more practical matters. He fetched a handful of moss from another room by touch, found his way back and put it under the baby's bottom, then gave the other end the rest of the milk. He waited for dawn.

He was sleepless, uneasily rocking the baby in his lap, when the first grey light filtered into the room. He milked the goat again, but she had not much to give and she was hungry, tugging at her woven grass tether with that rolling look in her eye, so he let her out down the steps.

Abruptly he retreated into the shadows, appalled at what he saw. He hissed for the goat to come back, but she kicked up her tail and kept going. Across the swamp, the reeds waving and clicking in the wind, shapes were moving out of the trees, first a line of filthy men in ragged leather, then a motley collection of bad-tempered women carrying baggage on their heads and shoulders, complaining to each other in harsh, sneering voices. This was what his parents had lived in fear of more than anything else: marauders. They did not seem weary enough to have been going for long; probably they'd endured a night of wind and rain on the heath and were seeking lower, more sheltered ground. The weather promised no better, uphill was hidden in a lid of cloud, and below them the Thames lay like a grey worm wriggling in the marshes, no boats, no houses, no smoke, no fields. The women came into the clearing grumbling loudly to each other that those menfolk of theirs had better be sharp about finding them some-where nice, like right here for instance, if they wanted a warm welcome tonight. Their calls and mocking laughs, faint at first but growing, sounded to Rufus like the ugly screeching of birds swept along by the wind.

He shrank into a dark corner, staring through the bright door-way. He hissed again for the nanny goat to come but of course she did exactly the opposite, crossing the tussocks in the stream with small delicate jumps, wandering out of sight between the mounds in search of greener grass.

'Go away, then!' he hissed, sure that would make her return, but she didn't, and perhaps that was lucky for him. Most of the men coming closer had swords or long daggers and some of the women were carrying shields for them. The women were prisoners, or they had started off that way and now they were making the best of it. There were no older children, but he saw a baby and a youngster not quite old enough to walk yet too heavy to carry. A woman bent under a burden kept on picking the child up and trying to stagger on with it, then putting it down – a red-haired girl, Rufus now saw, with a terrible scar up the side of her face as though one of the men had tried to do her in.

Leo whimpered and Rufus realised he was squeezing him.

Ahead of the women, the men gathered by the stream and stood scratching their sides, deciding where to camp. Their hair was dark or reddish – British. One hefted his skins and pissed in the stream, trying to hit the balls of foam flowing by, and the others made wagers, knocking him when he ran dry too soon. Rufus could hear the squelch of their boots in the mud – a couple were wearing wooden clogs bound with leather straps to hold them on, and one carried his arm slung across his front, injured or broken. He only pretended to laugh with the others, painfully. The leader was the biggest, and stood with his hand ready on his sword, which was longest, but Rufus reckoned the injured man was the brightest. He kept jerking his sharp face towards Rufus's hiding place – camp in there, keep dry, let's be sensible. But the leader shook his shaggy hair uneasily, and the others followed him to the wall in the rubble. The women were grateful just to drop their loads. They set to work like a team, stretching skins for shelter from every available point, getting smoky fires alight, sorting through their stuff for bits of food while the men climbed the wall. The leader reached the top first and threw down a brick or two, sending the others scattering, but the sharp-faced man had seen it coming and kept away.

'What do you see, King Vindomarucius?' he called in British, but only after starting the first word in Latin. He clenched his teeth, cradling his arm.

'Chop it off, Emrys!' called down the man on top of the wall, chucking a brick that made the sharp-faced man skip.

'It's better,' Emrys said through gritted teeth.

'We'll chop it off for you, won't we, lads! Yes we will!' King Vindomarucius bellowed from his vantage point above their heads. Then he pointed out over the slope, the treetops, the river, as though they were his own. Between the banks of rainclouds drifting in the distance, the clearly-defined shape of a town, one straight length of it lapped by the river, was visible on two hills. 'That's the place? What did you say it was?'

'The people who lived there said it was London.'

'There we are then!' cried Vindomarucius, then gave a shaken roar of laughter as the wind tried to gust him away. 'Food!' he yelled furiously as he scrambled down. 'Give me my bloody food and my bloody bitch!' The woman with the biggest breasts embraced him with one arm, offered him a joint of skinned hare in the other, and he looked at her as if he didn't know what to start on first.

Rufus felt sick. The nanny goat must have wandered into the trees or she would have been seen by now. The trouble was, when she wanted milking, he knew she would return.

Rufus looked for a back way out. There wasn't one. He returned to the doorway, staring from the shadows at the figures moving across the stream. The women were concentrating their efforts on one fire now, gathering firewood in groups while the men struggled to bring back a huge tree branch, toppling it on the flames with shouts of joy to see the sparks shooting up. The flames gusted hungrily, and the buxom, red-cheeked woman with the baby went down to the stream to fill an old pot with brown water. Rufus knew she was doing it in case one of the precious tent-skins caught fire, which it would if the men kept up their pranking. One of the women was telling them off with a wagging

308

finger, the rest had turned their backs.

The woman with the baby looked through the doorway straight at Rufus. He held his breath and shut his eyes lest she see them gleaming. He turned to stone.

When he drew breath again and opened his eyes, she had turned away and was plodding back to the fire.

The men quietened down and did not move again all day, Emrys sitting away from them, the woman with the baby finding a place halfway between him and the fire. Once she went over and looked at his arm, but he kept shaking his head. The wind blew their hair and skins and they must have been cold and uncomfortable, but they preferred their own company to the others'. Several times they looked across at the bath-house, straight at Rufus, it seemed, and he waited in an agony of suspense in case they crossed the stream towards him. But they would not defy Vindomarucius.

Leo was growing hungry. Rufus murmured to him, cuddled him, soothed him by pressing his little finger like a nipple into his mouth, kissing him on the lips during the louder cries, but soon nothing worked. Rufus was starving, but Leo's hunger obsessed him and he could hardly think of himself. He retreated to the innermost room where they had spent the night, hoping the thick ragstone walls would muffle Leo's cries. Leo had got wise to the little finger trick, stopped his frantic sucking and began to scream, purple in the face, as though he would never stop. But the wind was rising again, whining in the roof holes, and dark clouds scudded across the doorway. Finally Leo exhausted himself with his hungry complaining, fell into a whimpering doze, and Rufus peeped from the door. Emrys and the woman had moved close to the fire, which flared brighter as the day grew darker.

Rufus wondered if he dare risk a run for it – he would have to run in clear sight round the front of the building, and a boy carrying a baby would have a hard time running in the heavy undergrowth that must lie behind.

He never thought of simply abandoning Leo. Not once.

With pernickity steps, the nanny goat came from the trees, crossed in plain sight of the men lazing, whittling wood, arguing or lying on their women in the shelter of the wall, then picked her way delicately through the rubble field. Rufus tried to hiss her away. Her udders swinging beneath her were swollen with milk, too heavy to run. Rufus watched with tears in his eyes, he so badly wanted the milk for the baby. But the men saw her and chased her with roars, circling her and falling over, catching her on the edge of the bourne and cutting her throat.

Rufus watched them eat.

He went back to the inner room and lay down beside Leo, waiting for darkness.

When his eyes opened, it was as if they were still closed, he could not see his hands. He found Leo only by reaching out towards the hungry cries. That noise no longer mattered; the wind whooped like a demon outside, rain rushing in squalls across the roof, beating invisible wings in the dark, then flying on. Rufus made his way carefully to the door, finding it by the wind whistling through the gap and the speck of firelight it held. As he watched, building up his nerve, the bonfire seemed to blossom, blowing out to one side, then fanned into separate flying pieces. Logs and embers and sparks were sent whirling through the air. A dull *crump* carried to his ears. Dozens of scattered logs burned where they tumbled, freckling the darkness like candles. There were shouts, curses, groans. Then Rufus heard a woman shrieking and shrieking. She would not stop.

Dawn found Rufus slumped in the doorway not knowing he slept. He was terribly thirsty, and in his dream he heard the bourne flooding yellow-brown in front of him, but he had been taught by enough cuffs round his head from his father never to drink water, except from the holy well flowing from its bottomless pool down the slope – and that ran only after heavy rain, and then only slowly, clear but tasting of chalk and minerals. And it wasn't really bottomless; he'd lowered a stone on a piece of twine into it once, and it was barely deeper than a man standing with his arms over his head. But he dreamed of the rich taste of it now, hearing the sound of it splashing like footsteps, approaching.

'So she was right after all,' a voice sighed wearily. 'I should have known, knowing that one.' Rufus's eyes snapped open at the first word, and now he tried to jump up, but the baby was bundled in his lap. A sword tip was pressed to his chin. Rufus looked up its gleaming length to the sharp-faced man, Emrys.

'Boys is fast,' Emrys said sadly, and Rufus knew he was about to die. 'I had a grown-up lad of my own, once. Point would you have it, or edge?' He pressed with the point, drawing blood – the blade was fine steel and must be very old, perhaps passed down from father to son. 'We kill people who spy on us, see. Keeps us safe.'

But he did not thrust, and he seemed so sad and exhausted that perhaps he would not; there was a withdrawn look in his eyes, behind his pain, which might have been kindness.

'I need milk for my baby,' Rufus appealed to him. 'You killed the goat,' he added fiercely.

Emrys flicked open the woollen swaddling, noticing the way the boy flinched. '*Your* baby? You're hardly old enough to shave.'

'My mother's. I'm looking after him.'

'Are you, indeed? He's a noisy one.' Emrys winced and cradled his injured arm, wrapped in leather crusted with black blood and pus. 'We needed the meat. Any more of you, would there be? The truth now,' he threatened abruptly.

All at once Rufus saw how to answer. 'I wouldn't be doing woman's work like this if there was anyone else.'

Emrys grinned, showing ghastly yellow fangs at odds with his thoughtful eyes. 'You're a cunning boy, I see, and you may be worth it.' He thrust his sword through his belt, held out his hand impatiently for Rufus's rusty blade and took that too. Using his good arm he heaved Rufus to his feet with surprising strength.

'No trouble from you, boy,' he warned amiably, 'or I'll kill the baby.'

Taking the bundle and propping it casually against his shoulder, he splashed across the stream without waiting to see if Rufus would follow. Emrys smelt as bad as a badger, but he was no fool. Rufus followed.

The gale had blown the wall down. The falling bricks had caused terrible injuries, but most of those caught had died and, beyond earthly torment, looked peaceful. The little girl with the scarred face sat holding her foot, which was twisted and badly swollen. Other survivors shuffled among the ruins, picking out things they had lost, a boot sticking from the rubble, a bent sword, a piece of tent-skin that stretched longer as two women struggled to extricate it from the weight of brick. King Vindomarucius lay beneath a similar pile, only his barrel chest and shaggy hair visible, cursing weakly for help through the blood that ran from his mouth, but Emrys ignored him, just as he ignored the dead he stepped among. They had already been stripped naked by the women's quick, sensible, passionless fingers.

Emrys scrambled over the rubble towards a woman who was weeping loudly, then jumped down to her on the grass.

'Stop it now, Saturnia,' he said, thrusting the bundle at her – she was the woman who had looked straight at Rufus. 'Here's another one for you.'

'I don't want another one,' Saturnia wept. Her tears had trickled clean pathetic lines down her filthy face and neck to her heaving breasts. The rest of her was matted and smeared with blood from the soft, broken shape she cuddled to her. 'Where have you been? You're all the same, you left me alone when it mattered.'

'Quiet now!' Emrys said.

She wouldn't. 'I want my own back,' she said dully. 'I want my own dear darling back. Even if you don't care, I do.'

'You can't feed her,' Emrys said gently. 'Here. Here. This one is living, and needs your milk.'

'It can starve,' Saturnia sulked, but she glanced at the baby when Emrys shoved it under her nose, then turned away.

'A boy,' said Emrys, going round her, showing her. 'Here, you don't have to let her go. You can feed him warm on one side while you hold her body to the other.'

'I don't know.' But Saturnia looked again, and her eyes softened. 'He is rather sweet. He looks strong. He's so small!'

'He was born yesterday,' Rufus said. 'I'm his brother.'

Saturnia settled Leo to her breast, her dead baby to the other, which looked quite horrible and wrong to the two men, even to Emrys who had suggested it. But Leo sucked at once. Saturnia put back her blunt head and gave Emrys a satisfied look. 'I told you there was someone there, didn't I? Didn't I?'

'And how right you were, my sweet, as always.'

'You must remember that the next time I tell you something.' After a few minutes Saturnia reluctantly laid her own cold child down and transferred Leo to the other plump breast. 'He's drinking too fast, this'll give him awful burps. I suppose I shall have to look after him.'

'He makes awful messes,' Rufus said.

'You shut your mouth and collect my things together,' Saturnia said sharply, 'before that lot run off with them.'

'He's my baby too,' Rufus said.

Emrys scrambled to the top of the mound. 'I'm the leader now,' he called out to everyone. 'This is a bad place for us. If we hurry we can be in London tomorrow, rich and fat. Who's with me?'

'He's all brains and no brawn, that Welshman,' yawned one of the men who wore his skins fur outwards like Vindomarucius. 'Spent too many years away from his mountains, on the moors of Dumnonia.'

'I'm not Welsh, I'm British,' Emrys said angrily. 'I fought against the pagan English at Arthur's side by Mount Badon, when he was an old man. And I've worshipped on my knees by the Tor at the church of Our Mother Saint Mary the Virgin, built by the Christ's own hands at Glastonbury.'

A woman with the first streaks of grey in her hair put her hands on her hips and spoke up. 'We'll go with you, Emrys, until we find someone better. He's right, this has not been a good place for us.' There was a murmur of agreement. Then she held up something that shone in the morning light. 'We found these on the ground. Shall we carry them?'

Emrys went over. 'It's a hoard,' he said.

So it's true! Rufus thought. The old fireside stories are true after all!

He bit his lips tight.

'It must have been buried in the wall,' Emrys said.

'There was a stone with something on it.' The woman prodded with her foot.

Emrys crouched. 'It's Roman writing. *Toherus fecit*. Toherus built this.' He looked around him at the swamp and moss and scattered stones, then shook his head. 'What use is silver? We'd have done better to keep the goat, at least we could have bartered a goat.'

'Better to have a belly full of red meat,' glowered the man who wore his fur outward.

'Gather up the coins,' Emrys decided. 'They're worth carrying.'

'Carry me!' Vindomarucius called. 'I'll be strong again. I'll lead you.'

313

'I'll do him,' offered the girl with the longest hair and biggest chest and before anyone could stop her she drew a dagger from her thigh and thrust it to the hilt into Vindomarucius's mouth. 'There,' she said with satisfaction. 'That's stopped his hole.'

'No more,' Emrys said, shaken. 'We move on *now*.'

Saturnia knotted the grass tether, all that was left of Ylas the goat, round Rufus's neck lest he should snatch the baby and run away, and told Emrys to knot the other end round her wrist. When Rufus walked faster than her hip-swinging plod she jerked him back, and sometimes she jerked just to let him learn who was boss. The track climbing between the trees of the hanging woods was treacherous with a jumble of old road stones and they had to weave between them from one side to the other. They passed beneath a ruined archway, then crossed through the old village cemetery – some said it was just the one family, the stones all with their heads to the west in the Christian style, softened with weather and many knocked over. Some of the deeply-carved names were still legible: PAUL. LUCIUS. LUNARIS. COR-NELIUS THE ELDER . . . None of them meant anything, and the ragged party tramped between them without stopping.

They left the valley deserted behind them.

Nothing moved but the rooks that circled above the oaks, dropping now to feed in the green silence. Tiny red squirrels scampered along the motionless tree branches clasping acorns, a young deer parted her stilted front legs and lapped soundlessly from her reflection in the holy well. And then the slight figure of a young girl slipped out of the trees, limping slowly to the bodies where the rooks feasted, jostling and cawing noisily as she approached. After a while she shooed them up in a racketing cloud. Sitting by the body of her father, she pulled the dagger from his mouth and cleaned it on her dress. When she felt stronger, and her foot gave less pain, she would use the blade to dig his grave, but for now she turned her eyes, bewitchingly slanted and dark as sloes, towards the abandoned bath-house. It looked pretty, she thought, its shape softened and garlanded by flowering honey-suckle. The boy had hidden there, it must be safe whatever the old women niggled and fretted with their old wives' tales. The girl limped wearily towards the gaping doorway.

On top of the heath the weather was too harsh for trees,

although today, Rufus noted thankfully, the wind was catching its breath after the storm, and the sun stood on legs of light between clouds that hardly shifted all day. The band made fast time.

Rufus had never been so far.

The gravel of the Roman road had mostly worn away, and in places the stones beneath had either been washed out or carried off; the road dipped and rose through new marshland. New paths, easier to walk on than the rough stones, had sprung up along the line of the old road. The ragged party, less than twenty of them left now, more than half of them women, hurried uneasily, knowing how dangerous travel of any sort was, the roads always claimed by this or that king to exact dues or tolls or steal the best women. But the plague had hit the British hard this close to London, Rufus knew, and the farmers from Jutland kept themselves to themselves. Their odd huts, no higher than a man because of their sunken floor, barely long enough to sleep in, with two flat straw walls tilted together to meet at the top, were few and far between and none of them were lived in. A road was dangerous not only for travellers, but also to live near, and what few tendrils of smoke they saw came from the midst of deep, inaccessible woodlands. They saw no one else on the road at all.

'Anyone seen Natalina, the little runt?' Saturnia called suddenly. 'The one with the mark on her face Vindomarucius did when he was drunk. Where's her mother?' Someone made a throat-cutting sound. 'She's skipped us!' Saturnia swore, giving a good hard jerk on Rufus's rope as though it was his fault.

'She hurt her foot,' Rufus said hoarsely. Drawing breath hurt.

'She's no loss, doesn't matter,' Emrys called back.

'She *does* matter,' Saturnia muttered. 'She was worth something even with that face, the daughter of a king.' But Emrys just laughed.

They camped on the slope above London that night. No lights whatsoever showed through the darkness within that enormous boundary of walls and forts across the moonlit river; even the shoreline was fortified by battlements taller than any ladders or masts Rufus could imagine.

In the morning silence they tramped downhill towards a few threads of smoke rising among the islands of the south bank. Saturnia walked with Leo clamped first to one breast then the other, jerking Rufus sharply whenever the fancy took her. 'That's the way to bring them up,' clapped one of the older women approvingly. 'Gets the boys used to doing what they're told.' The marshes had flooded the Roman cemeteries along the road, and Rufus saw monumental weather-stained fragments standing out of the reeds, part of a stone horse, a stone woman without arms, curlews and oystercatchers fluttering and whizzing among them in the shallow lakes. The causeway had subsided in several places and they had to wade through the water.

'Here's the place,' Emrys said as they came to the south bank of the river, a rural and deserted frontier shored up by the remnants of great wooden quays. The wood was bleached white by the sun and splitting, the rising tide sluicing smoothly between the ancient wharves and over revetments of stakes and wattles, spilling into channels and marshlands beyond. A few buildings with walls and roofs stood dotted on the islets and they paused outside a small place, ignoring the man who watched them, arms crossed, leaning in the shadows of his doorway.

Across the marsh on their right rose the pillars of a smashed pagan temple which had been converted into a Christian church, also doomed – birds flew inside its shell. By the inlet on their left the outline remained of some sort of Roman building. No one had bothered to steal the stone, and grass grew from the clay walls fallen inside.

'They'll be back,' called the man in the doorway beside them so suddenly that the travellers, men and women together, jumped like one person, then turned towards him in confusion.

'The Romans will come back,' the stranger repeated patiently, his eyes pale in the shadows, keeping his gaze on them as he nodded at the ruin. 'And they'll bring their money back with them and I will be a happy man.' He pushed himself upright, towering over them – no one except Rufus noticed he was standing on the step. 'The headquarters of the Military Guild, that old place was, and very good for business!'

'You can't be that old,' Rufus said, and Saturnia choked him with a meaty tug on the rope, not easing off until he writhed.

'No, I'm not so old that *I* remember, boy,' the man answered Rufus, 'but my blood remembers.' He bunched his fist, slammed it against his heart. 'My father's tongue told me, and my grandfather's who could remember the German mercenaries we British paid for, who betrayed us, and through being our servants became our masters. British, are you?' he asked innocently. 'Like myself?'

'And proud of it,' Emrys said, not to be fooled. 'British you may be to us, but I'll wager you're a Saxon to the Saxons and English to the English. And a Christian to Christians.'

'You're right, I'm a survivor.' The stranger's unpleasant blue eyes appraised them one by one with a pale, penetrating gaze, settling on Rufus, then he unfolded his great slovenly arms and yawned, scratching his belly, contemptuously dismissing them as refugees.

'What rogue are you?' demanded the man wearing his fur outward, pushing forward his lower lip aggressively, but the stranger's gaze dismissed him, seeing he was not the leader.

'I wish there was more in this belly of mine,' the stranger said, making his move and stepping from the shadows. He'd quickly picked out Emrys as the one in charge. Widening his eyes slightly, he took in everything about his prey, that hurting arm, sharp hunted face and nervous eyes, the muttering people behind him. He smiled. 'Isn't that the only truth that matters to your people, my friend? Food for your belly and beer for your head!' he called over Emrys's head to the others.

'What's Emrys waiting for?' Saturnia asked one of the other women loudly. 'Why don't he stick him? It's always talk with Emrys.'

The stranger grinned. There was not a single reason why any one of these ruffians should not slip an iron blade under his ribs and take everything they wanted, if only they realised they could, but they had been lulled by his air of authority and powerful voice telling them what they wanted to hear. 'With me you're safe,' he reassured them. 'Welcome and safe. The Saxons only pass through, these wet islands remind them too much of where they came from, and London frightens them. It is London you've come to see, isn't it? A little looting perhaps. Nothing wrong with that, everyone does it.' He flicked them a conspiratorial wink, his gaze lingering on the prettiest girl, who looked away and shook her long hair over her face.

'It's true we've travelled far,' Emrys admitted, aware of the impatience growing behind him. This stranger was offering them what they most desired, repletion, a few hours of peace, forgetfulness from the harsh realities out here in the sun.

'Travelled far! Then doubly welcome!' boomed the stranger with a laugh. 'The further you come, the greater my welcome!' He threw his arm round Emrys's shoulder. 'I am *Magister* Wittle, but inside the inn I am your servant. Here in the Tabernacle my fat body and shrivelled soul are yours to command.' He guided Emrys to the doorway with a welcoming sweep of his arm, deferential and yet commanding. Then, as Emrys was on the brink of stepping into the welcome shadow, he was stopped. *Magister* Wittle spoke quietly. 'I could not accept payment from you naturally, sire. A great leader such as yourself. Except what you wished to shower upon me in the fullness of your generosity. But what of your people?'

'We don't pay, we take,' Emrys said, sniffing the sweet, dark strength of warm beer inside, trembling with pain and his need to rest, knowing he had met his match. 'And we know our friends.'

'Then you know me,' said the big man with amiable menace, moving Emrys inside but not releasing him from that great ponderous paw of a hand. 'I am your best friend, Emrys, for you I piss beer and shit bread and meat, and in the night my eyes are your lamps. I am your warm fire and your woman, any woman, and your contented slumber. I am anything you pay for.' He stopped suddenly. 'But how will your people pay me?'

'We have money.' Emrys clicked his fingers.

Out in the sunlight one of the women unrolled the apron wound up at her waist, revealing a puddle of silver pieces in the belly of the materials, a few of which fell out in the dust when she sneezed. She picked them up and dropped more by doing so, then swore and knelt on cracking joints to retrieve them, and the lot slid into the dust.

'Money buys nothing,' *Magister* Wittle snorted.

Emrys was quick. 'Ah, but when the Romans come back, as you said they would, you'll be sitting pretty. You'll be—' he used an archaic phrase – 'a rich man.'

For a moment *Magister* Wittle looked both greedy and doubting. 'If you threw in the boy as well . . .'

'Right, he's yours.'

'I'm not!' Rufus shouted, and *Magister* Wittle grinned. He liked spirit, and cuffed Rufus's head with the back of his hand, but affectionately. He had been cuffed and bruised and demeaned throughout his own childhood, learning his trade in the outhouses, but he prided himself on doing things differently, on becoming a better man than his father, of being a better man than he instinctively felt himself to be. He was a hunter not of deer or boar or fish but of passers-by, his hook and spear being the hospitality he lived by, a man who prospered by his wits. Besides, the lad was not his own flesh; the runts and bastards of *Magister* Wittle's loins were snotty sulky creatures without a spark, either too skinny and tall or too short and fat, all with different mothers but all unwashed and reprehensible, who slunk about the shadows keeping out of his way. But this boy had an open, honest look and a freshness that he found fascinating, because it was so rare. Look how he held his head! The child had class. *Magister* Wittle had recognised it instantly. Undeniable class.

'Emrys is such a fool,' Saturnia was complaining to the other women. 'You won't let that brute take my baby, Emrys!' she called. 'I like him.'

'Keep your baby!' shrugged *Magister* Wittle, with a sniff of offence, then looked surprised as Rufus tugged his elbow, hard.

'Leo's not hers,' Rufus said fiercely, staring up, pulling against the rope with his hand to keep his air. 'He's *not*.'

'Well, I wouldn't know,' *Magister* Wittle said with gravity, 'would I?'

'He's mine now,' Saturnia appealed to the women.

'That's right, he's hers!' they chorused obligingly. 'Poor girl lost her own kid!'

'If you take me, take in the little one too,' Rufus begged *Magister* Wittle directly, speaking low. 'He's my brother.'

'A baby? Am I a fool?' laughed *Magister* Wittle. 'Only women like feeding useless mouths, I won't have it here!'

'He's all I have,' Rufus said, with quivering lips and eyes wet with appeal.

'We'll cure you of such feelings,' *Magister* Wittle responded amiably. 'But I'll tell you what, I'll have that girl – you, long-hair, pretending not to look at me. It's your lucky night.'

She pouted.

'One night only,' Emrys said. 'She's strong. We need her.'

319

'We'll see how she feels in the morning.' *Magister* Wittle nodded his satisfaction with the conclusion of negotiations, spat on his hand, and led them into the inn's single room.

The creaking floor, spread with a thick mulch of straw to hide the gaps, was speckled with stars of sunlight streaming from the roof and walls which had been patched with split planks, obviously robbed from old jetties. It was the first proper house Rufus had ever been in, but even he could see it had once been much larger. In the centre of the hovel rose a set of steps cobbled from jetty planks nailed to gnarled trunks, the bark still on them, but above head-height it stopped abruptly at a landing without railings, overhanging and worn smooth, covered with sheep droppings. There was nothing else, no second floor, only thatch hanging from the roof. The steps were draped with drunks sleeping off last night. One of the men turned over in his sleep and fell a couple of feet without a murmur.

'One way or another,' *Magister* Wittle told Rufus quietly, taking his rope, 'one way or another, they always pay.'

Like shadows, the Wittle children thieved around the margins of the sleeping, stuporous band until they were driven away, chirping and scuffling, by a few whacks from the flats of swords. All the long miserable night, it seemed, *Magister* Wittle himself pounded the girl with the curves, panting heavily to overcome her. Rufus, tethered by the neck to a stair post, heard no sound from her across the room where she lay under her burden as still as though she was dead, except that she occasionally reached up to scratch her scalp.

The early light of high summer at last gleamed its patterns on the walls, casting its weave across the floor and the tumbled figures snoring and twitching around Rufus. The thieving children had long faded into the walls, back to wherever they slept, and now *Magister* Wittle was blaming the girl in a low, repetitive voice for not being more involved, and kept slapping her awake, infuriated by her sleepiness.

Saturnia was still snoring.

Rufus inched over to her until he reached the limit of the rope, then lifted himself on hand and hip, looking down.

She lay with baby Leo clasped to her fleabitten belly under both her filthy hands, his clean frizzy baby hair and little bunched fists barely visible. His tiny body rose and fell rhythmically with her breathing. He looked insignificant and fragile enough for one of those great hands to crush him without thought or meaning, but instead they stroked him lightly with each breath.

Rufus reached out and touched that fine cap of hair, but Saturnia's hands tensed rigid to protect the baby immediately, and he saw her studying him from beneath her lashes. Rufus knew he could not look after little Leo as she could.

With a sigh, unwinding his mother's leather thong from round his neck, he took off the talent he wore and slipped it over the baby's head. Saturnia neither turned away her steady glowering gaze nor stopped him, then she gave a tiny nod and closed her eyes, and he realised she understood.

'Promise you'll look after him,' Rufus whispered.

'As if he was my own,' she grunted – to her, her love was obvious.

'Tell him about me, one day,' Rufus said.

'Ah,' she said, her eyes glinting possessively, 'I don't promise that much. That's a bit much.' She turned over, huddling the baby to hide him from Rufus.

'His name's Leo,' Rufus said doggedly. 'Tell him the sound of it just like that, Lay-o. Promise.'

She grunted.

Across the room there was a sudden shout and *Magister* Wittle rolled off the girl. He cursed and clutched himself, then cursed her and reached out with sweeping blows, but she slipped away from him and stood up, then plaited her hair unconcernedly. *Magister* Wittle roared and slammed his fists on the tables, which were made of upended tree trunks. Emrys sat up and drank from the wooden pot of beer he had been working through last night, and everyone began waking and yawning, or groaning and holding their heads. 'Get rid of her!' cursed *Magister* Wittle. 'Take her with you and be damned.'

'Told you, I did,' Emrys said righteously. 'She's a proper flirt, that one, isn't she now.' He whacked some bodies with the side of his foot and the women packed up. Rufus was sent down to the cellar for more beer, and when he returned everyone was gone and the tavern stood silent and empty, apart from a few sleeping men he did not recognise, a dog grating its teeth on a bone by the cold hearth, black and white hens pecking at the straw.

Leo was gone.

'Let that be a lesson to you,' growled *Magister* Wittle when he returned from outside still holding himself, then examined himself carefully. 'Never trust them,' he grunted, 'especially the pretty ones.' He looked up in amazement. 'What are you blubbing for?'

For Leo, of course. That was another thing *Magister* Wittle, who thought he knew everything, would never comprehend about Rufus.

Though he treated Rufus better than he had ever treated anyone, he received little in return. The boy was loyal and polite, but kept to himself. He'll come round in the end, the innkeeper told himself. For the moment, his respect was enough.

The one thing *Magister* Wittle loathed was work. He loved the cut and thrust of being with people, the social exuberance of his job, or rather, of his job in better times such as his grandfather had remembered. An innkeeper's lot was *Magister* Wittle's vocation and pleasure. Welcoming guests, striking deals, sniffing out trouble and sorting it out with the speed of his hand or the weight of his belly or the power of his personality, strolling up to the river on a sunny morning to check his salmon nets and see what opportunities were to be found among the folk there – that was not work. To him it was joy.

He had boys for work. If he decided the place needed sweeping, there were always boys to roar at, filthy scampering scavengers who appeared and disappeared according to his rage, keeping out of his way in one of the crumbling barns or outhouses round the back, watching and waiting, biding their time. Such a training for life hadn't done him any harm; he looked at them, and saw himself as he had been. But now the boot was on the other foot.

He hated them for being younger than he was, and one day the strongest would take over, as he had. He hated the idea of not living long, of his time in command being taken away. There was no deal to be struck with time, no negotiation. Each year slipped away faster than the year before, his fingers could not grasp it, or claw back what was lost. Grandfather Wittle had hung on until he was senile, not a tooth left hanging in his head but never raunchier than in decay; Father Wittle had died much younger, after only a few years in control, and now *Magister* Wittle, in what would once have been called middle age, was the oldest man he knew. He hated that, too. And the beer that had given him strength in his youth now pickled his cock, and even a girl could not pleasure him.

What a bitch that one had been!

And now the inn was silent, the shell of its former glory. *Magister* Wittle could still walk along the foundations of a Roman wing – as it must have been, to judge by pieces of tile floor remaining – but the wing itself was long gone. And once there had been an enclosed courtyard round the back, but now a traveller could hitch his horse anywhere – not that there were any travellers nowadays, or any horses. British folk emigrating to Normandy departed from what was left of Arthur's towns in the west, and snivelling British bishops on pilgrimage to their business in Europe passed through on foot in fear of their Christian lives among the Godless tribes of English, or took one of the Byzantine ships returning from Putney, if the Pope stood them passage money.

High tide lapped the outhouses. Knowing his children were asleep, *Magister* Wittle took out the coins from behind the counter and unwrapped them, looked at them and yawned, then wrapped them up again and tossed them back.

At first, when Rufus was his prisoner and not his friend, *Magister* Wittle slept during the day; the days passed so quietly it had become his routine. The thick beer he drank made him sleepy and cantankerous, and though he was never visibly drunk he was most alive, and most approachable, when he had just begun his early mug. When Rufus first arrived that was at the start of the day, then there was another opportunity in the middle of the day, the early evening, and finally the late evening. Between drinking bouts *Magister* Wittle strolled out to tend his teeming salmon nets in the inlet or to do a little business here and there among the smallholders, such as selling out his children to them in return for brewing barley, cow's milk, butter. From foreigners passing through or beaching their boats on the easy south bank on the way up the Thames, *Magister* Wittle had acquired an English taste in food – oysters, and salmon fried in butter. Iron frying pans were no longer made, but there were plenty rusting away in London.

There was only one rule. Rufus must not move from the inn.

Sometimes, *Magister* Wittle saw Rufus looking across at London as though he expected his baby brother was still there somewhere. What a fool the boy was! Those wanderers were long gone, or had had their throats cut by now. But Rufus would stand staring at London, his head held back in the way he had, unaware of anything going on around him, one foot raised sometimes, and *Magister* Wittle learned to recognise that tense, yearning look on his face. Or he'd gaze across the south-eastern marshes to the far hills, especially when sunset brought out the distant colours clearly, green and violet, the shining threads of streams sewing the rolling hills together. Just staring. *Magister* Wittle learned to recognise that look too. It was homesickness. The boy had been taken from that way apparently.

'Come on, my boy!' He would spit on his hands jovially, slap Rufus's head and give him work to cheer him up, hoping to see that light in the boy's eyes for himself. It hadn't happened yet. Yet *Magister* Wittle kept Rufus by him, closer than his own children, and let him into his heart more than he let any woman, treating him less like a slave than a favoured guest. The innkeeper was lonely, his great ponderous carcass no longer as sure-footed as it once was, his pig's head of bristling greying hairs a prey to longings and uncertainties he could not put into words. He heaved great good-natured sighs, following Rufus everywhere with his squinty blue eyes.

Rufus fetched water, swinging up the bucket from the decrepit timber-lined well in the yard. Nothing else moved. The children were asleep wherever they slept, which was wherever they could not be found. A girl was gathering flecks of grain from the dust. Beyond the church the willow trees stood in their shadows along the riverbank, and on the other side of the water was London.

London, anonymous behind its great wall. London, hiding everything inside itself behind those stones, except for a few jutting rooflines. If any people lived there, they never showed themselves. Occasionally streaks of smoke betrayed a camp fire somewhere below the wall, especially last winter, and lately during the summer sometimes a great pall billowed up, as though a building had caught fire spontaneously, with no one to put it out. The bridge had fallen into decay, as had the single gate through that seamless immense wall, left hanging on one hinge.

Rufus wondered if Leo was still alive somewhere inside the deserted city, still clasped to Saturnia's breast – no, that was his imagination, old memories. Leo would be weaned by now, and toddling, repeating whatever words Saturnia let drop, and perhaps like many mothers she had knotted a short rope at her knee for him to hang on to. Rufus stood on tiptoe, staring over the outhouses. On the hill to the right, the forum and basilica, distant but enormous, lifted their broken roofs against the sky, standing in their imperial reflections in the river below.

From the inn's yard Rufus stared at London, and from the doorway Wittle stared at him, then returned soundlessly inside. Checking he was alone, he went to the counter, made of a single split tree trunk with the bark still on its sides, unwrapped the coins on top of it and stared at them, miserable dusty things.

Amazing, *Magister* Wittle grumbled to himself, this affinity he felt for a young man who was not his own blood. He could have handed on to Rufus what he knew, and Rufus was bright enough to learn, but he just wasn't interested, and *Magister* Wittle didn't know how to unlock him, get the lad going. He was a serious one all right, did everything he was asked, but he was not part of the inn. Behind those deep brown eyes he was somewhere else, and where was no secret: he was with that little brother of his. No, no secret, but certainly a mystery. Why should a young man with his whole life in front of him care about a baby brother he hardly knew, had held in his arms for only a couple of days after his birth? *Magister* Wittle shrugged to himself. He couldn't imagine.

He flicked a coin over in his fingers.

Should he let Rufus go to London to search for his brother? Would that get it out of his system? Would he come back?

Magister Wittle had always prided himself on his cunning, his insight into other people. But he couldn't see into Rufus.

He polished a silver piece on his sleeve – it came up with a really nice gloss, showing his face looking back at himself. He popped it back in the bag as Rufus returned with the bucket and doused vomit from the table where an ulcerous old man, paying for his beer with his son's carefully garnered surfeit of peas which, he

325

was supposed to exchange for a fish for the family's supper, had puked. The stink was terrible.

'You don't like me, do you,' *Magister* Wittle called, keeping his gaze averted, scratching the hair in his ears.

'Why shouldn't I like you?' Rufus answered evenly.

'That's a question, not an answer.'

'I have no reason to dislike you. I'm your property and you've treated me well.'

'Oh, get out,' the innkeeper snapped, then poured himself his beer to celebrate the middle of the day, drank the top half and left the bottom to settle, then called Rufus back, feeling more genial. 'All right, you can go into the town and see if he's there.'

'Thank you, *Magister*!'

'And then come back. You must come back.'

'Of course, *Magister*.' The boy dropped the bucket, then put it neatly in the corner and skipped out before the old man changed his mind.

'He isn't there no more, he isn't,' *Magister* Wittle called, but no reply came back.

I wonder if that odd one really will come back? he wondered sadly, spreading out the coins again, helping himself to more beer and polishing the things to give himself something to do. One day the Romans will return and these'll be worth a fortune. He sat thinking bleakly, no, he'll only come back if he's a fool.

Then he thought: I was a fool to let him go.

In front of Rufus the clear blue waters of the Thames lay swollen and motionless with high tide under the baking heat, and from the far side the ragstone wall beat back its smooth implacable glare. By contrast the timbers of the bridge on which he stepped felt rickety and ancient. The central span had fallen in and a rope bridge now stretched across the gap. It swayed dangerously and in the middle almost swung Rufus's feet into the water. He had to climb up with his fingers and toes jammed between the slats to reach the far side of the bridge. Below him the wharves of the north bank were being swallowed by mud, and beyond them the tide lapped the wall – and he saw to his amazement that it was made of sculpted human heads, pagan statues, effigies, blocks of stone with writing on, headstones, anything, crammed together and cemented here for eternity.

Rufus crossed himself and passed through the empty gateway into the empty city.

It *was* empty; one glance and he felt it. The silence was solid. Now that the walls enclosed him, the one-way system for vehicles to pass through the gate silently screamed its emptiness because it was so obviously designed to be busy. In the shadow of a curved bastion the entrance gate of the governor's palace, inset with the London Stone, rose hugely from the ruins of the houses around it, dry fountains behind, and bald rooms showing off decaying sun-faded frescoes smudged by rain. Empty and silent.

Rufus inched along the street, his feet sending up puffs of dust, wanting to meet another human yet at the same time afraid to. He looked about him at the strange sculptured buildings, the windows staring down like empty sockets, their glass and shutters long gone, the cracked walls stripped of tile and thatch. Yet once the place must have been so busy, so full of people and teeming with noisy life that he could hardly have pushed his way through.

He trod slowly forward on loud footsteps, then jumped across part of the roadway that had collapsed into a sewer below, realising with awe that there must be other such channels, a whole network of tunnels and cavities sprawled beneath the town but as empty of use as the veins of a dead man. He could hear his heart thudding.

'Leo,' he whispered, then cleared his throat. 'Lay-ooo!'

No wonder the English and Saxons passed this place by. Rufus's rapid, anxious walk sent echoes clapping behind him, so that he kept stopping to look round, and when he called Leo's name it sounded like the cry of an animal. And there were animals here. He had expected to see rats, but there were also holes to fox and badger sets burrowed in the rubble, and round a corner a pack of scavenging dogs appeared, one on three legs. Rufus drew his pathetic food knife; its puny blade glinted menacingly in the sunlight and to his immense relief the dogs turned out of sight as one. But then Rufus's skin crawled, sensing someone behind him. The hairs stood up on the back of his neck and he turned with a shout.

Magister Wittle, sword drawn, winked at him amiably.

'Cowards,' the big man grinned, sheathing the weapon, then chuckled – he was only really happy when the person he was with was caught off balance. 'Didn't imagine I'd leave you here on your ownsome, did you? You cost me too much beer.'

'I thought I left you counting—' Rufus stopped. He suddenly realised that *Magister* Wittle did not know that he had seen the silver coins and knew where they were kept beneath the counter. It occurred to him that his knowledge might prove very dangerous. 'Counting your blessings,' he finished lamely.

'This way.' *Magister* Wittle shrugged, taking him by the elbow. 'I'll show you that there's nothing to see, I know London like the lines on my hand.'

The houses they came to on the slope were low and newer but very tumbledown, with fields overgrown beyond them, and the road turned to grass. Together they climbed up to the forum and from its steps surveyed the empty shimmering space around them.

'There's people here within the walls all right,' *Magister* Wittle admitted, blowing out between his lips, 'else how would it be remembered this place was called London? They're people like me, I reckon, barely making ends meet, scratching a living in their way, keeping their heads down and waiting for the good times to roll back. We haven't done anything wrong.' He pointed to the south-eastern tower and a huddle of buildings in the corner beneath it. 'Hallowed ground. Monks. You can hear their dogs barking sometimes. Probably heretics, can't tell these days, can you? But once, my boy, they were so powerful.' Rufus was staring at him raptly, and *Magister* Wittle basked. 'They led the Christian mobs what broke down the pagan temples, built up the walls with the blasphemous faces to put them to some good, and dragged the headstones from the ungodly cemeteries, even broke the crossroad shrines.' He crossed himself superstitiously, taking both sides at once. 'Seen enough?'

'Not until I know where Leo is.'

'What's behind this?' *Magister* Wittle asked flatly. 'Why do you have to hurt yourself? You have that regal, down-your-nose way of holding your head, like we're all dirt.' The anger left his voice. 'Rufus, by now he wouldn't want to go with you. Listen to me. He's part of another family now.'

'That's something he'll have to tell me himself.'

'Forget him. Look what I'm offering you. I've put you in front of my own children, they're the bane of my life, rubbish on 'em.

328

You're an aristocrat, I said you have that way of looking, for all you're dressed in rags. I'll find you fine clothes, I can do anything. But *him*? You wouldn't even recognise him. In a year or three he'll be whatever that lot make of him, and you saw what they were like. They're just ordinary people, not like you and me. Why do you have to make it difficult?'

'Why don't you want me to find him?'

'Did I say so?' *Magister* Wittle bunched his great fist. 'I wish I was young again like you, boy, and there's the simple truth!' He concealed his emotion almost as quickly as it had appeared, plodding down the steps, expecting Rufus to follow him.

But Rufus pointed into the valley below them, to the west. 'What's that?'

'Only the stream they call the Walbrook. There's a few farmers down there, in the summer anyway, but nothing for you. Come home, boy.'

He says he owns me, Rufus thought, and he does. Yet he likes me, so he wants me to like him.

Rufus realised that he was the old man's one weakness. Except for drink of course, and occasionally women.

'This way,' he pointed, and *Magister* Wittle sighed and grumbled, then plodded after him complaining about the heat and flies.

They found the huts by the stream empty; the only stone ruin was a temple to Mithras, demolished by fanatic mobs. They waded between the reeds then picked the leeches off each other's backs, climbing the hill on the far side past bath-houses and market halls and other great buildings whose purpose was forgotten. At the airy summit, crowned by noble villas – most of them converted into flats before falling into decay, their courtyards overgrown by ivy – lay a Christian church in ruins. A wreathed pagan shrine had been set up at one end as the old beliefs returned, every pool and tree and glade once more cared for by its own comforting, guardian presence.

A blond man dressed in blue trousers and a beige top came wandering from among the roofless structures, looked at them without curiosity, then tucked the rusty iron grate he carried – scavenged from a bathroom furnace perhaps – casually under his arm and sauntered away. Rufus called, but in a few moments the man was gone as though he had never been.

'Best not to call attention to yourself in London,' *Magister* Wittle murmured. 'You never know whose attention you're calling.'

'Lay-oh!' Rufus called. '*Lay-ooo!*'

'I reckon there's hundreds of people picking up bits of this and that around London,' *Magister* Wittle muttered. 'If we keep out of their way, they'll keep out of ours.' He tugged Rufus's shoulder. 'Your friends are long gone, boy. They took what they could rob and were air within a day or two. This is a dead place.'

'Wait,' Rufus said.

Above the church, beyond a cleared space, rose the gigantic curved and tiered walls of the amphitheatre, throwing a long shadow to the north. From inside came joyful cries.

'Children,' Rufus said. 'Children playing!' He walked along the broad roadway that led to the entrance, then ran, and stared through.

Boys and girls were playing a game he could not comprehend, running in circles. The boys carried wooden swords, and the girls squealed and wanted to sit by themselves, or play some other game not involving boys. One boy sat crying with his arms wrapped round the neck of his dog. Their language was strange, sounding without form, like farmyard animals.

'English,' *Magister* Wittle grunted.

He cupped his hands and gave vent to a terrible roar that echoed back from the banks of empty stone seats encircling them. The children ran away screaming, and Wittle nearly choked himself on his own laughter. On the far side, the children regrouped and stared back nervously, clutching one another. Wittle roared again, and they disappeared, pushing each other aside, ducking through the tunnel where once lions and elephants and men about to die had walked out. Their cries faded and silence returned.

'There,' *Magister* Wittle said. 'Gone. Told you.'

The counter was not a safe hiding place for the coins, Magister Wittle decided. Rufus might have seen him hide them there – or worse still the children, devious observant little monsters incapable of keeping their noses clean, who sooner or later got to learn of almost everything, and doubtless kept a running total of their birthright in their greedy little heads just as he had.

But Rufus was different, wasn't he? He knew of them of course; he himself, as well as the coins, had been the price those vagrants had paid for all the beer they could drink, all the mutton they could stuff in their bellies.

Rufus had shown no interest in them since. Not a word. But there were limits to how much you could trust anyone.

It was his own children *Magister* Wittle feared most. Now that they were growing up, he could hardly talk to them, and he feared the day when they would be stronger than he was. He saw too much of himself in them.

These thoughts began to fret back and forth inside his head, as they always did when he started on his third mug.

The trouble was, under the counter was just too convenient a hiding place. He couldn't help taking them out once a week, or twice, opening the bag and gawping at them, giving them a rub just for the sake of it. Not that they were worth anything right now, but they meant something to him.

They allowed him to dream. Dream of the days when silver would once again be worth something.

They'd be worth a fortune one day, and when that time came he would be a great man. He'd set himself up in fine clothes and women like a lord, or whatever it was the Romans called their lords these days. And he would purchase jewellery, not little bits of stamped gold broochware like snuffling English women wore but hunks of the stuff that impressed by their sheer weight, massive ornate settings round carnelians and rubies as red and rich as blood.

Magister Wittle looked around him slyly, then reached in the niche hacked under the counter and pulled out the bag, stroking the silver with his fingertips.

But what if he could never put them to good use?

What if his children, not he, were the ones to benefit from his stroke of luck? The strongest or hungriest or angriest or most cunning of them would one day inherit the Tabernacle Inn just as he had – even nowadays a deed of ownership scribed in real Latin like an ecclesiastical document counted for much. The silver was different. He was the one who had had the wit to bargain for them and win them. No one else. They were his personally, won by his own effort, not some easy inheritance.

Suppose the brats stole them?

He dared not warn them off with bellows and roars as he would usually do; that would simply arouse their curiosity. Once they knew there was something to look for, they'd never give up searching.

He must find a proper hiding place for his hoard.

Where was Rufus? At this hour tending the vegetable patch, or pining for home as usual, gazing across the marshland with that motionless look about him.

Magister Wittle lit a flambeau and lifted the trap door to the cellars. With the bag swinging from his fist and the flambeau upraised in his other hand, he descended the creaking steps. These shadowy rooms were huge, seeming greater in extent than the inn above, as if made to serve a much larger place. They were deep, the walls lined with clay and the floors with brick. Dim chambers led away from him, some of them stone-arched, echoing and dark, others streaked and speckled with light leaking through the boards above. Apart from a few mossy casks of beer placed conveniently near the steps, they were mostly unused now except for endless rubbish, mostly broken clay pots of some very odd, foreign shape, made for dragging not carrying, which must once have contained wine. Wine!

Magister Wittle panted, licking his lips. Those days would come again. Paid for in silver.

The wine store must be one of the oldest parts of the cellars, it still had an earth floor.

Kneeling, he selected a shard of broken pot and dug. It was hard work at first, but after a finger's depth he was through the compacted earth and into the soft yellow sand below. He wrapped a cloth round his hands to protect them from the shard's sharp edge and dug with a will. The fine dust made him sneeze and the flame flickered irritatingly, but the hole was almost deep enough when he struck something.

He paused, then lifted out a couple more scoops of sand.

A human skull, a scream locked in its open jaws, stared back at him from enormous sand-filled eye sockets. He had dug into a shallow grave beneath the floor.

Magister Wittle swallowed. Small, a woman probably. Her skull was full of sand that had crept in where her mind once had been. It lay at an odd angle: her neck had been broken. Sand grains grated between her vertebrae when he touched her.

What a sad death. Her hands were open as though she had fought. As though she had known the man who killed her. He must have been very strong.

Magister Wittle felt leather crumble between his fingers, scooped down, let the sand slide from his palms. He was sweating; the sand stuck to his sweat.

Silver. A silver coin identical to the others he already had beside him.

He stared, scratching his head with his gritty fingers, totally baffled.

Mint condition, too, except for the hole she had made for the thong. And such workmanship. No doubt about it, the very same. Good Christ in His Heaven, what a lucky man he was. Blessings would be falling on him out of the skies next.

How long had she been there? Impossible to tell. Whatever had happened here was nothing to do with him, but someone else might think it was – and they'd be right in a way, now that he knew about her. He'd better get these buried quick and the hole filled in. Adding the new coin to the hoard, he dropped it into the hole. As he did so he touched something else lying against a vertebra.

Something else she had been wearing.

He picked it up, then pouted because it was valueless, a wooden plaque black with age, with a bit of writing on it. He shrugged and slipped it in his belt.

Upstairs, Rufus came into the back of the inn shaking rainwater from his hair. He did not call out as he usually did, wanting to give the besotted *Magister* time to shovel the coins that fascinated him back into their sack and the place under the counter. The heavy raid had startled him with its suddenness, driving him from the vegetable patch to seek shelter indoors.

There was no one at the counter. It seemed very quiet inside the inn, except for the sound of rain and the drip of raindrops finding their way through. Rufus saw the open trap door, reckoned the innkeeper was fetching beer, and went down a step or two to offer his help. What he saw made him skip lightly back up, go to the back door, and stand outside in the rain.

Down below, *Magister* Wittle covered the hole then heaved himself from his knees. He stamped the earth down until no sign whatsoever remained of the disturbance he had made and kicked pot shards over the place to make it blend in. He surveyed his handiwork with satisfaction. Taking the flambeau, he climbed up the steps and finished off his beer leaning against the counter with a lighthearted air, happier than he had been for months.

A weight had been taken off his mind and he felt so much better that he surprised Rufus when he came in soaking wet by making him drink beer with him like a customer. Several times he couldn't help chuckling to himself, but Rufus didn't seem to notice. Why should he? He didn't know anything! It was *Magister* Wittle's own personal gloating secret, safely buried.

He forgot about the wooden plaque for several weeks, then it fell out when he changed his clothes. *Magister* Wittle knew enough of writing to realise the shapes were not Roman, and the matter bothered him in case it was a secret message, a solution to the mystery, until one wintry morning an idea made him slap the side of his head and sent him slogging across the slushy marsh. He took the path through the willows, along the highest ground, to find the miserable Byzantine who lived, shipwrecked, in the ruin of the temple. Zosimas, a devout Christian with a learned manner but very little idea of where in the world he was except that he wished he was anywhere but here, eked out his existence trapping salmon, which he detested as a common fish, from the loop of the River Neck nearby. Throughout the winter he lived on smoked sides of the fish, which had gradually permeated his body with a very strong fishy smell.

'Old friend of mine!' *Magister* Wittle boomed, welcoming himself since he would receive no other welcome, and pushed his way through the ranks of gutted smoked salmon strung between the pillars, protected from the birds by nets. Zosimas, wearing a ragged white robe still bearing tattered gold trimmings, sat in front of his barrel, in which he lived quite cosily, watching his arriving guest without a change in his gloomy expression. He could see the river from here, and he lived with his eyes fixed almost constantly on the empty Thames in the hope of seeing one of the slim stately galleys of Byzantium. On the rare occasions when such a vessel did appear he would run out across the mudflats whooping, hoping to catch a berth home. Zosimas knew himself to be a stranger in a very strange barbarian country, and this man *Magister* Wittle was the most barbarian of the barbarians.

The innkeeper brought beer dredged from the bottom of the cask with him, which the Greek detested. 'Drink deep,' Wittle said cheerily, pouring the disgusting brew. 'Cheer yourself up, it will!'

Zosimas knew that in this country something was never given for nothing, there was always an exchange. 'What can I do for you?' he said wearily, cutting up fish tails into very small pieces and throwing them to the birds, which he called *beccaficos*. When he was alone the birds would even take fish from his lips. Between the broken columns swirled a whole twittering aviary of them. The ancient paving was now white and slippery with bird droppings, and *Magister* Wittle stepped carefully.

'It's about nothing really,' he said, not finding anywhere to sit but lowering his big rotund backside onto the slime and sitting anyway, looking very comfortable. 'Just friendship.'

'I'm sure there must be something I can do for you,' Zosimas offered insincerely, praying that his unwanted guest would go soon. He cut off a thick wedge of smoked salmon, transparent with age, and handed it across with the air of one conferring a great delicacy.

'I hardly like to bother you,' *Magister* Wittle said through the fish he was trying to chew without breathing.

'Please do,' Zosimas encouraged him.

'You haven't drunk your beer.'

Zosimas drank, then pulled his lips back from his teeth. 'Excellent vintage!' he choked.

'It's just this.' *Magister* Wittle passed the piece of wood across. 'I'm only a simple man. I wondered if you . . .'

Zosimas turned it over and saw the writing. 'It's Greek. Trifosa. It's a girl's name.'

'That's all?' *Magister* Wittle covered his disappointment by swallowing. 'It doesn't mean anything?'

'Why should it? It's just a pretty name for a girl. It means dainty, or delicious. Delicate.'

Yes, and she died of a broken neck at the very least, *Magister* Wittle thought. Her screaming mouth and her head full of sand.

Well, you started off with only one, but you've got a whole treasure trove in with you now, Trifosa, whoever you were.

'Thanks,' he said, getting up. 'That's all I wanted to know.'

'Surely I can do more,' Zosimas said unhopefully. 'A marriage is in the air, perhaps?'

'What, me? No, that's one girl I don't know,' *Magister* Wittle threw over his shoulder, setting off home along the slushy riverbank. 'She's nothing to do with me.' He sent the little tag spinning into a stream running across the mudflats, where the tide swept it away to the sea, and he never again thought of her name.

London, the haunted city. Rufus prowled the byways and backways of cold imperial stone, the damp grassy streets giving way suddenly to vistas of open fields within the encircling walls, searching for Leo his brother. By now he had lost all hope of finding him, but he could not stop looking. He could hardly imagine, in fact, who it truly was he hoped to find – a young man by now as old as Rufus had been when the child was born. He would have long ago lost his baby-blue eyes and pale cap of baby hair; his eyes would be Fox brown, his hair red, those tiny bunched white fists grown into hands as large as Rufus's, no doubt. Perhaps even a beard the fiery colour of Rufus's. It was incredible to imagine that Leo's shape had been formed and set by the blood of a family he had never known. Bearing himself like Rufus perhaps, probably as tall as Rufus – and spindly like me too, Rufus imagined. Although working at the inn had put muscle on him, his constant yearning search and short food and sleep had kept him as thin as a youth even in his twenties. Would even his personality be like mine? Rufus wondered.

He knew what he wanted, and that made life hard for him. The easiest thing would have been to roll with his fate and settle down here. But the Tabernacle was not his place, not a day passed when his surroundings did not seem strange to him – and strangest of all to him was *Magister* Wittle. He showed such authority and cheerful confidence in public, welcoming travellers to his inn and unctuously attending to their every whim, yet this was the same man whom Rufus saw muttering and grovelling on his knees when he thought no one was looking, scrabbling among the shards in the wine cellar.

Rufus carried out his duties, but he was waiting without really knowing it. Perhaps Leo was looking for him.

Rufus kept himself to himself, and would not lie with any of Wittle's daughters, though one or two flaunted for him. Aella almost succeeded in seducing him in the hay store round the back of the byre. Using the oldest trick of all, she said tearfully she'd lost her brooch and he followed her like a lamb. Instead of looking, she gave an impatient sigh at his stupidity and took his cheeks in her thumbs to make him look at her, right into her slanty blue eyes with their long soft lashes; then she kissed him with a smile Rufus was sure her father knew all about. Aella was the sweetest of her bunch, but Rufus didn't love her and had to tell her so.

She looked at him with utter contempt. 'There's nothing wrong with *me*,' she said, tossing back her filthy blonde hair. Everyone said her mother had been English.

'You don't love me either,' Rufus pointed out, but she spat at him.

'Spoken for, are you?'

'No, of course not!'

'Who is she, the bitch! You've been leading me on, keeping her a secret!' Aella went wild. 'What else are you hiding? Frightened of me, are you? Of all women, I bet!'

'I'm not frightened of you,' Rufus said with dignity. 'But I won't deceive you simply to pleasure myself. I do not love you.'

'Saving yourself for another?' she jeered. Then she taunted him, knowing other ears were listening. 'Thinks he's better than me, he does!'

She squeezed herself between her thighs. 'Know what this is called? *Can't*!' she shrilled mockingly. 'Can't! Can't! Don't you touch me!'

Rufus stumbled into the inn, her taunts ringing in his ears. *Magister* Wittle, leaning on the counter, looked at him blearily. 'Straw in your hair!' he chuckled in a thick voice, then gave Rufus a playful push. 'Sly dog, you are. Got you in the hay, did she, one of the sweet serpents of these old loins of mine? Now you've bitten her apple you'll settle down soon enough, no doubt.' He helped himself comfortably to more beer. 'Watch your back with the boys, that's all I can say.'

The boys were watching him, Rufus knew. He felt their eyes on him. He was the privileged one, the outsider who had worked his way closer to their father than they ever could. They whispered that Rufus was plotting to take over their inheritance. Pathetic birthright though these four bent walls made, it filled their hopes and dreams. It was theirs, they did not have to work for it. But that was exactly what Rufus, brought up close to his mother and father, used to working with them both until his father's disappearance, did automatically. All his memories of his childhood grew sharper as they became more distant, seen in his mind's eye as clearly as tiny faraway Valle Dei washed by rain. And all those memories were of loyalty – loyalty to the family name, loyalty to the family's place, loyalty to the family's memory. *Your great-grandfather, Count Valens of the Saxon Shore, rallied to Arthur's banner in the west . . . Grandfather Patrick has red hair just like yours, Rufus . . .* His father's voice came to him in the darkest hours of the night, when everything seemed clearest. *Red as flame it was, yet the time I'm speaking of was so long ago you weren't even a twinkle in my eye . . . Once there were open fields instead of a forest . . .*

Once, Rufus thought, a whole hoard of silver talents just like my mother's was buried in a wall. Lost to the family now. Buried in *Magister* Wittle's cellar.

The past could not be brought back, but it was part of what he was. It pumped in his veins and arteries, in the blood of everyone, even Aella, if only she knew it or cared.

But Rufus cared.

So it was loyal Rufus, the outsider, who draped a blanket over the old man when his last drinking bout of the day was done, unclenched his fingers from the empty mug, doused the welcoming flambeau that Wittle insisted on mounting over the door to draw custom, then closed the door and blew out the few smoky tallow candles. The other young men watched him jealously, but did nothing themselves. Once a door slammed almost on Rufus's fingers, sometimes a pot of water was poured over his bed, but nothing was ever said. Only grinning smiles hiding hostility.

A man could not afford to be thought weak. The longer Rufus kept to himself, the weaker he was thought to be. If he helped about the place, he was a scheming arse-licker, if he did nothing he was a lazing free-loader. Though he was the strongest individually, he could not stand up to them all, and the girls would not take his side now, especially Aella, because he would not let them use him.

In a way, Rufus acknowledged, I am looking for myself.

So whenever he could, he swung across the bridge and prowled the streets of London. But he never found Leo.

Leo found him.

It was not the best morning to slip across the river but not the worst either, with the hilltops curving out of the slowly moving mist and the sun glowing hazily. More important, Rufus knew, was that *Magister* Wittle had hidden himself down in the wine-cellar and shut the trap door over his head, his sign that he absolutely must not be disturbed, and he would stick down there gloating and mumbling to himself for hours, dreaming of the days when the Tabernacle would again be a great meeting place.

Alone, Rufus climbed up the far side of the bridge.

On the Corn Hill in front of him the forum and basilica stood out like black bones above the valley of the Walbrook, filled with mist. Rather than go down and lose his way, Rufus walked westward along the top of the Thames wall, four times a man's height above the river, the walkway crumbling in places, mist wreathing his knees. On his right the amphitheatre rose up sharp and clear, and beyond it bulked the impregnable Roman fort from which all the walls ran. The parade ground and barracks had been patched up as a *civitas*, whatever that proud-sounding word meant – everyone tried to use Latin to bolster their authority, but no one knew the exact meaning of the impressive words, they had become as softened by time as the paving stones and ancient buildings. Scattered among the cobbled-together hovels were occasional thatched halls and huts. When there was enough food and not too much disease, they were used by the kings and under-kings of Kent, Sussex and the smaller kingdoms as neutral meeting places for trade and treaty, if they could find anyone to write. Some folk said the place had been called Lud's Hill and was put to such use even before the Romans came, and now, after more than four hundred years, the old name was once more in use. Lud's Hill. The memory of a people, Rufus thought longingly, is stronger than the words of scribes or the actions of conquerors.

He climbed the broad bastion at the south-western corner of

the wall and stared between the battlements. Fish jumped in the misty River Fleet below. Upstream, the broad Thames began its long loop south to Thorney Island before winding westward again, showing blue flashes of its distant course here and there through the forest. Following the river's loop ran the broad sandy strand where the English, who avoided walled London, which they feared as the work of giants, beached their boats. Between bouts of drinking and sleeping they traded hides or oysters or whatever they had spare with the likes of *Magister* Wittle, who had learned to bark their language like an Englishman. They called their emporium the 'Wych', meaning port.

Rufus gazed at their ragtag huts dotted haphazardly along the dry river terrace below him. There was a holy well about halfway along which sanctified most trade, so the men hung around there, bargaining or watching bargains being struck. Elsewhere the women in blue woollen skirts worked bent over, red elbows protruding, the blonde braids of their hair brushing the sand, their backsides looking as broad as coracles. Dogs, children, cats and chickens scrambled everywhere.

Rufus was on the point of walking on when he saw a group of men running – a sort of game, he thought at first, but then he saw the flash of iron. There was a pause as the pursuers backed away and others pushed into the back of them, and in the confusion their prey escaped.

Rufus leaned over the edge of the wall, trying to see. The banks of mist obscured his view infuriatingly.

Then the running man came weaving between the huts. There was a furious scrimmage outside one dwelling as one group of men who had gone round the back of the hut was set on by another group who had gone round the front. Everyone piled in with staves and blades, with the fleeing man caught somewhere between them.

Then suddenly he burst through the side of the hut and ran off like a madman, trailing fronds of weeping willow behind him. He fell over a chicken coop, arms flailing, then jumped up, tearing the greenery off him. He vaulted a fence and sent sheep scattering noisily in every direction, slowing the men who were following. One woman screamed at him and threw an iron pot which caught the young man on the shoulder; he ran on with his clothes steaming, and she put her hands to her head realising she had thrown away her husband's meal. Dogs ran after him yapping wildly. Now he had got ahead he looked over his shoulder and shouted insults at the older men, who were slowing down or stopping, panting with their hands on their knees.

Rufus bit his lip, sure the over-confident red-haired youngster was bound to trip on a tussock or run slap into a tree. But he dodged and skipped with a charmed life, then plunged down into the valley of the Fleet and disappeared into the mist below the wall.

Rufus could see nothing of him, heard only the sounds of him sliding down the slope, his curses as he tripped over the grassy tussocks, then a splash. The men walked down more slowly, standing on the edge of the mist throwing stones into it. From below echoed a shout of pain and the men, encouraged, picked up more stones.

But still they looked at the walls of London fearfully.

Rufus ran down the steps inside the wall, jumping from the first landing onto the accumulated rubbish below, into which the steps disappeared. To the north the double gateway now called Lud's Gates was shrouded in mist below the curved breastworks; the right-hand exit gate was blocked by rubble and overgrown with shrubs, but the left-hand side still showed a tunnel. He ran through crouching, his shoulders brushing the rounded roof, but his feet made no sound on the mulch of decaying ancient garbage that lined the tunnel.

The walls seemed much higher from the outside. Perhaps there had once been a bridge here, but there was none now.

Rufus hissed to attract the attention of the figure wading towards the bank. The young man looked at him and Rufus held his breath. He could have been looking at himself at the age of fifteen, sunburned skin, fiery red hair and fiery curly beard doing its straggly adolescent best, same nose as his own, almost the same cheekbones – as good a view as he could ever get of himself in a mirror. Except for those extraordinary, unfamiliar blue eyes, still as blue as a baby's.

'What's your name?' Rufus demanded, his heart in his mouth.

The boy in the water would not give away such a valuable secret and merely replied cheerfully with a question of his own. 'Are you one of that lot?'

'No, I'm one of you,' Rufus said. 'Look at me, can't you see how alike we are?'

'What's that got to do with it?'

Rufus took a deep breath. 'I'm here to help you.'

'Is that right?' the boy said lightly.

'This way, quick,' Rufus called impatiently, 'before the mist clears and they start shooting arrows. What did you do wrong, you idiot?'

'Oh, I got caught, that's all,' the young man said, grinning as he waded forward without a care in the world. 'This water's like ice! My balls have wrinkled up as far as my neck.' A stone plopped into the water nearby. 'You from the city? No, not me, neither.' His white knees showed through his torn trousers in the clear water. Rufus ducked as a pebble whizzed out of the mist and clattered against the stonework behind him, then came a clattering rain of them, thrown blind. He reached down urgently.

'I'm Rufus. Hurry, we won't keep lucky much longer.'

'Won't we? My name's Leo.' He pronounced it *Lay-O*, just as Rufus had told Saturnia to say it. The tears sprang to his eyes.

'I know,' Rufus said, 'I've been searching for you all your life.'

Leo winced as a pebble splashed past him, then grabbed his brother's wrist and heaved himself onto dry land.

'I didn't ask you to help me,' he said, sounding offended. 'It's your choice.'

'Is Saturnia still alive?'

Leo picked up some of the pebbles and flung them back. 'This is rather fun, isn't it? Are you enjoying yourself as much as I am?' He put his arm round Rufus and they scrambled back to the gate, Leo contorting himself to suck his clothes at the shoulder where the cooking pot had struck him. He rolled his eyes. 'Oyster and mussel soup. Divine.'

'Stop a minute. I've got something to tell you.' Rufus pulled him to a halt. He told Leo who he was.

'I don't see what difference it makes,' Leo said when Rufus had finished. 'Why do you keep looking at me like that, brother?'

'Now you know who you are.'

'I knew who I was before. I don't need you to tell me who I am. I still feel exactly the same.' He looked around cautiously. 'Let's get away from the gate.'

Rufus reached inside the young man's shirt, sliding the silver coin hanging there into his palm. 'Did you never wonder, Leo? I put that round your neck when you were a baby. It belonged to our mother, and to generations of our family before her.'

They walked in silence, two shadowy figures in the mist, London rising around them in gigantic ruins.

'Searching for me all your life?' Leo shivered. 'Why weren't you having a good time? Is that why you look so glum?'

'I do not look glum.'

'Miserable lines here, and here.' Leo touched his own smooth skin where his beard had not reached.

'I promised our mother, *our* mother, that I would look after you. It was the last thing I said to her.'

'Was it a sworn oath?'

'A promise.'

'Yes, but it was a promise to a woman,' said Leo comfortably.

'Our mother,' Rufus said dangerously.

'You do take yourself awfully seriously, don't you? I suppose it's kept you going.'

They stopped in a weedy, overgrown square surrounded by houses. 'Do you have no sense of responsibility?' Rufus burst out. 'No children of your own?'

Leo looked at him blankly. 'How should I know?' He rubbed his arms. 'Let's have a fire. Have you got anything to eat?'

Rufus was determined to bring him down to earth. 'What if that lot come in here after us?'

'My noisy pursuers? No, they're English, and the English are frightened of London.' Leo winked and pulled a flint out of his pocket. 'Come on, just a little fire.'

He pulled some wooden frames from a window and broke them over his knee, telling Rufus to go round the corner and keep watch. When Rufus looked back, the whole house was burning and Leo stood in front of it holding his hands palm out to warm. His clothes were steaming, and he turned his back to dry them, lifting his long red hair with his hands to get the heat to the bugs.

That hair. The talent. He really is my brother, Rufus thought with wonderment. After all these years, Leo is alive, and I've got him back.

Leo saw Rufus watching him and gave a broad smile. 'What now? Eat?' He pulled some wet bread from the belt at his pouch, impaled it on the longest stick he could find, and toasted the bannock at a flaming window. There was an apple tree nearby, its fruit small and sour this early in the season, but he nodded to Rufus to climb up and chuck some down, then roasted the apples to soften them. Sitting cross-legged, juggling the hot apple between his hands, he ate with enormous pleasure and not a care in the world. Beside him, Rufus nibbled.

'So you've just been living from day to day,' he said. 'Getting a meal where you can.'

'Isn't that what everyone does?'

Rufus wondered if Leo had ever slept between four walls, under a roof, the way of life that seemed so natural to him at the Tabernacle. 'What did the English catch you stealing?'

Leo raised one eyebrow. 'She was lovely.'

'A *woman*?'

'Someone's wife, actually.'

'You don't want to go back for her or anything?'

Leo frowned. 'Why should I do such a stupid thing?'

'But you must feel . . . you must be . . .' Rufus thought of *Magister* Wittle – he could not welcome a woman to his establishment without coveting her as soon as she was beneath his roof. 'Tell me her name,' Rufus finished lamely.

'Why should I have wasted time asking her name?' Leo frowned, wiping sticky apple juice from his hands onto his shirt, sucking strands of his beard. 'We both knew what we wanted. Besides, I gave her a chicken. Her husband was going to get a special meal out of her bit of hokey-pokey, so he was getting something extra as well as her. She was a good wife.' He sighed at Rufus's expression. 'What have you been doing all these years? Living a sheltered life?'

Rufus didn't know how to answer. 'I always knew I'd find you.'

Leo squeezed Rufus's shoulder. 'You know, Rufus, you're not at all as I imagined you. Tall and strong and capable of anything. All I knew of you was your name. But of course that was all Saturnia knew.'

'Did she pretend she was your mother?'

'She told me the truth one day. When she was dying.'

'Did you believe her?'

'Don't people always tell the truth when they're dying? And I looked nothing like her, or poor Emrys One-Arm.'

'You have a British lilt to your voice.'

'Let's get moving,' Leo said, jumping to his feet. Rufus followed.

'I didn't think well enough of Saturnia,' he said. 'She was such a brute, I never thought she really would tell you.'

'I've made my way well enough since.' Leo kicked at a paving stone. 'People aren't really brutes, you know. She taught me to turn my hand to anything.' They came to the bridge. 'Where are we going?'

'A place called the Tabernacle first,' Rufus said. 'Then home.'

'An inn!' Leo said. 'Beer!' He skipped and helped himself cheerfully to raspberries growing among the brambles on the bridge railing as they crossed.

He looks like me, Rufus thought, but he isn't like me at all. He's so irresponsible and full of fun. Perhaps he's as I should be – as I would have been but for him. He has everything I lack. I must learn from him.

So Rufus smiled, and tried to skip too.

Magister Wittle was standing with one hand on his hip on the bank of the inlet upstream of the bridge as they approached. He stared at them grimly.

'Who's this?'

Rufus told him. 'I've found him at last!' But the *Magister* wore his most remorseless glare and Rufus faltered. 'Aren't you pleased?'

The innkeeper Wittle summed up Leo with a measuring glance. 'Why should I be? Took you long enough to find him, he'd better be worth it. He looks such a lazy piece of rope he can't even stand up properly, and why's he wearing that silly grin?'

Leo lost neither his tall, easygoing slouch nor his smile. 'What are you hiding?' he asked pleasantly.

Magister Wittle went quite pale and looked quickly at his inn across the marshes. He did not like to leave it at all now, even to tend his nets, wondering who might be digging up his wine-cellar while he was out. 'Me? Hiding? Nothing, I swear it!'

'What are you holding behind your back then?'

Wittle breathed a sigh of relief. He showed the fat brown fish he was holding by the tail, so fresh that its flesh still quivered, its eyes clear as glass. Water dripped enticingly from its lips.

'A carp!' Leo exclaimed. 'How magnificent! I've never seen one in the Thames before.'

'They're not common,' *Magister* Wittle agreed grudgingly.

'The largest I've seen,' said Leo admiringly, nudging his brother's ribs.

'I suppose so,' Rufus admitted, who knew he wasn't going to be offered any of it.

'It's a matter of skill in the catching,' *Magister* Wittle told Leo proudly.

'I can see that, it's a monster! How many meals of smaller fish he must have eaten! His meat will make you very strong.'

'So like your brother,' said *Magister* Wittle thoughtfully. 'Yet he's not like you, is he, Rufus?' Rufus was silent. 'Well, then, Leo, you shall join me at my table,' continued the innkeeper with a broad smile, smacking his lips then wiping them, for a moment looking a little like the carp. 'You shall eat with us too,' he told Rufus.

Magister Wittle poached the fish with the last of winter's turnips, showing Leo how it was done, adding a spill of beer to impress him, and enjoyed watching his new guest eat as much as he enjoyed eating the meal himself. 'That Rufus, I almost think of him as my own son by now.' He grunted with amusement, pointing with his knife at Rufus. 'Not that he's ever been grateful.'

'I'm sure he is really,' Leo said.

'You can never tell what he's thinking,' *Magister* Wittle said suddenly. He drank noisily, then stopped, frowning. 'He's a good boy, don't take me wrong, I'll never let him go.' He put down his beer and dropped the flat of his hand on the table. 'But he should think better of me.'

'Never let me go?' Rufus said, looking from Leo to the *Magister*. 'But—'

'Rufus speaks most highly of you,' Leo said, with a warning glance at Rufus.

'He does?'

'Master, he has done nothing but speak of you in the highest terms all day,' Leo said smoothly. 'He knows how much he owes you. He could never repay you all your kindness.'

'He could. He could marry Aella,' grumbled the old man.

Leo sucked a bone. 'Aella? What a sweet name.'

'And a sweet nature,' Rufus said, with a warning glance.

'You shall both be my guests,' Wittle said decisively. 'You shall both work for me. I am a lonely old man and grown sad. None of my own children are worth anything, in spite of all that I've done for them.'

'A man's children can never live up to him,' Leo sighed, for all the world as though he'd fathered dozens of brats already in his short life.

Perhaps he has, Rufus thought. I wonder what he thinks of me. For all these years he's known me as just a name. Is he disappointed in me now he's met me?

The *Magister*'s large head had fallen forward, but now he looked up through his greying, tangled hair. 'Rufus, clear away these things.' He covered Leo's hand. 'There's treasure here, you know,' he slurred.

'Not real treasure,' Leo said.

The innkeeper winked. 'Let's say I have seed corn for when the spring comes.'

Later Leo stopped Rufus in the doorway. *Magister* Wittle was snoring in the corner, slumped over the table, a half full mug of beer beside him. It was already dark outside. 'Don't you ever stand up to him?' Leo asked conversationally.

'How?' Rufus said, miserable. He hated the way Leo and the old man had played along together. 'You don't know what he's like. He's so friendly at first, but inside . . . I don't know. Inside him there's a terrible storm. He just sucks everyone in.'

'I know the type. I won't let him get me,' Leo said amiably, picking his teeth with his knife. 'I've made kin in a dozen different tribes and nations, remember, living on my wits. Innkeepers are just servants with a high opinion of themselves. Everybody's servant instead of some particular body's. What did he mean, when the spring comes?'

'When the Romans come back will be a great day for the Tabernacle.'

'He's right too. But treasure?'

Rufus pointed at the trap door into the wine-cellar. 'He thinks no one knows about it, yet he can't keep it to himself. It represents all his hopes and dreams for the future, but it's just a handful of coins like your own, part of a set that belonged to our family. Emrys bartered them, and me, for food and a night's lodging.'

'Mine has always brought me luck,' shrugged Leo. 'Or maybe it's the hare's foot I wear. I've been very lucky since—'

'Until the Englishwoman's husband caught you giving her the chicken!'

'That was good luck,' Leo said, looking Rufus straight in the eye. 'Don't you see? Otherwise we would not have found each other. I'd be in Glastonbury by now, or among the middle Saxons or east Saxons or dead or making love to some farmer's daughter. And you would still be alone. Learn to recognise luck when it happens, Rufus.' He nodded his young head at the door, hearing footsteps. 'What's through here?'

'The yard and outhouses.' Rufus broke off as one of the loutish boys pushed past him with deliberate heaviness. In a flash Leo was on top of the lad, jumping on him with his knees between his shoulder blades, pressing the point of his knife into the boy's dirty ear.

'Don't let him stick me,' the boy whined to Rufus, wriggling round. His eyes were liquid circles of fear. Even *Magister* Wittle's beatings only induced a look of wary boredom, but now the boy gave a terrified shriek, writhing under the motionless knife. 'I'll be a good boy,' he squealed. 'I'll do anything for you, Rufus. Tell him. Rufus, tell him. I'll clean your room, cook you a special meal.'

'Leo!' Rufus hissed. Leo tensed his muscles to thrust. 'He's only a child,' Rufus pleaded.

'Next time I'll kill him,' Leo said. He let the boy up slowly. 'Dust down your clothes.' The boy did as he was told, then scampered away rubbing his ear and looking over his shoulder. When he was safe he stuck out his tongue and jerked up two fingers in the Evil Eye, then ran from sight.

'He won't forget that,' Rufus warned. 'The story will be around them all in three deep breaths, and they never do forget or forgive.'

But Leo only smiled, tapping the point of the knife against his teeth. 'Sleep together, do they?'

'In one of the old haylofts, usually, or above the byre where it's warm.'

'See you in the morning!' said Leo, giving Rufus a cheerful slap on the back and heading towards the yard.

'Don't you want me to find you somewhere you can sleep?'

'Oh, I'm used to finding out a place for myself.' Leo looked back from the yard and one of his pale eyes winked in the dark. 'The boy said he'd clean your room, not mine. Cook you a special meal, not me. They look up to you, don't they, Rufus? In their way.'

'I don't know what I've done to deserve it,' Rufus said.

The beer he had drunk was devastatingly strong and smacked rotten in the throat the morning after. Rufus dipped his hands in the bucket of water resting on the side of the well and splashed his aching head, groaning at the sun in his eyes. A door creaked then banged. Holding his head, Rufus winced round to see Leo crossing the yard towards him, prancing along like the cock of the walk. He was not alone. His hand lay on Aella's swinging hip as though stroking an egg, and she swayed beside him hardly taking her adoring eyes off him, a faint flush visible through the dirt on her cheeks. Rufus, aghast, pulled Leo to one side.

'What do you think you're doing,' he hissed, 'getting involved with that one?'

Aella sat on the wall round the well kicking her legs and running her fingers down her jaw, flashing Leo glances.

'I haven't got involved with her,' Leo said casually.

'That's not what she thinks. Look at her!'

'She's just being sensible. I'd do the same if I were her. And any man would do the same as I did. Well, no,' he said sadly, 'perhaps you wouldn't.'

'Now we'll never get away from here!' Rufus almost hopped, he was so furious. 'You heard the *Magister* say last night he wouldn't let me go – we can't sneak away carrying her with us.'

'You've got a lot to learn,' Leo sighed, tapping the side of his nose. 'One look at Aella sighing and simpering and he'll be sure we're staying.'

'But we aren't,' snapped Rufus.

'We don't want him to know that,' explained Leo patiently. 'If you want to get on in the world you have to look at things from other people's point of view, Rufus, not your own. You'll live longer, too.'

'Poor Aella.'

'She doesn't think so highly of you,' Leo retorted.

'But you don't feel a single thing for her.'

'I felt quite a lot of her last night,' Leo said with that sly wink, then returned to his look of blue-eyed innocence. Aella cleared her throat impatiently, lifting herself from one buttock to the other.

'We leave tonight,' Leo said in a low voice. 'No goodbyes, Rufus.'

'But I owe the old boy a debt of gratitude. He took me in and looked after me.'

'For treasure, Rufus. Our family's silver. It's not his.'

'But I can't just—'

'I'll tell you who you owe more than anybody,' Leo said patiently. 'You owe yourself. Think of yourself for once. Never mind me, never mind anyone else. Only you. You owe it to yourself to get away from here with your life, Rufus.'

'But—'

'Don't worry about him,' Leo said flatly. 'Don't listen to him, look into his eyes. You're right, he is a brute. He's mad like a dog with loneliness and mortal fear. And his mind's down in that wine-cellar. One day he'll bite.'

'What are we to do?' Rufus said miserably.

Leo laughed. 'That's easy,' he said. 'See you when it's dark.'

Rufus passed the day unhappily, feeling he was betraying the old man yet knowing Leo was right. Leo didn't even notice the problems that were so complex for him.

That evening Leo swept everyone along with that easy smile and carefree air of his, helping *Magister* Wittle to his evening beer, letting drop what a fine girl Aella was. 'Best of the bunch!' mumbled the old man, drunk enough to look cunning for a moment. 'You like her, do you?'

'Well, I've hardly spoken to her of course.'

Rufus snorted, and the *Magister* threw him a scowl of disapproval. 'I'll call her then,' he said. 'Aella!' But there was no reply. 'She sleeps during the day,' he said apologetically, then dropped his head into his hands, too drunk to keep his eyes open a moment longer.

'It'll be dark soon,' Leo whispered. 'He won't wake again

tonight. I told Aella we'd meet her near the old temple.' Seeing Rufus's expression, he sulked. 'She's got to come. I can't live by bread alone, Rufus, I just can't. I've got to have a woman around or it's not worth being alive. You're a good fellow, none better, but living with you would kill me with boredom.'

They spent half an hour serving beer to the regular customers, farmers who had spent the day pushing down a row of ramshackle buildings along the road, long abandoned, and ploughing up the soil to put it to use. They often turned up old coins, plates, rings that they brought in as curiosities, looking them over in their dirt-clotted fingers, making weary, grunting talk before staggering off home.

'Come on.' The last farmers tottered together in the doorway, supporting themselves unavailingly with their arms round each other's shoulders. Leo pushed them out and followed them. It was a fine starry night, and in a few moments the road was silent. 'It's an amazing thought,' Leo admitted, 'living in one place.'

'You'll get used to it,' Rufus said. 'It's called home.'

They walked round by the old quays to keep out of sight of the outhouses. The islands rose like the backs of huge black animals on their right. 'I've forgotten something,' Leo said, giving Rufus a cheerful pat on the shoulder as he turned back. 'Catch you up in a minute!' Rufus walked slowly along Bermond's Eyot. The tide was gurgling up the waterways between the islands, still channelled by banks of ancient oak planking. The small bridges were rickety but intact. He listened to the farmers' dogs barking. Leo was taking a long time.

Rufus took the path that avoided the temple ruin where Zosimas's single yellow candleflame guttered beneath the blue stars. A shadow moved on the footbridge in front.

'Oh, it's you,' Aella sulked, folding her arms again.

They waited awkwardly for Leo, not hearing his footsteps until he was beside them. 'Got them,' he said, white teeth grinning.

'What's that?' Rufus frowned.

'What's ours,' Leo said, pushing the filthy bag into Rufus's arms. 'Or rather, elder brother, yours. You lost it, you take it back.'

'You dug them up!' Rufus shouted.

'Sssh. And I covered up my marks afterwards, and sprinkled the pot shards back on top!' Leo giggled. Then he was serious, gripping Leo's wrist tight. 'I'm a member of the family now, aren't I!'

'What about me?' Aella pouted for Leo, understanding nothing of this.

'Oh, you'll do,' he whispered, squeezing her waist, and she hung onto him tight as they followed the old road between the willows. Keeping the Saxon island settlement belonging to Rethra, called Rotherhithe, well on their left until they came to the spa, they stopped in the shelter of the old baths and temples to rest. Rufus climbed a sloping pillar that had fallen against another, dutifully keeping watch while Leo and Aella rolled and stroked on the dewy grass below. He shut his ears to their gasps, telling himself he was the lucky one. He, not they, saw the first beams of dawn coming to illuminate London with a beautiful glow. The deserted town seemed to hang honey-coloured in the air above the azure river winding below. He stared in awe as a white ship, its high eastern stern trimmed with gold, moving silently under banks of white oars, appeared and passed beneath the rope bridge. As it emerged downstream, the mast was raised and set in its tabernacle. The square sail caught the dawn wind from the west, bellying and clapping above the creak of the oars. Then the sound of a tiny human shriek carried to Rufus, and a skinny figure sprinted from the old temple of Isis. Waving his arms, cavorting like an insane stork along the quays and across the mudflats, Zosimas threw off his clothes and plunged stark naked into the river, swimming after the ship. Rufus could not be sure, but as the galley turned towards the gleaming sun, perhaps a rope was thrown, perhaps this time the old man was hauled aboard.

Leo woke with a yawn, disentangling himself from Aella. 'Poor Rufus. What a night you missed. Anything of interest?'

'Not a thing,' Rufus said, staring from his vantage point after the disappearing ship. He had never seen anything so beautiful.

Leo looked up at him, shaking his head. 'Let's get on with it,' he said.

From time to time Aella dropped back, pouting and sulking to draw attention to herself, but in fact she was as strong as Leo – who was not above a bit of pouting and sulking himself – and almost as strong as Rufus, and they made good time. They kept off what was left of the main road for as long as they could, in case

Magister Wittle happened to search that way, and saw only a couple of peasants hunting duck or geese – London's hunting rights went as far as the Cray. Then they entered the dense, spreading woodlands now called the Great North Wood, and climbed to the high heath that stood clear of it.

The family cemetery was what Rufus recognised, though now so overgrown he found it only by the stone archway standing among the trees. But the feeling of coming home, of familiarity, was very strong, and he knew this was where he belonged. He stopped, breathing hard, feeling the excitement rush in his blood and bones.

Leo looked up at the archway, jumping to pull down some creeper, revealing the inscription. ' "VALLE DEI," ' he read. 'Come on!'

'I didn't know you could read,' Rufus called after him.

'Emrys taught me. You'd be surprised what I can do,' Leo said cockily, leading the way.

But Rufus hung back by the headstones. Something has changed, he thought. The change was not in himself, he felt exactly the same as the boy who had been dragged from here on a halter, but small details were not quite as they should have been. The moss had been delicately wiped from some of the headstones, revealing the names in white. The path seemed a touch too clear of leaves and branches to have been used only by animals, yet whoever had come this way had left no sign.

Cared for, that was it. As if a spirit had cared for the place while the humans were absent.

Rufus shook his head at his imagination. He followed the stream down past the silted pools overgrown with weed to the clearing. Leo, with the skill of long practice, was already busy erecting gable posts for a hut. Rufus helped him dig down the floor to keep out draughts and make good headroom, Aella wove wattles and collected moss for the roof sides, and they were ready long before sunset. Leo collapsed with a yawn on the long grasses Aella had cut and spread out to dry as bedding. She regarded this as a great adventure, and sat with Leo's head on her thigh, stroking his cheek.

Rufus sat weaving grass into a trap for hare, looking around him as he worked. Was it possible for the land to look after itself?

The old bath-house was as decrepit as he'd expected, mighty trees sprouting everywhere through its shattered roofs, yet the doorway was strangely clear of leaves and dirt. It could have been the wind, but . . . The rubble had sunk into the ground and was visible only as green bumps and hollows; even the great wall that had fallen and killed the people had become as much a part of the ground as the bodies were now. But some of the old crops had re-emerged, waving green brushes of barley and wheat, and the place seemed to have been planted with flowers and herbs. The old apple trees also looked cared for, pruned and trimmed, heavy with fruit.

'*Valle dei* is the only Latin I know. It means valley of the gods,' Rufus said suddenly.

'That's because my Leo's here,' gushed Aella, 'he's my god,' and Leo opened one sleepy smiling eye for her, running his little finger up her thigh.

Rufus went off to set the trap before the pair of them made him sick. He looked round at them but they were too busy fondling one another again to notice him, and he slipped away through the woods. Here he was in his element; he moved without a sound between the trunks, scrambling over the old field boundaries overgrown with tree roots, loping through the small secret glades he remembered from his childhood. Faster-growing limes, ash and beech were giving way to slow, massive oaks now, as if some long-forgotten plantation was reasserting itself from acorns fallen many summers past and patiently growing through the seasons. A great circle of them seemed to enclose the knoll. He slowed his pace as he came near to the tooth of barn wall sticking up between the trunks, where his mother Pascentia had died in childbirth, and where her mossy bones must still lie.

He wanted to bury her properly.

A great oak, blown down in a storm, lay across a hollow in the ground, obscuring his view of the glade. Rufus stopped and stared. In the hollow, cleverly using the trunk both for shelter and concealment, a moss-covered hut had been skilfully built. It blended so well with its surroundings he had almost walked straight past it without seeing it. No path led to its door of woven twigs and grass.

Beyond it, he saw the fragment of wall standing in the green silence of the woodland, and in front of it a wooden Christian cross, planted in a patch of grass which had been kept short. Rufus crept forward with his throat tight, and caressed the smooth wood with the palms of his hands.

From the corner of his eye he saw movement. Someone had been hiding in the shadows of the hut. The hair prickled on the back of his neck and he whirled.

The girl slipped away like a red deer, bounding across the tree roots breathtakingly fast and light, thin white ankles flashing beneath her shift and her red hair flying over her shoulders like a bird's wing. Rufus went after her, heavily and without her grace but as fast as she was, crashing through bushes and shrubs while she dodged round them, twisting away from him this way and that, until finally he crashed through a bramble bush and grabbed a handful of her shift. He tripped her with a sweep of his foot then pinned her on the ground between his legs before she could roll over and away.

She stared up at him through the deepest, widest brown eyes he had ever seen. Their faces were close enough for his dangling hair to touch her. Her breaths were quick and frantic, feeling like heartbeats quivering between his thighs.

'Don't. Don't make me hurt you,' he said. 'Don't run away.'

She held her breath. For the first time he noticed the scar down the side of her fragile, delicately-boned face, running jaggedly from her temple to her jaw.

He lifted his leg and got off her. She wore a dagger in a grass rope round her waist.

She drew a breath at last, staring at him. 'I know you,' she said in a pale, gentle voice. 'You're the poor boy.'

Rufus didn't touch her. He sat beside her, drinking in her beauty while she talked.

Her name was Natalina, she said, and she was about twenty or twenty-one years old. She was the daughter of King Vindomarucius who had died trapped in the wall, and her mother had been one of the women who died somewhere beneath him. Natalina had always slept alone, away from the others, and she remembered waking with the fires blowing away from her, and then herself running after the roaring flames as though to catch them, the slow thunder of the wall falling behind her and great clumps

355

of masonry thudding and bouncing by her, flaming boughs turning over and over above her head, dropping in brilliant trails all around her. She'd hidden among the tree trunks, her head between her knees until the daylight came. She had twisted her foot in the dark and couldn't walk properly.

She did not mourn her father. When his concubine drove the knife into his mouth, Natalina watched, her eyes steady. She made up her mind then. She would not leave with the others and she crept back into the trees. She didn't think she would be missed until it was too late, and anyway her foot hurt her . . .

Rufus listened to her. He saw himself through her eyes, muddy, desperate, caught in the ruins, the baby snatched from him. Natalina had seen that he could have escaped and left the baby, but he had not, and watching him allow himself to be dragged away, she had thought of him as the poor boy.

For fifteen winters and sixteen summers, she said, she had lived alone in these woods. She was not without resources, able to occupy herself with her mind as well as her busy fingers; her mother had taught her to count, being once of a high-born family with estates by the Darenth River, claiming descent from King Lud. Most British people did that these days, Natalina admitted with a smile, and since by now his descendants must include just about everyone, the claims were probably true.

She never went hungry. Her hands were quick and nimble with traps and she knew which berries and mushrooms to eat, and of course there were apple trees everywhere. When after a few days she found this perfect glade and the body of Pascentia, Rufus's story had been plain to see. It was Natalina who had buried Pascentia and planted the cross. She had made her home here, had become part of the life of Valle Dei.

'Were you not frightened of being alone?' he asked, sitting opposite her on the moss with his arms round his knees, their toes almost touching.

'I have never been frightened of myself, only of other people,' Natalina said in her clear, low voice.

'Have other people come here?'

'Hunters, sometimes, in the woods. And there are other people who sometimes live in the glades for a day, or a month, or a year. More than I see. People who perhaps remember the village that was once here.'

'And you're,' he tried to lower his voice to the level of hers, 'frightened of them?'

She put her chin between her raised knees. 'Yes, a little.'

'Are you frightened of me?'

'Yes,' she said. She lowered her eyes.

'Why?' he asked gently.

'Because I know what you feel for . . . for what you see.' She looked up. Herself. 'You don't hide it. Everything about you shouts it. Even your toes.'

He caressed the top of her foot lightly with his big toe. 'I broke my shoe chasing you. You know I've fallen in love with you. From the first moment.'

She spread her hands and smiled, putting her head on one side, and a flush came to her cheeks. He laughed delightedly but she twitched her face away, upset.

'Why do I frighten you?' he asked, hurt.

'Because love is frightening. Especially yours. I've been happy here, with myself, I've had so much.' She tried to explain. 'I know myself. I *am* myself. I don't want to lose anything.'

'What have I done wrong?'

'You are the sort of man who falls in love only once, and then for ever.'

'Are you not worth it?'

'I can see I am,' she said, looking at him straight.

'But not me?'

'You are the same person as the boy I saw dragged away,' she said tenderly, hugging herself. 'But a man capable of love is a frightening creature.'

'How could I ever hurt you?'

'Not you personally. The feelings you arouse in me. They're so simple for you but complicated for me. They intrude. *You* intrude.'

'You would rather be without me?'

'No.' She shivered. 'But I'm afraid! I've counted more than a hundred different colours of butterfly in these woods. Life is so silly. I don't want to lose myself.'

They sat watching each other fade into the background as it got dark.

'But I love you,' he said.

'Don't touch me,' she said. 'Give us time.'

Rufus looked round with a jolt as a light showed between the trees, then stood and rubbed his arms against the evening's chill. 'Leo's got a fire going,' he said. 'Come on down and join us.'

She looked longingly at her own hut.

'Come on,' Rufus cajoled her. 'He's the sort who'll have caught supper by now and he'll have his girl, Aella, busy cooking it. We'll all talk. You can't spend your life alone. It'll do you good to come.'

'You're such a kind man,' Natalina said, 'but you don't understand, do you?'

He helped her up for the pleasure of holding her hand, and they went down to the clearing.

'What have we here!' Leo whistled, slapping his forehead with the flat of his hand and looking enchanted. 'Rufus, you knew she was here all the time.'

Rufus shook his head shyly, but Leo pretended not to believe it. 'Don't know what you see in an old wrinkle like him,' he said, putting his arm round Natalina and sweeping her to the fire. 'What d'you think of this? Hot enough for you? You sit there, best place. Aella, you're putting us in your shadow, shift over, there's a girl. I thought you didn't like women, Rufus?'

'I do now,' Rufus blushed.

'Perhaps everything Rufus has done was for you, Leo,' Natalina murmured, almost too quietly to hear.

'Nonsense,' said Leo cheerfully, then spat out the piece of hare's leg he was chewing. 'This is raw.'

'Ask her to cook it then,' Aella scowled, sitting on her hands.

Leo chuckled and took his arm from round Natalina, blowing on it as if it burned. 'I won't even speak to her! You might get her to fetch us some stuff though, would you, Rufus? She must have salt somewhere. Beer.'

'What's hers is hers,' Rufus said.

At the end of the evening Natalina disappeared into the woods like a wraith. 'Aren't you going to keep her warm?' Leo yawned, taking Aella on his lap.

Rufus shook his head. 'I love her,' he said.

Leo laughed and put his hand up Aella's skirt, and after a few pouts and slaps, she forgave him and she let him have his way.

'Looked after bloody Rufus like my own son, I did,' *Magister*

Wittle slurred, wrapping his arms round his mug, gazing blearily at the drunks consoling him, his friends. 'In fact better than my own sons, that worthless shower.'

'Worthless,' agreed someone. 'Still, you aren't the only father let down by his sons. My own—'

'Nothing was too good for him, nothing I didn't do for that wretch,' the innkeeper consoled himself with a blubbery sigh, 'but he always had his nose in the air like I didn't smell fine enough for him.'

'Snooty,' someone said. 'My own—'

'This is the time a man learns who his friends are,' Wittle said heavily. 'Who of you's with me? We'll search them out!' He shook the oak stave he often used nowadays to support his great weight, banging it so hard it threatened to go through the floor. 'Flush them out and break their heads!' Then he gave vent to deep, helpless sobs, a terrible desolate sound, belly and shoulders heaving.

When he had calmed his grief he peered around him suspiciously, because everyone was quiet. 'Don't any of you care?' he demanded. 'Who's my real friends? You, Cerdic? I got you herbs when your daughter was ill, and I couldn't charge you enough . . .' But everyone was calling good night and staggering out.

'Can't I trust any of you?' he shouted, then settled back.

Customers. They were just customers. When it came to it they didn't care about him, just came here to drink his beer. They wouldn't have minded if it had been his blood, the leeches. He'd make them pay. You couldn't trust anyone these days.

He poured himself another mug and in a few moments, it seemed, the mug was empty. He was utterly alone, it was the middle of the night and he was as cold as death. 'Took my daughter with him,' he whispered tearfully, 'my dear, sweet Aella.'

But there was something even more urgent. The realisation of all he might have lost struck the old man like a bucket of cold water.

Suppose . . . It was impossible, Rufus was a man of honour whatever else one might say about him, and even in his ingratitude he wouldn't sink so low, but *suppose* . . .

He could hardly bring himself to articulate the thought.

Suppose they've taken my silver? he gobbled, panic-stricken.

Clutching his heart, he grabbed a candle and stumbled to the trap door, kicking aside the hound that slept on it, thrusting his staff through the iron ring and levering it up, then thumping down the steps in a shower of dust and rotten wood.

He squinted around him with his lower lip thrust out.

Holding up the candle, he drew a deep breath of relief. His secret was safe. The shards of pot he had so cleverly scattered across the place his precious hoard was buried were undisturbed, even the little hair spider was exactly where he had placed it so carefully. No thief would have been clever enough to notice it or cautious enough to replace it.

It was not that Leo grew bored with Aella, he had never been interested in her, except that she was fun at night. He was quite content to allow her to lead her own life, as long as she did what he told her and kept his meals on time, and as long as she entertained him after dark. By the same token, he did not expect to be tied down or harried by her or asked where he was going and for how long and why. The feel of her eyes fixed suspiciously on his back irritated him when he slipped into the woods to hunt or when he went to find a sun-dappled patch to have a nap in peace. Aella pursed her lips if Leo even smiled at Natalina, which made him more aware of Rufus's girl than ever. Aella was so jealous and possessive. She did not understand his masculine nature, Leo told himself.

Or perhaps, he admitted to himself but not to her, she understood him all too well.

'Aren't they fools?' he murmured, lying back with his head in his hands, watching Rufus and Natalina collecting apples, Natalina holding out the front of that long straw-coloured shift she wore for Rufus to toss them in. Showing her knees, the lovely curved backs of her legs, unaware of how beautiful she looked to Leo, unaware of his admiring glances behind her. From behind, he didn't have to see that disgusting scar on her face.

'They're not fools,' Aella murmured enviously. 'They're in love.'

'You're going soft in your old age,' Leo yawned, turning his nose into her lap, rubbing her.

'Look at the way she walks,' she sighed.

'I'd rather look at you,' he said insincerely.

'Thinking about him all the time, she is.' Aella shifted uncomfortably. 'And herself too. He makes her aware of herself, you can see.'

'I bet he gives her a good knocking all night.'

'Don't,' Aella said fiercely. 'You think you know everything.'

'Hooo!' He sat up, alerted. 'What's got into you?'

'You mocking,' she said. 'They're not sure of themselves yet. I think it's lovely. She's waiting until she's ready.'

'More fool Rufus, to let her,' Leo grunted. 'He might lose her.'

'Never, she's in love, and so's he.'

'Why's he making such a big thing of it? It's not manly, picking windfalls. That's woman's work.'

'You haven't taken your eyes off her,' she said.

'It was you who said look.'

'Look at me, Leo,' Aella whispered, then smacked his face. 'There, you see, you did it again! You always look at my tits, and don't think I don't know just what's on your mind! Why won't you look at *me*?'

'I like looking at the best bits of you, that's all,' Leo said incorrigibly. He took her nose between his thumb and forefinger and pinched, hard, until the tears came to her eyes. 'And don't you ever think you can get away with hitting me.'

'I like it here,' she sniffled when she could talk again. 'But there's trouble and I think it's you, Leo.'

He smacked her rump and sent her back to the hut. He stayed where he was, still watching Rufus and Natalina.

Aella was right, he decided. Natalina was in love, and the two of them were quite extraordinary to observe. It was like watching one person picking up apples, not two. They hardly seemed to talk, yet finished off sentences for each other, their eyes wide and bright, full of glances. Aella had never looked at Leo like that; no girl had, ever.

He watched them take their apples back to Rufus's hut, near the edge of the knoll where the stream cascaded over the brink, London gleaming in the afternoon air beyond them, its east boundary a dark line of shadow but the river wall brilliant. Leo straightened. The bridgeworks were burning, looped with a daisy chain of pale flames and thin smoke. But the lovers didn't even

361

notice, he saw with contempt. Now the English ships would have easy access to their wych.

When darkness fell, the crescent of camp fires along the river was like a curved, glittering sword extended westward from the dead, dark city.

Leo chatted cheerfully during supper, eaten communally as always, then watched Rufus walk Natalina through the dusk to her own hut in the woods.

'They must,' he said.

'They don't,' said Aella. 'Why don't you think of something else?' But he didn't touch her. Aella nodded when Rufus came back alone, very soon. 'Told you!'

'It isn't safe for her, living alone,' Leo murmured. 'She's asking for it. Why won't Rufus look after her properly?'

'Do you think she's helpless?' Aella sniffed. 'She looked after herself long enough.'

At dawn only the bridge pilings remained standing, like a row of tiny black teeth in the river. Leo hadn't slept. He was filled with hunger, an angry, dark hunger that made him restless and unable to sit still. He saw things simply now: Rufus didn't know what a treasure he had and Natalina was too shy to get him in her bed. Of course, someone had hurt her early in her life – that scar, which turned Leo's stomach. She needed someone to give her confidence.

Leo knew who. He set about helping her, small thoughtful things, a straw mat to put in the mud in front of her door, winning her trust. She thanked him with a smile, eyes downcast. When he brought her the skin of a red deer, he said, 'You don't have to look away when you thank me, you know.' He put it on her shoulders. 'The same colour as your hair.'

'Thank you,' she shrugged, but politely. She was such a slim, controlled, dainty little thing compared to Aella. It wasn't true that all women were the same, Leo realised dimly. He gazed at Natalina until she cleared her throat, and he grinned and waved goodbye. He'd find some other reason to come back tomorrow.

He watched Rufus carefully for a sign that his designs on Natalina had been discovered, but Rufus was as friendly and ignorant as ever. Leo shook his head. Love was blind; but no one should be as lucky as Rufus was. Envy filled Leo's mind like cold water.

362

Rufus had known their mother's love, he didn't deserve more. Nobody had ever loved Leo. For the first time he realised, really *felt*, everything he had missed.

If Natalina really loved Rufus, she could spare a little for him.

'Don't you like me any more, Leo?' Aella murmured, lying on her back, staring up at the ridge pole. 'What's the matter with you? I'm not having any periods, I'm clean.' She spoke her fear. 'Do I bore you, or what?' When he did not respond she grew angry. 'You haven't even noticed I've worn my top differently to make my breasts look bigger for you!'

Leo went outside before he hit her.

At the edge of the knoll, he saw Natalina coming out of Rufus's hut as though it was the most natural thing in the world. It was only halfway through the afternoon. The lovers looked so happy and so innocent that Leo turned away, appalled.

He had to wait for his moment. It seemed Rufus was always in the way. But then they discovered that some people were living out in the woods uphill and across a bit – Aella, who had sharp ears, had heard an old man's voice and what she thought was a woman calling her children, and they had all seen smoke weaving above the trees. Old villagers, perhaps, drawn back here by half-memories, Rufus thought. He understood such things and decided to go and see what they were like. Did Leo want to come along? Leo did not.

Leo slipped alone through the flame-coloured woods of autumn. Natalina was alone by her hut, and he watched her from behind the crumbling tooth of the barn wall. She wore her straw-coloured shift, not the deerskin he had given her; her white ankles showed beneath the fraying hem, sandals of woven straw, a leather thong between her toes. Leo almost tripped over the cross as he came forward. 'Why aren't you wearing the skin?' he said, close now.

She looked round with a smile, because she trusted him.

She laughed at what she thought was a joke, because it was a warm day. Listening to her laughter enraged him. She was the first girl Leo had ever really cared about, cared enough to hate as well as to desire, and she was completely vacant about what she was doing to him, what he felt.

'Look at me,' he said.

She looked at him with an affectionate twitch of her eyebrows. What did he want?

Leo reached out, taking her shoulder, and pushed her inside her little hut. It was dark in here beneath the tree, hardly room for the two of them, but enough light filtered through the open doorway to show everything around him neatly laid out in self-sufficient little rows, bone needles, thread of hair or grass, a very old hand mirror with the glass cracked and distorted, probably dug up out of the ground somewhere but lovingly rubbed clean, a many-pronged silver candlestick. Nothing masculine, not one thing, except Leo himself blundering about holding her in his arms, warming himself against her.

'No,' Natalina told him.

'It's your fault,' he said, pushing her, and she went down before he hurt her. Straddling her body, he bunched the shift between his fists and in one jerk split it from her navel to her knees, dropping his own hard knees between them to keep them apart. Between her legs she was red as a fox, the hair beaded with moisture as he dripped his saliva on her, and he sank down on her. 'Don't make a sound!' he shouted, slapping his hand over her mouth, then looked over his shoulder, fearful lest Rufus should have heard him through the woods somehow. There was nothing to her, no tits, no cries. He was possessing nothing but he could not stop. She kept putting her head on one side, infuriatingly, showing her scar, and he kept pushing her face the other way to see the perfect side. His spirit emptied into her and she closed her eyes tight, trying to twist away.

She lay with both hands over her mouth, breathing through her nose with tiny whistling sounds.

'If you say a word I'll kill you,' he said angrily, standing over her. 'I'll come back until you love me.'

Leo flung himself out of the hut and let the door bang down behind him. He stormed away through the forest.

Aella came out from the shelter of the barn wall where she had been watching. For a moment there was no expression on her face. Then, slow, dignified and decided, she went into the hut and took Natalina in her arms. The girl seemed to weigh nothing at all.

'Suppose Rufus finds out?' Natalina sobbed, terrified. 'You mustn't tell him. You mustn't.'

'There there,' Aella said, hugging her tight.

Aella stayed until the hottest hour of the afternoon, when Natalina dozed. Instead of going back to the clearing she cut through the woods uphill, following the way Rufus had gone earlier. Where the path divided and she was unsure of her way, she waited. She could hear Leo calling for her below, but she crossed her muscular arms instead of replying, flattening her breasts, her blonde hair hanging to her elbows in greasy coils, and eventually his calls faded away and stopped.

Rufus surprised her. He came down the path to her left, but his footfalls made no sound on the dry leaves, never breaking a twig to give himself away – he was a fine woodsman, the craft he had learned as a child. His childhood was still with him. Aella jumped noisily when he appeared.

'There's an old man, his daughter and her children,' Rufus said without bothering to greet Aella or ask why she was there. He didn't like her and she couldn't blame him for that. 'The old man remembers what was left of a village here – those hollows by the stream were fishponds—'

'Rufus,' she interrupted him, and Rufus stopped. Aella drew a deep breath. 'D'you love Natalina?'

Rufus stared. Aella ploughed on. 'I know you don't think much of me—'

'I don't think of you at all,' Rufus said. 'If you've got something to say to me, walk beside me.'

Aella, shaken, plodded on with the words she had rehearsed. 'If you love her, I can't do no harm with what I'm about to tell you. But if you're lying to her, it will kill her.'

'What's happened?'

'Your brother, Leo,' Aella said. 'He's happened. Do you love Natalina?'

'You know I do!' Rufus shouted.

Aella told him everything.

Rufus flushed red, then went as white as a sick man.

'I've brought it on myself,' he said in a dull, awful voice, like someone who has seen he has done everything right, yet now realised he has wasted his life. He drew his sword. The blade flashed. They had come into the clearing and Leo stood looking at them from a distance.

Aella turned in front of Rufus. Her slanty blue eyes held an expression that was almost motherly in their concern for him, and her raunchy, kissable lips had thinned to a hard, resigned line. She looked twenty years older, her girlishness quite gone – Leo had taken that from her today. She looked mature and forceful, and determined.

'Long ago you showed me that love matters,' she said. 'I didn't believe you, I spat at you for saying it. Well, I'm ashamed of myself. You were right.'

Rufus pushed past her. 'I'll cut off his balls,' he roared. 'Leo! *Leo!*'

'Rufus, it's too late,' Aella whispered. She squeezed her belly. 'I've caught.'

Rufus swung the sword from side to side. The blade whined in the air. 'I've got to do something,' he said.

'Go to Natalina,' Aella said. 'Go to her. Forget Leo, you can't do nothing about him, but I can. Oooh, I can. He's mine. He's not a great thinker, but good or bad he's mine, and I'll see to him.' She pushed Rufus's sword back into the scabbard with her hand, not caring that she cut herself. 'Natalina's yours.'

She watched Rufus hesitate, then he plunged away towards Natalina's hut, stumbling over the windfalls and rotten boughs, scattering leaves around him, making a terrible noise, all thought gone except concern for Natalina. Aella went down to where Leo stood.

'You didn't tell him,' Leo smiled, but as he looked at her his uncertainty grew, his eyes lost their easy blue confidence, and without his confidence he no longer looked innocent.

'I'm going!' he said. She slapped him with her open hand, spattering him with her blood. He stared, appalled, at the drops down his chest, and his fingertips came away smeared when he touched his face.

'What did you do that for?' he whined. 'Look at me.'

'You aren't leaving,' she said. 'You useless good-for-nought, you'll learn to stick with me.' She smacked him again.

'You can't do that,' he said.

She picked up the switchbroom, hazel twigs bound round an ashwood handle, that Natalina had showed her how to make, and pushed him with it in the chest. Leo fell back. His foot plunged in the fire with a soft powdery sound followed by a sharp crackle, and he howled.

'Cook your own supper,' she said. 'Things are going to be different between us from now on.'

In the hut deep in the woods, beside his mother's grave, Rufus lay beside Natalina. She would not touch him or look at him, lying with her back to him. He told her he loved her, patiently, over and over, too many times. At last she responded, shaking her head – at least, the back of her hair moved. He stroked her hair with the palm of his hand. 'That's better,' he said. 'I love you. Believe me.' But while he stroked her hair he was thinking, could you have fought harder? Just a tiny bit more, just one more push away? Should you have spat in his face, could you have screamed louder, would that have made a difference? Could you, should you? Or would that just have made Leo hurt you even more? He knew she was thinking these thoughts too. That was what made it even worse.

Some time during the night she curled herself into him, her hair tickling his nose and his feet cold, but he didn't move, and he didn't let her go. It was dawn before she wept, hugging him.

There's something inside us, Rufus thought. There's something terrible inside all of us, every one.

He stayed with her the next few days, until she smiled, and the smile came back into her eyes too.

That first morning she slept late, arms up over her head, and Rufus got up and unbuckled his sword. He left it where she would see it so she would know nothing was wrong. As soon as he was out of hearing he walked noisily through the woods. With long strides he crossed the clearing towards Leo working by his hut, packing up a heavy load for his back, moving out. Leo's face was pale and bitter.

'She's got her mind set on it,' Leo said as though nothing had happened, with a jerk of his head towards Aella at the stream. 'I don't know what's got into her.' He gave his grin.

Rufus grabbed his brother's hair, punching Leo's face until it was soggy with blood, until he felt the bones cracking against his knuckles, then he let him go. Leo fell into the stream and stayed there to keep Rufus away, but Rufus made no move to follow him.

Aella spoke into the silence. 'See, there's an old man called

Briginus Ammius, his daughter and her brats live uphill a ways, where the old village was. He's expecting his sons, and there's stones there we can use, where this good-for-nought,' she tossed her head indifferently at Leo, 'can set himself to something useful for once.'

Leo sat up, spitting out a tooth as though it didn't matter. 'Come on, Rufus. Nothing happened. Almost nothing. You can't believe a word they say, can you?'

'If you're afraid of hard work, Leo, you can run away,' Aella said doggedly. 'But wherever you go, I swear I'll follow you. Back to the Tabernacle, for example. Would you like to go back there with me, Leo?'

Leo threw her a venomous look and she folded her arms, content. He believed her threat.

Rufus spoke to Leo for the last time. 'If I ever see you near Natalina again, I'll come after you again.' He plunged into the water and tore off the silver coin that he had placed round Leo's neck sixteen years ago. It had looked so big on the baby and now seemed so insignificant on the grown-up man. 'And next time I'll bring my sword, I swear it.' He turned his back on his brother with the tears streaming down his cheeks. 'And I'll kill you. I tried for you, Leo, everything I did was for you. You are no longer my brother. I wish you'd never been born.'

As Rufus passed Aella, she put out her hand. 'What more is wrong?'

'Natalina is pregnant,' Rufus confessed in a low voice. 'She feels it. I trust her feelings.'

Aella put her hands to her head. 'Then whose is it?'

'How can we know?' Rufus said desperately.

Leo gave a high, painful laugh. 'A child!' he cried. 'Rufus's, or mine?'

Aella sat weakly. 'We'll hope and pray it will have the best bits of both of you.' She cursed Leo roundly. 'What mercy have we broken, that we do such terrible things to ourselves of our own free will?'

'It's mine,' Rufus said. 'You'll see.'

But Leo just laughed. 'A child of two fathers!' He leaned back on his elbows in the stream, laughing through the blood staining his face. 'I'll settle for that!'

V

Tully and Tyrell

John Fox's Family Tree continued
July 517 – 29 December 1170

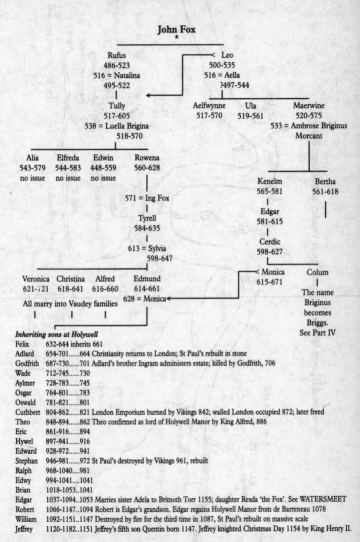

John Fox
★

Rufus
486-523
516 = Natalina
495-522

Leo
500-535
516 = Aella
?497-544

Tully
517-605
538 = Luella Brigina
518-570

Aelfwynne
517-570

Ula
519-561

Maerwine
520-575
533 = Ambrose Briginus
Morcant

Alia
543-579
no issue

Elfreda
544-583
no issue

Edwin
448-559
no issue

Rowena
560-628

571 = Ing Fox

Tyrell
584-635

613 = Sylvia
598-647

Kenelm
565-581

Edgar
581-615

Cerdic
598-627

Bertha
561-618

Veronica
621-721

Christina
618-641

Alfred
616-660

Edmund
614-661
628 = Monica

Monica
615-671

Colum

All marry into Vaudey families

The name
Briginus
becomes
Briggs.
See Part IV

Inheriting sons at Holywell

Felix	632-644	inherits 661
Adlard	654-701......664	Christianity returns to London; St Paul's rebuilt in stone
Godfrith	687-730......701	Adlard's brother Ingram administers estate; killed by Godfrith, 706
Wade	712-745......730	
Aylmer	728-783......745	
Osgar	764-801......783	
Oswald	781-821......801	
Cuthbert	804-862......821	London Emporium burned by Vikings 842; walled London occupied 872; later freed
Theo	848-894......862	Theo confirmed as lord of Holywell Manor by King Alfred, 886
Eric	861-916......894	
Hywel	897-941......916	
Edward	928-972......941	
Stephan	946-981......972	St Paul's destroyed by Vikings 961, rebuilt
Ralph	968-1040...981	
Edwy	994-1041...1041	
Brian	1018-1053..1041	
Edgar	1037-1094..1053	Marries sister Adela to Britnoth Torr 1155; daughter Resda 'the Fox'. See WATERSMEET
Robert	1066-1147..1094	Robert is Edgar's grandson. Edgar regains Holywell Manor from de Barreneau 1078
William	1092-1151..1147	Destroyed by fire for the third time in 1087, St Paul's rebuilt on massive scale
Jeffrey	1120-1182..1151	Jeffrey's fifth son Quentin born 1147. Jeffrey knighted Christmas Day 1154 by King Henry II.

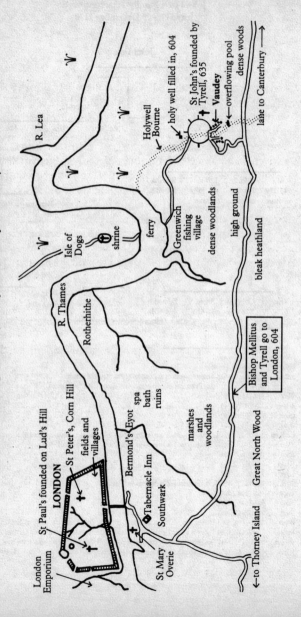

Tyrrell and Bishop Mellitus journey from Vaudey to London, 604

R. Lea

Holywell
Bourne

holy well filled in, 604

St John's founded by
Tyrell, 635 **Vaudey**

overflowing pool

dense woods

lane to Canterbury

Isle of
Dogs

shrine

ferry

Greenwich
fishing
village

dense woodlands

high ground

bleak heathland

R. Thames

Rotherhithe

Bermond's Eyot

spa
bath
ruins

marshes
and
woodlands

Bishop Mellitus
and Tyrell go to
London, 604

St Paul's founded on Lud's Hill

St Peter's, Corn Hill

fields and
villages

LONDON

Tabernacle Inn

Southwark

London
Emporium

St Mary Overie

Great North Wood

to Thorney Island

When *Magister* Wittle died, his son, Aella's half-brother who had soon forgotten his young sibling with slanty blue eyes and blonde coils of hair, dutifully laid the corpse of their father out on the counter.

The Tabernacle had lost almost all its trade to the Thorney Island crossing since the burning of the bridgeworks, and his offspring had no friends to help them. It took the strength of four of them to lift up the old man's bloated, rigid carcass onto the trunk of wood it had spent so many hours leaning against in life. They wedged him there with mugs, leaving a full one by his head.

They performed these acts not out of respect but from hope that he would talk to them from death, that he would not after all take the secret that had filled his life and given him hope to the grave.

The Tabernacle could not survive by itself, without people, and his heirs could not even make any repairs to the place, as without the bridge no more pilfered stone could be brought across from London.

They left the mouth unstrapped, gaping open, so that the corpse could speak.

Everyone knew of the hoard of silver coins the *Magister* had buried in the walls (some said) or beneath the floors (according to others). Within minutes of his death the place was ransacked by his family, friends, and once-regular drinkers from the outlying farms of Bermond's Eyot and Rotherhithe, anyone who knew the legend of the place. Holes were knocked in the walls, furniture broken. No one had ever seen the treasure, they only knew that it was as substantial as its owner. In his last years, blotchy with disease, shambling from place to place, the floors creaking beneath his weight, the secret took over the old man's mind. Chuckling and gloating, he would tap his finger to his nose at what he knew and they didn't. In the yard perhaps? When he was dead they dug it up. They dug up the cellars too, where he had spent so much time muttering to himself, choking on the sand and dust, finding nothing but shards and an old skeleton, which they threw away.

Had he been cunning enough to drop it down the well? They drained it and sent the littlest down, but nothing came up, only a few pots and skulls, odd shoes, a copper or two of an unknown design. They returned to their vigil beside the corpse.

Even beyond death, it seemed, their father continued a dreadful kind of life. His muscles relaxed within a few hours and his arms flopped down from his chest where they had been crossed devoutly, and his livid hairy hands, already eagerly relieved of their rings by his heirs, swung down and almost brushed the floor. While his sons stared at him and each other and broke up the place whenever a new idea for a hiding place occurred to them, the dogs crept in with ears flattened and tongues lolling, licked the old man's swollen fingers, and made off with one or two.

Although it was winter, the flesh bloated and stank in no time at all, probably rotten inside for years, sweet as apples and strong as fish. The eyes sank into the head but still the hair and fingernails grew, and black stains trickled down the sides of the counter as the belly swelled.

'If he won't talk,' the eldest son announced, flexing his long arms, 'we'll have to put him out. And no coin in his mouth, he can cross the bloody River Styx by his bloody self.'

They stared at the gaping mouth, but still it did not speak.

Laying a sail on the floor, they flopped the body down without dignity and dragged him out, dropping him into a soft wet hole in the marshes.

'It's here,' said his heir, a tall skinny young man with a face like a blade and his father's calculating, fawning, callous blue gaze, looking around the Tabernacle, now his own. 'It's here somewhere, and one day we'll find it, and it's mine.'

Rufus Fox named Natalina's son Tully, in memory of his great-grandmother Tullia, it was said, and maybe that was true; memories had been longer in those great days. And women had been greater, too, for it was said that Tullia had run the estate while her husband fought with the dragons in the west. She birthed her son Patricius, or Patrick as some said the name. Patrick's son was

Viventus, a good Christian name, whatever Christian meant. Viventus's only son had been Rufus.

All this was memory and rumour; none could read, none write.

In the village you still heard the whispers – gossip so common that it had become truth – that Leo had once been Rufus's brother, renounced in disgrace. Disowned. Pathetic shambling figure he now was, bent double with sticky-bone and his flesh dragged into wrinkles and clefts of bitterness, cowering under the lash of his wife's scolding tongue. And the deeper he sank into his misery, the greater Aella's strength grew.

It was whispered, too, that Leo, not Rufus the loving husband, was the father of Natalina's son.

Rufus never admitted it and Leo was not in a position to, even when he was younger, for Aella would have killed him if he breathed a word. Words had once come easy to Leo's silver tongue, but she had bound him up in himself in her revenge, breaking his nerve with her indomitable will. She never let up, she never rested, she never forgave. She took Leo and had her own daughters by him, her own smiling shrewish darlings brought up in her own image, any one of them capable of going for their father like a stoat, so thoroughly were they suckled and steeped in their mother's sour milk in distrust of their father. There was only one way, Aella understood, to treat Leo. Her first daughter, Aelfwynne, had been conceived in the days when Leo had done what he wanted with her, whenever he wanted, and no please about it. Not so the others. They had been conceived with her firmly on top; *she* had been in control of Leo's helpless, squirting seed, not him.

Tully was Leo Fox's child, Aella was sure of it. From the first the whisperers had called Tully not by his name, but mocked him as Natalina's son, or called him the child of two fathers. Aella herself, scorning Leo, had blurted that out in her cups, another stick to beat Leo with, but it had never been forgotten by the ears that overheard her raised voice.

In the village, as the years passed, such was Leo's reputation for sadness and bitterness, living in Aella's shadow, that he ended his life not as someone pitiable but as a figure of fun. Children threw stones at him, but he would just grin at them like a desperate animal in his loneliness. Everyone despised him, and Aella hen-pecked him cruelly for his weakness in not throwing the stones back.

But Natalina and Rufus were different. They were truly in love.

Natalina bore no more children after Tully. She and Rufus lived alone with their only son down in the clearing, at the edge of the knoll, apart from the village. The village grew but their household did not. There was something sad about them, Aella thought, seeing them so aloof and serene down there in the distance. Perhaps their lives had been too hurt by what Leo had done ever really to recover.

Natalina, despite her inner strength, had always been frail, and she died when Tully was five. The Christian cemetery up through the trees, beyond the gateway, was long disused, forgotten like the mystery of its religion, and Rufus buried Natalina on the slope below the knoll, near where the holy well bubbled up, always a precious place to him. Aella, a silent witness to Rufus's grief, would long remember the boyish uncomprehending figure of Tully standing beside his father's sombre form, obviously itching to run away and play, his child's hand enfolded and almost lost in his father's.

If Rufus really was Tully's father.

Aella, watching alone from the trees, had cried to see them together. She was not entirely without feelings of guilt herself about Rufus. She still winced as she remembered clutching her loins and shrieking *Can't!* at him. Later Aella sent down little gifts, cheeses, Aelfwynne or one of her neighbours' older girls to help clean the place in the mornings. They always returned to say it was clean already; the girls just spent their time larking with Tully. Rufus, they said, hardly spoke a word, neither friendly nor unfriendly. Already he seemed part of another world, hardly seeing this one.

Less than a year later, his heart broken to live without Natalina, Rufus followed his wife into the soil. Faithfulness had always been his strength.

But that left Tully with no one.

Aella stood at Rufus's graveside, looking down at the boy whose little hand she held in her own. Could she take him into her home? But that would have meant trusting Leo, which she would never do.

Tully glanced up at Aella with a roguish wink, as though he saw her thoughts. He had a face full of freckles and fire-red hair – hair just like Leo's, though Leo had no freckles. And Tully's eyes were his mother's brown, not Leo's blue. A deep and innocent brown with glints in them.

'What are we going to do with you, child?' Aella sighed.

'I can think of lots of things,' Tully said. 'Shall I live here alone?'

'No, that's one thing you won't do.' Aella made her decision. 'Come on with me to the village. We'll find you somewhere friendly.'

'I'll stay with you, won't I?' Tully chirped, bobbing beside her.

'No, you can't do that. And don't ask why not.'

'Why not?'

'I said.' She smacked his head.

'Why mustn't I ask? Is it because of Uncle Leo?'

Aella stopped. 'What do you know about him?'

Rubbing his head, the little boy shrugged. 'What the girls say.'

'Don't listen to that load's gossip.'

'Why not?' The little boy grinned. 'Words can't hurt me.'

'You're ahead of me,' Aella grunted. He was a spirited little runt, small like his mother but not delicate. Something tough as leather in those eyes.

'Are we kin?' Tully piped up.

'Definitely not,' Aella said.

'Brigina Luella said I had two fathers. And she said it was even worse.' Tully gave a delicious shiver, all the while searching Aella's face for information. 'They weren't just my fathers, they were *brothers*.'

'Don't worry about what she says,' Aella said, confirming the rumour without meaning to.

'I don't,' Tully said, relieved, because now he knew where he stood. 'Whichever one of them it was, I'm a Fox, you see, and that's all that matters.' Aella stared at him. He knows his strength, this one, she thought. And he's more like Leo than Leo himself.

And yet she saw something of Rufus in him too, Rufus who had, after all, brought him up to this age. Something flashed between the laces of Tully's shirt: so Rufus had handed on the family talisman, laying claim to Tully as his own proper son whatever the truth of it.

'I shouldn't let Leo see that,' she said.

Tully smiled his lovely smile and slipped his hand back in hers to get his own way. 'Can I play all day?'

'As long as you learn your responsibilities,' Aella said, because Rufus would have, 'and as long as you keep quiet and respect your elders. In a village there's other people, see, and we have to live together.' She tried to lighten her strict tone. 'Never could stop children playing,' she admitted grudgingly, trying to be friendly to the little boy, knowing how frightening her bulk must seem to him. 'What games do you like playing?'

'Chasing girls,' Tully said. 'I like chasing Aelfwynne. She squeals.'

This won't do at all, Aella thought as she plodded up the hill, crossing the stream on the tree trunk the men had felled across it: Why do I like him so much? Tully put out his arms and walked over the tree trunk with his eyes closed. 'I'll ask Briginus Ammius if he'll take you in,' Aella told him.

'Good,' Tully said. 'I can play with Luella.' Throwing up her arms, Aella groaned, then laughed.

And so Tully Fox came to the village, but part of him remained always back there on the knoll, the clearing where his grand-mother Pascentia had birthed his father, where his grandfather had been born, and his great-grandfather, and other men and women of his family for time immemorial. That was all Tully needed to know, and it was not something he knew so much as felt. He was one of the family, a Fox, and this was his place. He would fight to keep it.

Briginus Ammius and his sons and daughters and grandsons and granddaughters, all living under one roof, were a kind family, but they were not *his* family. Tully won them over with ease, they had not the remotest idea how to control him. He was old enough to carry Rufus's battered old sword now, and worked hard at using it. They had never met anyone like Tully.

'Vain and arrogant, like a great warrior,' chuckled the old man, sitting outside his whitewashed cottage in the evening sun. 'A natural leader.'

'Big-headed,' said his wife, holding out her hands from her ears.

'Clever and quick, and keeps us young.'

'I thought *I* kept you young,' his wife said.

'He'll be king of our little valley one day, you'll see.' The old man pulled down a piece of thatch to chew wisely.

'He'll be trouble when he's older,' opined their daughter who tried unsuccessfully to keep her own children out of Tully's influence. 'I never know where he is, and they follow him. You think he's silly, don't you, Luella?' she said hopefully.

But Luella, sitting under her grandfather's knee picking grains of oats out of the wheat, blinked her large brown eyes and said nothing.

On the clearing was a ruin that Rufus had called a bath-house. Tully, like the other children, neither knew nor cared what a bath-house was. The villagers had stolen the stone from its walls and soil had grown over the floors, so that almost nothing remained between the tree trunks. But Tully came here because Rufus had told him about it; the ruin had meant something to Rufus and so it meant something to Tully. This was all, Tully understood without bothering about it too much, part of his responsibility. After heavy rain, a spirit haunted the place, rumbling deep in the ground, a vibration that Tully could feel beneath him. Every grove and glade and well and stream was holy in its way, but this was a special place. He knew it because he felt it in his hands and feet, and if he lay on the ground, he felt it in his heart.

'What are you doing here?' said Leo's voice behind him, and Tully sprang up so quickly that the worn talisman his father had given him swung out of his shirt. Leo stared, then looked around him, smiling when he realised they were alone. He advanced with his hand out, but he was twenty-five years old and had to use a stick for his arthritis, and Tully danced back easily. 'It's mine,' Leo whined, reaching out. 'Give it to me.'

Tully held it at arm's length. 'Since you want it so much,' he grinned, 'I don't think so.'

Leo took a step, and Tully threw a stone. It thumped on Leo's ribs, surprisingly loud.

'Please,' Leo said. 'It's my good luck. It will make me better and end my troubles.' His lower eyelids gleamed with moisture. 'My life is a terrible hell.' He shrugged, and his shoulders cracked audibly. 'It's called a talent, you know.'

'I know,' Tully said.

'And . . . there are others.'

'I know,' said Tully. 'My father told me. He was my father, wasn't he, Leo?'

Leo reached back to some memory of the dim and distant past, the words of Emrys One-Arm on his deathbed, rambling on about King Arthur, and Jesus Christ, and Glastonbury, ancient memories and myths much older even than Emrys himself, passed down round the camp fires. Some of the words stood out powerfully in Leo's mind.

'Have mercy on me, a sinner,' he said. 'Forgive me, Tully.'

He took another step, hand out, eyes fixed on the talent, and Tully threw another stone.

That was the start of it. Leo believed that the wafer of silver worn inside the boy's shirt would heal his guilt and crotchety bones, and for this he'd walk after Tully through a hail of stones and turds flung by other boys; he would endure their jeers and blows, his eyes fixed only on Tully, his face wearing that terrifying, grinning rictus of submission to Tully.

'When I was young,' Leo cried, 'I too could do anything. By the blood of Christ's sweet mercy, Tully, forgive me.'

Leo never got better. But even when he was a cripple, crouched jagged and bent by his cottage door, his stick higher than his head, and Tully came striding by with the other young men, Leo would croak out a friendly call and his eyes would light up and follow them hopefully.

Then one day, all by himself, without Aella's help, Leo got himself to his bed, pulled up the blanket to his chin, and held his breath until he died.

Aella found him. She scolded him for being asleep, then slowly realised he was dead. She walked round his body in silent confusion, round and round, wondering what she would do without him.

Men laughed at the wonder of such a death, and mothers hushed their children who copied their fathers as always, and between themselves they wagged their tongues eagerly about what Aella would do now. There would be no rush of suitors after her, that was sure. Only Tully was quiet. He would stare into his mug of honeyed beer, then smile when he was jostled and pull a girl onto his lap, burying his head in her bosom to hide his face.

People said that was the only time when the garrulous Tully, always first to push forward with an opinion or loudly lay down the law, used no words where ten would have done.

Some men said Leo's death changed Tully, but they didn't know him. The people who knew Tully best were Tully's women, and the stories they had to tell about him were never repeated in front of their husbands.

Tully was a different man among men, a rogue, vain, extravagant, a bully, their leader. King of the valley. No man could stand against him because no man in the village of Vaudey – Valle Dei slurred on the tongues of this illiterate generation – could brag as loud or as long as Tully. Tully's camp fires were always noisy, with plenty of laughter, drink and showing off, and the occasional sudden, snarling fight to ease the tensions that always grew up in a village, best brought to a head in a way that could be controlled.

Tully knew this.

He knew how to make men do what he wanted, one way or another.

There was a feminine side to Tully that his friends and followers never saw and would not have liked. But the women saw. Tully was intelligent. He had the clever, quick, quiet intelligence that a girl like Luella, his first girl and his dearest, noticed in his silences and by what he left unspoken or only hinted at, but that a man would never bother to understand.

She saw plainly what he really thought by the way he listened, and when he said nothing she saw how often that meant more than words. She also saw how he roared with laughter and slapped backs, dribbled beer down his chin, played practical jokes with flaming twigs or bowls of water, his eyes gleaming in the firelight, being just like any other man.

He got better at it, too. He learned to do it.

That was how he led them, Luella saw, and why they followed him: because they thought he was like them. But they didn't see his cleverness, as she did, watching him without a word from beyond the male circle of firelight. He knew when to touch his sword, when to draw it, and when to laugh. He knew when to speak and how to make his words count, and how to use those silences of his too, which she thought was the greater gift. Tully knew when to wait and when to strike, swift and without mercy.

He was a child of his times, and the times were disorderly. Up on the moor, the land fell under the sway of this king or that with his laws and taxes, but in the valley Tully kept them out of trouble.

There was one thing that Luella did not know. While she thought she had been watching him unobserved, Tully had been taking in every detail about her. He had always behaved towards her with respect, almost coldness, as though he did not quite like her but, being shy, Luella was used to having that effect on men. He never treated her to the friendly slaps and winks he reserved for her friends – she would have died for him.

Now Tully stepped out of the firelight as though to relieve himself, but instead he touched Luella's wrist lightly with his fingertips. The moon hung mottled and huge over the treetops below them, looking like a huge biscuit, she thought, and wondered if Tully saw it as she did.

'You have big eyes,' he said. 'Even as a small child you had them.'

'They haven't changed,' she said.

'They have,' he laughed, hardly touching her wrist, not holding her. He was entirely different from the young man who knocked the other young men about down by the fire. 'You no longer ignore me.'

'You *are* big-headed,' she said.

'You like that.' Tully wandered up to the pool where the stream cascaded from the oak trees, not asking her to follow him but knowing she would, so she did. Below them the overflowing water made a silver line between the cottages and poorer huts of the village, then reappeared meandering in the clearing on the knoll. London was as black as the hills on which it stood, except for a few sparks of light in the old fort and from the cottages of the Wych scattered along the strand.

'You've been watching me,' he said, going down on one knee, dipping water from the pool into his cupped hand, offering it to her. He smiled. 'What goes through that mind of yours?'

Luella drew back, knowing if she sipped she was lost.

Then, careless of her hair falling forward, she put her head down and drank from his hand.

'You know what I'm like,' Tully said.

'Yes, I do. No one else would put up with you for long.'

He looked startled, then laughed. Deep in the clear water they could see a huge mossy stone that the moon made pale, seeming close enough to touch. By an old wives' tale there was a terrible face carved beneath the moss, and when it woke, and moved, the valley would be changed for ever. Luella took Tully in her arms and their cold mouths, beaded by the water, touched. She twined her fingers in his hair and pulled him down on her, staring into his eyes by the light of the moon as she felt him.

'Luella,' murmured Tully afterwards, stroking her hair. 'Wife.'

He was never faithful, of course, it was not in his nature to be. He bedded half the women in the village, and half their red-haired, brown-eyed scamps and sluts were his too. But in his way Tully was absolutely faithful to Luella. He never loved another woman, and whatever blandishments he whispered into other ears, she was sure they were not the same he whispered to her.

Within a few years she had her daughter, Alia, to share with him, and no father was ever kinder or happier to play with a child than Tully.

'Boy next time,' he said, rubbing noses with Luella, and she knew exactly what that meant: he took her upstairs while the house cow chewed and belched among the roosting chickens below, keeping them warm against the winter wind.

But the child was another girl, and Tully grinned. 'You're just practising,' he chided Luella.

'What name shall we call her?'

'Elfreda,' he said.

Elfreda was four years old before her mother fell with child again, and this time, to Luella's inexpressible relief, it was a boy. Tully was transformed. He shouted the news through the wind bars on the window and ran out holding up his new son above his head. Luella smiled tiredly, hearing his voice echoing from the muddy street. 'I've called him Edwin,' Tully shouted. 'He's Edwin Fox!'

Fox. That was the name that meant everything to Tully. Alia and Elfreda stood looking out jealously.

'Go and tell your father,' Luella murmured, 'that he's not to let his son get cold.'

But Edwin was always cold, and it seemed every winter might carry him off. He grew up thin and pale, the very opposite to his father who had put on weight round his belly and ruddiness in his cheeks, and was so remorselessly full of life that Edwin paled even more by comparison. Tully took the boy with him everywhere, rubbing snow into Edwin's cheeks to redden them and make him look powerful, but Edwin trailed after him like a pale shadow. That the child was pathetic was obvious to everyone but Tully, but it was more than anyone's life was worth to say so. Tully's temper did not improve with age and drink, and he was fierce in defence of his son, guardian of the family name. 'As soon as you're old enough, Edwin,' Tully said, 'we'll find someone for you. Liven you up. Bit of red blood in your veins and you'll be like me, eh?'

'Yes, Father.'

'Don't you yes me in that tone of voice,' Tully threatened, slapping the boy round the head, stamping his foot in frustration when Edwin cried. 'And stop that snivelling in front of everyone or I'll give you something to cry about all right.'

He tried desperately hard to be kind to Edwin, but his son just looked at him with flat, suspicious eyes. One day Tully took him down to the fishing village at Greenwich, to the old wharf called Billingsgate, to buy live carp to stock one of the old fishponds that Tully's men had dug out. The boy wore a ridiculous straw hat against the sun; Tully hid his irritation and did his best to get close to him. 'You're a Fox, you see,' Tully explained, but Edwin stared at him blankly from the shadow of the hat. Tully showed him the battered silver coin round his neck. 'One day this will be yours.' Edwin stared. Tully's voice rose. 'Isn't that exciting?'

'Yes,' Edwin said, sneezing.

'He will understand,' Luella whispered to Tully that night. 'When he grows up, he'll understand.'

When Edwin was eleven years old, almost old enough to be a man, his cold went to his chest and, flushed with a high temperature, he lay in bed crying like a child. He was frightened of dying, drowning, his lungs filling with moisture, and there was nothing they could do but watch him.

'He'll be fine,' Tully said. 'I've shaken this off myself a dozen times.'

'Yes,' Luella murmured, 'but he isn't you, Tully.'

'What will happen when I die?' Edwin choked.

Tully said nothing. 'You'll always be with your mother and father,' Luella said.

Edwin's death left Tully devastated. He drank himself stuporous, and Alia and Elfreda kept well away from him. When Tully finally roused himself, he went to find Luella and fumbled limply between her legs. 'We did it once,' he told her, 'we can do it again.'

'We were both younger then,' she said gently.

'Help me, damn you,' he swore tearfully, squeezing his eyes shut. 'I want a son, I want a proper son.'

But the child was a girl.

Tully took one look at her and howled, flinging himself out of the house. Luella called her last daughter Rowena; she was too old and too exhausted to have any more children, and lay with her eyes closed.

'The baby's got a funny foot,' Alia said, seventeen years old and a beauty. Tully had said he'd cut the throat of any boy who touched her.

'It's lumpy and wrong,' Elfreda said. She was quiet like her mother, pretty enough but a little dull.

'Don't tell your father,' Luella said, holding her baby tight.

Tully took so little interest in the girl that he did not notice the truth until Rowena toddled, late, rolling and twisting her little body over her clumping foot.

'Club foot!' Tully said, aghast.

'It doesn't hurt her,' soothed Luella, watching Rowena's cheeks flush with her exertions, her slanted brown eyes darken with determination at each step. She reached the far wall and smiled.

'What will people think about me, siring a malformed brat.' Tully turned on his wife. 'It's your fault.'

'It's nobody's fault,' Luella said, kneeling and stroking her daughter's rosy hair. Rowena was half the size of other girls her age.

'There's no club feet in my family!' Tully roared. 'I'm the grandson of a king! Never!'

'Then it must be mine,' Luella said meekly.

Tully rumbled. 'Useless mouth,' he decided. 'We'll see what we can get for her.'

For the first time in her life, Luella put her head back and defied him. 'You will not sell her,' she said.

Tully went brick red. 'I will do whatever I want!'

'Over my dead body you will.'

Tully glowered, then his shoulders slumped. 'Probably wouldn't get anything for a cripple anyway,' he grumbled. 'Sparky little face she's got, though. You take responsibility for her!' He stared along his nose at Luella as though the word 'responsibility' would make her back down.

'All right,' Luella said calmly.

Tully looked at her carefully, shaking his head at her wilfulness, then laughed, and Luella never admired him more. The irony was that Tully probably had plenty of sons, but none of them by the one woman he loved, none of them bearing the Fox name.

Tully Fox was growing old with no one to follow him. He had grey hairs now and was slowed by a belly too fond of honeyed beer, but among his followers he was as cunning and ruthless as ever, his bullying manner masking his subtlety, and he was still king of the valley. Faithful little Rowena hobbled after him like a slave, though he never showed the slightest sign of appreciating her. Several times he knocked her over because he hadn't noticed she was there. Rowena adored him, slipped his stool under him without being asked, a small, silent presence topping up his mug at the fireside, stitching his boot without being told.

He kept a tight grip on his two marriageable daughters, Alia and Elfreda, showing no sign of choosing husbands for them, and a successor for himself. But the young men and louts were already fighting themselves, Luella knew, to prove who was strongest, waiting for the day when Tully gave way. A man was old at forty, and he was fifty-three; but a man who lived to fifty-three often lived to sixty-three, and a man who saw his seventieth birthday was quite likely to survive his eightieth, even though toothless, blind and wracked with infirmity. So young heads waited for Tully to slip, and the older families in the village courted Alia and Elfreda for their sons and grandsons. And how Tully enjoyed playing them along, Luella knew, and she straightened her back with a sigh. Poor Alia, poor Elfreda.

She looked round, startled, as Alia burst in behind her, brilliant sundown shadowing her in the doorway.

'There's an army up on the heath!' Alia panted, always the most emotional, flinging back her hair. 'Father says to get out, get into the woods, now, run!'

'Where's Rowena?' asked Luella calmly.

'We've got to put all the fires out!' Alia cried over her shoulders. Huge blond men appeared in the lane, flames leaping up behind them as vivid as the sunset. Alia shouted, seeing Rowena hobbling slowly in front of her. One of the giants fixed on Alia, saliva swinging from the braids of his moustache. He tore her dress from her shoulders, and Alia screamed and screamed. A farmer's boy she vaguely recognised sank his hoe into the warrior's back, then looked at Alia with shining pride. The warrior gusted his last breath into Alia's face. Rowena ducked under his toppling bulk, sinking her little eating knife into his foot. Alia screamed again, holding up her dress, then snatched up her ten-year-old sister instead and ran for her life, stumbling and falling into the darkness among the trees.

Tully and Elfreda found them, and Tully wrapped them in his arms, saying not a single word all night as they watched the village burn. The raiding party stayed to rape the women and drink whatever they could find, then disappeared uphill dragging their slaves and booty.

'Most of my people got away,' Tully said. 'Most.'

'Mother,' Rowena said, and both the elder sisters turned on her savagely.

At dawn the survivors came out of the trees and wandered through the wreckage. Luella was where Alia had left her by the doorway, killed by a single sword thrust through her neck, her clothes undisturbed.

Tully turned to the people gathering behind him.

'Is there anyone here against me?' he said dangerously, hand on sword. No one said a word.

'None of the men has the guts,' said Maerwine, Aella's youngest daughter. She was holding her dead son in her arms, his children clutching at his dangling hair and feet, their faces terrified, another generation.

It was a hard winter. The village was a mess of cottages shored up among those left empty and unrepaired, their fire-blackened timbers rotting, sunken floors abandoned as pools for the rain. From these, insects swarmed everywhere in the summer, and a new pox, never seen before, struck at children and adults indifferently, leaving those who lived terribly scarred. No one left in his bedraggled kingdom opposed Tully; alone among their tired, worried faces his beamed optimism. At night he slept like a dead man.

Alia crept through the trees. She was still beautiful, she knew, but she lived in terror of her looks fading – of looking her age. She was twenty-eight, the grey flecking her temples daubed with red clay to conceal it, and her teeth were yellow and loose. When she smiled it was with her lips closed. She was afraid of dying without loving, without leaving a child; of being, when she died, as though she had never been. But she did not dare defy her father, and so she worried.

Alia worried about not having enough to eat; she worried about being too fat, or not fat enough. But most of all she worried about what was beyond the trees. In her imagination huge armies camped on the heathland. She would creep uphill and watch out for them, and worry, planning her route back through the forest to warn the village, worrying in vain. For a year she had seen almost no one on that flat, windy expanse.

But today, long before she reached the edge of the trees, she heard the heavy crash of shields, cries and shrieks. She crouched on her knees with her face between her elbows, her hands over her head, until the sound at last faded.

A man came through the trees.

He wore a dirty tunic made of a sheep's fleece, and leather leggings. He was very tall and his blond hair had a strawberry tinge to it. His face was covered in blood; his scalp had been gashed to the white bone and as he walked he wiped at the dripping blood. He seemed very calm. An arrow's feather stuck from his side, and he came straight towards her.

Alia ran, and he ran after her.

'Ing,' he called, then foreign words.

Alia screamed as she ran into the village and mothers herded their children towards the safety of the trees, chickens fluttered in their coops as the men tried to catch them, goats and pigs squealed as they were driven into the woodland.

The stranger collapsed behind Alia, crawling. When he lay still she found her courage and went back to him.

Tully came up, his eyes searching the woods. 'Anyone else?'

'I think he's alone. There was a fight and he's hurt.'

388

'Did anyone else follow you here, you silly bitch?' Tully shouted, and Alia burst into tears. Tully muttered, drawing his sword, then dropped to his knees and pulled back the foreigner's head by the hair.

'Is he an Englishman?' Rowena said. 'Isn't he horrid.'

'He's *huge*,' Elfreda said.

'I found him,' Alia said, wiping her nose and pushing in front. 'He was calling for Ing.'

'That's their god,' Elfreda showed off her knowledge. 'Ing of the Inglish.'

'I wonder if he's got a woman,' Alia said.

Tully sat back on his haunches, his eyes moving from the blond giant with the feathers in his side to his two daughters, and back again.

'All right,' he decided. 'If he lives, he'll live.' He beckoned to a couple of men strutting bravely from their hiding places. 'You two, carry him to the empty house beside mine, with the hay in. If he makes trouble,' he added, 'we'll burn him alive.'

In the hayloft Alia and Elfreda sat beside the giant for a while, washing his face so they could admire him better. 'I shall call him Ing,' Alia said.

'Just because you give him a name,' Elfreda said, 'doesn't make him yours.'

'We'll see.' They went down the steps, pulling them down behind them so that rats could not get up or the Englishman down. 'We'll see.'

'He'll be dead by morning anyway,' Elfreda said glumly.

In the last of the light, Rowena slipped inside. It took all her strength to prop the ladder, still blackened from the old fire, against the edge of the loft, and she hobbled up one step at a time, her club foot swinging. She stood looking down at him, her lips sucked in, for she was always in pain herself.

'You poor beast,' she said.

What an ugly beast he was, too. He even smelled different, and when she opened one of his eyes with her thumb it was dark blue. His fist was clenched round the feathers in his side, they sprouted between his fingers. She sat down beside him, always busy, and opened the fingers one by one, then plucked out the feathers from the notches in the wooden shaft. Placing the palm of her hand against the shaft, she gave a good hard shove, and the fleece tunic rose in a peak on the other side of his chest. Untying the straps – strange knots, even! – showed the bloody arrowhead poking out through fine golden curls. She dried it on her skirt to get a grip, then tugged hard and it slid out smoothly without touching any bones or jamming in the sticky bits between them. His eyes popped open.

'Hello, Ing,' Rowena said, pulling up his belt round him and tightening it so that the wounds were bound. 'Bet it doesn't even hurt.'

He seemed to understand her words, and gave a gasping laugh. No blood on his lips: missed his lung then. He'd live.

She tweaked his nose and swung herself clumsily onto the ladder. 'Sleep now,' she said, and a moment later the ladder jerked down out of his sight.

The Englishman drifted off to sleep, haunted by nightmares of his dead wife and dead children.

In the morning Elfreda, sulking, found the ladder already in place and Alia up there beside him. 'He opened his eyes and looked at me,' Alia preened. 'He must have got the arrow out by himself. What a man.'

'Have you looked at his thing?' Elfreda said.

'That's what I mean.' Alia stroked her hair. 'What a man.'

'Oh, you,' Elfreda said crossly. 'I wonder if he's got anyone. I wonder if he *is* anyone.'

'He isn't now. He's ours. You don't think Father could ever let him go.'

They looked at the sleeping blond with satisfaction.

That night Rowena returned, grunting to put the ladder in place, and climbed up with some meat and a little bread, first her round brown eyes appearing to his view, then her button nose, then her small down-turned mouth. The Englishman seized on the bread as a precious gift.

'*Hlaford?*'

'That's right,' Rowena said, standing on one foot, cocking her head to one side. '*Hlaford*. Bread. You eat it.'

She watched him touch it to his forehead, a strangely submissive gesture, almost one of allegiance. A jumble of other words followed by *hlaford* again.

'Rowena,' Rowena said, pointing at herself.

Ing grinned, then nibbled hungrily at the bread.

He was sitting within a few days, and the harvest was not in before he was standing. Manpower being so short, Tully went up to see him.

'You work,' he said, putting leg fetters round the Englishman's ankles. 'You work, that's the deal. No run.'

The Englishman knelt, with difficulty. '*Hlaford*,' he said, reaching out for Tully's sword, and Tully skipped back and nearly went over the edge, cursing. Ing waited patiently.

'His wits are curdled,' Elfreda snorted, her eye on Alia.

'I don't care,' Alia said.

Ing said the word again, laying his hands meekly on the blade of Tully's sword.

'It's true,' Tully snorted. 'They really do bark like dogs.'

'*Hlaford* means *lord*,' Rowena said. 'I think so, anyway. His life is yours, father,' she added in her self-effacing way, so as not to provoke her elder sisters' irritation. 'The English do anything for their lord, it's said. Die if he dies.'

'I'm his lord all right,' Tully said, pleased. Ing stood up, his blond hair touching the rafters. 'Phew,' Tully breathed. 'Puts you back a bit when he gets to his feet, don't it? Out into the fields with you, my lad. Get to work for your *hlaford*.'

The whole village turned out, but the crop was small as usual. After the oats, weeds and herbs had all been painstakingly picked out, half the wheat had to be set aside for next year's seed.

Tully watched the Englishman work, and he watched Alia working beside him. They didn't say much, but she swung her arms and made sure the Englishman couldn't ignore her. Working harder than she had ever worked in her life.

On the way to the fields Ing had taken no interest in the ruins of the bath-house or London in the distance, though he had given that respectful bow of his towards the shrine of trees of the Isle of Dogs. But he had pointed at a vast square area of brushwood and lower growth below them, beyond the holy well. '*Mick*,' he said to Alia, walking beside him. 'Great – great field. Mickfield.'

'So what?' Alia said.

'Good,' Ing said. 'Work.'

Tully watched them thoughtfully. This man was no fool. Then, as soon as Alia went, Elfreda appeared.

Tully's eyed took on a cunning, dancing light.

He called the most important men round the fire that night – rather fewer of them than there had been before last year's raid. He sat Ing on his right hand and handed him the best fillets of venison from the tip of his own knife. Ing cheerfully returned the compliment with slices of liver and offal. Tully chucked them over his shoulder as soon as he could politely do so and Rowena caught them before the dogs, eating hungrily.

'I've been thinking about our guest here,' Tully said, getting to his feet a little unsteadily. 'Now, listen. There's only one of him – for now. But there's no end to these Englishmen.'

'Good!' Ing said, looking round for approval.

'I think where there's one,' Tully went on, 'next there's hundreds. They'll burn us again, and maybe they'll stay, and then it'll be us in fetters.' He looked at their glum faces. 'That's what I think.'

'Sad,' Ing said. 'For all of us.'

'Let's kill him now!' one of the Briginus boys said.

'Might as well burn the village ourselves in that case,' Tully said. He let the silence stretch out. 'No, it's obvious to a wise man like me what we've got to do. We've got three choices. Fight 'em as hard as we can, fly from 'em as fast as we can, or marry 'em.' He held up his hand. 'Fight and we lose. Run and where do we run to? Wales? Dumnonia? Living in caves like animals. No thank you. We can't beat the English, we got to make 'em like us.' He put an arm round Ing's massive shoulders. 'Next time they come, they'll find us led by one of their own. Strike his fetters off. More beer for him – right to the brim, girl!' He pushed Rowena aside and pulled forward Alia and Elfreda from the darkness. 'Make your choice – go on!'

'Both?' Ing said, baffled.

'Our honoured guest don't quite comprehend our customs yet,' Tully beamed. 'You may choose just one of my daughters.'

'Her,' Ing said without hesitation.

Tully's face struggled. 'That one? But that's not a proper one!' He pulled Rowena round, making her hop. 'See? A cat scared her mother. And she's not twelve years old yet.' He pushed her over and stepped across her, fluffed Alia's hair, turned Elfreda's face to best advantage by the firelight. 'You're what I've been saving 'em for! Now, Alia's the beauty, if you'll excuse a father's pride, but Elfreda has a lovely singing voice and a kinder nature.'

'I wait for Rowena,' Ing said, bending down and holding out his great hand, the back of it covered with golden curls like his chest. 'Rowena.' He dwarfed her hand in his, drawing her to him. 'Rowena shows no fear. Rowena is strong, like a man. Rowena is silent, like a man should be, Tully Fox. And she looked after me, when everyone else thought only of themselves.' He looked at her tenderly, touching her freckles. 'She speaks little, but her words count. What more could a man ask? I marry her now and we sleep and have children when she has years enough.' He looked at her, then smiled.

Tully waved Alia and Elfreda away; they fled weeping. He dropped himself weakly on a log. 'You had it all worked out, Englishman. From the very first days, you did, working it out in that quiet way of yours.'

'It is, as you say,' Ing frowned, 'obvious to a wise man.' Lifting Rowena without effort, he embraced Tully too. 'Father!'

'Son!' Tully grunted, but that cunning look was still in his eye. The two men raised their mugs to each other's lips, drinking, looking steadily into the other's eyes. Tully ran out of breath first, blew froth. 'Rowena it is, my boy,' he burst out joyfully, 'and Ing Fox you are!'

Ing and Rowena's marriage, celebrated immediately, was not consummated for another five years, but their first and, as it turned out, only child was not born until eight years later, when Tully had almost given up hope of his blood continuing; both Alia and Elfreda had wasted away as spinsters, without children. The baby's cry and Tully's cackle of victory sounded on almost exactly the same note, and Ing named his son Tyrell in honour of Tully. 'Brown eyes, red hair!' Tully quavered proudly. 'Looks just like his mother – except he's perfect.' Even now, Tully had not forgiven Rowena for her club foot, but he was prepared to love his perfect grandson, Tyrell, uncritically.

Ing slipped away down to the clearing, the fields he had come to know so well silent in the moonlit dark around him, the Mickfield cleared and ploughed below him, and dropped his head in his hands.

'Why me?' he wept in English. 'Why am I so happy and have so much when my other wife and my other children are dead, and I can hardly remember their faces? Gone as though they never mattered, and I can't bring them back.' He went down to the holy well, knelt, and drank from the holy water bubbling up – all water was holy, all trees, the earth, sky, holy in its way. Suddenly he plunged his arm into the icy water to the shoulder, opening and closing his fist helplessly, but felt nothing down there in the dark, nothing to grasp, no answer to his cries or succour for his grief.

Tully watched him. 'You're a bit of a mystery, Englishman,' he said to himself, 'but you're almost as good as a son. I got a better deal in you than in Edwin, I think.' He sighed. 'And I'm still the one in charge.'

Tyrell grew up with something bitter in him. Rowena, who had gained more happiness from the world than she ever imagined, never understood why. Perhaps he had been born with something wrong, an invisible twisted limb inside him, which was something she could understand. She had overcome her own difficulties, but he seemed unable to do so, he held them in him where it hurt. It never occurred to her that she was the cause.

Tyrell adored his mother, and it was her judgment and strength of character, her solid lack of imagination so unlike his brooding, helpless father or manipulative grandfather, that he learned to value. He hated Tully because of the one thing Rowena could not see, it had become so much a part of her life: Tully's callous treatment of her. When she was ill, suffering terribly from infections and ulcers in her bad leg, Tyrell smouldered that Tully never sent round the gifts or honey or poultices that he had doted on Alia and Elfreda to their dying days.

Tyrell was lanky, his eyes darting suspiciously under the long forelock of hair that he kept brushing back with his freckled hand. He was a tall, thin presence seeming always to watch people, ceaselessly observing, his arms wrapped round himself as though he was cold, tucked tight into himself.

Tyrell said little, but he thought a lot, and he was good at what mattered.

He could drink.

The mother's boy drank as deep as his father and his grandfather, and gradually a tight grin would spread across his face, and his eyes beneath that hair narrowed as the quarrels began.

Ing and Tully were always fighting, and the fights were always serious. Tully was old – nearly eighty years old by the time Tyrell joined seriously in drinking that honeyed beer, sweetened to preserve it – and at first he loyally took his father's side against the old man. Ing had not had Tyrell taken into another household because he did not think he was tough enough, and instead tried himself to teach the boy to fight. The crushing blows with long sword and axe that put spirit in a man came easily to Ing; with a weapon in his hand this quiet giant became a terrifying fighting machine. But Tyrell would cringe and retreat under the hail of blows, dropping his sword as though it was red-hot.

'You're only frightening him,' Rowena said firmly. 'He's not a warrior like you are.'

'What other way is there for him to be?' Ing had answered.

But it was useless, and as he grew older and drank more, Tyrell, at first flinching and fearful, took against his father too. The shouting matches between the three drunk men ran occasionally to blows, Tully squawking like a chicken. Afterwards Rowena would quietly oversee the reconciliations, which lasted only as long as the men's tempers.

Ing was intelligent, but it was a simple, straightforward intelligence that lacked Tully's cunning. Whatever Tully wanted was enough for Tully; Ing wanted something more, more even than his adopted tribe, but it was vague; when he reached out to touch the dim vision, nothing was there. Sometimes he woke, flushed and sweating in the early hours, with Rowena stroking the tears from his blond cheeks. 'I don't know what ails me,' he'd whisper.

'Forget your life before,' she'd murmur. 'Forget where you have come from. Think only of where you are going.'

'But where am I going?' he'd cry, and for that Rowena had no answer.

The people of Vaudey were Ing's people now; he was chief in all but name, under that conniving rogue Tully. He was not by nature a tiller of the earth, but his family and his fixed tribe of villagers kept him in the valley; he could not roam or go off fighting as his blood longed to do. His yearning covered his unhappiness, his sense of not belonging and his temper, like dangerously thin ice. He passed his evenings drinking quietly, observing quietly; he showed no interest in other women.

Tully, his eyes almost white now with the affliction of all old people, was obsessed by the future of his bloodline and was always trying to find a suitable wife for Tyrell, now fired with this maiden, now that, never satisfied.

Tyrell bided his time. He knew that without the old man's baleful influence, his father would be weak. Ing was not interested in ruling the valley. Rowena, half his size, with her rolling gait on her crippled foot, was the strong one. It was just a matter, Tyrell reasoned to himself, of waiting for Tully to die. Better still if they killed one another. Under English custom, the son took his father's widow to wife: Tyrell would rule the valley with his mother. It could happen, because when Ing got drunk he hardly knew himself, he would lash out in that nameless grief that possessed him, and Tully was so senile he hardly knew what he was doing at the best of times. Even on such a cool, windy night as this, he'd insisted he be carried to his place by the communal bonfire, just a bag of bones though he was. But he put back his head like a monarch and drew his rags about him like greatness.

'Quiet as a little mouse, your son!' he squawked at Ing, who was hunched over staring into the smoke. Tully had slept all day and his tongue had stored up its acid.

Tyrell, ignoring the insult, stayed silent.

'What goes on in that quiet head of his?' Tully cackled, too canny to be fooled by Tyrell's silence. 'Plots and plans, I'll bet! A cunning Fox!' This too was an insult, cunning not being a manly virtue.

'Just like you once, I'll bet.' Tyrell smiled his tight grin, refilling his father's mug and his own.

'We've fallen so far,' Ing sighed, glancing up, and Tyrell realised he was deep in one of his black moods of anger and despair. *It might happen*, Tyrell thought with a young man's impatience, barely able to hide his excitement, *it might happen tonight!* He threw Tully a quiet, goading smile that Ing could not see, and Tully's tongue ran away with him.

'I'm amazed the boy doesn't still cling to his mother's skirt,' Tully shouted, his voice rising. 'Perhaps he does!'

Ing raised his hand. 'Enough.'

'Amazed he doesn't hobble like her!' Tully mocked his grandson, his poor eyes not seeing Ing's frown deepen. 'Hop, hop, hop!'

Tyrell touched the hilt of his knife, but Ing covered his hand with his own. 'Never mind,' he muttered.

'He's talking of my mother!' Tyrell hissed. 'Have you no pride?'

'I have my pride,' Ing said in a thick voice, wiping the sticky dregs from his mouth with the back of his hand.

'Why doesn't your son treat me with more respect?' Tully demanded. 'You've raised a wretch, you have.'

Ing looked at him, his gaze steady now, and spoke with slurred dignity, the firelight glittering in each of his dark blue eyes.

'A father may insult his own daughter, even though she is married to another. You may not insult my son.'

'You aren't one of us,' Tully sneered recklessly. 'It's *her* strong British blood that has come through in him, Rowena's, not yours. Look at Tyrell's hair, look at his eyes, nothing of you—' He squealed as Ing jumped up, throwing off the sheepskin he wore, the muscles tense beneath his gleaming skin.

I could strike him, Tyrell thought, staring up at his father's lowest rib. I could do it now, and become great.

Ing drew his sword, swinging it with a hiss through the air.

The old man held out his beaker as though to ward off the wild blow, falling backwards off the log he used as a throne. The long blade knocked the beaker along the ground with a clatter.

'Help!' Tully squealed. 'Help! Help!'

Tyrell stared at the dagger that was warm in his hand. One thrust would do it.

Ing lunged at Tully crawling away holding a blanket over his head, and by his own movement came close to impaling himself on the point of Tyrell's dagger. But then he whirled, venting his fury on the fire, scattering the fiery logs with great flashing sweeps of his blade, and a terrible numbness flowed up Tyrell's arm.

'Father,' Tyrell moaned. He reached for his hand with his other hand but found nothing there, only his torn sleeve.

The men stared at what was left of Tyrell's arm.

Ing dropped his sword. 'What were we fighting about?' he cried. He clapped his hands over his face and pulled his hair.

Tully lay on his back, pulling the blanket off his head. The dagger had landed by his eye on the ground and he threw it away without thinking about it, where one of the children found it in the morning and used it to impress his friends. He got slowly to his feet. 'What have you done?'

'By the gods, I didn't mean to,' Ing said.

Tyrell staggered. The joint of his wrist stuck out from his forearm, the gristle moving as though he was moving his hand, but there was nothing there. He collapsed to his knees. Ing snapped a cord from his boot and bound the upper arm tightly.

'That won't bring it back,' Tully said.

Weeping, Ing looked at the thong round Tully's neck and the talent swinging from it. He pleadingly held out his hands for the magic talisman, symbol of the family's leadership and fortune. Tully handed it over. Ing knelt and rubbed the dented silver reverently over Tyrell's bloodied wrist so that its spell would make the hand grow again, undoing the terrible wrong that had been done.

Tyrell shrieked and screamed, and the men kept looking, but nothing happened.

In the shadow of the trees, a man wearing the long woollen gown called a pallium, which hung from a narrow band round his neck, put his scrawny fingers on the bridle of his horse to silence it and stared at their pagan worship.

'Savages!' he said. 'Disgusting savages!'

His name was Mellitus.

He waited until dawn, praying on his knees, then woke his shivering *acolutus* and had his beard and hair combed, and vestments properly brushed and arranged – it was important to strike the right impression. He strode from the trees towards the cold ashes of the fire. The lowest of the low were sleeping there without shelter, snoring men and their filthy women who had scavenged the leftovers and the dregs of the beer, pigs snuffling around them in the glow of dawn light.

Mellitus stopped. In the distance, for the first time, he saw London. Illuminated by the first low rays of the sun, the town hung above the treetops and the river like a vision.

With an effort he dragged his eyes back to the earth, resisting the impulse to cover his nose at the stink of the people, his eyes from the sight of them, his ears from the sound of their snoring and snorting. The unsaved.

He rapped his shepherd's crook – for men were sheep who must be led to the Lord – loudly on the ground. 'Awaken!' he cried.

The scum rolled blearily to their feet, mumbling, then fell back from him. The swarthy Italian stood with the dawn behind him, his shadow streaming over them, the sun framing his hair. 'Awaken, I say!' he cried. He was not richly dressed but immaculately brushed and clean; even his sandalled feet showing beneath that simple robe were clean, and his toenails neatly trimmed – something the common people found particularly curious. He was dressed neither as a king nor as a property; they didn't know what to make of him.

Mellitus tolerated their examination as he had at a hundred other ignorant, fleabitten villages in the realm of King Athelbert and his French, Christian wife, Queen Bertha – names of which these people were almost certainly as ignorant as they were of the Kingdom of God above their heads.

'Whose people are you?' he asked.

'Who wants to know?' someone replied in that slow country speech that was so difficult to comprehend.

Mellitus put muscle in his voice, impressively. 'I am Bishop Mellitus, consecrated by Archbishop Augustine at the old Roman church of St Martin's in Canterbury, sent by him to preach Christianity to King Sabert, son of Ricole, sister of our good Christian King Athelbert. Further I am charged by King Athelbert to found an episcopal see in London, and to build a church there that will stand for ever as a monument to the glory of God.'

'Which god?' someone said.

'There is only one God,' Mellitus explained, talking to them like children, the dangerous, dirty-minded children that all men and all women were beneath their skins. 'God made the world, and made you. All men, even kings, bow down before Him.' His flesh crawled as he approached the man who had cut off his son's hand. The blond giant pulled his son forward beside him, the arm tightly bound up in leather. In the night Mellitus had heard the women wash the wound in the pool in the trees, and the young man's face was still grey as ash from loss of blood. The near side of the pool had still been laced with red when Mellitus washed there, fastidiously, from the far bank.

'If God made everything,' Ing said, 'he can make my son Tyrell's hand grow back.'

'Nothing can bring Tyrell's hand back, ever,' Mellitus said, 'because he is a sinner. Since Adam's Fall, to be born is to be sinful. We are enslaved to sin, to ignorance, and to death. Every choice we make leads us inevitably to do wrong. He must repent, but he is unworthy.'

'I am,' Tyrell said, remembering his murderous thoughts last night, unable to look his father in the eye in the sober light of day. 'I am a sinner. Everything was my fault.' He would never be a warrior now; he had no need to lie. The admission, despite the sickening pain in his arm, felt like a breath of freedom, and his heart lifted.

'Yes, I am a sinner, but I do repent, and I would live my life a different way.'

'I will do anything for him,' Ing said simply.

'All I can do,' Mellitus said loudly, 'is bring you to God, through God's gospel word, and the death and resurrection of His Son, Jesus Christ.'

A very old man pushed forward, his eyes almost opaque but still cunning, his crafty face a wizened mask behind long white hairs.

'Are you God?' he squinted, pushing his finger against the bishop's chest.

'I am only His servant,' Mellitus told Tully patiently. 'Above me is our blessed Augustine, first archbishop to the English, appointed by His Holiness Pope Gregory, successor to the Roman Emperors, who stands closest on earth to God.' He flinched from the pagan amulet, still smeared with blood from last night's business, swinging from the old man's neck, and could hold himself back no longer. With an expression of revulsion, Mellitus seized the talent and, snapping the thong, flung it in the stream as though it would burn him. 'The first commandment our Lord, through Moses, gave to us is "Worship no God but Me".'

'I will believe,' Ing said, 'if He will give my son his hand back.'

'I'd like my talent back,' said Tully peevishly.

'He will have his hand in heaven, in God's glory, when he has repented and paid for his sins,' Mellitus intoned. 'If he has been brought to God.'

'Brought to God?' Tully said, distracted.

'Baptised. If he has not been baptised he cannot enter heaven. To disappear beneath the water is a symbolic death, burial, and resurrection to a new life.'

'Then we will be baptised,' Ing said. 'We can pay you in sheep and goats, a pig or two.'

Mellitus hesitated. 'I am on a journey,' he said reluctantly. 'I cannot stay. For the moment, your faith will be sufficient payment.'

'Then I believe,' Ing said.

'He is a good husband, a good father,' Rowena said, limping forward. 'Whatever he does, I do. I too will be baptised into a new life.'

'Will you, too, do your best to lead these people – even of your own gender, woman, as did our Lord Jesus Christ – to repentance?'

'I will,' Rowena said.

'I will,' Tyrell said.

Tully was silent.

Mellitus was fired by an odd kind of exultancy; his morning's work swept him along, gave him new strength, simply because it was so successful – almost miraculous. Even the great Augustine in his room at the Abbey of St Peter and St Paul, scourged in secret by self-doubt as any man must be, admitted privately his misgiving that the more remote rural peoples could ever be Christianised. The Church could convert kings and through them the aristocracy and perhaps the fighting men – everyone had been encouraged to believe the white bread used at Mass conferred strength – but the common people remained obstinately wedded to their ancient nature religions. The Pope, mindful of the first commandment, had forbidden the worship of water and trees, but wherever possible the Church took over old shrines and customs and quietly converted them to its own belief.

'The overflowing pool,' Mellitus said. 'Is that your holy place?' The sun was already high and Mellitus realised that he had been speaking for hours, and that he was hot in his scratchy pallium.

'No, lord.' Tully sucked his gums. 'Some say there's good spirits there, but some say there's a terrible bad one.' He pointed across the fields of the knoll to where the land dropped away. 'Down there's our holy well, and it's been there for longer than any man can remember. Even my father—'

'That will do,' Mellitus said hurriedly, clicking his fingers for his acolyte to accompany him. They followed the stream between the fields to where it cascaded over the rim into a broad ferny gully. Tully led the prelate to one side, the crowd following them, to the well at the top of the Mickfield.

'It's said it's bottomless,' he cackled, pointing into the depths.

Mellitus gave him a stony glare. 'I have no place for super-stition,' he said, blessing the water and making it truly holy, and this a Christian place, 'only faith.'

Ing, undressed by the acolyte, stepped forward to the edge wearing only his loincloth. 'If I am to die, and be buried, and come to life a new man, I will require a new name,' he said, 'a Christian name. Who is the greatest Christian?'

'Pope Gregory, I have told you.'

Ing said, 'Then Gregory I shall be.'

Mellitus made him kneel and held his shoulders. 'If you believe with all your heart, you may be baptised.'

'I believe with all my heart.'

'Say, I believe that Jesus Christ is the Son of God.'

'I believe that Jesus Christ is the Son of God.'

Mellitus pushed him in and the water settled, then Gregory's white outstretched hands appeared, then his head. 'I touched bottom!' he shouted. 'I touched bottom and it was there!'

Mellitus pulled him out and made the sign of the cross on the Englishman's shining, water-beaded face. 'I baptise you Gregory in the name of Jesus Christ.'

Tyrell stepped forward nervously. 'Your Grace? You said you were on a journey.'

'To London.'

'I would go with as as your acolyte,' Tyrell said meekly. 'One head, one heart, one hand.'

'I shall think on it. If you believe with all your heart, you may be baptised.'

'I believe that Jesus Christ is the Son of God.'

Mellitus baptised him and Rowena stepped forward. When she was lifted from the dark water, her face shining in the sun, Tully cleared his throat.

'Now me,' he said.

Mellitus looked surprised. 'Are you sure?' He glanced towards London. The sun was passing its peak and he sighed. 'If you mean it. If you believe with all your heart, you may be baptised.'

'I believe that Jesus Christ is the Son of God,' Tully said. He disappeared into the water with a red splash. Mellitus drew back, appalled at the red speckles marking his pallium, and a woman screamed. The water was laced with threads of blood, slowly rising up from below. Tully came up splashing and coughing.

'Blood!' Mellitus whispered. 'Is the Devil among you?'

They stood round the edge of the well, watching the darkening water spread from below, stepping back lest it wash over their feet as it rose to the top and trickled away.

'It's not me,' Tully said anxiously.

'Fill it in!' Mellitus hissed. 'Have your men break in the sides, and fill this place in with earth.'

Slowly the water cleared and ran pure again.

'It's just Tyrell's blood,' Tully said. 'Soaked down from the upper pool last night, that's all. There must be some sort of connection underground.'

'I cannot believe such a thing,' Mellitus said, with a shudder. 'This is a cursed place, and you are all cursed!'

'I'm honest,' Tully appealed to him. 'I'm a bad man and a sinner, it's true, like you said earlier, but I'm an honest Christian. I'll prove it to you.' Scampering like a goat, he led Mellitus up the slope to the knoll. 'My father always used to call this the bath-house,' he said, pointing at the ruins sticking out near the head-land of a field, not worth breaking down and trying to plough over. 'I remember when it was all trees here,' Tully said sadly, 'when I was a lad.'

They pushed through the creepers and Tully dropped to his knees, in prayer Mellitus thought, but then the old man began to dig, scooping aside the soft soil in his cupped, blackened hands. Soon a strange mosaic appeared, vertical as if on a wall, but they were below the level of the walls. It was a pit lined with mosaics.

A jumping fish.

'A dolphin,' Mellitus breathed. 'In the time of Our Saviour on earth men must have made this a swimming bath.'

'Oh, I wouldn't know about that,' Tully said. The hole was sizeable now and Gregory knelt to help him, then jumped down, pulling out great handfuls. 'I was younger when I buried this,' Tully puffed, 'it didn't seem so deep.'

'The earth rises,' Mellitus said absently. He stared at the fish, a shoal of them now, caught in mid-jump by the skill of the long-dead artist, far beyond anything possible in these times. 'It covers us all.'

With an exclamation of victory Tully pulled up something corroded and rotten from the pit. It was a bag of heavy sacking, the tail of an earthworm hanging from a hole in one side. Holding it into the sunlight, where his old eyes could just make it out, Tully brushed away the soil that clung to it.

Then he put down the bag and let the neck flop open.

'For you,' he said.

Mellitus, staring at the silver gleaming in the sunlight, knew he was being offered a fortune.

'For the Church,' he muttered. But he got down on his knees, careless of his pallium, and counted the coins one by one. 'Twenty-six. I've never seen anything like them. The Church thanks you, Tully. You will surely go to heaven.'

'I can hardly see them,' Tully said sadly, 'but I remember my father Rufus showing them to me. He was a wonderful man. How I loved him. I thought they were the most beautiful things in the world, but maybe I'm remembering him.'

Bishop Mellitus rode up out of the valley on his short-legged horse, his two acolytes walking respectfully in his shadow. The silver coins that the old man had called his talents – how dare such a mere man and a sinner, his breakfast still clinging to his mouth, call things of such beauty his – jingled in the saddlebags of the Church now. Coming to the bleak heathland, his horse stepped over a fallen archway, and Mellitus glanced down: he could read the letters 'VALLE DEI' etched in the Purbeck marble. He rode on with a shrug; the people called the place Vaudey. He shook his head wearily. How often, how very often he was called to lead ignorant swines, filthy, conniving, ugly beyond redemption, *human*, who did not deserve his ministry. Still, the sound of the strange coins and the thought of their beauty comforted him.

Tyrell looked back for the last time, then hurried after the prelate swaying on his horse towards London.

Behind them, men working with poles and shovels broke down the ancient wicker lining of the well and filled it with stones, chalk boulders and earth which they trod well down.

A few days later, in the ruins of the bath-house, water began to seep into the hole Tully had dug. Slowly the level rose until once again the mosaics of leaping dolphins, eels and seaweed were underwater, then the water leaked out into the surrounding soil. That was always the most fertile end of the field.

Mellitus decided not to pass on the medallions to the Church, partly because he felt guilty about the one that he had flung into the stream. The set was incomplete, imperfect, and he could not give the Church an imperfect gift. The loss nagged at him because the ones he had were in such beautiful condition, whereas the bloodied charm he had torn from the old man's neck had been wafer-thin, bent, a hole knocked through it for the leather thong. But it had been the most important one, he now realised, the one that completed the set. Bishop Mellitus believed in perfection and hated imperfection.

Clouds covered the sun and a cold rain fell; his saddle rubbed his thighs unmercifully, giving him such pain that finally he sacrificed his dignity and walked. The strap holding his sandal broke, so he limped for a while, then had himself lifted back into the saddle and endured that agony. The bag containing the coins fell open and deposited them in a ditch, the boys had a terrible time finding them, and all the while the rain trickled down the back of his neck. When they moved on, the rain stopped and people started coming out, the clinking hoard attracting their unwelcome attention.

Tyrell, looking around him alertly, learned his duties.

The party sheltered at an inn overnight, and the innkeeper who welcomed them, kissing the bishop's ring and leaving a gob of saliva clinging to it, offered the services of his children to clean travel-stained clothes, feed and water the horse, prepare quarters, bring ale as late at night as His Grace wanted. Nothing was too much trouble, and in the morning, after politely enquiring after the state of his Grace's groaning bowels, the innkeeper fawningly offered the services of an elder son as a ferryman across the river. His Grace declined the offer, preferring to use the bridge. It had been repaired with tree trunks roughly flattened with adzes and laid across the old pilings.

They crossed beneath the walls and entered the green fields of London. Dusty lanes wove round the boundaries of each village, Tyrell saw, and here and there people were digging for the stone that lay beneath the grey clay. The amphitheatre straddled two smoky villages, its vast arena the venue of public punishment, parliament and royal ceremonial. A few houses were being built against its outer walls. They followed the lane curving past it towards Lud's Gate, the clopping of the horse's hooves thrown back by the huge columns of stone, then they came under the walls of the ancient fort where King Sabert kept his *sele* or hall. And there, while his Grace's bowels recovered, they waited. His Majesty might arrive tomorrow, or in six months' time. A king's court had to move to eat, one step ahead of disease, always in fear of being toppled by rebellion. A Christian king, however, would have the Church behind him. King Sabert saw the wisdom of this at once, especially since it came from his Christian uncle King Athelbert, who would even pay for the church that Mellitus would build.

So Mellitus, the first Bishop of London since the Romans had left, in due time baptised King Sabert, his earls, and then his warriors old and young, on the dais in the centre of the northern *cavea* of the amphitheatre. At Easter he began to build his church on the very peak of Lud's Hill, exactly halfway between the Walbrook and the Fleet. The wooden building would be consecrated to St Paul.

'Beautiful!' Mellitus said, clapping his fingers. 'The perfect place!'

When the workmen began the foundations, they dug through the remains of an older church, also of wood, its outlines sunk in a grey clay of collapsed daub walls and showing the marks of fire. Below this, to Mellitus's dismay – it being too late to change the site he had agreed to the glory of God with the king – the workmen began turning up richly dressed and carved marble, now almost impossible to obtain. Among the blasphemous and explicit statues was that of a naked woman with a bow and arrow: this place had been a pagan temple dedicated to Diana. And they found bones, human bones by the thousand, as though a whole congregation had been torn apart by terrible forces. The workmen scattered them, and Mellitus ordered the statues smashed.

He began to wonder about the value of old Tully's gift, except as a weight of silver, and considered melting them down for candlesticks.

'They've been in my family for as long as anyone can remember,' Tyrell said.

'They're the Church's now,' Mellitus said spitefully.

He forbade the labourers to dig any deeper, and put the carpenters to work. Within a month, from elms felled along the lanes of London, his beautiful jewel of a church in fresh yellow wood, St Paul's, stood proudly on its hilltop. God's message was clear to see.

The workmen digging out the porch for the *porticus* altar called the bishop over. Ox heads bearing the marks of sacrifice lay in the earth pit. Whatever religion it was, it was so ancient that they had turned to stone; even the forelock of hair still clinging to each skull had fossilised. Mellitus shuddered. 'Cover them up,' he said quietly, 'cover them up. My church is built on a profanity.' He walked away without looking back.

'Poor old boy,' the foreman sniffed, pulling his thumb from his nose and examining it before getting back to work. 'Takes it all a bit seriously, that stuff, don't he?'

King Sabert died and in such uncertain times the talents were hidden under the altar. Mellitus instructed Tyrell in Holy Orders and he was ordained as a priest. 'You're so full of hope,' Mellitus said longingly; the new king, and thus everyone else, had renounced Christianity, and the two men barely escaped with their lives when St Paul's was burnt by the mob. They slipped away across the ramshackle bridge in the early hours with what they had saved of the church silver. Mellitus abandoned his robe of office. In disguise they hired a horse and a donkey, all that was to be had in Southwark, paying for them with a silver talent, and fled to Canterbury.

The years were hard for the Church; Augustine had been taken to God and Laurence was the second archbishop when King Athelbert died. When his son married his mother in a pagan ceremony, most clerics fled, leaving the Abbey of St Peter and St Paul almost empty. While the Pope took his time deciding on the legality of the marriage, Laurence succeeded in baptising the new king, but died in the winter an exhausted man, and Mellitus followed him as archbishop.

'I still think of you as a young man,' he told Tyrell, calling him to his room. 'But I am old. You may be archbishop one day. There's few enough of us left, God knows,' he added bitterly.

'Mighty oaks grow from acorns,' Tyrell said.

'Justus will be primate when I die.'

'Not for a long time yet,' Tyrell said loyally.

'Imminently,' Mellitus said, holding up his hands: his finger-nails were blue despite the closeness of the weather. 'My patron-age will not sustain you much longer.' He went to a locker and lifted the heavy carved lid with an effort, picked out something which he closed in his palm, and let the lid drop carefully. Turning to Tyrell, he opened his hand. In it lay a silver medallion, as shining as if newly minted, though there were several heavy knocks around one edge. 'Taken as a gift to the Church in Roches-ter, and from there it has found its way here. But not to me, I think. To you.' He held it out. 'Take it. It's yours, not mine, not the Church's.'

Tyrell examined the talent, marvelling. 'But where—'

'Strange how the things one covets most in one's life matter least at the end. You don't remember the mounts we purchased at such an exorbitant price in Southwark? In ten years who knows how many hands it has passed through. But one heart in Roches-ter was truly devout.' He shivered with cold. 'Take all of them, Tyrell. Take them back home.' He closed his eyes. 'I'm super-stitious in my old age. Let people believe what they will. I've had enough.'

Archbishop Mellitus was laid to rest and Justus of Rochester was consecrated in his place, bringing his own priests with him. Tyrell went into the town to his wife, Sylvia, and four children – Edmund was already old enough to want to follow his father into the priesthood – and they talked.

They decided to walk to Vaudey, a brave decision, for the lanes winding back and forth over the route of the old Roman road were considered dangerous. But although Tyrell hired no armed thugs to protect them, having little money, they were not molested.

And so Tyrell came home.

Tully was long dead, of course, and Gregory's hair was a fine nimbus to his shoulders, neither blond nor white; age had stooped him but it had not changed his kindly blue eyes. He held out his hands then embraced Tyrell so tight his bones cracked. Rowena's fiery hair was stark white, making her overflowing eyes very dark.

'Never thought you'd come back,' she said, not looking at his missing hand.

'I'll kill the fatted calf tonight,' Gregory said. 'There's the biggest old carp in one of the ponds that you ever saw, long as your leg and fifty years old if he's a day, one of Tully's original stock, I'd wager.'

'My husband will bet on anything!' Rowena laughed to Sylvia. 'He's become almost completely British!'

It was a lovely summer's day. Gregory fetched his long-handled net and he and Tyrell set off for the fishpond. Tyrell picked up an acorn left by a squirrel scampering from his approach, dibbled a hole with his finger in the soft soil and dropped it in. Gregory enjoyed a few wild raspberries on the way and soon they crossed the stream feeding the top fishpond. Careful to keep his shadow from the surface, he laid the net under the water and the two men waited sitting on tussocks among the reeds. From his pouch Gregory took pieces of wheat porridge, rubbed them into balls and smeared them with a few drops of raspberry juice, then dropped them expertly in the water over the net. 'Bait,' he said. 'He's clever, your carp. Suspicious. And he knows we're here.'

They waited in companionable silence, the sun hot on their heads.

'Is it true?' Gregory said, kneading more bait in his palms, then casting it.

'Is what true, Father?'

'I should call you Father, Tyrell, shouldn't I? You being a priest. It's confusing.'

'I'm always your son, whatever I'm called. What do you mean, is it true?'

'Miracles. You've been in many places, I can tell. Have you seen any?'

'Only hard work. But one must believe.'

'I've often wondered about that day,' Gregory remarked conversationally, 'and everything Mellitus told us, if it really is true that Christ walked our earth in the flesh.'

'I believe so with all my heart.'

'But is it true? That He left His footprints in the sand and the waves washed them away. That the world is five thousand, eight hundred and eight years old. That Heaven is above us and Hell below.'

'Yes, it is the truth.'

409

Gregory put out his hand for silence as silt and bubbles rose in front of them, and a burly shape showed its fins in the shallows, snapping up the bait eagerly into its gaping mouth. Gregory waited his moment then heaved up the net, the ashwood handle bending alarmingly, and swung the thrashing fish onto the bank.

'I wonder,' he said.

The feast was held in Gregory's hall, the firelight flickering on the undersides of the rafters. Tyrell's son Edmund sat high up there watching the gaiety below, the carp displayed at the centre on its huge bed of seethed turnip. Beside him sat a sloe-eyed girl of his own age who said her name was Monica, swinging her skinny legs and pointing out everyone she knew below them. 'Look at them!' she said. 'Isn't it exciting? Isn't it marvellous! Isn't that the biggest fish you ever saw?'

'In Canterbury we behave with more dignity,' Edmund said.

'But you're staying here now,' Monica chattered. 'I heard it.' She gestured into the murmuring shadows around the doorways of the hall. 'All these people will be yours.'

Below them Gregory rose to his feet. 'My son is home,' he said, and handed his sword to Tyrell.

Tyrell blessed the carp and raised the sword in his single hand, then brought it down and cut off the head of the fish. There was a loud clink.

'What was that?' squealed Monica, and would have fallen from the high beam in her excitement had Edmund not caught her arm.

Tyrell put down the sword and reached through the bones into the carp's head.

He pulled out something that flashed.

He held up in his hand the worn, battered charm that Bishop Mellitus had torn from Tully's neck and thrown into the stream all those years ago. It had never been lost.

They say beauty, like time, lives in the eye of the beholder. An hour in torment lasts a lifetime, but for lovers dawn comes in the blink of an eye.

Edmund's youngest sister, Veronica, lived for a hundred years, and she was no beauty.

In her dotage, an icon of the family surviving from a time few could by then remember, this savage wrinkled creature noddingly attributed her longevity to clean water, and perhaps she was right. In Greenwich or London, both places once more in clear view as the hedgeless, open fields spread, the townsfolk lived little beyond thirty years. Veronica had birthed seven children, five of them girls, and later knew twenty-seven grandchildren by name and birthing day; but the time she died she owned great-grandchildren beyond knowing or naming. Their bright laughing faces flourished and in turn became dust.

The sons and daughters of the Fox family, like those of most others, spread beyond all recognising, carrying their name with them or without it, sons seeking their fortune, daughters good marriages, sometimes in the village, sometimes as far as their fate took them.

From the village of Vaudey, and the fields of the knoll below, called Holywell, the children who remained glanced up as they grew old, and saw much but understood little. They shook their grey heads, and turned their eyes back to the soil on which they worked and to which their bodies would return. And on the fearful Day of Judgement, their souls would rise to Heaven or fall to Hell.

In the distance St Paul's was rebuilt in brick with side chapels, and the eastern end, pointed towards them, was rounded in the popular style. The London Emporium – the Wych where the ships were beached, its busy markets serving people arriving by land and sea – spread westward from the walls of the City, along the great curving strand of the river, almost as far as Thorney Island. From time to time the peasants toiling in the Vaudey fields, or the priest in the church founded by Tyrell in the dell and consecrated to St John, noticed that the distant buildings and churches of the emporium were again being swept by smoke, but they just shrugged; the houses were always rebuilt within weeks, it was God's will. The priest hung the mistletoe at Christmas because it had always been done, and baptised children into the Church at the overflowing pool where baptisms had been held from the beginning of time, as far as he knew. Many believed this was the holy well from which the place took its name, though some old wives still swore – without knowing quite where they had heard the blasphemy – that there was a terrible spirit in the pool too. Nothing died harder than old stories; neither the Church's

411

mockery nor its condemnation could kill them, and as many common people believed in the sanctity of trees or ponds as believed in the transformation of holy wine into blood and holy bread into flesh.

Each generation of Vaudey priests, some more capable of reverence than of counting to such a high number, tended the twenty-seven silver coins laid beneath the altar of St John's by its founder; and each eldest son of the Fox family wore one round his neck for good luck on the day of his marriage and the bedding of his wife, as had been the case with amulets for time out of mind in this western outpost of Kent.

And in Surrey south of the river, the emporium of the Borough of Southwark, with all its squalid inns and cheaping markets lining the lane, spread like a dark cloud from the squat wooden tower of St Mary Overie. The church and convent had been built beside the inlet by the wealthy ferryman whose landing place it was – a man named Wittle – conveniently placed for City folk wanting the stews and brothels of Bankside. As Southwark's trade with the City grew, the rickety bridgeworks that were cobbled together and came apart were replaced with a more substantial structure dovetailed into the Roman pilings, and the ferryman fell back on his inn for his living.

And then the Danes came.

In Dumnonia in the west, the descendents of Toherus the builder of Valle Dei and Veronica his wife, now absorbed into English ways as the Torr family, fought for King Alfred in the inhospitable shadow of Exmoor.

At Vaudey, a great army camped on the tableland of the heath, and down in the valley the Fox family negotiated tribute to their new, temporary masters, and their peasants laboured to pay it. They saw Southwark burning within its defensive ditches, and London Bridge pulled down with grapnels from longships, the ancient pilings rotten beneath the water and snapping off like decayed teeth, carrying bridgeworks and defenders alike to the bottom of the river. The Wych was burned and everyone slaughtered. King Alfred drove back the Danes from the Borough of London and gave the manor of Greenwich to his youngest daughter, Elstrudis, at the same time confirming the Fox family in the manorship of Holywell. The office was hereditary, passing down from father to eldest son, with the priesthood falling to a younger son, in the three classes of society: those who fought, those who prayed, and those who worked.

And the innkeepers, of course, shuffled back to Southwark. Times changed and rulers changed, but people never changed. With the money they made from ferries, they rebuilt their inns, while the Bishop of Winchester, in whose diocese Southwark lay, enlarged St Mary Overie and added a college for priests. It was built of stone, with rows of dank, dark cells. A new bridge was opened, and burned, and St Paul's was again burned and rebuilt; when the Danes struck camp the common English always re-appeared as though out of the ground, setting up shops and thatching their ruined houses, dogged and indomitable. In their quiet, persistent, pragmatic way, they never gave up.

On Thorney Island (the river could only be forded here now at low tide, and then only on horseback) King Edward built his West Minster abbey church to St Peter to match the East Minster, St Paul's, already rebuilt within the City. These were the largest buildings seen since Roman times, and in their holy shadow peasants lived in squalor.

At Holywell Manor, one rainy day, a middle-aged man came past the watermills of the stream running through the demesne, grinding corn, and at the manor door asked for shelter from the storm. The westerly had defeated the efforts of his ship to reach London, and he was making his way overland on foot. To the lord of the manor, Edgar, he introduced himself as Britnoth of Torr. He was a doughty campaigner, a mercenary soldier of some renown, having fought in the pay of Earl Siward of Northumberland to defeat Earl Macbeth at Dunsinane. Edgar, young and new to his inheritance, at once warmed to the older man with his terrible scars and quiet, self-effacing manner.

Torr was tired of the fighting life and planned to take ship round the south coast to the Borough of Barnstaple, and there walk the Harepath into his homeland, to settle near his brother's farm at Torworth in quiet retirement. 'You shall not hang up your sword or leave here until you have taught me all you know of its skill,' said Edgar with a smile, and Torr, his fierce look dissolving, agreed. He had seen Edgar's elder sister Adela watching him. She had lustrous red hair and the most amazing, long-lashed chestnut eyes, and Torr had lost his heart to her in the one glance.

When Britnoth of Torr finally left Holywell Manor, autumn had turned to spring, Edgar was a fine swordsman, and Torr was accompanied by Adela, now his loving wife, who brought with her a fine dowry sufficient to open up land for a farm, and a silver talent hanging from a silver chain round her neck, a gift from Edgar. Within a year they had built a farmhouse near Torr's brother's, in one of the few warm, south-facing valleys in the north of Exmoor, and their daughter was born. They named her Resda, and she grew up to be a great beauty.

In London, King Edward's English heir and English nobles were swept away within a generation. The common folk kept themselves to themselves against the new invaders who came to rule them from the south: proud, stirruped, chain-mailed conquerors on horseback, descendents of the British aristocracy who had fled the English with the fall of Rome, settling the peninsula of France in such numbers it was called Brittany. King William built his White Tower on the south-eastern corner of London's Roman wall and had himself anointed with holy oil, becoming sacred. His peasant army trickled back to France but he paid his earls and lords with the fiefdoms, lands and manors due to conquerors, among them the Maner de Holywell which was granted to Ranulph de Barreneau.

De Barreneau and his pack of armed soldiery never learned English, and his subjects never learned French. He was known as the Wolf for his violence and rapacity, and such a reputation, brought to a head by the notorious rape of an English nun, was too close to the sensitive markets of London for the patience of King William's portreeve, Geoffrey de Mandeville. De Barreneau handled money matters no better. He soon found himself in debt to his ears with the usurers of the City – his two sulings of land at Vaudey brought him barely £12 a year. His debts were quietly settled by his own reeve, the wily and knowledgeable Edgar de Fox, and de Barreneau was granted the hostile wilderness of the Exmoor Forest. There he fell in love with Resda Torr, the Mistress of Watersmeet.

Meanwhile in Vaudey, in no small part due to Mandeville's gratitude, the Manor of Holywell reverted to the Fox family. Walking that day by the old English church of St John's, Edgar dropped his scarred sword hand onto the shoulder of his young grandson Robert. His own sons had been killed, one at Stamford Bridge, the other at Hastings, and Robert was now the repository of all his hopes for the family. 'We've got our land back again,' Edgar sighed, looking around him. 'It's still ours.'

'It won't be if that old oak tree falls on the church roof.' Robert pointed. 'It should be chopped down before it falls down.'

'That would be bad luck. The tree is supposed to have been planted by St John's first priest, St Tyrell.'

'How did you raise the money to pay off that monster de Barreneau, Grandfather?' Robert asked suddenly. 'You must have raised ten times what the estate was worth.'

Stonemasons were putting the finishing touches to the square Norman tower commissioned, but not paid for, by de Barreneau. With a wince for such modernity, the two men, young giving way to old, passed through the creaking door into the church, paused with heads bowed, then approached the altar. Lifting the altar cloth, Edgar revealed the twenty-six silver coins. 'I gave these to a Jew on Corn Hill as security. I never thought I'd see them here again. But he brought them back, a greasy disgusting fellow with a long beard and eyes like stone, but a robe as fine as a gentleman's. He said he was a rich man and the money I had borrowed meant little enough to him. They meant *more* than money to him, you see, but when I asked him what he was talking about he put his finger to his lips – or perhaps he was pointing to something on the one he held. You know what they're like, close-mouthed lot! Never understood them, those people.'

Edgar shrugged, and let the cloth drop back.

'Still, I'd chop it,' Robert said as they returned outside, squinting against the sunlight streaming through the oak branches.

But he remembered his grandfather's words and he never did cut it down, though he lived long enough to see his grandson Jeffrey sire five baby sons.

It was the week before Christmas, the old oak tree was black and bare and the mistletoe was cut. The girl who walked past the new lych gate with her eyes downcast crossed herself – crossed herself, it seemed to the young parson who watched her while tending his geese in the churchyard, as much in obeisance to the tree as to the

415

church. Though he frowned in disapproval, his lips tightened with hunger for her and his breath grew short.

Quentin Fox, red of beard and brown of eye, fifth and last son of Sir Jeffrey in the manor house, glanced around to be sure no one else had seen the tiny nod she had given him. Her pace quickened as she turned uphill towards the woods, a hot-tempered, luscious, irresistible girl of fifteen, the hem of her cloak flapping behind her in the frost like an invitation, and he knew she had garnered an hour to herself, as he had begged her at confession.

Quentin dropped the pail and flung the last handfuls of grain haphazardly, his loins already hot beneath his rumpled gown, then set off after her along the houses by the church as if on some other errand, his hands clasped prayerfully in front of him to hide his erection.

'Dear Nicola,' he hummed to himself as he climbed the lane, thinking of the silky feel of her dark brown curls, her mouth on his, his hands busy elsewhere.

Nicola Franks glanced over her shoulder when she reached the trees, and smiled, showing her sharp white teeth, to see the priest with his soft red beard hurrying obediently after her.

She was of French Norman stock, something that only her free status and surname recalled; her Christian name, Nicola, was unusual but her father prided himself on his unconventional turn of mind. His disregard for the conventions manifested itself in more than just his daughter's name. It had been his idea to build Vaudey's first windmill. Everyone said it wouldn't work, but the white canvas sails of his extraordinary *molendinum ad ventum* now circled slowly in the breeze that always blew on his land at the edge of the knoll, near the sheer stone walls and arrow slits of the manor house.

Nicola slipped away quickly between the oak trunks, knowing Quentin would hurry as soon as he was out of sight of the village. He had no patience, thank God. She soon found the old track, sunken and long abandoned. This was glebe land belonging to the Church from the days when baptisms, it was said, were performed here; nowadays in summer it was a place where boys swam and showed off and girls lost their virginity, but today it was winter and deserted, the black water encircled with ice like the white of an eye. She paused where the stream overflowed, keeping the water free of ice here, and stopped to brush her hair in her reflection as though she had all the time in the world. She did not want to be thought waiting, and soon she was absorbed in herself.

'Don't lead me on,' Quentin groaned, dropping to his knees beside her. 'I beg you, Nicola, sweetness, give me all of yourself, I must have you!'

'Is that all?' she said, hiding her elation behind a yawn, but he turned her by her hips, putting his head inside the front of her cloak, squeezing her loins with one hand then kissing her there so that even through her apron, her linen smock, her fine linen underhose, his youthful whiskers sent a warm shiver through her. Despite herself Nicola pulled him closer with a small hiss, leaning down so that his hands sliding up her belly could reach her breasts. 'You mustn't,' she said. He said he must, putting his arm round her knees, pulling her down against him, and she allowed herself to drop. He grunted as her knees pressed on his hips.

'It's wrong,' she said, kneeling on him.

'It's not wrong.' He wanted to kiss her nipples but the tight row of buttons defeated his fingers.

'It's lust,' she said, leading him on. 'You just want to pull my breasts about and have your way with me. It's the Church you love.'

'No it's not,' he said deliberately. 'Not like I love you. That's a different sort of love.'

'It would be, if I believed you,' she said, stroking his hair. 'But what of my self?'

'I'll do anything!' he groaned. 'Just let me be your lover and have all of you!'

She sank down a little further, so that her knees were apart on the ground and she was braced over him, his mouth nibbling into the warm corner of her neck.

'Anything?' she murmured.

'Anything,' he cried, kissing her neck, her jaw, the luscious curve of her lower lip.

'If you want me,' she said, 'give up your Church for me, and take me in my marriage bed.'

A priest could not have both the Church and a wife; the archbishops had enforced vows of celibacy for a hundred years.

Quentin stopped his kissing. He leaned back on his arms, his eyes searching hers looking down at him. She could feel his muscles trembling beneath her hands on his shoulders.

'But—'

'I won't be your hearth-wife,' she lectured him. 'No more fumbling and squeezing and being afraid of being found out. You know what you feel, don't you? I do,' she said provocatively.

'Then you do love me,' he cried.

'Enough to be your wife,' she said, 'if you're man enough to do what you must.'

He looked up appealingly, wanting to misunderstand, trying to thrust with his hips, then his face fell. 'Marriage? Marriage! But what would I do for a living?'

She lifted his head against her breasts and he inhaled the scent of her body.

'Think on it,' she whispered to the top of his head, and her eyes shone as she looked out between the trees. Sir Jeffrey Fox's son! Quentin's brothers were married, or in distant wars, or dead; Nicola could not expect to travel beyond her village, and this was her only chance to marry above herself. Once she had Quentin in her bed, as his wife, she could soften him and mould him in all the ways a woman knew, and live a fine life. For now she let him stroke her, bringing him on, but as soon as his fingers found the stiff strong gusset between her legs – she had come prepared – and tried frantically to work through the stitching, she rolled away from him. His cock stood up through the urine-stained gap in the front of his gown. He looked so ridiculous that she laughed, and he withered away at once.

Quentin dropped his head in his hands.

'Remember,' she said, clasping him fondly and giving him a little kiss to keep him warm, 'I am yours, but only when we are married.'

Quentin knew when he was beaten. He looked up. 'I'll do as you say. I'll give it all up. Look what a mess you've made of me!' But then his eyes widened as the sound of horses came to them through the trees. 'We're found out! God save me and forgive me! It's God's justice.'

They listened, white-faced and staring, as the harsh jingle of many horses grew louder, scattering birds, and the thud of hoofbeats reverberated through the forest floor.

'Quickly!' Nicola jumped to her feet, brushing down her cloak swiftly in her businesslike way, then pulled Quentin up. 'Marry me? Whatever happens?' she insisted.

'I will,' Quentin said simply.

For a moment, probing him with her cold gaze, she wondered what he'd be saying now if she'd let him have what he wanted. But perhaps she'd underestimated him. She turned away with a shiver. Perhaps, for Quentin Fox, love really did exist.

He blew her a kiss before running into the woods downhill. At least they would not be seen together; they could not be accused of fornication. She picked up her comb to give her hands something to do, her expression looking back at her calmly from the clear water as the riders dressed in purple, gold, white and aquamarine came flickering through the trees, then swung into open view. Reining in, the old men stared at her suspiciously. Nicola, who was no fool, kept perfectly still, recognising some as Cistercian monks, others as men senior in the Church by the colour of their gowns, and several men-at-arms who rode forward with swords. The horses were lathered by hard riding, champing at the smell of water. Packhorses and donkeys followed, their panniers jingling with gold and Church plate.

'Break the ice and let them drink, by God's mercy,' commanded a voice.

The man who rode at the centre of the group and spoke so authoritatively, towering over them all on his white horse, was about fifty years old and unbearded, the top of his head shaven in a tonsure. He wore an unbleached shirt as if travelling disguised as a plain man, but when he dismounted, leaning wearily against a tree with the reins dangling in his hand while his horse drank, his height gave him away at once to Nicola. Everyone knew Thomas Becket was as tall as two women.

Two *short* women, she decided with a sniff, precise as always; but even so, though she was taller than all her cousins, Nicola stood no higher than his chest. If only she could see him dressed in all his finery – his magnificence was a byword. She pursed her lips in disappointment.

Two friars, unarmed but with hard eyes, dismounted and shoved Nicola away so that she should not disturb the great man's peace.

'Leave her be,' Becket said. 'I would not have more enemies

than I already have.' He heaved an angry-sounding sigh. Even after years in exile in France he radiated nobility.

Nicola whispered to one of the friars, 'Is that really the Archbishop of Canterbury?'

'Aye, he will not give it up whatever King Henry says.'

'How much gold did I scatter on the streets of London?' Becket said to no one in particular.

'A fortune in alms, your Grace,' replied one of the bishops.

'Enough to buy the crowd,' sneered the leading monk, who wore the finest clothes and did not dismount while his horse drank.

'Send the men-at-arms back to London and my good Bishop of Winchester,' Becket grunted. He had spent the morning in prayer at the abbey church of St Mary Overie in Southwark. 'If I am not to be safe in Canterbury, I am safe nowhere.' He noticed Nicola for the second time, standing beside her reflection where the smooth water overflowed.

'The lady of the lake.' For the first time Becket smiled. He looked at her with the eye of a man who appreciated women. 'Are you?'

'Your Grace?'

'The lady of the lake,' he murmured, taking a step towards her, 'pure and without sin.'

He looked into her eyes, and her legs shivered. He held out his hand and his ring for her to kiss.

Within the week Thomas Becket was dead, in sanctuary in Canterbury, the top of his head cloven from his skull by a sword stroke from one of King Henry's knights.

VI

Maurice and Jack

John Fox's Family Tree continued
15 April 1387 – Easter 1812

John Fox
★

Sir Jeffrey 1120-1182

The Manor				The Soil
Henry	1139-1201	Patrick	Richard	Gilbert	Quentin 1147-1182

The Manor

Henry	1139-1201
Reginald	1174-1231
Hugh	1215-1281
Thomas	1246-1283
Rolph	1269-1321
Rowland	1297-1353

Patrick   Richard   Gilbert
These three sons marry but die young,
without issue

The Soil

Quentin 1147-1182
= 1171 Nicola Franks 1155-1235
Much 1181-1261
Vincey 1253-1269
Harold 1270-1316
|
= No.1 1288 Mildred d. 1310
No issue
= No.2 1310 Agnes

Miles	Maud	Eleanor
1319-1367	1320-1344	1321-1357 >

Nicol 1314-1355

Miles
|
= Alison 1366
|

= 1342 Eleanor
|

Maurice + 2 elder sisters
1345-1389
= No.1 1361 Gemma de Rokesley 1347-1362
|
= No.2 1363 Katherine de Kidbroke 1336-1389
|

Jack 1346-1416
= 1360 Joan 1346-1411
|
son by another man, 1359

Kay
1368-1436
= 1389 Elaine ◄

Elaine
1371-1445

BRIGGS FAMILY
Philip	Elias
1313-1386	1326-1369
	Oliver
	1347-1389

Peregrine	1390-1449	inherits 1436. Marries Joy Briggs 1412 ◄
Lambert	1414-1471	1449
Daniel	1431-1472	1471
Edward	1457-1527	.......1472 Edward's cousin Richard Fox becomes

Tom 1373-1412
= 1389 Adeline
|
◄ Joy 1391-1460

Bishop of Winchester at Southwark

Peter	1493-1577	.......1527 Due to his longevity, Peter is succeeded by his grandson
(Ralf) Noll	1546-1609	.......1577 1602: Ebenezer Wittle buys Tabard, much decayed, for £124
Guy	1575-1620	.......1609 1620 plague: Guy and sons die. His cousin James, innkeeper of
		The Pope's Head on Vaudey top green, inherits Holywell Manor on death of
James	1581-1626	.......1620 Guy's dwarfed, brilliant sister Bess
Charles	1596-1677	.......1626 Vaudey depopulated and deserted. St John's a redundant church
Francis	1630-1677	.......1677 *The Pope's Head* is renamed *The King's Head*
Josiah	1657-1719	.......1677 1676: part of Tabard Inn destroyed by fire, rebuilt on old plan
Percy	1679-1755	.......1719 1766: the Sign of the Tabard over the Borough road ordered removed by
		Parliamentary Act; placed in Pilgrim's Room
Noel	1706-1793	.......1755 Born on Christmas day
Thomas	1752-	.......1793 Second son, by Noel's third marriage. Joins Royal Navy as midshipman.
		Elder brother Matthew dies 1793 without an heir; his daughter Alice marries
		Capt. O'Neill, and moves to Ulster

No male issue

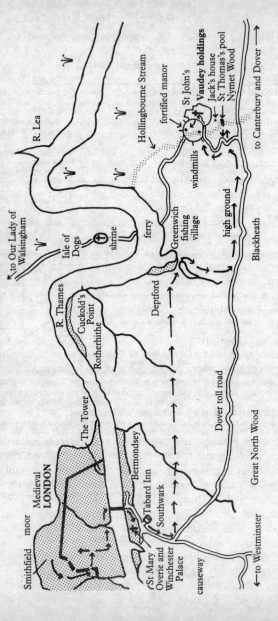

Sir Maurice's journey from Smithfield to Holywell Manor, 15–16 April 1387

to Our Lady of Walsingham

R. Lea

Isle of Dogs

shrine

ferry

Hollingbourne Stream

fortified manor

St John's **Vaudey holdings**

Jack's house

St Thomas's pool

Nymet Wood

windmills

to Canterbury and Dover

Greenwich fishing village

high ground

Blackheath

Deptford

R. Thames

Cuckold's Point

Rotherhithe

The Tower

Medieval **LONDON**

Smithfield moor

Bermondsey

Tabard Inn

Southwark

St Mary Overie and Winchester Palace

causeway

Dover toll road

Great North Wood

to Westminster

Among the noble cities of the world which Fame celebrates, it is said that the City of London, seat of the monarchy of England, is the one which spreads its fame more widely, distributes its goods and merchandise further and holds its head higher than any other.

Sir Maurice Fox, his business with the moneylender concluded unexpectedly quickly, gazed over the sea of colourful woollen, fustian and beaver caps of the crowd at the weekly Smithfield horse and cattle fair. Men and women and animals pushed and shoved their way inside the barricade of the fairground by St Bartholomew's Priory, amid the shouting and neighing and lowing, and hounds barking and fighting. A student shouted rhyme doggerel of King Arthur, or he would declaim the Fall of Troy or the gory murder of St Thomas à Becket for a small fee, his voice half drowned by cockerels crowing – a sound that always made Sir Maurice twist to look over his shoulder, as though expecting to see something frightful waiting for him there. Above all the tumult rose the piercing cries of the stallholders touting their wares, hot pies, cold pies, plump chicken drumsticks and sauce, spiced wine, fiddles and psalters, your shoes fitted with the latest fashion of buckles while you stand. The drought of March had not yet broken and dust drifted in the air like smoke, mingling with the smell of blood and food and dung.

How quickly the common people forget their sins, thought Sir Maurice with a sour twist of his mouth. Hardly half a dozen years had passed since the peasants' revolt had fizzled on these very fields and the plague had last emptied London, yet still the people flowed back the same as always, their empty heads loud with chatter and foul breath, their hearts full of lust and gluttony, and not a thought for God until they heard the dread rattle of bones, and bought absolution by the grace of Mother Church with dolorous confessions and silver pittances.

Young men eyed Sir Maurice seated above them on his palfrey, eager for employment, hopeful of making their name in his service. He was a short, stern man with sad brown eyes and reddish hair, his small chin-beard already stranded with grey. He wore the short sleeveless surcoat called a tabard over his clothes to keep off the dust. His legs were bent in the stirrups so that his pointed shoes (the length of their points proclaimed his rank) almost brushed the London paving – the streets now spreading, since the plagues, into the healthier moorland beyond the walls of the City. His hands holding the reins gripped the horn of the saddle-bow jutting up between his legs, and his young page hung tight against his knee, jostled by the crowd and coughing in the dust.

Suddenly, a course was cleared and in front of them the horse race began, the riders, mostly boys, leaning their faces forward almost into the ponies' flying manes, sticks flashing. One lad, leading in a blue hat, came off on the corner, breaking his arm with an audible crack. He scrambled up holding it with an exult-ant grimace to show his bravery, but half a dozen who had bets riding with him set about him with their caps, and one with a stick, who must be the owner.

Sir Maurice, without a change of expression, broke the wooden tally for the wager he held on the blue hat.

He rode to the Horse Pool by the clucking racket of Chicken Lane, strung with racks of fowl hanging by neck or claw, and allowed his mount and straw-haired page to slake their thirst while he drank wine, good fortified Lepé wine too, as though he had all the money in the world. The boy, Tristan, was still cough-ing; his voice was not yet broken, and again Sir Maurice looked behind him, not liking that harsh, high sound. He was reminded of his own boyhood, of something he had made himself forget, had put into the back of his mind many years ago, when he was a child.

All at once the crowd swirled towards a gibbet by the great elm trees. A cart came into view and everyone began to run towards it, touts selling space on boxes to those who arrived last, purse-snatchers sliding between the people as slickly as eels. After an interval of repentance and prayer greeted with impatience by the crowd and roars from those who had been robbed, the cart abruptly pulled away, leaving a figure thrashing in the air from a rope. Wagers were taken on his longevity. When his kicks were finally still he was not cut down but lifted up even further, a hook on the crossbar jammed into the back of his neck. The body would be left on the bar until it was stiff. Sir Maurice had no idea who the man was and neither did the folk he asked. He had been brought from the Newgate Prison, was all that the good citizens could tell him, and that his immortal spirit undoubtedly burned in the fires and unspeakable tortures of Hell.

When the field was empty but for the sound of the wind in the elms, Sir Maurice rode across and stared up into that anonymous face on its hook, a crow already perched in the hair.

'May God have mercy on my soul,' he muttered, then kicked his heels and turned his horse towards the walls of London, following the stinking curve between the shacks of Cow Lane where an apprentice was loading a wagon, swinging a calf's head on each arm, his fists jutting from the mouths. Sir Maurice's horse picked its way fastidiously between buzzing mounds of heads and cloven hooves, huge tubs of flyspeckled pudding with the guts hanging out like grey serpents, piles of skins roped up to be sent to the tanneries, buckets of blood topped with yellow scum. A skinned carcass seemed to walk ahead of him by itself, a man's legs sticking down beneath.

Sir Maurice paused to watch the archers competing with their longbows at the butts by Holborn Bridge, allowing himself to be drawn into a wager. He rode on beside the Fleet River poorer by a penny, having once again proved to himself his weakness and sinfulness, a mere man in the shell of his brightly coloured clothes.

Next to the reddened, inflamed skin of his chest and back he wore a roughly woven shirt of horsehair. The prickly hairs rubbed and tickled and itched his belly and shoulder-blades horribly, that he might achieve God's mercy through his private suffering.

Rather than enter London through Newgate, past the vicious gaol, Sir Maurice rode down the Bailey to Fleet Street, turning from the noble houses and inns of the bishops and abbots that were going up everywhere, dotted along the Strand to Westminster, and passed under Ludgate. He flinched from the clutching hands begging from the ventilation gratings of the debtors' prison; a man in debt must live on charity, and if charity was not given, then in God's name that man must die, for he had brought his punishment on himself. The riots of that class had convinced Sir Maurice of the justice of this view, and the vile language shrieked at his back confirmed it.

Going down Bower Row past the great mound in the garden of the Dominican priory, all that was left of the keep of Montfichet Castle, Sir Maurice found himself in the dense swarm of the City. He kept his purse well above grabbing hands as his page, the elegant form of his legs outlined by his tight royal-blue leggings, walked ahead of him now, clearing a path through the human river thronging beneath the overhanging gables.

On St Paul's Cathedral workmen were busy restoring the facade of the south transept, while lawyers touted for business in the portico. Above their neighing voices the awe-inspiring steeple rose into the air like a spike to pierce the clouds. Because of the London law of providing for widows at the expense of children, he saw children everywhere, muddy grasping urchins foraying from tenements left vacant by the plague, nagging and brawling and thieving, their numbers so large and so nimble, like flocks of birds, that the common sergeants seemed helpless to do anything about them.

Instead of going through St Augustine's gate into the markets of Cheapside, Sir Maurice turned to the right past the bishop's palace into the west fish market, empty but for its lingering taint this late in the day, and from there down to Thames Street. The Roman river wall had mostly fallen into the river or had its stone stolen for buildings, but some of it still remained to impede the busy chaos of alleyways winding to the river. In the part of Thames Street called the Vinetria, by the wharves where in the season the wine fleet from Gascony arrived under the drawbridge of London Bridge, he haggled with a vintner for a pint of wine which he got for a penny, good value. Drinking three-quarters, he handed down the dregs to his page, then rode on.

The Walbrook stream was timbered over with houses and workshops, some with decaying watermills attached, the wheels turning sluggishly in the rubbish floating down; the Dowgate was a beach of collapsed masonry wedged solid with rowing boats, the oarsmen and scullers readying themselves for the evening crowd to be pulled across to Bankside. But because he was riding, Sir Maurice must take London Bridge.

Some said there had been a wooden bridge here once, built and rebuilt in elm many times, like the churches of olden days, but no one could now imagine anything but London Bridge as it was, one of the wonders of the world. Its nineteen stepping-stones stood against the racing slopes of foaming tide, the chapels and houses over its twenty narrow archways rising six or seven storeys high, towers and chimneys and flags bannering above them, except over the gatehouse, which wore its necklace of boiled and tarred heads.

More money must change hands, and the horse plodded on. A benefaction to St Thomas's chapel in the middle, and then Sir Maurice endured the intolerable crush of hawkers and priests, pardoners and summoners, flagellants and penitents and pie-sellers on the drawbridge, which creaked dangerously beneath the weight of the faithful as always. London Bridge pulled people to it like flies to honey, a small town in itself, a bridge not only to join but to keep apart, a buttress under the jurisdiction of the City to keep Surrey, with all its different laws and customs, separate from the pride and wealth of London. Once over the drawbridge, however, he was in the parish of St Olave's. He ducked as he passed beneath the Stone Gate, even more careful of his purse now, into Southwark.

On his right, the road led to the pleasure houses and brothels of Bankside – Sir Maurice could not for one moment believe the rumours that they were owned by the mayors and aldermen of the city and their wives – it had long been closed as a right of way, which accounted for the busy traffic of rowboats now sculling like spiders across the river from Queenhithe and the Dowgate. The Bishop of Winchester had secured all the land of St Mary Overie as his sanctuary, called the Liberty of the Clink, and it was a tedious and dangerous walk round the precinct borders. Sir Maurice paused to admire the wealth and magnificence of the building's size. The bishop's palace, with its rose window three times the height of a man, had been repaired after the riots, and it was said that beneath the cellars of the great hall criminals were now imprisoned in deep oubliettes to put them closer to Hell. A cocking stool for dunking wicked women had been set up in the stream running into St Mary Overie's dock, and on a platform by the whipping post Sir Maurice saw with approval that a new, special pillory for women, called a *theu*, had been put up, and that the heads sticking out had been shaved in further sign of their guilt. More debtors shoved their scrawny fingers through the gratings, whining for money, and Sir Maurice turned away furiously, clutching his purse.

With his page running after him, he rode past St Thomas's Hospital as though he had the Devil on his back, cloak flapping. Swerving to avoid a cartload of dung being emptied into the ditch that ran between the inns lining the High Street, carrying its slow stinking cargo of slurry to the Bridge Yard Sluice into the Thames, he slowed and recovered his composure. Opposite Foul Lane was the Pope's Head Inn, and then the sumptuous St Margaret's Church filled the middle of the road on its island. Just past the George Inn and the chapel of the Abbot of Hyde, opposite Counter Street, he came to the finest and oldest inn of them all, the Tabard.

Sir Maurice knew the place well, having stayed here often on his way home. In his youth it had acquired a wicked reputation and was called the Tabernacle, but after a disastrous fire left the owner destitute the ruin was snapped up by the Member of Parliament for Southwark, Sir Harry Bailey, a wealthy wine importer. He was a sociable host and spared no expense – which he would well afford – rebuilding the place from the cellars up in timber, four storeys high to the cock lofts, with wide chambers, and a gallery running round the yard to the second storey. The day-to-day business of the place he sensibly left to an innholder, the original owner, who knew his trade backwards, having been born to it. The inn had been in his family a hundred years or more, he claimed.

And perhaps it was true; Sir Maurice knew that innkeepers, like tenant farmers, went on for ever. Once they had a piece of ground, they never moved off it – at least, that was the way things used to be. Sir Maurice did not like the man, Richard Wittle, although he could not have explained his reasons. Master Wittle was always polite and humble in his welcome, and made his guests feel as though they were being invited into a private household.

The Tabard, so called to appeal to the common traveller, after the popular fashion in such garments, had always been special. Sir Maurice's father had stayed here under its old name, and his grandfather too. An enclave of private land tucked among the

430

properties of the Archbishop of Canterbury, the Bishop of Winchester and the various abbots, the Tabard's timbered front wall with its tiny windows stuck defiantly into the King's highway by one foot, narrowing the road, for which privilege Sir Harry paid His Majesty one penny each year, due on the first day of the Christmas Fair. Above the centre of the road, hung from a massive beam, swung the sign of the Tabard: a drawing of a surcoat like Sir Maurice's, a hunting dog of the breed called a talbot, a hoard of scattered silver coins.

Staring up at the sign, Sir Maurice shivered as though a cold wind blew through him despite the warm stillness of the Southwark evening.

His page tugged his leg. 'What ails you, my lord?'

'Someone walks over my grave,' Sir Maurice said, shaking himself free of the horrid feeling as he dismounted. He forced a smile for the boy's innocence. 'That's all.' Townsfolk with no respect for their betters brushed past them without courtesy in the busy lane between the inn and the church. He watched Tristan walk the horse across the straw and ashes of the inn's yard, where tonight he would feed on horsemeat, bread and ale with the ostlers and other servants, if he was lucky.

Taking off his gloves, Sir Maurice went inside.

The dark-parlour, as it was known, was full of men of the commonest sort, their pocked flesh souring the air with old sweat and rotten teeth, the cheeks of even the youngsters collapsed inward on their gums. Their loutish eyes summed him up with unfriendly glances. Sir Maurice hesitated, taken aback by the numbers. The room used always to be nearly empty. Where did these men get money enough for the Tabard – good shelter, and white wheaten bread, though only second-service quality ale?

The inner door opened and a huge man shoved through.

'Me good Sir Maurice!' Dick Wittle thrust out a gigantic hand in greeting, each finger thick and bent into its neighbour, hard as horn with calluses, and bowed as well as he could over his gross leather-clad belly; his head had not spied his feet for many years, no doubt. By sheer force of personality, and a faultless memory – he never forgot a face – he swept his guest towards quarters more fitting to his rank. 'In there is not for 'ee, me lord, not at all – oh, not at all!' He guided the knight effortlessly through the parlour to the broad inner door and along a hallway. Beyond this lay the Great Parlour, a long series of rooms looking out on the yard which could be glimpsed through the open shutters on this warm April evening. The Great Parlour, too, was full of people; of the seven classes of society, these were perhaps better than those in the dark-parlour by one degree, hurrying through their food at rough tables, rough talk on their tongues and roasted chicken spitted on their knives, plates of whiting or smelts jammed between their elbows on beechwood platters, cash jingling in their purses.

Sir Harry Bailey, who had an ample belly himself, came forward with a true vintner's salutation. 'Welcome, sir—' he read Master Wittle's lips – 'Sir Maurice. A crust, and what wine will you drink?' Dick Wittle did not allow the knight to answer, calling jovially for malmsey, the most expensive. His veined blue eyes were always restless, seeing trouble before it appeared, nodding to the maids to clear away empty platters or replace them, indicating whose ale to water, all while Sir Maurice's attention was distracted by his host. The knight seemed a little threadbare to him – Master Wittle always distrusted pale men who arrived smelling of wine. Still, the thickness of Sir Maurice's purse was Sir Harry's business.

Sir Harry had noticed his guest's frown. 'These worshippers of Mammon are a low sort,' he confided, drawing Sir Maurice, his cup of malmsey in his hand, through a further, windowless, room where a friar and three priests sat quietly in opposite corners, like counters waiting to be moved, a table between them with a candle set on it. The flame flickered as the two men went past but the occupants did not stir.

'You find us busy?' Sir Harry enquired cordially as he crossed the hall beyond.

'Unexpectedly so.'

'Place always wanted money spent on it,' Sir Harry said briskly, slapping the fresh beams of good English oak. 'No shame in attracting trade, I beg pardon to say. A man who is not born to it has to make a living.'

'I do not regard a gentleman as an item of trade,' Sir Maurice huffed, and drank his malmsey.

'But his custom is. That's how matters lie these days. No slight

432

intended,' said Sir Harry cheerfully. Even the accent of London speech had changed, Sir Maurice noticed, grown harsher as people came south from the Midlands seeking their fortunes. His own Kentish accent sounded lilting against the babble issuing from the doorways around them. 'I have given Master Wittle free rein,' Sir Harry continued, 'and not regretted my judgment for one moment. Given my money and his experience, the Tabard, to be blunt, is once more the premier inn of the Borough, head and shoulders above all others.' He put his hand on the latch of the final door. 'We provide for all. Here is company more fitting to your taste, perhaps.' He swung the door open. 'You too are on pilgrimage to Canterbury, Sir Maurice? You will accompany us on the morrow?'

'Only as far as my manor at Holywell.'

What a mixed bag were gathered in this room, Sir Maurice noted with disdain, women as well as men, of all orders and degrees of life, the high pushed together with the low, the holy with the lay classes. How they would hate each other after a week on the road! He reckoned there must be twenty or thirty pilgrims altogether. A knight still wearing the smudges of armour on his poor fustian clothes bowed courteously to him, a woman with the voice of an eagle ticked off a servant; everyone had left a clear space round a dirty, scratching man, who had flour engrained like glue in his rigid red hair which stuck up like a spade.

Sir Maurice drew back. 'I would prefer to eat in my chamber.'

But Sir Harry was not to be put off. 'There is one you must meet, a poet travelling with his wife on pilgrimage to St Thomas at Canterbury. They have fallen on hard times,' he added in a low voice. He beckoned Sir Maurice to a heavyset man sitting uncomfortably on a stool at the fire, by whose flickering light he wrote. 'A scribbler of illiterate stuff,' Sir Harry introduced him patronisingly but proudly, 'but a vintner's son – why, there's hope for us yet! Sir Maurice Fox, Sir Geoffrey Chaucer, knight of the shire of Kent.'

'You can tell by his insults that we are good friends,' muttered the poet, raising his eyes. They were brown and soft as a hare's in his paunchy, drink-veined face.

'I write myself,' Sir Maurice said.

'Better than he, I'd wager!' laughed Sir Harry cheerfully. 'He's doing the story of these folk here, that was my plan, but his dreary rhyming isn't worth a turd.' Sir Harry was called away, leaving them alone. A thin, hungry-looking boy positioned himself beside Sir Maurice and refilled his cup, expertly topping it up from the jug he held whenever Sir Maurice took a swallow.

While he drank, Sir Maurice examined the poet with a fixed stare. He was dressed in parti-coloured red and black breeches and shoes long-toed to the point of indiscretion. On his finger he wore a gimmel-ring with its pair of tiny jewels symbolising two lovers side by side.

'You cannot seriously be interested in common folk,' Sir Maurice said. 'Have you really been writing of them?' Without reply the other man turned the piece of paper on his knee so that Sir Maurice could read it. He frowned at the difficult writing. 'All that is given, take with cheerfulness. To wrestle in this world is to ask a fall. Here is no home; here is but a wilderness.'

Reading the words for the second time, Sir Maurice realised the poet was watching his reaction with interest.

'May I keep this, Sir Geoffrey?'

'No, sir.'

'You write of me. This loneliness of which you write is me.'

'The ink is mine.'

'I shall remember the words,' Sir Maurice said. He was feeling dizzy, the sweet, strong malmsey thick in his throat. 'I think . . . I must go to my chamber now.' He held up his arm for the boy to assist him.

The flames flickered on the fresh, new firebricks, scattering the poet's shadow as he stared after them.

The boy was willowy and not very strong, and his arm under Sir Maurice's did not keep the knight very steady as they came outside into the dark. 'Deep breaths now, me lord,' the boy said. 'Steps ahead of us now. Foot next to mine, hup. Now t'other, hup. Hup we go.' They wove their way along the outside gallery, the yard swaying like a bottomless black pit below them. 'It's like being on a ship, this, I imagines,' the boy said. 'You'd know more about that than I. Has'ee been to the Holy Land, me lord?'

'Many times,' lied Sir Maurice, then put his fists to his ears. 'No, never. Never.'

A girl appeared and backed in front of them, holding up a

candle that lit blue flames in the boy's eyes.

'I would go to the Holy Land before the end of me life,' the boy said wistfully.

The girl knocked open a door with her hip and stood aside with a curtsy, having made up the room earlier with sheets and a counterpane. The man and boy staggered past her. Sir Maurice stood swaying at the bed post, trying to appear sober. 'Food,' he said. 'Pie. I demand pie.'

'It's late,' the boy said, glancing at the girl, his younger sister Blanche.

Sir Maurice turned on them. 'A good hot pie, by God's dignity!' he cried. The children scurried out, then stared at one another on the gallery.

''E'd better not make a mess of me clean sheets,' Blanche said, arching her hands on her scrawny hips, then flounced off. The boy flew down to the kitchen to beg a pie from the cook, and received a ladle round his head for his pains.

'Who do these gentlemen think they is?' cook stormed. 'Them and their fancy parley-voo! Cold pie he'll have, to teach him!'

When she was gone, swearing at her knotted apron strings, the boy slipped the pie in the oven himself.

Standing upright by the bed, Sir Maurice waited impatiently for the boy to return. The girl had left a candle on the little table and there was a chair, still new. The chamber was spacious, and he was not expected to share it; he could not find any fault.

'At last,' he said when the boy reappeared, scampering. The pie was visibly steaming; Sir Maurice could not object. He ordered it to be put on the table. The ale was first service; the bread was white and soft. He sat reluctantly. 'Where is my page?' he demanded with irritation. 'How am I to undress?'

'He be dead drunk, my lord,' the boy confessed, sharp enough to admit the lesser crime: he knew that by now the page, a servant freed of his master, was probably having sport in a hayloft with ale, cheese, and Blanche.

'How old are you, boy?'

'I don't know, me lord.'

'I judge you about eleven years.' Sir Maurice cut the pie with his knife and ate.

'If 'ee says so, me lord.'

'I was eleven once,' Sir Maurice said, then looked behind him. 'It is the age we become aware of sin. I had a friend. He was a year younger than you.'

The boy said nothing.

'Master Wittle's son, are you?' Sir Maurice asked, mouth full.

'Yes, I be one of his brats, me lord. We all be out of 'im, what with the price of work and so many dead of the black plagues, or frighted. It's being a family business what keeps the place cheap for Sir Harry. Does the food please 'ee, me lord?'

Sir Maurice stopped eating. 'Is this Jack-of-Dover pie?' he asked suspiciously. 'No, my lad, I think it does not please me.' The old, fearful rage filled him, squirting acid into his stomach. 'By God's breath, I asked for hot pie and you've given me Jack-of-Dover!'

'I'll take it back right off, me lord.'

'Reheated pie!' said Sir Maurice in a rising tone. 'I ordered fresh, hot pie! Those very words!' He slapped his hand on the table, because now he had started to complain he had to go on. 'Really, do you call this good enough? Landlord!' He waved the boy away, longing only to get to bed and snore.

But a huge shape filled the doorway, wrapping the boy's arm in fingers as hard as horn.

'Trouble, me lord?' growled Dick Wittle politely.

'Do you usually serve stale, reheated pie to your guests?' Sir Maurice prodded the crust with his knife, but he could not look away from the fear in the boy's eyes, his shoulders squirming in his father's grasp.

'Never, me lord knight.' Dick Wittle did not so much as glance down at the pie. 'I'll rouse the cook to prepare 'ee fresh, and punish the boy.'

'Don't bother,' said Sir Maurice petulantly. 'I'm not hungry now. Forget it, it doesn't matter.'

'It matters to me,' Dick Wittle said. 'A complaint has been received.' He scooped up the tray, bowed and backed out of the room, closing the door with his foot.

Sir Maurice sat staring at the table, seeing himself in that frightened boy, remembering himself at that age. The sound of blows came through the door, and the boy's cries.

Sir Maurice, who was a humane man, wished he had not complained.

He got up, picked up the candle, and pulled open the door. 'Stop, man, in God's name,' he said, squinting past the candle flame that flickered in the night air, then recoiled as he trod in something soft. It was the pie, thrown down the gallery with such force that it had splashed everywhere, pieces of meat and gravy trickling down the timbers.

In the shadows, Dick Wittle bent over his son, pounding him with his great fist.

'You're killing him,' Sir Maurice shouted.

Dick Wittle lifted the small flopping figure, then tossed it over the rail like a cock of straw. There was a moment's silence, then a soft sound below.

'God save us!' Sir Maurice cried, holding his candle out. Below, in the yard, he saw the boy's body sprawled on its back.

The blue eyes caught the candle flame in their fixed stare.

'The boy fell,' Dick Wittle said.

People ran out below, a semicircle of smoking rush-lights gathering round the body, white faces looking up.

Dick Wittle leant against the railing. ''E fell!' he cried. 'Me son, me son!'

Sir Maurice stumbled back into his room. The pie he had eaten came vomiting out of his mouth and nostrils; it felt as though a great fist was squeezing his stomach. The pain stabbed into him as if he was being eaten up inside by his own juices, and the final strands of spittle were laced with blood.

Sir Maurice lay face down on the bed, his knees drawn up, his shoes dirtying the counterpane, remembering when he was eleven years old.

It was the night they broke into the church.

Maurice was eleven, but Jack was only ten. The two boys were young enough still to be friends despite the different level of their birth, and they were cousins. Maurice insisted he was the leader, but even in those days low-born Jack had a vitality and a saucy look in his deep brown eyes – Fox eyes – that attracted people. Maurice, though of the true blood, could not compete.

The village beyond the churchyard had fallen dark and quiet around the two boys, and Jack struggled to hold back his cough.

'Can't you stop?' Maurice turned furiously, bitterly regretting getting himself into this silly, terrible dare. It was all Jack's idea, as usual – Jack's fault.

'God a tiggle in my froat,' Jack quavered, grinning at Maurice's nervousness.

'Got a tickle in your throat,' Maurice said. He was a knight on crusade and Jack was his squire. 'Hold your breath. And speak like a grown-up.'

Jack hid his grin. Nervousness made Maurice strict on campaign. This was not the first time Jack had wheedled him into playing the game. On one occasion they broke into Master Franks's close to steal his finest cabbage from directly beneath his window – they could hear him snoring inside. Another time they let the rabbits run free from the coney warren built by Sir Rolph near the fishponds, which had caused a terrible uproar in the village. Had it been summer, the swarming rabbits would have devoured the common crops, and many families in the village would have gone hungry. That too had been Jack's idea, but he allowed Maurice to think it was his, as he claimed it was once risk of being caught was past. If the boys had been caught, Maurice would have been informally thrashed by Sir Miles, but Jack would probably have been hanged by the Circuit Court.

Tonight Jack had got Maurice involved in something even more dangerous. Twenty years had passed since Sir Miles had married, a length of time so much longer than their young lives that neither boy could imagine it: twenty years since Sir Miles, in front of the village and the priest, had worn the sacred amulet round his neck and sworn his marriage vow. It was part of village lore that the silver amulet was one of a set, the rest having been hidden in the church. Maurice had boasted that the legend was true, but Jack had scoffed at him. Prove it, he said.

And so tonight they intended to break into the church and establish the truth.

Hiding behind the gnarled trunk of the massive old oak by the churchyard, its huge branches creaking with leaf above them in the dark, the two boys shivered with fear, though neither would admit it. It was the darkest time of night, between the setting of the sun and the rise of the moon.

Jack blew out through his lips. 'Maurice,' he said.

'*What?*'

'How can I hold my breath *and* speak like a grown-up?'

'If you make another sound I'll kill you,' Maurice said.

'*I* be not frightened,' and Jack chuckled to prove it. His face was so grubby from his toil in the fields that only the whites of his eyes showed in the dark.

'That's because you've got me to look after you,' Maurice asserted. 'Anyway, we aren't doing anything wrong,' he murmured to calm his stomach.

'It's more fun to think we is,' Jack said eagerly.

'It wasn't wrong of King Arthur's knights to search for the Holy Grail,' Maurice continued to justify himself. Everyone knew that after Christ's Passion Joseph of Arimathea had come to England, bringing the Grail with him to hide in Glastonbury.

'Let's play being King Arthur's knights!' Jack said, slashing the air with an invisible sword.

'You can't ever be a knight. You're just plain Jack Fox and you always will be. The church door's always open,' Maurice added uneasily. 'It's not as if we were really breaking in.'

'Yes, we do be,' Jack said simply. 'Tonight our souls may be dragged down to Hell by red-hot demons.'

'Stop it,' Maurice snapped nervously.

He crept forward from the tree, slipping through the hedge and across the wet scythed grass, until he came to the stone sepulchre of his grandfather. Sir Rowland had not been buried in the family vault in the crypt but outside because he loved the sky – and also, it was said, because he'd had enough of his family in life and did not wish to sleep with them until Judgment.

Maurice beckoned Jack with a pale wave of his hand. They were close to the church now, close enough to inhale the dark smell of its ancient timbers. They could see the steps leading down to the door, as though the earth had risen since St John's was built.

The church was at the centre of the village, as was right and proper, for St John's was older than the village; the vicar, Philip Briggs, eldest of the Briggs brothers, preached so in each of his four sermons of the year. And it was the centre of their lives. Its rituals baptised them, married them, buried them, and one day, Maurice knew, the stuttering vicar would anoint him lord of the Manor of Holywell, hereditary in the Fox family since the year

1078 according to the rolls, and possibly (so fireside legend ran) even before that.

Over lifetimes the houses, cottages and hovels of villeins and free men had grown as though organically round this little building with its squat wooden tower, straggling along the pale, dusty lanes that stretched down the dell beside the stream to the knoll and the manor house. The village continued up the roadside towards Blackheath, towards fields and pastures and meadows, finally out to the assarts, the clearings looking like black mouth bites in the forest.

'Look!' Jack pointed as a scratch of light crossed the sky.

Maurice jerked round. 'Where? What was it?'

'I see'd an angel,' Jack said.

'No you didn't,' Maurice muttered. '*I* didn't.'

A cockerel crowed, marking the hour exactly, as it was the God-given nature of such birds to do.

When they were older, the cousins, close enough for their hands to touch comfortingly at this moment, would know how utterly different everything was between them; but for now they were still children, made one by the fear and mystery and innocence of childhood.

Maurice Fox would become a knight the instant his father exhaled his last breath, and all the duties and responsibilities of the Manor of Holywell, which included the village of Vaudey, would become Maurice's. He would take and he would give. Each son stood on his father's shoulders, and to Maurice would go the power of appointing the bailiff, the beadle, the sergeant, the reeve, the hayward and the steward. Maurice would take the rights of heriot, with first choice of a dying tenant's finest animal or possession, and to the Church would go the second choice. His word would become law, with rights and privileges of infangenethef and outfangenethef, of pursuit and confiscation. He would hold in his possession, and pass on to his own son in due course, the fortified manor house and all its carucates of demesne land, its woodland pannage for hogs, its well-stocked fishponds. He would also obey, as his father had, and his great-grandfather, the customs of the manor laid down from time immemorial. Among many other strictures he must maintain in his household his own chaplain, a post laid down by ordinance, for a payment of five shillings a year. The rent of a windmill would pay for the Saturday night candle, but money for the chaplain's clothes, his daily loaf of bread and flagon of ale would be paid from the parish tithes. Maurice would own the serfs of the manor and care for them, giving them land, the richest of them virgaters with thirty acres or more. But he would leave free men, like Jack's father Nicol, to fend for themselves, often in desperate circumstances, clawing a living from a few acres of rooty assarted land, forced to take up some trade or other to make ends meet.

Jack would also grow up free, but he would live a life as hard as a punishment for his freedom. The fact that his mother, Eleanor, was Sir Miles's youngest sister was no advantage to him, since she had defied Sir Rowland and disgraced herself by marrying beneath her, taking to her bed the man she loved, Nicol Fox. His surname being the same as hers was no advantage either. Under the Kentish laws applied to ordinary folk under 'Borough English', cleared land was passed down in gavelkind, from a father to all his sons equally, so his children did not move away from the village as those of the noble classes so often did, leaving only the eldest son to inherit the estate. As a result, over the years Fox had become an everyday surname in the county, distant kin, no doubt, of the thin haughty strand of the family in the manor house but utterly beneath their noble blood.

Sir Rowland had reacted with predictable horror to his daughter's madness. He beat Eleanor, he shut her away and starved her on bread and water, he even arranged a suitable marriage for her, but she escaped. Her behaviour was incomprehensible. She had always been a strange one, eccentric, wilful, and the more her unfathomable obsession was opposed, the more defiant she became. For all his power, Sir Rowland was helpless in the face of her wrath and love. Finally he cut her hair, disowned her, and discarded her to do whatever she would. St John's was denied them on their wedding day, so Eleanor wed Nicol in the stand of oaks round the overflowing pool and became his common-law wife, and from that day to this she had spoken not a word to either her father or her plump brother Sir Miles, now growing arrogant in the manor house in his turn. Her single son was Jack.

Since Nicol's accident, Jack was her life. She would have hated his friendship with Maurice and forbidden it, had she known of it; since he did not wish to feel the twigs of her besom slashing his arse or to be starved on bread and water, Jack made sure she did not know of it. A boy's friends were his own, and in his way he was just as stubborn and determined as she was. She only had to look at him to recognise herself.

Jack whispered to Maurice, 'Are you going first or do I?'

The boys crossed into the shadow of the church together as the moonlight, creeping down the tower, touched the dovecotes under the eaves. The villagers hated the doves, which grew fat on their corn.

The cockerel crowed again, and Maurice looked round from the church door with a terrified start. But Jack reached out for the latch and Maurice had to open the door to keep ahead. The oak hinges creaked loudly enough to wake the whole village.

'Go on!' Jack hissed.

The floor was beaten earth, hard and dark as iron. Jack slipped the door shut quickly and quietly behind him. They were alone in a room the size of a barn. The scuffing of their feet on the straw echoed around them as they crept along the nave. The walls were crude and rough and the floor gave off its strong human smell of Sundays. Each tiny arched window on the east side, to their right, cast moonlight the colour of water. Even the lepers' window at floor level cast a frightening, barred glow. A few steps up, and they passed beneath the oak screen onto the flagstones of the chancel, which were warped and hollowed by the passage of pious footsteps towards the altar.

Maurice knew he was in terrible danger. Broad though the shadow of the Cross was, the shadow of the Devil was even broader, encompassing them all, requiring no confession. Behind him on the chancel arch was the painting of Christ meting out punishment on the dreadful Day of Judgment, the demons at His left hand seizing sinners with flesh-hooks and pitching them like cocks of hay into the flames and everlasting torment.

The two boys held hands, feeling each other shiver. The Devil walked the earth; many in the village had seen him flitting in the dark, or found his signs in the morning dew, or heard his whispering voice haunting the ponds and deep forest.

Maurice advanced towards the altar. The saying of a Mass could strike the iron fetters from an innocent man charged of an offence and enable a sick man to receive the Host through his side, directly into his heart. Scattered on cabbages, the Host would keep off caterpillars. Maurice knew that these things were as miraculous as the known power of a magnet to attract iron, or the power of a little fish to hold back a ship, and he feared them all. He crossed himself repeatedly as he approached the altar steps.

Jack hung back. By the smell of him Maurice had soiled his clothes but still he advanced, ever the chivalrous knight-to-be, honour bound to finish what he had started. Jack crouched in case Maurice was struck by lightning.

On the altar rose a heavy seven-pronged candlestick worked in silver, very old, said to be Roman. No one knew what it signified, but its holiness had become part of St John's.

Going up the steps, Maurice dropped to his knees, feeling his strength drain away. He looked round for Jack but couldn't see him, then with trembling fingertips he lifted the ornate vestment that covered the altar to the ground.

His shadow made everything dark; he moved until a beam of moonlight struck past his shoulder, illuminating the gleaming interior. Silver!

Maurice stared back at his own terrified face, multiplied many times.

'*Oh my God,*' he whispered, and the cockerel crowed and marked the hour.

Sir Maurice, forty-one years old and lying face down on his bed in the Tabard Inn, had never forgotten that awestruck moment of revelation, by far the most potent memory of his boyhood – until, at least, the events of the day he married Gemma. He'd long ago forgotten his first blood, the brawls that were expected of young bucks such as he had been. And he could not even remember now how Gemma had looked, still a child, younger than he was, the first time his father brought them together in the great hall of the manor and told Maurice that she would be his wife. Had she been pale? Had he?

But he remembered perfectly that moment in the church. Crouched on his knees in the moonlight. Holding up the heavy altar vestment, stunned. There were so *many* of them, and they

443

all reflected his own face, grotesquely, with what seemed like every possible shade of expression between horror and compassion, love and despair, confidence and guilt. And behind him came Jack's whisper, over and over: 'What is it? Is anything there? Is it true?'

As he stared at the multiple reflections of himself, Maurice saw everything he might become: good and noble like his father, a steady-eyed chivalrous knight with the fires of Jerusalem burning behind him; low-browed and brutish like the village peasants; possessed like the screaming, flagellant priests on London Bridge; evil like the rapists whose souls burned in Hell.

He dropped the vestment and jumped back as though kicked in the stomach, and then he ran.

Jack caught him in the graveyard and stared into his face, laughing, excited, full of questions. What had happened? What had he seen? Was the legend true? Maurice gibbered, white as a ghost, totally unmanned. His hair literally stood out in spikes, and he smelt like a cesspool.

After the night of Maurice's humiliation, the boys had no more adventures together. Their closeness ended and they never met as equals again, no longer children, no longer friends. Maurice grew up and never spoke of what he had seen; never, at least, until the day of his marriage.

But Jack had paused as he left the graveyard, quietly watching Maurice walk away beyond the lych gate, and the expression on his peasant face was thoughtful. And curious.

Jack had no bed.

He lay on a bag stuffed with straw which pricked him through the canvas and accounted for his rough, wealed skin and the itching flea bites. He lay scratching them in the dark, his mind elsewhere. His sheet of nettle-linen was long enough to cover him on top but not underneath, and over it lay a counterpane of scratchy dogswain. The log beneath his head was softened only by his thick ginger hair. He was lying stretched out, stiff, listening to the rain that had been falling all day. Under such thick clouds, evening, and therefore time for sleep, had fallen early.

But Jack could not sleep, and an hour of dark was twice as long as an hour of day.

He hated his life.

Now that the last glowing ember had faded from the cooking fire on its iron plate, the darkness around him was complete. No moonlight like last night. The wet sound of the rain hitting the thatch and dripping down one slimy wall filled the room. He lay dabbing his big toe in the water trickling across the earthen floor.

The cottage had only two rooms; the sound of the rain drowned his mother's snores from the small back room. Eleanor would sleep, exhausted, until dawn. This was the life she had chosen, all for love of her husband. Jack knew she did not regret her decision even now God had taken Nicol, his father, from her.

I didn't choose this life, Jack thought. I was born, that's all. Everything that Eleanor did, and the style with which she did it, showed him that there was more to life. She gave him everything she had, and a mother's love too. But Jack had no prospect of getting back what she had given away for Nicol. He did not really want to be a knight; despite the ballads and romances, he knew it was impossible truly to escape servile origins, malicious tongues always remembered. But he wanted more than he had.

He lay in the dark, scratching.

Jack wanted his life to be worth living.

There was no hope for him; none at all. He had been born free to work the soil, and when his work was done he would die; his body would return to the soil that had broken his back, like his father's back before him, and rot away. His father's death had taught him how unimportant an ordinary person like himself was in the scheme of things; only lords and ladies really mattered. Jack, whose wits were sharpest when he saw his advantage, didn't think someone like him would be bothered with very much on Judgment Day.

What had Maurice seen there in the church last night?

Maurice hadn't answered his questions. But oh, the look on his face! He had seen something, all right. Perhaps something valuable. But something valuable to a boy brought up to be a gentleman wasn't necessarily valuable to a peasant.

Jack sat up and grinned, always ready for a bit of fun. 'But you never know, it might be worth a try,' he said to himself. 'Just a look, then slip back home.'

Rolling to his feet, he felt his way to the wall. It creaked. He fumbled along it, pausing when his hand fell into the open space of the window and dislodged two chickens roosting there. There was a short, plaintive squawk and the flapping of wings from the dark. The window hole was just large enough for Jack to wriggle through, but he was growing up and knew that the rotting stick and daub – Sir Miles allowed only his favoured villagers to collect extra wood – could collapse beneath his weight. He moved to the doorway which had a short door jammed in it, and wriggled through the gap at its foot which allowed the cat out to hunt and the dog in to sleep.

The sound of the rain filled the night around him. It was as dark outside as inside, but cooler, and he pulled his smock over his head as he splashed down the path. The cottage was built on assarted land out at the very edge of the village, near the overflowing pool. Finding the paling gate by touch, Jack followed the rush of the Hollingbourne Stream to the fishponds, where he turned towards the church and paused under the shelter of the lych gate.

Here he had waited, only a few months ago, for what seemed an endless time beside his father's poor body. A youngster of nine waiting with his hand enfolded in his mother's, while the sun's shadow inched round the style on the church wall and the appointed hour for the funeral passed. Waiting while the mourners trickled away to the wake and got drunk, and Eleanor went to find the priest, who had arrived as drunk as his parishioners by now were, and Jack, looking at that smiling apple of a face, had felt real anger and real hatred for the first time in his life. Strong as a taste in his mouth, he had wanted revenge.

Jack had never felt alone or afraid since. And now he was ten, grown up and looking after his mother.

Standing in the lych gate, the huge drops from the oak tree above smacking on the shingle roof, Jack crossed himself to his father's memory. Relinquishing his grip on the heavy oak gate, he slipped across the churchyard and by touch felt the steps down to the church door. It opened as easily as last night and he went inside, closing it behind him, and suddenly he could not hear the rain. The silence was total, there was only the smell of old, wormy wood. His heart thudded as he walked forward. When he felt the oak screen, he took the two big steps up into the chancel, the stone floor cold under his toes.

He held out his hands in the direction of the altar until he bumped into it.

The heavy vestment felt smooth and rich under his palms.

Kneeling, he took a deep breath. He spat on his hands for luck, then quickly lifted the material and ducked into the space beneath.

There was a loud chinking, rattling noise. Coins!

Coins, that was all.

And there was nothing holy about them; he had not been struck by lightning. He felt them sliding under his knees as he moved, but not nearly as many as he had hoped. He picked one up, turning it in front of his eyes which could see nothing, bit it. Harder than gold, silver probably. He had seen silver coins once, bent and tarnished but still good, when his father had sold the milch cow. These coins were very large, though, each as large as a child's palm, which might mean they were worth so much he could not use them without giving himself away.

Jack chuckled, the idea appealing to his childish humour – so valuable that they were useless!

He scooped them into the front of his smock, including the one which felt as though it was encased in a claw and had a chain on it – he might as well be hanged for poaching a sheep as a lamb.

He ran home through the rain, and buried what he had stolen under the compost heap at the end of the cabbage patch which was his responsibility.

He wriggled under the door, pushed off the dog which had claimed his bed, and fell into a dreamless sleep.

He was young. He had plenty of time to think of a way to put the coins to work.

Face down on his bed in the Tabard, Sir Maurice, fully clothed, did not realise he had slept until he woke. The bolster seemed suddenly hard under his head, and stank of vomited meat and sweet malmsey. Last night he had fallen into his bed certain that in Dick Wittle he had seen the Devil himself. Even now he still saw the body of the boy outstretched in the yard below, the fixed eyes reflecting candle flame; he saw it as clearly as a dream while his page bustled around him brightly, like the new day. Tristan knew nothing of the events of last night – put two cups of

Southwark ale under his belt and Tristan fell in love, and that was all there was to that drone.

Listening to his chatter, Sir Maurice wiped the sleep from his eyes and hobbled to the doorway. He stared across the first-floor balcony outside, freshly mopped and swept, and then dropped his gaze to the yawning, scratching travellers moving in the yard below, some finishing off meat bones or crusts of bread, throwing them to the dogs which growled and fought, while swearing ostlers tugged horses from the inner yard and hitched them to the posts, groomed and saddled in the early hours – the usual highly-organised commotion of an inn yard. The dead boy was gone as though he had never been, horses contentedly munching hay where Sir Maurice thought he had seen the body lie; it was difficult to believe the yard could contain anything but these noisy, genial pilgrims preparing to depart for Canterbury.

In a fresh surcoat, but with a thumping head, Sir Maurice went down to the yard's archway. Under its shadow two nuns plucked primly at their rosaries; they'd obviously heard no evil. Sir Maurice was beginning to doubt what he had seen when his shoulders were encircled by a great arm and a stubbly face was thrust forward, staring into his own.

Sir Maurice opened his mouth to speak but Dick Wittle got in first.

'Say nothing of last night, my lord, or of my private grief, I beg 'ee.' He nodded at the pilgrims filing from the dark interior of the inn. 'Look at them! Observe how happy they are, my lord. What would they care for my poor tragedy?' A tear slithered down his rough cheek. 'Pity me, my lord, for my dear dead youngest boy, useless though he was, what fell.'

'Did he fall?'

'Do not make my agony worse for me by doubting me. How could I harm my own son?'

Sir Maurice hesitated. He himself had only one son by his second wife, after Gemma's tragic death, as perhaps the landlord knew. A son was more important than anything, a man's name would live on through his son; daughters cost a family's fortune in dowries, then lost their bodies and even their names to another man, becoming as anonymous as seed trays within a generation or two. A son was everything – especially if land and property were involved. Nowadays a good draught ox cost thirteen shillings – if a man to work the beast could be found; plagues had taken the best workers and to get good men was expensive, but the income of Holywell Manor had not risen at all to compensate for these terrible expenses and scarcities. These days even a knight must parley with moneylenders, and not in the fine Italian agencies along Lombard Street either, however proud his coat of arms and family motto – *Corruptio optimi pessima*, when the best is corrupted it becomes the worst. An impoverished gentleman must seek deals in alleyways or the back rooms of inns, and pay usury for the privilege. Sir Maurice shuddered. Only yesterday, behind the booths of Smithfield, he had to borrow against this year's harvest to keep hold of his property.

A sudden loud shout from one of the ostlers brought Sir Maurice's mind back into focus. Dick Wittle's unsettling blue eyes probed his face. As if finding what he sought, the fat inn-keeper smiled.

'There's no charge to pay,' he said. 'No charge for 'ee last night. You was disturbed, I received a complaint, and you had just cause. We'll forget the matter of the one shilling and sixpence board and lodging you owe me.'

'One shilling and sixpence!'

'And half a gallon of malmsey.' Dick Wittle removed his arm. 'Agreed?'

Sir Maurice said nothing. He had agreed. The other man gave a low bow and wandered off, hitching up his trousers.

Putting his hand over his mouth, Sir Maurice walked quickly through the archway and stood in the road. His stomach tightened and acid rose in his throat. Swallowing, he crossed into St Margaret's church, an island of peace within its thick walls which silenced the carts rumbling around it, though the shrill cries of the Winchester geese, the Bishop of Winchester's whores, touting for business at the crossroads echoed after him through the open door.

Sir Maurice threw himself on his knees in prayer, still swallowing, then confessed and repented his love of gambling, and paid a penny into the beautiful silver bowl for the priest's benediction. Rather than waste time muttering the penance, he paid another penny, not telling the priest of his hair shirt but holding it very much in his mind and scratching himself pointedly once or twice. He re-emerged into the racket of Long Southwark, blinking in the sunlight. On impulse he crossed to a stall and spent one shilling and fourpence, a fortune, on a piece of scarlet silken cloth for his wife, imagining Katherine's face when he held it up. She would probably wear it wimpled on her head – she loved clothes. Tucking it carefully in his pouch in case folk thought he was living as sumptuously as a merchant, he returned to the inn yard.

Everyone who would ride had paid their shilling for a horse and were already saddled up, and he had to press aside as the mounts came prancing past him, the riders ducking beneath the arch, those who would walk following in the dust with varying degrees of humility, the younger impatient souls running to get the clear air in front, their elders hobbling well back where the dust had settled. If the summer kept up like this, Sir Maurice told himself, then given a sprinkling of rain occasionally he would make a fine harvest.

Sir Harry Bailey reined in beside him. 'Why so glum, my lord knight? You will ride with us as you promised, to St Thomas's watering place?'

'I will ride with you a way, but I am not familiar with any such place.'

'That road keeps my flock of pilgrims clear of the blackguards of Greenwich! Why, we'll tell stories to keep our minds off the sad accident last night!' The vintner laughed and clapped the cruel rowels of his spurs to his horse, reining back to make it prance in a fine show, parting the crowds, then spurred forward. The man whose hair stuck up like a spade followed him half on, half off his horse, reeling a screeching, merry tune on bagpipes.

Sir Maurice watched the yard empty. As silence fell, he saw a blue-eyed lad, thin as a stick, leading a pony not wanted back to the stable, and remembered the other boy's words in his room last night. *Yes, I be one of Dick Wittle's brats, me lord. We all be out of 'im, what with the price of work.* Sir Maurice called out to the lad. 'He wasn't the only one, was he? Your poor brother?'

'Didn't see nothing, me lord,' the boy said, frightened.

'How many sons are there?'

'Me lord, we can't count,' muttered the boy, tugging the pony away, and escaped with relief. Sir Maurice stood almost alone, only Tristan and his own horse remaining, both of them half asleep in the sun. He kicked Tristan awake and swung into the saddle, swearing that he would never come to this place again, and rode out through the archway with Tristan running after him. But Sir Maurice had given Dick Wittle his victory. He would do nothing, and Dick Wittle would roam the warren of parlours and hallways of the Tabard scot-free. Even as he rode into Long Southwark, Sir Maurice felt the landlord's eyes fixed on him from the darkness of one of the upper windows, gloating, his arm encircling a woman's shoulder, sitting on the bed no doubt, where he would probably spend his morning siring what Sir Maurice himself most desired and could not have: another son.

His son, Kay, twenty-one years old now, was effeminate and frightened of shadows, not a patch on his father, who was ashamed of him.

The easterly sun struck in his eyes as Sir Maurice turned off the causeway and took Tabard Lane across Snow's Fields into the marshes.

'It's time!' roared Sir Miles jovially.

Young Maurice, sixteen years old and his bride-to-be fourteen today, scrambled from sleep, cringing under the flat of his father's sword blade across his bare arse. 'Time to make a man of you!' thundered Sir Miles happily and strode through the great hall, pulling Maurice after him. Despite the arthritis in his back, and the infection that made a slimy pink funnel of his left ear, Sir Miles preferred to sleep on the cold floor alongside his men, where the conversation was manly and the memories of past glories flowed with the ale. The half-timbered rooms upstairs, built as an afterthought on top of the stone walls, were left to the ladies and what he dimly imagined, from his infrequent visits to his wife's bed, was their pampered life of spinning wheels and chatter. 'Keep up!' he roared, and farted like a war horse. 'Excellent!'

His father's burnished shoulder plates of Milan steel shone in the bright sun that speared the window slits, and his tabard with its scarlet holy cross was white as snow beneath the greasy fingerprints of last night's mutton. Sir Miles's plain, filthy cloak – no sumptuous merchant finery for him – was held by a white enamelled clasp, showing his vowed allegiance to King Edward, whose badge it was.

Under the stone chimney the fire roared though it was summer, and the tapestries on the walls collected more soot. Maurice tried to cover his buttocks with his free hand while Sir Miles whacked his sword along the line of men muttering their way from the dregs of sleep, cursing them cheerfully while they cursed their hounds, their stiff bones, their aching heads. Sitting up, they began eyeing the maids with appreciative glances, though at this time of day any man's grasping paw was met with a sharp slap.

The serving girls, awakened hours ago with the sun, scurried under Sir Miles's eagle eye to prepare the festivities for Maurice's wedding day. Lads with girlish faces in tight colourful clothes carried in the high table and spread it with a white cloth, then set out bare trestle tables below, pointed respectfully towards where Sir Miles would sit. The girls flustered past them with culinaries prepared overnight by the cook: cold glazed carp and pike and trout, birds boned and stuffed with smaller birds, bowls of walnuts and dishes of butter and cheese, loaves baked into wonderful fancies of ships and swans, and fragile subtleties baked in the latest fashion, with sugar. The hot roasts and pies would be carried in shoulder-high with a great show later, after the ceremony. Even the lowest bond villagers would be allowed to have all they could carry in their napkins. Sir Miles, Maurice knew with some dread, was incapable of holding back on anything. He and his new wife must sit at his father's right hand while their guests consumed the wedding breakfast, entertained by minstrels and bawdy doggerel about marriage beds.

Maurice wondered how he could survive today.

Sir Miles had fought at the Prince of Wales's side in Gascony, defeated not by the French but by the weather; he had returned home in a state of rage, to find his young son softened by the years with his mother and almost a stranger. Even now Maurice could not hope to live up to the older man's brutal energy on the chase, or inspire such affection among his men.

Maurice pulled up his tight black hose to cover his backside, then tried to recover his dignity by fretting out the wrinkles from his sea-green woollen cloak, which he had used as a blanket in the draughty hall. His mouth was dry with fear.

'All for you.' Sir Miles, looking around him, clapped his mailed hands on Maurice's shoulders. 'My only son. Don't let me down, will you? Well?'

'Never, Father.'

'It's an important day for us. John de Rokesley's daughter, by God! Greenwich is worth a hundred shillings a year to him, clear profit, and his Deptford watermill as much. What a catch she is!' He clicked his fingers, forgetting her name.

'Gemma, Father. I know my marriage to her is important. I mean, that we are important.'

'What? Of course, he only leases the place from the Abbot of St Peter in Ghent, and it needs money spent on it. But, by God's honesty, what a dowry he promises!' Sir Miles looked down, examining his son's face. 'You'll do your duty,' he said. 'Get yourself ready!'

Maurice was silent. The de Rokesley family had allowed Greenwich pier to rot and few ships now used it; even Vaudey sent its wool to Flanders through Woolwich, the wool port a few miles downstream. And John de Rokesley had not yet paid Gemma's dowry.

'I will, Father!' Maurice vowed loyally.

His father waved a gauntlet in dismissal, looking proudly after his son. 'He's a man all right,' he told anyone who was listening – and everyone listened to the lord of the Manor of Holywell if they knew what was good for them. 'Yes, he's a man all right – if he's anything like his father!' Sir Miles banged his codpiece and roared with laughter.

Miles stood alone in the pissoir, staring through the draughty gaps at the green moat below, its foul weedy surface fed by a small diversion of the stream. He wiggled his own yellow stream to make patterns drop through the air, just as he had as a boy. All that was behind him now, and he made his face firm and commanding, as much like his father's as he could.

Sir Miles was a harsh father and an even harsher overlord. It was fear more than loyalty that had kept most of the villagers of Vaudey from being infected by the various bands of roving, seditious peasants who were always rising up and complaining about this or that. Of course some lazy criminals and their families had succeeded in slipping away to the ragged encampments that sprang up from time to time on Blackheath, drifting towards London, but anyone who fled was seized, dragged back, and fined. Sir Miles was incapable of understanding why they should want to evade their serfdom. When the knotheads muttered that they no longer wanted to work on his fields, Sir Miles had their rents assessed in cash not labour, and his cellarer seized their goods to the value of what they could not pay – and a little more, to ensure their future good behaviour. At the moment Sir Miles charged a crushing fine of forty shillings for a widow's permission to remarry, and twenty shillings for allowing a man to employ his brother.

You'll do your duty! Maurice felt the terrible burden of his responsibilities stretching ahead of him, all that he must live up to. And take for wife a girl he had hardly met.

Hearing voices below, he knelt and peered through the gap, but all he could see were horses' legs stamping on the embankment, then the rackety wheels of a closed cart for women passing by. He heard the rich Kentish lilt of the de Rokesleys calling out. The wedding party had arrived early from their most important manor, at Lullingstone. They dismounted – Holywell was too small for an inner court – and Maurice, striving for a glimpse of his bride, stood on one of the seat planks to peep over the top of the balustrade.

And there she was, the woman he would marry.

Gemma de Rokesley was plumper about the hips than he remembered her as a young child. He could not see her face; she wore an obscuring silken veil, with a very tall, high-crowned hat that gave her short form some elegance. She must be wearing satin shoes, for her feet crossed the little drawbridge without sound. Maurice imagined her, and smiled. Full hips and dainty feet! He liked her already.

Someone yelled for him and he ran inside to prepare himself. A goblet of wine was thrust into his hand, his coat brushed more effectively than he had done, and lewd advice was shouted at him from all quarters. When the time came to ride to the church, Maurice felt quite drunk and far removed from the proceedings. He mounted up beside Sir Miles, who now held a kerchief to his infected ear for the pain, and they set off. Fortunately the horses knew the way.

The dusty lane wandered between the hedgeless, treeless field strips of the demesne. Separated from the lord's land by no more than sticks and stones lay the strip holdings of serfs, who were held to be descended from Roman slaves, and villeins who had fallen into servility later. The tiny properties of free men were scattered beyond the boundaries. On their right, on the far side of stony fields that had once been the most fertile but were no longer so since their springs had dried up, rows of windmills creaked and spun along the westerly, windward edge of the knoll. Through the twisting sails Maurice glimpsed London, there and gone, there and gone, under its banner of smoke, and the spire of St Paul's, looking tall enough to touch God.

A shimmering dot appeared in the lane ahead. As soon as he recognized the bumbling figure, Sir Miles spurred forward angrily. 'Why in God's name are you here and not in your place, Father Briggs?' he roared.

Maurice could see that the village priest scuttling along towards them was terrified. His red hands were clenched in front of him, his watery eyes looked up at them appealingly. He flung himself on his knees.

'Gone!' he cried.

'Stop stuttering, blast you to Hell!' thundered Sir Miles, flinging his kerchief. 'What's gone?'

Briggs forced himself to stand calmly. He pursed his lips to control his stutter – a stutter was the Devil speaking.

'All of them,' he said, and the tendons stood out in his neck, and he cringed.

But Sir Miles did not strike him. He just stared.

'No one would dare,' he growled. 'No one would dare.'

Beside him, Maurice felt his bowels freeze. He tried to swallow and could not. His throat simply would not co-operate. The reins slipped out of his numb hands and he croaked, 'Stolen?'

'Didn't you hear the man?' roared Sir Miles.

Maurice cringed. The memory of himself staring into the grotesque reflections of his face in the church came back to him with a force that left him breathless. He felt guilt rush into his face and stain his cheeks red.

'I didn't steal them!' he panted. 'I swear to God I never touched them!'

455

Sir Miles paid no more attention to his son than usual. 'Of course you didn't,' he said irritably. 'No one touches them, except a Fox, on his wedding day. Why should anyone disturb the old rubbish at any other time, or even look?' He glanced round, adding, 'Your cheeks have caught the sun.' He tried to be kind in his blunt way. 'Don't worry, boy. You're always worrying. It's just a bauble.'

'It's a tradition,' Maurice said.

'Wedding nerves!' Sir Miles scoffed. 'You'll feel a different man after tonight, *that* I promise you!' He winked at his followers, then glared at the priest, sending him ahead of them back to the church.

So Maurice was married in front of the altar at St John's, his bride at his side, without wearing the talent in its golden claw, hanging from its golden chain, suspended from his neck.

He held Gemma's hand warm in his.

'When I find out who stole them,' Sir Miles promised during the feast, 'I'll wring his neck until he pisses.'

Gemma lifted her veil to eat, though she ate as little as a mouse. She had a pleasant round face with plump cheeks, that dimpled pleasingly when she smiled. She said little, only looked at Maurice with her amused brown eyes.

'What's funny?' he hissed at last.

'You,' she said. 'You're much nicer than I remembered.'

Maurice glanced at his father, whose good right ear was pointed towards them. 'What are you talking about, wife?'

'Gemma,' she said comfortably.

'Gemma,' he muttered.

'More human,' she said, and smiled that smile. 'Nicer.'

'You'll find out,' he growled.

Having eaten hardly anything, Gemma was swept away by the twittering women to prepare herself for the most important part of her most important day: the bed. Maurice remained below eating and drinking, slouched at his father's side at the white table. Finally the peasants came in to offer their stumbling good wishes, caps in hand but bringing the stink of their unwashed flesh with them. They ignored the broken sugar swans but eyed the buckets of meaty leftovers and gravy like starving men, and their brats lined up behind them, and their women too, all with their eating knives in their hands. Sir Miles waved benevolently for them to go to it. The wedding party, drunk enough to vomit, went upstairs to the women's quarters, jostling and shoving each other on the steps, followed by the bawdy minstrels and the acrobat.

Gemma lay quiet and alone in the panelled room with its glazed window, only her head showing above a beautifully embroidered counterpane. She had worked on it since the day her marriage was arranged, years ago. It was her childhood memory of home.

The men elbowed each other behind Sir Miles as Maurice came through wearing a nightshirt, carrying a candle. He sat in bed beside Gemma, bolt upright with eyes downcast, and there was a muffled silence for prayers, punctuated by the sound of someone being sick down the hall. As soon as Briggs stopped his Latin, the crowd surged forward and Maurice lifted the covers and dropped on top of his wife. Her arms went round him. His backside made a bump under the counterpane and willing hands pushed him.

'Is she blooded?' Sir Maurice demanded.

Maurice looked down into Gemma's eyes. Her fingertip crept to his lips. Almost a smile.

'Yes,' he grunted over his shoulder. 'It's done!'

'Then they're wed,' Sir Miles said, and held out his arms for everyone to leave. He winked approvingly at Maurice and slammed the door behind him.

Maurice and Gemma lay together.

Someone had hung a drape over the window and the room was full of wood-coloured shadows.

'You said what you said for me,' she whispered, caressing his smooth jaw. 'You risked embarrassment for me.'

'I had thought I wouldn't like you,' he said, reclining beside her.

'I felt the same about you!' They touched thumbs, then Maurice looked round as the boards creaked beyond the door. 'They're waiting,' she said.

'What for?'

She nudged him. 'You know. The noises. Oh!' she cried.

He looked at her admiringly. 'Oh,' he said.

'That's it.' They scrambled up, covering each other's mouths against their laughter, facing one another cross-legged on the

457

sheets. 'Oh!' Maurice bumped to make the bed creak. 'Oh. *Oh!*'

They heard Sir Miles slapping his hands to scatter the eaves-droppers, then his hearty whistling as he went off to find his own wife.

Darkness fell and Maurice lost himself in his bride. The candle burned out but still he lay in the dark, stroking her face, marvelling at his luck.

'No man was ever more happy,' he swallowed.

Somewhere distantly on the estate a cockerel crowed, and he sat up with a start. But Gemma breathed slowly and deeply, and he lay back beside her, pulling her hair over his throat, nestling her head warm in his armpit. But now his mood was broken, and he stared up into nothing.

For the first time since the Conquest, certainly, and perhaps long before, a Fox had been married without the talent that tradition dictated he wore around his neck. The tradition was the important thing. Who could have been so envious or vengeful that they stole a family's tradition, even if they could not use it themselves?

Maurice sat up slowly.

Jack, he thought. *It was Jack.*

He was up and dressed before dawn, black rage and humiliation obliterating every thought except Jack's name. *Jack stole them*. Gemma could not stop him; Maurice pushed her aside and flung himself through the empty rooms, his sword clattering on the steps because he was so short, so damned short. He wrenched at the scabbard as he strode past the men still snoring amid the ruins of yesterday's feast. Kicking an ostler awake, he had a saddle thrown on his horse and rode away from the sleeping manor house without seeing Gemma waving from the top window.

Galloping headlong across the fields of the knoll, Maurice almost unhorsed himself jumping the bank into the sunken lane, then spurred uphill past the labourers wandering dozily from their houses to start work with the sun. The horse slowed uphill, lunging and wheezing under the spurs.

Jack's few acres were protected from the sun's fiercest heat and drought by the cool damp shadows of the oakwoods behind, but in the open his crops were already catching the early sun, turning golden. Maurice rode a swathe through them. Jack's cottage, just outside the border of the church's glebe land, stood near the overflowing pool on the ground cleared by his father, Nicol. After Nicol's death, Jack had cleared the rest himself, digging out huge roots and tracts of bramble with amazing energy and persistence for a boy, especially one looking after his mother, Eleanor, who had been sick to dying. Perhaps he had been desperate for something to do.

Maurice would not bring himself to sympathise with Jack's feelings; he could not.

'Jack, come out!'

Maurice slid down from his horse and kicked open the paling gate. Striding up the path to the cottage, he drew his sword and thrust the blade through the wall, hacking straw and twigs out of it, then kicked the door with his boot. But though the wall cracked, and bits drifted down from the roof, the door stuck fast.

A dog barked.

'Jack, I know it was you!' Maurice shouted through the gap. He stopped, panting, resting his forehead on the sun-warmed wood. He was trembling with rage, but more important was his feeling of betrayal. Jack had been his friend, his trusted friend.

'I should kill you for what you did,' Maurice said quietly.

The door creaked open and Jack, with a smile, came out wearing only his dirty nettle-linen shirt, showing everything Adambare from his belly button to his toes. Those dark eyes took in everything at once, as always, particularly the fact that Maurice was alone. Jack pretended to wince at the brightness of the sun, sleepily scratching at the straw in his hair.

'Maurice,' he said, sounding pleasantly surprised. Maurice blinked. Jack's voice was deep.

'Hello,' Maurice said.

Jack was friendly and unafraid. 'And what brings you here this hour of morning, my good sir knight, my lord?'

'Do not mock me,' Maurice said, and pushed his sword against Jack's throat.

Jack would be fifteen now, and the rest of him had changed as much as his voice. He had filled out and slowed, acquiring this casual motionlessness that was so difficult to provoke. But when he did move, he was sharp and quick as his eyes. Those Foxdark eyes.

459

'Don't provoke me, I warn you.'

'My best wishes on your marriage,' Jack said sincerely, though he was speaking along the blade of a sword. 'She'll bear you fine sons.'

Jack's diet of pottage had made him shorter even than Maurice, but he held himself as though he could spring much taller. Maurice pressed him against the wall with the sword point to keep him down.

'Where, Jack?' he said.

'Where what?'

He knows I won't hurt him, Maurice thought. 'Tell me where you hid them,' he said, 'or I'll . . .' He pressed harder, merely to threaten, but drew a bead of blood. Jack put his fingers to his neck and glanced at them. He rubbed them, and Maurice withdrew a fraction. Only a drop, but there was blood between them now.

'Hid what?' Jack said contemptuously.

'You went back into the church that night. You went back and stole my family's most precious possession from holy ground.'

'No I didn't.'

'Liar.'

'I swear it on my oath I didn't go back into the church that night.'

'What does a peasant like you know about oaths or truth?' Maurice accused wildly. 'I don't believe a word you say!'

'Take me to the manor court,' Jack invited, changing to an altogether more dangerous tack. 'I'll swear it on the bones, in front of the cellarer, or we'll wait until the circuit judges of the eyre court are due in the village, if you prefer. But I seem to remember that you were in the church too, weren't you?' he added innocently. 'What did you see there? You never told me.'

Maurice pushed past him toward the cottage, but Jack gripped his arm. 'What *did* you see? Was it really anything?'

Maurice dragged himself away. Taking a deep breath – he would never have dared behave like this if Eleanor had still been alive – he kicked the door and knocked his way inside the cottage.

A girl screamed and sat up on the filthy straw bag that passed for a bed. She had very long blonde hair through which her nipples peeped like soft red cherries. Her eyes were deep blue, slanty and insolent. She held back the yapping dog by its scruff.

The two pathetic rooms of the cottage were lit by the sunlight pouring through the window holes. Ignoring the girl, Maurice raised his foot and knocked over the single wooden chest, scattering the ragged clothes and cloths it contained.

Jack stood in the doorway. 'It's not fornication,' he said, and nodded at the girl. 'That's Joan, and she's my wife. We're as proper wed as you are.'

Maurice tipped her off and slit the bag she had been sitting on, ignoring the dog and the crouching nude girl. He slashed the straw this way and that with his sword, but nothing clinked. He knocked over the cooking pots but nothing rolled out of them. There were clay pots and mugs on a shelf and he broke them, then the shelf came down by itself and smashed all the plates too. Maurice stepped over the shards fastidiously in his long pointy shoes, ripping his sword blade down the walls, but no secret cache was revealed, and the roof was empty but for roosting chickens. He ran his hand along the rafters and felt nothing but dry, dusty chicken shit.

He crumbled it between his fingers.

'Seen enough?' Jack said, putting his arm round his terrified wife, who clutched her threadbare shift in front of her. Maurice roared like his father and smashed the stools and table, then thrust past them into the sunlight.

Jack followed him, sweating slightly in the sun but watching quietly as Maurice slashed the cherry tree and apple tree, slashing even at the ripe apples as they tumbled around him, then dug his sword along the line of vegetables, leeks and beans, garlic, even the cabbages finally, then jabbed the blade back and forth into the compost heap at the end. Nothing.

'You can't do this to us,' Jack asserted. 'We're free.'

Maurice turned, panting. 'On my estate no one is free, not even me. I've nothing but custom this and responsibility that—'

'I'll want an apology from you,' Jack said. 'And damages.'

'I'll take you to hell first!'

'If not from you then from your father,' Jack said calmly. 'I got damages from him when them men of his jousted in my field and flattened the crop.'

Maurice sheathed his sword. His shoulders slumped.

'Where did you hide them?' he said. His voice rose. He knew

he could never explain about traditions to a type like Jack. 'Please, Jack, I just want them back again, by God's mercy.'

'Don't know what you're talking about,' Jack said, and Maurice didn't know whether to believe him or not.

After a week or two, bound by the custom of the Manor and his father's own laws, Maurice paid up for the damage he had caused.

Nine months later, Maurice's son by Gemma was born. A woman came plodding downstairs when the shrieks ceased, crossing towards Maurice who waited by the fireplace. Her footsteps echoed on the flagstones. She seemed to take ages, and Maurice knew what she was going to say. But Sir Miles interposed himself eagerly, turning his right ear to hear her – his left was a dripping vortex of decay that no poultice could control.

But the woman pushed past him and stood in front of Maurice.

'Your wife is dead,' came her voice. 'Your son was stillborn, with a club foot. He wouldn't have lasted anyway.'

He wouldn't have lasted anyway . . .

Even twenty-five years later, the pain was no less.

Sir Maurice rode his palfrey. On the horse's forehead swung the small bronze pendant, enamelled with the Fox coat of arms, whose irritating jingling had recalled him from his reverie. *When the best is corrupted it becomes the worst.*

How true that was.

Sir Maurice twisted and looked back as though expecting to see something terrible following him – his fate, his punishment. His whole life had run wrong since the night he broke into the church.

But he saw only the pilgrims on foot, who had fallen well behind. He could just make out his page, Tristan, no doubt playing sweet and meek, trying to latch to a girl who was not a nun.

Sir Maurice squinted into the sun ahead of him – his eyesight was no longer as good as it once was – and saw the mounted pilgrims riding in a tight group ahead. Their voices carried to him in the warm, still air; he could hear one of the pilgrims telling a story to while away the journey.

'Lord, hear my heartfelt prayer.' Sir Maurice closed his eyes. 'I beg you, forgive me, and bless me with a good harvest, that I may then pay off all I have borrowed to keep me till that day. Let me keep Holywell, do not let my creditors seize me, for I have risked everything. If You will do this for me, Lord, I will never lay another wager again, ever, or borrow again. This is my oath. Do not let me be the one to let my family and the memory of my parents down.'

How childish prayers sound! he thought. Most childish when most true. His words had come from his heart, not his brain.

The truth of the matter was that the de Rokesley family had lost their money, lost Greenwich, lost Deptford, and Gemma's dowry had never been paid. Without that money Sir Miles, rather than dismiss his men, had let the manor house fall into disrepair and hastily married Maurice to Katherine de Kidbroke – 'What a beauty!' But he pilfered her dowry and the money ran away through his trembling fingers and senile brain, made rotten by infection. Her fortune wasted, Sir Miles could not even afford to take a horseman with him to Spain, where he died at Najera.

Maurice inherited all his debts.

At first he hardly noticed. Then as now, Katherine was indeed a beauty, a great beauty – milk-white skin, with the face of a lazy cat, those wide sleepy eyes over a tiny pouting mouth. She'd captivated Maurice. Even after they were wed, like an illicit lover she came prowling into his bed whenever she fancied, filling him with herself, shrugging him away with a sigh when it suited her. And the more she rejected him, the more he lusted after her. Sir Maurice never desired another woman, his own perfumed wife filled his thrusting dreams.

But it was not love.

Sometimes he thought of Gemma, and even after a quarter of a century the memory of her was still wonderful, and her loss cruel. In the nine months they'd had together, he'd learned to love her. His soul still loved her, without her he was only half a man. Katherine was here in body, and she had given him a son, but she could never give him the love he had lost.

Sir Maurice's head drooped as he rode, and he dozed. His sleep at the Tabard last night had not refreshed him but drained him, haunting him with the poor boy's murder for which he felt partly responsible, and he was ashamed of his cowardice this morning in not facing up to that monstrous villain Dick Wittle.

He jerked awake. The pilgrims ahead had turned uphill, away

from the black waters of the River Ravensbourne where it widened into Deptford Creek, avoiding Greenwich – the village was a notorious haunt of thieves and beggars since the pier had collapsed. Sir Maurice followed them, winding among the watermills lining the river banks and then up into the trees where the slope steepened for the stiff ascent to Blackheath. At the summit the horses were lathered and snorting, especially the priest's hack, and Sir Maurice thought the pilgrims trailing on foot must be finding it a hard toil. The riders, who having paid for horses intended to make the most of them, did not wait but pressed forward along the broad spine of the heathland, chattering and gesticulating, obviously enjoying themselves. To his surprise, they turned left into Hanging Wood where it had been his own intention to go, and he followed their hoofprints down the leafy, sunken lane towards Vaudey, his own village.

But they did not go as far as the village; instead, under Sir Harry Bailey's guidance, they scrambled up the verge and went twisting out of sight along a path between the oak trees. Sir Maurice frowned and spurred his horse, following the path into the forest brilliant with wild flowers, ducking beneath the branches where birds fluttered. Through the tree trunks Sir Maurice glimpsed the overflowing pool, the still waters holding the reflections of the oaks standing around it as perfectly as a mirror.

He stopped; he had forgotten how beautiful this place was. He had not been here for years. In his day this was where young men came to lose their virginity before they took marriage vows and must be chaste. And still was, for all he knew. Perhaps something should be done about it.

As he rode forward, he heard a deep voice calling. He would have recognised it anywhere.

It was Jack's voice.

'Welcome to Saint Thomas's Pool!' Jack called, striding forward from the open-fronted hut whose roof and three walls were a mass of fragrant honeysuckle. His figure was full with the muscles and belly of middle age but spritely, and his eyes were everywhere at once as he took the bridle of the leading horse. 'Blessed good afternoon to you, Sir Harry,' he winked, then turned to the others.

'Blessed good afternoon to all you good pilgrims. Get you down! Rest you!' The horses drank, rippling the waters of the pool with their muzzles. 'Any poor of heart, any sick need help?' Jack reached up willingly to help one lady down, grunting as she transferred her weight wholesale from her saddle to his arms. 'My,' he cried, muffled by her bosoms, 'one of you's enough for me!'

'Hold your wicked talk,' snapped a dour-looking tonsured pilgrim. 'I've heard a sufficiency today, more I cannot forgive.' The woman's warm look suggested a ready willingness to forgive Jack his wickedness, and she simpered at him when he seated her on the bench by the pool.

'My, how overheated you poor souls do look!' he cried, coming back to the others. His leather workman's breeches, Sir Maurice noted, were humble rather than poor, as was his forest-green smock and hood of soft wool which he wore dropped back on his shoulders. And there were rings on his fingers, which distinguished him, though one was of base bronze, worked with a pattern as a seal, revealing he could not write. The pilgrims were dismounting, staring around them at the pool in the glade. 'Is it not a beautiful place?' Jack said quietly.

Then he was back at his stallholder's patter again, moving busily among them, stretching his limbs as if to give them example. He held their attention in the palm of his hand. 'Wearied by your travel no doubt, you are. Walk round, free your legs up! No, my good master, pray don't bandy your legs like that, it makes my own thighs hurt to see you so sore! They do say the first day's always the worst in the saddle – only four more long, long days to go to Canterbury! You must ask me about my herbal salve – or try the healing magic of Saint Thomas's Pool. No charge, I'll sell nothing to such devout folk as yourselves.' He handed round mugs. 'Pure, fresh water. Scoop it from the pond yourselves, taste the holiness of Saint Thomas's Pool!'

Sir Harry Bailey sat relaxing in the shade of the hut, drinking a mug of wine. He had heard Jack's patter many times, and he chatted familiarly to the girl who served him.

Jack, her father, stood on a tree trunk that had fallen half in the water, spreading out his arms so that his audience fell silent.

'Valle Dei, 'tis said, these lands were once called, in old King

Lud's time mayhap. Valle Dei, that's Latin, meaning Valley of the Lord, known to my common tongue as Vaudey.' He paused as a large pilgrim with a headache refilled his mug and drank noisily. 'One winter's day my great-great-grandmother came here for solitude in her prayers. And here, as she stood where you are standing now, on the water's edge, her hands clasped before her in devotion, and cold as ice, I expect, who should appear before her eyes?' Jack's own eyes widened as though he was seeing what he described. 'The saintly figure of our Thomas Becket, with a halo about his head, in only poor clothes, his way of showing Christ's poverty. He was on his way home to Canterbury, to his martyrdom, foully slain in holy sanctuary! But these here were his last moments of peace, I like to think. And he called her the Lady of the Lake.'

He knelt down, and plunged his hands into the water. 'This lake. Ever since, this water, where Saint Thomas stopped and drank on his last journey, has been named Saint Thomas's Pool.' He raised his eyes towards them. 'You have just drunk the same water he did.' He paused to let that sink in, then slowly stood up.

'I have a few relics and mementoes of that day that my daughter will show you in the hut – even to the actual mug Saint Thomas held to his lips, and a silver cokebell that for her piety he gave to my great-great-grandmother as a gift. Do not attempt to buy them, I beg you, they are too precious to me.'

Then as they milled towards the hut, he called at their backs, 'But I do have some pilgrim hat badges, and Saint Thomas brooches and rings . . .' They were soon busy looking at the merchandise, drawn in by the more expensive sights to purchase the cheaper. Jack, watching them holding out their pennies to his daughter Elaine, gave a happy grin and dried his hands on the front of his smock.

Sir Maurice rode over quietly and looked down at him. 'I am as devout as any man here, but I do not believe a word of your tale.'

Jack stared back calmly.

'Church land!' Sir Maurice said, enraged by Jack's watchful stillness. 'I'll have you off it!'

'It's mine,' Jack said.

Sir Maurice glared at him.

'I bought it,' Jack said levelly. 'I can't read, but I can count, and I know a good thing when I see it.'

The man was incorrigible! Sir Maurice dragged on the reins, snapping the horse's head round, and gave a good jab with his spurs to get the beast going. He soon had to slow down as the next batch of dusty pilgrims, the ones on foot, filed through the woods behind the beckoning arm of Sir Harry's servant. Sir Maurice grabbed Tristan and turned him back, chivvying him ahead of his horse. By the time they reached the lane, he could hear Jack starting his harangue again, greeting the newcomers with the same words he had used before.

Jack gazed after the tabarded knight disappearing into the woods. Sir Maurice with his nose in the air, returned from London unexpectedly soon!

And nearly caught him out. While the cat was away, the mice would play. Holywell's lord had spent much time away during the past few years.

Jack was sweating. By God's breath, that was close! How had he kept so calm? He could actually see one of the big silver coins on clear display, shining at the back of the hut on the top shelf. If Sir Maurice had only demeaned himself to look inside, he would have seen it.

Jack had never actually sold one, but the bright gleam drew the pilgrims inside to examine its glory more closely, making the stock spread out below look twice as rich, and twice the value.

If Sir Maurice had seen the talent, representing tradition and family and all the things Sir Maurice believed in, for sale . . . Jack didn't have to imagine hard: the knight would have drawn his sword and Jack would be lying here disembowelled, his blood staining the water.

He drew the back of his trembling hand across his forehead, dashing away his sweat. His venture was so successful, he was growing careless. He must not let greed make him foolish, Jack realised.

His wife came hobbling round the side with a huge tray, its weight taken by a leather sash slung from her neck, laden down with trinkets to replace the depleted stock. To his eyes Joan had lost none of her beauty, though her brassy hair was cut short now, and well salted with grey. Jack went to her and embraced her without a word.

'What's brought this on?' she exclaimed, pleased.

'Oh, I just remembered how much I love you, that's all.'

'Kissing in front of our daughter,' she scolded.

'Elaine knows about kissing well enough herself,' Jack muttered. He didn't like the way the village boys followed her with their eyes. Elaine was a beauty, and Jack knew exactly what was running through those boys' minds, having been quite a lad himself. The fact that his daughter was too shy to take any pleasure from the effect she had on the male sex did nothing to appease him.

'It's not her fault those ale-house lads are always calling at her,' said Joan defensively. 'You mustn't think wrong of her. A girl can't help the way she walks.'

'*You* couldn't,' Jack winked, slapping her ample haunch.

'I've never regretted you,' she replied simply. 'In all our married life, you've only kept one secret from me.'

'Aye, and that I will, too,' Jack said brightly. His wife was the only person who knew he'd stolen the talents, but even she did not know where he had hidden the remainder of them. 'It's sinful to think a man or a woman can know everything about each other. 'Tis the sin of pride.'

'You don't know what sin is, husband!' she scoffed, then glanced after Sir Maurice. 'What did he want?'

'That poor unhappy man doesn't know what he wants,' Jack said dismissively. Sir Maurice was Jack's sore spot.

'I've never forgot the day he came to our house,' she shuddered, lowering her voice, 'and you swore that oath – about you not going back to the church the night when you was boys.'

'No less than the truth.'

'I know you told the truth, Jack,' she said patiently. 'I still think you're going to burn when the trumpets blow, and the pity and glory of it is, you don't know it.'

'I went back the *next* night,' Jack grinned. 'Would I ever lie?'

'And this story of yours,' she spluttered, though she wouldn't have had him any other way, 'this about your great-great-I-don't-know-how-great-grandmother being the lady of the lake! Have you no shame?'

'No, and my own father, Nicol, told me,' Jack said, looking injured. '*His* grandfather could just remember her being talked about, a very old woman with no teeth, no mind, bedridden. And even if it isn't true, my love, think on it – can't we afford to eat meat now? And don't we have enough now for a dowry of sorts when our daughter marries? Elaine's happiness would be worth lying for, wouldn't it? Doing anything for,' Jack said fiercely.

'Ah, you used to speak like that to me,' she nudged him, 'when you was a young man.'

'Even when we was almost starving.'

'Everything changed for us since you put *that* out,' Joan said thoughtfully, nodding at the gleam amid the shadows of the hut. She plucked with disdain at the tatty pieces for sale on the tray, the ornamental scrolls containing written pardons for minor sins, lucky St Thomas medals and St Thomas amulets, St Thomas pins, St Thomas badges, the St Thomas holy rings of cheap sapphire-coloured glass cobbled up by their neighbours as evening work, which pilgrims making the journey of their lives snapped up by the hundred as symbols of their devotion. Equally popular were the tiny lead flasks of water from St Thomas's Pool, stamped with a small image of the sainted archbishop with his middle finger upraised in blessing, and etched with the words 'St Thomas is the best healer of the holy sick' by the same scribe who provided the pardons. Lately Jack had learned that not all he sold need be cheap. This year he was selling rings of real silver with a real amethyst, and the stone could be turned to unlock it, revealing a saintly fragment of bone, or a drop of dried blood underneath. Such workmanship had to be imported from London. The important thing was that the pilgrims believed in these trinkets. Though Jack was well aware it was pig's blood and bits of chicken wishbone, he did not think he was selling anything false; belief could make anything true.

Elaine had done her best business with the souvenirs and was selling ale now, and for those who could afford it wine in St Thomas goblets. Even the goblets were available for purchase.

'You've never let on where you've hid them,' Joan murmured. 'Suppose you died? We'd never know . . .' But Jack grinned, not to be drawn. 'For years I was sure it was the compost,' she confessed, 'judging from the way you sweated when anyone went near it. You always sweat when you're guilty, did you know that, Jack?'

'I do not!' Jack said, alarmed.

'I remember,' she taunted him innocently, 'how you sweated when he dug his sword in that compost.'

'Aye, well maybe they were hidden there once.'

'But not now?'

'Every husband is allowed one secret,' he reminded her. 'But not his wife,' he added.

She remembered the son she had borne out of wedlock, when she was a frightened girl of thirteen years old, before she met Jack. She had given her baby away to a childless woman in Greenwich, far enough away for her to never know of him or meet him again, and she would not have recognised him if she had. Yet every night of her life, before she drifted off to sleep, she wondered if her son was still alive. That was her secret.

'You're right, as always,' she said, giving Jack a peck.

The next batch of pilgrims arrived, footsore and weary, and thirsty. Jack scooped up a mug of water from the pool and his voice rang out. 'Blessed good afternoon to all you good pilgrims. Sit you, rest you! Welcome to Saint Thomas's Pool!'

Sir Maurice rode down through the Nymet Wood to Vaudey in a fine rage. It was all too much for him: seeing Jack flying so high above his station in life – that mock-humble lambswool smock had been bought with money, and not cheaply – while he must scrape for every shilling and spend it to show his status over the lower classes.

Coming from the trees and riding along the sunken lane, his head bobbing just above the verges, Sir Maurice spied the weeds and boulters, yellow and purple, already festering in his smooth strips of green wheat and oats. And where were the women, supposed to be out on the lord's land snaring birds for his table, and their children with slings and stones driving away the magpies thieving his seed? Nowhere to be seen! But as always, he saw, his serfs contrived to keep their own little strips in better condition than his, the sly devils! Back in his father's day, most of them had purchased themselves clear of the 'lord's boon' days, when the manor could call for extra work from the peasants. The small influx of capital from the purchases had been useful at the time, but now it was exhausted and Sir Maurice must pay through the nose for every stroke of work – if he could find someone to do it.

If.

The world was turned upside down, the bottom rising to the top!

Sir Maurice felt his stomach clamp tight in a flood of sour juices. This harvest must succeed. This must be the best harvest Holywell Manor ever had. His head spun with the intensity of his prayer.

Strange, that name, Holywell. There must really have been a well here once, holy, presumably . . . The pain in his stomach squeezed mercilessly, like a clenched fist inside him.

Sir Maurice set his face as he crossed the Hollingbourne bridge and clattered into the village, riding high and haughty in his rage and agony. Now he was so near home he held himself as his father had, trying for that impressive presence, tall in the saddle, legs straight, one hand round the pommel of his sword, and believed he achieved it.

But the more he thought of Jack, the more his anger grew, and his stomach fed on it. He belched as sharply as the bark of a dog.

Rubbish in the street was buzzing with flies. Will Norris, the reeve, should have slipped word in the offenders' ears long before this – serfs, no doubt, like Will himself. They were all hand in glove here, so near the servile centre of the village. Oliver Briggs, the estate steward, must make an example of them – look at this mess!

Sir Maurice rode on with increasing fury, finding fault with everything, scattering children and chickens, trying not to think of Jack.

Jack, who had looked at him as though he was lord of the manor himself.

He rode past the green where free men straddled the benches outside the top alehouse, not taking the mugs respectfully from their mouths when they saw him but carrying on drinking. He saw others playing some sort of game on the grass with a willow stick and ball of shrunk leather as though he was not there.

He told himself that his Vaudey had at least fared better than most villages, praise God for His mercy; with his own eyes Sir Maurice had seen estates further from London, at Ightham and Lullingstone and countless others, where two houses in three stood deserted and tumbledown – and how quickly they decayed, like bodies with the life departed. The dilapidation was dreadful to see, dreadful; such a waste. For time out of mind, steady reliable tenants, the salt of the earth, had followed their fathers onto the soil in the lord's service, but the plagues had killed off many of the old and loyal tenants, and in doing so had blighted the living as much as the dead. Whole families of good folk had upped sticks for London, only stopping off where they were offered a better deal by the local lord. Nowadays Sir Maurice must compete among his equals to employ low-born labour! And there was always some lord, dragged down by his responsibilities, with fields running riot with weeds and barns falling down, desperate to improve the offer though it cost him his life's blood.

And above all stood London, bloated on the horizon, drawing all in with her promise of wealth, and London citizenship granted after only a year and a day within her walls.

Travellers would work at Vaudey only until they had saved enough to continue their journey. Sir Maurice no longer owned them, their work was no longer his own, their possessions were no longer his own. And Jack wearing lambswool and rings on his fingers like a merchant, one of them of amethyst, as good as any of Sir Maurice's own handed down to him by his father; better even.

With a mottled face, Sir Maurice reined in by the lych gate as he spotted the parson, newly appointed. 'What's this about the sale of Church land to Jack Fox?' he roared. 'You'll tell me it's a lie!'

The man came over politely, but without hurrying. He was thin and neat – no fat and jolly face like old Parson Briggs's sticking roundly out of a dirty cassock, hardly able to read the Creed and so shortsighted he once baptised a baby's bottom. No, Father Sterre was one of the new breed, not to be intimidated, coming from outside both the village and the family, thin, pale, and ambitious. For him, too, Vaudey was just a place on the way to somewhere else.

'You didn't really sell the overflowing pool to that renegade!'

'Overflowing pool, Sir Maurice?' The priest frowned politely. The oak tree waved its shadows over them; since his arrival it had been at the back of Father Sterre's mind to have it chopped down, but though the branches overhung the churchyard, strictly speaking it was the property of Sir Maurice since its trunk grew from the verge beyond the churchyard. 'I fear I'm still unfamiliar with some local names. Oh, you mean . . .' He clicked his fingers, and Sir Maurice gritted his teeth.

'Ancient glebe land, Father Sterre.'

'Church land is the Church's business,' the thin man frowned.

Sir Maurice's jaw dropped at such disrespect. 'The church and manor are different sides of the same thing!' he shouted. 'That's the way it's always been.'

'These are more spacious times, Sir Maurice. The pool and woodland waste was part of my benefice, but was earning no income. It was useless.' The priest took his explanation a step at a time, as though Sir Maurice was just another one of his flock. 'And then Master Fox, who is a devout man—'

'Jack's not a devout man, he's fooling you!' Sir Maurice exploded. 'He doesn't even know what religion is.'

The priest held up his hand patiently. 'After Vespers last Michaelmas, Jack came to me, kind enough to mention my impoverished situation, and proposed a solution whereby my living might be improved. He applied to my lord the Bishop of Rochester and offered a most generous price—'

'Jesus's blood! Under canon law? Lease or copyhold? How long for?'

'Freehold, in perpetuity.'

'Where did he get the money from?' Sir Maurice wondered feverishly.

'He must be the wealthiest man in the village, after yourself, Sir Maurice, since his connection with Saint Thomas was revealed.'

'The lady of the lake,' Sir Maurice sneered. 'It's all made up, you know, there's nothing to it. He's deceived you.'

Father Sterre tightened his thin lips. 'Jack pays his tithe without complaint – almost uniquely, I may say.' Sir Maurice coloured, and the priest cleared his throat. 'Sir Maurice, on another subject, may I mention the vexing matter of this oak tree—'

'No you may not, sir priest!' Sir Maurice grabbed the opportunity to assert himself. He hated educated men with rolling phrases and cold hearts who felt nothing for the soil. '*My* land is *my* business,' he snarled, and spurred his horse on.

Alongside the stream, the desmesne lands stretched around

473

him on the knoll. As Sir Maurice rode past the Stonefield, so
enduring and familiar was the sight of home that his mood
improved and the pain in his stomach eased. But what a shame
the manor house looked now, reflecting his own shame and the
fall in his fortunes: ivy gripped the crumbling walls and no candles
glimmered in the narrow arrow slits of the first three storeys of
the tower. The living quarters were perched on top, half-timbered, and the broad windows once thought fit only for women
were holding the sunset in their glass. Over London the drifting
smoke looked like a shield painted with wonderful colours, he
thought, and the sun gleamed through like lances of light. Perhaps
Katherine was looking out, and he waved just in case. Riding
quietly across the grass and drawing up in the shadows, he called
for the coistrel to groom his horse. But only the stableboy came
out, looking first sleepy, then startled to see him. Sir Maurice slid
down from horseback and cuffed him. 'Where is everybody?'

'Didn't think you'd be so soon back, my lord,' the lad mumbled,
rubbing his head.

Shaking off his weariness, Sir Maurice strode across the little
drawbridge now fixed in position by grass and weeds. His hunting
dogs greeted him in the great hall, skidding on the rushes and
slobbering on his legs. He glanced up, feeling quiet eyes on him,
his pleasure evaporating.

Kay, his son, was watching him from the circular stone steps of
the turret, his body skinny as a rake below that white pimply face.
His shoes ridiculously pointed, his sleeve enormous, his breeches
so London-tight that they showed every wrinkle of his genitals.
Taller than his father, the boy – boy! Sir Maurice had first been
married when five years younger than Kay now was! – looked to
weigh nothing. Skin and bone, dry of blood or passion, Kay had
made no friends, had no followers to impress and urge him on,
but instead lived in his own room, shy as a girl. What could one
say to such a poor sort? Still Kay had not even greeted him, and
Sir Maurice longed to whack him with the flat of his sword, put
some colour in him.

'I could knock you down with one blow of my fist,' Sir Maurice
growled, and turned his attention back to his dogs.

'Yes, Father,' Kay said evenly – he never stood up to his father
– and Sir Maurice sighed, feeling betrayed by his own loins.

Perhaps his first son, with the club foot, would have turned out the real man. But Sir Maurice had looked at the talents, and ever since his life had been a punishment and a trial.

At the age of six Kay had been adopted out to another family to grow up with the knightly arts that would make a man of him. No good. Now that he had returned home Kay clung quietly to the margins, not interested in swordplay, hiding behind chivalrous manners in the company of the women his father arranged for him, living celibate as a priest. Other young men learned to heft a proper hunting bird like a peregrine or merlin on their wrists, but Kay carried an owl as if in defiance, much larger and very shaggy, its claws dug deep into the leather, its winged eyes inscrutably waiting for dark.

Kay's own large brown eyes were fixed on a point over his father's shoulder.

Is he merely insolent, or afraid of me? Sir Maurice wondered, not without a certain domineering pleasure.

'By God's mercy, *do* something!' he spluttered, kicking away his dogs, and climbed upstairs.

Again he glanced round, sensing Kay's eyes on his back.

But Kay was gone.

Does my son hate me? Sir Maurice unbuckled his sword as he climbed the next flight of steps, and then the thought slipped through his mind before he could stop it: exactly as I hated my own father?

The thought filled him with shame. He had loved his father.

Why am I the person I am? he asked himself, not for the first time. No one else doubts themselves like I do, no one thinks against their self as I do, or suffers as much as I do.

His shoes made a light shuffling sound on the timber floor as he came to the top, crossing to Katherine's rooms. No maidservant appeared and curtseyed to him, the ante-room was dull and empty. Taking the gift of silk he had bought in Southwark Market, he laid his sword on the table and reached for the latch of the inner door, then knocked instead. There was no reply. He knocked impatiently, irritated to come home and find her out. 'Katherine!'

He thought he heard a flurry of footsteps beyond the door, but it was not opened.

'Katherine?'

There was a sound like a window banging. He raised his hand and knocked again. Who was in there? Was someone with her?

Suppose he went in and Katherine was there, alone now but panting and terrified to see him, guilt written all over her beautiful face?

He lifted the latch and let the door swing open.

Katherine was lying in bed, the drapes half pulled to keep out the draught, the glorious counterpane depicting Jesus's Nativity and Christ's Passion in gold and silver thread pulled up to her chin. Her black hair was unpinned and lay across the bolster. She was quite motionless, as if dead, and his heart gave a quick thud of fear. Then her eyes fluttered and opened.

'I'm not well,' she said, moving her head to look at him. She gave a weak smile and tried to rise dutifully to greet him. Sir Maurice sat beside her, concerned, and Kate let him touch her forehead.

'You're not running a fever,' he said. There was a man's smell in the room.

'I feel a little better now,' she smiled.

God, she was still lovely, though his elder by nine years; she wouldn't feel her fiftieth year again. He could see dark streaks of hair dye on the bolster and she smiled with her mouth closed so as not to show her terrible teeth. But still her smile was bewitching, a cat's pouting come-hither-if-you-dare smile. She always had this effect on him: he wanted her. And yet they were not close, even in the dark, even when most intimate. Sir Maurice knew what men were capable of, including himself, especially himself, and because he desired her, he knew other men must desire her too.

She never shrank from his lust but embraced him eagerly, which always made him a little suspicious; and the more he desired her, the more suspicious he became.

But suppose it really was true, not just his fearful imagination?

'You're silly and possessive,' she scolded him as if she read his mind, then laughed weakly, her knuckles at her temples to show she was favouring a headache. 'Look at you, red to the tips of your ears with jealousy!'

'I'm not,' he muttered.

'I like it,' she said earnestly.

He gripped her soft white hand.

'I suppose you think you nearly caught me with a lover,' she chided him, then embraced him with growing strength. 'You're the only man who plants in my garden, husband.'

'I know that and I've never, ever doubted you.' Of course he had, but once he openly admitted he doubted his wife, where would he stop? He glanced at the open window.

'The draught cooled my fever in the heat of the day,' Kate said quickly. 'I feel better now. Shut it and come to me.'

Sir Maurice crossed to the casement and closed it without looking out at the flat roof below, because he was afraid of what he might see. Perhaps it was Jack. No, that could not possibly be, Jack would not have had time to run down from the woods.

He must stop thinking of Jack.

He turned. He felt as though he was hanging on to life by a thread; he could hardly bear himself. He swallowed repeatedly before he could speak.

'Your maidservant was not attending you,' he said. 'I thought – I thought—'

'Alice? She's probably off with the stable lad somewhere. I'll beat her if you like.' With a wink Katherine held up her arms to him, milk-white. 'You sent her away so that you could be alone with me, didn't you?' she reproved him enticingly.

He held out the silk he had crumpled in his hand, and it was on the tip of his tongue to tell her everything. But she took his gift with sparkling eyes as though it was the world to her, and as though he was too.

Sir Maurice closed his mind to the truth, closed the drapes round the bed, closed his eyes, and wrapped himself in her with a hot heart.

While his childhood friend willingly mistook some other man's sauce for the wetness of his wife's passion, Jack Fox was busy at St Thomas's Pool.

He did not look as if he was busy. Had anyone seen him, he looked to be peacefully fishing.

He sat on the tree trunk that had half fallen in the water, sucking a piece of straw comfortably in his mouth, and between his heels a line disappeared beneath the surface of the pool. The pilgrims who had left earlier would be struggling to reach

Crayford before dark, but it was perfectly peaceful here. Joan had finished marking tallies for the stock she would need to fetch tomorrow and gone home to clean the house – although they now had a servant girl for such tasks, since employing her Joan was never satisfied with matters of cleanliness. By now, Jack knew, Joan would be preparing a piece of rich fat bacon and the first peas of the season for his supper, which she did not trust a slut to do properly either. Joan had found a very waspish tone of voice now she had someone to boss about.

A slow smile spread over Jack's face as he jiggled the line. That just meant she bossed him less and gave him another shift to try his hand up. What a fine home he had, and what luxury he lived in, meat twice a day if he wanted, and the choice of mint or tarragon on his peas. He could even afford the expense of a pinch of saffron in his fennel soup! He had paid Vaudey's new freeman carpenter to add two rooms behind his house, one for Joan and himself with a proper bed, the other for Elaine, both with oak floors and glass windows, so that the old front of the house was now not half so fine as the back, which faced towards the woodland around the pool. Fifty acres was his own property now, more than any servile virgater's holding – it took more than half an hour for Jack to beat the boundary ditch of his freehold. He knew because he had tried it, timing himself by the church dial down the vale. And he never needed to go cap in hand to beg a favour from other men; he could afford to pay money, if the price was right. Jack's smile broadened. He would go to bed with a full belly tonight, rummage Joan cheerfully while he dreamed of the slut, and had every prospect of providing a fine dowry for his daughter Elaine. He was truly a free man at last.

And so, smiling, he sat with his rod in his hands in case anyone was watching, absorbing the stillness of the woodland, waiting until he was sure he was alone.

Jack was not fishing for fish.

Elaine finished shutting up the hut, yawning enormously and stretching her long body, then laughing at his protective frown. 'I don't think you're ever going to stop looking after me,' she smiled, then went over when he patted the trunk for her to sit beside him. They sat in companionable silence, her head resting on his shoulder in a cascade of nut-brown hair.

'Parson Briggs said he never caught anything here in his life,' she murmured. 'He said there weren't any fish in here, even when he put some fry in. Perhaps there's a pike who eats them, a patient old pike too cunning to catch.' His shoulder felt her head move; she was a wonderful mimic. 'His teeth toothy and his eyes slitty, and his scales too slimy to hold, as old as time.'

'You're making my flesh crawl,' Jack said.

She chuckled, breaking her own spell. She didn't really believe there was anything down there.

The warm sweet smell of her reminded Jack of his youth. 'Nut-brown maid,' he said. 'You be careful who you sit with like this,' he warned her.

'Why?' she said.

'Never you mind. Just don't you do it.'

Elaine laughed. She had her mother's slanty eyes, though a lighter blue, and she had Joan's way of looking at him straight in the eye, too. But her smile was entirely her own.

'I've been so lucky with you,' Jack said suddenly.

'But don't you wish I was a son?'

'Yes,' he said. 'Of course I do. But you aren't. And if I had a son, maybe I wouldn't have had you.'

'You're kind,' she said, then laughed as she got up, brushing the bark from her legs, and pointed at the line which hadn't moved so much as a ripple. 'But you're an unlucky fisherman!' She slitted her eyes, showing her teeth. 'Unless you catch *him*. Or he catches *you*.'

'Tell your mother I'll be home soon.'

Elaine waved over her shoulder.

As soon as she was out of sight, and he'd waited long enough to be certain no one else was about, Jack got down to business in the failing light. He measured the distance from the fork in the tree branch beside him with his elbow, then dropped the line into the water exactly below that point, weighted, hanging straight as a plumb. The straw fell from his mouth unnoticed, such was his concentration. He jiggled the line carefully, a hand's breadth from side to side, until it went tight, then lifted carefully, delicately. It stopped, caught on something, a tree root perhaps, or a stone, and he jiggled it until it was free. He looked around him, checking he was still unobserved, then pulled up the line quickly, hand over hand.

Perhaps, in a strange way, it was his respect for the water that had made him choose it as his hiding place. It was deep, twice his height or more, and he could not swim.

A big bronze hook appeared beneath the surface, too large and heavy to be a fish hook. Its generous curve held a stiff loop of rope which was attached to the top of a wooden box. Tying off the line on a branch, Jack lay on the trunk and reached down into the water.

His hand touched nothing. The box was not where his eye saw it. Neither was his hand. The water was playing tricks. He reached out further, as far as he could, his hair almost touching the surface, and pulled the box to him, scrambling backwards with it.

He sat on the tree trunk taking deep breaths, the box in his lap trickling on him, then opened it and wondered what Maurice had seen in the coins to disturb him so much. They were pretty enough, and Jack was grateful to them because they were the source of his fortune, they'd changed his life. When the St Thomas's Pool idea first struck him – he neither knew nor cared whether the family story passed down through his father was true – he'd used them as security to borrow against, risking the whole lot. But they'd paid off, and he'd repaid the usury. And now they drew people into the shop. But his mother had taught him it was wrong to be greedy and, a more practical consideration, Maurice's unexpected appearance had shown him the wisdom of caution, so now Jack returned half those he'd kept at the back of the hut, in the mistaken hope of a sale, to the box.

Despite the dusk, the coins seemed to shine brighter together, and he looked at them with affection.

Without the talents to get him off the soil, Jack knew, he'd probably still be breaking his back grubbing a living off three miserable acres, as his father had. He might well be dead by now, an exhausted, broken man like his father – Nicol had died at exactly Jack's present age. With Jack dead, Joan would revert to the servile status that had been her lot before marrying him, a free woman only as long as he lived; as Sir Maurice's property she would have to remarry whomsoever he chose, and pay the fine for it too. And what of Elaine? Jack could hardly bear the thought.

He had been staring at the coins for a little while. He began to notice that they were not all, as he had thought at first, identical. The more he looked, the more he realised how different they were. The one in the gold claw and chain stood out of course, the one which by tradition Maurice should have worn at his wedding, and Jack did feel a little guilty about that. But now he noticed that some of the coins were thinner that others, as if worn down by the finest sand, or cloth, or even skin. Worn by love, perhaps. Or by hatred. Was that blood he saw, engrained into the milling of one, its silver worn thin as paper?

The coins themselves were nothing, Jack thought. It was the use to which they were put that mattered.

And now, examining them in his fingers, peering at them closely in the gloom, he began to realise that even the ones in mint condition were not quite the same. Each one came from its own mould. Each of the finest craftsmanship. But each one was subtly different from its brothers.

Unique.

Jack yawned and slammed the lid. He didn't have time to care. The night was dark, Joan would be worrying, and she was quite capable of letting his supper get cold *and* giving him a whack from the wooden spoon, rich man or not, if he was late home.

He measured his elbow against the branch and lowered the box into the water at the exact place. When the line went limp he paid out a little more, then swung it to one side and pulled the hook up empty. On his way home he reached up and dropped the coiled line into a hollow tree.

As he hurried out of the woods, an owl hooted.

Sir Maurice, lying on his back with his eyes half-closed, sated but still dressed in his shoes and tabard and fustian, heard the owl hoot. He could not sleep and his hair shirt itched him without mercy. He wondered if Kay was out hunting.

'I wonder why God makes people so different,' he said, thinking of Kay, then grunted when Katherine tugged at him below.

'Because without it there'd be no children,' she said. He flushed, ashamed as his body responded to her.

'I didn't mean that difference,' he said coldly.

'No hope, no future, no laughter,' came her warm murmur. 'No pain, no suffering, no joy. We'd die of boredom.' Her eyes flashed in the dark. '*I* would.'

He sighed to hear her chatter. In bed, especially after they had

481

made love, Katherine was his equal; it was the only time they talked openly, and most of him hated it. Her point of view was always the opposite of his own, being a woman, yet so often she said things he had never thought of. Didn't want to think, perhaps. Tonight he had stayed with her instead of stumping off to his own small room and hard bed, and she drew him on.

'Even a child like our Kay? He wanders around looking thin and miserable as a woman.'

Katherine paused. 'I didn't hear you shout at him when you came in.'

'I didn't shout at him. He's nineteen and it's time he grew up.'

'Time he was a man,' she said dismissively, then worked on him subtly with her hands, softening her hard words with her caresses. 'You want him to be a man, like you. He's in awe of you, Maurice.'

'Good!'

She persisted. 'In awe of your frown, even of your smile.'

He preened himself, thinking of how everyone had been in awe of his father.

'Because of the way you behave with him. Angry and domineering. Not the man you really are.'

'Katherine, he hates me!'

'Kay doesn't hate you,' she whispered, her hands still now. 'He despises you.'

He spoke in a strangled voice. 'What do you mean?'

'You never talk to him,' she explained quietly. 'Only you know what he feels, Maurice. You've been where Kay is. Why do you never talk of your childhood? He is so much of you. Show him.'

'Show him what?'

'That you're not an ogre,' she said. 'Show him you're like him.'

She lay listening to his breathing. She felt him sit up and thought he was going to run away back to his room, as usual. Men were such little boys. Such dangerous little boys.

Then the bed creaked as he lay back again.

'I'm not an ogre,' came his voice.

'I know.' She kissed his chest, her lips feeling the raised outline of the Holy Cross embroidered on his tabard. She put her hands beneath to peel it off, wanting to be closer to him. He always took her while he was wearing his clothes, or a heavy nightshirt, and she hated the coldness of it, the distance, as if he was afraid of really touching her with his whole body, of letting her feel all his warmth. She knew he'd say something about sin and the Church forbidding love more than once a night, but more than that happened: every muscle in his body jerked away from her.

'Don't!' he cried. 'Don't.'

She stopped too late. 'God's breath!' she murmured, appalled by what she felt scratching her hands. 'You're wearing a hair shirt! You must be in agony!'

'Now you know,' he said.

He pulled the counterpane off her as he rolled over, turning away from her.

Katherine lay staring at where she knew him to be. She could not see him at all, and she shivered: she had thought her husband a soft, malleable man, but he wasn't. Beneath, he was as hard and mysterious as stone.

'Kay *is* like you,' she whispered. 'He's like you were – not the man you have become. You weren't born guilty, Maurice. You learned.'

But he didn't turn back to her. He lay breathing evenly, as though he was asleep.

'My life's a misery,' Elaine said, opening her heart. She knew she was letting her father and mother down, slipping from her room like this and flitting in the dark to her lover like one of the worst village girls. But still she did what she was doing, whatever the risk, driven by a force beyond her self-control. And although she was ashamed of herself, she was not sorry.

Her voice was low.

'I work all day for my father at the hut but nothing matters except thinking about you, because everything I touch feels of you. You're part of me, I dream of tasting you and feeling through your tongue, seeing through your eyes, feeling everything as though I was you. You matter more to me than I do to myself.'

They sat an arm's length apart on the old piece of wall by the headland of the Stonefield, where the meaningless fragments of mosaic kept emerging from the ground as the earth dried and shrank. Beyond the windmills the ground fell away into the Mickfield. Elaine sighed. The scurrying farmwork of daylight seemed almost infinitely distant here under the peaceful stars, the gleaming spray of the Walsingham Way arched above them like a huge saintly finger pointing towards Our Lady of Walsingham far to the north.

Elaine dragged herself back to earth. Kay's owl hunted around them in the dark, its beating wings invisible, heard but not seen.

He had not kissed her or even touched her.

'When I first saw you, you were so quiet that I thought you were nothing,' he murmured.

'I *am* nothing,' she told him earnestly, 'away from you.'

'You're everything to me.'

He reached out. She took his hand.

'Now I'm happy,' he said.

At first Elaine had been terrified of her own feelings and of Kay, knowing what was supposed to happen. She'd been on her own shutting up her father's stall at the overflowing pool one day last year, and a group of boys had come to douse their sunburn and sweat-matted hair in the cool waters, making the woods echo with their good-natured shouting and ducking. Arguments were sudden and violent, with fists and blood. Elaine's friend Adeline, whose brother Berry was always in trouble, said that afterwards, all friends again, the boys would turn on the girls, even the ones they'd been friendliest with. Most Vaudey girls knew it was better to give way than be raped, but giving way accounted for half the births in the village, and a few of the marriages too; plain rape accounted for a good proportion of the other half. Elaine's heart had bumped in her mouth as the bushes rustled in a shower of leaves, but when Kay's tousled red head appeared, they had just stared at one another as he disentangled himself, then he nodded and went past. On impulse she brushed a leaf off his shoulder.

Soon he worked out when Elaine would be there, and he would make sure he was there too, just happening by with his enormous brown eyes and his shy, curious smile. Kay wasn't like other men, none of them were as sure of themselves as he was, as strong. Kay did what he wanted, at peace with himself until he met her. They began to talk – no boy of her own age had talked to Elaine before, only at her. Casually at first, step by tiny step, they became friends. That was all they were. As if he would not be lord of the manor of Holywell one day, and she was somebody.

Kay could never belong to her, nor she to him.

484

Elaine would have given herself, if he had taken her; he had not, but she had given him her heart, quietly and without fuss. She'd said so tonight.

'I couldn't bear to be no longer friends with you,' Kay said simply. 'I'd die.'

Now he was at peace only when he was with her.

There was a flurry of wings and some small animal squealed. The sound spiralled away above them, fading.

On St John's Day the new priest, Father Sterre, refused to lead the ancient annual procession of villagers holding aloft flaming brands lit from the need-fire round the fields of corn. The Church's new breed of clerics no longer tolerated such pagan beliefs; heresies were everywhere and they were determined to overcome them. Few attended the church service held instead, but Sir Maurice, praying for rain, was one of them, sitting on his privileged bench in the chancel, with Katherine sitting beside him and Kay beside her. Behind them the nave held none of the usual infuriating murmurs and farts and coughs, it was almost empty of peasants, except one or two drunks lounging about who had forgotten what day it was. Sir Maurice looked anxiously at the altar, wondering if God would blame him for the villagers' non-attendance and send down a wind to ruin the crops. Damn them, they were spoiling everything, he'd fine them until their noses bled! And the pittancer would be given a note of their names, too, to hold against them when they begged for help. It was not enough to be needy, he told himself with desperate self-righteousness, they must be devout too.

'Let me keep Holywell, Lord, and I will never lay another wager again, ever, or borrow again. This is my oath.'

His shirt, woven from strands of horsetail, itched and scratched and prickled his skin at the slightest movement.

He twisted round, hearing footsteps. Jack was standing behind the screen, his head bowed in prayer, his shoulders padded out with fine clothes, his wife and daughter standing well-dressed behind him, nobodies, yet with the air of people of quality – except the daughter. He didn't know her name. Her rosy complexion did not suggest a diet eked out on oatmeal porridge, and she was tall but she held herself like a mouse, eyes downcast. Kay stared straight ahead, but Katherine twisted and looked round too, then sighed at her husband's obsession with Jack. Maurice was so tense that the tendons stood out in his neck.

'*Ite, missa este*,' Father Sterre intoned, ending the service.

Sir Maurice broke his oath, of course. The summer stayed so sunny and fine that the harvest came early, dried out, but because the wheat had to feed so few people since the plagues Sir Maurice did not quite suffer a disaster. The Company of Bakers in Billingsgate took his excess grain but still he had to go on up the road to Jewry, by the Tower of London. He had long ago sold the war horse that had carried his father's armour back from Najera; now he sold that proud suit of finest Milanese steel and all the memories it contained, and paid back his sympathetic moneylender enough interest to borrow a little more.

It would not be enough.

At the next session of the court-leet, Sir Maurice settled himself on the shabby, creaking dais of the great hall, with his beadle, steward, reeve and hayward ranked below him, and to one side the travelling clerk with a quill, who had arrived late. Kay sat like a pale shadow, supposed to be learning – this would be his duty one day. Sir Maurice groaned at the thought and knocked the boy awake. Kay must be awake all night, he thought irritably, for he slept all day.

The business dragged on as usual, petty beyond belief, but important because it allowed the lord to show his authority. Offenders who let weeds grow on their garden path or let their house fall into disrepair were fined a penny, someone guilty of cutting a branch from one of the lord's trees with an axe instead of pulling it down with a hook paid a fine of twopence . . . the list was long. Sir Maurice looked up as a latecomer arrived and stood at the back of the hall behind the serfs. It was Jack.

He wondered if Jack knew which villager had been sleeping with Katherine. Perhaps several men were cock-holding him, he fretted, taking their pleasure with her whenever his back was turned. Such was his worry that he rarely went to London any more but instead sent loyal Oliver Briggs, the steward, as his agent whenever possible. He looked at the villagers suspiciously, wondering if his cuckolders were here now.

Why was Jack here? The queue of dreary plaintiffs seemed to

486

grow longer, not shorter, and every time Sir Maurice glanced up Jack's eyes were still fixed on him. When at last Jack stood before him, Sir Maurice stared at him coldly.

'What do you want of me now, Jack?' he said.

'I be afraid of dying,' Jack said.

'You too.'

'No, not for myself, see, but on account of my wife Joan.'

Sir Maurice grinned nastily. 'How can that small matter bother you? I'm told you are the wealthiest man in the village now. Undoubtedly you can pay for prayers.'

'Yes, I know the way things work,' Jack said, 'but I want to be certain of something that works in this life, what I can see and touch. I mean what can't be revoked or fiddled about with.' Someone laughed, and Sir Maurice glared. 'See, if my time comes first, my lord, Joan will revert to being your property, and it's been dogging my mind.'

'Enough talk, get on with your plea.'

'I want to pay in advance to buy her freedom in her old age, just in case. And I want her manumission entered officially in the court roll.'

'Since you want to pay, pay you most certainly shall!' Sir Maurice's cold staring eyes made him look like a hungry fish. 'One hundred shillings!'

There was an audible gasp, but Jack came forward and paid up without a word, waited to witness the transaction entered in the roll document, then bowed and took away a white tally as his receipt.

Thoughtfully Sir Maurice watched him leave. One hundred shillings into the estate coffers, easy as pie – he should have demanded twice as much! Jack hadn't batted an eyelid, so he must have more.

Over the next few days and nights, Sir Maurice's mind clicked busily. What a shame Jack was unassailably free. Wealthy men who could be shown to be serfs were a rich source of income for an embattled lord; he could seize and claim them, their heirs and blood, all their lands and tenements, goods and chattels. Still, perhaps drops could be squeezed from Jack Fox somehow or other, for the good of the manor.

Sir Maurice had a word with faithful Oliver Briggs. Enquiries were made. Jack was found guilty of adding two rooms to his house without permission, hauled before the next sitting of the court and fined twenty pounds by Sir Maurice – and then fined another hundred shillings for being dressed in clothes above his class.

Jack paid. When he came home, he did not seem at all upset. 'See, I know why he's doing it,' Jack said, but that was all the explanation Joan could get from him.

She watched her husband suck his soup from a silver spoon, so sure of himself that he hadn't taken her into his confidence, and kept her own mouth shut.

Sir Maurice, Jack reckoned, must be all but bankrupt. The lord of the manor was a good and gentle man who wouldn't do these bad things from choice; men did bad things, sometimes awful things, because they were driven to them.

But when Jack was found guilty of walking along the balk of raised earth that marked the boundary between two holdings, that particular balk not having right of way as a footpath according to the custom of the manor, and he was fined according to his wealth in movable goods, assessed by jury then multiplied by ten by Sir Maurice, he saw red.

Jack hired his neighbour's horse and rode to London – he did not need Sir Maurice's permission for the journey, since he was free – and began making enquiries about his old friend, now his enemy. Moneylenders were a close fraternity and he met only blank stares in Lombard Street. The afternoon found him in Old Jewry and the shadow of the Aldgate, being fobbed of by the shrugs of poor-looking men with long side hair. But in Harts Horne Alley he struck lucky. Sir Maurice's name was known here, though not personally: a different man was described. 'Oliver Briggs?' Jack guessed. 'Tall, stern-looking, little hair but still dark?'

'Like a tonsure,' the moneylender said smoothly, 'as though a priest. A face one trusts.' Bowing, he took Jack's elbow and guided him into a room of the Hart Inn, staring at him with motionless eyes in a slant of dusty sunlight from the mullioned window. No drink was called for.

'And mine?' Jack said.

'Yours is a face of business.'

'Then I'll get down to business,' Jack said briskly. 'I'm not borrowing, I'm paying. I want to know how deep the lord of Holywell is in, and I'll pay to know.'

Jack left the tavern with his head reeling, and not from beer – and not because the sums the moneylender had told him were large, but because they were so small. To his great humiliation and at some risk to his estate, Sir Maurice had borrowed four or five hundred pounds. Jack was amazed. For this mean-spirited amount Sir Maurice had let the shingles rot on the roof of the manor house and the rain in, so that now all the timbers were going to the devil. For this, he was so small-hearted that he saved pennies by burning smoky tallow tapers instead of fine wax candles, as a man in his position should. For such a paltry sum, in his despair and self-contempt, Sir Maurice had sold his father's armour at a time of peace, when it would fetch a pittance.

'My brother in Smithfield,' the moneylender had added unctuously, with a flick of his finger, 'also advanced him a little something. Sir Maurice is a man who likes a wager, you see. He's not a man of spend and show. Wagers are his weakness.'

'How do you know this?'

'Money is blind, my friend. A moneylender must see everything.'

Jack rode towards home, cutting through Bermondsey to avoid tolls and footpads, then skirted Greenwich which had been sucked dry by the new lord of the manor, Sir Nicholas Brember. Coming to the path leading down from Vaudey to the ferry, he stopped to buy some fish and refresh himself at the Grange Inn, where he was greeted like a lord. Jack plumped himself at the best table and ate a platter of whitebait, looking round him with approval while he quaffed his ale – last year he had purchased an interest in the place, seeing the potential. From St Thomas's Pool he directed pilgrims journeying from Canterbury to other shrines to follow the path downhill, and here at the Grange Inn they would stop for a meal and a night's sleep, and a good simple breakfast too. In the morning the ferryman, who paid a commission to the inn, rowed them across to the Isle of Dogs, a pleasant place of meadows and pasture now the marshes had been drained, and they walked to the old tree shrine left high and dry on its islet in the middle, rebuilt as a chapel. Having offered up their prayers, and purchased a profitable memento of their devotion, they continued up the Ferry Road on their pilgrimage to England's Nazareth, the exact replica of Christ's house built by command of the Virgin Mary at Walsingham in Norfolk, and passed out of Jack's life – until the next year, when those who could afford it sometimes repeated the tour. And of course trade came back the other way too. Some of that pious lot were old friends by now, and they always left their money sticking to Jack's fingers.

He chuckled to think of it, then shivered, remembering Sir Maurice's despair, that terrible lost look in his eyes, and how they had once been friends. Jack's expression fell serious. This bad blood between Maurice and himself could not be permitted to run its course; Jack was not fool enough to think he could win against someone who, in the end, had all the resources of class and the law at his disposal.

He spurred up the combe to Vaudey and came home, throwing the fish cheerfully to the slut and even enjoying the inevitable arguing between the women that ensued, because they didn't have a copper large enough to poach them, or any almonds or ginger for the sauce. He stopped Joan's mouth with a kiss, so glad to be with them again that he didn't notice Elaine moping but gave her a kiss too.

The next day rained, but Jack walked down to the manor anyway. Sir Maurice received him in the great hall, no fire burning, wearing his sword.

'What is it this time?' he said. Jack diplomatically offered to lend Sir Maurice money until next harvest. Sir Maurice said he would see Jack roast in Hell for his insolence.

It would be a better harvest than last year. Sir Maurice depended on it.

Both men waited and watched from the fallow strips as the green shoots of wheat, rye, barley and oats emerged and began their yearly battle against weather, weeds and disease. Though neither man acknowledged the other, Sir Maurice stiffly riding by on horseback and Jack on foot with a straw in his mouth, both men were gauging the effect of every twist and turn of the sky on the coming harvest, the outcome of the wager that Jack, without putting it so, had made. In May rain fell, late but not too hard, and Sir Maurice wore a smile. In June the sun shone but not too harsh, and in July the weeds and thistles were pulled, but not so industriously that the crops were trampled.

While the two husbands watched the crops, their wives watched them. 'Children!' Joan snorted, hands on hips. 'I'm sorry, my lady, they're worse than little children, both of them is!'

'Silly little boys,' Lady Katherine agreed, not normally at ease with other women but now finding a warmth of companionship where she had least expected it. 'I don't think they ever grow up – the Lord be thanked,' she added beneath her breath, thinking of her lover's ardent pranks. 'They can't see what really matters even when it's held up plain in front of their faces.' They looked through the window to the lane, where Alice the maidservant held Lady Katherine's horse, and Kay and Elaine earnestly ignored one another. 'If they turned, those two,' Katherine snorted, 'they'd bang noses!'

When Katherine left, Joan watched her ride away with admiration. Lady Katherine calling by her little house and sitting at her table! She'd held herself beautifully, her skin too delicate ever to have worked, and rose perfume had graced the air around her. At first Joan had been flustered out of her wits by the unexpected visit and almost knocked over a chair as she curtseyed. But Katherine, having noted the silver mugs and plates, and a fine new copper generous enough to poach the largest salmon, didn't stand on ceremony. She came straight to the point. 'How much do you know?'

Joan's first instinct had been to play the innocent. 'About what's that, my lady?'

Katherine frowned impatiently. 'About the only thing of importance, of course.'

Joan swallowed. 'You mean about my Elaine?'

'And my Kay. My only son, your only daughter.'

'She could never even dream of marrying so high!' Joan burst out.

'But the dowry she would bring . . .' Katherine had sighed, looking again into the lane. 'And we see what we see. It would be a love match. But our husbands do not see it.' She turned back with a smile.

The eyes of the two women met. They understood one another

491

perfectly. Money would marry breeding – with love as a bonus for the youngsters. Both families would benefit from the arrangement.

'I'm sure there must be a way . . .' Katherine purred, and Joan lay awake that night, scheming pleasurably.

In the drowsy afternoons of August, the ears of standing corn, too fragile for a man to walk among, turned first golden then gradually darker, almost ready for the scythe. About two weeks before the harvest the wind blew in the night, shaking the roofs, and no one slept. When they peered out at first light, they saw the crops lying flattened as though by sweeps of a great hand. The grain would rot if left on the ground, and so had to be harvested where it was, with great difficulty and labour, and fed to the pigs.

Sir Maurice sat on horseback, watching the rows of toiling peasants. His windmill had blown down, the centre post found rotten through, so he could not have ground his flour for his bakers to bake anyway; the private millers and bakers would take over that work, and they would feed his peasants and get their hooks into them. He left without a word.

Jack walked to the manor house for the second time. He was kept waiting in the passage, then Oliver Briggs came out past the iron-studded door.

'Hello, Jack.' The two men were friends, but Briggs's loyalty to his master was absolute.

'Tell him,' Jack said, 'tell him I'll buy the Stonefield from him, freehold.'

'He never will,' Briggs said.

'Tell him, Oliver, that's all.'

In no time Briggs returned, looking amazed. 'It's yours. He's demanding a high price, but—'

'I'll pay,' Jack said.

In the next months Jack nibbled up several holdings as they fell vacant with folk moving to London. Now he was in, he paid a lower price each time, and took only the best land, touching nothing that would not yield his farm labourers twelve bushels an acre. The woodlands were encroaching on the village now, and as the dwindling numbers forced Sir Maurice to charge his villeins the same rents as the free men, undergrowth took over first the poorer strips, then whole fields until even the Mickfield lay fallow for a second year, and London grew fat.

One morning Sir Maurice, the daily service in his own chapel long discontinued and his father's deaf and blind old chaplain dismissed from his pension years ago, rode to matins. His brain buzzed like a swarm of bees, and he was no longer quite sure what he was thinking. He stopped as he found Father Sterre tugging at his stirrup.

'You!' the priest shouted. 'You and this stupid feud! It's your fault!'

Sir Maurice looked around him at the confusion which he had not noticed. 'I told you,' bellowed Father Sterre's unpleasant voice. 'We warned you for years. Your fault . . . your fault. . . .'

The oak tree, said to be as old as the village, planted by St Tyrell, and which everyone had been too superstitious to chop, had finally fallen across the churchyard and where the church roof had been lay a tangle of branches and beams. Jagged cracks ran down what could be seen of the walls, crushed timbers poking through the windows. All the precious glass was gone, exploded outwards among the headstones like a glittering, multi-coloured frost. The stone tower was unharmed, but what remained of the nave and chancel held up the massive trunk at an angle. The smell of earth and splintered wood hung on the air.

'I didn't even hear the wind,' Sir Maurice murmured.

'There was no wind,' someone said, and Sir Maurice felt the eyes of the crowd on him. He had never seen so many coming to church as came to see its end. The stonemason, wearing his tools in a leather apron under his belly, waddled forward. He didn't even bother to lout, being a free man from Somerset, and Sir Maurice wanted to strike him down, but he felt too weak.

''E'll 'ave ter be rebuilded in't stone, now, zir, woan 'e?'

'Not by me,' Sir Maurice said.

'I'm sorry for the way I spoke to you just now,' Father Sterre said. 'I was upset. Forgive me.'

'The firewood is mine,' Sir Maurice said. 'Remember that.'

He rode back towards the manor house, then dismounted and walked the rest of the way. Everything made perfect sense to him. Not only everything that had brought him down, but everything else, life itself. His life, anyway. Sir Maurice saw himself clearly. One man, one life, one chance.

493

The church would be rebuilt, he supposed. But not by him.

Coming into his house, he took a deep breath and ordered Oliver Briggs to bring Jack Fox to him.

It was evening before Jack could be found; he came forward into the shadows of the great hall, his feet crunching on the rushes, until he saw Sir Maurice sitting on the stone steps that rose behind him to the upper part of the house. Damp streaked the walls. Jack shivered, wondering where the draughts came from, then realised the arras tapestries had all gone.

'My lord, you sent for me,' he said at last. The feud between them seemed suddenly very sad.

'No, I asked for you to come.'

Jack cleared his throat. 'If it's about the Mickfield,' he said, 'I can't afford your price.'

'Come up here, Jack, and sit down beside me.'

Jack stared. Sir Maurice smacked the stone with the flat of his hand, sending the echoes clapping around them. Jack went up beside him, sweeping his coat beneath his buttocks against the coldness of the stone, and sat.

Sir Maurice heaved a sigh. 'Jack, promise you will tell me truly.'

'I will whatever I can, my lord.'

'What did you see that night, at the church?'

Jack was surprised. 'But I saw nothing.'

'The truth, now.' Sir Maurice turned his head slowly and looked at Jack.

'Nothing!'

Sir Maurice groaned. He rested his chin between his bent knees, looking down between them as if noticing his feet for the first time.

'Your life's turned out so well for you, hasn't it, Jack? Everything you wanted.'

Jack waited for him to say more, but there was no more.

'Yes,' Jack said. 'Yes, I suppose it has. I've worked hard for it,' he added.

'Did you steal them?'

Jack stood up. 'I think we've talked enough.'

'Oh, I don't care about it any more.' Sir Maurice picked at the loose threads on his shoes. 'I'm like you, Jack, I don't care. I have no soul. I hear nothing. I see nothing.' He looked up, moving his head slowly, as though it carried a great weight inside it. 'Sit

494

down. Jack.' Then he shook off his lethargy. '*Sit down!* Listen.'

Jack sat.

'Jack, you'll never own the Mickfield,' Sir Maurice said, 'but your grandchildren will.'

'I'm sure I don't know what you mean.'

'It's been right in front of our eyes and we never saw it. When did you last look at your daughter's face?'

'Elaine?' Jack was baffled. 'I see her every day!'

'Really look and see her. We don't, do we? The ones we really love. We don't see.'

'You're a long road ahead of me, Maurice.'

'My wife tells me that my son wants to marry your daughter.'

Jack swallowed; it was exactly as Joan had dreamed, but he had not believed it possible and scoffed at her. Now it had come true. 'Kay and my Elaine?'

'Elaine is not your property any more than Kay is mine. But they and their children will inherit this property. If you agree.'

'My own girl will be Lady Elaine,' Jack whispered. 'I can't believe it.'

'Have you not seen them, Jack? What fools we've been. They're in love.'

But Jack's brow furrowed, his sharp business brain probing for the catch. 'What dowry do you want?'

'Five hundred pounds. That clears the estate of all debts. They will come into it free.' He gripped Jack's elbow. 'Now talk no more of money.' But Jack's mind was still working busily: such a marriage was made in heaven, much more that he had dared figure on for Elaine, but what could go wrong? Might the Church forbid it? He counted on his fingers the eight generations that separated Kay from their common ancestor, Sir Jeffrey, and the dividing of the Fox family's bloodline between the manor and the soil. Seven generations lay between Sir Jeffrey and Elaine; once that would not have been enough, marriages being forbidden between kinsfolk to the seventh degree, but nowadays canon law allowed marriage after the fourth degree. Jack tapped his fingers. Through Eleanor, his own mother, Elaine's grandfather was Sir Rowland Fox; she was related to him in the second degree. Kay was Sir Rowland's great-grandson, related in the third degree. The Church wouldn't allow it.

'It won't work,' Jack said.

'Father Sterre is not a local man,' Sir Maurice said. 'He will not know what he is not told. More than half my serfs in the village are intermarried by now, and who do you think would dare stand up and gainsay me?'

Jack drew a deep sigh. 'Then let Kay and Elaine marry for the good of both of us.'

'No,' said Sir Maurice. 'Let them marry for love.'

The wedding was held in the spring, the most popular time. All sixty families of the village of Vaudey would wait outside the chapel wall, by permission of the lord of the manor, to cheer the bridal couple, and Elaine's tall figure and train would be attended by bobbing bridesmaids, anxious, preening girls who would be allowed to keep their posies and striped silk underwear – for weeks their mothers' fingers, dirty or fine, had worked in a frenzy of stitching and Englishwork to prepare for the day.

On the morning of the wedding, Jack led a wheezing donkey to the manor house and paid the dowry in gold. It was all the money he had and all he could raise, but nothing but pride showed in his face.

'There will be no bedding ceremony,' insisted Sir Maurice privately, coming out into the hot sun on the drawbridge, frowning at the rusty chain. His manner was calm, but Jack saw a strange light in his eye. 'After their betrothal they will be escorted to the house I have had built, where they will live in peace, left to themselves, until my time is past.'

'Your time won't be past for a long time,' Jack said as politely as he could.

'Sooner or later,' Sir Maurice shrugged. 'Sooner or later, Jack. There's no distance between us and our children at all.' He pinched his fingers to demonstrate. 'Not the smallest gap. I know everything they must be feeling, don't you?'

Jack walked the poor blown donkey home rather than ride. No, he didn't know what Elaine was feeling; looking forward to getting cleaved, he supposed, remembering himself rutting like a pig with Joan and how she'd said it was fun, drawing him on; but they'd got married a few months after because she kept crying and Jack was soft-hearted at root. Elaine had lived like a nun for more than a year to get Kay, as far as he knew.

To save time going through the village, he cut across the knoll on the balks dividing the Stonefield on his right, taking pleasure in his own possession, checking that the barley and vetches were being properly sown in the finely-harrowed soil. The Nymfield of the demesne lay to his left, where the serfs were busy at their demeaning work. Sweating, furnace-shouldered ploughboys were working the strips after the pulling of the last winter vegetables. Will Norris's son Wat whipped his team to show he was the reeve's son and would be first to turn at the headland and complete his furrow. It was late in the season for such heavy work and the lord's oxen staggered under Wat's lash, lathered under the midday sun, enduring the first real heat of the year.

By his house Jack put the donkey in a stall until the air should cool and went into his house. Elaine was sumptuously dressed, her hat wimpled and veiled by finery reaching almost to the ceiling, so that she had to duck double, guided by bridesmaids, beneath the low doorways of Jack's house. That would not be a concern, he thought, through the arched doorways of the manor house or its chapel.

'My daughter, gone up in the world!' Jack said, hugging her, wondering why she was crying. 'You're a real beauty, you are. A sleeping chrysalis what's turned into a beauty of a butterfly. My Lady Elaine.'

'Not yet,' Joan said, consumed with nerves now that the scheme she had laid with Katherine last year was so close to fruition, terrified it would fall through at the last moment. 'Don't count eggs afore they're chickens, Jack Fox.'

'Why's our girl tearful?' Jack demanded.

'Because I'm happy!' cried Elaine.

'Get out of our way.' Joan fussed her husband to the door. 'We've got confession and prayers and there's a crease down the back of her dress . . .'

Jack went outside scratching his head. That haunted look in Sir Maurice's eye came back to him, and suddenly the reason for it struck him: the coin in its claw that the eldest son wore on his wedding day, the tradition broken by Sir Maurice and now by Kay.

Jack saw how he could bring even more happiness to this happy day.

Quietly he strolled off, as though passing time, up the lane. As soon as he was in the woods he hurried, then paused to listen. There was no sound but birdsong and the flutter of blackbirds foraging among the dry leaves.

He reached up into the hollow tree for the hook and coiled line hidden there, then looked around him carefully. Seeing nothing, he slipped between the oaks to St Thomas's Pool.

As soon as Adeline pulled away from him Wat Norris knew how it was going to go: she was going to run, she was going to scream, because he didn't have his friends with him and she thought she stood a chance. Wat was heavy but he was not slow. He came after her in three quick paces, his wooden-soled boots crunching on the acorns the pigs and squirrels had missed in these quiet, sacred woods. He reached out for her, but as he grabbed her her dress tore and the material slipped through his sweating fist. She was almost free, elbows pumping, but he pulled his boot back on her ankle, tripping her. That dealt with the running. She lay stunned on her face in the moss, her hair flown about her. He flipped her on her back so she couldn't scramble, then dropped on her. She came to herself and clawed his sunburned back, slick as a fish in his grasp.

'Lovely,' he said, slapping his hand over her mouth to silence the scream. He put his face in her ear. 'When a ploughboy's work is done, all 'e wants is 'is bit o' fun.'

She lay still, so that he wouldn't kneel on her.

'Good girl,' Wat grunted, seeing she knew what would happen now. He unlimbered his breeches with one hand, sliding himself out of the sweaty leather, muzzling her lips with his panting mouth. She twisted her head aside, closing her eyes.

'I won't fight you,' she whispered.

'I knew you liked it,' he said in contempt. 'All they said about you's just right. Open for business, whore.'

But then Wat looked up, hearing dry leaves rustle, and he dropped his weight on Adeline so that she could hardly breathe, crushing her motionless and clamping her mouth again with his hand. Jack Fox was coming through his wood, looking around him – right at Wat; it seemed impossible he would not see him.

But then Jack strode on unconcernedly, and Wat stared as he

shuffled out along a tree trunk half in the pool and dropped a hook into his reflection in the still water.

Wat gazed at what Jack pulled out.

Opening the lid, Jack took something shining from the box. He closed the lid and lowered the box back into the water. Reeling in the line, he looked around him again, then strolled from sight whistling softly.

Wat Norris forgot about the girl.

Whistling innocently, Jack crossed the great hall of the manor, almost empty now that everyone was assembling outside the chapel entrance. Kay was in the hall, sitting for a last few minutes alone. That earnest, pale young face didn't notice him at first, then he jumped up, his manner wretched.

'You are a yeoman of the shire, sir,' Kay said, 'and in a few minutes you will be my father-in-law. You are a man of business who understands how matters stand or fall, I think.'

'What worries you?'

'I'm afraid of letting my father down,' Kay said simply.

'By marrying my daughter? Not likely!' Jack said cheerfully. 'All you've got to worry about is deserving Elaine.'

'I don't,' Kay said miserably.

'Wedding nerves.' Jack held out a goblet of wine in one hand, and while Kay drank, reached round and lay what his other hand held quietly on the bench. 'For better or worse, Elaine believes in you,' Jack said, 'and that's all that matters. She loves you, so be someone for her. There's nothing else.' He took back the goblet, finished it off with a smack of his lips, and belched.

Kay watched him go, and cringed, remembering his father's voice: *They're peasants! How can they know anything of themselves? The estate is clear and free of debt, that's all that matters. And they're ours now – she's yours, Kay . . .*

Kay loved Elaine and she loved him, but his father's voice ranted in his memory, the endless childhood confrontations, trying to stiffen Kay's backbone, obviously considering him weak. In the end Kay believed him.

But Elaine . . .

Kay sat, then jumped up with an exclamation, staring down. He understood immediately. Jack had stolen them after all.

Kay gazed at the claw and coin gleaming beneath a mess of gold chain on the bench, then picked it up and rested it in his palm.

The usher put his head round the door. It was time. 'Wait,' Kay called, about to drop the chain over his head. He changed his mind as a better thought struck him, and went out with his neck bare.

The ceremony in the chapel was small, almost private, and after the oaths were taken and gifts exchanged, and Kay and Elaine were husband and wife, he stopped her kneeling for prayers and looked into her eyes, noticing for the first time the faint, deep flecks of blue in them. How little he really knew of her.

'I love you,' he said.

Sir Maurice witnessed the look on their faces, and his own was pale as death.

Kay took the talent and hung the chain round her throat. Made for a man's physique, it hung long, and the coin rested in the cleft between her breasts, drawing his eyes down there.

'Kay,' she murmured, and the colour flushed into his cheeks.

'Let us pray,' Father Sterre intoned sternly in Latin. The Church laid down that marriage was not to be physically consummated until three days were spent in prayer and fasting, and as far as he was concerned it would not be.

Kay and his wife came out hand in hand into the sunlight, received the bows of the most important people in the line waiting at the foot of the steps, the steward and the reeve and the hayward. Behind them the villagers beat their hands and threw up their caps half-heartedly, then touched their knives ready for food. As the wedding party passed, only the oldest villagers understood what Elaine wore and applauded the tradition. The younger women turned their mouths down, thinking it rather a poor piece of jewellery.

Will Norris, prodded in the back by his wife, was looking aggressively around him for his son. Unlike the boy to miss the opportunity for filling his belly; but as he searched the crowd he realised Wat and the lads who trailed him everywhere were not to be found. Mrs Palin was also calling for her daughter, Adeline.

Adeline lay as still as though she was dead. Wat Norris shambled away from her, still half out of his breeches, scratching himself thoughtfully as he stared into the water. The scarlet weals torn by her nails stood up on his sunburned shoulders. She hardly dared breathe in case he turned and saw her, and remembered what he was about.

The smell of the leaf mould and decay was very strong where she lay. She could not open her left eye for the dirt; one-eyed, snot trickling down her nose from her tears, she watched as Wat came to the tree trunk in the water. His muscles bunched as he pulled himself up.

Adeline wondered if she could run.

Wat bounced, testing the strength of the wood, then walked along the rough bark and stood leaning on the branch, looking down into the water below him.

'Fall in,' she prayed, then remembered that he could swim. Stupid Wat Norris wasn't afraid of anybody, not even Jack Fox. No quick splash in the shallows of the Hollingbourne for him after a boiling day's work; if Wat wanted a swim, he swam, Jack Fox's private property or not. She'd always admired that sort of disregard for others before, and in the village she'd even let him notice her looking at him once or twice. But though Wat's brain was stupid, his muscles were clever. They rippled beneath his skin like oil. She realised he wouldn't fall.

Wat's hair dropped over his face as he stared down.

Adeline inched backwards. She felt a root beneath her knee. Now part of a tree trunk obscured her. She pushed herself back and risked wiping her left eye, then scrambled to her feet, one shoe missing, her dress torn, and limped away. After a few paces she tried to run.

She almost escaped.

She bumped into the chest of her own brother, Berry. He caught her to him. 'Eh, what's this, Adeline?' She struggled frantically; Berry never went anywhere on his own, and she glimpsed figures gathering around her. ''S Adeline!' Berry cried. He shook her then gripped her at arm's length, looking at her in disgust, his mouth half open. ''Ee's dirty as sin, Adeline, and where's 'ee lost 'ee shoe?' He frowned. 'What's 'ee done, girl?'

Adeline wept.

Nick, Hector, Roger and Tom Briggs were all boys she knew. And here came Dickon following on behind as usual. 'Look at that ''un,' Dickon whistled. She hated their smiling faces.

'Adeline, our mother'll kill 'ee,' Berry said, letting her go as she was pulled by the others.

'Berry, you go piss in the trees,' Dickon said.

'I don't mind,' said Berry, scratching his neck and following them.

'Where's Wat?' laughed Nick. They had a skin of ale with them.

''Ere!' called Wat from the trunk, still staring into the water.

'Pulled her through the 'edge arse back'ards, Wat did!' Roger said.

'Ay, wed 'er good'n proper,' Wat bragged, but his mind was on the pool. He stripped off his breeches, showing himself dark and shaggy like a bull where it mattered but white as a virgin about his hips. 'Your keep 'eeselves busy, lads.' He plunged into the water, gasping pleasurably at the cold, then duck-dived and did not reappear for a long breath.

'What's 'e doing?' Hector squealed, holding one of Adeline's feet as the youths wrestled and grunted over her, but looking over his shoulder backwards. 'There 'e is!'

Wat came up shaking drops of water from his eyes. He hung onto the trunk, heaving deep breaths. 'There's something down there. 'Ector, 'ee'll 'ave to wait to take turn with 'er. See if 'ee can find a 'ook and line what's hidden.'

Adeline, writhing free, crawled towards Berry. He backed away. 'I'll look,' he offered.

She shouted, 'Berry!' He turned and walked quicker and didn't look back.

Hector blew out his cheeks, relieved.

In the background Wat splashed and dived.

Adeline lay still. The tree shadows moved on her face. Roger covered her and she held his head close against her own so that he would not hurt her unless he really tried.

Wat surfaced, spluttering. He hung onto the bank and snorted water from his nose. 'It's down there,' he said. 'A box, but deep, and caught under a big stone or something, what's got shapes on it I could feel.' He sucked the finger he had skinned trying to lift the stone.

'Give it the Wat Norris ox-heave,' Tom Briggs said, keeping his eye on the girl for his turn. She looked at him with the tears running from her eyes, and he felt a twinge of shame at what he was going to do to her, but he couldn't back down in front of the others. Tom was a free man, son of Oliver Briggs, whereas the others, even Adeline, were servile, and he had to keep their respect.

Berry shuffled back from his quest. 'Can't find nothing,' he called, holding out his empty hands.

'I'll do it the hard way.' Wat Norris took a deep breath and plunged, his white arse bobbing bright then showing as a pale, wavering shadow going down beneath the black water.

Sir Maurice looked up at the dark sky as he and Jack escorted their son and daughter to the edge of the knoll. He wondered how the clouds above them could go one way while the wind blew across from the other direction, bringing a sharp tang of London smoke with it. Kay and Elaine's house, a pretty dwelling with mullioned windows and properly seasoned and tarred half-timbering, had been built a short way downhill near what the local people called the Sabrina oak. The name, if name for the tree it was, had been scratched simply in the bark, more enduring than a carving in stone. Now more than thirty feet in girth, the Sabrina oak was supposed to be older even than the tree that had fallen on the church, if that was possible. Sir Maurice doubted it; these days folk legends abounded everywhere, each more fabulous than the last, grown no doubt from only an acorn of truth, if that. But last night his sleep had been haunted by a dread that the tree would fall and enmesh the young lovers in their wedding bed.

Sir Maurice thought he was going mad. But as they came to the edge of the knoll and looked at the Hollingbourne cascading down its gully past the house, he could not help eyeing the tree and mentally calculating trajectories and the angle of fall. The clouds blew against the wind. Lightning flashed over Essex.

'How small London looks!' he said.

Kay embraced him. 'I shall see you in the morning, Father,' he promised, but Sir Maurice's eyes were fixed on the chain leading to Elaine's breasts as she reached up and kissed her father goodbye. He watched them leave with his face as white as death.

Jack and Sir Maurice walked back to the manor house without a word, then, at the drawbridge where Jack would turn for home,

Sir Maurice stopped him with a hand on his shoulder.

'*You* gave it!' he said.

'I don't know what you're talking about.'

'Then swear to me for the last time, Jack, that you saw nothing and you didn't steal them that night.'

'Nothing,' Jack said.

'Give them back to me,' the knight pleaded. 'Perhaps when a new church is consecrated. They could be left quietly beneath the altar. Nothing need be said.'

Jack bowed, his face perfectly blank.

Sir Maurice watched him set off for home. 'Nothing,' he said to himself. Life had given Jack everything he wanted, and he took it all for granted, even perfect health. Did Jack Fox ever get down on his knees and humbly thank God for all that he had been given? Not likely.

Nothing.

Sir Maurice, rubbing his ear, crossed into the great hall. He had told Katherine that he would pass the evening at prayer in the chapel. No one was in the hall, only his hunting dogs scavenging among the scraps. He drew his sword and raised it as they fawned around him, then lowered it slowly. He could not bring himself to kill them in cold blood any more than he could have killed himself.

He touched the blade, and flinched. He had not sold his father's sword. It was too heavy to carry for long in one hand, well-balanced but more than three feet in length, each honed edge of Damascene steel sharp as a barber's razor.

Sir Maurice carried it slowly upstairs, step by step.

Katherine's voice carried to him, then her laughter.

At the top he saw two people, a young man and a girl, listening at the door. They were giggling and for a moment Sir Maurice could not for the life of him remember their names. Tristan and Alice. Of course. His page and Katherine's maidservant.

'Who's in there?' he said calmly. He watched them run, then waited until he could no longer hear their footfalls.

Sir Maurice opened the door and stepped inside. Closing it behind him, he crossed the ante-room. The laughter was louder now. Katherine's, and a man. The man's laugh was deep and familiar.

Sir Maurice reached out his hand and the door seemed to open

504

by itself, swinging slowly. The two people standing by the table in Katherine's bedroom with their backs to him did not notice him at first. The small of Katherine's back was a delicious curve picked out in tight-laced velvet, the man's strong fingers casually holding her there.

Oliver Briggs towered over her, the light from the window shining across the top of his head. For twenty years he had been Sir Maurice's estate steward, for twenty years his loyal and most trusted right arm.

The door creaked and they turned as one.

'Alice! I told you—' Katherine stopped. She put her hands to her mouth. 'Maurice,' she said.

She moved forward. 'We were working on some papers,' she said, and gave her high, excited laugh.

'Don't,' Oliver Briggs said. 'He knows.'

Katherine turned savagely. 'Don't tell him anything!'

'He *knows*,' Oliver Briggs said, looking along the sword calmly. He must have known this would come one day, but that hadn't stopped him. He reached out his arm and held Katherine back. 'I couldn't help what I felt, my lord. Everything I have done for you, I have done to be with her.'

'My love, don't,' Katherine begged.

Oliver Briggs said, 'It's true.'

Sir Maurice held up the point of the sword and took two paces. Oliver Briggs grabbed at the blade but it slid through his hands, through his breastbone, effortlessly into his heart. His fingers hung limply, the tendons severed, but his palms clung to the blade. He groaned as the broad brass pommel thudded against his ribs, and Katherine screamed. Sir Maurice let go of the weapon and her shrieks rose. Tottering backwards, Oliver Briggs tried to turn towards her and plunged through the window.

The room was suddenly brighter, though showing only the dark sky and the crumbling ragstone battlements surrounding the flat roof below.

The wind set the papers rustling.

Suddenly Katherine rushed to the window, dragging herself away when Sir Maurice tried to pull her back. Scrambling onto the sill, tearing her dress and legs and breasts on the jagged glass as she slid over, she fell near her lover.

Through the window frame Sir Maurice watched her pull herself onto her elbows, dragging her broken bones painfully the few paces to where the body lay outstretched, and cradle in her bloody arms the man she loved.

Sir Maurice jumped down, putting out his knee in a brief flare of pain, and limped to her.

He stood listening to her weeping.

He looked around him at his property, all that was his.

He lifted Katherine in his arms and walked with her to the battlements. The drawbridge was far below. She clung to him with all her strength, afraid he was going to throw her over. But he went with her. He walked straight on as though there was solid ground beneath his feet instead of nothing.

They went down through the air together, over and over, holding each other as tight as they could.

Sir Maurice remembered Gemma.

All that is given, take with cheerfulness. To wrestle in this world is to ask a fall. Here is no home; here is but a wilderness.

Sir Maurice remembered being in love.

'Your turn,' Roger said. 'Come on, Tom, show some balls.' He staggered over to the fallen tree and hung against it to show how she had taken his strength.

'She's crying,' Tom Briggs said.

'And it looks like rain,' yawned Dickon. 'Oh me, oh my, I might get my arse wet.'

'She's not crying, she's all right,' Hector said, offering himself hopefully. 'I'll keep 'er dry.'

'Any of 'ee lads seen Wat?' Nick's voice called from the water's edge.

'She just lies there,' someone commented scornfully.

'Her name's Adeline,' Tom told them firmly.

'Who cares what 'er name is?' Nick called. He pulled his smock over his head, the only other one of them who could swim. 'Wat can 'old 'is breath long enough to down a quart of ale.'

'And kiss the wench blue afterwards,' Dickon called. It was Wat's favourite brag.

''E's been down near that long.' Nick plunged in. Dickon wandered over with Roger, and they sat on the tree trunk to watch, swinging their feet over the expanding ripples.

Back in the trees, Hector twisted Tom's wrist. 'I'll do 'er, if 'ee's not man enough,' he whispered viciously, 'and I'll make sure it's known 'ee was the odd one out.'

Tom got on her.

'I'm sorry,' he murmured, stroking her eyebrows. 'I can't help it.'

Wat looked up. The pool was deep and everything was distorted, not quite where he thought it was. The surface was a dim and silvery circle shimmering overhead and seemed very far away, but everything else was terribly close, enlarged as though by a dark glass. His hands passed in front of his face, enormous, his fingers wrinkled like an old man's.

He grabbed at a root to hold himself down, missing the first time, then held tight. His body kept trying to rise.

The box was still snared under the ledge, the loop of rope squashed flat so that he could not get a grip and he could not reach in far enough to get his hands round the back. But once Wat started something he never stopped, and he had a reputation to keep up.

Pulling himself down, he slipped his legs between the old rotten roots and caught again at the edge of the stone, his bare feet squeezing down into the ooze as he took the strain.

He straightened his back, hauling with all his strength, giving it the ox-heave.

Something moved.

The stone lifted a finger's width. He pushed his fingers deeper to get a better grip. A hand's breadth now. Bubbles came streaming past his face, marsh gas or trapped air flushed from beneath the stone, or even his own breath leaking with his enormous effort.

A shadow moved past him and someone grabbed his shoulder. Nick. Wat bobbed his head at the stone, and Nick nodded, looking comical waving his arms, his cheeks puffed out and his feet higher than his head.

Nick pulled himself down on Wat, who arched his back, the muscles standing out across his shoulders like a chain.

Wat gave the stone his strongest ox-heave.

Nick lunged underneath to grab the box.

Suddenly the stone turned up easily, coming up far larger than Wat had imagined, longer than a man, rotating as its far edge twisted deeper in the silt, falling away.

The screaming stone face of a devil-god rose up between Wat's arms as though it would drop on him.

Wat fell back, then overbalanced forwards as the stone tugged him down with its weight. He slid helplessly over the dreadful stone as something gave way below.

Bubbles thudded in his ears.

Nick's legs kicked. They stuck out, trapped beneath the stone, kicking and jerking like an insect's legs. More bubbles gushed out. Nick must be screaming. The bubbles tailed off to a thin streak.

Then there was nothing except his legs still kicking, and his shoes hanging off. One of them drifted away.

Wat saw a silver coin lying in the silt, thrown from the box by Nick's struggles.

He stared with bulging eyes at the clouds of silt flowing over the coin, being drawn away beneath the stone.

All the mud and ooze and silt that had been thrown up was being sucked down beneath the stone, he saw, and clear water was being swept after it, and now pebbles and pieces of chalk appeared beneath Nick's thrashing legs.

There was a deafening roaring sound. The box was whirled away. The coin lifted suddenly, then flipped over towards the stone.

Wat grabbed it, and kicked for the surface.

'You can't think much of yourself,' Tom said.

'Let me run,' whispered Adeline to his face above hers. 'You don't have to be like them. If they catch me I'll say it was my fault, not yours. I'll say I hurt you.'

'Then they'll make me hurt you more,' Tom said.

'Give me the chance, that's all I ask.' She threw a terrified look at Hector, but Hector had turned away as Wat's head and shoulders came out of the water.

Wat's face was white with fear and horror. He whooped for breath and threw something on the grass. Still whooping, he hung onto Roger's foot dangling from the tree trunk.

'Hoi, get off it,' Roger whined.

'Something's wrong,' whispered Tom to Adeline.

'Nick,' came Wat's voice, coughing, then he belched vomit. 'Stuck.' With a savage look he dragged Roger into the water.

Roger tried to haul himself out on Dickon's legs. 'I can't swim!' they heard him squealing.

'One arm round the branch, tight.' Wat hit his friend with his fist and Roger sobbed. ''Ee pull up when I pull down'ards, right?'

Hector laughed from the grassy bank. 'Nick's stuck?'

Wat went down without a word. Roger hung onto the branch with chattering teeth, submerged to his nipples.

'Nick's not really stuck, is 'ee?' Hector called.

Tom whispered in Adeline's ear, 'Roots, mayhap.' Then he pursed his lips, coming to a decision, and drew back from her. He nodded at the trees. 'Go on. Go!' he hissed.

But before Adeline could move, Wat's head burst from the water. 'Christ!' he shouted. 'Christ!'

Rain began to filter through the trees.

Wat whooped a breath and went back under.

Hector pulled the hood of his smock half over his head to keep himself dry.

'Jesu, help me,' Roger cried, wrapping both arms around the branch as he was jerked down, then jerked again. Beneath the water Wat must be lifting Nick, pulling on Roger's legs.

The branch bent.

Roger looked terrified. He stared around him. 'Dickon!' he wept, and Hector ran along the trunk to help him, grabbing his clothes as Dickon was tipped forward by the angle of the bough.

Roger wriggled, trying to kick Wat off him beneath the water.

On hands and knees on the grass, Tom and Adeline watched open-mouthed as a broken twig began to drift in the water round Roger, round and round.

Nick's ankles stuck up motionless from beneath the stone. Silt and weed and pebbles rolled towards the gap, speeded up, were wrenched down.

Wat grabbed one warm ankle in his right hand and clamped his left arm round Roger's legs.

But instead of pulling Nick out or lifting the stone up, Wat was being dragged down.

He gave a mental shrug and let Nick go. Nick's legs rushed then squeezed into the gap, his flesh rippling and quivering. His kneecaps caught, then they were gone and even his feet were gulped from sight.

Nick was gone.

I've drunk the quart, Wat thought doggedly, and the wench has kissed me blue. He'd had enough, just hanging on was taking all his strength, his head was spinning and the urge to fill his lungs with sweet air was all that mattered to him. His mouth opened with a desperate effort and he looked towards the surface.

His feet were drawn towards the stone by the current.

Wat kicked.

The silt gave way beneath him and the water rushed down. He clung to Roger's legs with both arms. His bare feet were sucked against the stone, then into the gap.

Wat kicked, breaking his toes on the stone.

He looked up, still kicking, smashing his ankles, his mouth gaping wide for air.

The bough broke and they were all plunged into the dark.

The overflowing pool had ceased to overflow, though it was raining heavily now.

'What happened?' Tom said, aghast.

He and Adeline stood on the edge, the rain plastering her hair to her shoulders.

'Whose is this?' Tom picked up something silver lying on the grass, a coin.

'Who cares?' Adeline said.

They looked at the water. No heads bobbing up.

'The level's going down,' Tom said. He faced up to it. 'They're dead.'

But still they waited.

Nothing happened.

'What will we say?' Tom asked. The warm rain had turned cold and their teeth chattered. It was growing dark.

With trembling hands he draped Adeline's sodden clothes over her shoulders.

Lightning flashed, sending a huge illumination down through the trees, white and black. After the thunder, only the hiss of rain falling around them.

White streams were cascading into the crater from uphill, but still St Thomas's Pool was draining down almost visibly; the grassy banks, once flush with the surface, stood up like muddy walls, and ancient roots began to stick through the surface.

Eventually they sheltered in the open-fronted hut, water streaming like a curtain from the thatch. 'It's going to take days,' Tom said.

'What is?'

'Before we find their bodies.'

'Good,' Adeline said.

'One day, it'll look as if everything we knew wasn't here. All this.' He shivered. 'What are we going to do?' he said helplessly.

There was a crack as the tree in the water dropped further, its weight no longer supported.

'We was never here today,' Adeline said, deciding for him. 'We're going to forget we was ever here, that's all.' She put her finger firmly over his mouth. 'No one would believe us – and would you want them to, anyway?' She looked at him. 'Would you, Tom?'

'Adeline,' Tom said after a while.

She put her head on one side.

'I believe in God and the Devil,' Tom said. 'I do believe in them.'

All night the rain fell. Kay lay with Elaine, listening to its sound, feeling he had been made a man by her love, happy and not alone for the first time in his life.

Down the gully by their house, the Hollingbourne had lost half its force, carrying only the run-off from the knoll. The lovers were too bound up in each other to notice its muted note, and would not have cared if they had.

Up at the manor house, Maurice, Katherine and Oliver Briggs lay in the chapel, where their bodies had been carried by the order of Jack Fox. And he had given strict instructions for silence about the dreadful accident.

'Accident!' Tristan exclaimed and looked at Alice. They had been given the task of washing the faces.

'Accident was what it was,' Jack said. The truth was best hidden. 'They fell, that's all. Sir Kay and Lady Elaine are not to know. Not until morning.'

No one need know the truth.

Jack went home. He didn't want to think about anything at all. He kept his mind blank by worrying about his business affairs, but still he could not sleep. Something was wrong. Something that had been with him all his life had gone; he could feel its absence.

Below him in the vale the village slept with full bellies this happy wedding night, three hundred and three souls in all, the tapers glowing in a cottage where a child lay dying, and further along the lane a woman in labour, her mother with her.

Further down near the centre of the village, in their old dark houses, old men and old women lay apart in their dark rooms, never fully awake and never fully asleep, waiting for the dawn of a new day.

In her dark house Mrs Briggs lay cursing the clouds that obscured the moon, fretting for her husband Oliver and her son Tom, and both of them for boxed ears when they got home.

Will Norris sprawled in his dark bedroom beside his wife, their snores drowning the weary crying of the new baby in its cradle, and their grown-up daughter snoring too among her brothers, and all of them happy that there was more room without Wat so they didn't all have to turn over when he turned.

First light found Jack Fox staring from his window. The slut pushed past him with a simper, but this time Jack ignored her, then sent her irritably to fetch bread from the baker. When Joan came out yawning, he was still standing there.

'The stream's stopped running,' he said. 'I wondered what it was. It kept me awake.'

She ran her fingers through her hair to comb it.

'But it can't stop,' she said.

Jack turned slowly. 'You're right,' he said.

He threw himself out of the house and ran uphill, not waiting for her running after him, though he heard her calling his name. Breathless now, he ran through the trees until he saw St Thomas's Pool ahead of him, then stopped, staring.

Nothing was left, only a huge muddy crater dotted with tree roots and long-drowned trunks. Very small fish flapped in the remaining pools, drying in the sun, and the fins of a great old pike circled the largest pool, round and round, exploring his shrinking, shallowing domain.

The streams feeding the crater ran away under the mud. Jack jumped down but his precious box was nowhere to be seen.

'It's gone,' he shouted when Joan arrived. 'Gone! Gone!'

'So that's where you hid your hoard. Good job you kept seven of them things back,' she said, practical as always. 'Pity you didn't keep them all out. How many you lost?'

'Eighteen,' he said, knowing nothing of the one Wat had thrown ashore. He cheered up a little, remembering his gift to Kay. 'I suppose I could always ask Elaine for that one back.'

'You dare,' Joan said. Then she put her hand over her mouth as the implications sunk in. 'The pilgrims won't come here without the pool, will they, Jack?'

Mullioned sunlight poured through their bedroom window over Kay and Elaine, who knelt by the bed praying together for the joy of it, not in hope or fear of anything, or for anyone, but simply for the happiness they felt. She wore a gown of pearly damascene silk worked with figures, his gift; Kay, who could never be persuaded to wear the fashionable colours of each year, wore black with small trimmings of white fur, and a short black cape.

Her hand held in his, they went outside. Around them the pale grass was steaming in the early slants of sun, men working already in the Mickfield holdings. They crossed the stream, which was very low, and took the path uphill to the knoll.

More men were gathered by the muddy channel of the Hollingbourne across the Stonefield, scratching their heads, and Elaine now followed behind her husband, obedient in public, as his wife.

The manor house stood tall and ungainly in front of them, its shadowed side towards them, one rusty chain of the drawbridge glinting. 'Walk beside me,' Kay said, holding out his arm.

'What's 'appened to the stream, master?' one of the men called. 'There's something fair funny about it.'

'I heard the ground shake,' said one man who lived a little apart from the village.

The others chuckled, but one of the old men said, 'I heard it too, though my ears aren't so good. Rumbling, like.'

'Like something below,' said the first man. 'Magic.'

'A sign,' the old man said wisely. 'Whose been sinning?'

'Not I!' said a youngster, flushing bright red.

'Best get Father Sterre to tell you,' Kay smiled, letting nothing spoil his marvellous day, but the men rubbed their lips at the mention of the priest's name.

'What does 'e know about the fields,' one muttered. ''E's too clever, that one, 'e's a book-reader.'

'Look at the headland on the Stonefield,' pointed the old man. 'That old spring's started up again, what my father used to speak of, and his holding were no good when it went dry.'

'But I did feel it shake,' grumbled the franklin, who lived on a freehold outside the village bounds.

'One of 'ee's stupid,' said the youth, giving him a hostile shrug, 'and the other of 'ee's deaf.'

'But I can feel it now,' said the old man, 'and I can hear it, too.'

As Kay and Elaine walked on, Jack, looking flustered, his shoes splashed with mud, hurried from the manor house and came towards them across the drawbridge. The rusty marks on it were not rust; they were blood. His face was terrible, with dark bags under his eyes like a man who has not slept for a week. He bowed to them.

'Sir Kay,' he said simply, 'Lady Elaine.'

Kay understood at once. 'What—'

'There's been a terrible accident,' Jack said.

'Listen out!' somebody yelled. 'Can't—'

The men behind them shouted, then scattered in all directions. One of them dropped headlong into the old stream channel and clawed his way out covered with mud.

Where they had been standing the ground bulged up as though pushed from below, the tussocks of grass separating, showing gaps of stones and dust, then wet black soil bubbling up between them. In front of Kay and Elaine and Jack the patchwork mound subsided then blew upwards in a fountain of water, the falling drops dousing them all. A big block of masonry heaved up slowly, then broke into pieces as it thumped down.

Kay bent and picked one piece up, turning it over in his hand.

'Mortar,' he said. Mortar, deliberately mixed and set, but crumbly with age. One side still bore the whorled marks of wood-grain, where the wet mixture had been poured onto a plug of timber. There must have been a hole in the ground here once, and it had been stopped deliberately. He saw no sign of the timbers, they must have rotted away, probably centuries ago.

Kay crumbled the mortar between his fingers. 'I never knew this was here,' he said. The mortar contained tiny pieces of tile and mosaic, like those the ploughmen cursed everywhere in the Stonefield, and organised their children to throw away.

Kay took off his wet cap, getting drenched in the fountain of water. He laughed, and Elaine, watching him, began to laugh too. They stood watching the water spout into the air, surrounded by grief, with their heads turned up to the sky and the fountain pattering down on their faces, laughing for the wonder and joy of it.

'*I never knew this was here*,' Sir Kay Fox marvelled, crumbling the Roman mortar in his hand as he stared at the fountain spraying from the smooth grass he had walked over a thousand times, solid ground; and he understood for a moment how little people really know of where they have come from, and what has gone before them.

He gave instructions for the fountain to be plumbed, and when the weighted line was blown out by the rush of water, he ordered a pole thirty feet long to be thrust into the hole by three strong men. When they struggled he helped them, soaked to the skin and laughing. The pole went down as far against the water as they could push it, then rose up into the air like a spear when they had to let go.

'More than thirty feet deep,' Kay said.

'Bottomless!' the men said, and that was what they told around the ale-house, and so that was what people believed.

Kay and Elaine's son Peregrine, a clumsy sickly child, grew up a handsome man, but the infected bones of his club foot never would knit properly. He married Joy Briggs, Tom and Adeline's daughter. Joy was the first of several in the Briggs family to carry that name, and her smouldering red-haired prettiness matched her hot temper, so different from quiet, thoughtful Peregrine who loved her uncritically; but she never let him down, and did what she could to ease the awkwardness of his foot. Rather than endure the steep stairways of the manor house, he and Joy lived quietly in the Sabrina cottage.

Kay had the decrepit manor house knocked down and gave

orders for it to be rebuilt while he was travelling in Spain and Italy. Peregrine oversaw the work with a practical eye for detail so fine that it must be inherited, or so the herdsmen who watched him said, understanding bloodstock. They were reproved by the new priest appointed by the Bishop of Rochester, who told them that since the gift was a marvel, it was God's will. Peregrine limped in agony around the construction site personally shouting orders – much of the seasoned oak for the heavy timber beams, bressummers and curved tension braces, beautifully worked by the freemen carpenters now living in the village, came from the tree that had fallen on the church. The stones were picked from the Stonefield, formed long ago, some still with mosaic clinging to them. When Kay returned from Florence he had a stone pool built around the fountain, similar to those he had seen abroad, and a conduit led over the edge of the knoll so that the old gully by Sabrina cottage took the overflow just as, it seemed, it always had.

Raising money where he could – usually from Jack – Kay, with Elaine, saw St John's parish church rebuilt to the glory of God, rising up white and new in the vale as though it would never age, and would stand for a thousand years. Three decades passed before the work, after wars and delays, and running out of money, was complete – time enough for the lower stones to have weathered grey. It was worth the wait. Despite the heavy Norman tower nothing like the tall windows and slender pillars of the new, enlarged nave of the church had been seen by most parish folk before. It was provided with a gallery for the orchestra and benches to seat the worshippers so that they could not so easily slip out to the alehouses at the top and bottom of the green. Sir Kay and Lady Elaine sat at the front in fine woollen clothes and high caps, readily seen and setting an example, and prayed with humility in the source of their pride.

St Thomas's Pool was never filled in, but sometimes Jack Fox could be seen staring sadly into the overgrown green hollow, as though something had gone out of his life. He never felt so lucky again, and though his fortune grew he never lost his nostalgia for the old days. At first he cursed himself for all the talents he had lost, imagining the opportunities he might have made with them – he was not quite sure what, but they might have brought him more than he already had. He could never be satisfied. He moved his business to London, but after Joan died of cholera he just sat in his house listening to the street below. Few in Vaudey would have remembered him now. He lost his money as easily as he had won it, then evaded his debts by ending his days at a ripe old age in the Marshalsea debtors' prison in Southwark, halfway between the Tabard Inn which sent in his ale and roast meat, and St George's church which took his soul. The Abbot of Bermondsey was an honest man and Jack's body was sent home to Vaudey for burial as he had written in his will, and what personal possessions he had not sold were laid into Elaine's hands intact. Among them were seven silver coins. She put them away in a safe place, but only the talent she already wore in its golden claw round her neck, Kay's gift, was ever precious to her: his love. Elaine, quiet, virtuous and dutiful, praying in the church in sure and certain hope of the Resurrection with the growing numbers of her children and grandchildren gathering around her, had long had all she wanted from life.

And when she died, she knew she would live for ever.

People never change. Their babies were born, the children grew up and grew old, forgot and were forgotten. The land settled on their bones, moss and frost and sun erased their names from the stones.

The land did not change, because everyone thought it had always been as they saw it now, with their own eyes. Some old men said the fields had once been cut up into tiny strips, and everything was different. But the stones never changed, or the sun on bent backs, or the white snow of winter. Hedges grew up along the balks between freeholds to stop their owners' sheep and cows wandering, and as the freeholds multiplied so did the net of hedgerows, until it seemed the land had always been like this, a fretwork of green ribbons round the vast acreages of open, ancient common. And across the river, the Isle of Dogs had always been that rich pastureland spied in the distance all people's lives.

But the Thames was rising, pushing its tides even past Westminster now, and when the embankments collapsed the Isle of Dogs was once again marshland, and the chapel stood on its mound with water lapping at its door. Soon it had always been that way.

London never changed, growing on its accumulation of rubbish above the Roman streets and buildings preserved ten, fifteen, now twenty feet below each new layer of roadworks and new buildings lifting above the old. The work of the Roman stonemasons, and the generations of farmers and businessmen who came after them, were long forgotten as London stretched from the two hills along the highways that covered the wall – too tough to knock down, and anyway long submerged by debris – but the great, many-times-great grandchildren of those folks, spreading like a single heedless, instinctive organism, swallowed the villages outside so that they, too, became Londoners.

Soon even the ancient gates fell, or were copied until the copies fell to decay, and were forgotten. No one remembered St Paul's with a spire to scratch the sky, its point often blunted by cloud on a dull day, struck by lightning and gone; generations of people believed its short blunt tower had been built that way from the beginning. Plague and fire swept London as always, and soon people felt as though St Paul's with a dome, fading dark with soot, had stood for ever. It was part of their lives.

London Bridge was still falling down, as it had been throughout the last two thousand years, though this last one had lasted for fully one-third of that span of time. Icebergs had swept away some of its arches, but they were always rebuilt, and many times fire almost destroyed the structure, but it was always set right. There was talk of knocking down the houses and shops to save the broken backs of its ancient arches, which were held up by Roman stone from the demolished gates, but there had always been such talk.

And the Tabard Inn never changed; it grew as Southwark grew in the good times, and held its ground in the bad times, a steep pile of roofs rising in every direction above its filthy, swarming stableyards surrounded by shacks, hovels, and oil-houses for lamps. In the street outside were the well and the pillory as they had always been, but fewer pilgrims arrived to hire a horse to Canterbury, or returned with a 'Sign of St Thomas' hanging from their necks. By the time St Margaret's church on its island opposite the inn was suppressed and turned into a courthouse, no pilgrims remained and only the sign over the road remembered them: 'This is the Inn where Sir Geoffrey Chaucer and the nine and twenty pilgrims lay, anno 1387.'

518

Sir Harry Bailey's ownership of the tavern passed to the Mabb family, who threw the Wittles on the street; but Ebenezer Wittle, whose father ended his days sweeping the yard of the Soldier and Citizen (known as the Salutation of an Angel and Our Lady in those papist times), kept his eyes open. After John Mabb died in 1582, Ebenezer wheedled himself a job at the Tabard with Mabb's widow, and when he convinced her he knew what he was about, Good Queen Mabb felt free to live in Bull's Head Alley near the Bear Garden, the theatres, and her playwright friends. She kept her share in the Tabard but spent no money, so the timbers cracked, and the roofs of the haylofts and attics became as bent as her own spine. After she died her son put the place up for sale and Ebenezer, who had been skimming the profits for years, bought the Tabard for £124 in partnership with the local Preston family. The dark-parlour, the hall, the dining-room and the Great Parlour were all rebuilt with Preston money and extended, as were the outside staircase and the rooms on the first floor. The Corner Chamber and the Middle Chamber, Master Hussy's Chamber and all the other new rooms were stuck on or built up wherever there was space, as trade required. Further up lay the New Chamber, the Entry Chamber, the Flower de Luce, Mr Russell's Chamber, the Knight's Chamber, all with cock-lofts over them, and garret windows sprouting from the split shingles of the roof. Around the yards far below, warehouses were added, and stables, and rooms were rented out to smithies, and stores to grain merchants or oilmen. A deep coal hole was dug, revealing a warren of forgotten cellars, soon put to good use filled with casks of sack, claret, and port; an oven house was built to ease the risk of fire, and stables were added and had oat lofts and haylofts put over them. Carriers and carters who came from Westerham, Cranbrooke and Benenden in Kent, and soon as far away as Lewes, Petworth and Uckfield in Sussex, lodged themselves four to a bed at the Tabard, and their cargoes in the yard.

Within a few hours one windy Tuesday in the month of May, five hundred Southwark houses were consumed by flame. Only part of the Tabard could be saved by blowing up, with gunpowder, the tenements cramped and crowded between its walls and the walls of the Queen's Head further along. As the fire spread from across the street Wittle's children and grandchildren scampered out of back windows, slid down the roofs, toppled to their deaths or horrid injury; the courthouse in the middle of the road was blown up, but still the fire came rushing over the street, leaping between the overhanging storeys, flashing the market stalls to flame, igniting debris from the explosions and even the horse dung lying on the roadway. At the last moment before the fire would have blown across the Tabard and into St Thomas's Hospital which lay behind, a change in the wind saved them both.

The City of London paid for a new Town Hall in place of the court-house, and a statue of the King for its colonnade. The homeless poor must make do as they could; villeinage had ended but the Poor Laws begun, and the rich would not owe to those they did not own.

The Tabard, with much scrimping and saving, and money got however it could be come by, slowly rebuilt its destroyed timbered frontage in fireproof brick, but the rear quarters remained as they had been, ancient, timbered, cobwebbed, a dirty maze of attics and cocklofts and murky corners and stairs down and stairs up, and creaking rooms where Mr Wittle had sired his dead children, and now sired more.

In the year 1619, Don Orazio Paz, a proud and pointy-bearded grandee, whose family had long been loyal in the imperial service, sat in the gilded stern of a galley sweeping him from Whitehall Stairs between the eel boats, their nets raised on long poles, and sculls and pinnaces crisscrossing the Thames like insects in every direction. His sensitive nostrils picked out the stink of the queen's weed, or tobacco as it was called, drifting from the teeming shores and the fishermen who watched them pass. Don Orazio had a long aristocratic nose and he looked down it at the brown, blotchy water, wishing his young wife would leave her undignified position by the rail and return to the raised, padded chair, almost a throne, by his side. But Donna Gloria adored London uncritically, almost to the point of being unpatriotic. Her father's years as a favoured captive at Watersmeet in Devon (scandal had it that Don Juan Delgadillo de Spes was the true father of Sir Lionel Barronet, the noted English sportsman and parliamentarian) seemed to have left their mark. Don Delgadillo had doubtless filled her childhood with stories of his happy stay in this country and infected Donna Gloria with a love of the place. She even wore her dress in the English style, hanging well-nigh from neck to the deck without folds, displaying her bosoms liberally, with tight sleeves and no waist at all. He sighed, but it was Donna Gloria's saint's day, and he had promised her a change from the ornate tedium of the Residence.

He cleared his throat, unable to tolerate her back turned to him any longer.

'Donna Gloria!' he said loudly, and she jerked from the view she found so interesting. Her eyes faded, then she pushed her broadening hips between the creaking arms of the chair, and sat like an icon at his side. The less she was given to do, the more she ate.

'Remember who you are,' Don Orazio said rapidly in Spanish – he could speak not a word of English. 'People will judge your country by you.'

'They can't see us out here!' she said irritably, and twitched the bowing servant a nod for another sweetmeat, candied orange wrapped in marchpane. Don Orazio tried to work at his papers.

'Oh, look!' she cried, pointing along the inlet of the St Mary Overie dock, infuriating him by knowing everything before he did, 'that's His Grace the Bishop of Winchester's palace, you know, that poor old man we met last week – or the week before that.' Don Orazio compared the tumbledown structure, which looked like a cross between a shambles, a pigsty and a prison – all three of which in fact it was – to the shimmering episcopal palaces of home. 'When the Protestants were in power they tortured Catholics there,' Donna Gloria said.

'Appalling barbarians,' Don Orazio grunted, but she chattered on.

'And when the Catholics were in control, they hung Protestant bishops up on hooks and burned them with red-hot irons.'

'Excellent,' grunted Don Orazio.

'Monks were put in cold oil and boiled,' Donna Gloria said. 'Are you listening?'

Don Orazio stared her. There was something very strange about his wife.

'A lady should not know of such things,' he said, and she huffed. She was young enough to be his daughter and Embassy life bored her silly. The gulf between them was as deep as between two different countries.

The loyalty of old Don Orazio Paz to his King, and his unrepaid loans to the imperial treasury, had been rewarded two years ago by his appointment as Spanish Ambassador to the Court of King James. He could well afford the huge expense. His retinue was dazzling, his rowers sweating in scarlet velvet, their muscular legs encased in hose of finest white silk, their shoulders glittering with gilt as the dignity of Spain required. Don Orazio's grandfather has bought shares in a small but hopeful mining venture in South America, called Potosi. Potosi was now the largest silver mine in the world, the Eldorado. But as always with Eldorados, the more silver the labourers mined, the more the price of silver fell. The agents had not passed on this small fact to Don Orazio, and he would not have listened with understanding had they done so. A gentleman was always a gentleman.

Now that she was freed from the cage of the Embassy for a day, Donna Gloria could not keep her face stiff and formal. 'How fascinating everything is!' she exclaimed, trying to interest him as they slipped safely beneath London Bridge, it being slack water at high tide. Even so, he pulled her back beneath the canopy in case the people on the bridge spat down on them. Spain and England were now officially at peace, but only yesterday one of Don Orazio's staff had been caught by a mob and rolled in the mud, lucky to escape only with bruises. 'What a wonderful, busy country!' Donna Gloria cried.

Don Orazio thought of the fragrant, clicking orange groves of home, the harsh perfume of heat and dust.

He thought of his first wife, Esmerelda, and his eyes burned.

'It is dirty,' he said with distaste, 'and they are a dirty people.' He dipped his quill, turning his attention to the report he was writing on the mother-of-pearl inlaid travelling table in front of him. London appalled him. Even under their sniggering Scottish King, the English were a race of thieves and heretics – dirty thieves and heretics. They passed the stinking tanneries of Bermondsey, and then on into Rotherhithe where Donna Gloria pointed out another old palace, now in busy use as a pottery beneath a billowing chimney. The willow trees were all being chopped down to feed the fires. The ambassador thought such lese-majesty entirely typical of such a race.

'This people is very badly off for water,' he wrote, 'although they have an immense supply. They raise it artificially from the stream even by windmills, and force it into all the fountains throughout the suburbs, but it is so hard, turbid and stinking that the odour remains even in clean linen. In the heart of the city, however, they have fountains supplied by conduits, where the water is clear and tolerably good. Thither flock great crowds of women and porters, who for hire carry it to such houses as desired, in long wooden vessels hooped with iron.' He stopped, realising Donna Gloria was reading over his shoulder.

'But it's not like that,' she said, so upset that she alarmed him. 'You've missed everything out! How they run and call and slop their water about, the way they skid on the corners and push and shove at one another, how they try to trip up their friends! And how cheeky they are, Don Orazio, and how they pop the coins in their mouths for safekeeping when they are paid.'

He looked at her sadly. 'The longer I know you, Donna Gloria, the less I understand you. It must be your English blood, not only the difference in our ages, that sets us so far apart.'

'But I haven't got any English blood!'

'Your joy in all things English, then.'

She squeezed his arm, and Don Orazio realised he sounded jealous. He could hardly keep up with her. She must be so unhappy.

The breeze off the water was cool, and he snapped his fingers for her heavy woollen shoulder-cape to be brought, then turned back to his work. The first highly delicate, and secret, negotiations for the possible marriage of the Prince of Wales to the Spanish Infanta had begun.

The falling tide more than the efforts of the rowers was sweeping the galley rapidly past the huge dock called the King's Yard, then the jumbled shipyards of Deptford and the tall mast-house, a vessel being warped beneath it to be shipped with new masts, the old ones rotted perhaps, or lost in a storm. Such chaos, so organised! Donna Gloria knew all the names of these places – there had long been seafaring links between Devon and the busy ports and yards beneath these hills. Here, not in Plymouth, Francis Drake had first learned seamanship. She pointed as the roofs of Greenwich came into view beneath the park, now enclosed by an enormous redbrick wall behind the redbrick, riverside palace of Placentia, Duke Humphrey's tower still standing above on its high green knoll. All that her father had heard described during his captivity, Donna Gloria now saw in the flesh.

She wondered when she should tell her husband her secret.

Don Orazio was still engrossed in his work. She reached up and touched the large, intricate silver frame of the brooch on her left breast. Inset in the florid Potosi silver, at the centre of a star of diamonds, was a precious emerald, white inside, carved with a bas-relief cameo of her likeness, as though she had been mined from the earth.

The jewel was the gift of Don Orazio. It was cleverly hinged, like a locket, and the compartment held the gift of her father. In there was the most precious thing.

The most precious thing. Dying, her father had murmured those words to Donna Gloria in English – just as the young English wife who had loved him in his prime and bore his English son at Hellebore House had whispered it to him, perhaps. It was Rebecca Barronet's parting gift, pressed into his hand by hers the night he stole away from Watersmeet. She had known they would never meet again. She even put up his headstone in the woods, the Barronet family, for their crimes, not being allowed onto consecrated ground.

And so Don Delgadillo had smuggled himself away, coming home to Seville a hero, and a hundred fathers competed to offer their daughters' hands in marriage. He married Donna Maria in 1593 and Donna Gloria was born three years later. When she was eighteen her bright spirit was betrothed to the greatest local widower, Don Orazio Paz, still in the depth of his grief for his first wife.

The galley swept them slowly down Greenwich Reach, the knolls and combes of Vaudey rising above the marshes. Don Orazio wrote busily. A case of plague had been reported there last week, and she wondered if he knew.

Donna Gloria touched the image of her face with her thumb. The emerald moved on its hinge, and beneath it she saw her *fortuna*, as Don Orazio called it. But Donna Gloria always thought of it by the English name her father had used, sliding it into her hands from his deathbed: her talent. *The most precious thing*, passed down in the Barronet family for generations.

To Donna Gloria, remembering her father, it meant simply love.

She picked up a sweetmeat between her white velvet fingers and pushed it into her mouth. She wiped her lips on the back of her glove.

Donna Gloria had not married her husband for love. She did not love him now. She drew deep breaths into her lungs. In fact she hated Don Orazio. He stifled her, so that even sitting out here beside him in the windy air on the wide Thames she felt as though he was suffocating her.

Mudflats had thrust through the falling tide, and on one she saw the beached remains of Captain Drake's ship. The *Golden Hind* had sailed round the world and returned home laden with looted Spanish silver and aromatic spices. The hulk looked exactly, she thought, like the sun-bleached ribs and bare skull of a dead horse.

'Orazio,' she burst out, 'I am to bear your son.'

Don Orazio did not display even the compliment of surprise.

'You are with child?' His mouth turned down. 'I thought I was too old. . . .'

She shrugged. 'You underrated yourself.' She hid her satisfaction: the less he was interested, the more influence she would have over her child. 'Or perhaps you underestimated me,' she added coldly.

He ordered the boat turned round at once, the rowers plugging and sweating against the tide, and instructed the servants to erect screens – it was most important a pregnant woman be kept out of the air. 'It may not be a boy,' he admonished her through pinched lips, 'and it will not be born in London.'

Don Orazio was wrong on both counts.

The child was a boy, and Juan was born in London. The family did not return to Seville until he was three, when English was already set into him as his first language. As Don Orazio passed into old age, Donna Gloria got her wish, bringing up her son in the way she had determined upon. After Don Orazio's death, the family's income declined rapidly, the silver mines pilfered and exhausted, no investments made to replace them; Juan worked in the colonial office from necessity where his father had from choice. The emerald was sold and the silver setting melted down, but not the most precious thing; Donna Gloria insisted.

In his old age, in the company of Esteban his grandson, Juan toured England and visited Hellebore House, remembering all his mother had told him long ago; but since fighting the English Civil War on the losing, parliamentarian side, the Barronet family had fallen into eclipse with the restoration of King Charles. Sir Lionel Barronet's heir showed his well-spoken Spanish guests very amiably round his house with no idea of their connection to him, and sufficient treasures remained in the warren of rooms that Juan, ever the diplomat, saw no need to mention the provenance of the silver amulet worn by Esteban.

Spanish diplomats' hopes of a Roman Catholic king of England were dashed by the Glorious Revolution a few years later, and as Spain's alliance with France flourished, Esteban and his sons found their careers sidelined in Madrid. They spent the time usefully, making money and building influence, and Esteban's grandson Eduardo became an experienced and wealthy diplomat, though employed only in minor postings. Then, at the age of fifty and the peak of his powers, the long war with Britain ended abruptly, and Eduardo Paz found himself smartly appointed the first English-speaking Spanish Ambassador to the Court of St James for many years.

The year was 1783, and since his wife had died he brought his daughter Esmerelda with him to satisfy the social protocols. Esmerelda was a brilliant girl, ravishingly beautiful but easily bored, and she knew her mind when she fell in love. She married an Englishman, a Devon man who had come to London to make his fortune, Mr Summers, a fabulously wealthy speculator in City securities. They were married at the Ambassador's country residence in Hampstead Lane, called Spaniards. At her smooth neck, white as a swan's, Esmerelda wore a gold locket on a finely-woven chain of gold. Flick the hasp open, as Mr Summers did on their wedding night, and it revealed her face painted very prettily in miniature on a coin-sized circle of china, smiling with eyes as brown as her hair beneath the glaze.

'Beautiful, but not as beautiful as the original,' said Mr Samuel Summers Esquire (as he signed himself) touching her real face. '*Amor mio*,' she whispered. 'My own true love, my sweet love.'

'*Con ti mio*,' he murmured, and she laughed. Three years later he cradled their English daughter and only child, Eve Summers, her eyes as blue as his own, lovingly in his arms. Esmerelda died before Eve's sixth birthday.

And so it went on.

Their story hadn't ended; it was hardly begun.

The mass of London's streets and people swamps the rivers. Where once the Fleet and Walbrook flowed, serving the busy sunlit wharves, now only sluggish and foul water trickles far down in the dark, and they and the streams that once divided the sandy islands of Southwark – the Overie, Neckinger, Earl's Sluice – are haunted by sewer-hunters who crawl in the dark maze from the quicksands of Cuckold's Point as far as the Tyburn beneath Parliament. Above them people hurry along the pavements, or sit at desks, or are served in bright shops, the roads busy with horses and carts. But in the darkness below, these half-blind creatures probe and scratch for sovereigns and half-sovereigns, false teeth and hairpins and wedding rings, finding bodies, babies and dead dogs, copper pennies by the score and lumps of metal by the ton.

However great London grows her largest sewer, the Thames, remains open to the sky, its water lifeless and stinking to high heaven. Londoners drink the water, cover it with bridges, drown themselves in it, hold regattas on it, and depend on it for almost all their livelihood. The Thames is part of them every day of their lives, a thoroughfare of masts snaking from London Bridge to Greenwich and Vaudey and the whole world beyond. The oak masts make a forest which grows thicker as trade grows, and without them London could not have existed, or any of its people.

BOOK THREE

VII
Sam Wittle

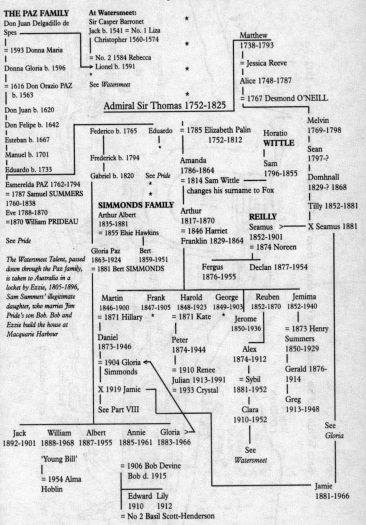

John Fox's Family Tree continued
Easter 1812 – March 1918

John Fox

THE PAZ FAMILY
Don Juan Delgadillo de
Spes
= 1593 Donna Maria

Donna Gloria b. 1596
= 1616 Don Orazio PAZ
b. 1563

Don Juan b. 1620

Don Felipe b. 1642

Esteban b. 1667

Manuel b. 1701

Eduardo b. 1733

Esmerelda PAZ 1762-1794
= 1787 Samuel SUMMERS
1760-1838
Eve 1788-1870
= 1870 William PRIDEAU

See *Pride*

*The Watersmeet Talent, passed
down through the Paz family,
is taken to Australia in a
locket by Ezzie, 1805-1896,
Sam Summers' illegitimate
daughter, who marries Jim
Pride's son Bob. Bob and
Ezzie build the house at
Macquarie Harbour*

At Watersmeet:
Sir Casper Barronet
Jack b. 1541 = No. 1 Liza
└ Christopher 1560-1574

= No. 2 1584 Rebecca
→ Lionel b. 1591
*
See *Watersmeet*

Admiral Sir Thomas 1752-1825

Federico b. 1765   Eduardo
                      *
Frederick b. 1794

Gabriel b. 1820   *See Pride*

SIMMONDS FAMILY
Arthur Albert
1835-1881
= 1855 Elsie Hawkins

Gloria Paz   Bert
1863-1924   1859-1951
= 1881 Bert SIMMONDS

Martin   Frank   Harold   George   Reuben   Jemima
1846-1900   1847-1905   1848-1923   1849-1903   1852-1870   1852-1940
= 1871 Hillary   *   = 1871 Kate   *   Jerome
                                                1850-1936
Daniel
1873-1946   Peter   = 1873 Henry
                        1874-1944   Summers
= 1904 Gloria ◄   Alex   1850-1929
Simmonds   = 1910 Renee   1874-1912
                        Julian 1913-1991 = Sybil   Gerald 1876-
X 1919 Jamie   = 1933 Crystal 1881-1952   1914
See Part VIII   │
                                         Clara   Greg
                                        1910-1952   1913-1948

Jack   William   Albert   Annie   Gloria >
1892-1901   1888-1968   1887-1955   1885-1961   1883-1966   See
                                                                     Gloria
'Young Bill'
│   = 1906 Bob Devine
= 1954 Alma   Bob d. 1915
Hoblin   Jamie
            Edward Lily   1881-1966
            1910   1912
            = No 2 Basil Scott-Henderson

Matthew
1738-1793
= Jessica Reeve
Alice 1748-1787
= 1767 Desmond O'NEILL

Melvin
1769-1798

Horatio   Sean
WITTLE   1797-?

Sam   Domhnall
1796-1855   1829-? 1868

= 1785 Elizabeth Palin
        1752-1812

Amanda
1786-1864
= 1814 Sam Wittle
changes his surname to Fox   Tilly 1852-1881

                                    X Seamus 1881

Arthur   **REILLY**
1817-1870   Seamus >
= 1846 Harriet   1852-1901
Franklin 1829-1864 = 1874 Noreen

Fergus   Declan 1877-1954
1876-1955

See
Watersmeet

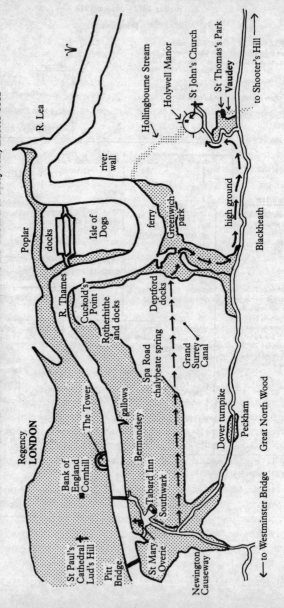

Sam Wittle and Sir Thomas Fox take coach from the Tabard to Holywell, Easter 1812

to Shooter's Hill →

St Thomas's Park
Vaudey
St John's Church
Holywell Manor
Hollingbourne Stream

R. Lea

river wall

high ground

Blackheath

Greenwich park

ferry

Isle of Dogs

docks

Poplar

R. Thames

Cuckold's Point

Rotherhithe and docks

Deptford docks

Spa Road chalybeate spring

Grand Surrey Canal

Dover turnpike

Peckham

Great North Wood

Regency
LONDON

Bank of England
Cornhill
The Tower
gallows

Bermondsey

Tabard Inn
Southwark

St Mary Overie

St Paul's Cathedral
Lud's Hill

Pitt Bridge

Newington Causeway

← to Westminster Bridge

'Hit's a gennelman for you, Sam, hit is!' piped Smidg'un far below, his little voice faltering up the many stairwells of the Tabard Inn, coming finally to the garret with a cracked, grimy window where Sam Wittle slept.

Except that Sam was not really sleeping. Life ran too fast and hot in Sam Wittle. He dozed like a cat, curled in the corner on a blanket thrown on the bare boards, hardly breathing – almost purring. He looked less as if he was sleeping than waiting.

Sam was always hungry.

Everyone called him Sam-in-the-middle, because he was older than his smaller brothers and younger than the bullies bigger than him: he knew his place. Sam-in-the-middle had been born hungry, hungry for more than his mother's milk, which he probably never got, hungry for her love which he certainly never did. Sam had no mother, at least not one to own up to him. So he regarded all women equally, with a suspicious, slitted eye behind his grin. Any of them coming and going about the place could have had the honour of bringing him into the world, even one of his elder sisters got into trouble, but he knew they'd never tell him – *he* wouldn't have.

'Sam! Hit's a tuwible haccident, paw gennelman!'

Sam had gone to bed hungry, and now the child's shout woke him hungry. His eyes flashed open, an honest bright blue with dark lashes. His tawny hair had a slight tinge of strawberry that gave his curls a glow, and his wide generous mouth stretched into the easy smile that set the hearts of girls and their mothers fluttering alike; and had broken more than one or two, as his own had been long ago.

He rolled to his feet and slipped into his jacket in one smooth movement, and had silently opened the door before he was properly awake. But there was no need to run; the landing was empty, only dusty floorboards. Knowing which ones did not have their nails loosened to squeak like nightingales, he went to the stairwell and peered down the angles of steps falling crankily away below him. Anyone coming up would have seen him looking neat and fresh as a daisy, except for his grubby face and grubby fingers.

But no one was coming up.

Sam put his hands lightly on the railing, then glanced along the yellowed corridor to his right, which turned away to another set of banisters. This crowded jumble of nooks and crannies at the top of the building, where all the stink of the tobacco smoked below ended up, made the Easter sunlight slanting through the row of windows strike thick and heavy.

No one was there.

Still, Sam was sure he had heard Smidg'un calling; and Sam had prospered, relative to some others here at the Tabard, by not missing out on anything that was to be had. Self first, self last, and if there was anything left over, self again, was his motto.

At his throat Sam wore a smart yellow kerchief, speckled with red dots, tied with the nautical reef knot taught him by sailors from St Mary Overie dock. Sam's jacket definitely flashed it away, navy-blue, stolen from the laundry in Red Lion Street, sporting impressive tails that touched the backs of his calves when he walked with a swagger, as he invariably did – nothing by halves. He kept the buttons hanging loose, broad pale yellow lapels spread out like butterfly wings, his thumbs skewed in the pockets of his garish scarlet and azure waistcoat, his mouth slowly chewing a quid of tobacco. Below his knee breeches Sam's silk hose, carelessly left unpacked by a gentleman's servant one morning, was of the finest quality, as were his shoes, though the buckles were pinchbeck. Humility was not Sam's strong suit, but he was clever enough to show, having drawn people's attention, that he knew his place better than anyone – except perhaps his father, Horatio Wittle. Sam could make a guest's stay easy or difficult, comfortable or worse than they could possibly imagine.

Sam always gave good value.

He often got the best tips. A shilling was rewarded with a look man to man and remembered with the memory of an elephant. That customer would receive the smoothest service next time, and the best bed. To a copper penny, Sam was polite; to nothing, he backed in front of the customer to set them on their way, bowing to the ground and knuckling his forehead, uttering loud embarrassing cries of 'Thank'ee, thank'ee!' Then he would call after them until they were gone from sight, bright red about the ears. 'Thank'ee! Come back, come back, vy don't you, next time I'll know how to treat you!'

Besides, Sam knew, glancing at the cheap pinchbeck, silver buckles were apt to be missed. One choleric traveller sent his man back from as far as Rochester to find a silver stock button Sam had taken a fancy to; he turned it up lost beneath the bed, of course.

Beneath his showy clothes, Sam was thin as a stick. His brothers and sisters (if that was what they were, and he supposed everyone's great-grandfather had fought at the battle of Hastings, it was only common sense) did not ache with hunger as Sam did. However much he ate, Sam was always hungry for more.

'Sam, vere are you!' The excited cry came from below, then a breathless scampering sounded on the stairs at the corridor's far end, and the high-pitched cries came closer, along with the scuttling noises. 'Hit's a veal gennelman, Sam!'

Sam crossed to the window. In the yard lay a grey-haired man, from above showing a circle of pink pate normally concealed by an admiral's casque which was tossed on the cobbles, complete with gold braid and a dog-vane cockade, in signature of his rank. The old man was struggling to rise from the donkey's breakfast – a mattress of canvas and straw – on which he had been laid by well-wishers hoping, apparently in vain, for a reward. Faintly through the grimy glass Sam heard the admiral roundly cursing everyone who approached him, both hands clasped round his knee.

'An hadmiral, Sam!' Smidg'un cried.

Sam turned slowly as the urchin skidded into view along the corridor, and sternly held up his finger. 'Steady there, young Smidg'un, my young colt. Halt.' Smidg'un halted. 'Approach with decorum,' Sam ordered.

'A veal hadmiral, Sam!' squealed Smidg'un, wringing his cap in his filthy hands, his eyes huge and appealing. He dared approach, cringing. 'You said you'd give me a copper Johns!' he lied.

'Sixpence? I said I'd give you vun penny for vot I ought to know. I saw the old salt horse from up here avore you did,' Sam said, also lying.

535

'You promised!' snivelled Smidg'un, creasing his face into a picture of woe, still keeping out of reach.

'How old are you, sprog?' Sam said dangerously.

'Old enough to know better!' Smidg'un wept.

'Let this be a lesson to you,' Sam said, then flicked the boy a farthing in passing. 'Quicker next time.'

Smidg'un's face lit up and he scampered loyally behind Sam to the stairs. 'His horse threw a shoe, then threw him, except the old Harvey's foot got stuck in the stirrup and spurred the old nag on faster the faster he dragged him.'

'Lucky to be alive, eh?' Sam said, doing up his buttons, going downstairs.

'Wery lucky, Sam,' Smidg'un said obediently, snatching a brush off the windowsill and brushing Sam's shoulders. 'Vot with all the market stalls, and him towing the rigging and the canvas after him, an old lady caught up rolling after him like a skittle, ev'rything going ev'rywhere. And all the volk running after him, they all fell over him ven he got his boot free and stopped, bang. They were hoping for a reward for catching the horse. Never find it now,' Smidg'un added wistfully. 'It won't stop bevore Mr Edwards's tenter ground.'

'Vot's that brick on your shoulders?' Sam said, coming down into the main hallway.

'It's my head, Sam!'

San kicked a carter's hound that was pissing on the newel post, then turned and smoothed the creases from his lapels. 'Vot's the first place a City horse would stop?' he lectured Smidg'un severely. 'Bet you a copper John you'll find the nag grazing his head orf in the first grass he spies. Where's that?'

Smidg'un groaned at his own stupidity, having exchanged a sure reward for a poor bet. 'The yard of the old Marshalsea prison.'

'Bring him to me!' Sam said authoritatively, and Smidg'un scampered off. By the counter a yawning tapster in the inevitable blue apron was pulling wax out of his ears, and in the corner Sam spied a serving girl excitedly adjusting her Trafalgar garter, thinking she was not watched; even the most sensible maidens became completely silly when a sailor was in the offing. 'He's a copper-bottomed hadmiral, not a common tar-hat for your sort,'

Sam told her irritably. 'Where's the guv'nor?'

'Mr Wittle's at Smithfield, buying beef – and you mind your own business, Sam snottynose. Your sort, yourself,' she flounced.

'Get your head from out them clouds,' Sam barked, bullying down as he was bullied from above, 'and sweep that floor!'

He pushed open the door and strode into the yard, knocking through the crowd of hopefuls from the kitchens and balconies who had gathered to cluck round the old gentleman. 'Vot's all this?' Sam roared. 'Get avay from him, give him air!' He thought they would scatter like hens, but everyone was shouting suggestions at such a volume that they could not hear him, and they were getting in each other's way, serving girls and kitchen maids and parlour maids and chamber maids milling around in their dirty white aprons, bonnets or kerchiefs knotted hastily over their heads, any excuse for excitement and a moment snatched in the sun, paying him no attention whatsoever. Sam frowned, his pride injured, not one to accept such an affront lightly, and surveyed the chaos with tightening, whitening lips.

'Quiet!' he yelled, but their noise redoubled.

One of the girls, Mary – they were all called Mary, just as all manservants were called James – this particular Mary was crying because the departing mail coach had torn her dress with its greasy hub, and now the yellow branch coach was coming in from Westerham. The two huge, overladen vehicles locked together under the archway, passengers hanging onto their tall beaver hats, then clinging to the roof like spiders as the teams knocked and plunged in a tangle of horses and harness. Above, a bald man in a nightshirt leaned down from the window of the house over the arch, shouting he could get no peace. Everyone shouted back at him to hold his tongue, he was well off out of it up there.

There was a loud clang and silence fell.

Sam gave the fire bell a second clang, contriving to look them all in the eye. 'That's better,' he said. 'Now, hold it like that. Hold it like that!' He crossed the silence, winked up at the driver of the mail coach. 'Vun moment, master,' he said and unhooked the bridle of the lead horse from the wooden trace of the branch coach. The mail coach departed. Sam went back to the staff. They stood around looking shamefaced. 'Vot you scum doing here?' Sam demanded quietly. 'Go back to your vork, all of you, avore I lose my temper. Avore I lose my temper!'

He watched them disperse quietly, even the girl who had torn her dress, too frightened to make more fuss.

'Give 'em an hinch,' Sam said to no one in particular, 'and they'll snatch a mile.'

With hands on hips he stood watching the yard empty, as much as the yard of such a popular hostelry ever did: at any time of day or night there was coming and going, coaches and carts parked everywhere round the walls, squeezed beneath the galleries. The farrier was working as a mechanic on the broken wheel of a wagon in the corner, its hooped canvas hood inscribed 'William Parkhust, Horsham, Sussex, Common Stagewagon to the Tabard Inn, Borough'. Each stable half-door showed a horse's head nodding over the top of it, the animals so closely stabled that they were separated by smooth round balls to prevent chafing. With coach trade growing at such a rate – even the eight-wheeled coaches pulled by teams of six powerful horses were no longer a sight for amazement – nowadays the inner yard and even part of the outer was used as a laystall, spread with dung and straw.

Sam turned, hearing a groan behind him. 'Ahoy there,' he greeted the prone admiral, friendly, but with gravity. 'Now, vot's the trouble here?' Bending at the waist to keep the advantage of height, he tutted at the knee, shaking his head slowly, but of course he was looking at more than the injury, noting that the admiral's grey hair above his epaulettes had been roughly cut. Sam was very particular about such matters and walked to a guilded barber in a proper house in Foul Lane, no itinerants for him; and though he was not old enough to shave often, producing only a pale strawberry down, he noted nicks on the admiral's gravelly cheeks as though the old codger had shaved himself, and in a storm too, or pitch dark at the very least. Where was his man? Why was he in such a hurry? A full admiral, travelling on horseback!

Interestinger and interestinger, Sam thought. Coming to a decision, he knelt. 'Let's have an eye on this terrible vound,' he said, sticking out his hand like a gentleman, which was ignored.

'Wound! It's nothing, damn you, James! Help me on my feet, damn—'

'Does it hurt?' Sam took no offence at the oath, for his hand

538

was quietly slipping into the admiral's pocket for what it could find. He prodded the wound with his finger to cover his exploration.

'Ah!' cried the injured man, slumping back.

'Yuss, right enough, that's nothing,' said Sam agreeably, prodding again, palming some small change and a small roundish object he had filched from the pocket, unable to tell what it was but restraining his curiosity. There were more of them in the pocket. 'Vy, this knee's just wrenched, my lord,' he reassured the admiral, 'not broke. And scraped a bit on the ground vhere you vas dragged, got a bit o' dirt bedded in the beef. And ve doesn't vant that to itch, does ve?' Sam answered his own question. 'No, sir, ve does not.'

'It doesn't itch. It hurts like the devil.' The old man was weakening, losing his airs. He bit his lip, and in truth his knee was a dreadful mess, poking crookedly between his hose and breeches, which smelt of sea salt.

'Best have a dig.' Sam scraped out fragments of roadstone from the flesh with his fingernail, grinning cheerfully. 'Best bound up in the blood, my lord.'

'I'm not your damned lord, blast you!'

'I don't know who are you, I was just being perlite,' Sam said indifferently. 'Sam, sir, that's my name, and I'm no James. Don't cry out so, whoever you are, it disturbs my vork.' What were those peculiar things the odd codger had stuffed in his pockets? Not metal, so not money, or pieces of shot.

'I have not *cried out*, God rot you,' hissed Sam's patient through pinched lips. 'Sir Thomas Fox, Admiral of the Blue.'

Sam chuckled, binding up the wound with a length of rag. 'Sam Wittle, at your service.'

'And what have I said that's so amusing, my man?'

Sam paused. 'No, sir, no, that I can't tell you, you'd be hangry with me, you vould.' He tied off the knot, tight, and made to go. 'You've been rude to a fault as it is – God rot me.'

Alarmed at being deserted on his mattress in the middle of the inn yard, the patient lifted himself on his elbows. 'I am never angry with an honest man, and that I see you are.'

'That I am, sir, hexcuse me, 'nest Sam, known fer it. See, Admiral of the Blue, round here, Admiral of the Blue's our name for a tapster.' Sam gave a conspirator's wink without a touch of insolence. 'Let me help you up onto this bench, you'll be more comfortable,' he said solicitously. 'Fetch you a glass o' best port, sir?'

'Yes, no. Oh, very well, but bring the bottle, I don't trust a glass.'

'This is the Tabard Inn, sir,' Sam said, injured. 'Ve don't sell no tap-lash as top quality here, sir,' he lied. He went inside and, while the tapster fetched a bottle from the cellars, Sam examined the item he had acquired from the gentleman's pocket.

It was an acorn.

Sam carried the bottle and a clean glass outside, a napkin over his shoulder, and wrapped it round the neck of the bottle as he sprang the cork. He worked in silence.

'You're a jack-of-all-trades,' Thomas Fox observed.

'No, sir,' said Sam, 'I'm a Sam-of-all-trades.'

Thomas drained his glass and had it refilled, a little more comfortable now. 'Doubtless one has seen the last of one's horse, in an area like this.'

'This is a fine neighbourhood, sir,' Sam said with dignity, 'and your horse is already been sent fer.'

'You're a proud and touchy fellow!'

'Me? I can afford to be, sir,' Sam said, who had splashed his last farthing on Smidg'un and would have been penniless but for his swift forage in the admiral's pocket. He poured a third glass. 'Still itching, I hexpect, sir?'

'Not at all.'

'Feeling much better?'

'So-so.'

As though the thought had just struck him, Sam said, 'Your man was not a-travelling with you, sir?'

'My man was cut in half by Boney's chain shot. And I'm travelling alone for . . . for a more personal reason.' Thomas had closed his eyes and was resting his head on the wall behind the bench, hardly realising who he was talking to – talking to himself. 'My squadron blockading Portugal, watching Wellington's back . . . change of command, hauled down my flag, received my terrible news by letter aboard the *Borealis* at Portsmouth . . . rode post-haste, passed last night at Nerot's Hotel in St James's Street . . . damned uncomfortable bed and with fleas.'

'Oh, shockin'!' Sam drawled.

'The gas lamps shining in Pall Mall like the glare of Hell.'

'You're tired out, sir,' Sam said, shooting his cuffs over the flea bites on his own wrists. 'Best get a bit of shut-eye, I'll have you carried inside. No fleas at the Tabard.'

The old man's rheumy brown eyes popped open. 'I must continue my journey today. I have been at sea for nearly five years.'

'Strike me!' Sam exclaimed. 'You know your bawbard from your starboard by now, I daresay.'

'The sea is another world, Master Sam.'

He must be bawdy as a straw-yard bull, Sam thought, not seeing Mrs Admiral of the Blue for five year, sixty month, God knows how many thousand days, with not so much as a fondle – cherry ripe!

'By the god of war, the land is a strange country to me now, Sam.'

'I 'spect that's true,' Sam said agreeably. 'Steam engines, and steam ships with giant paddles. Just last week on the Thames—'

'At first light I placed my reports before my Lords of the Admiralty. Now I must hurry home. I must hurry!' He gripped Sam's wrist powerfully. 'You will help me. I must have my horse.' His eyes faltered, then closed, and he breathed raggedly.

'Poor old feller, it's something vorse than the bottled port, I reckons,' Sam said to himself, sentimental for a moment. 'He's fretted himself thin 'bout something. And vy such a scrambling rush?' His face hardened as Smidg'un arrived leading the horse. Sam went over and flicked him a sixpence acquired with the acorn from the admiral's pocket. 'Where I said?'

'The brute wouldn't've stopped so soon as the Marshalsea yard 'cept he threw a shoe,' Smidg'un said in disgust. 'He's lame. Vot an old nag, Sam! You won't get a reward off this one.' He nodded at the sleeping man, then his face broke out in a grin as he pocketed his sixpence. He'd finally got one over Sam.

'With that knee, you think that old boy'll be a-goin' further on horseback?' Sam bunched his fist and Smidg'un scampered inside, squealing.

Sam walked slowly round the horse, which was ribbed and mangy, and sufficiently hungry to munch the straw bedding of the laystall. Not a gentleman's mount, and not even hired out by

Nerot's Hotel, which had no livery: the brand on the rump was the sign of the Blue Bell Yard, St James's. Sam unbuckled the saddlebag half expecting to find more acorns, but a sheaf of opened letters lay inside, carefully refolded and tied up in a red ribbon. Sam looked round him innocently while his fingers worked busily. A proper wax seal would not have deterred him; Sam could replace the contents of an expensive bottle of port or sherry with something altogether less demanding without disturbing either the seal or the cork. The pair of half-hitches securing the bundle delayed him not a moment.

The opened letters were arranged in order of receipt, two dozen or more of them covering a period of five years – Sam's fingers riffled them expertly – all written by the same hand, except the last. Sam's reading was not as good as his stealing; he made out the words with difficulty, moving his lips. They were addressed to Admiral Sir Thomas Fox, aboard the *Borealis*, and each letter was signed 'Your loving wife, Elizabeth'.

The first letters wished him well, Elizabeth referring to various extra clothing and little gifts sent out, a brace of pistols, a volume of Walter Scott's *Marmion* that she hoped he would like, and she was sorry that he could not abide the Byron . . . Sam shrugged and skipped ahead, put off by the cool aristocratic tone that left everything important unspoken. He could tell they loved one another but she wasn't saying it; her real feelings were in what she was not saying, hidden, unadmitted. Sam grinned, shaking his head. That was women for you! Him of course being an expert on the fair gender.

She lived in a big house in the country, obviously, and she gossiped about boring things that Sam had no idea about, names and a way of life he could hardly imagine, something about the Hunt, and the laying out of a rose garden according to her husband's wishes – he was obviously sending her letters and instructions for the home life he could not enjoy himself. There was a big gap in the dates of the letters, then she was writing to tell him of the King's Head public house being pulled down after the land was sold to speculators, and houses built all over the place, and adding with sudden warmth, almost gushing by her standards: 'You will notice such a change in our little village when the moment I pray for comes, the blessed day that brings you home to us safe and sound.'

Sam tapped his front teeth thoughtfully at the change, and that 'us'.

Elizabeth was dying. Her failing handwriting, not her doggedly cheerful tone, told him that. She probably wrote the later letters from bed or somewhere awkward, Sam thought, but only her pen scratchily and painfully crossing the page betrayed her. The lines turned down at the end as though each was a trial of strength, each completion a small, terrible victory. Her gossip of the garden, the futile roses obsessing her because they had been important to her husband, could not conceal the fact that she was housebound, bedridden, in great pain. These letters must have been a torment to receive, Sam reckoned; all her worries were for her husband's danger and discomfort at sea, not her own anguish, in her own bedroom.

Postscripts had been added to the jagged script of the later letters in a different, flowing hand, the salutation simply 'Father', signed 'Yr dutiful, Amanda'. Added without the invalid's knowledge, Amanda telling her father coolly and calmly of the cancer that was eating her mother's stomach, and her decline.

Sam reckoned that between Amanda's efficient nursing reports and Elizabeth's frantic warmth – all the things she felt, dying, that she was trying to put into words now it was too late – they had spared their man at sea nothing.

The last letter, in Amanda's hand, was dated only ten days ago and had reached the *Borealis* in Portsmouth. There was now no hope of a recovery. Her mother's crisis would come at any moment. *Yr dutiful, Amanda.*

Sam closed up the letter, wondering what it was like to have a mother and, having her, to lose her.

He retied the knots perfectly, then replaced the letters in the saddlebag and buckled it tight. He looked around him, seeing everything he knew: the sun striking across the Tabard yard, the gloomy windows, the beggar who must be kicked away before the lunchtime rush, drivelling his grief at the people coming through the arch, who skirted him fastidiously or brushed him aside or did not see or hear him. The tapsters shaving themselves smart, parting their hair and polishing the mirrors. The stink of cooked lunches being made ready, trolleys of stews and pies and piles of buttered smelts being trundled across the yard to the parlours for the top-table trade, chops to be served with shredded

543

shallots and gravy, barrels of oysters delivered fresh from Billingsgate this morning, cuts of smoking roast beef as big as a man's body, carried on platters on the heads of boys. Scratched wooden platters of bread and cheese for the low tables, and bowls of bone soup. From somewhere upstairs, a girl's trilling laugh. This was all Sam knew.

'All right,' he drawled, 'I'll help you.'

Sam cheekily rode inside the heaving, creaking coach, lolling on the red leather as though it was his natural place, not perched uncomfortably on the roof where a manservant should have been, at best beside the driver, at worst on the postillion's step perfectly placed to catch the mud thrown up by the spinning rear wheels. Sam had decided not to know his place. If for his insolence he was sent back by his unexpected employer, that was fine by him; the coach was hired from the farrier in Sam's name, not the old man's, and it was not Sam who would find himself abandoned on the roadside. His guest seemed to understand that this was the normal way Sam set about whatever matter came before him, always to his own advantage, for he was not frowning; there was even a trace of amusement in that steady, appraising brown gaze looking into Sam's blue eyes opposite him.

'You're a rascal, Sam,' the old man sighed.

'But not an idle rascal,' said Sam, still wondering about the acorns.

He had arranged everything, not only the hire of the coach but hopping the old man across to the drain to relieve himself, fetching a bowl of hot water to wash his face, then lifting him into his seat, setting his uniform straight and brushing the straw and road gravel from the white facings, called wash-boards, as best he could. Smidg'un was sent to return the nag to the Blue Bell Yard, and the coach had pulled out towards Newington Causeway, between the mass of shops and tenements lining the road, before turning left.

The admiral flicked Sam a coin to pay the toll. He must have been suffering, but still he said nothing of his wife. His injured leg lay on a board placed across the footwell onto the seat beside Sam, jolting on the cobbled junctions or slipping from side to side as the coach swayed in the ruts of the open road. Sam sat holding the foot as they travelled, feeling a peculiar intimacy in its warmth. In front of him the great man was helpless, his face again pale with the pain of his accident, the port wearing off now. There was little traffic; Sam could have leaned forward and performed the sensible act, struck him in the face with his fist, rifled the old man's pockets and pouches, stripped him of what he wanted, and left him naked in a ditch. He'd have to cut in Nathaniel Stair, the driver of the coach, with a sovereign and maybe the sea boots, and then they would turn round and no one who mattered would know they had been gone. Back at the busy Tabard the admiral was already forgotten, and nothing more of him would ever be said.

Away to their left, above the fouled waters of the River Neckinger oozing like slurry into the Thames, four tiny dolls swung from the gibbet, turning as lightly in the wind as though made of straw.

'Pirates,' grunted the admiral with satisfaction. '*Suspensus per collum.* Not dropped, hanged until dead.'

For the first time in his life Sam, trying to appear casual and as though he knew it all, saw countryside. Beyond the rattling window glass, flatlands opened up, crisscrossed with fields and hedges and ditches, and beyond them woodlands dotted the hills. 'Don't it strike strange!' he exclaimed.

His guest pulled down the glass by the strap. 'Clean air! No stench of tanneries.'

'Never noticed 'em,' Sam drawled. 'Grew up takin' matters for granted as they are, I s'pose. This here air smells of shit to me, sir, beggin' your pardon.'

The coach bounced and Thomas groaned. A bead of sweat trickled on his forehead. 'I remember when woodlands lay beside Neckinger Road, Sam, and open fields stretched between Mile End and Wapping, and the Isle of Dogs was not drawn round with that misery of shipwrights' yards, and docks, and shacks for the navvies who'd dug them, and windmills, and white-lead yards, and those smoking chimneys.'

'Seems nat'ral enough to me. Vot's to be had out here? No lights to see at night, and no sound o' the early carriers, no shouts o' people falling their vay home from the inn. And no int'rest,' he added.

'You've heard too many different voices in your short life, Sam, and seen too much in that busy tavern. Where's your innocence gone?'

'Hinnocence!' Sam scoffed.

'Yes, and wonder. You've grown old too quick, Sam, too sharp.'

'I has not, sir,' Sam said with dignity, 'had the hadvantage of being born a gennelman, hunlike some.'

The coach banged, and the old man gritted his teeth. 'But you are a survivor, quite obviously.'

'Yuss, sir,' said Sam fiercely, 'but that was an hadvantage I had to learn.'

They fell silent for a while.

'My wife is dying, Sam.'

Sam thought for a while. 'You knows I know it, sir.'

'Any other man would have denied the petty thievery.'

'I denies it too. I didn't steal nothing,' said Sam, sounding injured.

'My private grief is my own business.'

'Not at the Tabard Inn, sir,' Sam said. 'Not at the Tabard.'

Thomas gave a short laugh. 'An incorrigible rascal! You'll end up with them, Sam, if you aren't careful.' He jerked his thumb at the distant, swaying figures silhouetted against London. '*Sus. per coll.*'

'I'm sorry about your wife, sir,' Sam said. 'It's a tuwible home-coming for you, that it is.'

'If only I had not tried to journey at such frantic speed, I might have been home by now!'

'It won't make no difference, sir. Just you rest yourself quiet-like and gather your strength.'

The old man closed his eyes obediently.

'There is one further thing to menshun, how'ver, sir,' Sam said, 'vot I vould like to get a handle on, so to speak.'

'And what is that, Sam?'

'Please 'ee, sir, I refers to the matter of the hacorns.'

'Hacorns? Acorns! So you know about them too.'

'Nat'ruly, sir. That's my job, sir.'

The old man rolled one between his fingers. 'I picked them up at every inn where the post-horses were changed. Why does an old gentleman weary of the sea pick up acorns? The future, Sam.'

He flicked it from the window into a ditch.

'You're planting *trees*, sir?'

'No. I'm planting masts.' The admiral pointed at the huge mast-houses rising against the sky over Deptford. 'This war will end, but another will be fought by your children and your grand-children, Sam. And they will require masts.'

'I don't have no children, sir,' Sam said, probably untruthfully.

'Neither do I, Sam,' the old man said sadly, and Sam cast him a a sharp look, knowing of the daughter's postscripts and her letter. 'Well, there is Amanda, but no children who matter, you see.' He shrugged. 'The great virtue of a boy's sex is that the family name lives on in him. A girl is useless.'

'You could always take another wife, sir,' Sam said, 'hafter a decent interval, 'course.'

'By God's truth, Sam, don't speak to me of that now!'

'Perhaps she vill magically recover, sir. Such cases do hoccur, I believe.'

The admiral spoke quietly. 'Elizabeth, my wife, is the only woman I have ever loved. Even if the worst happens, I will never marry again. The name Fox ends with me. After more than seven hundred years, Sam. The Holywell manorial rolls survive from its grant to Edgar de Fox dated 1078, shortly after the Norman Conquest. I am the last of the line.'

The coach bumped across the Grand Surrey Canal at Black Horse Bridge and turned along Broomfields Street into Deptford, running between rows of terraced houses. On one side of the coach a child smiled and waved. 'Look out!' Sam said, knowing the trick, and a moment later a mud ball, thrown by a child on the other side, struck the side of the coach. 'Missed,' Sam said comfortably. 'They aims at the winders,' he explained, putting up the glass. 'Right mess it makes if it comes inside.'

'They don't know who I am,' Sir Thomas said irritably. 'Why—'

'Oh, they does know, sir,' Sam said. 'They knows you're a gennelman, and that's all they cares about.'

They passed shops with broken windows now, even along this main road made prosperous by the war. Yellow and black war-ships filled the busy docks, their masts and spars overhanging the rows of chimneypots, every dockside tavern busy and brawling. Sam, watching the admiral's face, guessed he knew nothing of the hovels hidden in the filthy side streets behind, the starving folk caught up in the bread and potato riots – human scum who were so poor, Sam knew, that they had taken to swarming onto the main thoroughfares after dark, if they thought they could get away with it. Women and children mostly, their men having been pressed into His Majesty's service. Probably ripped apart by chain shot and the lash by now; at best those breadwinners would return home toothless with scurvy, broken men, made vicious.

'Poor people,' Sam said, and shuddered. Not to be poor was worth paying any price.

'Sometimes I wonder,' the old man said, 'why I have fought for them, why their betters have died for them. I could have been home with her, Sam. Perhaps there was something I could have done for her.'

The docks and the heady odour of rum and pitch fell behind them as the coach crossed into Greenwich, the horses toiling up Crooms Hill beside the park. The Easter Fair was a disappointing business this year, though through the picket fence Sam spied an alarming steam-boiler on wheels chuffing round a circular track, towing a coach behind it. But there were few crowds come to picnic on the smooth grassy knolls rising to the Royal Observatory where workmen were busy installing a new telescope. He saw other workmen converting the old mansions that lined the road into endless terraced housing that people in ordinary employment could afford, where even undergarments fluttered in plain view, hung out to dry. Sam watched enviously as in the park a few young bucks, not so much older than himself, ran their richly-dressed young ladies down the slopes until they tumbled on the grass, and lay scandalously together, giggling.

'Not a patch on our Christmas Fair,' Sam sniffed as they passed the town well. 'Much further, sir?'

The admiral knocked on the roof. 'Hurry!'

The horses plodded uphill and turned left on the broad straight road cutting across Blackheath Common, picking up a trot on the level ground. 'The Duke of Montague's place,' grunted the admiral, pointing at a building as fine houses gave way to open land. 'Some say this is the old Roman road from London. Straight, you see. That's how you can tell.'

'She'll be all right, sir,' Sam said.

'You've been a good friend to me today, honest Sam. I won't forget it.'

'Well, sir,' Sam muttered politely, 'gennelmen always *says* that, in my hexperience.'

'There's five pounds in it for you, at any rate.'

'Too mightily gen'rous, surely,' Sam said, who had planned very definitely on more.

'Not at all, Sam,' muttered the old man. He roused himself to nod at a long ride of trees and ornamental ponds. 'Used to be Ridley Marsh. The building at the end is Morden College. It's their investment fund which is behind the damned speculators.'

'Speckerlaters?' Sam said, with interest.

'Men like Loat and Royal, buying up every roadside field, every hole in the woods, putting up houses wherever they can.'

'Tsk, tsk,' tutted Sam between his teeth.

'I am something of an antiquarian, as you may have guessed.'

'A hantiquarian,' Sam said seriously. He cleared his throat. 'A collector of waluables, vould that be, sir?'

'Not of items that you would consider of much value, Sam, I think, but that are of interest to an educated man.'

'Vell beyond such as I,' Sam said modestly. '*Wery* waluable, vould they be?'

'It is a fascinating study but one for which I have had too little time. The collection was my brother's, God rest his soul.' He sat upright, staring. 'Vaudey? But this was all trees!'

The coach had turned left into Holloway Street, dropping downhill between bow-fronted shops, each with its sign – butcher, baker, and, Sam noted with approval, a barber's pole. The narrow pavements had been made secure from traffic by cast-iron bollards. Proper shops, not stalls. Sam sniffed, inhaling the rich scent of ratepayers.

Around the old field boundaries workmen in round black hats, with large hands as red as pickled beetroot, pushed wheelbarrows full of rubble, planks or spades along boards laid over the mud, toiling to level new building plots down to the chalk. Their rough Irish slang – half of them had probably been convicts, and the other half should be – rang loud on the English air, stealing work from honest English workmen. Sam saw bricks arriving on carts, fired elsewhere. Carpenters – not craftsmen working in proper premises – knelt outside the walls as they went up, cobbling together windows to fit, glaziers following them tacking in panes of shoddy glass. Yet the centre of the new village, a cluster of shops and the St Thomas à Becket Church of England School, already looked weathered and pretty, Sam thought. He could see the right sort of people would want to live here, not your riff-raff, vagrants or sailors on the rantan, or light-fingered wharfies with their children in tow as foulmouthed as their parents. Vaudey was too far from the river trade for that. No, Sam could tell, this here was for people with steady incomes, and standards. Quiet people, retired folk maybe, Vaudey being in the country but close enough to take carriage to London in a couple of hours if need be, not out of town life entirely but safe from the City's high prices, drunks and street gangs.

'Nothing was here!' Sir Thomas said.

'It's here now,' said Sam. These men Loat and Royal knew how to seize an opportunity, obviously. From a covered cart, furniture was already being shouldered into one house, the windows not yet painted and the plaster probably still damp. Money in the bank.

There was even a small piece of parkland laid out as if for proper gentry, a hollow of greensward kept down by sheep and trees dotted round a pond. Sam could see how it would go. Enclosed by iron railings, only householders would be provided with a key. No beggars, no itinerants, no servants allowed to bother the ratepayers.

For all its airs, this place was no different from anywhere else, Sam realised. Only one thing mattered here, and that was the same as anywhere: getting on top.

The old man stared at his fingers, flexing them. He looked unbearably nervous. They passed a church standing in the middle of nowhere, old and unimpressive, its grey stones almost black with soot. 'Vaudey was depopulated by the Black Death plague of 1620,' he murmured. 'I believe the houses were once down here, but everything is gone. Only the name remains, and my feeling. And St John's Church, which is the ruin you can see.'

'Now, sir, you keep yourself composed,' Sam said, hefting the saddlebags. 'Vhy, I'm sure in a minute or two you'll be laughing for vorrying yourself into such a state.'

The coach turned up a white gravel drive bordered by a line of oaks on each side. They came out into the open on a knoll with steep slopes on three sides, and treetops waving below. It was all as Sam had imagined it would be: men were kneeling on the lawns, short-scything the grass with the first cut of the year, plucking out weeds expertly with the curved blade tips as though they had been employed on this task for ever. Beyond them, in the centre of the elegant carriage circle, rose a stone fountain in the usual fashion for owners of this quality, water splashing from its peak into the ornamental pool below.

And then there was Holywell Manor, rooks circling between the tall redbrick chimneys, half-timbered walls glowing in the sun, its many leaded windows holding an immense panorama of London in their reflection.

Sam jumped out before the coach stopped, swinging the saddlebags neatly over his shoulder, and helped the old man down onto the gravel. The water splashed loudly.

'Amanda!' the old man called in a trembling voice.

At the top of the steps, the door of the house had opened. A girl, her face perfectly calm, stood there against the dark interior. What a dull sort she was. As she took a step, blinking, into the sunlight, Sam saw that she wore a plain blue dress to the ground, no bonnet, her hair hanging stark red on each side of her indoors-white face to her white shoulders – white as a prisoner. Her eyes were brown and very large, and lines pinched round her mouth. The lines and the way she stood put her age, by Sam's guess – and Sam was good at guessing the secrets of women – in her middle thirties, if she was a clever liar. But Sam thought she was not a liar – he had never seen such a withdrawn face. The look in her eyes did not come forward enough to lie.

'Papa,' Amanda said blankly, as though she could not comprehend the frail figure below her, not having seen him for five years.

'Give us an hand down here, miss!' Sam called urgently.

She crossed awkwardly to the steps as though she had one foot set in mortar, dragging herself with a strange rolling gait. Sam wished he could see her legs. With one hand on the balustrade, she limped slowly down to them.

'You're too late, Father,' she said, without weeping. 'Mother died this morning.'

A parlourmaid – no male servants to be found indoors in what was, until now, a wholly female household – helped Sam support the old man upstairs, half insensible and inconsolable with grief.

The admiral was laid on his bed and Sam was busy at his work before anyone could think he should not be – pulling off the master's boots and unbuckling his saddlebags with quick efficiency as though he did this every day. No stranger to settling people in rooms, within moments he had made himself at home, throwing open the window for air as assertively as a chamber boy greeting a guest, then thoughtfully fretting the drape half-closed against the light in the invalid's eyes.

The parlourmaid watched him nervously. Her place was downstairs, but she had no one to tell her to return to her duties. Amanda stood aside from the scurrying servant girls roused from the house by Sam's roars, obviously taking it for granted that they would earn their keep while she oversaw matters from a distance, ladylike. These few moments were all the opportunity Sam needed to push his face. Calling the little parlourmaid over to him in the dressing room, he gave her a firm but friendly smile from above, brushing a strand of hair from her forehead with the back of his finger.

'Vot's your monnicker, Mary?'

'Beg pardon, sir?' the parlourmaid lilted. A village girl, then, unfamiliar with town ways.

'You call me Mr Sam,' Sam said authoritatively. 'Your monnicker, girl, your real name!'

'I'm only Dora, I'm afraid, that's all I am, sir, what they call me.'

'Mr Sam.'

'Mr Sam,' she blushed.

'Vell, Dorrie, you shouldn't be wearin' a white apron in a house in mournin'!' Sam laid out hairbrush and comb very professionally, unwrapped shaving tackle from the towel. 'Let me see you in a black rig-out immediate-like, and show some respect for the dead!'

Dorrie's lower lip trembled. 'But I haven't g-got a black one, Mr Sam. We don't, usual, here.'

'Go to Cook and tell her to dye you one,' Sam said. 'Chop-chop!' He jerked his head to show what he meant, and she said 'Oh!' and ran.

Sam whistled cheerfully under his breath. So far so good.

Going to the door, he summoned the skinny upstairs maid,

pulled his weight with her too, found that her name was Euphemia and called her Effie, and finished by issuing instructions for tea. She dashed off obediently, flushed and thoroughly put down, and Sam preened himself. He was a cat among the pigeons and no mistake.

He glanced into the bedroom. The old man was leaning back against the pillows on the bed, his head in his hands. Sam thought ahead. He'd want to see the dead woman, of course.

Sam turned, hearing a shuffling sound. Someone was coming up the grand oak staircase step by step. The crippled Amanda, no prizes for that guess. Sam made sure his waistcoat was buttoned then jerked the travelling creases from his coat and showed himself over the top railing.

Amanda's white face, her eyes like brown holes, looked up from below. And that hair, distressing to witness. She staggered.

Sam ran down and took her elbow, but she flinched. 'I need no help from you!' she said, and in that moment they became enemies.

Sam shrugged and released her. 'Your father does, from you.'

'I'm going to him now.'

He watched her pull herself up another step, then another.

'I was only trying to be kind,' he said.

She neither looked back nor replied.

'Sam,' Sam said boldly.

She stopped, gripping the banister so tight that her knuckles stood up like white peas. 'I am quite worn out with helping my mother. She is at peace at last and so am I.'

Sam caught up with her in two quick strides, taking the steps two at a time. 'I took the liberty of ordering tea—'

'You cannot. We take tea only at mealtimes.'

Sam cut to the nub of the matter. 'Is she presentable?' he said flatly.

Amanda looked at him properly for the first time.

'Vashed,' Sam said, knowing he sounded out of place; every stableboy and table waiter at the Tabard knew that the upper classes spoke their own upper-class, educated dialect quite different from that of ordinary folk like himself. Here the walls were pale yellow, the carpets soft, the gallery windows cleaned to sparkling, and suddenly he saw himself as she must see him, classified by his accent. He struggled for a 'w'. 'Washed. Persent'ble . . .' He cleared his throat, forcing himself to pronounce the vowels. 'Presentable, you know.' He supported Amanda's elbow in his hand and she took another step not realising he was helping her.

'He cannot possibly be allowed to see her!' Amanda said, forgetting Sam's accent and understanding his suggestion now. 'Out of the question!'

Sam waited a couple of steps.

'Vy – *why* – why not, miss? If she only kicked it this morning she can't be swellin' or smelly yet.'

Amanda gave a horrified shout. 'Let go of me. Let go!' She pulled away her arm, her expression of hatred making her face, for the first time, rather interesting to him – life in her eyes after all. But that lank hair. Sam couldn't take her seriously.

'If that's the way you want it, miss,' he shrugged, and she fell back against the railing, shaking with anger. Her dress had ridden up over her ankle and revealed her misshapen foot, the twisted flesh stuck in a woollen sock and a clumsy platform shoe. She made no effort to hide the horrible sight.

'How dare you!' She turned and continued up the stairs, Sam following at a respectful distance.

At the top, she rested and Sam stood quietly to one side.

'My mother had a growth in her stomach—'

'Sam.'

Amanda spoke with admirable levelness. 'She died of agony and starvation over many months.' She put her hands over her face. 'It would be indecent to show . . . to allow him to see . . . what became of the woman he loved.'

'Loves,' Sam said. Her shoulders shook. Her weeping was terrible, he thought, sounding like rusty, unused machinery breaking out of her. 'You take your time,' he said, watching her, then stopped the upstairs maid's trolley and poured a strong cup of tea, nothing elegant, and held it out. He summoned to mind some of the thousand gentlemen he had shown to a room, the sound of their voices, and stepped into their shoes.

'Drink this, Miss Fox, I beseech you. The beverage will compose you.'

It was easy.

554

'I'm so very ashamed of myself.' She stopped her tears by sheer effort of will, and returned doggedly to her obsession. 'There is so much still to do, you see. The doctor has signed the certificate. You've been very kind, but I don't know what to do next – send for the vicar from Westcombe, I suppose, which has long been amalgamated with our parish—'

Her father came out onto the landing. He and his daughter stood looking at each other like strangers.

'Not Westcombe, Amanda.'

'No, Papa,' she said obediently.

'Our family have always been laid to rest in the churchyard of St John's, in Vaudey.'

'Yes, Papa,' she said, bowing her head.

'I'll arrange it, sir,' Sam said, lapsing into his own voice with the old man, who was not so easily fooled. 'And the flowers and ev'rything, som'thing himpressive, just as you vould do it yourself, or as Miss Amanda vould have.'

Sam watched them go together into the dead woman's room, then turned away, whistling tunelessly under his breath. He was in.

Years later, gossiping tongues whispered about Sam: *We know what we know.* Nothing had changed.

Uphill in the new village of Vaudey, class-conscious and competitive as villages had always been, Londoners who had moved only five years ago into the first Regency houses already referred to themselves as old blood, and brought their old ways with them. Everyone who could wanted to move out of London, and the old blood vetted their new neighbours with the social inquisition of the Morning Call, *de rigueur* with them until afternoon tea became a more fashionable and even more fertile breeding ground for gossip and innuendo. These sharp-nosed, impeccably mannered folk sensed at once who was not one of their own and who was letting the side down. All these well-educated people knew it was a saying going back to the time of Chaucer that one bad apple spoiled the barrel. Tongues hissed beneath the polite conversation and elegant rustle of crinolines in the front parlour, knowing glances were exchanged, deductions inferred, conclusions drawn. Nothing need be said for a gentleman's reputation to be ruined.

But Sam was not a gentleman.

Later the women decided that Sam had deliberately planned everything that happened. Such success as he had must be born to, could not possibly be deserved – must be stolen, a cheat in some way. Sam *must* have worked everything out beforehand, they concluded, stealing his way into the heart of Miss Amanda Fox as cold-bloodedly as a worm, because someone so quick, so vivid – and so poor – as he was, a manservant, could not possibly fall in love with someone so cold, so ugly, so deformed – and so rich!

Miss Amanda Fox, they reasoned, should have known better. Surely her father warned her?

Sam had moved easily behind the several young local men at the burial, his betters who were eyeing the pretty girls who always looked prettier in black – the coming colour for mourning – especially in the skimpy dress that was the fashion, showing the tops of their breasts like curved, corseted peaches, all the more luscious for the severity of their restraint. He watched them try their luck with the new elfin-eyed schoolmistress from Vaudey, Miss Carpenter, for all that she had arrived on foot and was plainly poor as a church mouse. Her beauty alone, if she did not give away too much, would enable her to marry above her. But as soon as Amanda appeared it was she, wrapped in herself like a woman in bandages, eyes downcast and her face ten years older than her age, without a care for herself or her clothes, whom the young men followed and paid court to as though she was the greatest beauty of them all.

As, of course, she was. Sam understood her suitors well enough. Money was beautiful. Money was power and comfort and self-esteem. Money was Holywell Manor and all the fields and trees it owned. Money, Sam could see, was the Fox family.

Money bought everything, Sam mused, looking at the old man and his daughter standing, heads bowed, by the bier. Everything but health or happiness or a son.

Had the Fox family always been outsiders? The squire had spent more than half his life at sea, an admiral not a magistrate, not part of the village. Everyone deferred to him and to his family because they had lived here longest, but even in olden times the village had been separate from the manor house.

He bowed agreeably to Miss Carpenter.

One day Holywell Manor would fall to Amanda, who cared least for it, who had the lowest opinion of herself, and it would automatically become the property of whoever married her. With corn at war prices, and with builders who would pay ten times the agricultural rate for a leasehold, the admiral's property was said to bring him five thousand pounds a year. He had his dead wife to thank for it. It had taken Sam a very few days, quietly undertaking his duties about the house, becoming familiar with every nook and cranny, to understand this.

Only a generation ago Sir Noel, keeping his head above taxes for the American War, had been forced sell the family's London house among the bookshops of Holywell Street to the Lord Mayor. With the money left over he purchased, for a song, the riverside marshes where the Hollingbourne Stream – which had its source in the overflow from the artesian fountain in front of his house, piped from there to the edge of the knoll before being allowed to go on its way – rushed downhill, and finally wandered across the marshland to lose itself in the Thames. He had no scheme of draining the marshes for building, trade being beneath him, but only erected towers for the comfort of shooting parties to bring down the enormous flocks of shelduck and pochard.

But as fashionable Greenwich crept eastward behind the river wall, what had been useless marsh became valuable building land. The admiral might lament such encroachment during his absence, but it was Elizabeth's foresight in taking advantage of it that enabled him to complain in comfort.

After the service, there was a moment of confusion, the lych gate squealing loudly, unoiled, condolences offered to Sir Thomas and Amanda, villagers milling in the hope of a word before setting off home, and Sam took advantage to find himself, as though by accident, blocking the way of the schoolmistress.

'Miss Carpenter.' He took off his tricorne hat, new, and twisted the corners nervously as he spoke to make himself look innocent, so that she would not step round him. 'Does I have that 'onour, miss?'

'You do indeed,' she laughed daintily, new to the village, her pretty cheeks colouring, 'if it is an honour.'

'I'm Sam Vittle, ma'am, man to Sir Thom, beggin' your

557

pardon, and he's a wery busy man, so I've only a moment to speak.'

'Pray do so.'

'Sam,' he said, shuffling and squeezing his hat.

Miss Carpenter glanced into his eyes, amused and unafraid, made confident by his demeanour. 'I pray you, Sam, unburden yourself.'

'You bein' an heducated person, miss, I vondered,' Sam drew a deep breath, 'if you vould teach me Henglish!'

She trilled with laughter, absolutely trilled. 'Oh, I'm not sure that would be proper, Sam. Considering our opposite gender.' But he noticed that the fingertips of her gloves were threadbare, darned.

'You lodges with old Mrs Chandler, doesn't you? I overheer'd,' he explained, not adding that he had also overheard she was more than half blind with glaucoma, poor old lady. 'With fine summer evenin's comin', and her gard'n with the apple trees, and her to vatch over your good name from the back window, vy, ma'am, you could learn me to speak like I should.'

'And what, Sam, is that like?'

'Like a gentleman,' Sam said. He nodded eagerly. 'Termorrow evenin', less'n the weather's bad?' He looked at the sky: settled as could be. 'Done!'

Whistling beneath his breath, Sam watched Miss Carpenter's slender figure walk away, small steps and swaying hips. She put her parasol up, throwing her upper half in shadow, but he could imagine everything about her. She was divine.

Sam returned to the gig – the house was too far for Amanda, with her club foot, to think of walking. She and her father sat miserably in the back, drained by the funeral, the blunt Norman church tower bobbing behind them as Sam swung into the driver's seat and clicked his tongue, setting the horse trotting. From time to time as he drove he threw out his right arm or his left. For almost five minutes his passengers said nothing.

'What the devil are you doing, Sam?' the old man demanded at last.

'Planting masts, sir,' Sam told them cheerfully over his shoulder. Neither smiled, but when he looked back later the old man was pointing at one of the barns, some work to be done, and

Amanda was nodding. That was better.

The wagging tongues were quite wrong about Sam, of course. Miss Amanda Fox had no reason to know better, for it was no part of Sam's plan to marry her. And her father saw no need to warn her, for he himself was the object of all Sam's attention.

Sam was the best, most attentive manservant the old man ever had. These were hard, empty days for a man in one breath thrown into retirement and a lonely old age as a widower. Sam had seen it all before among the thousands of faces that had passed through the Tabard, and he knew what the old man was going through, and how to take advantage of it. He filled the old man's life, 'the hadmiral,' as Sam would have put it in those early days to Miss Carpenter, 'that I 'ave so much come to hadmire, you might say.'

'*Admiral*,' Miss Carpenter corrected him. '*Admire*. Really, Sam, I sometimes suspect you of putting it on.'

'Comes nat'rel to me, miss,' said Sam, with that peculiar honesty in those blue eyes of his. If Sam believed in nothing else, he believed in himself. There was something wild about him, something not Holywell, nothing to do with the stifling social life she suffered in Vaudey.

'Then, Sam, you really must learn to speak *un*-naturally,' she lectured him, endeared.

Sam picked an apple and handed it to her with a wink. 'Exactly,' he said.

Sam quickly found that the old man woke with the bells of the night, as though he were still aboard ship, and Sam always made sure he was on hand during the dogwatch with a sugared drink and a biscuit. 'You're at home, sir, and all's well.'

When the old man woke in the morning, it was always to Sam breezing around him, unfailingly cheerful if his employer's mood demanded it, biding his time in silence otherwise, bringing steaming coffee and a second cup without being asked. At sea the old man had acquired the odd habit of washing daily under a pump and he had a shower fitted on the ground floor, by his private study, with an enormous fall from the artesian cistern in the roof. Such cleanliness made other people smell and so Sam, without being asked, stepped out of line and begged permission to use the shower too. The old man was delighted to have made a convert, and greeted Sam like an old friend when he came from under the icy blast shivering like a dog. 'Excellent, what?'

'Puts ten years on my life, sir,' Sam said loyally. Next day he stood fully clothed by the noisy water, picking his teeth, then splashed a few drops over his hair to make it wet.

He knew without being told, recognising the signs, if the old man would go out riding. Sam would already have laid out riding boots and kicked the stableboy to life, and the horses would be waiting in the yard. Sam rode behind his master on a pony. He carried money in his pocket in case the old man made a purchase, and a pistol in case they were waylaid. Soon the old man asked him to ride alongside and talked to him, if not as an equal or a son, at least as a grandson.

'You've changed, Sam,' he remarked one day. 'Do you remember the person you were, when you first arrived here?'

'No, sir. Don't embarrass me,' Sam said.

'You even talked differently.'

'You've taught me so much, sir,' said Sam. 'I could never thank you enough. Getting me away from the town. The smoke. My early life was rather miserable, sir.'

'But you're happy now, eh?'

'In your service, sir.'

The old man laughed so hard his horse was startled. 'No, no, Sam. I know who's making you happy.' He tapped the side of his nose wisely before spurring on, and left Sam pondering how much he knew about Miss Carpenter, whose first name was Sarah.

After pulling off his master's boots and ordering Dora to take refreshments to the private study, 'Chop-chop, Dorrie!' and giving her a quick slap behind to make her squeak, Sam walked the horses back to the stable. Leaning against the hitching rail with a piece of straw nipped between his teeth, he swore at the stableboy to remove his own boots, threw him his riding coat to be brushed, and threatened the snivelling lad with the fires of Hell if the job wasn't properly done. 'I'm keeping my eye on you, Skyvey, my lad,' Sam warned, and the boy threw him a look of absolute terror, good jobs being so hard to come by in the locality. Skyvey did all the cleaning work Sam sent him, without complaint and without payment. Sam picked a dandelion growing between the cobbles and nodded once, contriving to fill his every action with menace in the boy's eyes.

Smiling broadly, he went up the back stairs where he ran into

Euphemia, the upstairs maid. She was coming out of the linen cupboard with a pile of dirty sheets bundled in her arms. Leaning against the doorway, he twirled the dandelion under her nose. 'Oh, Mr Sam!' she said, not trying to get past. 'I'm up to here with work!'

'I was out riding and I thought of you, Effie.' Sam could not for the life of him bring himself to call such a skinny nonentity Euphemia. 'I did think of you,' he said seriously.

'Liar,' she said, but he could see she wanted to believe him, and he snatched a kiss over the top of the sheets. Now she'd think of him all night, and tomorrow he might get his hand up her leg, even to her garter. Then victory would be in sight, and he would feel his way to heaven the next time, or the next. Then it would be over, just as it had been with Dorrie, his desire satisfied and fled. But even Dorrie, pouting, still squealed and gave him that hot, resentful, respectful look when he whacked her rump, which was just as it should be.

Sam whistled cheerfully as he gave Effie the nod and went on his way to the dressing room where he slept – he could hardly bed down in the maid's quarters in the attic, and the moon-faced scullion, Perdie, slept on a straw pallet in the kitchen, with her dirty toes almost touching the glowing range. Alone on his truckle bed in the corner of the dressing room, Sam was in hearing should the old man call unexpectedly in the night.

The maids were not the centre of the house, they were just something to get into, no better than they should be and deserving the genial contempt and occasional viciousness with which he treated them. The dining room was not the centre either, nor the broad entrance hall with its oak-parquet floor and oak-panelled walls hung with an ancestor or two, Sir this and Sir that. Nor was it to be found in the front parlour with its heavy lace tablecloths, heavy lace lambrequin, heavy overstuffed furniture and dark walls, where at the far end Amanda did her sewing quietly near the oriel window, the eight-day clock standing behind her in its mahogany case as tall as a man, the slowly-swinging pendulum sending forth its tocking as heavy as honey in the silence.

No, Sam thought, the centre of the house was the old man. It went wherever the old man was. And usually he was to be found in his private study.

Sam had glimpsed the room first from the outside, through the traceried window. He'd known at once it was the place to be. 'Something of an antiquarian,' the old man had said. 'A collector of valuables.'

To Sam, valuable meant gold, silver, jewellery, anything that could be stuffed in a turkey bag and hoisted to safety up the chimney.

The heavy bars across the windows confirmed it. Sam sucked his teeth, circling the flower beds as if looking for something lost, getting the angle of the sunlight streaming inside, straining his neck to see. The room was crowded with artefacts, display cases, glass-fronted cabinets, swords on the wall, muskets. Over the next few days Sam happened to notice, by dint of much hanging about in the hall, that the old man opened the door, which was mahogany, three inches thick and as strong as steel, with two full turns of an iron key.

Whatever was inside must be worth a fortune. Sam knew plenty of case-hardened cracksmen and clever shins, but none who could break into that room except by cutting the old man's throat for the key. Such a price made what the room contained even more valuable.

'You look like a bird-dog what's just seen the bird!' Dorrie trilled as she came out with the hearth brush, and Sam snatched a kiss to keep her quiet.

'What's in there?'

She looked surprised. 'Mouldy old rubbish,' she said, and wiped her mouth.

Sam took the bull by the horns, breezing in with a tray and a cup of hot chocolate as if he had been invited. He crossed to the desk by the fireplace, nimbly weaving between the cabinets and tables as though he was familiar with everything in the room. 'Put it down here for you, sir?'

The old man grunted.

Sam made the morning chocolate his routine, and noticed more every day. The huge china vases were useless, the old-fashioned muskets and rusty swords too, ten-a-penny down any Bermondsey market. The butterfly collection that the old man was working on, left him by his brother, was worthless too. There were a few yellowed skulls from up by the Blackheath road, as though there had once been a cemetery there, a fragment of marble with DEI carved on it in letters as large as a sign, quite without meaning now, and a mosaic of some sort of fish coming together out of a jumble of pieces, many of them missing – probably fetched in some farmer's apron. But there were one or two wonderful items, including a seven-branched silver candelabrum of a very odd, heavy-looking design, that had been dug out of the ground.

'Roman,' the old man said, mistaking Sam's interest. 'One of my tenants found it near the edge of the knoll. Was it hidden or was it lost? We'll never know.' Sam picked it up, weighing the silver. 'This will amuse you!' the old man said, showing Sam a few cracked fragments of red pottery, battered coins. 'Samian ware and coins of Claudius, found near the site where the Tabard now stands. I have a theory that between London Bridge and St George's Church was once a Roman street lined with villas and inns.'

'Too old to be valuable, then,' Sam said.

'Valuable to me. I see you are not struck with wonder, Sam. The sheer wonder of the past, of all our lives – not a secret, Sam, but a mystery. But pieces can be found, you know, the puzzle put together – who we are, where we come from.'

'I don't even know who my old ma is,' Sam said, and realised he had made a confession. It had come out of him suddenly, and hurt him as it came. He cleared his throat to hide the ache.

'Sam, Sam!' The old man embraced him, tears standing in his eyes and lips trembling, going senile, Sam thought. 'One day we will know everything – scientific enquiry reveals everything, just as Maskelyne's *Nautical Almanac* tells us all we need to know of the thirty-six fundamental stars, and with an accurate clock reveals exactly our position in the world.' He scattered the coins with the back of his hand, including seven or eight larger ones, one of them gripped in a copper claw. 'Knowledge, Sam. Everything can be known. Even the secrets of the human heart, one day.'

'Really, sir?' Sam said uneasily.

'Look at this – cheap copper. But look closely at these glittering specks, what do they tell us? That once it was expensively gilded with gold foil. My brother believed it was displayed during family marriages. Look at it, Sam. Did they believe it was solid gold, perhaps? Cheated by some goldsmith! Now the gilt is quite rubbed away, even the decorations, runes, whatever they were, worn almost smooth.' He perched glasses on his nose. 'Microscopic examination may reveal them.'

'Not worth much then,' Sam said.

'I'm holding *time* in my hand,' the old man laughed, 'and you talk of money! Feel it, Sam! History, our story.'

Sam laughed too.

When he came out of the barber's in Vaudey High Street, Sam looked sleek as a duck, his hair pulled back and secured by a particoloured ribbon, his jacket undone – the weather was hot – revealing a waistcoat as bright as ever, azure and carmine to make anyone's eyes water, and he walked as cocky as a cockerel. A few paces downhill took him to Mrs Chandler's door, where she took ages to answer his knock, must be going deaf as well as blind, and he went through to where Miss Carpenter waited in the garden, beneath the red apples, to give him his English lesson.

'Sarah!' he murmured. She knew as well as he why they were really here.

'Don't!' she whispered, struggling, but not too hard, as he took her in his arms. She was dressed in pale chiffon against the heat, not the heavy wool she wore to school, and as the gossamer material caressed his hands like a draught of air, he sensed the heat radiating from her body beneath. With a fingertip he brushed again, as though by accident, into the slim form of her hidden curves, and again she sighed, 'Don't!'

She was the most delicious thing he had ever held. 'You're divine,' he murmured, burying his face in her hair which smelled of the hot sun, and she put back her head.

'You don't know me,' she said.

'I want to know you.' He kissed her pale neck.

'You mustn't.'

'She can't see us,' said Sam. 'What do you want me to say?'

'Oh, I don't know,' she said, with longing.

'I love you,' Sam said. 'There. I love you and I'm burning up in the flames of Hell for you, divine, divine, Sarah.'

She took pity on him, and let him kiss her lips. She truly was beautiful, he thought, staring at her as he kissed her, filling himself with her, those elfin eyes of hers closing, the lashes quivering as the sunlight struck across her soft eyelids, her eyebrows darker than her hair, quite the most beautiful girl. He let his weight pull him down on her, kissing her mouth, her throat. 'I love you.' Her breasts revealed themselves to his hands, then he had all of her, slithering into her heart, and suddenly there was nothing. It was over.

She wanted to hug him, of course. Bits of fresh always did. 'Thanks for the English lesson,' he said.

She pulled his cheek. 'Tell me again you love me. I love you,' she said, as though they were going to get married.

'I should have thought you know how I feel by now.'

'I feel so wicked. Show me I'm not wicked, Sam.'

'Let's do it again,' he said, and she sat up, horrified.

Sam walked back to the manor eating a ripe red apple and tossing another in his hand. He felt drained, given, taken, marvellous to be no longer in need of her. Having possessed her flesh, the divine Miss Carpenter was now merely flesh, and he was free.

As he crossed the rose garden, a female's voice called out to him. It was a formal place, with little lawns, steps and balustrades, and heated walls that made the place startlingly green even in winter. Now it was drowsy with high summer, the shrubs overblown and wilting in the muggy heat, and only when she waved to catch his eye did he see Miss Amanda Fox. She was doing gardener's work pruning an espalier rose latticed to the wall, wearing a broad-brimmed hat from which a white veil hung down over her face to protect her from the wasps attracted by the nearby fig tree. As he came towards her, she turned back to her task, then snatched away her finger, lifting her veil to examine it.

'Every rose has its thorn,' Sam said.

She spoke without looking at him, drawing a deep breath. 'Mr Wittle, it is our duty to become friends.'

For the first time in his life Sam was lost for words.

'My father instructs it,' she told the roses, adding vulnerably, 'Surely it is not too horrible a thought?'

'But—'

'You know how my father feels about you. He is an old man made frail by a hard life, and you have made yourself indispensable to him in his failing years. You have wormed your way into his heart – don't deny it, Mr Wittle. After a lifetime at war, peace is what my father craves above all else, and I treasure his happiness above all things.' He did not think so highly of her, Sam knew, remembering the admiral's casual dismissal of his daughter, 'a girl is useless'. Though the old man was perfectly polite to his daughter, that was all it was, and now that he thought about it Sam could not recall a single show of affection between them, only good manners.

A thrill ran through Sam. She must be desperately lonely! He knew he must be able to make something of such repression, for she had shown little sign of it. Except that he remembered her shaking with anger on the stairs.

'I'm sure he has your best interests at heart,' he said smoothly.

'Do you really think so?' she scoffed, catching Sam out, and he wished he had paid her more attention. She stood up to her full height. 'He is thinking of the family. I am willing to do my best.' She glanced at Sam Wittle as though there was a bad smell under her nose. 'There. I have said my piece. If I have ever offended you, I apologise.'

'Well, don't fall over yourself with pleasure about it,' muttered Sam, his complaint seeming cruel when she staggered as she turned, and he visualised that bloated lump of deformed flesh beneath her skirt as clearly as though she were resting her club foot in his lap.

'I revolt you, don't I?' she said, looking at him straight. 'I revolt everyone, I can see it in their eyes and smiles, the way they don't look. Except your eyes, Sam Wittle. But perhaps you're just a very good liar.'

No woman had ever spoken to him like this, browbeating him and succeeding, and he hated it.

'Let's not be enemies,' he compromised, with the awful feeling that he was supposed to kiss her hand. He took her fingers and bowed his head over them.

'You have lice in your hair,' she said, and Sam looked at her with a forced laugh, his vanity reddening his cheeks. She nodded slowly, looking right into his eyes, and Sam was diminished by her force of personality, realising she thought him even more imperfect than she thought herself. 'Carry in my vegetable basket, would you,' she said. 'And, Mr Wittle, there is just one condition. Just one.'

'Yes, ma'am,' Sam said.

'You must never let me see you lie.'

He followed her obediently. 'That's all?'

'That's everything,' she said.

From then on, Sam was expected to do more than simply acknowledge her when he saw her in the front parlour; they must make polite conversation about the weather, the flowers, the frost, whether such and such a piece of embroidery should be this shade of blue or that. Her earlier reluctance to admit that she needed help from anyone, especially Sam, had changed to a positive insistence that he help her all the time. He must exchange a few words whenever they passed on the stairs. He must carry her basket, lift her into her carriage or onto her horse, all tasks she could do for herself perfectly well but which she deliberately made him perform. She was making him more than a servant, more than a suitor. She was domesticating him. Revealing herself to him. Intimidating him. Amanda had chosen a man at last – or rather, had had him chosen for her.

Sam was well aware of the scandalised whispers in the village – Amanda even made sure he was seen out riding in the afternoons with her, she sidesaddle on the large, steady roan called Boulder, he on the infuriating little pony, cantering alongside like a faithful puppet to her ladylike trot – but the truth was that he felt nothing for her. He worked Dorrie's and Effie's affections mercilessly, so that they scrapped for a kind word from him like dogs for bones, but he could not manipulate Amanda because he could not simulate affection for her. Sam's vanity was such that he could fall only for a pretty girl, and then only for a day. Away from Amanda he had a fine life, but not with her.

Perdie on her straw mat in front of the stove was his, and now he had his eye on niggling the red-cheeked buxom girl in the buttery, round the back of the saye, who had a button missing from her blouse. Her name was Ginny.

But Sam would have been outraged to know that the show Amanda made with him stemmed wholly from her loyalty to her father, who watched them leaning from the study window or waved to them from the balustrade round the fountain as they set off, taking pleasure in their apparent pleasure. The truth was that the closer Sam and Amanda appeared, the further apart they were. The more they talked, the more their words estranged them

from each other. The more Amanda trusted Sam with her foot –
'It's what the doctors call *talipes*, Sam' – the more she repelled
him. 'When I was a child they manipulated it, and broke the
bones, and reset the joints. But it's part of me.' She looked at him
plainly. 'It's what I am.'

Sam lied perfectly.

The old man's knee had never really healed, and sometimes he
cursed its grating stiffness as more trouble that if he'd had his leg
off, but still he limped out to wave goodbye to the young lovers or
to greet them on their return. Amanda was right, and the wagging
tongues in the village quite wrong: Sam had wormed his way into
her father's heart, not hers.

Sam still dreamed hungrily of that private study stocked with
treasures. He knew now that there was jewellery kept in those thin
drawers, not only Elizabeth's but family stuff going back for
generations. Rings and brooches lay loose among scuffed prayer
books and crucifixes of silver and gold. The yellowed pages of an
almost illegible masque called *Cardenio* were pressed under a
great weight of medieval church plate, hidden in the garden when
the Puritans came to ransack St John's Church, ugly but worth a
fortune melted – an accumulation of the fabulously worthwhile
with the worthless.

These were the things Sam thought of when he lied. And an
income of five thousand a year, and this fine house with its
windows shining like the sun, and owning that iron key.

One afternoon, riding past the school in Amanda's shadow,
Sam saw Miss Carpenter on the other side of the railings, and
remembered her for the first time in months. He touched the
brim of his hat with his cane in salutation as he had learned to do,
and cantered on. A few weeks later, someone told him she had
applied for a teaching post elsewhere, and for a moment he could
not even recall her first name. Sairey? Sarah. All he remembered
of her were the apples.

A few days later, it might have been a week, a message came
with Skyvey, who lived with his grandmother opposite Mrs
Chandler, that Miss Carpenter wanted to see Sam about his
English. In the stable yard Skyvey, cringing, tried desperately not
to look knowing or sly. 'I must've forgot to pay her bill,' Sam lied
instinctively, gave Skyvey a cuff round the head for good measure,

and rode up to Vaudey. It never crossed his mind that anything was wrong.

It was a windy, blowy evening, dark smears of cloud flying overhead but a blade of clear sky rising over the bowl of London, and he could smell the smoke of Newcastle sea coal, the smell of London, and a wave of nostalgia swept over him.

He dismounted and hitched his pony to an iron bollard. No one was about, and what with the noise of the wind and Mrs Chandler's hearing, his knock on the door was not answered. He pushed the latch and the door swung open.

The old woman was sitting by the fire, asleep, a lantern gleaming brightly on the table beside her, showing up the dark indoors. She was snoring, blowing out the fine pale hairs around her mouth, and her breathing did not change when Sam coughed politely. He took off his hat, striding nimbly up the narrow staircase in the corner – even bareheaded, he had to duck at the top against the angle of the roof which showed a greasy oblong where everyone caught themselves.

There was no reply to his tap on the door. Was it the girl's way of saying he should have thought of her more often? Sam began to wonder if this might be Miss Carpenter's petty revenge on him – a wasted journey. He knocked again, louder.

'Miss . . . Sarah?' How ridiculous they could be in their spite, and his impatience turned to irritation that she was wasting his time. 'This isn't funny, Sarah,' he called.

Something creaked. She was there.

Sam pushed the door and stepped inside.

A shadow crossed the window, then crossed back again. He watched for a moment, thinking calmly. She hadn't understood that he would feel nothing.

Sam knew exactly what to do.

He stepped quietly downstairs, tiptoed past the old woman and fetched a candle from the scullery. He lit it from the lantern's oil flame. The old woman still nodded by the fire, snoring unpleasantly.

Holding up the candle, Sam climbed back to Sarah Carpenter's room.

Her sash window faced him, open. She had hanged herself, fully dressed, in clean clothes, with the window open to hear the wind in the orchard. The rope creaked. She had struggled dreadfully.

Sam moved round her carefully, holding up the candle. Black blood had burst from the corners of her eyes, the veins standing across her temples like claws. Sam held her hand, stiff and hard as ice, to stop her swinging.

Her bed, neatly made, was fitted into a niche on his right. Against the wall on his left was her dresser. In front of him was her overturned chair – she must have tried her chair first, but found it not high enough. She had clambered onto her dresser and tied the rope round the roof beam. She must have crouched there very awkwardly between her pitcher and her washing bowl, with her bottom against the mirror, tying the rope round her neck. It was a child's skipping rope, the handles painted with bright red stripes, easy enough for her to pick up or confiscate at school.

Crouched on the dresser like a swimmer on the edge of cold water, thinking of him.

And then she had slid forward. *Suspensus per collum*, by her own hand, the bitch.

Sam wasn't frightened, he was angry, he was as angry as he had ever been. Did she think to haunt him? He had done nothing wrong. She had understood men not at all, not one thing about Sam Wittle. She should have married another schoolteacher and raised children.

Sam touched her cold, swollen belly.

The wind blew, and she twisted and turned, her hands still clamped together in the death agony of her last prayer, her tongue sticking out like a lizard's about to strike.

On her pillow Sam saw a piece of folded paper, weighted by the wax stamp that sealed it. He sighed, having seen all this before at the Tabard. They always left notes.

He picked it up but did not read it. For all he knew she had left the folded paper blank, as blank as she felt her own life to be. Sam never knew or cared. He slipped the folded corner into the candle flame and watched it burn, turning it in his fingers as it blackened, then letting the ash blow from the window.

Standing on the chair, he took her weight – not much – and unknotted the skipping rope from the beam, then from her neck, and laid her on the bed. She lay like someone in the grip of a ghastly nightmare, but soon that would not matter.

Sam left the skipping rope coiled on the chair, where it was innocent. He left the window open, and the door, cupping his hand to protect the candle flame as he went downstairs. The stairway made a natural chimney.

He found cooking oil in the scullery and splashed it around the downstairs rooms, then a jug of lamp oil which he poured carefully round the old woman, knocking over the lantern too so that its reservoir spilled across the table – the obvious cause of the fire, if anything at all was left.

The oil spreading over the table caught in a soft white flare, raining fiery drips on the rug. Threads of sooty smoke boiled up at once, then dense billows that made the fire dim, catching the back of Sam's throat, and he held his breath as he backed to the door through the crackling gloom. The smoke billowed across the ceiling toward the stairwell, sucked upstairs.

Sam opened the door and let himself out into the street. He latched the door carefully and returned to his post at Holywell Manor – supper would soon be served – without looking back.

In the stable yard he dismounted, having circled round and come in from the opposite direction, beside the buttery. Skyvey was sleeping on a bale of straw. Sam took the lobe of the boy's ear between the nails of his forefinger and thumb, pinching hard. Skyvey woke, struggling like a fish.

'I haven't been anywhere,' Sam said, twisting his pinch, breathing close over Skyvey's face. 'You have not seen me.' Twist. 'Or I'll have your lungs out.'

'I haven't seen you, Mr Sam.'

'That's right.'

'That's right, Mr Sam,' Skyvey whined, and Sam walked away pointing at a glow uphill. 'Looks like someone's chimney's caught fire.'

Skyvey threw him an admiring glance, sure that Mr Sam had just had his way with that worthless smut in the buttery.

Going inside, Sam changed his clothes in case they smelt of smoke, and went down to dinner. When Dorrie leaned against him to place a silver dish on the table while the others were absorbed at the window watching the tragedy of the distant flames, he took the opportunity to pinch her behind and cast her his irrepressible wink.

It would be difficult to think of any way in which matters could have turned out worse for Sam. Had he been caught – seen riding away from the burning house, for example, if the flames had been visible at that time – and if he had confessed (which he would never have done) he would merely have been arraigned at Maidstone Assizes and hanged by the neck until dead, and everything would have been over.

Had he been less proud and kept to his original plan, breaking into the private study to take his pick of anything worth having, he would have vanished back to the Borough long ago, or like as not set himself up in merry Bankside as a man of property, with wives a-plenty and never the same one twice, and no nagging tongue to make his life a misery, and children to be sent out to work instead of pampered.

It is an eternal truth, of which Sam was jauntily aware, that people such as he do not get caught. After his childhood at the Tabard Inn, survival in this pleasant haven was easy; he was a pike among the minnows. In front of the Vaudey villagers he shed the proper tear for Miss Carpenter, but not too much, for she had been no more than his English teacher, he could hardly have known her, could he? He took flowers to her grave, but no more than the schoolchildren, who placed them with serious faces then ran away to play. Sam knew he was innocent, he had done nothing wrong.

Sam could not believe in his own guilt, only other people's. Such men as he did not run foul of the law, it was always on their side.

Soon the fire was just another minor tragedy, the two bodies placed in the earth charred beyond recognition, covered over and forgotten, the one presumed to be Miss Carpenter's in a deal coffin and an unmarked pauper's grave, for she had left no will, the plot grown over with grass and weeds within a week or two, and the withered flowers stolen for later burials. Within a couple of months even the tacky wooden cross was gone as though she had never been, and by winter the gravediggers cursed to come across her unknown bones, there was never enough room.

Between her hips lay another tiny skeleton, part fish, part reptile, part monkey, like a first rough sketch for a human being. Still cursing the frost and their wasted effort, the diggers looked for another place, and left the bones to embrace their unborn child until Judgment Day.

By next summer the unsightly gap of blackened timbers between the houses of Becket Street had been plugged with another dwelling, thanks to the property speculator Mr Loat. A new family moved in, the proud young mother placing a vase of daffodils in the bow window, so that once more the facade of the street was regular and proper.

Meanwhile, at the manor house, everyone got what they thought they wanted. Sam got an income of five thousand a year, Holywell Manor with its windows shining like the sun, and that iron key – more than he had ever dreamed of possessing, though to get it he must take a wife whose appearance repulsed him, whose personality made him feel small. The admiral's crippled daughter Amanda got a husband at last, though that was altogether different from a friend or a servant, and fulfilled her duty. The admiral would get what he wanted more than anything in the world, even more than long life in his uncomfortable old age: an heir at last for his blood if not his name. His grandchildren would be the old man's immortality.

'Give my permission, my boy? Delighted!'

Sam kissed Amanda on the lips and they stood awkwardly for a moment in the parlour, their hands touching, the clock ticking loudly. Amanda covered her mouth with hers on pretence of a cough, and did not return it. Sam put his behind his back, wishing he could sit down. He must marry the one woman who could see through him, and instinctively he pulled apart. The old man gave a clap and pushed them together again, so that Amanda staggered. 'Young things!' he chuckled, not noticing.

'It's a great honour you do me, sir,' lied Sam. 'I never dreamed—'

'I can't pretend I'm not pleased, Sam.' The old man hobbled to the painted Adam cabinet and unlocked his private stock, kept safe from Dorrie's tippling. The moment had come when Sam was almost one of the family, and it was time for frankness. 'Forgive me, but you see, Sam Wittle, the very things that would usually be against you – a nobody, to be frank – work to your advantage. You have no name to mention, unlike some of the young hopefuls of this district, whose country stock goes back with ours for hundreds of years. And you have no income, unlike they. On the other hand, you have no debts, as they surely do.'

'Heaven forbid, sir,' Sam said.

'And you will treat Amanda better than if you were her equal, for you will not be her superior.'

Sam swallowed.

'The best went to sea,' said the old man. 'The butcher's bill, you see, Sam. The terrible butcher's bill.'

Amanda laid her hand sympathetically on her father's arm, then sat quickly on a fauteuil.

The old man waved Sam to a couch. 'There's just one condition,' he said. Sam sat instantly motionless and watchful; Amanda had used exactly the same words seeking his friendship in the rose garden. The Fox family always kept their sting in the tail, it seemed, and suddenly he hated them for it, their arrogance, their self-confident superiority.

'Anything, sir,' he said politely.

The old man turned, red-faced as a squire should be and jovial, and handed Sam a small glass of smuggled brandy.

He spoke implacably. 'If you are to marry my daughter, Sam Wittle, you will change your name to hers, not hers to yours.' He clicked his fingers as though flicking the worthless name Wittle from under his fingernails.

'Agreed,' Sam said at once, before everything he had won slipped away from him, and tossed back his brandy, then sat there twirling it as the old man and his daughter stuck their long noses into their balloon glasses, snifting and swirling the fine brandy before taking tiny sips. Sam watched comfortably. Everything would be different when they were married. He would have to learn to be served, how to be a gentleman.

He would give the orders.

'Agreed, then,' said the old man. 'There is one final point. On my death the house passes, not to Amanda, since women cannot own property, but straight into trust for my grandson.'

Sam swallowed. 'What if there is no son?'

'Look on the arrangement,' smiled the old man, 'as an

encouragement. You will possess, Sam, but you are not truly of the Fox blood. You will never own Holywell Manor.'

There was a long, long moment of silence. Then Sam held out his glass. 'I was wrong about you, sir. You're not so much a gentleman, more a fighting man.'

'My family and my name.' The old man shrugged as though it was obvious. He refilled Sam's glass. 'These were worth fighting to the end of my life for.'

Sam drank the brandy in one. It tasted bitter as dregs.

'Then you own me, sir,' he said.

Sam decided not to care. He had wooed Amanda without caring where it led, just as he had arrived at Holywell without caring where it was, living from opportunity to opportunity. When he took Sarah Carpenter, or Effie upstairs or naughty Dorrie with her soft curves held in place by her dress and apron strings, or Perdie or the girl in the buttery who had resisted him enticingly, he cared nothing for their hopes and loves. So now he married Amanda without caring, and lay with her without caring.

But Amanda would not allow him to be indifferent to her.

'Look at me, Sam,' she said, sitting up beside him.

'What's there to see?' Sam surprised, pushed himself back in the soft pillows. 'Stop treating me like a child. I'll be the one in charge here. You'll learn.'

'You've never really looked at a woman before, have you, Sam?' she said as if he had not spoken, and Sam shrivelled. Did she know about Dorrie, Effie – even Sarah? How much did she know about him?

Sam tried to laugh it off, but he couldn't manage that friendly slap on the rump to put her in her place. He just sat there hugging the sheets round him.

'*Look* at me, Sam,' Amanda said, showing herself.

He looked. He started to make a joke, intimidated, but Amanda stopped him.

'Hold me,' she said.

'Come off it,' he laughed. 'What's all this about?' Amanda limped round the bed and sat beside him, holding him in her arms. 'My poor husband,' she said, rocking him. 'My poor, poor fool. To think you could get away from me.'

Their only child, Arthur, was born three years later. He had lovely deep eyes and red hair, and grew up with everything that a child could ask for. Arthur was the exact opposite of his father and Sam had no time for him. Where Sam dealt himself a fortune in slick but apparently above-board speculation with such men as Loat and Tyler and knew how to be lucky – and would have raffled the manor itself for a fortune if he could have got his hands on it – Arthur who was born with everything was always unlucky. And though Arthur, unlike Sam, never did anything wrong, he always, always got caught.

Evening had fallen, dark with rain, and it was the same old London story: without warning Jemima's train slowed, rattling, then the brakes squealed and the third-class passengers began to curse, even the women standing around Jemima, who were leaning back as though against a slope.

'Strewth!' one man shouted, jumping from his seat. 'Not the bleedin' points a-bleeding 'gain! Can't they get *anyfink* right?' As the brakes came on hard he lurched forward, then, when he tried to get back to claim his place, a pert girl had already slipped onto the hard wooden slats. 'Oi!' he complained.

''Ard cheese! Finders keepers.' She rested her feet with a groan. 'Yer didn't want it nuff ter sit on it, chum! 'Smine now.'

'Out of it, or I'll put yer face inside out,' the man said. He started pulling her arm, and Jemima watched, horrified that none of the other passengers noticed, as the man dragged the girl off her seat and gave her a shove down the carriage. Helped by the brakes, she almost fell, then caught herself by the door and pretended that was where she had wanted to go, keeping her dignity. The man settled himself on the seat and looked around victoriously. 'Cracked!' he asserted. 'She was bleedin' cracked!' Jemima wondered why no one told him to watch his manners, or called the conductor, or sympathised with the girl, who was rubbing her bruised arm.

Jemima had never ridden third-class before. Now she would ride third-class for the rest of her life, unless the talents saved her.

The train stopped with a loud grating noise, throwing sparks that illuminated the rain in white bursts, freezing the scene outside like a photographer's flashpan: endless rows of rooftops and ranks of chimneypots marching line after line into the overhanging smoke of a London winter's evening.

'Bermondsey, bleedin' Bermondsey, more bleedin' Bermondsey,' came a girl's voice. She leaned morosely over the seat back, her chin almost touching Jemima's shoulder. 'Spa Road ternight, juss like last night, an' stuck points, if yer believe *that*. I don't know what they'll fink of next.'

Goaded, Jemima responded tartly, 'I'm sure the London and Greenwich Railway is not in the habit of telling fibs.'

The girl put forward her head and looked round at Jemima as though she was mad. 'When was you born, yesterday?' She pushed back a wet papier-mâché flower drooping from her Rosemary Lane rag-market hat, and Jemima dismissed her as a common woman of no importance. 'Nah, the bloody sods, they don't care, do they?' the girl went on, having a friendly chat. 'I should sit leanin' ter the left if I was yer.' She patted a bead of rain that had dripped from the roof onto Jemima's shoulder. 'Cor, that's a nice bit of old velvet, I should watch yerself going fer best like that round 'ere, they'll 'ave it off yer back. Not a tart, are yer?' She came round and pushed herself on the seat, wriggling to get comfortable, as friendly as though Jemima was one of their own. Jemima shuddered. The girl, who obviously considered herself quite well off, shrugged and wiped her nose with a sniff at not being answered. 'I'm sittin' 'neath the drip fer yer!' she pointed out.

Jemima said nothing. She was seventeen years old, and though she did not have much experience, she felt this must be the bleakest hour of her life.

She'd left the green valley and Holywell Manor on its knoll for the last time, left her privileged childhood behind her; she had grown up and now, she feared, she might become just like the girl beside her, if she was to survive.

But she remembered her grandmother's favourite saying: *Something always turns up. You never can tell, Jemima, you never can tell. Lucky is as lucky makes.* With a nostalgic half-smile Jemima recalled walking beside Grandmama in the rose garden, a child earnestly adjusting her stride to suit Grandmama's clumping foot. In those days her father, Arthur, could still afford the gardeners who kept the grass smooth, and Amanda could still walk.

Jemima stared from the train window, which was as dirty as a disease.

Her long red hair had fallen over her shoulders, but she dared not pin it up in case she drew even more attention to herself. She clasped her embroidered handbag tightly in her lap, afraid to look inside at her dead father's pocket watch in case it was stolen or, worse, in case the silver curiosity that lay beside it was stolen. Amanda always called it a talent, saying the word as though it promised something wonderful, and Jemima, growing up, had had a child's belief in such promises: that there was something wonderful worth growing up for. In those days there had been eight of them, kept in Arthur's private study, but one of them had been stolen, supposedly pilfered by the notorious Irish hop-pickers who, having drunk their train money, footed it back to the rookeries of London, keeping themselves in cider by breaking into places as they went.

Only seven were left.

'Is it really magical, Grandmama?'

'There never is anything to such curiosities, my dear,' Amanda had replied, but reluctantly, as though loath to disappoint a child's sense of wonder, bringing Jemima gently down to reality. 'It's a family story, that's all. Once there were supposed to be twenty-nine of them, something to do with Chaucer. The twenty-nine pilgrims in the *Canterbury Tales*, I suppose – excluding Chaucer himself, of course.' She had added, as adults do to children, 'I don't think it's really true, do you?'

But at the age of seven Jemima had known magic was real, and she remembered herself saying fiercely, 'I do believe in them, Grandmama. They *are* special. I *do*.'

Amanda had laughed in the sunlight and tousled Jemima's hair, her youngest of seven grandchildren and her favourite, the only girl. 'It's strange,' she said. 'None of the others feel about them as you do, you know, none of the boys . . .'

This afternoon, before catching the train at Combe Forest Station near the bottom of Vaudey Hill, Jemima had stood in front of Holywell Manor. Nothing had moved; the oak trees were bare, black nets. She had been saying goodbye. A white-haired man carrying some planks under his arm had crossed the drive towards her, but she ignored him.

No light had reflected in the windows – the sky was already dark over London behind her – and the great house looked silent and still for the first time she could remember. The rooms had always been so full of life, not the dull dusty caverns they now were but vibrant with laughter – with such a large family it was bound to be a lively place, children running everywhere, nannies calling, servants giggling behind their hands at the children's naughtiness, and then Mother coming out both angry and fearful at once, a finger to her lips and her eyes turning towards the study door: '*Sssh, your father's working . . .* '

Father hadn't been working, Jemima knew now. He'd been drinking. Or rather, he always worked with a small glass of whisky at his elbow – to help him think, Mother always said, refilling the glass understandingly. It wasn't for drinking but for reassurance; Arthur actually drank very little, the level took ages to drop. He was never drunk. Harriet had gone to her grave believing this, so convincingly had she lied to herself about her husband.

'It's my fault,' Amanda had said, leaning on Jemima's shoulder by the graveside in St John's churchyard, watching Arthur, forty-seven years old, place his top hat carefully on his head, fold his gloves in his left hand, and walk steadily away from Harriet's life and the past, his six sons in tow behind him like a row of geese.

Watching them go, Amanda, nearly eighty years old, had shaken her head and whispered, 'You're the only one I have to talk to now, Jemima. We're the oldest and the youngest, the closest. The end of the circle and its beginning. I was going to say all my friends are dead, but that's not why I'm so lonely. The truth is, I never had any friends.'

'I like you to talk me, Grandmama. You had Arthur, didn't you? But he was only a child, I suppose.'

'Your father was a wonderful child.' Implicit in the old woman's praise, Jemima realised, was that, despite her constant prodding, Arthur was unable to live up to her dreams for him as an adult; only a Second at Cambridge, and only minor lapses of business judgment, but as consistent as a flaw in the mirror. Arthur had inherited his father's propensity for lying, but he was a bad liar; he never made a promise without breaking it, raining with the clouds and shining with the sun. 'Children are always wonderful, always worth the price. If only I could have had him without marriage.' Amanda could say this now, looking calmly at the headstone a few paces away, an ostentatious and sentimental slab of black marble with gold leaf and Cockney cherubs flying and angels blowing horns, beneath which Sam Fox had lain for ten years.

'An illicit relationship!' Jemima said, shocked, very straitlaced at the age of twelve.

'You'll understand one day. Sam changed all this, you know, like a breath of fresh air.' Amanda pointed around her with her stick. 'Paid for the renovation of this ancient church, bullied and chivvied for it to be reconsecrated. He saw that St John's could once again be the centre of the village.'

'He must have been very far-sighted and religious,' Jemima said, thinking that was what the old woman wanted to hear.

'Sam was very greedy, child. The fields around it were all his – I mean Arthur's, of course, when he came of age. Sam wheeled and dealed sheep pasture into villas for the up-and-coming classes as well as the wealthy. The railway from London Bridge to Greenwich was one of the first proper lines in the country, you know, so that suddenly a banker or lawyer could travel to the City to work and come back to his home here in the evening. Sam saw all this, and invested in it. He made and lost several fortunes. Money stuck to him and slipped away. He loved money. That was all he loved.'

'But my father is not like that.'

'No, they had nothing in common. They could hardly speak to each other, but Sam didn't hate Arthur. He was jealous of him.'

'Of his own son? But Sam was so successful!'

'Sam came from nowhere, he had no childhood, no training for love. But Arthur was born with a silver spoon in his mouth, everything was handed to him on a plate. Everything that was so hard for Sam is easy for Arthur. Sam grew old young, he could never unlearn his lessons from the Tabard Inn – yes, my dear, your grandfather was a common tavern boy.'

'Oh,' Jemima said, her cheeks colouring.

'Of course he was envious of his son! However hard he tried, Sam could never be a gentleman, he could only cut a dash to show he was rich, buy whatever clothes or horses or, my dear, women that he fancied.'

'You mustn't have allowed it!' Jemima said earnestly.

'Mustn't I? I'm talking of real life, child, not what is supposed to be. Yes, I know. I connived, if you will. I asked no questions, and I was told no lies. That was our arrangement, and it was perfectly satisfactory. Arthur would be born a gentleman, brought up a gentleman. But it was too late for Sam. He knew it.'

'But you loved him.'

'For more than thirty years we did not share the same bedroom.'

'But you must have been proud of him.' Jemima struggled to understand the strange world of grown-ups that she was coming to. 'The way he died, a hero, breaking into a burning house and jumping from the window with a child in his arms. Everyone knows that.'

Amanda had looked at Jemima sadly. 'My dear, Sam died with my arms round him, apparently of his burns, which were dreadful. But in reality he was already dying of syphilis and he was losing his mind. He had been making love to the boy's mother. He whispered to me that the fire was his fault, he had knocked over a lantern on the table. Those were his last words to me. "I knocked over the lantern, and its reservoir spilled across the table." And then he died.'

The fountain splashed loudly in front of Jemima, the empty house beyond. The old man dropped one end of the planks on the ground, getting out his hammer.

'Yes,' Jemima said, 'finish your work.'

She watched him drag the planks up the steps to the front door and begin hammering the planks across.

Suddenly, Jemima wished she knew more. She'd almost cried out, 'Stop!' Wished she could have known everything. But it was too late.

The old man finished and walked away.

In the dead silence, the cheerful splashing of the fountain, which never stopped, had seemed almost obscene.

Mortgaged and repossessed, Holywell Manor had been gutted. Last week she and her brothers, working in a frenzy ahead of the bailiffs, had thrown away the old bits of pottery and mosaic – no one had offered a brass farthing for them. The manorial rolls and the St John's parish registers, worthless in themselves but going back hundreds of years probably, had been bundled up in string and sent away to the Greenwich Local History Library in Mycenae Road. No one had ever looked at them at Holywell, but as soon as they were absent Jemima had felt their loss. The virtuoso butterfly collection had been left, the cabinets claimed by the bailiffs, but the children came across the seven talents in one of the drawers. They were hidden right at the back, as if to resist temptation – the temptation to pawn or sell them, perhaps, because Arthur had pawned or sold everything else, silver candlesticks and Grandmama's jewellery, even their mother's jewellery, to the jewellers in Becket Street, and a whole library of books to the Greenwich secondhand bookshops.

But the seven coins were safe, and Jemima had clutched them in her hands, feeling their warmth.

'Strictly speaking,' Martin had lectured her, 'they belong to the bailiffs. It's stealing.'

'Whose side are you on?' she'd demanded. 'They're *ours*.'

'She's right,' Reuben said, less than a year older than Jemima; their mother Harriet had said they were almost twins. 'Besides, Martin, what does it matter if it is stealing, if it's the only way to get on?'

Seeing the light in Jemima's eye, Martin compromised. 'We'll share them out equally, by value if they have any, which they don't. Drop them in with any other stuff, Mimmy.'

And so Jemima, simmering at his use of her pet name, had written to Spink's and made her appointment for a valuation in a week's time, determined to prove her eldest brother wrong. Over the next few days she and Reuben had worked to finish up before the family was scattered for ever. Reuben found their father's gold pocket watch behind the wainscotting, still ticking. It was then that they had begun to find the bottles, just one or two at first – whisky bottles, empty. The hiding places were exposed one by one as the furniture was removed, pictures were taken down and bookcases were pulled away from the walls. Jemima and Reuben even came across their father's bottles sunk in the ornamental pool of the fountain.

Arthur had claimed he was suffering from a touch of jaundice. After his death his liver was found to be completely yellow, hard as stone, made cirrhotic by alcohol over many years. He was fifty-three.

Arthur had been born with everything, but it hadn't been enough.

The house had seemed so empty as she had walked through the echoing rooms for the last time. Part of the structure was supposed to go back to the fourteenth century; the great windows and the staircase had been put in by Bess Fox in Elizabethan times – Jemima ran her hand over the banisters, their oak worn smooth by time and the hands of generations of children running up and down, or sliding when they thought they could get away with it, as she had done . . .

The wind sent the rain sheeting across the rooftops of Bermondsey below the viaduct, and Jemima dragged herself back to the present, staring at her own face in the glass.

Someone hawked and spat on the floor of the railway carriage. Ahead of her the locomotive growled and muttered quietly to itself, like a sleeping dinosaur. The sparse oil lamps dotted the unheated wagon with yellow pools of illumination, each one filled with heads, hats, shoulders, more than she could count, and Jemima realised that she had never really seen these people before. For the first time in her life the cloth caps had faces beneath them, they were real people, Jemima realised, all in the same hurry as she was and all with the same fears and desires that she had. The man opposite her ate his way slowly through a stump of cheese.

She felt her bag for the hardness of the talent inside.

Something always turns up. You never can tell, Jemima, you never can tell.

'Lucky is as lucky makes,' she muttered.

The train lurched forward, but nobody cheered.

She did not realise until many years later that Phineas Murge must have followed her back across London Bridge to the Tabard, where she was late meeting her brothers. And as she pushed her way through the smoke and smell of the inn's parlour, she did not notice the girl working there stare at her as if she recognised her, and then duck down behind the counter.

Her name was Tilly O'Neill.

Two years before, at the end of the hop-picking season in October 1868, Tilly had been not quite sixteen, her birthday falling in the middle of December. She knew nothing of this, being unable to count higher than twelve, or read, or write, and having no birthdays that she knew of. From the age of eight she had been sent out with a tray of useless things to sell, single matches or watercress or whatever was in season, but her wan, hopeless face and drab manner did not attract customers; they hurried past without even seeing her. The more she returned home with her tray only half-empty, or her money stolen, the more her father beat her. Everyone said he had justification, she was such a dull and careworn creature. The more she was beaten, the more she attracted beatings, until just seeing her forlorn face was a provocation to him.

Tilly was no beauty; she was thin, her nose was too long and her eyes were too wide, and they were sort of slanty, which he said made her look like a bloody liar.

Tilly had wept later, knowing he spoke the truth. As soon as he heard her moans, he beat her again.

Domhnall knew how to take everything the wrong way, he did it deliberately. It kept his family, the two of them that remained, in their place.

All the O'Neills were born with the feeling that things ought to be better for them than they were – long ago, they were supposed to have been part of a great family – but Domhnall felt it as a grudge. Everything was against him. He begrudged being poor and blamed the rich, he begrudged feeding Tilly's mouth, he begrudged the Catholics that surrounded him in the stinking, swarming rookery at Lisson Grove on London's northern boundary, making him doubly an outsider: shunned by the Catholics because he was a Protestant, shunned by the English because he was Irish. And the more they treated him with contempt, the more he felt contempt for them, white-hot.

Domhnall hated everyone, it burned his guts.

To Tilly, hatred was normal. She could imagine nothing else, though she didn't feel it herself. She didn't feel anything. Of course Domhnall beat her, like he beat her mother, chasing her round the room or out into the street to give her a knockabout, then sorting out Tilly too, nothing too rough, bending her arms until she screamed obediently. Domhnall had a history of strength. At the age of fourteen, strong enough to try, he'd beaten his father to a pulp, closing both his eyes, and then carried on knocking him from side to side across the street until old Sean wouldn't get up. Domhnall went back to the pub, and when he barged out spoiling for a fight again, the street was empty. His father was gone.

Everyone agreed old Sean had got what he asked for.

Domhnall O'Neill was a huge man with huge hairy fists, and he used them to keep order against the chaos all around them. Tilly's elder sister had got out by marrying one of the Ryans, from the frying pan to the fire, that was, so only Ma and Tilly were left. Fortunately for Domhnall he had no sons; sooner or later they would have had their revenge, for as he grew older his muscle was turning to beer froth, but his women's submissiveness excited him, and made his grudges and his cunning rages more frightful than ever. In his youth, it was said, Domhnall could lift a horse across his shoulders to shoe it, and any girl would have fallen for him, Ma admitted. Even at the age of forty he was more than a match for any woman. Domhnall kept himself clear of fights with other men nowadays, preferring to be a big fish in a little pool within his own four walls.

''Tis me good luck ye're an ugly bitch,' he told Tilly. 'Ye'll never get a husband.'

Tilly would walk along the street with her head down so that she would not be seen. She never looked up, and there was not a thought in her head, for she was frightened to think. Her spirit was broken and she was an absence, like a shadow without a real person in front of it. If anyone asked her a question, they had to bend down and ask twice, her voice was so low.

Every year there was one event that brought the warring factions of Lisson Grove together. At the start of September the whole Irish community, Domhnall and his women in train, set off through London, joining forces with the flood of vagrants and navvies pouring from the other cunny-warrens of slums that flourished between the main roads. They roared songs and swore at passers-by as they strode towards the countryside of Kent.

The hop-picking season had arrived, and so had they, put up by landowners in rows of makeshift shanties, with food stewed in a flint hut and water dragged from the well.

Hops were Domhnall's yearly excuse (and he was not alone) for a six-week drunk holiday paid for by his menials. The enormous five-bushel baskets were filled with hops by the two women and only delivered by him the last few paces to the collection point, his palm out for the shilling. And then there was the pub to drink, and maybe a donnybrook with villagers, fists, staves, knives sometimes. Tilly and her mother turned up afterwards to steer him back to the hut, and feel if he had a penny caught in the seam of his pocket for anything to eat.

But that year there were strikes and riots, the season being so poor. Some crushers of the Kent constabulary were crushed, and it was said that the Chief Constable had sent by electric telegraph for a hundred troops from Shorncliffe Camp. A battle loomed, and the women decided to return to London while they still had some money left, and spend it peacefully before their men got back with broken heads and raging thirst. But the Ship and Billet was nearby and the crowd of ladies stopped for a tipple, and started scratching and pulling hair, no better than their men, then found they had drunk or lost the money they had saved for clothes, and everyone started blaming everyone else's children for the theft, and chasing them and falling over. By the time the men found them it was near dark. They knew a real fight was coming so they slammed a scheme together to pack the platform and board the train in a rush, get to London Bridge for free in the confusion.

But at Combe Forest Station the crushers were only allowing Irish to the ticket office one family at a time, and they were scrutinising faces with bull's-eye lamps.

'Aye, this is no fun,' Domhnall said, drawing back, and Ma began to cry, she was so tired and depressed, so he gave her one with the back of his hand, then a good crack frontwards with the palm. Rather than fight him or run from him, she gave up and tumbled limp in a mess of skirts. He kicked her, infuriated by her stillness, but she didn't move. He grabbed Tilly's shoulder and dragged her back. 'No ye don't,' he muttered. 'This way wi' ye, we'll meet ye ma back home, she always comes up sunshine, does Ma. Best lie low and let the crushers cool.'

Tilly walked half a pace behind him, tugged up the lane by his hand, almost fainting with hunger. Domhnall had the instinct of a hare when in trouble: he always ran uphill, knowing searchers always search down. Tonight the crushers would be baton-ready and on the lookout for Irish in every flatland riverside pub from

586

the Ship and Billet to the Half Moon and Calf's Head, but they were all for an easy life, and they'd never lift their eyes to the dark hills.

As his head cleared, Domhnall grew more cheerful. 'Heh!' he said, his black bulk nodding at the lights gleaming in the large houses around them on the slope. 'Let's do a panney!' While Tilly trailed listlessly after him, he dodged into driveways, staring in the bright windows at servants yawning in luxuriously unoccupied rooms, casually tasting the food they were putting out, finishing off leftovers or just looking out picking their noses, thinking they couldn't be seen. But Domhnall was grinning in the dark below them almost close enough to touch.

''Tis all right, this!' he said.

He shook Tilly and tugged her on to the next house. She glimpsed elegant women in beautiful dresses, brilliant colours that made a woman shine, jewels at their necks, and the man of the house like a priest conducting a service at the head of the table. The children, scrubbed, with slick washed hair, ready for bed – a whole bed for each, no doubt – being marched in by an old woman to say good night, then marched out again. It was a world totally beyond Tilly's comprehension, not for her. So there really were people like this, she thought, bored people letting their food go cold while they made conversation, a fortune in silverware on the table. They had so much that she gaped, unable even to feel envy. In another window a gentleman and a lady argued, their voices noiseless, and she struck out with her glass, but he caught her hand, like a kind of game. In the rustic below, Cook worked in a mass of steam, the butler combed his hair and grinned slyly, and a whole fish was brought back to the kitchen table with only a couple of portions cut out of it, enough thrown away to feed a whole family for a week.

'Kill 'em all!' Domhnall grunted. 'Kill 'em all, an' burn their bones.'

He moved on, hissing for Tilly to follow, then grabbed both her hands tight in one of his, hearing a dog bark. Other dogs took it up, the sound spreading like a wave. Domhnall dragged Tilly across a field until the noise faded behind them. She squealed, feeling a dead bird strung on the fence, and Domhnall bent her wrists for making him jump.

''Tis only a crow, ye bitch,' he hissed, 'for frightening the others away.'

They crossed a drive beneath huge trees, and Domhnall took to the soft lawns to avoid the rustling of dead leaves. The house ahead of them was large and solitary, many of its windows dark, the lighted ones streaming green squares across the grass towards them. A fountain splashed, burying the sound of their footsteps crossing the gravel to the wall. Domhnall stood fearlessly at the bright glass, scratching his lip.

The lower sash was raised to admit the night air, but strong vertical bars, painted white, kept him out. In the room beyond, a gentleman sat at the desk, dressed in white tie and tails, ready for dinner. He was not reading or doing anything. At his elbow was a glass containing a half-measure of whisky, no more.

He sat for some minutes without moving, and Domhnall, watching him outside, did not move either.

Tilly's eyelids drooped and she settled against the wall, her elbows on her knees. Her eyes closed.

Domhnall dragged her up. 'Lookit,' he hissed. Tilly shivered; for the first time she felt cold, and now a fine rain drifted like mist past the lighted windows. She huddled her shawl closer round her shoulders, but she always did as she was told.

Inside, the gentleman had reached into the knee panel of the desk. He took out a bottle and filled the glass to the brim, then drank it in two gulps, carefully leaving only the original half-measure. He drew a deep breath, replacing the cork and the bottle, then ran his hands through his ginger hair. Standing, he crossed to a cabinet. For a moment he did no more than look at it, his back to them. 'The fool keeps doing it,' Domhnall hissed.

This time the gentleman opened the drawer, felt in the back of it, and took out something. Tilly saw a flash between his fingers.

He looked round, hearing some sound in the house she could not, quickly returned whatever he had taken, closed the drawer. He crossed to his desk and picked up a pen.

Tilly stared.

A beautiful girl, the most beautiful grown-up girl that as a child Tilly had ever dreamed of being, with long lustrous red hair curled over the white skin of her shoulders – she was wearing an evening dress, the hem barely above the parquet – was coming into the room. She went to the desk laughing and must have been telling the gentleman he had forgotten the time, for he looked at the clock and knocked the heel of his palm to his forehead. The girl leaned over his shoulder, lifting the pen from his hand with an affectionate shake of her head, making her hair gleam in waves as though it was alive, like flames falling down. Tilly stared with her tongue stuck to the roof of her mouth. She had never wanted so badly to be somewhere, anywhere else. She knew she would always remember this moment.

The gentleman was standing and the girl, who must be his daughter, took his arm. Smiling, she nodded at his whisky glass, and he shrugged, as if noticing it for the first time, then drained it dutifully. They walked together elegantly, arm in arm, to the door and went through, out of sight.

Tilly's face crinkled up, almost blind with longing.

''Tis empty. Ye can do it,' Domhnall said. 'I cannot, but a skimpy little thing like ye . . .' He was talking about the bars, standing on tiptoe to test them through the window. 'Up ye go.' Seizing her beneath the arms, he lifted her. 'Quick, girl!'

She put her hands round the bars and pulled herself up the rest of the way, kneeling on the broad sloping ledge. It felt precarious, her knees slippery with the rain, and the hard stone hurt her bones.

'I can't,' she said. Most of her would slip through easy, there was nothing to her, but she was frightened of getting her head stuck between the bars.

'Do it or we know what I'll be doin' to ye,' Domhnall said, knocking her foot into the gap. 'In the cabinet. Ye saw. Quick sticks, now!'

Tilly wriggled through, twisting her neck to slide her ears past the bars one at a time, and dropped down onto the floor. She pulled off her clogs quickly, so as to leave no marks, feeling the carpet soft beneath her toes, then the cold parquet as she crept over to the cabinet. The study door was half-open; she glimpsed a broad hallway beyond. A servant crossed it holding an empty tray, returning downstairs to the rustic, then everything was quiet except for the clink of cutlery. The meal had been served and they were eating.

Tilly slid open the slim drawer and slipped her hand inside, grasped something on a chain and pulled it out, a coin in a copper claw. She had never seen anything like it before.

It flashed, and she saw her face.

A door creaked on its hinge and Tilly started round, terrified. As footsteps tapped rapidly in the hall, she slipped the drawer closed, grabbed her clogs and fled on her toes to the window. She sprang on the windowsill and put her leg through, twisting her body after it into the dark, tearing her ears agonisingly on the bars when they stuck.

She tried again, the breath whining in her throat.

'Throw it!' came Domhnall's voice hissing from below.

Tilly let her clogs drop, and he caught one.

'Bitch!' he swore.

The footsteps were very loud. Tilly forced her head back between the bars, not caring if she tore her head off, almost falling from the slippery wet ledge, and in the same instant the girl came through the doorway.

She didn't see Tilly. She came straight towards the sash window where Tilly was kneeling in the dark outside, the rain sounding noisily now, and pulled the frame down with a heavy thud. She pushed the catch closed to lock it.

Tilly stared at her through the rain-starred glass, not daring to move, their faces only inches apart.

The girl pursed her lips at the raindrops speckling the inner sill and wiped her fingertips across them. Then she looked into the glass, straight into Tilly's eyes.

Tilly knew she was caught. She heard her father's footsteps running away, leaving her in the lurch. The sound of barking dogs started up again, closer.

But still Tilly did not move.

Inside, the girl studied her reflection in the window. She raised a hand to her cheek, lightly rouged.

Outside, Tilly held her hand to her cheek.

The girl wiped away an imaginary speck then turned away back to the door, and in a second she was gone.

Tilly crouched there in the pouring rain, her hand to her cheek.

Rainwater trickled and dripped down her face, pattering around her.

'Give it me now or I'll split ye,' came Domhnall's voice. He must have circled round, pulled back to her by his greed, but the dogs were barking thick now, and lamps bobbed between the trees of the drive.

'Did ye see her?' Tilly said. 'For a moment I thought I was her, Father, and she thought so too. 'Twas a lovely thing!' She tried to explain to the angry blur of his face: 'I was lovely!'

Domhnall pulled her down into the soft flower bed and rolled on her, holding her with his weight, his face grunting against hers while he fumbled for her hand, pulling at the chain hanging from her clenched fist.

'No!' she cried.

Domhnall banged his head down on hers, giving her a fearful crack. Instead of scratching and clawing, she clung to him tight, face to face, catching his nostrils in her teeth. She felt the fine slippery hairs against her tongue. He shrieked, jerked himself back with all his strength, pulling her up.

She bit, hard.

Domhnall screamed. He slapped his hands over his face and rolled away, howling.

'Why do you hate me?' she cried. 'Why didn't you tell me the truth? I'm not ugly! Can't you see it?'

Domhnall was still howling, the rain spreading the blood over his face.

'*I'm beautiful!*' Tilly screamed at him.

She backed away from him, her hands in her hair against the rain.

Pulling on her clogs, she slipped the coin over her head on its chain, so that she would not lose it, and ran into the dark as the dogs came.

Having ducked down behind the counter, Tilly stood up, smoothing her dress, staring after the visitor. It was the same girl, she was sure, the same girl come here to the Tabard from her fine country house, a coincidence so extraordinary it was almost frightening.

The girl Tilly had dreamed of being.

Tilly never knew what had happened to her father that night, or why such terrible people as he were allowed to flourish. She never saw her mother again either, and sometimes wondered if she had survived the night. Perhaps Domhnall was sent to prison, perhaps he won pity by some line of blarney or other, perhaps he was never found. Whatever the case of it, she'd known that London was large enough to hide her from him. Many people came to London to lose themselves and were never found.

Tilly was a free woman, she had won her freedom, and she could live as she wanted. Yet here was the girl again.

Tilly got one of the others to take over her duties, and went quietly up to her room. She wanted to be alone with her thoughts.

It was long hours at the Tabard, but the girls were all friends, except over men, or food, or tips. She had a fine long room in one of the lofts, and sometimes she took a pleasant man into her bed for a little extra, nothing dangerous, nothing involving – she was happy here, and she didn't want to spoil it. The Tabard sprawled enough to accommodate all types and there were always new people to meet, but she never expected to fall in love, or thought that love truly existed. Such a wonderful thing was strictly for the penny broadsheets, she thought. And she believed that for more than ten years.

Tilly sat on her bed and pulled at the chain that hung round her neck. The silver coin in its copper claw flashed as it emerged from under her gown.

Phineas Murge looked from the talent in his hand to Jemima's figure climbing the stone steps to London Bridge; and back again to his hand.

Above him, Jemima came into view high on the arch above. The moon illuminated the silver loop of the River Thames, appearing motionless and eternal, curving into the distance round the dark island of Southwark.

Phineas Murge ran away from her.

He ran like a madman. He felt as though the whole world had gone mad, that he was the only one with his sanity. He ran with his coat tails clapping the back of his legs like the seconds of passing time. He ran with nowhere to run to but could not stop himself any more than he could stop the thumping of his heart. Common sense was no help. I could have saved Reuben's life. Been on the quick-smart somehow. Shouted the alarm, got her thanks. Be walking with her now, and her in my debt.

But he was not an heroic sort of a person.

It would be me lying there now, Phineas realised, and Reuben still alive, tossing the coin in his hand above me, saying, 'You were right, Jemima. It brought me luck, because *you* believed it.'

Reuben standing looking down on Phineas Murge's body cut from ear to armpit. 'I wonder who this poor fellow was? I wonder why he followed us.'

Phineas ran pell-mell the length of Bankside, his tall long-legged figure, hatless, startling lovers in doorways and drunks curled up in any old hole, thieves and dogs and foxes scavenging. He forced himself to walk as he came onto the three huge iron arches of Southwark Bridge, trying to catch his breath – the police were always on the watch for suicides. Beneath him he saw the bridge lights streaming down into the water to an infinite depth. He faltered, staring. A quick vault over the parapet into those silken reflections, going down and down . . . The hairs prickled on the nape of his neck, and he held tight to the coin, remembering his partner's sneer.

Why, Mr Murge, should anyone make such an expensive forgery so easy to detect?

Because it's real, Mr Slippole. It's as real as real can be.

Phineas Murge was too clever to be happy, and he was cursed with imagination. He knew he would never know enough to make sense of everything. The parapet drew him to it as though by magnetism: he'd read Brunel's lecture on the foot tunnels beneath the riverbed now being converted to railways, and knew that far beneath the bed of the modern Thames flowed, like a knife that had cut deep into the earth, its ancient channel. Once these low hills of London hung on the edge of a gigantic chasm, the great canyon looping between them like somewhere in Africa, with elephant and hippopotamus grazing and the Thames foaming three hundred feet below.

Invisible now, filled in with thousands of years of flood-gravel as the sea rose, but still there. Phineas saw himself standing on the bridge high over the abyss, throwing himself out, falling.

He couldn't do it.

But he could throw the coin.

When the talent was gone it would be as if tonight had never happened. Phineas would go home and his wife, when the child had stopped crying, would put his supper in front of him, and nothing would have changed.

But Jemima Fox had said, '*Once there were twenty-nine of them.*'

Phineas raised his arm. But he couldn't let it go any more than he could let himself go.

A lighted train clanked and squealed across the railway bridge below him, sheeting sparks as it passed between the towers into Cannon Street Station, billowing smoke against the vast glass span of the roof to make everything dark again.

Phineas put the coin in his pocket and walked calmly to the far end of the bridge. The dome of St Paul's swelled above Lud's Hill like the rim of a rising moon, and a policeman moving in on a destitute woman eyed him, but said nothing. Phineas crossed the roadworks of Victoria Street, picking his way between the trestles and fresh gravel, trenches all around him for the sewers, and climbed the hill to the cathedral.

The evening service was over, people filing past him, but many others remained. Phineas sat for a while resting his head on his knuckles, listening to the whisper of prayers.

He had seen a man murdered tonight. There had been no reason for it, that was what horrified him. It seemed there was no room left in the world for anything clean or pure, no room for love, only sickening violence, and sex, as though men and women were animals.

People had made themselves filthy in this filthy city, too busy to care for anyone but themselves. Nothing to light their way.

Everything was a lie.

Phineas knew that he, too, was a lie. He would go home to his wife Nancy and lie to her about where he had been. He would lie about what he really felt, about what had really happened today. Her smell, her dull pudding-basin face, revolted him as often he was allured; her slowness and indifference to him since baby Tom came between them stuck in his throat. And soon there would be another baby, as if they loved each other. Perhaps they did. But it wasn't enough. It wasn't nearly enough.

Along with a hundred others, Phineas Murge left the cathedral and turned his steps through the dark for home.

Elias Slippole never knew whether or not Jemima Fox did eventually return to take up his offer of a silver shilling for her coin. Made wealthy by a lifetime of cheating those who could least afford to be cheated, Slippole endured his final haemorrhage before the end of the month and died in the New Year.

594

Before the day was out, Phineas nailed up a new shop sign proudly above the lintel: 'Murge and Son, Coin Dealers, Expert Valuations Undertaken, Gold and Silver Purchased'. The baby was still crying.

In January 1871, Martin Fox was contacted by a Mr Wittle of the Tabard, through the name and address given on the booking for the Pilgrims' Room, and received an offer from Murge and Son, coin dealers, that sent his eyebrows shooting into his hair. 'What's mine is mine,' Martin had told Jemima, but the offer of £250 for 'a certain coin in his possession', followed by a precise description of it, was another matter entirely. Martin raced on foot all the way from Bloomsbury Square to the lodgings of his fiancée, Hillary, in the Borough High Street, where he caught her leaving for her shift as a Nightingale nurse at Guy's Hospital. 'You know what this means,' Martin gasped. 'I can afford to buy the chemist's shop, and we can live in the rooms above when we are married.' He followed her, waving the paper. 'Exactly the price the Church Commissioners are asking.'

'There must be a catch,' Hillary said practically.

'Yes, there is,' Martin said cockily. 'A fool and his money are soon parted!'

'And you nearly let that sister of yours talk you into giving it to her for nothing,' Hillary scolded. 'I'd like to see her face when she finds out.'

'It's a condition of the sale that it is not revealed.'

'You can't possibly leave her believing that they're fakes,' Hillary admonished. 'They can't be, if someone is prepared to pay such a huge sum.'

'Who cares? It's paying for our future, Hillary. Our children.' He embraced her. 'Give me a kiss!'

Hillary returned his kiss holding his cheeks between the palms of her hands, right there in the street, which set the clerks gobbling their sausanmash in the Tabard's window hallooing, and made Martin blush to the tips of his ears.

Jemima never did find out, and to the end of her long life she believed the talents were worthless forgeries. But, if anything, that increased their sentimental value to her. They were not worthless to her, they were her scattered family. She had the two given her

595

by Frank and George as well as her own, a little collection of three which she kept safe in the drawer in her writing desk at Abbey Place, St John's Wood. She always had a feeling about them, woman's intuition. A marvellous feeling at first. And sometimes, later, a terrible feeling.

After crossing London Bridge that first evening, Jemima made her way to Crooked Street and found shelter in Mrs Smith's lodgings. She set her sights on the young medical student boarding there, Henry Summers. She was much the stronger personality and he did not stand a chance. Paying her way by teaching at the church school, within a month she was walking Henry to St Thomas's Hospital and then waiting outside when he finished as well, whatever the hour or the weather, in a mackintosh if it was raining, and carrying a dry one for him. By the time spring arrived, she was sending him in with packed lunches, and they would eat supper together in a dining room somewhere. She was poor but he was handsome and debonair, with a fine doctorly manner. Mrs Smith was related to the family somehow – on the wrong side of the blanket no doubt, Jemima thought tartly. His father, George Summers, had recently passed on, and his elder brother had died a hero's death in China, when the Royal Navy captured a Chinese steamship. A large house in St John's Wood would be Henry's as soon as the formalities were completed.

They were married two years later, and Jemima moved into Abbey Place as Mrs Summers, the wife of Dr Summers, the up-and-coming young gynaecologist with a room in Harley Street and his eye on the wealthy *enceinte* of Society. Not until after the birth of her own children, Alex and Gerald, did Jemima hear by chance that Reuben was dead. Jerome told her. He'd heard about it from a local policeman, now retired, who remembered the case. 'It happened years ago,' Jerome said with the brutality of one who has observed much suffering but has a message to bring, setting himself in his clerical grey on one end of the conservatory sofa. 'Probably that very night, just after you left him.' Jemima put the back of her hand to her mouth, the tears springing to her eyes, because she had sensed nothing; for half a dozen years she had blamed Reuben for not writing, imagining him too busy with his girl in every port, or fighting storms off Cape Horn. All the while she thought of him, eating her breakfast or combing her hair,

Reuben was dead. Several times she had answered the doorbell with an instinct that it might be him. Now she knew it never would be.

'It's not your fault,' Jerome said, misreading her.

'How could it be my fault?'

He sniffed, looking around him at the rich surroundings. For some years Jerome had been a preacher at the Tooley Street Baptist Chapel in Bermondsey, his gingery hair already thinning. 'There was nothing on the body to identify it at the time. Talent, money, purse, all were stolen, even his handkerchief. So many people have nothing . . .'

Jemima opened the drawer of her writing desk. 'Reuben's last words to me were that he was the luckiest man in the world.'

'The sin of hubris,' Jerome said insensitively. 'Arrogance – the ancient Greeks, you know, believed nothing offended their gods more than human arrogance. I have seen such poverty and degradation in this city, Jemima, it would move a stone to pity. To some poor souls a dirty peajacket, a pair of shoes, a silver coin and a handkerchief are a fortune worth killing for.' He stood briskly and called the maid for his hat and cape, then went to Jemima at the desk where she sat looking at her three talents. 'You really must stop this foolishness. Blaming yourself – you could not have changed our father's death, Jemima.'

'I know. You're right of course. But that isn't what it feels like.'

He looked at her blankly. 'Any more than you could have prevented Reuben's death.' He followed her eyes. 'Those coins exert an unhealthy influence on you, my sister.'

'You spend your days and nights among people frightened of the afterlife, telling them what they should believe,' she said, then turned on him. 'It's changed you.'

For the first time he laughed. 'Oh, Jemima, I fear you are beyond saving! You would have to give up all this. Easier for the camel to pass through the eye of a needle.'

'I am not rich and I do not feel comfortable.'

'Remember the first commandment.' He lifted her fingers from the three coins and closed the drawer reprovingly. 'Worship no god but me. Do not make for yourselves images of anything in heaven or on earth or in the water under the earth. Do not bow down to any idol or worship it, because I am the Lord your God and I tolerate no rivals. I bring punishment on those who hate me and on their descendants down to the third and fourth generation. But I show my love to thousands of generations of those who love me and obey my laws.'

'You're quite right,' Jemima said loyally, as she showed him out. But from the driveway Jerome looked back at her, then gave a barking laugh, shaking his head.

'Shall I never really bring you into the fold?' he asked.

'I wish you could,' Jemima said, by way of farewell.

None of them could bear to go back to the house where they had been children. Yet they could not forget it. Jerome never married, but the others whispered bedtime tales of Holywell to their own children – Martin, struggling to make the chemist's shop pay, passing them on to his only child, round-eyed Daniel, Jemima to Alex and Gerald – tales of their lost birthright. 'My God,' Jemima realised one night, 'I sound so *bitter*.'

Yet it was better, the adults thought, to remember Holywell this way, in a kind of make-believe, a child's story, than to forget. The reality must be very different and unpleasant by now, the house dirty, unsafe, the walls fallen in or knocked down by contractors. Fairy tales were kinder. But there was another side to the adults' well-intentioned hiding from the truth: their children grew up believing that the past had been better than the present, a golden age before the grubby realities of their own time, the struggle to make a living, the family's slow inexorable decline and fragmentation.

Holywell, with its shining windows, always clean, and cheerfully smoking chimneys, the fire always lit, should have been theirs.

Alex grew up and married a debutante, Sybil, for her beauty and social connections; he kept a town house in London and a country house in Devon. His singleminded brother Gerald studied dentistry at Guy's and moved into Harley Street, on the corner near their father's premises. It was in those rooms that Alex collapsed with blood-poisoning after the removal of a tooth by his sibling. The newspapers got hold of the story; Alex lost his life, and Gerald lost his career. Unable to practise, he plunged into despair, married a fine girl despite himself, and only finally succeeded in drinking himself to death soon after his son Greg was born.

In 1904, Martin's son Daniel married Gloria Simmonds, a piece of stuff as bold as brass, with a lively blue gaze that caught Jemima straight in the eye. Gloria was the eldest of a brood fathered by a common railway carter from Lisson Grove, now a delivery driver for Leibig's Emporium in Old Bond Street. Estranged from her parents, who did not attend the wedding, the girl made ends meet by selling cheap toiletries door to door. She married Daniel at St George's Church, near the chemist's shop in Southwark which was now Daniel's living, such as it was, and the reception was held across the road at the Tabard.

Jemima took the wedding as a heaven-sent opportunity to bring the family together after more than thirty years apart, but she found it a shock.

Everyone, she thought, looked so old. They were all in their fifties. Harold, gentle, lucky, willowy Harold, had become a beefy Suffolk squire, hard-bellied, his face mottled by good living and high blood pressure – what Henry called an apoplexy waiting to happen. Harold had cultivated a booming laugh, and his wife Kate was only letting him quaff the tankards of beer to keep him off the spirits. 'Never felt better!' he boomed at Jemima, then confided, 'Kate's a worrier, you know. Couldn't live without me, bless her.' Jemima could see no trace in him of the boy he had been.

'Did you keep it?' she said.

'Foundation of me fortune, dear gel!' Harold said with avuncular jollity, slightly false.

'I thought you were going to give it to Kate.'

'Took it back. That's how I bought my first Guernsey. Now the herd's world-famous. She doesn't mind. Kate, I said you don't mind. Look at those round her neck, they're not glass, believe me.'

'How much for? To whom?'

He looked uncomfortable, allowing the guests milling through the rooms of the Tabard to sweep him away. 'It was a condition of the sale that it should not be revealed . . .'

Jerome looked thin and haunted, with only a few grey strands strapped primly across his bald pate. His work among the poor obsessed him, aged him. Almost nothing of the ambition of his youth remained, and his lips pinched in disapproval of Gloria's bright laughter. Jemima herself had greying hair which she called silver, and she supposed fresh girls of Gloria's age would think her old. Jemima kept away from her at first, not wanting to meet her.

No one knew what had happened to George. Frank came back from Canada, supposedly a rich lumber baron and supposedly happily married with wonderful children and wonderful grandchildren, all living in great houses. He tried to sell everyone life insurance and tomorrow would have to borrow his passage money home from Jemima.

Undoubtedly wealthy, however, was the solid banker, Winston Prideau. The Prideau family had been on nodding terms socially with the Summers since Winston's grandfather had married Eve Summers, the cousin of Henry's father, nearly a hundred years ago. On Winston's arm, in a strangely individual choice for a City banker, clung his blatantly colonial wife Emma with her twangy laugh, a Tasmanian Australian of no breeding. She greeted Henry with a wringing handshake, grateful to see someone she knew; though Emma was in her mid-forties, her wispy daughter Trilby in tow behind her was only eight years old. After almost twenty childless years of marriage to Winston, Emma had thought herself barren and sought Henry's professional advice. 'There is nothing physically wrong with you, Mrs Prideau,' Henry had said, steepling his fingers. 'Have you heard of Mendel's work? Perhaps you do not have a propensity to conceive – characteristics can be passed on in humans, it seems, just as they can in plants or animals.' Winston would have been horrified to hear his wife and himself referred to as animals, and Henry had changed tack. 'What do you know of your family, Mrs Prideau? Your maiden name was Pride, was it not? We stand on the shoulders of our ancestors, you see. Perhaps I should be examining your marriage, not you.' Henry had stood. He was a fine doctor. 'Good day to you, Mrs Pride – I'm sorry, I meant Mrs Prideau . . .'

When Emma fell pregnant, Henry had been supposed to attend the birth, but before she could call him the baby had popped abruptly into the world during the climax of the play *Trilby* at the Haymarket Theatre. Inevitably she had been called Trilby.

Jemima chatted to them for a few minutes before moving on.

And then there was the bride, Gloria.

Gloria dominated the rooms of the Tabard with her wedding dress, her exuberance, the strength of her presence – as powerful as Jemima's own, though the girl was hardly into her twenties. Something in those bright blue slanty eyes, straightforward, familiar, almost intrusive in her appraisal of the people around her, showed that Gloria had lived a great deal, perhaps too much for poor sheltered Daniel. Jemima wondered if Gloria was marrying the man she loved. It was hard to imagine that she could be marrying him for his money, for he had none. Even the ring that he had given her was secondhand, though she flashed it proudly – knowing no better, no doubt.

Jemima should have disliked Gloria, ignored her, or put her down in the way women of Jemima's class knew very well how to do. But Jemima did not. She could not help liking Gloria.

They met alone for the first time in the Pilgrims' Room. No one knew what they said in there – Daniel nearly fell through the door trying to eavesdrop – but the two women came out firm friends. Gloria, though she dropped her aitches to the end of her long life, had been approved by Aunt Jemima.

There was one thing that Jemima could not know about Gloria. Out of sight, a coin hung on a fake gold chain between her breasts. A young man called Jamie Reilly had given it to her in token of his love for her. ''Twas me own mother's, 'twas Tilly O'Neill's,' he'd told her. It was a coin in a copper claw.

In truth, like all unloved houses, as soon as it was alone, Holywell had begun to die.

The fountain still chuckled cheerfully above the ornamental pool but there was no one to listen to it. The house was silent, the gutters, blocked with oak leaves, had overflowed down the walls and streaked them with damp. Birds nesting in the roof dislodged tiles, and in no time it was the sort of place Vaudey mothers warned their children to keep away from, which naturally encouraged the youngsters to play there. For a little while girls played ring-a-ring-o'roses on the grass growing through the carriage circle, seeming no larger than dolls reflected in the gloomy windows. Pirates and cowboys played on the lawns until they were too overgrown, the grass giving way to thistles and brambles. Later, truants came sneaking up the drive to throw stones and break the windows, which gave the house a gap-toothed look below the ragged roof.

In the old rose garden, roses ran riot from a tangle of weeds in a glorious, unseen display for a few years. Then the creepers strangled them and grew over everything, submerging even the balustrades beneath a growth of green fingers, turning brown in winter.

And each year, as the vegetation rotted, the earth rose another inch.

The infants who had once played here grew into adolescents in grey flannel shorts and blue blazers, miching off on their way home from the Nemeton Grammar School, stopping by at the Old House for a secret rebellious smoke, prising the nails carefully out of the planks boarding the door so that they could be replaced, leaving no sign except very short cigarette butts. One winter's day, having acquired a bottle of whisky and some cigars, they started a bonfire in the vestibule and frightened themselves when it almost got out of control, and one boy running away down the drive cut his foot badly on a shard of tile. After this scandal the mums in the new Oakwood estate complained to the Vaudey Parish Council, and the legend conveniently grew up that the place was haunted, and the windows and doors were thoroughly blocked over using two-inch timbers and four-inch nails.

Still, a scullery back door was overlooked, and several young men and women of the district, whose fathers had outgrown the grey flannel shorts and whose mothers had cut off their schoolgirl plaits for fashionable shingles, and who later lived lives of the utmost respectability, were said to have been conceived in the large, dark rooms of the Old House after closing time at the King's Head.

Speculators bought it for an hotel, then it was sold on as a golf course, but the company went into liquidation. Then the house was to be knocked down and a housing estate built over the knoll, but work went forward on the Holmdene estate instead. More than half of St Thomas's Park was given over to heavy machinery, lorries bringing in tons of topsoil to level the slope, the steam cranes and bucket engines of S. Reilly & Sons, Building Factors, filling in the pond. Then the houses of Holmdene Close were built over the place, and another, smaller pool dug where there had been none before, in the remaining corner of the park.

Just in hearing of the piledrivers, though more than a mile away, the fountain in front of the manor house died away to a trickle.

The water fell silent. A few last drops came from the spouts, not clear but dark with soil, then nothing moved. The pool drained away through its forgotten conduits. Dry leaves rustled on the stones.

No one noticed the change; there was no one there to notice, and no visitor would have known the difference.

Holywell Manor stood empty behind its dry fountain.

The London County Council purchased the house for a teacher training college, but the plan was shelved at the outbreak of the Great War. Then it was to be a convalescent home for soldiers, but that plan too was shelved because of the cost. The truth was that the place was good only for knocking down; no one in their right mind would buy such a ruin.

For forty-eight years Holywell Manor had stood deserted. And then something wonderful happened.

VIII

Julia

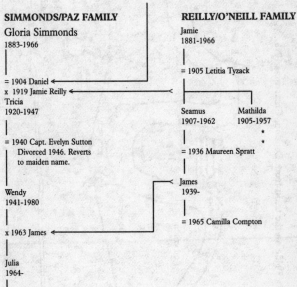

John Fox
★
★
Daniel Fox 1873-1946

SIMMONDS/PAZ FAMILY

Gloria Simmonds
1883-1966

= 1904 Daniel ←
x 1919 Jamie Reilly ←
Tricia
1920-1947

= 1940 Capt. Evelyn Sutton
　　Divorced 1946. Reverts
　　to maiden name.

Wendy
1941-1980

x 1963 James ←

Julia
1964-

REILLY/O'NEILL FAMILY

Jamie
1881-1966

= 1905 Letitia Tyzack

Seamus　　　Mathilda
1907-1962　　1905-1957
　　　　　　　　★
　　　　　　　　★
= 1936 Maureen Spratt

James
1939-

= 1965 Camilla Compton

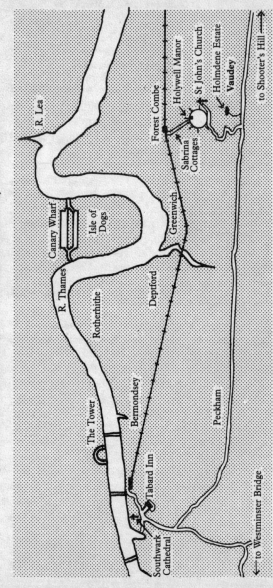

Julia Fox and Esmeralda Pride on the train from London, Christmas 1998

Something wonderful; and something dreadful.

'Why don't you have any children, Aunt Julia?'

'Let's get one thing clear,' Julia said, stopping dead among the commuters crowding homeward across London Bridge. She forced herself to smile, so as not to frighten the child. 'Don't call me Aunt.'

Through her smile, Julia could feel the dark wings of her depression flapping and lifting ominously around her.

'Sorry,' Esmerelda said meekly. 'Julia.'

'That's better. Then I won't call you god-daughter.'

Julia continued to smile as they walked. It was the sort of depression that pills hid but did not cure and alcohol made worse, a bleak windy darkness inside her. A year of emptiness had passed since Cameron died. If she had been asked before it happened, it would have been the most dreadful thing she could have imagined happening.

It really had happened.

'I like it when you hold my hand,' Esmerelda said. She finished off her ice-cream Cornetto – in December! – as they came down into the Borough High Street.

Julia wiped the ice-cream from the child's face – it amazed her that in these sophisticated days children still loved ice-cream. Esmerelda had very properly refused the sweet tooth-rotting jellies that Julia had ordered from the office canteen, refused equally damaging sweets from the vending machine, but she'd wolfed Julia's potato crisps (which she called chips), Julia's prawn and mayonnaise sandwich, then finished off with a huge ice-cream sundae. And now, as they passed beneath the railway clock, Esmerelda begged for a banana split from the London Bridge Station franchise.

'Julia, don't you have children because you're thirty-four years old?'

'Who told you my age?' It was true. Julia tried to keep her mind on what Esmerelda was saying. The exact place was along the platform ahead of her. The rails were exactly four feet, eight and one-half inches apart, the distance between the neck and ankles of a man of average height. Cameron had been of average height. The slab yellow front of the train had been doing only twelve miles an hour, but with a thousand unstoppable tons behind it. Julia focused all of her attention on the child, like a liferaft. 'Thirty-four's not exactly old age, you know.'

'It is when you're five. Mummy told me she's twenty-eight. I'm the only one who talks to you like this, aren't I, Julia?' Esmerelda said happily, glad to have Julia Fox properly to herself to the first time today. In the Fox Pharmaceutical Company's City building there had been too many distractions competing for Julia's attention, and for most of the office hours Esmerelda had been saddled with a secretary, Miss Slippole, with beautiful wavy hair, and the Gloria Fox Smile that Smiles, who had given Esmerelda the tour of the clean-rooms and laboratories and been very pleasant – though all too wise to the ways of a wilful child, having several of her own. Nothing had been too much trouble. Between shoots in the tiny floodlit studio where models tested new colour lines for the camera's eye, the expert had made up Esmerelda's precocious five-year-old face to look at least as adult and mature as a young lady of twelve. 'I'm nearly *six*, you know,' Esmerelda had complained, offended by their chuckles, and wouldn't look at them, sulking when they snapped a few shots for her to take home to Mummy.

A faint gorgeous memory of the lipstick still tasted on Esmerelda's lips even after the ice-cream, and she knew she must find a way to get to bed tonight without having it washed off, so she could go to sleep with its adult fragrance still clinging to her.

The attention of a secretary was good but the full and undivided attention of the boss was better. Now Esmerelda had Julia to herself, and she savoured her opportunity to the full, skipping cheerfully from Julia's hand, looking up adoringly at Julia with eyes as bright as new pennies.

Esmerelda Pride worshipped Julia. She longed to grow up to be Julia more than anything else in the world, to be thirty-four years old like Julia, with her deep velvet-brown eyes and her hair like curled flame, to walk like Julia and wear a one-piece lemon-yellow lambswool dress to just below the knee like Julia, and a long broad-lapelled overcoat that felt as soft as though it was woven of the same material. She wanted to stand out effortlessly from the crowd as Julia did – it felt to Esmerelda as though they were walking alone among the mass of people moving onto the platform.

Why's she looking at me like that? Julia wondered. Children were very strange; as strange as another country. Julia had never had the knack of being easy with them. The dark wings flapped around her; it was here, this very place, where Julia passed by twice each working day, that Cameron had been pulled onto the track by the suicide he had been trying to save, and Julia's life had ended.

That was what it felt like. Losing Cameron McBarb had felt like a kind of death for her too.

'Does it cost a lot to have done?' Esmerelda asked.

'What, children?' Julia said brightly.

'Your hair.'

'I just comb it.' And Esmerelda pouted, because Julia had spoken as though her mind was somewhere other than on her.

'You mean just with a comb?' Esmerelda gave her a little tug. 'Don't you colour it? Don't you?'

'No.' Julia put her hand to her hair without thinking, then broke into genuine laughter. 'I'm what they call a throwback!' She flashed her season ticket to the woman in the booth, whose ankles were wrapped in tubigrip bandages because she stood, or almost stood, all day, but Julia had eyes only for Esmerelda now.

'I know all about throwbacks,' Esmerelda said importantly. 'We had one in my folks, back home in Oz. I've seen pictures of the old Anzac, that's what everyone called him, but his name was Larry. He was a great swimmer but he drowned when his wife was drowned, because he wouldn't live without her.'

'You aren't a very sentimental child, Esmerelda.'

'I never knew him, did I! That was in the harbour.' The Pride family still kept their mansion in the Wilderness of Tasmania, on the southern shore of Macquarie Harbour. 'In those days the water was still good to swim through and you could see down to the bottom. Are you really a throwback?'

'Every so often something the parents don't have comes out in

611

a child, Esmerelda. A grandmother's eye colour perhaps, or the shape of a great-grandfather's ears, or even further back, to someone or other nobody remembers.' For the first time in years Julia thought of her slightly thickened left ankle. Back in the nineteen sixties the malformed foot she was born with had been treated by a series of corrective operations and she never noticed it now. In thundery weather the broken and reset bones sometimes ached, that was all.

'My hair's brown, just like my mummy's,' said Esmerelda, flourishing it across the back of her hand, but leaving a sticky smear of banana. As they settled in the compartment, Julia's face was so tense, like a clenched fist beneath her composure – Esmerelda thought of it as her office face – that Esmerelda was afraid of being ignored again.

'Let's ride coach!' she suggested eagerly, jumping up. 'I hate it here, Julia. There's no one to look at. We could stand, I don't mind standing.'

'That's why it's called standard,' Julia said. 'It used to be called second class.' Julia had never ridden second class in her life. 'My ticket's first.'

'I haven't got a ticket at all,' Esmerelda said.

'Well,' Julia said guiltily, 'you don't look five.'

'Scrooge. Come on! My mummy says two wrongs make a right.'

'Eve Pride,' Julia muttered as she followed, 'you have a lot to answer for.' To her surprise they did get seats, opposite a fat man with an enormous crotch who sat with his legs apart, and a girl in Gloria Fox lipstick, who looked as if she'd put on her eyeshadow that morning with the heels of her palms in the rush for work. They rocked as the train rocked. No one else looked about them, only Julia and Esmerelda.

'My mother's hair was sort of goldy,' Julia said, 'with dark strands.' She gave up trying to see from the filthy window as the train took up its soporific rhythm above the rooftops of Bermondsey. 'She wore it long, like a hippy – in those days a hippy was something good. My mum believed in peace, and flowers, and doing her own thing. My grandmother, Tricia, had black hair, but I never knew her. She made a disastrous marriage during the war, divorced him and reverted to her maiden name. She died when she was quite young. My mum was about your age at the time, I suppose. A little older.'

'*I'm* old,' Esmerelda insisted. 'Nothing hurts me. I'm a Terminator.'

Julia's lips gave that tense little twitch and she half-closed her eyes. 'Ezzie, you do not look like Arnie Schwarzenegger, not even since he's been building down.'

'Don't call me Ezzie,' Esmerelda said seriously. 'It's not my name. And *my* mummy and daddy love me.'

The fat man took out an orange and dropped the peel on the floor, feeding the segments into his mouth with fingers so pudgy and bent that it was difficult to tell where man ended and orange began. He stared at Julia and she realised she had been staring at him, breaking one of the thousand unwritten codes of train travel.

'Of course Jim and Eve love you, Ez – I mean, Esmerelda,' Julia said, sounding slightly embarrassed because the man was listening.

'I came from between mummy and daddy when they rubbed themselves together, because they love one another so much. That was just before they went sailing on the *Ezzie* and were shipwrecked on King Island. But my mummy says you didn't have a daddy and that's why you're like you are.'

'Ouch,' Julia smiled lightly. 'What am I like?'

'You're so unhappy you're screaming,' Esmerelda said.

Julia looked across the carriage. The windows down that side held the broad empty curves of the Thames, the buildings of Canary Wharf standing like fireworks in the last of the sunset, night darkening behind them. Lights were coming on in the dormitory settlements of the Isle of Dogs, and all along that north bank the Docklands Light Railway ran above the waters of the abandoned wet docks, crossing the dull orange streets below on stilts. The dismal flash of speed cameras and junction cameras sent flickers rippling along the shoreline from Island Gardens to the Tower. Beneath the glare of surveillance floodlights and the shadows with rifles moving watchfully on the rooftops, the City checkpoints were busy. Another normal London rush-hour.

'Mummy says it's because you don't know where you come from, Julia. Anyone could have been your daddy. Anyone at all.' Esmerelda stared at the man eating the orange.

'I've had enough of this conversation,' Julia said. She'd been intending to make a joke about little girls with too much imaginations; but then, she had been the same once. Esmerelda was half-English – her mother Eve had been born Eve Summers, Julia's friend Buzz-wuzz from school, and their mothers, Wendy and Carrie Paz, had also been schoolgirl chums – but Esmerelda's other half was the Wilderness Australia of Jim Pride, her father. Esmerelda was a little girl caught between two worlds, as Julia herself had always felt herself to be: caught between who she was and who she wanted to be. 'I'd rather talk about ice-cream, even,' Julia said.

That was a poor attempt at a joke, and Esmerelda did not attempt to laugh. The man got out and she shifted to his seat.

'You don't relax even when you're relaxing,' she said.

'You don't like me at all,' said Julia.

Esmerelda was horrified. 'But you don't understand, it's because I *do*!' She slipped her hands earnestly under Julia's coat, under her skirt, onto her warm knees. 'When I'm with you, I feel so alone. As alone as I do at our house at Farmer's Cove, with the wilderness everywhere.' The prehistoric caldera of Farmer's Cove hid, with its grassy slopes, the gigantic mining extraction works taking over the shores of Macquarie Harbour. Deep below the sea bed of the Harbour *graben*, sixty-ton Komatsu ore-trucks plundered the ancient trapped lens of minerals, gold, copper, silver. The mother lode.

'Sometimes it seems out there is the only time Mummy and Daddy come together,' Esmerelda said tearfully. 'And sometimes they're not really together. Mummy says he's changed. Daddy says she's not a bloody realist.' She looked up hopefully, as if Julia would explain what a bloody realist was.

Julia smiled reassuringly. 'Esmerelda, all grown-ups have disagreements.'

'That's the same as bloody shouting matches, am I right?' Esmerelda frowned, then cheered up, and flashed her magpie's eye. 'Look what Mummy gave me to show how much she loves me.' She pulled a battered gold locket out of the neck of her coat – she had worn it all day, along with various plastic beads and a Polly Pocket bracelet. 'Mum and I found this when we were clearing out the attic when Dad was away. It was awful old stuff and dusty and made you sneeze, but Mummy called it Victorian. Fetch a price, she said. Old letters and papers, a funny-looking writing desk, old photographs all gone an odd colour and none of them of anyone we knew. And there were bracelets and necklaces and rings that didn't look much because they were so grimy, but Mum said it was because they had lost their point – she said she meant the people who had loved them were long dead so the life had gone out of the objects. And there was this.' She flourished the locket, then leaned forward almost into Julia's lap and flicked the hasp. 'Look at her, Julia.'

Julia looked. Inside was a miniature painted on china, cracked and old: a girl with eyes as brown as her hair.

'Who is she?'

'She's me,' Esmerelda said.

Julia laughed, surprised. 'Well, I do see a resemblance.'

'Dead on,' Esmerelda said, snapping it closed. 'But *she's* grown up.'

The train's brakes began to squeal. 'Here we are. Button up your coat, it'll strike cold. Combe Forest.' They got out and crossed between the glaring advertisements to the taxi rank, which was empty. Julia thought about calling out Mrs Morrison with the little car, but it would take the old lady twenty minutes to find the keys and get herself together, and she always drove in an overcoat, hat and gloves, her nose almost touching the windscreen. In twenty minutes they could walk it. Julia buttoned Esmerelda's lapel closed and they set off through the pools of orange light along the main road. All the houses had their curtains tight closed, car boot lids already starting to sparkle with frost.

'I'm not unhappy because I have no children,' Julia said.

They turned into the uphill side road to Vaudey with its old-fashioned wrought-iron lights.

'I never met the right man,' Julia said, 'that's all.'

Esmerelda said slyly, 'You must have been in love.'

'No, never.'

'For one minute.'

'It doesn't happen like that, Esmerelda. Or not usually. Not real love.' They drew back from the kerb as cars tore past, using this as a rat run, the experienced using headlights on full beam to intimidate those approaching the width restrictors from the other direction. Their tyres skidded on the frost, then it was quiet again. 'I don't think real love ever happens. It's just in books and films. I think everyone's unhappy, more or less, that's why we cover our faces.' She patted her smooth, pale cheeks. 'Realising that was how my great-grandmother made the family's money back again.'

'Have you rubbed yourself with a man?'

'Eeeuuuch. It sounds horrible. Who'd want to?'

'I bet you have, all grown-ups do. Mummy rubbed herself with Daddy,' Esmerelda said gloomily. 'That's when the trouble started.'

'Oh, Jim and Eve are one of a pair!' Julia said loyally.

'She believed that when they were married he would always tell her the truth,' said Esmerelda, repeating without rancour something she had been told. It was amazing what a mother would whisper to her child, thinking nothing would be understood.

Julia looked up through the black trees. Above them and the glum V of the Sabrina Cottages estate loomed the dark bulk of the knoll, and through the fuzz of the trees' top branches she saw the lights of Holywell Manor gleaming as if in welcome. As always, it was as if she was coming home to warmth and peace from somewhere dreadful. Every day, on her way to work and leaving work, she must pass the place where Cameron died, but here, here at Holywell, was where they had been happy. For a month, or two, or three. Here at Julia Fox's home.

The wonderful thing had happened a long time ago – long before Julia was born. In 1919 Gloria Fox, Daniel's wife, after fifteen childless years of marriage, had used her cosmetics fortune to buy back Holywell Manor from the London County Council. It was in a derelict state but she'd had it rebuilt to its original condition in original materials, the fountain now fed by a recirculating electric pump, sparing no expense, by her friend the builder Jamie Reilly. All for Daniel. She'd made it Daniel's surprise Christmas present that year, all but wrapping it up in a red ribbon for him, typically Gloria. She'd have his child here: Tricia. Julia's grandmother.

Gloria always got her way, one way or the other.

And so Holywell Manor had come back into the Fox family.

Blonde Gloria, ginger Daniel. And Tricia with her hair as black as Jamie Reilly's.

Daniel had died in 1946, Tricia the year after, when Wendy was six years old. By that time the affair, if there ever had been one, between Gloria and Jamie had long cooled over. They didn't meet for years. Then in the early nineteen sixties Jamie's crippled wife died.

Gloria and Jamie were both old by then, but Wendy had looked at her grandmother, who had been the most important person she could remember in her life, with a bright glint in her eye: the old hen loved partying just as much as Wendy did. And Wendy knew all the right parties.

Wendy drove like the wind. Gran sat beside her in the Mini-Cooper called Horace with her feet planted firmly on an imaginary brake, wishing, no doubt, for her awful crotchety stick. But Wendy had been very firm with Gran on that subject. 'You won't need that where you're going.' She'd helped Gran down the steps of Holywell, the lights of London spread out from horizon to horizon below them, a map of orange street lamps with the parks showing as dark holes, St Paul's and Westminster floodlit. The lights of an airliner winked overhead. The whole scene flickered and twinkled magically, and Wendy's little white car waited at the foot of the steps.

'Do I ride in it, girl, or on it?' Gran asked.

Wendy held open the door, not taking no for an answer. 'Gran, you promised.' She tapped the party invitation with a fingernail. 'It says "and friend".'

Gran sat in the little car, watching Wendy by the streetlights flashing overhead. She was eighty and it was difficult to tell what the old woman was thinking or feeling, if anything. Every time Wendy changed gear, Gran looked at her mini-skirt, her tight white bra-less halter-neck, shiny white PVC belt, her lucky amulet swinging and bumping between her nipples as the car raced round the corners on its rubber suspension.

'I always drive fast,' Wendy said as they came into Belgravia, 'and I *always* get a parking space.' She was well aware she was showing off, but that was in her nature.

'Wendy Fox,' she gave her name to the dopey orang-utang on the door.

'It's hot in here,' said the orang-utang in a muffled voice, 'and this thing's got fleas. All right, pass two.'

Wendy drew Gran inside the lovely marble hall, a natural dance floor, with a chandelier and a staircase round it and rooms off it, all of them packed with people having fun, the older ones trying to talk over the DJ. Some of the rooms had tables covered with food, and the walls hung with black or blood-red curtains, but Gran had the good sense to stay in the hall with the older folk, holding court as always, getting everybody around her, and Wendy shook her head in admiration as she passed through the other rooms. She felt her body twist to the music and somebody brought her a Bacardi and Coke. It was the orang-utang.

'How's your fleas?' she said.

'How's yours?' he said, taking off his head and shaking out his long black hair, which was tied back in a queue. It was James Reilly, the clothes designer and grandson of Jamie Reilly whose house this was, and he gave her a kiss for her amazement. 'You know I'm always up to monkey business!'

'So I've heard, James.' She put her hand on his chest. 'The band's *groovy*, by the way.'

'You're so cool, Wendy.' He had a dark, handsome face, all strong lines, straight black eyebrows.

'You're so sweaty. And I think that thing *has* got fleas.'

They found themselves in a small room with flashing coloured lights, a couple kissing on the floor, others smoking. James unzipped the top of the orang-utang and stepped out of the legs. He was wearing what appeared to be black silk pyjamas.

'Black silk pyjamas?'

'Japanese martial arts this year,' he said, fishing out a cigarette case, and offered her the plump shapes.

'Pot!' she said, impressed. 'Ready-rolled!'

He put his arm round her as they inhaled. 'Did you bring her? Was that her?'

'Signed, sealed and delivered. But I don't think there's anything to it, do you?'

He snorted smoke. 'What do you expect? How could there be, at their age?'

'You're right,' Wendy said.

He glanced over the top of the staircase. 'Let's dance.'

His body felt like hot silk and he liked touching her, she could tell. In a break in the music he went over and had a few polite words with Gran, came back with his eyes flashing humorously and one eyebrow raised, so Wendy reckoned he'd met his match.

'Quite a lady,' he murmured and fetched another Bacardi and Coke.

'Look,' said Wendy.

White-haired Jamie Reilly had come down to join them. He crossed the dance floor halfway, then stopped and held out his hands. Gloria went to him.

The youngsters couldn't hear what they said.

'It's rather sweet,' said Wendy, watching them dance.

'I reckon there was something between them,' James said. He lit another smoke. 'And now here they are, too old to enjoy it.'

'They keep looking at me,' Wendy said, fingering her bangle nervously.

'No, it's me looking you're feeling,' James said, dancing Wendy round the side of the stairs. 'You're a fine and pretty girl. You're the only one here.'

'The only girl? You must be blind.'

'The only one that means anything to me tonight.' James opened a door and beckoned her into a passage, gave her his smoke and watched her draw it in. She leant back against the wall and he kissed her, breathing in the same breath. His hands became part of her, slipping under her halter-neck without touching her belt, the stretch nylon accommodating his hands in much the same way it accommodated her breasts. 'Mary Quant hair,' he said.

'Pearl Mist lips. The rest's all me.' James glanced along the corridor and suddenly she was afraid he'd stop, look amused and say, 'I'm sorry, Wendy, but you're not letting me seduce you fast enough, we really ought to get back to the party and do something more interesting.' She sank a little, pushing her hips against the lump in his black pyjama folds, and knew she'd won. Reaching behind her, he opened a low crooked door, a cupboard under the stairs, and they tripped inside. With the door closed, there was no light at all. She leant back against the long smooth broomsticks, lifting her leg into his hand. She was wearing only silk knickers and they didn't matter at all. She was so tense she would have scratched him if he had backed away, and imagined her moisture like a necklace of jewels for his cock to thrust through. James didn't disappoint. 'Oh!' they grunted as one, then he said, 'My God! My God! Oh Wendy, what a sweet girl you are. You'd better stop off at the loo on the way back to the party.'

And so Julia was conceived. Wendy always supposed so. She hoped so, because it was her most memorable sex at a party that month. Later she drove Gran home. 'Who'd've believed it!' Gran murmured. 'Old Jamie Reilly's still alive, and nothing's changed. Did you enjoy yourself dear?'

'The usual,' Wendy yawned.

Gran and Jamie passed the last years of their lives together, between Holywell and Belgravia, which suited Wendy just fine as a strong-minded single mother. She saw James Reilly again, when he was married to a girl who got her face in *Country Life*. Before Julia could walk she had lived with Wendy on a commune in India and a kibbutz in Israel; wherever Wendy went, backpacking in the Himalayas or fishing for the pearl of Gilgamesh in the Gulf, her sunburned child in tow, Wendy always had a great time. Julia behind her, the throwback. Julia, the quiet child. Julia, the illegitimate child. Julia the bastard.

Julia, the heiress.

'Everything that most people spend their lives working for was handed to me on a plate, Esmerelda. But the one thing many people take for granted, a father and a mother, what you have, Esmerelda, I did not have. My mother was sleeping in the garden on a summer's afternoon and a bee flew into her throat. She suffocated within five minutes, the gardeners trying to push a length of watering hose down her windpipe. It's a terrible world. For every one good intention there's a thousand, evil, actual ones.'

'So there *was* someone special,' Esmerelda said with that sly, disdainful note a five-year-old couldn't help when talking of love. Starting to disbelieve in Father Christmas. Julia held the little girl's hand tight, warm, and their breath followed them in grey puffs as they climbed through Sabrina Cottages – suddenly blindly white as a car streamed past, then tail-light red, then grey again in the silence. No one else was moving on the pavements, which were very narrow. People who bought these houses did not like people walking through.

'Yes, Esmerelda, there was someone special.'

'And you did love him. You told me a fib,' Esmerelda said cheerfully.

'Cameron McBarb was the husband of my best friend. I couldn't love him. He couldn't love me. He loved his wife. Everything we felt we could not say, we couldn't hurt Debbie. You've no idea how we went round and round, being so . . . *nice*. The only real time we had together was the few months when Debbie's mother was dying. Debbie nursed her. The happiest time of my life. His children . . . and yet we felt what we felt.' Julia drew a breath of frost and coughed. 'There was an accident and Cameron died. Debbie married again within six weeks. *Six weeks*. They went to live in America. I got a few letters and calls, then nothing. My whole affair was nothing. The whole huge balloon had burst and there was nothing inside. I knew Cameron so well, but I don't think he knew her at all. He was gentle so she thought him weak. When he was kind she took him for soft, and of course he gave her anything she wanted. He was the perfect husband. She just used him, she never cared for him.'

Esmerelda walked in silence and Julia realised she must be getting tired. Her bitterness must be passing very much over the child's head; they ought to be talking about Big Bird, for goodness sake, or Johnson and Friends. 'We're nearly at the top now.'

'I'm not tired.'

'Almost there.'

They came to the top of the knoll and saw the lights of Holywell Manor shining through the trees ahead of them. There was an ancient and usually exceedingly irritating right of way that cut across part of the lawns, but tonight the stile by the huge old oak was a welcome short cut, and Julia swung the little girl across with a puff of pleasure.

'But Mummy says you can't have any babies,' Esmerelda said. 'She says you *can't*.'

They came at last onto the gravelled drive and looked down the black ride of trees to the house. Julia reached down her hand to the child.

'There are some things, Esmerelda, that you can't do anything about when they happen to you,' she said. 'This is one of them. I have tubes inside me called Fallopian tubes which are blocked. They're just scars, solid and tough as gristle, and nothing is ever going to help. So your mummy is quite right, Esmerelda.'

'I've been ever so puffed, but I didn't tell you,' Esmerelda said proudly as they came to the carriage circle – car circle, now – round the fountain that splashed from its ornamental peak. Submerged lights gave the effect of a Christmas tree, filling unlighted windows with a kaleidoscope of starry reflections of the cascade. Behind them simmered the enormous lava field of London. 'I knew you weren't strong enough to carry me.'

'I'm stronger than I look, kid,' Julia said out of the corner of her mouth.

'I wish I was you,' Esmerelda said simply. 'I have done for every minute of today. It's been the most wonderful day of my life and this has been the very best part of it.'

'Such praise!'

'You don't treat me like a kid.' She ran ahead up the frosted steps, all but skidding flat on her face.

Julia stared at the small, pricey peach-coloured BMW parked by the fountain. Mrs Morrison opened the doors and Esmerelda dodged past her into the hall, flying into the library to find her mother.

'Good evening, Mrs Morrison,' Julia murmured. 'Who's our visitor?'

'Visitors, in the front parlour, dear, sitting. Him and her.' Mrs Morrison looked stormy, giving the door a heavy slam against the cold; she did not like these visitors. 'Then they got itches in their britches and started wandering about, so Mrs Pride took them into the library to catch her 'flu.' Mrs Morrison's seamed features showed a trace of pleasure. 'Let me take your coat, hen, you must be frozen. Don't tell me you walked all the way.'

'Christmas and taxis.'

'And the poor wee bairn and all.'

'The poor wee bairn,' Julia said, relinquishing her coat with a fluid gesture that was almost a dancer's, 'is stronger than I am.' She called over her shoulder, 'Tea and crumpets?'

'Fresh not five minutes past. *They're* eating them.'

'You still haven't told me their names.'

The old woman clicked her fingers. 'Oh, he's an odd one. Mr Murge.'

Taking the card, Julia went past the Christmas tree that reached up the stairwell into the second floor, opened the library door and slipped quietly inside. It was her favourite room, a fire halfway down the left wall, deep rugs and plenty of clutter. The man moved among her things almost bumping into them; his manner suggested he could pick them up if he wished, he'd been offered plenty of stuff as good or better. Julia guessed him to be about seventy years old but his movements were very spritely and assertive, he kept his head back and his neck stretched. He wore his tight bird-breasted navy pinstripe suit over a matching tightly-buttoned navy waistcoat with a silver chain, and his scraped-back silver hair gleamed dark metallic grey in the licks where the hair gel was thickest. He had a tall red face. 'Ah,' he called, raising his arm, 'the lady of the house.' He lowered his hand into hers, gave Julia a man's handshake. 'Maxwell Murge. You've kept us waiting, madam.'

'You have an appointment?'

'Oh, I know all about getting appointments with the Fox family, don't I, dearest!' he said, gesturing to the woman who had been making twisting, primping conversation with Eve. Eve was sitting with a blanket over her knees by the fire, Esmerelda now kneeling beside her, whispering excitedly in her ear. Whether the woman was his daughter, girlfriend or floosie – Julia thought she was anything but his wife – Maxwell Murge repeated, 'I *said*, my dear, I know all about—'

'Of course you do, Max dearest, don't go on about it. He does it to embarrass me,' she told Julia with a naughty-boy smile.

'Adjana,' Max introduced her with gruff pride.

Adjana was a white-faced woman of about forty-five, with glassy chestnut hair and a snap-on skirt of the same colour. She wore lashes and suede boots with fur tops.

'Adjana's the love of my life, you can see that,' Maxwell Murge told them with dignity. 'I know a great golden piece of good luck when it happens to me, like she has. How old do you think I am? I'm seventy years old. Going to end my days as I'd lived, a bachelor, I was. And then I met her and everything changed and here I am. My Adjana.' He put his hand on his heart and reached out for her. 'I'm selling up. Going to end my life having the time of my life, all the things I dreamed of doing and never did, wasting away as I was in that little shop. The Greek islands. Drive down the Croisette in my own Bimmer. My father wasted his life. So did my grandfather. Not for us, eh?' He tugged Adjana tight with a look of genuine love, affection, need. 'An apartment in the Algarve.'

'You'd never believe he was seventy,' Adjana said.

Julia sat down politely and held out the tray of buttered crumpets, but only Esmerelda, leaning back against Eve's chair, took one. 'Don't get butter on anything,' Eve warned, then sneezed. Julia was glad her friend was here. Eve was the daughter of Sammy Summers, who was either in HM Prison for embezzlement again or recuperating. She had not been born to money – or at least, only to money that was stolen. She'd been to a dozen schools by the time she was sixteen. She was supposed to have Spanish blood, the hot carmine streak showing across her cheekbones, but her eyes were dark blue. Her loveliness had saved her, and a certain ruthlessness which Julia admired but did not like. Eve had supposedly slept her way to the top with the banker William Prideau, twice her age, before her twenty-third birthday; then, seeing that he was about to lose his empire in the huge tussle over Project Zain, the Macquarie Harbour mining development, she jumped horses (or, as it was put in London, swapped beds) and went over to Jim Pride's rival consortium. She loved him and believed in him; when he married her, Jim had promised her he would save the harbour. Such a promise flew in the face of all commercial logic. But Eve had believed him.

She saw Julia staring and looked away.

Maxwell Murge placed himself with his back to the fire, his hands behind him, raising himself on his toes. 'I'm selling everything,' he said abruptly. 'Everything must go.'

'You seem to think I know who you are, Mr Murge,' Julia said. 'You talk as though I know what you're talking about. I don't and I do not know you. As far as I am aware, we are strangers.'

'Mr Murge is a coin dealer,' Eve said, looking about to burst with laughter. 'He has explained it all to me – at the cost, probably, of catching my Beijing 'flu.'

'Then obviously he must consider it an important matter,' Julia said. She was much cannier about people than Eve.

'A most important matter,' said Maxwell Murge. 'I thank you for your seriousness, madam. Let me put it square. I have in my possession three immensely valuable Roman silver coins of the Emperor Tiberius.' Surprisingly, he turned for a moment to Eve.

'In 1870 your great-great-grandmother, Jemima Fox as she then was, came into my grandfather's shop shortly before Christmas, just as it is now . . .' He paused to let this selling point sink in as he turned back to Julia. 'She attempted to sell him a Tiberius coin of which she claimed there were once twenty-nine, by legend called the talents. But he refused her. Later my grandfather, Phineas Murge, changed his mind. He followed her. He found out everything about her. In fact the talents became his obsession.'

Adjana reached up the corner of her handkerchief and wiped a tiny fleck of spittle from his lip.

'They ruled his life. He vowed to himself to track them down, all twenty-nine – on this subject he was quite mad. They were a challenge to him, a dare. Mere mention of them provoked him. My father, Tom, would not see him for months at a time, and Mother took in washing to make ends meet. Phineas would return half-starved – his eyes driven inwards. I would say he was a haunted man. It turned out he was offering immense sums to your great-great-grandmother Jemima's brothers – typically two hundred and fifty pounds, a fortune in those days. Money that he begged, borrowed or stole; he certainly did not have it. He lived until he was almost a hundred years old, you know, killed by a bomb at the end of World War Two. He was a cadaver of a man and those haunted eyes seemed to look into you and stab your soul.'

'Perhaps a little brandy,' Adjana said.

Esmerelda jumped up, wiping her hands on her dress, and fetched the bottle – she loved the shapes. Adjana poured a tiny drop into a snifter glass. Murge braced his hands round its generous curve with authority but did not drink.

'My father was afraid of him. And yet he became a little like him, in the way that, you know, sons do follow their fathers whether they like it or not. By the time of his death Phineas Murge had acquired three talents, purchased from Harold and Martin Fox, and one . . . lost . . . by Reuben. We know Phineas travelled as far as Perth, Australia, to find a fourth brother, George, but he had already given away his talent to Jemima.'

'Good for him,' Julia said.

'Come off it, for a battler that bit of extra could have made all the difference,' Eve said.

'But my grandfather never contacted Jemima – Lady Jemima Summers as she was by then. He rented a room where he could spy on her house. I think his obsession was with her as much as the talents. Whatever the truth of it, she died before he did, in the late nineteen thirties, I believe.'

'She died in nineteen forty,' Julia said, with a nod at the framed portrait on the wall.

'Handsome lady.' Maxwell Murge swirled his glass. 'Tom, my father, took over the business. He toyed with selling the talents – Gloria Fox was at Holywell Manor in those days, as you know. Maybe he couldn't think of a good enough line to spin her, and anyway, with all her wealth and success, why should she have known or cared about them?'

Julia said, 'She had one of her own.'

'Did she?' Eve exclaimed. Maxwell Murge took a gulp of brandy.

'In a copper claw,' Julia said. 'She was holding it when she died, like a hand in her hand.'

Eve drew her blanket round her. 'Must be my fever,' she said. Julia dropped some coals on the fire with the brass tongs.

'You ought to be drinking honey and lemon,' she said.

'I'm up to my nose in honey and lemon.'

'And madam still has the object?' Murge interjected.

'I'm not prepared to comment at this time.'

'When my father, Tom, died in the nineteen sixties at a very venerable age, the three coins were found still in his possession. To me the situation was ridiculous. I wrote to Miss Wendy Fox offering them for sale. To a whole sheaf of letters I received not even the dignity of one reply.'

'Mummy wasn't very organised,' Julia said. 'And they weren't worth enough for you to sell on the open market, obviously.'

'Something is worth,' Maxwell Murge smiled, 'what someone will pay for it.'

'So,' Julia said, 'you have three coins in your pocket.'

Murge gave a secret smile. He turned up the lamp by the fireplace then held out the three coins across his palms. They flashed and caught the light. 'Tell me, ladies,' he said, 'tell me they're not beautiful.'

'They don't look old,' Eve said wistfully. 'That one's got a strange oily sheen.'

'I must've touched my thumb on the car key, it was serviced yesterday.'

'I've never seen anything like them,' Eve breathed. 'Have you, darling?'

Esmerelda said nothing, looking up under her lashes. Then she shook her head mutely.

'I bet you'd like to play with them!' Adjana winked.

'Dear, I'm working,' said Maxwell Murge. He laid the coins in Julia's lap, a salesman's ploy: let her touch.

Julia touched.

'Twenty thou,' Maxwell Murge murmured, 'but Father Christmas is coming.'

'Pounds?'

'Listen. Christmas offer. Fifteen thousand pounds for the three. I can't go lower.'

'You're whistling in the dark,' Julia said.

'You want them. That sum's nothing to you.'

'This is your apartment in the Algarve,' Julia said.

Adjana threw Murge an angry look. 'You said it's paid for.'

'It's a detail,' said Murge without moving his lips.

Julia laughed. She picked up the coins and stood, going round the piano to the bureau. 'Even you'll want to see this, Eve,' she said. 'Bring your mother over, Esmerelda.'

When they were gathered round, Julia pulled open the long drawer.

'Blimey!' Maxwell Murge said. He put up his hand.

'There's lots of them,' Esmerelda whispered. 'Hasn't she got *lots* of them?'

'Not really,' Julia said. 'It looks as if there's more than there are, that's all. It's the lighting in here.' She chinked one with her fingernail. 'When she died in 1940 Aunt Jemima willed the three talents she had accumulated during her lifetime to my great-grandmother, Gloria. In addition was the one left to Jemima four years before by her brother, the Reverend Jerome. I know his gesture of reconciliation amazed Jemima, and she always kept his talent separate, but they're all mixed up now. That's four. And this is the clawed one that belonged to Gloria and she gave to her children, which eventually made its way back to her. The fifth.' Julia cleared her throat. 'Hand in hand.'

Maxwell Murge saw his price going up.

'If five of the little buggers looks like this,' he murmured inno-cently, 'imagine what the whole twenty-nine must've looked like. Here,' he said, 'give me back my three.' He took them and held them against the others, smiling with his evenly spaced white teeth. 'Don't it make a show. Oh, who could resist?'

'I have a weakness,' Julia said. 'It's gambling.'

'Julia, don't be silly,' Eve said. 'Stop now. Julia, *don't*.'

'Eve is remembering Monaco last year.' The break had been Eve's idea, about a month after Cameron's death. The change that had come over Julia in those few weeks had been shocking; she had looked like a ghastly photograph of herself, the sort of holiday snap that goes immediately into the bin: eyes too staring, hair stark, and her weight loss had been horrifying, as though she hadn't eaten since hearing about Cameron. Which was very nearly the case. Eve's idea had snapped her out of it, and under the Mediterranean sun the old Julia had come back.

But changed.

Not much. Hardly enough to notice unless you knew her. But she laughed more brightly. When she drank, she drank more. And she was more determined, Eve noticed. Quiet, shy Julia could be angry now. She could be a shit when she wanted, and when she was provoked her face changed, as though her flesh wore a fist inside it, as though her skin and bone and muscle were remembering Cameron being pushed beneath the train, as though it was happening still inside her.

And Julia gambled.

She always had gambled, filling in the tabloid bingo and having a flutter on the big race days. But in Monaco Julia gambled more. In one evening at the casino, to Eve's horror, Julia had dropped three-quarters of a million pounds.

Eve had looked at Julia with new eyes after that. Quiet Julia. Shy Julia.

'I have in mind a small wager,' Julia murmured.

Maxwell Murge licked his lips.

'I will not pay you fifteen thousand pounds for those three coins. I will pay you twenty thousand for them, or ten thousand, depending on the toss of a coin.'

'Julia, you mustn't do this,' Eve said.

'This coin,' said Julia, picking up one of the talents. She didn't look at Eve. She pushed past her and cleared the table to make more room.

'Julia, stop it,' Eve said.

'Twenty thousand quid,' Maxwell Murge muttered to Adjana, who wore two high spots of colour on her cheeks.

Julia moved her hand under the light. On her thumb twinkled the talent. She flicked. 'Tails!' Maxwell cried.

The coin spun and dropped.

The head of Tiberius.

Maxwell Murge turned on Adjana. 'Ten thousand quid, that's not bad, it's more than you were reckoning on the way 'ere—'

'Your turn,' Julia said.

Murge looked at her.

'I'll pay fifteen thousand, or five,' Julia said. She pushed the coin a fraction of an inch with her fingernail.

'I don't know.' Maxwell Murge picked it up. 'Fifteen thousand, that'd get us back where we started,' he told Adjana.

'Are you sure what you're doing?' Adjana said fretfully. 'Oh, Maxie, I always trust you.'

'Course you do,' he winked. 'So you blooming should.' He flicked.

'The Menorah,' Julia said.

The coin spun, shimmered, stilled. The Menorah.

'Five thousand pounds!' Adjana said in a little voice. 'Oh, Maxie, what have you done?'

'Shut up!' he said. 'Not one more word. Not one.'

He raised his eyes to Julia's.

'Double or quits,' Julia said.

'Maxie!' wailed Adjana. 'You're always going on at me about how I should look after the pennies and the pounds will take care of themselves.' She found her little hanky that had dabbed his lip, and put it to the corners of her eyes. 'You're throwing away the pounds!'

'Shut your whining,' Maxwell Murge said.

'*You can't afford to lose!*' Adjana wailed.

'I'm not going to lose,' he grunted. 'The odds are way on my side now. Pick it up.' He banged the table. 'Pick it up!'

Julia picked up the coin, balanced it on her thumbnail, flicked.

'The head of Tiberius!' Murge shouted.

The coin spun.

Esmerelda squealed with excitement, jumping up to look.

'The Menorah,' Julia said. 'The seven-branched candlestick.'

Murge rubbed at his long red face.

'You've got the blooming things for nothing,' he said.

But Esmerelda piped up. 'No she hasn't,' she said, 'she wants to carry on. Look at her. Look at her face.'

Julia said calmly, 'Five thousand on the next throw.'

'This is insane,' Eve said. 'Julia. *Julia!*'

'It's his choice,' Julia said.

'She doesn't think she can lose,' Esmerelda said.

'I know better,' Eve said. 'I've seen how much she can lose.' She spoke to Adjana quietly. 'Dear, I really think it's best if you get him out of here.'

'There's too many women in this room!' Murge said loudly from the fireplace where he had gone to fetch his brandy. 'They're cursed, those things are. Whichever way I called, it would have flopped over the other way to spite me. Fate. I was fated to lose. You knew it, Julia. Those things want you.'

Adjana took his elbow.

'It's time you got me home,' she said. 'Come on, Maxie. There's a good boy.'

Murge paused, staring at Julia. 'Congratulations,' he said belligerently. 'You got eight now. More than anyone. I suppose you won't be satisfied until you've got the whole twenty-nine. I got news for you, Ms Fox. I ain't never been offered another one, and I been fifty years on the lookout in the business.'

'Oh, there's one in a little secondhand shop in St John's Wood,' Adjana said helpfully. 'The bow-fronted place, in Abbey Road, you know?'

'You never told me!' Murge said, aghast.

'I didn't think you'd be interested,' Adjana chattered, hugging his arm. 'You're always talking about money, and they were only asking ten pounds.'

'It seems you didn't lose so much tonight after all,' Julia said.

Maxwell Murge stopped by the piano and picked up a black and white photograph in a silver frame. 'The man of the house?' he said, then waved it petulantly. 'He's welcome to you, that's all I can say.' He was holding the photograph of Cameron. Julia went over and took it from him.

'Oh, Maxie, I don't like it when you're bossy,' Adjana complained as she guided Murge through the doorway.

Julia stood with her arms wrapped round the photograph. Something glinted in her eyes. Eve was amazed to see it: Julia was angry.

'If you want your flat in the Algarve, Mr Murge,' Julia called, 'you can always sell your BMW.'

The front door slammed.

Julia replaced the frame carefully on the piano.

'My dear,' Eve said, 'you're *shaking*. I've never seen you like this before.'

'More brandy!' Esmerelda said cheerfully, then quietly picked up the tongs she was not normally allowed to use, and tried to pick up a coal. It wasn't as easy as it looked.

'I'm fed up with being lied to,' Julia said. 'I'm fed up with not saying what I really think. I'm angry, Eve.'

'Goodness, I can see that.' Eve pulled the blanket up over her shoulders and shuffled back to the fire, then looked back. 'You knew you were going to win, didn't you?'

'I did!' Esmerelda said. 'I did. I saw it in her face.'

Julia wondered why she was having this happiest Christmas of her life. There was no particular reason for the undeniable glow she was feeling, but each morning she found herself again waking early, still tired from looking after Esmerelda the day before – Eve had relapsed to her bed, completely crook from the 'flu. Looking after the little girl was a tiring full-time job – but Julia found herself actually wanting to wake up, eager for the day to come.

Mrs Morrison had retreated to her brother's home for Christmas to look after her mother, so the days with Esmerelda were full. Julia usually had no interest in the kitchen, but Esmerelda loved making cakes and adding sultanas, and putting cherries on top. She was very decorative. They'd spent a couple of hours covering themselves with flour this afternoon and now they sat in one of the deep chairs watching something on television, the sort of show Julia never watched, Esmerelda sprawled across her, eating food that a week ago would have made Julia shudder: chocolate fudge, strawberry Mr Men, banana Hippopots. 'Try some.'

'I won't just now.'

'You can have my spoon,' Esmerelda said, and they stuffed themselves companionably, Julia filling herself out, while the sky grew dark outside the tall window. Esmerelda had fallen in love with Julia's loose-knit particoloured scarf and she wore it wrapped thickly round her neck all the time, even in the house. 'I prefer English winters,' she yawned in a voice of great experience. 'Back home it either pours with rain or sun. You can't rely on it.'

After lunch they'd muffled themselves up in coats, gloves and scarves, wellingtons on their feet, and gone for a walk. The stormy sky made even the stark leafless bulk of Blackheath look pale. They heard the siren of an ambulance or police car crossing towards Shooter's Hill as they went to feed the horses. Six years ago Julia had kept a dozen mounts, but now only a couple of the old faithful remained; there had been some cases of horse slashing in the area, bored kids going home from school envying Julia's fields. One of the Fox trusts set up by Gloria worked in association with the local authority to bus children from the mighty sprawls of Greenwich, Charlton, Lewisham, out to places like Oxleas Wood or Nymet Wood that they would never normally see, without walls, without streets, without levelled ground. Esmerelda stroked the horses' noses and fed them Polo mints.

'They like me!' she said.

The other stable block had long been converted to garages, Wendy's white sixties Rolls-Royce still inside, and they sat in the back, in the gloom. 'My mother had us driven to Saudi Arabia in this,' Julia remembered. 'I was younger than you.'

'The television doesn't work,' Esmerelda said.

'It never did. She wasn't interested in things actually working.'

Esmerelda removed a cobweb. 'She did a lot, didn't she?'

'Yes. My mother was never still.'

'Julia, what have *you* done?'

Julia walked across the yard. The car door slammed and Esmerelda ran after her, her footsteps echoing on the bricks then running silent on the lawn. She slipped her gloved hand into Julia's.

'Wouldn't it be wonderful if it snowed?'

'Yes, it would be wonderful.'

'We could build a snowman.'

'It doesn't usually happen at this time of year though.'

'I wish I could make you happy,' Esmerelda said. 'I wish I could force it into you with a spoon, like we did with the turkey.'

'I'm happy with you,' Julia said, and realised it was true. She wanted to squeeze Esmerelda against her and keep her and hold her against her all the time, but Esmerelda must leave in the New Year, return to Farmer's Cove with Eve, school in Tasmania, the other side of the world.

'What's this?' Esmerelda said, kicking at a tent rope.

It looked like a mess of jerry-rigged canvas and tarpaulins, all gleaming with frost. Duckboards stood frozen in the mud, wheelbarrows, markers and pieces of tape. 'Some students were looking for a Roman settlement around here,' Julia said. 'In the nineteen twenties Gloria had a swimming pool put in – I suppose they had huge poolside parties in those days, sunglasses and Jean Harlow swimsuits – but by the forties it was derelict. The bottom had subsided, a rare piece of bad work by Jamie Reilly. After Tricia died, Gloria let it grow over with weeds, and so it stayed, – until one of the bearded gentlemen stumbled across a mosaic of an eye, ten times larger than his own eye. They were very excited. They've found something directly beneath Gloria's pool, an old Roman bath-house. The mosaics are stunning. Porpoises swimming and plunging. A moray eel wearing gold earrings. It seems that Gloria built her pool over the exact place where a Roman pool stood two thousand years ago. There may have been a villa here. It's an amazing coincidence.'

Esmerelda was silent. Julia supposed it wasn't so amazing when you were five.

'It's wonderful,' Esmerelda said. She turned and put her arms round Julia's hips. 'It's wonderful.'

'Yes, it is,' Julia said, and realised it was.

'And it would be even more wonderful if it snowed,' Esmerelda said. 'Race you back to the house!'

Every ten minutes that evening Esmerelda went to the curtains, opened them, and pressed her nose to the glass. She was looking for snow. They watched a film and hung a huge fluffy red stocking from the mantelshelf for Father Christmas to do his job. 'Daddy says you've got to leave the poor old boy a whisky,' Esmerelda said, so Julia poured one and they turned off the lights and closed the door quietly. After her bath, and all the business with cleaning teeth, and finding the right pyjamas, and kneeling with Julia for prayers, Esmerelda dropped into bed yawning tiredly.

Julia kissed her.

''Night, Mummy,' Esmerelda murmured sleepily. She cuddled her bear and turned over.

Julia pushed her hands on her knees and stood. She adjusted the night light on its dimmer – Esmerelda liked it quite bright – then almost closed the door and stole quietly downstairs. She had the presents ready to put in the stocking, laying the ones that wouldn't fit on the floor beneath it. Sipping Father Christmas's whisky, she crossed to the window and pressed her nose to the window glass.

Outside it was snowing.

Going to the front door, Julia stood on the porch, watching the fat white flakes whirl down. The drive was already white, one smoothness with the grass. The fountain splashed and chuckled, illuminating the fluttering cone of snowflakes around it in the black air. Julia finished her whisky, coughed, and held out her hands to catch the snow.

Why had Esmerelda said 'Mummy'?

Nothing. No reason. A child going to sleep.

Julia whirled slowly in the snow, her arms outstretched.

The one thing I want, I cannot have.

She was certain now that running the Fox Pharmaceutical Company was not what she wanted. Harold's grandson Julian Fox and his wife Crystal, lifelong employees, had managed the firm during Wendy's years, Wendy not being noted for her attendance at the office, and by the time of their death in 1991 Julia had been old enough to take over. She could do it. She had proved that.

She thought of Esmerelda eating Hippopots. Winding the scarf round her face. Kicking at the tent rope. Yes, and it would be even more wonderful if it snowed.

Two tiny curls of scar tissue.

Julia sat with her legs apart in the snow, her face turned up to it.

I want a child.

There. It was said.

Esmerelda's face was magical in the morning. The two women watched her play in the snow, and Julia began to relinquish control

634

over Esmerelda back to Eve, who was feeling much better. Control, and closeness. Once more it was Eve who did up Esmerelda's shoes, Eve who fussed over Esmerelda's gloves. Julia felt her slipping away and knew she must not interfere. 'Have another carrot with your roast turkey,' Eve said.

'She doesn't like carrots,' Julia said.

'Don't let her spin you that one,' Eve said decisively, unskewering one from her fork. Julia wished she wouldn't feed the child from her own cutlery, then realised she had done the very same thing herself.

Esmerelda looked at her. She had left one carrot at the side of her plate. Julia understood immediately. It was the snowman's nose.

At the end of December she went up to the office for the day. It was an excuse to get away from the house and her feeling that she was coming between mother and daughter like a gloomy, meddling shadow. Eve did not make Esmerelda kneel beside her bed at night for prayers, as Julia had. Yet once Eve had believed in a better world. Once she had believed she could stop Project Zain, and anything bad she had done, she had done because of that.

All Eve thought of now was her daughter, and keeping her marriage together. She had her hair permed at Snips in the village, to look good for Jim.

Julia rode on the train, alone.

She paused as she came out of London Bridge Station, almost deserted, the rubbish shifting in eddies between the buildings. It was the sheer smallness of human will that was so infuriating. How clearly things were getting worse, yet everyone seemed powerless to make them better; every effort was swept away or evaporated like a drop from the ocean, at terrible individual costs – those tiny wars in the republics of Europe, smaller than nations, crossing borders, tribal wars almost, tribes of families fighting among themselves with a savagery unthinkable at the Pentagon or the Ministry of Defence, fighting tooth and nail for what they believed in. Julia had read once that the Roman Empire fell because the Romans came to prefer life with the barbarians to their own entrenched bureaucrats; the barbarians offered cheap, fair justice, low taxation and good beer.

She heard laughter and looked round. Down the street, on a

big road junction with traffic lights flashing, was an old public house called the Tabard. A young man came out, then a group of them spilled around him, pushed him down, and a struggle ensued. Julia pressed her knuckles to her mouth and looked around for a policeman, but knew this was the sort of incident the police considered trivial, she might get in more trouble for reporting it. An old man on a bike waited nervously at the lights, trying not to get involved – he wobbled then stayed where he was, afraid of getting flashed by the camera. It all seemed very close to Julia, though their voices were faint and she could not make out any words. Girls with drinks had come out to watch the ruckus, laughing, then one of them started kicking the boy who was down and had to be pulled away. She came back, kicking as hard as she could. One of the boys lifted her over his shoulder and carried her into the inn yard, the others rushing after them, someone flourishing a pair of trousers, and slammed the gate leaving the young man lying on the pavement.

Abruptly there was quiet.

He got up ruefully slapping his thighs, then pulled down his shirt tails and limped, missing one shoe, to the gate, where he started hammering on it with the flats of his hands. The lights turned green and the old man on the bike wobbled away gratefully.

The gate opened and a big blunt face stuck out like a rusty red iron, then a belly in a white apron, and massive arms. He looked the trouserless boy up and down, back and front, then pitched him contemptuously into the inn yard with a heave of his elbow. But he didn't return inside himself.

He stood looking around him. He looked straight at Julia. He looked at the empty pavements, then scratched his armpits. He seemed to notice everything. Then slowly he stepped back inside, until only his head was left looking through the gap. Then abruptly the gate was closed, and he was gone.

Julia walked across London Bridge, also deserted, and wasted her time for an hour at the office. There was nothing for her to do, as she had known, not even any post, and no one was there because she had not asked them in. The Christmas decorations looked sad. But she knew why she had come.

Julia pulled on her coat again, went downstairs, and turned

right instead of left. She managed to find a taxi.

'St John's Wood,' she said.

There was only one bow-fronted secondhand shop in Abbey Road, with basement steps going down on each side of it. It was called Daisy Pickwick's. Julia paid off the cab and crossed the pavement slowly. The windows, as grimy as the brick, were stacked with bits and pieces: a dusty Hornby loco coming out of a tunnel dotted with sheep, a black and gold Singer sewing machine, an original 1861 Mrs Beeton's, handcrafted jewellery, a child's stuffed tiger, a classic model car beautifully detailed in chromium, a silver coin.

Julia knew it with her first glance. It was real.

She didn't expect the shop to be open, but it was. The bell tinkled as she stepped down inside. Several clocks ticked at different speeds, then a head appeared out of a hatchway. 'I'm having my lunch,' said the man. 'Is that all right?'

'I'm just looking,' Julia lied.

She slipped round the hatstand and a large brass pot, and reached into the window to take the coin into her palm. It was very dusty and dull and she polished it on her coat. On the back was a cheap sticker on which had been written in blue pen: £10.

Maxwell Murge's girl had blurted the truth.

'Before you start your pudding . . .' Julia called towards the hatchway.

A door opened and a plump man came through wiping his lips. Wearing a sports jacket with leather patches and flannel trousers, he had the air of a retired schoolteacher. 'That was quick,' he said, peeling off the sticker. 'A woman who knows her mind!'

'Yes,' Julia said, 'I am.' She added, 'Do you happen to know where this coin came from?'

'We're a family shop. Known for it in the locality.' The man dropped the coin in a brown paper bag. 'It's from when the old Briggs place was emptied, I think – a lot of their stuff came through here. That was from there.' He pointed at a model of a canal boat, beautifully painted with flowers in tiny detail, wild flowers and rabbits and fishes jumping in flourishes around the boat's name: *Joy*. In the stern, holding onto the brass tiller, stood the wee figure of a girl, her hair tied back, her hand levelled over her eyes, looking forward as if against the sun.

Julia didn't know of anyone called Briggs in Vaudey – or rather, she suspected if she looked the name up in the phone book she would find dozens. 'Well, thank you anyway,' she said.

'My pleasure,' smiled the man, and the door tinged.

When she got home she went into the library. Mrs Morrison must have returned, for a fine fire was blazing. Julia took off her coat and laid it over the back of an armchair, warmed her hands at the flames for a while. The only sound was the flames. The decorations twinkled. Eve and Esmerelda must be out walking.

Julia took the brown paper bag from her pocket, then went to the bureau and opened the drawer. Kneeling, she dropped in the new one. The coins did look better together; they flickered by the firelight, hardly silver but reddish, but that was the flame. Or perhaps it was her hair. She moved her head slowly from side to side to see. She had nine of them now. Only a week ago she'd had only five, and been sure that was all there were. Reddish with her hair, and she could see her eyes in them too.

Julia turned.

Esmerelda was watching her from the door.

'It's amazing,' Julia said. 'I went to St John's Wood, and there was one.'

'I knew that was why you went,' Esmerelda said. She'd taken off her wellies but looked very top-heavy in her overcoat and all the layers beneath it, gloves, Julia's scarf, pom-pom hat, and a red runny nose between them. 'Mummy says this snow's getting dirty.'

'Well, maybe some more will fall.'

'You haven't been paying attention to me,' Esmerelda said. She looked at the open drawer.

'I don't want to get in your mummy's way,' Julia told her.

'Oh, she's a bundle of nerves about going back to Daddy,' Esmerelda said. 'I have a pretty free rein.' She giggled. 'Her hair! Do we *have* to do that sort of thing?'

Julia laughed and blew Esmerelda's nose, because they were close again.

At midnight Julia and Eve, slightly tipsy from the port they were drinking, stood in the hall looking up at the Christmas tree which was blazing with light; all the other lights were out. The two women had kicked off their slippers and were waiting to welcome in the New Year. From the library came the ghostly revelry of the television at high volume, and they danced slowly, holding their glasses at arm's length. Esmerelda came downstairs holding her bear, rubbing her eyes. 'Can I dance too?'

The three of them danced, Esmerelda hanging from their hips, then Julia put down the bottle she was holding and they picked her up between them. 'What New Year wishes are we going to make?' Esmerelda asked brightly. So that was what she had been thinking about up there in bed.

'They're supposed to be called good resolutions,' Eve said. 'Like giving up smoking, or swearing, or whatever it is.'

'That's boring.'

'It's a wish, and then having the resolution to make the wish come true,' said Julia. 'Not just talking about it. It's about resolving to do it and making it come true.'

'It's nearly time,' Eve said.

'What are you going to wish for?'

'That's a secret!'

They closed their eyes as the clock chimed.

'I know what she wished!' Esmerelda told Julia. 'She just wished Daddy would be there to meet our plane, and she'd still have a marriage.'

'Ezzie, you horror!' Eve said, outraged, but blushing. 'Go straight to bed. Now. Don't answer back. Go!'

Esmerelda went.

'I'll go and tuck her in,' Eve said, and laid her hand on Julia's wrist. 'She was quite wrong, you know.'

Julia knew that Esmerelda had been quite right. 'You know children better than I do.'

'Little liars,' Eve said, going upstairs. Julia went to bed.

The next day was Esmerelda's last full day and Julia walked outside with her. The little girl was saying goodbye to her horses and everything that was now so familiar to her. 'That sky looks like snow,' she said. It was amazing how quickly and how much a child learned, how naturally they became part of a place. Julia was sure that Esmerelda would remember Holywell all her life; hardly more than a week of her childhood, but Holywell would be true and real inside her as long as she lived.

The first flakes fell. 'I told you,' Esmerelda said.

It was a quiet supper, though Mrs Morrison had gone to the trouble of tying balloons to all the sausages. After Esmerelda's bath, Eve came down. 'She wants you to go up and say good night.'

Julia expected to find Esmerelda almost asleep, cuddling her bear, but she was kneeling at the window, the bare pink soles of her feet sticking out of her nightdress. 'I'm praying like you do,' she said.

'At the window?'

'That's because it's still snowing outside.' Esmerelda studied her seriously. 'You can't see it because the lights are on.'

Julia turned them off and the pale glow of the snow filled the window.

'And snow and snow so that I can stay here for ever,' Esmerelda finished her prayer. She skipped into bed and pulled the sheets to her chin, a little dark face looking up between the white sheet and white pillows. Julia kissed her.

'I'm a throwback too,' Esmerelda whispered. She blinked her eyes. 'Mummy's are blue.' She fumbled out the locket, opened it. 'Look. Mine are brown. Like hers. Mummy says she must be older than 1800. When you said on the train the other day that you were a throwback, I felt so close to you, Julia. Everything you said you seemed to be speaking about me.' Julia had to lean close to hear the little girl's voice, she was speaking so low, and suddenly Julia realised that Esmerelda was sharing secrets, coming close, her eyes searching Julia's by the light of the snow. It was the child's way of saying goodbye – and *I'll come again*, perhaps.

'Your mummy and daddy are going to be just fine,' Julia murmured awkwardly. 'They love one another, you know. They love *you*.'

'That's the whole business, isn't it?' Esmerelda whispered. She wound her hands warm in Julia's. 'I was right about Mummy's wish, wasn't I?'

'Spot on, I'd say.'

'I know what you wished, Julia.'

'I don't think you do, Esmerelda.' Julia rubbed noses.

'You wished for a baby.'

Julia was silent.

'You want a baby who will change everything in your life,' Esmerelda said simply. 'I saw your face. It's that face you have with a fist in it. Like when you look at those coins.'

'Do I look at them?'

'You know there's something between you, don't you?'

Julia licked her lips. 'When I bet Murge, I knew I wouldn't lose. I was on a winning streak. I could have carried on winning. That was what I wanted to do. I wanted to make him another bet – the original twenty thousand pounds he'd asked, perhaps, set against his car. I would have won.' She smiled. 'Come on, now you tell me. What was your wish?'

'I wished for your wish to come true, Julia.'

They squeezed hands, but Esmerelda pulled away. 'There's something.' She took off her locket and leaned forward into the light of the snow, working her fingernail under the back of the miniature. 'Mummy doesn't know, she didn't think to look when we found it. This is our secret, Julia. Promise.'

'Promise, promise.'

Esmerelda lifted out the little painting and laid it carefully on the pillow. Where it had been mounted a pale light flashed, not golden like the locket.

'It is, isn't it?' Esmerelda said. 'It's a talent.'

'My God,' Julia said. 'It is.'

'My mummy had to do a lot of research to help Daddy beat William Prideau,' Esmerelda whispered. 'Before eighteen hundred there was a girl called Eve Summers who *married* someone called William Prideau. The same family. Well, her *mother* was called Esmerelda Paz. I think this painting is of her. Esmerelda Paz. My grandmother's maiden name is Paz, did you know? Carmen Paz, but everyone calls her Carrie.'

Julia touched the coin with her fingertip. 'There's more, Esmerelda,' she said. 'Gloria's mother, who married Bert Simmonds. Her maiden name was Paz.'

Esmerelda pulled the coin out with her fingernail. 'I want you to use it.'

'I couldn't, Esmerelda.'

'So you don't forget me.' The coin popped out and she wrapped Julia's hand round it. 'I want it back. I want you to remember that, Julia. One day I'll ask for it back. But I know you really want it.' She opened her eyes wide. 'The way you look.'

Julia scuffed her hair. 'Cheeky.'

'Remember,' Esmerelda said. 'I'll remember.'

The driver of the Mercedes taxi took the M25 all the way round to Heathrow, white fields, houses and blocked roads lying motionless on each side of the yellowed, salted conduit. Julia hugged Eve and Esmerelda, drank a cup of coffee and watched their flight curve, flickering as though becoming unreal, into the snowclouds.

Julia sat in the back on the return journey. She had ten talents. It seemed incredible. Her eyes fluttered sleepily. She was woken by the driver swearing and a heavy jolt from the taxi. 'Pardon my English, ma'am,' he said. She realised they had left the motorway and were almost home, the back of the car fishtailing as the wheels spun in the ruts of Vaudey hill. The weather had deteriorated: ragged clouds, and the trees chucking their bare black heads in the wind, great heavy clods of snow showering down from them. The driver started the wipers. 'Go to the right,' Julia said, directing him up the well-graded modern road through Sabrina Cottages. It had been gritted – one dad was even cleaning his car in the drive, with a bucket of hot soapy water; these people were extraordinary. The driver got almost to the top, where the road was least used, then shook his head as the tyres whined. 'That's my lot,' he said.

Julia paid him and got out. The wind was freaky here on the edge of the knoll, many of the trees still heavy and bent with snow, others blown clear. She watched the Mercedes slither from sight among the rooftops, multicoloured Christmas trees, snowmen, then she trudged the last few steps uphill.

From here the view of London was immense, and London was immense, seeming to lie everywhere around her as far as her arms could stretch. The empty river was grey and ragged with the sky, the City a tiny jumble of spires that must once have seemed so important, Canary Wharf standing like a candle in the gathering sunset, streaming steam from its heating or cooling. There was a loud creaking, popping sound and Julia looked around her.

She sat on the stile to rest, buttoning up her lapels against the cold, banging her gloves.

There was a terrible groan, and the stile trembled. She jumped up with a cry.

The old tree, the one they had named Sabrina Cottages for,

was falling, and she was watching it. Half the young lovers in the district had inscribed their initials and hearts in the bark, and obscenities, and Nazi symbols. Snow sheeted from its upper branches as it leant downhill. The snow around its base began to leap and jump as though moles were digging in the earth beneath, the roots letting go with dull thumping sounds Julia felt in her feet. It never occurred to her that the tree might fall on her, but it might. The sound was terrible. The tree crushed the fence and thwacked down half across the road, its enormous black base and gnarled roots rotating into the air, flinging soil. A tiny fleck stung Julia's cheek.

Nothing moved.

Julia lifted herself across the stile and walked unsteadily the few snowy paces to where the black roots stuck into the air. The Sabrina Oak had survived the storm of 1987; it was supposed to be one of the oldest thousand or so trees standing in Britain. Except that it wasn't standing now, and Julia had seen it happen: the end of two thousand years or so of continuous history. The dendrologists would be able to count the rings and date it to the year. They would be able to state what the weather had been like here, exactly here, every single year since. But the tree was gone. Tears filled Julia's eyes. Her little squirreled store of talents seemed pitiful compared with this end.

She stared into the crater.

In the churned soil she thought she saw something. Slowly she realised it was bones; dark brown human bones, darker than tea, so old that they seemed petrified to stone. A leg bone; the lines of ribs.

But small. Not an adult's skeleton, or even a child's.

A baby's skeleton.

Julia slid down. 'A baby,' she whispered.

The head had been cut off. The skull had been placed between the leg bones, where they would appear during birth, symbolising rebirth.

'You were only a baby,' Julia said.

She pulled off a glove with her teeth, and dared to touch the smooth top of the skull between the fontanelles, which had not knitted. For ever a baby.

'Oh, you poor baby,' she said. 'Whatever happened to you?'

The bone felt so cold. 'Somebody deliberately buried you like this,' Julia whispered. 'Somebody loved you.'

The earth moved, trickling down, and the skull turned upwards under her hands, the eye sockets staring up.

In each one lay a silver talent.

Julia ran all the way home, her boots leaving great prints in the snow. Her tracks came to the ride of oaks bordering the white drive and went on between them.

Julia ran with soil clinging to her fingers, her breath puffing behind her, a talent clasped in each hand.

She ran past the fountain, up the steps, into the hall, then hopped through the hall prising her snowy boots off. Her scarf had got in front of her mouth and she blew it aside. She knocked open the library door with her shoulder, panting, and padded to the bureau.

She put her hands down on the tooled leather top and opened her fingers.

She was shaking.

She unwound her scarf and threw her coat over a chair, where it dropped to the floor. She knelt, panting, and looked at the two coins at eye level. They were the same.

She opened the drawer.

Julia didn't know what she felt. She thought she'd left the front door open. She thought she'd been chosen. It was impossible.

Two days before Christmas she'd had five of them, passed down by two women she'd never met, Gloria and Jemima, and had hardly thought of until now – she'd hardly thought of the talents either, not from one year's end to the other. They'd just been in a drawer.

But almost every day over this Christmas, something had happened. Something was happening that was more than a coincidence.

She had twelve talents now. They were taking over her life. The front door banged in the wind. Julia half got up then knelt again. She was making it happen.

But what did she want? What did she *really* want?

Julia put the two coins she had found – that had found her – in the drawer with the others.

'Join your friends,' she said.

She waited, but nothing happened.

Mrs Morrison came in to light the fire. 'I didn't know you were back, hen!' she said, surprised. 'I thought the milkman had left the door open, you gave me quite a turn.' When Julia said nothing, she lit the tinder, blew it to life, and put the guard in front of the fire.

Julia waited all evening. Nothing happened.

She wondered what she ought to do. What she normally did, she supposed. Everything was up to her; she could do whatever she wanted.

The next day she was back at work, looking up every time her secretary's phone rang. The day was nothing but normal; at five thirty she joined the usual gloomy rush through London Bridge Station feeling let down. The work she took home didn't help the way she felt. She knew the signs by now, the little Julia signs that seemed to exist almost outside her own identity, the black wings of her depression gathering until she could not see her way between them. The little yellow pill she took to blow them away was almost more frightening, because it made her feel as though her emotions were unreal, and yet she knew they were not. They were what she *should* be feeling. *A year of emptiness had passed since Cameron died. If she had been asked before it happened, it would have been the most dreadful thing she could have imagined happening.*

It really had happened.

Lying on her bed, she took another little yellow pill with a glass of water, and the thoughts evaporated. She found herself holding the eight-by-ten glossy photographs taken of Esmerelda, Esmerelda sulking, Esmerelda pouting, Esmerelda wearing secretary glasses. It was ridiculous. The adult needing the child so much. Julia hoped with all her heart that Jim had had the sense to meet the flight. She lay longing to pick up the phone but having the sense not to. She couldn't live their lives for them.

She couldn't live her own life.

Nothing happened with the talents. No phone calls offering her coins, no visitors. Julia decided she had been deceiving herself with the mysticism inherited from her mother. She plunged into her work.

She kept going, and day by day she forgot.

Up in the Holmdene estate, the fifty-four plots of solid nineteen-twenties half-timbered dwellings built by Jamie Reilly around St Thomas's Hollow, as the developer had so enchantingly renamed the large part of the park he had taken for his scheme, were the first houses in Vaudey planned from the start to have concrete driveways and half-timbered garages. It was an inspired idea. Although the driveway cut the front garden by half, and the garage increased the council rates also by one half, the speculator knew he was selling not houses but dreams. The essential point about living in Vaudey was to have a country home in the country-side. To enjoy the countryside, one needed a car. The advertise-ments promised golf courses, brambly wildernesses and nightingales; a three-bedroom semi-detached house with a garage could be had for under a thousand pounds – and with no road charges either, all roads on the estate being of concrete laid by the contractor.

Twenty-two Holmdene Close stood exactly halfway along the close, cupped exactly in the centre of the hollow. The hollow had once been a lake but no one would have guessed that now: it was a swoop in the road, and the kids pedalled hard down one side to cruise to the top on the other side. There was never any trouble with flooding; the water that naturally tended to run down here was carried away by a four-foot greywater main that ended up out of sight, out of mind – in the Thames, probably.

In the middle of January the intense cold snap was followed by an almost-thaw, and on that particular day the Reeds moved out of Number 22 and the Mr Barkers moved in. There had been a last-minute prickle about the mortgage, and then a sudden scare about dene holes – totally without foundation, Joanna Barker had joked with a levity her husband found incomprehensible. Mr Barker was a headmaster and he was used to being called Mr, it was his professional life. Even Mrs Barker called him Mr Barker when their children brought in other children who might be pupils, and so did Drew and Dawn. In this way Mr Barker's life was kept orderly.

The heavily-laden Coppers Brothers' pantechnicon that brought their household goods from Sevenoaks stopped behind

Mr Barker's white Audi in the close, where the kids were already jumping out and getting the dog out and running about. Mr Barker walked up the front path, the shining front-door key in his hand. The Coppers Brothers' driver, with more practical concerns on his mind, leant his elbow on the window and sniffed his hairy nostrils at the sky, where the rain was trying to snow. There was old snow everywhere, too, looking like flaky skin. He turned his huge vehicle across the road and backed it expertly up the drive.

A tiny crack ran across the concrete between the rear wheels.

Mr Barker did not notice it the next day when he got out his Audi.

When about a month later he did notice the slight double jolt, front wheels then back, as he was putting the car away, he assumed the crack had always been there. The weather was terrible, the snow hanging about in great filthy banks, ice everywhere – he wasn't going to spend his time peering at dirty patches of concrete.

The weather turned warm on Saturday night, with sheeting rain, and Mr Barker turned down the central-heating thermostats. He listened to the gutters: the snow must be melting at a rate and a half, and that terrific rain coming down too. In the morning there was a lull, with another warm front from the west not expected until roast-beef lunchtime, so he put on his scarlet anorak and green seaboots and ventured out to do his duty with the hose. His white car, one of Herr Ferdinand Piech's *polar* white cars, had to be kept clean. He backed the Audi out of the garage and gained a smooth feeling of pleasure from watching the brilliant polar white coming up under the combined ministrations of brush and hose.

The car leaned over.

'What's going on?' Mr Barker said, looking at the tyres. He wondered if he had a puncture.

The Audi dropped its nose on the concrete, making a grinding noise with the underside of the spoiler. Then the car cocked its tail slowly in the air, one back wheel actually coming off the ground. Mr Barker sprayed it. 'What are you doing?' he said.

With a roar the car fell from sight. For a moment Mr Barker sprayed where it had been. His drive was an enormous hole and he was standing right on the edge of it. He'd heard of this sort of thing happening but he'd never thought it would happen to him. He put down the hose carefully and knelt on the edge, peering down into the dark swirling slurry of water, clay and chalk, trying to reach the door handle as though to pull the Audi out and put it on the grass to finish cleaning it. Filthy water was spraying everywhere, making a deep glugging sound – the Audi was sinking through a four-foot greywater main drain, water pouring over its white roof from above now. To his horror Mr Barker saw dents appearing all over the white paintwork, and rivets popped with a sound like bangs from a tin drum. His BP vouchers were in the glovebox. Mr Barker slithered and swung from a root, realising there was a danger he might go with his car now. The front of the car dropped as though it had been seized, and suddenly the steering wheel slammed away from the invisible driver and the seatbelts sprang taut, just as they were supposed to in a crash.

The dog rushed to the edge barking. 'Get back!' Mr Barker shouted to his wife Joanna, and to Drew and Dawn who were running up. 'It's a dene hole!'

Joanna said something profoundly stupid. 'But that's totally without foundation,' she said. The same bad joke twice was unforgivable.

The car turned once more and dropped from sight beneath Mr Barker. Water from the ruptured main roared down after it into the funnel, round and round, round and round, like a vortex leading into the ground. It grabbed one of his boots. An edge gave way and the dog slid down as if it was playing, gave a startled bark, and was gone.

Mr Barker scrambled out, scraping his chest painfully on the edge. He sat on the grass in one boot, one sock, and began to weep.

'Something's happening,' Mrs Morrison said.

'I know,' said Julia. It was a strange sound; it seemed to come from underneath the house. 'I'm not sure I like it.' A photograph fell over on the piano, lay with its frame chattering on the rosewood. Julia went to the window. Mrs Morrison stood the photograph up properly.

Something had happened to the fountain, Julia saw. Along with the pure recirculated water, some dark stuff was coming out, then a terrific dirty spray as air blew out.

Julia ran for the front door, opened it, stood on the steps in her slippers. It was raining again, soaking the shoulders of her cardigan. She went down a step. More air belched from the fountain, spraying her. Her face was quite blank; she did not know what she was seeing. But she was excited.

'Come on!' she said. '*Yes!*'

A great weight of water poured from the spout, gulping and spewing above her in every direction. And it was dirty, too. It thumped down into the pool and broke the stones, sending a fan across the rotten snow of the drive. More of it sprayed into the air with a sort of whistling scream and then the bottom of the pool rose up and broke apart. The flood washed against Julia's ankles. She felt something hit her and she reached down.

She knew as soon as she touched it what she was feeling.

'Seventeen of them,' Julia said. She must look a sight: it was dark and she'd had the garden floodlights switched on, brought the cars over and made a half-circle of their headlights, and she was on her hands and knees with a torch. She'd put on a pair of wellies, some woolly long johns and a Barbour, but even so she supposed she was freezing. Her face was caked with mud and silt, she could hardly recognise her hands for her own. But here it was, her fingers finding it in a bank of silt with the water still running past it; the seventeenth coin that the ground had spewed out.

A hoard of seventeen talents beneath the ground. Waiting for her to find them.

No, waiting to find *her*.

Julia rinsed the final talent in the running water. The cold had made her hand like a claw.

She dropped the coin in her pocket with the others.

Mrs Morrison came down the steps and wrapped a blanket round her shoulders. 'Into the bath with you, no arguments,' she said angrily. 'You're as bad as a little child, playing in the cold with no sense!'

Julia lay in the bath. She looked through the steam to the coins lying wrapped in a towel on the stool. Seventeen. That made twenty-nine altogether.

She had the twenty-nine talents. For the first time in who knew how many years, she had them together. *She* had them together.

She remembered the night before Christmas, adding Maxwell Murge's three to the five: how much more than five the added three had made them look, how much more than eight. And then each of the others, the pile of twelve she had built up: how much more each addition made them look.

And now she had seventeen to add.

She washed them carefully, and wrapped them in a clean towel.

Unlocking the bathroom door, she went downstairs in her white towelling wrap, the new cherry-velvet slippers Eve had given her for Christmas coming in useful now (a roundel of King Island Brie had accompanied each one). She went into the library and opened the drawer.

She added the seventeen talents from the hoard in the water under the earth one by one. Her hand looked normal now, a bit wrinkled round the fingertips from her bath. She stopped for a moment and towelled her hair.

The more she added, the brighter the pile grew. She couldn't take her eyes off them.

She breathed through her mouth. Twenty-seven. Twenty-eight.

Julia looked round, wondering if someone had turned the lights down. It wasn't the brightness of the pile itself, she decided, but the way it concentrated her attention.

She was sure there hadn't been these many together for *ages*.

She added the final one. It flashed, and shimmered, as if it grew hot with the others.

Something moved in them, and she looked behind her again.

Then she laughed. It was only her damp hair slipping off her shoulder, she was sure.

Her laughter slowed.

She stared.

Her towelling wrap had fallen open down the front, warm in the fire. She could feel the warm play of firelight on her skin.

She picked up one of the talents. Her breasts felt very full in the teasing, flickering air. She touched the silver to her skin, slipping the coin into her navel. She swayed her hips like a belly dancer. The wrap brushed her skin as she swayed and the hot coin slid into the cleft between her legs. Julia pressed her knees together, swaying. The coin moved under her fingertip, sending a slow flower of warmth through her. She stiffened her thighs and the heat moved inside her, blossoming, spreading, filling her though Cameron was dead.

Julia stopped and the coin dropped into her palm. Scarlet to the tips of her ears, she drew the curtains, hurried back and put the coin with the others, then went and sat by the fire.

She sat looking from the fire to the bureau drawer.

She patted her cheeks.

Twenty-seven was half as powerful as twenty-eight.

Twenty-nine was twice as powerful as twenty-eight. She had felt it.

But twenty-nine wasn't enough.

Julia felt totally focused on herself. Her head turned between the fire and the coins. What dreadful, wonderful things they were. She didn't care about anything else. She knew what she wanted, and there it was, looking at her from the mantel mirror: what Esmerelda called her face with a fist. Her face was determination. She thought about the talents. *Two tiny curls of scar tissue*. She thought about what she wanted. Needed. Wanted so deeply she *knew* there was more to her life. There was another.

There was another one.

A thirtieth coin.

Thirty, twice as powerful as twenty-nine.

Julia couldn't imagine it. She was sure of it.

Thirty pieces of silver.

Julia had the water stopped. When the bulldozers turned off their engines she stared down into the hole that was revealed where the fountain had been.

'You get a lot of these in Kent,' the foreman said. 'Dene holes. Bronze-age men. Little bastards.'

Julia went down the aluminium ladder. She was wearing a yellow hard-hat with a torch on it. At the bottom, splashing into the mud, some young man handed her a heavy-duty accumulator. The place smelt heavy and silty, as though it had been submerged for a very long time, yet she thought she could hear running water.

'There's seven chambers in all,' said the girl from the Kent Archaeological Society, who was writing it up for the *Archaeologia*

Cantiana. 'Dug with antler horn five or seven thousand years ago, or more. Druidic signs.' She pointed to her right. 'That blocked tunnel once led up. There's a runestone, almost illegible, the Guardian of the Day, or the Guardian of the Sun, as he is sometimes called.'

Julia looked around her in wonder. 'I've lived her all my life, and I never knew this was here.'

'These caverns are not an uncommon feature.' The girl pointed her ballpoint uphill, and Julia followed her huge jeaned buttocks through the short tunnels joining the chambers.

'I never imagined. They were here all the time and I never imagined.'

'Used for chanting mostly,' the girl said. 'The rote memorising of poems, religion, a whole way of life. We can't guess – I mean we do, of course. Disgusting human sacrifice with gold knives. Mass burning in huge man-shaped wicker baskets on the earth above. Fertility rites. A whole credulous population in awe and subjugation.' She glanced at her watch, unzipped a triangle of Dairylea cheese spread and ate it. 'Here we are.'

The final chamber was much larger and higher: Julia's torch beam probed and illuminated a slow fountain spurting from near the peak into a pool of clear water by her, trapped between chalk rocks.

'This may actually be *the* holy well,' the girl said. 'Name evidence is one of the primary clues we have. Often it's right in front of our faces. Holywell, Hollingbourne: holy water. Nymet or nemeton, sacred grove.'

'St Thomas's Hollow,' Julia whispered.

'Oh, there's lots of them, I'm afraid. Hundreds.' The girl pointed her cheese wrapper. 'Somewhere up there at the top of the fountain, along various holy passages, is the Guardian of the Moon. That's where the poor man lost his Audi.' She sounded awed.

'You don't understand,' Julia said. She turned off her torch and listened to the water. 'This was here all the time.'

She knelt and drank the water.

There was a thirtieth coin. Julia was sure of it. She was sure it was not in the caverns; if it was, she would have found it – or rather, it

652

would have found her. She had complete faith in that.

She looked, but she was not disappointed not to find it. She was excited.

Each day she went to work on the train. The faces around her were quite unreceptive, jogging with the motion of the carriage, Walkmans on, one man working on a laptop computer, a secret writer perhaps, or an accountant filling out on private work; thin girls reading fat books, gent after gent after gent buried in the sports pages. Cunning old men in threadbare suits and sharp young men in Armani, shoulder to shoulder.

Julia kept her eyes open.

She knew it would happen. She had faith in herself.

She came out of London Bridge Station with a thousand others, crossing Tooley Street in a dominant stream, climbing the smooth slope past the flower sellers onto the bridge.

Julia stopped.

Across the broad bridge road, above the parapet and partly silhouetted against the four pinnacles of Southwark Cathedral beyond, she saw a sign – or rather, part of a sign. Only the top part of four capital letters showed: S-M-O-M.

People pushed past Julia. One girl swore at her.

She crossed the road and leant over the parapet. Stone steps fell steeply away below her, set in the side of the bridge, into the cathedral precinct. Down there was another sign: ST MARY OVERIE MUSEUM. Beneath it was a large painted arrow, pointing past the cathedral.

Julia took the first, steep step almost delicately, probing with the toe of her shoe. In the end she went down them crabwise until she stood in the quiet cobbles-and-grass enclave of the precinct. She felt miles away from the rush on the bridge, high over her head. It was quiet here; her shoes tapped on the cobbles.

She followed the arrow.

She remembered very vaguely hearing of this place. St Mary Overie had been intensively redeveloped in the last ten or fifteen years by Eagle Star Properties – through her business managers she owned shares in the company, which was probably how she had heard of the development. As the Victorian warehouses on the river shore were gutted, medieval buildings had been revealed within. She remembered reading in the newspaper about the rose window of Winchester Palace being found as part of a decrepit hospital wall. Beneath it had been found a collapsed Roman building, and a wall painting with figures and perspective miraculously preserved when the wall fell. There had been something else; the wooden revetments of a Roman flood embankment, or a fishing boat perhaps.

Julia walked along the narrow lane.

To her surprise, a sailing boat appeared ahead of her – the *Kathleen and Mary*, a nineteenth-century coaster from Bideford, now preserved in a wet dock, behind lock gates. Julia crossed the open space. This must be a signature of what remained of the old St Mary Overie dock. It would be a busy, pleasant place in summer, with tables out perhaps, and hurrying waiters.

She turned. Behind her was a modern brick building, wedge-shaped. By the door was a circular notice on a chromium-plated stand: *St Mary Overie Bookshop and Museum*.

Julia opened the door and went up the step inside. Entrance to the museum was free; they reckoned you'd buy enough at the bookshop, obviously. The walls were hung with maps, guides, local history books, big glossy London books.

Julia went through. A big florid man in a plaid suit regarded her genially. 'Goot morning!' he beamed, coming round the desk. He sounded foreign. 'My first of the day. My first ever, in fact.' He gave her a shy look. 'My first day in charge,' he said. 'Am I making sense?'

'Congratulations,' Julia said.

He came across to her, bowed, and shook her hand. 'Professor Eskild Eskildsen,' he introduced himself. 'This is a new experience for me. To be in a museum instead of contributing to it. Hands-on job, in contact with the public. It's only for a fortnight, while Tom is away.' He blinked at her, running his hands through tangled black hair that despite its white streaks made him look improbably young. 'My wife was going to help,' he said, 'but her mother is ill.'

'I'm sorry to hear that.'

'Well, guided tour?' he said. 'I haven't been round myself yet. I have connections with a little place in Denmark kilometres from the town, I'm known for my work on Borremose Man, bog burials. I was co-finder of the Gundestrup cauldron. My speciality is those strange Celtic stone heads that are built into the walls of so many Danish churches – when I get home I'm returning to my work at Bramminge Kirke, standing in a grove of oaks, on a holy well.'

Julia smiled politely. 'But meanwhile you're enjoying life in the big city,' she said.

'Very similar history!' he said. 'Take away the buildings and you have Denmark. You came from us – not the British, but you Anglos, you Saxons, you Jutes. Now, the guided tour?'

'I'll wander round by myself,' Julia said.

She knew it was here.

'Just shout, I'm here to help,' he said. His fingers, trying to find something to do, made a pile of catalogues.

Julia wandered. This river bank had obviously been busy for a long time; there were glass display cabinets showing battered swords and knives and nails, red Samian flagons, bronze neck collars and an Isis jug, all the usual museum stuff. The tip of a sword found inside a skeleton beneath the yard of the Tabard, discovered in 1994 when a new drain was put in, was mounted in such a way as to give a frisson to a younger audience. Julia moved past a copy of the Roman wall painting thought to have decorated the club room of a military guild, and came to the boat.

The boat was a one-third scale model of a Roman square-rigged sailing ship, and it was mounted in a little scene as though moored against a wharf, with little plaster men unloading pots of fish paste, others loading bags of grain, slaves, hunting dogs. The bulwarks had holes for oars. 'A boat was found here?' Julia called.

Eskild Eskildsen came over. 'During the excavations of 1990, deep under the mud of the St Mary Overie inlet. It is believed to have sunk, or expired, on a mud bank shortly after the Claudian invasion. It had been badly damaged in a storm. Many ropes were broken, and so was the mast.'

'What dated the boat?'

'It was built of cedarwood in the eastern Mediterranean style, probably in Joppa or Caesarea. The hills of the Holy Land were covered in Lebanese cedar in those days, not at all bare and dusty as we imagine them. Until the trees built the ships, that is. By radio-carbon we could date them as being felled in about AD 20.' He added, 'And there was a coin in the tabernacle – the box that

655

holds the mast – placed there for good luck by some traveller, no doubt.'

'It seems not to have had the intended effect.'

The professor looked confused, then gave a great nod of his head and a laugh for English humour. 'You are quite right. The mast broke. Well, the plans of mice and men. It was a coin of Tiberius.'

'I'm interested in coins. You have it here – not a copy, I mean the original?'

He pointed at the display case in front of her.

There it was. The thirtieth talent.

It was mounted with a number of other coins that had been found in the river and did not stand out particularly, though it was larger, and more regular, having been protected from the tides, pebbles and debris by the wooden box, and by the stump of the mast wedged over it for nearly two thousand years.

Julia laid her gloved hand on the glass.

She remembered Esmerelda, and heard the child's voice describing what she and her mother had found in the attic at Macquarie Harbour: *And there were bracelets and rings that didn't look much, but Mum said it was because they had lost their point. The people who had loved them were long dead so the life had gone out of the objects.*

'No one's loved you for two thousand years,' Julia whispered. 'You've lost your point.'

She turned to the professor. 'I'm most interested in this coin, but I don't have time to stay today. I'd like to come back next week and sketch it, most carefully, with your permission. Of course I'd be prepared to pay a fee—'

'I shall look forward to it, madam,' said Eskild Eskildsen, sounding uncomfortable at the mention of a fee.

'Perhaps a donation . . .'

'No, no, the museum is funded by the London authorities.'

'To a charity of your choice, then.' There was a Guide Dogs for the Blind box on the desk; Julia opened her purse, selected a twenty-pound note, and dropped it in. 'Until next week,' she smiled.

She walked out of the museum, out through the bookshop, crossed by the *Kathleen and Mary* and walked quickly through the cathedral precinct. Her heart was thumping. She could hardly believe her luck – but that was it, she *did* believe in it. She ran up the steps onto London Bridge. Her office was over on her left.

Instead, Julia crossed the road. The train for Combe Forest was just pulling out and she caught it, letting the rattling carriages take her home although it was hardly mid-morning. She took off her gloves and pressed her fingers to her lips to cool them. The most terrific excitement was running through her. She must remain very cool.

There was a taxi in the cab rank. She had herself driven up to the house. Mrs Morrison was hoovering in one of the upstairs rooms.

Without taking off her coat, Julia went into the library.

She opened the drawer and took one of the coins, slipping it inside her glove.

She walked into the village, the winding Vaudey High Street of quaint Regency bow-fronts and double yellow lines, and went into the silversmith's, Lorris and Dell, Established 1815. Mr Lorris fawned on her personally.

Julia settled herself on the seat at the counter and took the coin from her glove.

'I want you to make a copy of this for me,' she said. 'Not a cheap copy, a perfect copy. Pure silver.'

'Madam,' Mr Lorris assured her, 'nothing we do is less than perfect, and nothing cheap.'

'By next Monday,' Julia said. 'Good day, Mr Lorris.'

He held the door for her with a bow.

Julia walked back to the house. Her hands weren't shaking. What have I done? she thought, but the thought only excited her more. She was committed. Commitment was exciting.

'I don't know what's got into you, hen,' Mrs Morrison grumbled. 'Ants in your pants, is my guess. I never ken where you are these days.'

'My second childhood,' Julia smiled.

'You make me feel my bones when you smile like that,' said the old woman. 'Hen, it's no another man, is it?'

Julia smiled.

On Monday she drove the little car into the village and collected the coin. 'Let's put the copy in the box,' Mr Lorris said uncomfortably.

Julia looked at him in surprise. She could have told them apart at a glance. The copy was perfect, but dull.

Even so, she kept it apart from the others.

That afternoon she went to the museum, taking care not to arrive until after four, when the light was failing. Eskildsen jumped up at once, obviously remembering her – probably had not forgotten her for a moment, in fact. Julia put down her handbag, her gloves and her sketchpad, but kept on her ample furry coat. He had the key ready, and brought the coin across to her. 'Will there be any others? We have a very beautiful gold medallion of London welcoming Constantius Chlorus.'

'Thank you, but not today.' Julia traced busily.

He went and examined some files. Sitting at his desk, he asked her if she wanted some tea. Julia did not want tea. He turned the lights up, looking out through the narrow modern windows at the dockside, the lights of the City across the water. He grunted in satisfaction then worked on some papers. Julia shaded busily with her pencil. The phone rang and he answered it, then put it down. The man from the bookshop brought in his tea and they talked for a few minutes, yawning. Julia stood up, replaced her pencil neatly in its case, pulled on her gloves, and held out with a smile the coin that she had been copying. 'Here you are, Professor,' she said. 'Thank you very much.' She handed it back to him. 'You've been very helpful.'

'My pleasure entirely,' said Professor Eskildsen, snapping it up in his palm with a bow. 'Good night. Perhaps we'll see you again sometime?' He held the door open.

'Good night. Good night,' Julia called to the bookseller, and went out into the dark evening, the bright lights.

It had been so easy.

She held the talent warm in her glove, and wondered what she would have done if they had tried to stop her. She would have done whatever she had to do, that was the answer. She would have screamed rape. She would have punched and kicked, she would have run into the dark, and run, and run.

One way or another she would have succeeded.

She had not felt the slightest chance of failure.

She stayed at home the next day.

It was a hazy, sunny day and she lay in bed in her white nightdress, her hair over the soft white pillows, feeling herself.

She went into the bathroom and drew a bath, spending time on herself. Afterwards she sat on the bed with her hair streaming between her knees, and cut her toenails.

It was very quiet in the house; the twenty-fifth of March. Not a hoovering day for Mrs Morrison. None of the televisions were on. The doorbell had not rung all morning.

Julia trimmed her fingernails. She ate honey crumpets for breakfast, and drank hot black coffee by the fireside in her room.

She supposed she was quite mad.

She had not taken any of the little yellow pills, and the strange dark wings of her depression beat around her. She had not taken any little yellow pills yesterday, either – Prozac, she remembered the name now. Wonderful little pills that concealed all the bad things about herself from herself, and all the good things, and filled her with contentment. She had taken none of them the day before yesterday, or the day before that, and Cameron was dead. The wings beat around her. Julia looked through them to the coin on the glass top of her dressing table. The talent was neither bright nor dim; without point.

If you had the chance, she thought, would you take it?

I'd take it with both hands, she answered herself. I already have.

She dressed in white panties and bra, white silky shift, a simple dark blue woollen dress. Simple indoor shoes to match. She put back her hair in a plait, winding it quickly with her arms over her head, secured it with a dark blue band.

She drew the curtains, opened the window. She thought she could smell spring. The birds were singing. Even nightingales, perhaps.

Julia picked up the talent.

The day was right, the date was right, everything was right.

She went downstairs and crossed to the library, went inside, and closed the door behind her.

Mrs Morrison walked in the drive. The sun felt lovely, striking the first warmth of the year on the shoulders of her overcoat and the uppers of her shoes. There were strange cloud formations overhead, but there always were. It was the aeroplanes. She put a few flecks of seed between her lips and held out her arms, turning up her face to the sun.

There was a finch who was tame enough to feed from her lips. Mrs Morrison called him Jolly.

'Come on, Jolly,' she mumbled through the seed. 'Here, Jolly.'

She listened for the whirr of his wings, but they did not come, and no birds were singing.

Julia looked at the twenty-nine talents, then took them from the drawer one by one. She laid them neatly on top of the bureau, piling them carefully so that every one was visible. The sun shone across them. She thought that looked very pretty.

She held the thirtieth talent towards the pile. She was quite sure that they had never been together since that day shortly after the Roman invasion of Britain when a storm blew, a man gave a coin to be put beneath the mast for good fortune, and the ship sank.

They can't be used, she thought.

She held her hands towards the pile. *Use me.*

'Use me!' she said.

She put the coin with others.

Nothing happened.

Julia closed her eyes and clasped her hands.

Mrs Morrison put back her head, her eyes closed against the sun.

'Here, Jolly,' she mumbled. 'Here, Jolly, Jolly.'

She heard the whirr of wings.

'My God,' Julia said. She peeped from under her eyelashes. The lights were very bright and she was afraid the bulbs would blow. But the light was not coming from the lights. The sunlight was not coming from the sun.

Julia thought it was very important not to look, but she couldn't not look.

The talents were a silver glare stretching from floor to ceiling.

As she watched, the glare pierced the ceiling and illuminated the room above, which was her bedroom, and she saw her white towelling wrap lying across the chair where she had forgotten to take it back to the bathroom, and she felt guilty about it being so clearly shown. She could see everything in her chest of drawers, neatly piled, mostly, and her dresser drawers, which were a mess.

Julia knew she was having a vision. She could smell something and thought it was ozone – except that she had thought ozone was very pure air, and this smelt decidedly sharp.

'Oh my God,' Julia said, 'let what I'm seeing, what I'm *feeling*, be real.'

The illumination spread into the upper rooms, Mrs Morrison's room with a large teddy bear, incredibly, lying rather masterfully on the bed. Julia's eyes followed the light blossoming and flowing down the walls. The light went into the ground and she saw the soil, the chalk beneath, the huge network of tunnels, Devonian rocks, underground rivers that filled the earth beneath her, all illuminated. She realised she was surrounded by wonders; all the things that were around her all the time, but now she saw them.

Yet she was sure she was awake; the vision felt as real as a dream. She pinched herself, and it was absolutely real.

'*Something's happening*,' she whispered, her face radiant.

Tears filled her eyes; it was too marvellous to believe.

The light went out.

The colours rushed away.

The sound of wings fluttered, swirled, was gone.

'Come on, Jolly,' Mrs Morrison urged, peeping under her lids, 'don't be afraid now. I won't bite.'

Julia blinked. Only dim house lights in the room; only sunlight through the window. The talents were only coins. There was no magic.

'I believe,' she said in a frail voice. 'I do believe.'

It's a wish, she heard herself telling Esmerelda. *It's a wish, and then having the resolution to make the wish come true. Not just talking about it. It's about resolving to do it and making it come true.*

She heard herself say: *It's about telling the truth.*

What do you really want, Julia?

'I want a baby,' Julia said loudly. 'I want a baby who will change my life. Do you hear me?'

I wished for your wish to come true, Julia.

Julia held her hands in front of her. 'I want a baby who will change my life!' she shouted.

She waited.

She noticed that there was a storm over London. A smooth grey whirlpool of cloud rose above the spires, spreading, and beneath it were flashes of light seeming no bigger than footprints at this distance, each flash illuminating a dense swarm of streets, rooftops, flyovers. The storm expanded with frightening speed, rippling outwards, the lightning flashes striding towards her.

Julia went to the window.

Mrs Morrison was standing out in the rain as though it was dry. She had her arms out and birds were fluttering about her, feeding from her lips. The old woman's mouth widened in a smile as the lightning flashed and pounded round her.

She threw no shadow from the lightning, only from the sun, as if the sun was still shining.

Lightning and thunder crashed together.

Julia turned. She saw herself in the mirror, her teeth revealed, and gums, and eyeballs, her ridged windpipe, her pulsing lungs, all revealed to the glow above and below her.

Never had she felt such a sensation of peace.

Julia saw her beating heart, her womb.

Two tiny curls of scar tissue.

She felt herself fill with blood.

An illegitimate child.

She knew what she was seeing, but she didn't know what to call it.

The light rose up through the house into the sky, rose through the clouds which closed behind it, illuminated the clouds from above, slowly faded, faded. Julia strained to see until it was gone.

She closed her eyes and opened them.

Nothing had changed.

But it had. She felt it. Everything had changed.

Julia walked outside.

Mrs Morrison didn't tell her about the miraculous flock of birds. Such a moment came only once in a lifetime, and it was her own.

'I believe,' Julia said. 'I believed, and it happened. I believe it may be the most wonderful thing that has ever happened.'

'I believe in tea, hen,' Mrs Morrison said, plodding past her. 'And I'm going to put the kettle on now.' She left Julia alone.

'*But I do believe,*' Julia whispered. '*I do believe.*'